# The Sarah Roberts Series

# Vol. 34-36

by

Jonas Saul

PUBLISHED BY:

Imagine Press Inc.
Ebook ISBN: 978-1-998047-98-7
Paperback ISBN: 978-1-998047-99-4

The Sarah Roberts Series Vol. 34-36
Copyright © 2024 by Jonas Saul

## The Sarah Roberts Series

*Dark Visions (One)*
*The Warning (Two)*
*The Crypt (Three)*
*The Hostage (Four)*
*The Victim (Five)*
*The Enigma (Six)*
*The Vigilante (Seven)*
*The Rogue (Eight)*
*Killing Sarah (Nine)*
*The Antagonist (Ten)*
*The Redeemed (Eleven)*
*The Haunted (Twelve)*
*The Unlucky (Thirteen)*
*The Abandoned (Fourteen)*
*The Cartel (Fifteen)*
*Losing Sarah (Sixteen)*
*The Pact (Seventeen)*
*The Terror (Eighteen)*
*The Chase (Nineteen)*
*The Betrayal (Twenty)*
*Sarah's Return (Twenty-One)*
*The Hunt (Twenty-Two)*
*The Delivery (Twenty-Three)*
*The Trap (Twenty-Four)*
*The Ultimatum (Twenty-Five)*
*The Depraved (Twenty-Six)*
*The Condemned (Twenty-Seven)*
*Payback (Twenty-Eight)*
*The Unknown (Twenty-Nine)*
*Wrath (Thirty)*
*The Damned (Thirty-One)*
*The Game (Thirty-Two)*
*The Decoy (Thirty-Three)*
*The Disappearance (Thirty-Four)*
*The Whole Truth (Thirty-Five)*
*Alex (Thirty-Six)*
*Parkman (Thirty-Seven)*

*Darwin (Thirty-Eight)*
*Aaron (Thirty-Nine)*
*Remains To Be Seen (Forty)*

**The Jake Wood Novels**

*The Immortal Gene (Book One)*
*The Immortal Target (Book Two)*

**Standalone Novels**

*The Drowning*
*The Woman in the Woods*
*The Threat*
*The Specter*
*The Mafia Trilogy*
*A Murder in Time*
*Frequency of the Dead*

**Co-Authored Novels**

*Collision Course (Written with Gary Ponzo)*
*There Will Be Blood (Written with Rania Stone)*
*The Soulless (Written with Rania Stone)*

**Short Story Collections**

*Twisted Fate (Tales of Horror)*
*Twists of Fate (Tales of Hope)*

The Disappearance

Book Thirty-Four

# Chapter 1

MARIA CHRISTY EASED ONTO her shoulder to avoid bumping her broken fingers on the bars of the cage.

A part of her wanted to give up. Let them win. This was no way to live. Death was final, and once dead, the suffering would be over.

*If you find yourself going through Hell, keep going.*

She couldn't remember who said that, but it got her this far, so she couldn't allow herself the easy way out now.

The stench of the decomposing body in the cage beside hers made her gag at first, but with each breath, hope forced her to grow accustomed to it.

*Can you ever get used to that smell, though?*

Being right-handed, they chose to break those fingers yesterday, leaving her left hand unblemished.

They'd broken bones before. That's why she walked with a slight limp now and why her left wrist healed at a crooked angle, as well as several gnarled fingers. If she ever made it out and got back home, she wondered if these things could be fixed, or if she would always walk around slightly hunched over.

She only needed one hand to extend through the bars to touch Samantha's dead body.

The room was void of light, absolutely. When her left hand eased through the bars, it entered the adjacent cage of her dead friend.

Gingerly, Maria touched the bottom of the cage, feeling for Samantha's body, her hair. When she got nothing, she pressed her shoulder against the bars as hard as she could, extended her hand, and grasped at the air in the pitch black.

A moan escaped her lips as she pushed to the left, then the right. When her hand touched the bottom of the neighboring cage again, she thought she had touched hair.

Everything in her soul made her want to recoil.

Samantha had been dead for at least twelve hours now. When locked in cages as punishment, they were only fed once per day. But that morning, Alonzo had entered the old wine cellar, which now doubled as a cage for the slaves, and sliced Samantha's throat. Maria was left with images of Samantha's white face, the last of her life flowing from a large wound in her neck.

Then Alonzo opened Maria's cage, and as she cowered in the corner, he yanked her right hand toward him, clamped something onto her fingers, and snapped them all backward, audibly breaking each one. She screamed in pain and anguish for close to an hour after he closed her cage door, snapped the padlock, and left.

According to some workers, the rumor was that Samantha had attempted to escape and sought help from other slaves on how to do so. They were to work the fields, clean the house, and generally tend to whatever whim the family requested, as well as be available for sex whenever their body was needed.

Maria had tried to stop Samantha from trying to escape, warning her not to trust the others.

And now her only friend was dead. This place left her no reason to live.

Yet something urged Maria to try. At least death would come quickly if she failed.

If she succeeded, she'd be able to leave this life behind. Maybe even have men like Alonzo jailed.

She could only hope.

And that was what pushed her on.

Hope.

She reached through the bars again and, this time, felt the tips of Samantha's hair.

Closing the fingers of her left hand, she gripped the hair with the determination of a fighter on her last swing, a free diver with his last breath, and pulled.

Pulling all that dead weight was impossible. Wouldn't the hair simply disengage from the scalp?

She inhaled deeply, suppressed her gag reflex at the vile stench, and braced her body to pull again.

Without the advantage of sight in the blackened cellar, she could only determine movement through feeling, and sure enough, it felt like Samantha's body eased toward her.

She redoubled her efforts and pulled again.

This time, she was rewarded with a soft scraping sound. Perhaps she wasn't dragging the woman's entire body along the ground. She could only be straightening it out, bending it at the waist.

A sob escaped her, and salty tears—water she needed and shouldn't be releasing—slipped down her cheeks.

How could hope be stronger than the urge to die? This was surely Hell.

She released Samantha's hair, got up off her back, spun around until she was on her knees, then leaned down and extended her arm back through the bars.

The hair was where she'd left it, but this time, she could grab it and tug it toward her with more leverage. Inch by inch, she pulled, pushing against the bars on her side to get Samantha's head as close to her side as possible.

Then something gave way, and the hair in her grip split from the dead scalp of her friend.

Maria dropped onto her side, expelling a short burst of air.

She released Samantha's hair like it was on fire, then felt for the bars again. Once she found them in the darkness, she shoved her hand through.

Success!

She had been able to maneuver Samantha's head close enough that the pair of barrettes she wore was accessible now.

One-handed, Maria popped them and pulled them onto her side of the bars.

She edged her butt to the middle of the cage. With the barrette's thin tip clasped in one hand, she managed to find the lock on the outside of her cage, but with only one hand, she was stuck. She needed the other hand to hold the lock while she tried to pick it. Although, she had no idea how to pick a lock.

Each time they brought her food and opened her cage, she'd look at the lock assembly and memorize it. In her mind's eye, Maria easily saw where the key was inserted in the front of the teardrop-shaped brownish-gold lock.

She tried to stab the keyway, but the lock just kept moving against the bars, squirming away from her touch.

The sound of voices drawing near made her stop and grab the lock so it didn't clang against the bars of her cage.

Two men were just outside. They were close enough to hear words, but Maria didn't speak enough Italian to know what they were saying.

One man laughed. Then the other laughed along with him.

They'd stopped walking.

To avoid the blinding light when the door opened, she eased backward in her cage, bumping into the toilet pail in the corner. It fell over, spilling hours-old urine onto the dirt floor. The stench this close made her recoil and hold her breath.

When she got to the other side of the cage, she inserted one of the barrettes into her mouth and used her tongue to shove it up along her gums and inner cheek.

The other barrette remained open in her left hand, waiting to be used.

Something clicked above her, and a shaft of sunlight became a wave of intense brightness, erasing the darkness from the cellar as the swipe of a brush stroke would on a canvas.

Steps followed as the men, now silent, descended the ladder.

Maria kept her eyes closed, her head turned, listening to their movements. Both men sounded like they were breathing through their hands or a mask. Of course, they'd wear something to avoid the stench of Samantha's corpse.

The lock clanged against the bars. They were either feeding her or letting her out.

She opened her eyes to adjust to the small amount of light seeping past her arms. If they dragged her outside, she feared she'd go blind without acclimating her eyes first.

The door to her cell smacked open.

"Get out," one of the men ordered.

Maria put weight on her left arm and shimmied closer to the door, keeping her broken right hand close to her chest. Blinking away the light, she moved toward the opening with the hairpin still wrapped in her hand.

At the door, one man grabbed her arm and helped her to her feet, but she remained bent over.

"Help her up the steps," he said to the other man, his Italian accent thick.

The man started up the steps first, then stopped and leaned back to grab her right arm below the shoulder. She had to open her left hand to grasp the rungs, or she'd fall. When she did, one of Samantha's barrettes dropped to the dirt floor.

No one saw what she'd been holding.

The man's fingers dug into the small amount of flesh still covering her bones as he dragged her over the lip of the cellar hole.

She plopped her butt on the rim and breathed in the clean air, the blessed clean air. It was cool out this morning, raising bumps on her flesh, but it was a wonderful smell. A cleansing of the soul smell.

She wondered if this was what Heaven would feel like when they finally killed her. Death equaled freedom: no more suffering, no more pain.

What made life so valuable that she kept trudging along anyway?

"Move," the man bellowed from beneath her.

The other man grabbed her armpits and dragged her away from the opening.

She didn't care anymore. If a chance to get out arose, she'd take it. But otherwise, she would be a living, breathing robot until she died.

The second man climbed up and snapped the door closed, then rolled the grass back over the top and tapped it down with his foot.

The cellar door was so well concealed that it was impossible to know a door even existed below the sod.

Those hands lifted her again, but this time he dragged her toward a golf cart, the kind they used to access all areas of the compound.

Once she was secured on the rear seat, her right hand nearly swollen to double its regular size with all four fingers broken for over twelve hours now, she guessed at the time. The sun had been setting when Alonzo killed Samantha and broke Maria's fingers, so now it must be morning.

They started toward the main building, which she referred to as the castle. It resembled one, as it even had a turret on the left side.

As they pulled up outside, four other men were waiting for them.

"Get her inside and cleaned up. Cut her hair. Give her new clothes. Then she can wait for the doctor in the sitting room."

*The doctor?*

Two of the men nodded and grabbed at her, one turning away and scrunching up his face at her smell.

"What the fuck, boss?" the man whispered under his breath. "This one is bad."

"What did I tell you?" the driver shouted. "Of course, she smells bad. That's why you're supposed to clean her up. Now fuck off and get the job done right."

"Yes, sir."

"Doctor?" Maria muttered as they pulled her off the seat.

The man who unlocked her cage and then drove the golf cart swiveled to look at her. "Someone needs to set that broken hand. You have work to do in the fields. For several weeks, you'll work one-handed. Then you're back in the house. You need two hands." He rested his arm on the back of the seat. "Be grateful Alonzo didn't slit your throat, too."

Maria stared at him. There was no compassion, no empathy in his eyes, and she felt sorry for him. Not to feel in this world must be easy, but what sort of life did that offer?

She lowered her gaze as they dragged her away.

"I wish he had," she muttered.

Someone ripped the filthy piece of cloth from her body as they got to the front steps of the house, discarding it on the stones below their feet.

Naked, dirty, scarred, and broken, they hoisted her up the stairs and into the house, the front door slamming shut with finality.

# Chapter 2

SARAH ROBERTS CLUNG TO the steering wheel as she headed north of Barrie. When she left Toronto an hour ago, it was partly cloudy. But when she got to the Barrie area, she'd encountered snowfall. Early March still brought the threat of snow to this area, and she hated driving in it. So, she'd pulled over to buy a large coffee and something sweet to keep her awake on the road, praying it wouldn't get too bad.

Back on the road now, she gripped the wheel tightly and leaned forward, her headlights only offering a glimpse of snow falling about ten feet in front of her.

The plan was to get in behind a rig and use its taillights as a guide. Or drive behind a snowplow.

What boggled her mind were the idiots who raced by on the left. How they stayed on the snow-covered asphalt and didn't slide off the road made no sense to her.

She released one hand, grabbed the coffee cup, and drank some, her eyes never leaving the road.

The startling, shrill ringing of her phone made her jump, and she almost dropped the coffee in her lap.

"Damn it." She set the coffee in the holder, looked to the side quickly, then snatched up her phone. Eyes darting to the road, then the phone, then back to the road, she tapped the speaker option and set the phone back on the seat.

"Sarah?" Parkman said.

"Yeah," she replied, her voice raised. "You're on speaker."

"I called to tell you they forecasted a lot of snow up your way."

"Driving through it now."

"Stop."

"What?"

"Stop and get a room. Stay in Barrie for the night. It's not worth it."

"Parkman, I have to get to Parry Sound tonight. The map says it's just over an hour's drive. Even if I go fifty kilometers per hour, I can do it in two hours."

"I checked Parry Sound, too. You're driving into several more feet of snow. The authorities are talking about closing the highway."

"You're not helping. That forecast makes things worse. You know how much I hate driving in the snow."

"That's the point. I *am* trying to help by telling you to stay in Barrie. Turn around. Take a room. Get some wine. Wait until they've cleared the road, then go further tomorrow."

"I can't."

There was a moment of silence.

"Okay. Your mind is set. I get that. Nothing will change it but you."

"Anything else? Gotta focus on the road."

"Did you tell Aaron where you were going?"

"Parkman, Aaron isn't interested in my routine or my life anymore unless it's regarding visitation. Those days are over." Even saying the words stabbed her gut. This wasn't what she wanted, but there was no *convincing* someone to love you, to want you. That had to come from them, or it was useless.

"Wait, am I the only one who knows you're going to Parry Sound?"

Sarah thought about it for a moment, her eyes glued to the white road ahead.

"Yeah. You're it."

"How safe is that?"

"Safe?" Sarah blinked a few times to clear her eyes. "Parkman, I'm going to speak to a woman whose son has been missing for seven years. Then I'm coming home. That's it. How could I encounter trouble with this one?"

"Hey, when Vivian's involved, you never know."

"That was part of my deal with her. I'm only doing safe things from now on. I've got Willow to think about, and Aaron's only a visiting dad now, like a babysitter."

"Is she with him now?"

"Yes, she is. For the whole weekend."

"I haven't talked to him in a few weeks. Is he still pursuing full custody?"

"I got the papers a couple of days ago, on Thursday. Full custody on the basis that I'm an unfit mother. Especially after what happened with that diamond robbery thing we averted last summer. He claims I almost got killed by the suspects *and* the police."

"Sarah, do you think you'll lose Willow?" He spoke in a monotone voice.

She shook her head and suppressed the tears that threatened to come. "I don't know, but let's not talk about that now. I have to concentrate on the road, and it will only make me cry."

"I see why you didn't tell him you were doing something for Vivian if you only got the papers on Thursday."

"Yeah. That."

Parkman was quiet for a moment.

She reached for her coffee again as a yellow Hummer buzzed by. Her foot eased off the gas pedal to slow down and avoid the fog of snow his tires kicked up.

"Fucker," she whispered.

"What was that?"

"Oh, nothing. Just a huge SUV raced by, kicking up snow. Made me have to slow to thirty."

"Sarah, I'm worried. C'mon. Stay in a hotel."

"Too late. I'm already north of Barrie. I'll be there soon. It's fine."

"Okay, then call me when you get there. I'll be waiting for your call."

"I'll do that from the hotel."

"Right, you're meeting these people tomorrow. So, take it easy, get to Parry Sound, check in to the hotel, and relax."

"That's the plan." Her nerves were firing on all cylinders as the snow thickened around the vehicle. She wanted off the phone before

Parkman detected anything in her voice. "Gotta go. Must concentrate."

"Okay, I'll talk to you in the next hour or so."

"Bye." She glanced sideways and stabbed at the button to end the call.

After a minute, she took another sip of coffee, but now her stomach had turned, and the coffee was making her feel sick.

She could deal with angry men. Knives, guns, and martial arts had become part of her life. But weather scared her, and Canadian winters weren't something she'd gotten used to yet—if she ever would.

How the tires maintained traction in such slippery conditions baffled her. All she could do was keep it under fifty and stay in the soft ruts the vehicles ahead were creating.

She tried the radio for company, but the commercials grated on her nerves, so she turned it off.

Even though the clock said it was nearing four in the afternoon, it was already getting dark. Her headlights offered more light than the afternoon sun and visibility for oncoming traffic—they could see her lights before her car, which made things safer all around.

There had been no more vehicles since that yellow Hummer, so she had to assume they'd closed the highway south of her.

"That's just great," she said to herself. "What am I driving into?"

The wheels crunched the snow under the car as she continued north on Hwy 400. Most of the signs were covered in snow, with some of the bigger ones half-covered. Without GPS on—which she hadn't needed because Hwy 400 went directly to Parry Sound—she had no idea how close or how far she still was.

On a long curve, the back wheels threatened to lose traction. She eased off the pedal and dropped to thirty. When the road straightened out, she pressed down on the pedal softly, a whole body sweat now covering her.

How much damage could she cause at this speed? Not much, likely. However, that wasn't something she wanted to test.

The car climbed another rise, leveled out, then started down a long decline. She eased off the pedal again as her speed steadily increased with the hill. Tapping the brakes didn't seem like a good plan. The hill had to level out soon.

But it wasn't leveling out. And now the car was doing over sixty miles per hour.

"Too fast," she muttered, her nerves making her talk to herself.

She placed a foot on the brake and ever so gently applied pressure.

The end of the decline came into sight—at the exact moment when the back end of her car slid to the side.

Sarah tried to correct it by steering into the slide, but nothing worked. The car ended up completely sideways as she spun the wheel, trying to regain control but failing to do so.

Luckily, it was a two-lane highway heading north, so she hadn't moved into oncoming traffic, and the road was virtually deserted at the moment.

Without hitting anything, she slid to the bottom of the hill and came to a stop in the middle of the road.

Safe and secure—breathing like she ran a hundred-meter dash, her heart pounding in her chest—the tips of her fingers endured a pins and needles sensation.

Before someone burst out of the snowy wall south of her, driving like a madman and T-boning her, Sarah hit the gas, spun the tires, and got the car going in the right direction, then eased off to the shoulder to collect herself.

She put on the four-way flashers and rested her head back to catch her breath while the wipers fought to keep the snow off the windshield and the ice on the edges at bay.

Something told her not to move again. This parked-on-the-shoulder thing represented safety. Moving forward—any sort of movement—came with risk.

But she couldn't sit here all night. With only half a tank of gas left, she'd run out at some point, and there'd be nothing to heat the car after that, which meant she'd be walking in this shit and freezing to death.

The only way out was to keep going.

She checked her side mirror, which showed her nothing but whiteness—it was covered in a thin layer of snow. She lowered the window, brushed it off the mirror, then raised the window and checked the rearview. In the few minutes she sat on the shoulder of the highway, the back window had built up a layer of snow. The defroster for the back window fought against the elements but was losing the battle.

Her arm stretched between the seats until she reached the snow brush. After taking a deep breath, Sarah exited the car, bowed her head, ran to the back window to clear it with the brush, then hopped back inside and slammed the door.

She shivered once, tossed the brush in the back seat, rechecked her mirrors—not that the snow afforded much of a view behind her—and saw they were cleared enough to get going again. She put the car in gear and eased off the shoulder. This time she'd keep it to thirty or forty, and if she crested a hill, she'd ease off the gas and coast down it doing twenty kilometers per hour.

Having a plan of action was calming.

Now in the center of her lane and doing no more than twenty-five kilometers per hour, she reached for the coffee, touched the cold cup, and thought better of it. Besides, her stomach was worse now.

Ten minutes later, still driving past snow-covered signs, the light from the sun almost gone, it seemed that it was snowing even harder, if that were possible.

Maybe Parkman had been right. Thinking back, she should have taken a hotel in Barrie and driven up to Parry Sound on freshly cleared roads in the morning.

Signs were only somewhat visible as she passed them in this near-dark state. What was visible was the wooden stake they used to hold them up. The green reflective signs were covered in snow, so she still had no idea if she was half an hour away or ten minutes.

Would she even see the exit signs when she got there?

The night lit up behind her.

Headlights.

Someone was coming fast—well, at least faster than she was going.

The headlights came up quickly, then veered to the left to pass her. She caught a glimpse of the cab lights, which confirmed it was a huge truck.

And now they were headed down a hill again.

"Shit, shit, shit …"

She released the gas pedal as the monster rig passed on the left. Snow billowed up from under its tires, covering her car in a large puff of whiteness, removing all visibility for several moments.

That sinking feeling in her stomach tightened as all she saw was a wall of white brightened by her headlights. Nothing else was visible.

Aware that she was on an open highway and nothing would obstruct the road was of little comfort. All she could do was sit beside the truck and wait until it got ahead of her and stopped whirling snow up in her vision.

The truck's taillights crept by the driver's window, then the hood.

She checked her speed. Hitting thirty kilometers an hour.

*How? I'm coasting!*

Coasting downhill had increased her speed while she focused on the truck.

Then the truck moved ahead. The whirling snow was dissipating. The headlights had more reach. Not that that mattered. Instead of five feet of whiteness, they now showed twenty feet of white.

A complete whiteout.

She passed another sign and was sure it had an arrow pointing to the left, but she couldn't see the entire thing.

A corner? Coming up?

Her speed was too fast for a corner.

But after what just happened over ten minutes ago, she was too afraid to tap the brakes again.

The shoulder of the road moved closer to the right.

Everything was white. The road, the shoulder, and beyond the shoulder—all white. The only reason she could tell the shoulder edged closer was the small pile of snow from a previous plow that had cleared the road some days past.

She eased the car to the left with her foot on the brake and her hands tight on the wheel.

And lost control.

Frantically, she tapped the brakes harder, but nothing was stopping the car as she was still driving downhill—sliding downhill, as it were.

The shoulder slid under the car. The embankment grew large in her windshield. Then there was a punching sound, followed by silence as her car smacked into the pile of snow before going airborne.

Sarah screamed as she lifted out of her seat, her head pushing into the roof after having forgotten to reconnect her seatbelt again after getting out to clear off the back window.

There was a distinctive sound when the car was crunching snow beneath the tires. Now airborne, there was silence. What seemed like several minutes of quiet but was only a few seconds, the car hit the ground with a heavy crunch.

The airbags deployed and shot into Sarah's abdomen at the bottom of her ribcage. Her upper body was punched back into the seat while her legs extended outward beneath her after having been suspended in the air.

Something stopped the car instantly, and the impact shot pain through her chest, knee, and head when it connected with the windshield.

The car swung around whatever it hit, snagged something on the ground, flipped onto its roof, and flipped again with its forward momentum.

Inside, Sarah was tossed around like clothes in a dryer.

Glass shattered around her as the back window imploded. Both passenger windows broke out as a tree trunk ripped them from the car's frame.

The hood wrapped around the trunk of a tree, killing the engine and the lights.

At that exact moment, her head whacked the windshield again.

Blessed darkness enveloped her, cutting off her screams.

# Chapter 3

SCRUBBED WITH A HARSH brush, her body now clean but covered in red splotches, Maria sat in the sitting room of the Italian mansion surrounded by three large men as she waited for the doctor. A woman had come and brushed out her hair, but the men had dressed her, each taking an extra look and a feel while helping with her panties and bra.

After five years of being here surrounded by men, she had grown desensitized to their acts of moral turpitude. Her private areas were once special, desired by her husband, and something that also gave her pleasure. Now they were nothing but a tool for these men to be used based on their needs. It was also something to gain an extra bit of food, a favor, or even a small piece of comfort like a pillow.

Yet, as much as they'd stolen from her, they hadn't taken her soul, and she was determined to escape from this place, to get as far away as possible before they did.

The thick black bracelet around her ankle was removed when she was in the cellar. But now, topside and showered and clean, they'd snapped it back into place. Every step she took, everywhere she went, security was watching. She wouldn't make it ten feet from the front door without an alarm sounding somewhere in the mansion.

Stone walls surrounded the grounds she could never climb. There was no leaving this modern prison—or so they thought. She had an idea of how to do it, and if it didn't work, they'd kill her, so either way, she escaped them.

That was good enough for her. Alive or dead, she couldn't continue this way.

The men stared at their phones while they all waited for the doctor to arrive, with one of them playing solitaire.

Maria crossed her legs and placed her uninjured hand on her stomach. Pain was not something she'd gotten used to. How could someone get used to that? Her queasy stomach anticipated the doctor's visit, while at the same time, she knew it was for the better.

A buzzer rang throughout the front foyer.

"The doctor's here." One of the men got to his feet. "He's at the gate."

She was sure his name was Vincenzo. Everyone called him Vinny. Names were challenging here because several dozen men roamed the property at any given time.

The other men slipped their phones away and got to their feet to stand behind her. Maria rested her broken hand on the table to her right and waited, a slight tremor in her body at the thought of what was to come.

The question of how someone could be so cruel to another human being had long gone unanswered. Five years of indentured servitude on this Italian estate left her with thousands of unanswered questions, pain, and sorrow.

The front door opened, and the man who'd pulled her from the cellar—Alberto Baglioni, Alonzo's brother—stepped inside.

He stared across the expanse at her, then nodded once. "Good. You're presentable." He released the door and moved gracefully across the open space toward her. "The doctor is pulling up out front. Don't speak to him. Don't answer any of his questions. Don't signal him. Do nothing of this nature, and the doctor will walk away a free man. Jeopardize your position here, and the doctor won't leave the building. His burned-out husk of a car will be found tomorrow, one hundred miles from here." He nodded at her hand. "And your hand will still be broken." With a quick movement, he leaned forward and stared into her eyes. "Understood?"

Maria nodded, then averted her gaze to stare at the wall, knowing the man didn't want to hear her voice.

Alberto stood back to his full height, then moved to the side as

Alonzo, the torturer, stepped in through the open doors.

"There you are." Alonzo spoke in his signature eerie voice, sending a further chill through her core. "Still alive, I see." The man's face was a mask of distaste. Lips quirked up at the side, exposing yellowed teeth, brows scrunched, causing rippled skin on his forehead, eyes slitted above pockmarked cheeks, and a jutting chin. Alberto's brother is the son of the owner of this family-run business. The man who did whatever he wanted whenever he wanted without recompense.

"Watching Samantha die was your last warning, whore cunt." He spun around to look outside at the sound of a car door closing. When he swung his head back to glare at Maria, an evil grin pressed his lips back against his teeth. "Please, please," he whispered. "Signal the doctor. Do something so I can rip your beating heart out in front of the man, disembowel you, then send your body parts to feed our pigs." He spat on the floor, his eyes never leaving her. "I ache to watch your last breath, my darling. Please grant me this wish. One signal, one word. That's all I ask."

Then Alonzo stormed across the sitting room, ripped open another door, and disappeared inside, slamming the door behind him.

Maria gasped in a breath, having not realized she was holding it. When sitting under the glare of a predator, remain still, without breathing, and hope they move on to other prey.

A man in a suit with a black bag stepped into view at the open front doors.

"Is this the young lady I'm to see?"

He wasn't their usual doctor. Maybe something happened to him. Could it be why Samantha was dead? Did she signal their regular doctor, and now they're both dead? Was that violent rape just Alonzo's way of defiling her before he killed her?

Of course, slitting her throat in front of Maria and leaving her body in the cellar to rot alongside her in the cage was a message. There'd been enough *messages* over the years that Maria understood how these savages worked.

Alberto stepped forward and gestured at Maria. "One of our maids has hurt her hand. Please, come tend to her."

The doctor wiped a bead of sweat from his forehead as he approached. The temperature outside told Maria it was February or perhaps early March in Italy, so why would the doctor be sweating so much? Nerves?

The surprise on the doctor's face was evident as he drew closer to her hand and was able to see the injuries close up.

"But, sir, those fingers are gnarled in a way that'll likely take more than a splint. How long ago did this happen, ma'am?"

"She doesn't talk," Alberto said. "It happened yesterday."

"Well, uhm." The doctor wiped more sweat from his forehead. "We'll have to rebreak them to set everything correctly. The bones have already fused in the wrong position."

Maria swooned, feeling sick to her stomach at the doctor's words. This was definitely another lesson from Alonzo. Any bone he broke was never tended to for at least twenty-four hours. Everyone had to have their bones reset to correct them. That's one of the reasons for her limp. However, hearing it from the doctor still filled her stomach with a toxic soup, nonetheless.

"Then rebreak them." Alberto frowned. "What's the issue?"

The doctor gazed upon Alberto's face with a strange sort of scrutiny. "I can't do that here. I must take her to the hospital where it can be done under local anesthetic, and we can—"

"She's not leaving this house, and neither are you until her fingers are reset." Alberto nodded at his gorillas standing behind her. They stepped closer, each man producing a weapon.

"Yes, of course, sir." The doctor set his bag down, then plopped into the seat opposite her and leaned closer to examine her fingers with more care.

Maria followed a bead of sweat as it trickled down his forehead, stopped at the bridge of his nose, then disappeared as the doctor swiped it from his brow.

"Ma'am, I will give you a needle for the pain, but it won't be strong enough to eradicate all the pain—"

"You'll give her no such needle." Alberto crossed his arms. "And you will refrain from speaking to her. That is the second time I've warned you. There won't be a third." Alberto touched the doctor's shoulder, then pulled him away from Maria until the man leaned back in his chair, staring up at Alberto with a face reddened in fear. "Are you aware of how many doctors occupy Italy?"

The doctor shook his head.

"Well." Alberto released the man's shoulder. "I don't either, but I can assure you there are hundreds, if not thousands. But we chose you. So, if you cannot do what we have asked of you, please tell me, and you can leave."

The *and you can leave* part was code for you'll become feces once the pigs' digestive systems have dealt with your body parts. Maria hoped for his sake that he just got on with the task.

"This woman is under house arrest. See the GPS tracker." Alberto pointed at Maria's ankle, and the doctor nodded vigorously. "Her fingers are broken. Please set them, wrap them, and leave. You will be paid handsomely for your discretion." Alberto leaned close to the doctor. "You respect confidentiality, don't you, Doctor?"

Most people would crack something in their necks if they nodded as fast as the doctor did.

"Good. Now, no painkillers, no nothing. Just fix the bitch's fingers, wrap them, and leave. Are we clear?"

The doctor opened his bag like he was in a hurry, withdrawing several items.

Maria looked away and focused on a painting on the far wall. A ship cresting a wave, sailing on the sea somewhere. When this was all over, perhaps she could sail back to America, where she was stolen from.

Or perhaps Alonzo would get his wish, and she would die here.

Tonight was her last night in this wretched compound. Her heart would be beating when she left, or it would be still, but either way, this was the last thing they took from her.

Eyes on the ship across the room, the doctor touched her hand.

He whispered something she paid no attention to as one solitary tear slipped from her eye.

In the second before the doctor snapped her index finger straight and white-hot pain consumed her, she saw her husband on that ship in the framed picture.

He was waving at her.

*I'm coming home, my love. Please wait for me.*

Then she passed out.

# Chapter 4

PARKMAN FINISHED BREAKFAST, CLEANED his dishes, put them away, and then checked his phone for the tenth time.

Nothing from Sarah.

He'd texted and called her, and she hadn't returned his calls, nor had she seen his texts.

It was now nine in the morning. Something had to be done, but what?

Calling the police was too early. Besides, it was Sarah Roberts, and she had Vivian to take care of her.

She probably got to the hotel in Parry Sound and forgot to charge her phone. There had to be an explanation, some reason for her not seeing his texts.

Knowing that, and equally knowing she was likely safe, he still wanted to call Aaron to see if he'd heard from her.

He walked out to the balcony, took a seat, and then dialed Aaron.

"Hey, Parkman." Aaron sounded cheerful.

"You at the office or the dojo?"

"Neither. Willow and I are heading to see a movie. Sarah left Willow with me for the weekend, so I took the time off. What's up?"

"Have you heard from Sarah?"

"Why?" His tone changed from cheery to bothered. "Should I have?"

"It's a simple yes or no question, my man."

There was a pause on the other end. Parkman thought he heard Aaron stop walking. Then a muffled, "Wait here a moment," he said to

Willow. "Look, Parkman. It's not a good time for us at the moment. And by *us*, I mean Sarah and me."

"I'm aware of that. The papers arrived on Sarah's doorstep on Thursday. But none of that changes she's Willow's mom, and she still loves you."

"You picking sides?"

Parkman inhaled deeply to refrain from snapping at Aaron in anger. "No one is taking sides. Alex, me, Daniel, Darwin—none of us. We all love you both like a brother and a sister. This is about you two, and that's it."

"So, if you're looking for Sarah, what makes you think she'd call me?"

Parkman stared up at the sky and the darkened clouds that threatened more snow. "Because I can't reach her, and she was heading out of town yesterday."

"Out of town?" Aaron laughed, then stopped. "See? She didn't tell me a thing about leaving town."

"Look, I guess I was just thinking she might have turned around yesterday and come back, and if she had, she would've contacted you. But since she didn't, I have to assume—"

"Turned around?" Aaron asked. "The storm that dropped a couple of feet of snow was north of us. Are you saying she drove through that?"

"She was heading to Parry Sound."

"What?" Now Aaron's voice rose an octave. "What the hell for?"

"An easy task. Something about talking to people about their missing son. The parents might want to hire her to help find him."

"Did you call the parents to see if she arrived?"

Parkman rubbed his temple. "I don't have their contact info."

"So you don't know who they are, right?"

He sighed. "No, I don't."

"Isn't that reckless of Sarah?"

"Aaron, you know as well as I do that after we lost Benjamin, everything changed. You changed. Now Sarah takes only easy tasks and keeps to herself. Where's the danger in talking to a couple of grieving parents in Parry Sound?"

"The danger? Well, if something happened to Sarah, then I have a sneaking suspicion she found that danger wherever it was."

Neither man spoke for a moment. Then Parkman cleared his throat and leaned forward to place his elbows on the balcony railing as the cold air made him shiver.

"I'll call around and see if anyone else has heard from her."

"Look, Parkman. I'm not an asshole. Separation isn't easy. Feelings harden. And when I hear she's still doing the shit that broke us up, it's like I'm being hurt all over again, and I don't do well with pain. I lost my sister many years ago, and because of my temper and fortitude, a lot of people died, not to mention I got shot and almost died myself. In martial arts, there's a move, and then there's a counter move—there's *always* a counter move. There is no counter move with loss, so it's tough for me to manage."

Parkman was nodding as if Aaron could see him. "Okay, that makes sense. I get it."

"As much as I love Sarah and will always love her, I can't hear about her exploits without being upset. There's nothing I want more than the safety of my daughter's mother, but she puts herself out there, and I can't protect her. I can't save her. But the worst thing of all is I'm not a fixer."

"Sarah doesn't need fixing. Maybe that's where the disconnect is."

"I don't mean her. I mean, fixing things when shit goes down. What if she's missing, like that time when she disappeared from the hospital after a bullet to the head? And when we caught up to her, she thought, wait, was *convinced* you shot her. She almost killed you that day in Santa Rosa. I couldn't fix that, and I can't fix this. I can fight, though. That's one thing I know. I've lost fights, and I've won fights, but fighting isn't something that scares me."

"Then fight for Sarah." Those four words caused Aaron to make a hitching sound on the other end of the line.

"I've tried, trust me, I've tried."

In the background, Parkman heard Willow asking if her dad was okay.

"I have to make some calls." Parkman sat up straighter, then pushed up to his feet, spun on his heels, and stepped back inside the apartment. "I'll get back to you in a couple of hours."

"You do that." Aaron's voice was softer, gentler. "Let me know what you find out." Emotion laced each word.

He still loved her, probably as much as he always had.

Maybe he was just stubborn, and their relationship was heading down the wrong path because he wouldn't back down and just love Sarah for who she was instead of trying to get her to be something she wasn't.

There was plenty of time to examine their relationship when he found Sarah, though. So, for now, he plopped onto his couch and dialed Alex.

"Hey," Alex said upon answering.

"You heard from Sarah?"

"No."

See, that's all he needed. A straight-up fucking answer.

"Me neither. She went north yesterday in that storm. Now she's not picking up her phone."

"Then we need to go look for her."

*Oh, Alex, I love you.* "I'm thinking the same thing, but let me make a few more calls first."

"I'll come to your place. Make your calls. If you can't find her or don't hear anything good before I arrive, we leave right away."

"That works. I'll start making my calls now—" There was a click. Alex had hung up. "You little fucker. Always straight to business. Always willing to do whatever it takes to get the job done. Not a wasted word, and no issue with the work involved." Parkman shook his head. "Maybe Sarah should've gotten with you, my friend. How different would things be then?"

Parkman dialed Daniel's number with the idea that he'd reach out to Darwin last.

Darwin could track Sarah's phone. Perhaps even give him a last-known location.

When Daniel didn't pick up, he checked to see if Sarah had read his messages yet.

She hadn't.

He redialed her number, and it went right to voicemail.

Then he called Darwin.

It was time to find Sarah.

# Chapter 5

SARAH FELT THE UNBEARABLE cold in her bones. The pain seemed to be everywhere and racked her body, causing her to shiver on top of the shuddering the cold was causing. Was this what going into shock felt like? How bad could her injuries be?

Sarah moaned as she tried to move when the pain in her chest amplified.

Eyes open, she blinked in the darkness and only saw the soft illumination of white everywhere. The car's interior was dark, but a whiteness surrounded the area, softly illuminating the night.

Something had woken her up, something like thunder. When it came again, she understood it was a snowplow on the road.

How far from the road did she go? Had the snow stopped?

Was that why it was dark inside the car? Because it was encased in snow?

Without moving her chest or arms, she swiveled her head to look around and caught a tiny glimpse of light coming from the rear.

If that was the sun, then she'd been out here all night, and that couldn't be good. Would they start looking for her? Would they even know she was missing?

She closed her eyes and focused on her breathing to calm the tremors. A pervasive smell of coffee filled her nostrils. Of course, the coffee she didn't drink would've spilled all over the interior.

A soft breeze ruffled her hair gently. She opened her eyes and detected more light. The sun was rising. Everything was now cast in an eerie brightness. As soon as a minimal amount of light came to the area, the fresh snow made everything even brighter.

She lowered her gaze to take in her surroundings. The windshield was intact but broken in multiple places. A small smear of blood colored the glass in front of her.

"When I hit my head," she muttered to herself.

She moved her arms, which only caused pain in her chest. Maybe that was because she was draped over the steering wheel.

The airbag.

It shoved into her lower abdomen when it exploded. The damage to her bottom ribs made sense now.

Okay, broken ribs and a bump on the head aren't too bad. She could walk away from that. But then why couldn't she move?

She touched her forehead gingerly with her left hand but couldn't feel the contact with her fingers. When she brought her hand away from her forehead, her fingers were a bright red and difficult to bend. She checked her right hand. It was in the same state.

That sound of thunder came rolling closer—the snow plows. She tried to determine how far away they were by their sound alone. Sarah frowned at the distance. That didn't make sense. Could she have dropped fifty feet? One hundred feet?

Was she visible from the road?

Her jacket. It was in the back seat.

Without thinking, she tried to turn around, winced at the pain, and groaned. After a minute, when it grew tolerable again, she eased her right hand between the seats in search of the jacket. Since she had no sense of feeling in her numb fingers, she had to turn her face as far as possible to see where it might have gotten to.

Luckily, her jacket had fallen to the floor right behind her seat.

But now the challenge was to pick it up with fingers so numb they weren't responding well to grip it, and any tightening of the hand caused pain.

She pushed the jacket against the back of the seat and wrapped it around her arm, then slowly raised her arm, bringing the jacket with it.

When she angled her arm back through the seats, more than half of the jacket came with it before falling off and landing on the center console.

Gently, she brought her arm back to its regular position and breathed through the pain. Then, when she could no longer stand the cold, she used her elbow to drag the jacket onto her lap. Within one minute of painful maneuvers, her jacket was now covering her abdomen, forearms, and hands.

This had to make a difference for her hands. Otherwise, frostbite would set in, and that wouldn't make sense, because if this was supposed to happen, why would Vivian send her north? Couldn't her sister see what was coming and tell her about it? Have her bring thick gloves?

She glanced down at her covered hands. To get out of this predicament, she needed her hands; that much was for sure.

There was even more light now, certainly enough to see what had her stuck in her seat. Whatever the car hit that stopped it—presumably a tree, but she couldn't see through the snow-covered, broken windshield —she shot forward and hit the airbag with her chest, her head to the windshield, and her knees smacked the underside of the dash. Her left knee was so swollen that it was stretching her jeans to the limit. When they arrive and extract her from the car, they'll have to cut off her pants. There'd be no sliding these bad boys off her.

That line went through her head. *When they arrive and extract her*

...

Why hadn't they come yet? Where could *they* be?

If the sun was up again and as bright as it was, it had to be the morning of the next day. Even though she exited the highway in an unusual spot, wouldn't anyone be looking for her by now if she were missing overnight?

Slowly, to avoid inflaming her ribs, she turned to look outside the passenger windows. They were the only view to the outside as every other window was covered in thick snow, including the broken-out back window. Through the rearview mirror, she only saw snow piled high inside the back of the car where it had settled on the headrests of the back seats. It must've drifted up with the wind because the pile was so high inside the shattered glass that she couldn't see outside.

The broken passenger windows offered little hope. To the left were trees with an open space on the right. She needed to get out of the car, and if she couldn't walk, at least she could crawl through the snow toward the road. Whether it took an hour or five hours, she had to do it because even if they were looking for her, how would they find her here, covered in snow?

The rare sound of a car going by above could easily be heard in the stillness of the forest around her. She tried to determine how far the road was again, but couldn't by the sound alone.

Her phone. Maybe if she got to her phone, she could call for help.

It wasn't on the seat next to her. She leaned forward, scrunched up her face at the pain, then tried to go as far as she could to see the floorboards.

No phone.

She would swear it had been beside her when she was driving. Then she was airborne, came down hard, and stopped suddenly. Maybe the phone lifted into the air and dropped in the back somehow.

The tips of her fingers touched together, but she felt nothing under the jacket. They hadn't warmed to any degree yet, and any sort of feeling hadn't returned.

A knot of worry worked through her gut.

Stuck in the car with her knee jammed into the dash, the seat shoved forward, her hands frozen, and heading toward frostbite wasn't ideal. If something didn't happen soon, this could be the end. There would be no coming back from this.

The shivers hadn't abated, but they increased slightly with that thought.

She had to get out, and now was better than later.

The sound of a car raced by overhead. Distant, but there. Even if it were fifty or a hundred feet, she would make it. She had to.

Or, maybe in the act of crawling from the car, she'd locate her phone and call for help.

Sarah let her jacket slip away from her abdomen, moving it onto the seat beside her. Her fingers and hands were bright red. She brought her fingertips up close to examine them and saw no blackness, which was good—no frostbite setting in yet.

She tried to bend them but only got a slight movement out of her hand—a move that sent a wave of pain through her arm.

*This isn't good, Vivian.*

It wasn't easy, but she was able to get her fingers inside the door handle latch. Then she pulled, and the door popped open an inch. In the silence, it was louder than she expected. That was as far as the door would go, though. Something, likely a tree, blocked it on the other side.

"Shit," she muttered to herself.

She faced the passenger side and saw nothing had obstructed that exit except perhaps some snow.

But how would she climb through the broken window with her ribs aching, her hands frozen, and her left knee swollen to twice its size?

Without thinking more about the subject, knowing she had no choice, she placed her hands on the seat on either side of her, then pushed downward and tried to slide her butt toward the passenger side, keeping her eyes on her lower legs.

The pain turned to agony in that second, and she breathed through it, small gusts of visible air bursting from her mouth in the cold. It seemed like an all-over pain. Her leg screamed, her ribs hurt, and the breathing wasn't helping, and pain shot up from her freezing hands. Even her ankles protested at the movement.

She wanted to scream, wail at her sister, and curl up and cry all at the same time. How could this happen? *Why* did this have to happen?

Light-headedness overcame her. She tried to calm the rapid breathing.

If her left leg was stuck under the steering column, how was she supposed to get out? Waiting wasn't an option. She'd already been sitting out here for twelve hours or more. Spending another night was certain death. So she had to edge along the seat and climb out the window regardless of the pain. It was one or the other—pain or death.

When she looked down at the steering wheel, blood was in the center where her body touched it.

Remembering that she'd smacked her head on the windshield, she gingerly tapped her forehead with her left wrist, and it came away with dried blood.

She moved slowly to look at herself in the mirror.

Blood covered her face, reminding her of the posters for that Stephen King movie, *Carrie*.

"Well, don't you look pretty," she whispered to herself. "Okay, up and at 'em. This is the only way you live."

She leaned sideways as far as she could go without twisting her leg, then slumped down onto her right shoulder, her teeth mashed together to manage the pain. With her left hand, she clutched the edge of the door where there wasn't any broken glass and pulled.

Her body slid an inch, her left leg easing out from under the dash.

*Why did the seat have to be so close to the dashboard?*

When she pulled again, her ribs causing her massive discomfort, she felt her consciousness waver.

"No. Do not faint. Do not faint."

She rested for a moment, considering her next move, breathing through the moment of lightheadedness.

To live, she had to fight through the pain, make it to the outside of the car, and get to the road.

Simple.

Once that's done, someone will pick her up, place her in a warm vehicle, and take her to the hospital.

Warm vehicle.

That sounded so good.

With one last glance down the length of her body, she positioned her leg carefully so it would come up to rest on the driver's seat, then made sure her hand was firmly on the door—and pulled hard.

Her ribs screamed at the exact moment her wounded left knee bumped the bottom of the steering wheel.

Sarah's shout of pain was cut off when she lost consciousness.

# Chapter 6

PARKMAN HAD CALLED EVERYBODY.

No one had seen Sarah.

A friend in the Toronto Police Services had even called the RCMP in Parry Sound, but they had heard and seen nothing come in on Sarah Roberts.

His last call was to Darwin. He sat at his kitchen table and tapped a finger on the coffee mug in front of him, waiting for Darwin to pick up.

"Parkman?" Darwin's voice came through without static from his home in Italy. "How's everything?"

"Well, not so good."

"Talk to me. What's up?"

"We can't find Sarah."

Before Darwin responded, Parkman detected the sound of keys on a keyboard. "Fill me in on everything while I do a scan on her cell number."

Parkman told him about Sarah's trip to Parry Sound, his warning about the weather, and how she had gone silent since yesterday afternoon.

"No one has gotten a message or a call from her, and when I call her phone, it goes directly to voicemail." He lifted his mug, tested the coffee—it was cold now—and drank it anyway.

"I should have a hit on her cell in a minute." Darwin cleared his throat. "We shouldn't worry too much, though, or jump to conclusions. She's got Vivian."

"True, but things happen. Sarah's still human, and Vivian can't protect her from everything, I imagine."

"One second," Darwin said as if speaking to himself. "Got her!"

"Where?"

"The last time her cell bounced off a tower was yesterday, around five in the afternoon local time."

"Okay, that's not good. Where has she been since?"

"It's showing me she was on Highway 400 heading north."

"Yeah, to Parry Sound. How far did she get?"

"Last known signal pings her a little north of something called Crooked Bay."

"What's a little north? By how much?"

"Two, maybe three kilometers."

"How's cell coverage up that way? Is that something you can check?"

"Sure, give me a moment."

Parkman got up from his seat and moved to the couch, where he dropped in front of his laptop. Once it was booted up, he opened the Maps application and found Crooked Bay on Highway 400.

"Cell coverage appears to be spotty up that way," Darwin said.

"Meaning she could be anywhere north of Crooked Bay?"

"Yeah, up to about twenty kilometers, I'd say."

Parkman scrolled along the highway on his laptop. "That's a lot of area to cover."

"Sometimes it depends on the cell carrier someone's using. If they're piggybacking another carrier, coverage can be different. While some carriers will have at least one bar through that area."

Parkman dropped the little man onto the highway on his screen and scrolled north. "Could she have turned her cell phone off?"

"Sure, but why? In the middle of a snowstorm? If she did, why hasn't she turned it back on this morning?"

"True." Parkman kept scrolling.

"What are you doing?"

"Scanning the highway on Google Maps. Just wanted to get familiar with the area before heading up there."

"There are reports that they closed the highway last night, but it reopened at six this morning once the plows had a chance to clear the road."

"Time's a-wasting. I'll grab Alex and head north. We should be passing through the Crooked Bay area in just over two hours. I'll keep you posted on what we find."

"I'll be available night and day. I'm six hours ahead over here, but don't let that stop you from calling. In the meantime, I'll check hospitals north and south and see what I can find."

"Thanks, man. Call me with anything. Ciao."

Parkman ended the call, then dialed Alex.

"Yeah?"

There was an engine sound in the background—Alex was already in a car. "Alex, how fast can you be ready to head north?"

"Darwin had nothing?"

"I'll explain on the way. When can you be ready?"

"Less than five minutes."

"Okay, I'll come get you."

"No."

Parkman looked up and stared at nothing. "What do you mean, 'no'?"

"In less than five minutes, I'll be at your place. I'm in a taxi. When you called an hour ago, I got ready, canceled my classes at the dojo, and grabbed a taxi. When will you be ready?"

"Heading to my car now. Meet me outside."

The line died.

"Fuckin' Alex. Always the first to volunteer. Always the first to dive into a fight. And always the first to help Sarah."

He shook his head as he grabbed his car charger and ran for the door, leaving his cold coffee behind.

Maybe Sarah should've fallen for Alex.

Things would have been a lot easier for everyone.

# Chapter 7

THANKFULLY, THE ROOM WAS dark when Maria Christy woke with a headache. Opening her eyes otherwise would've been harder.

She was back in her usual bedroom, disrobed, and deposited in her bed, the covers up to her neck. Pain radiated from her broken hand. Did the doctor set everything? Was it over?

With her tongue, she gently tapped the thin wire of the barrette, still shoved snugly at the top of her gums against her inner cheek. How it didn't fall and slip out of her mouth when she was passed out and brought to her room, she didn't know.

She eased back the covers and swung her feet over the edge of the mattress slowly. They touched the hardwood floor as she righted herself while carefully holding her broken hand up so it didn't snag on the thin sheet they gave her for warmth.

The pain in her hand remained a constant throbbing, like a diseased tooth. Barely tolerable but certainly manageable to escape this place.

Feeling woozy for a moment, she pushed up to her feet, then crossed the room to the light switch.

When the brightness hit her, she had to scrunch her eyes closed. A moan escaped her lips when her headache flared.

A couple of painkillers would go a long way at the moment.

The closet held her work clothes—she didn't have any other clothes. It was work clothes during her hours of labor or naked in her room.

Alonzo owned them, body and soul. They were like property, something you'd own, to do with whatever you wanted. And the one thing he didn't want was sex. He only wanted to hurt people, torture them.

The rest of the men could take the slaves for sex anytime they wanted. She'd been handed around to the men hundreds of times, and if her work suffered for it, she was the one who got in trouble.

But Alonzo had gone too far with Samantha, so he slit her throat to watch her bleed. For Alonzo, owning a woman as a slave meant owning her sex, too. A woman named Jasmine arrived and was raped by every man on the property in her first week at the house several times. She tried to escape, and her throat was slit. Samantha was her replacement.

With the light on and her eyes adjusting now, she examined her hand.

The doctor had wrapped large white gauze around each finger. There were no metal holders, nothing to lock the bones in place, just gauze. Although, he'd used so much that she couldn't bend her fingers even if she wanted to. Maybe that was the point. Now the bones would fuse in place, and then she could start her physical therapy in four to six weeks.

Yeah, right. PT would consist of a trowel in the garden or a spade in the field. She saw the doctor once. That's all she was going to get.

None of that mattered anyway. Being caught in the act of escaping meant certain death. So, unless she were successful in getting away from these madmen tonight, she wouldn't live long enough to have to endure PT.

Without the use of her right hand, getting dressed was a challenge. Her pants had to be cinched, so for that, she placed one end of the string in her teeth and used her left hand to tie it.

The shirt slipped over her shoulders without too much issue. Worn-out shoes on her feet, sweater with moth-eaten holes over her shoulders, Maria moved to the door and allowed the barrette to slip from her mouth and into her hand.

The wooden door was thick, but the lock was old. Even though she'd never picked a lock before, no one was around to see her try.

With the tip of the barrette inside the keyway, she twisted it left and right, then held it rigid and turned it.

All she managed to do was make tiny metallic clicking sounds.

The lock didn't pop out of place. The door remained firmly immovable.

The odds were never high, but she had to try it.

Frustrated, she turned and stared at the small window. That wouldn't work because they placed all their slaves on the third floor. High enough that if they made noise, any guests on the first floor wouldn't hear it, and if they broke the glass in the window, they'd surely break a bone hitting the ground.

Jumping from the third floor would not be good for her ankles, knees, or legs, and she needed them all intact to run.

A key slipped into the door behind her.

Maria jumped at the sound and hopped out of the way.

The lock snicked loudly, and the door swung open.

Alberto stepped inside. Maria was so close to him that they now stood shoulder to shoulder.

"What are you doing?" he asked. "I saw the light on from the outside. You should be resting."

Her stomach spilled acid into her bowels, threatening to loosen them.

"I have missed my work." She glimpsed her hand. "I must do the dishes. Perhaps sweep a hallway. Something to please Mr. Alonzo."

Alberto shook his head. "He would be pleased to know you are healing and back to full capacity in a week." He nodded toward the bed. "Rest, then come for breakfast in a few hours. We'll find something for you to do to make you feel useful then—something one-handed."

Maria shook her head, letting the barrette stick out between her fingers where she hid it behind her thigh. "Please, let me do something now."

She moved toward the hallway and was almost through the open doorway when Alberto grabbed her hair, yanking her back into the room.

But not before she shoved the tip of the barrette into the tongue on the door, depressing it inward, then snapping the barrette off, leaving the tip in the door.

When the small hairpiece made a noticeable sound when it broke, she yelped in pain at the hair pull.

Alberto brought her face up to his. "Since when do you disobey an order, *chattel*?"

She'd never gotten used to that name. Alberto enjoyed calling them cows and chattel. Maybe that helped his conscience reconcile what they were doing on the grounds of this Italian mansion.

His breath caressed her cheek as he sneered down at her. "Answer me."

"I'm, I'm sorry. I only want to work."

"Then work at resting." He placed a hand on her right breast, squeezed it, then shoved her toward the bed. "Or I'll open those legs of yours and fuck you into tomorrow when Alonzo will slit your throat. Do not disobey me again."

She hit the side of the bed, curled inward to protect her broken hand, then dropped to her knees, a fake sob escaping her.

These sorts of men loved to think they were brutes and weakened the damsel in distress, so she put on the appropriate show as needed to survive the moment.

Out of the corner of her eye, she watched him adjust his pants at the crotch area, flick off the room's light, then exit her room.

He closed the door quietly, likely to avoid making noise on the slaves' floor at this hour, then walked away, the sound of his feet fading on the floor outside her room.

Back in darkness, she breathed rapidly, nervous and excited at the same time. Did it work? Did the hairpiece jam the tongue back so she could open the door?

If so, would she actually attempt to walk out of the mansion that had a dozen soldiers roaming the property all night?

And even if she did, could she successfully remove the GPS monitor around her ankle?

Questions for another time.

It was three or four in the morning. The majority of the house would be asleep.

If she were ever to make a break for it, this was the time.

She pushed up off the bed and strode to the door barefoot and silent.

Her left hand clasped the knob. She inhaled twice in anticipation, then pulled.

Nothing happened. It didn't move.

She pulled again.

Nothing.

Then she bent at the waist and yanked on the door.

It popped open, and dim light from the hallway spilled into the room. The tongue was still depressed, with only a millimeter sticking out. Just enough to catch and hold the door closed.

This was it—her only chance.

If they caught her, she'd be raped for hours, then killed.

But if she stayed, she'd be chattel for another five years or longer.

Either way, she was dead. The only chance to live was to get out of there.

Alive or dead, she would be free when she exited her room.

The first hint of a smile formed on her face.

Freedom.

Maria Christy exited her room, her head held high, and strode down the hallway of the third floor of her cage-house en route to the large kitchen.

# Chapter 8

THEY DIDN'T STOP UNTIL they got to a coffee shop near Barrie, about an hour north of Toronto. The roads were plowed but still snow-covered in some areas.

"I'm going to need a coffee." Parkman eased the car onto the exit ramp and slowed at the lights. He glanced over at Alex. "You're quiet. Everything cool?"

Alex nodded.

"Well, if you're worried about Sarah, I can tell you she'll be fine."

Alex gave him a sidelong look, then turned away to stare out the window. He'd had a long road back to recovery after a fight in a hotel room ended with him in the hospital. Sure, his body was wounded, but his ego had taken a solid hit. Thinking himself somewhat invincible for a decade caught up to him, knocking his confidence off a few notches.

Now, with the possibility that Sarah could need their help, Parkman figured Alex was eager to jump into the fray to prove himself, which could be dangerous.

He tried to discuss things with Alex several times, but he'd clam up. It wasn't exactly the silent treatment. It was Alex stating—without saying a word—that he didn't want to talk about it.

Parkman eased into the drive-thru at a coffee shop and turned to Alex. "You want something?"

"Large coffee. Three sugars, no milk."

Parkman jerked his head sideways. "You take sugar?"

Alex nodded once. "We'll be searching for hours. Need the boost."

"Hours? You think?" He eased forward as the line moved. When

Alex didn't respond, Parkman added. "Three sugars it is."

Fifteen minutes later, they were back on the road and drove in silence until they got to the Crooked Bay area on Highway 400. Parkman eased to the shoulder and put on his four-way hazards.

"Darwin said Sarah's phone was last spotted about two to three kilometers north of this area."

Alex adjusted his pant legs and sat higher in his seat.

"I'll drive along the shoulder with my hazards on. You keep an eye on the right."

Alex was already staring at the ridge of snow the plows had created running the length of the highway on his side.

"With no cloud cover today, it's bright. Let's hope it's bright enough to spot her car if she slid off the road. Otherwise, we'll end up in Parry Sound without a clue of what happened to her."

"A grim prospect," Alex whispered.

"Indeed."

Parkman sipped his lukewarm coffee and got the car rolling forward. The sides of the highway looked the same for several kilometers. Just a wall of snow piled high on either side, evidence of heavy snowfall with plows working all night, and new bright white snow deeper toward the trees on both sides. Where the area dipped into a ditch on the right, Alex leaned higher, using the door's armrest to get the view he needed.

"Anything?" Parkman asked.

They'd gone five kilometers past Crooked Bay.

"Nothing yet."

They continued north as the midday sun headed toward the west, where it would dip below the horizon in two hours. They were running out of time and sunlight. Worried that Sarah might be out there alone somewhere, he grabbed his cell phone and dialed Steve's number.

"Steve here."

"Hey, it's Parkman."

"You find your girl?"

"We're up on the 400 and haven't seen a thing. Look, I think we file this as a missing persons."

Alex spun around to look at him, then turned back to search the side of the road.

"When did you last speak with her?"

"Twenty-four hours ago. About this time yesterday. Her phone was last pinged in this area yesterday late afternoon. Nothing since."

"Okay. I'll write it up and file it. I'll see who can come from the local RCMP detachments for a search. You think you could stay up there and help set up a search party?"

"Of course. We'll do whatever is needed."

"Have everyone meet in Crooked Bay tomorrow morning—"

"Wait. What? Tomorrow?"

"Yeah, Parkman. No one will want to walk the ditches and shoulders of that highway tonight in the dark. It's supposed to drop to minus fifteen overnight."

"That's exactly why we need to search tonight. If she's out there somewhere, she'll freeze to death at that temperature."

"Parkman. Listen to me. I'll file the missing persons report. I'll make calls. I'll do everything I can, but I can't currently assure you that anyone will be searching tonight. If you want to be out there in the middle of the night, be my guest. Have at 'er. Until then, we'll see you in Crooked Bay in the morning. Six sharp."

The line died.

"Shit."

"When are they coming?" Alex asked without looking at him.

"Six a.m. tomorrow morning."

Alex lowered into his seat as Parkman slowed the car to a stop. "Call Aaron."

"Why? This'll just piss him off, and he'll whine that it's all Sarah's fault. If she wasn't listening to Vivian, blah, blah, blah." Parkman stared straight ahead, one hand draped over the wheel. "Not sure I can take that right now."

"Call him. Put him on speaker. He won't whine."

Parkman glanced at Alex and saw the muscles in his jaw flexing. He heard the stern tone Alex's words were delivered in and knew this side of Alex was the one that no one fucked with.

Parkman dialed Aaron's number without another word, then hit the speaker option. The ringing filled the interior of the car.

"Yeah? Parkman? What's going on?"

"Sarah's missing. I called in a missing persons report."

"Fuck."

Alex leaned close to the phone. "Call my class."

"And do what? Tell them you're canceling again?"

"Tell them to get dressed in warm clothes and carpool to Crooked Bay on Highway 400. We're going to search for our missing friend." Alex swallowed. "Aaron." If it was possible to speak a man's name and make it sound like a warning, Alex had accomplished that. "Call. Every. Student."

There was a pause. "Sure. I can do that." Aaron must have detected that warning tone, too, based on his response.

"Then load your car with extra hats, gloves, and a few blankets. Leave Willow with Daniel, and get your ass up here to help search. We will walk the sides of the highway until the sun rises, so bring flashlights. If you don't have enough, buy some on the way here."

"I'll call Daniel to see if he—"

"Aaron. Do this for Sarah." Alex swallowed, then stared out the windshield. "For everything holy in this world, if you don't do exactly as I've asked, I will hospitalize you for a month. This is Sarah we're talking about. This is the mother of your child. This is the one woman who gives selflessly to strangers. The least we can do is give her a chance. Get here. Do it now. Or I'll probably end up killing you. Now *fuck* off and hurry."

Alex's hand jerked up so fast that Parkman barely registered the blur. The call ended with a snap of his thumb. It was such a violent smack that Parkman dropped the phone on the seat and had to shake his hand as his own thumb had gotten twisted backward.

Alex's hands were tightened into fists now as he stared out the passenger window. "I'm sorry. About hitting your phone." He lowered his head. "I love Aaron like a brother. But this tug-of-war between them has to end, and it's all on Aaron to end it. Sometimes a brother can make you want to hurt him." Alex snatched a look at Parkman. "Lately,

Aaron has pushed me to the limit with all his talk about court dates, separation, and who is fit to care for Willow." After two inhales and exhales, Alex seemed to calm down a notch. "This will prove where his heart lies. And if it's in the wrong place, I'll need to move on from him. I refuse to lose Sarah." When he looked at Parkman again, Alex had a tear in his eye. "I will *not* lose Sarah."

At significant risk of personal injury, Parkman placed a hand on Alex's shoulder as a gesture of brotherly love. The problem is that not many people get to touch Alex—he wasn't much of a hugger.

Yet, Alex allowed that hand without recourse.

Parkman squeezed. "I'm with you, brother. I'm with you. Now, let's keep driving north for another hour. If we find nothing, we'll circle back and head to Crooked Bay to meet whoever Aaron sent."

Alex wiped an eye as Parkman eased off the brake, and the car began moving forward.

"I'd hate to kill the man, but Aaron had better be there. That's all I'm saying. He'd better be there."

Parkman took in Alex's rigid posture as the man stared out the passenger window. "He will be. Of all the people who know you, I'm not sure anyone would take what you said moments ago with a grain of salt. If I know Aaron, he'll be there."

Alex jerked his head once—his version of a nod.

Parkman got the car up to thirty kilometers an hour as they coasted north.

About twenty kilometers farther north, almost an hour later, having seen nothing to indicate a car had left the highway, he turned around on a bridge overpass, and they headed south back toward Crooked Bay.

Neither man spoke again.

Worry was too thick for words.

Sarah could handle herself against guns, knives, and bad guys, but the weather was something altogether much more powerful.

The elements kill without compassion or guilt. You're just another animal, a living, breathing chunk of meat out here. A plaything for that often fickle bitch, Mother Nature.

Parkman slammed his hand against the steering wheel as he drove them south.

*Oh, Sarah. Where the fuck are you?*

# Chapter 9

THE SHIVERING WOKE HER up. Why was it so cold?

Sarah opened her eyes and stared at the roof of her car. She was twisted at an odd angle, but before righting herself, she took in her position. Hands held tight together at her chest; body splayed out on the seat, legs draped over the front seat, still under the steering wheel. Then it all came back to her. She had been dragging herself toward the broken window on the passenger side when she hit her knee and passed out.

How long was she out? Minutes? Hours?

She glanced upward to see the sky. It was blue, but the sun was past midday and heading toward evening. So, maybe an hour. Maybe more.

This wasn't good. She needed to get warm, and she needed to do that while there was still sunlight.

But how?

Could it be the bump on her head that kept knocking her out and making her sleepy? Not to say the pain in her leg wasn't helping, but usually, people were only unconscious for seconds, a minute at the maximum. Why did she keep sleeping for so long?

If she went under again, she might not wake up. And then what?

She adjusted herself to get comfortable, and her leg responded by degrees. What was a four out of ten on the pain scale rose to a seven with every movement. Was her knee broken? A ligament torn? How bad was it to swell that much and knock her out every time she moved or bumped it?

Her hands were a deep red, but they weren't showing any signs of turning black yet. That had to be a blessing.

A thought struck her.

What if she simply opened the car door? Why did she have to climb out through the broken window?

She lifted her hand and slipped a finger through the door handle. Even though she couldn't feel her fingers, which were too cold to bend properly, she pulled on the door handle, and it worked.

The passenger door clicked open.

She breathed a sigh, then raised her hands over her head and pushed. The door got about halfway before slowing, likely because snow was bunched up on the other side. If she could slither through like a snake, she'd be out of the car and on her way toward the edge of the road.

*If* she could.

She doubted there'd be any *slithering* in her future.

Her bunched-up jacket lay on the side. With her right hand, she raised it to her chest because when she got outside, she'd have to find a way to get it on or at least wrap her hands in it.

The pain from the cold was slowly becoming unbearable. Combined with the pain from her injured leg, she pegged her odds of crawling away from this as low. But lying there and waiting to freeze to death wasn't an option she would indulge in.

As gingerly as possible, her gaze on her legs, she pushed with her right foot and edged along the seat with her shoulder blades. Inch by inch, she moved toward the door until her head was suspended over open air.

Then she nudged the door handle with her head.

The next step was to turn onto her right side, so her injured left leg wouldn't have anything to do but stay up and out of the way.

Without too much trouble or pain, except where her ribs were concerned, she was able to roll onto her right shoulder. That's where she paused to catch her breath while staring at the glove box.

Cars drove by on the road more frequently than before. They were moving faster than this morning, too, which meant the roads were even cleaner in the afternoon sun.

The snow had been melting to some degree. But overnight, the temperatures would drop again, and she couldn't be out here in that. Even if she didn't use her legs, Sarah estimated it would take her an hour to drag herself up to the highway.

But first, squeezing out the opening the car door afforded without passing out would be a challenge.

Pushing with her right foot, she edged out farther, then arched her back until her head was entirely out of the car.

With one last look at her legs to ensure the left one wouldn't make contact with anything, she pushed again.

Her shoulders exited the car.

She was almost out. A little farther, and gravity could do the rest.

Although she'd drop onto a bed of snow, which would be much colder than lying on the front seat of her car, she'd be out and ready to drag herself away.

The leg was the last step.

Clenching her stomach muscles and fighting the pain in her chest, Sarah curled inward and glanced down the length of her body. Then she raised her legs until they were on the seats, her right thigh resting across the center console.

Cold as she was, a sweat broke out on her forehead.

She breathed in shallow bursts to avoid expanding and contracting her chest, then edged out of the car even farther until her upper body lowered gently into the snow, and her legs followed like the tail of a worm.

Now, her right shoulder blade pushing down on the snow below her, both legs up on the passenger seat, she waited until the wave of pain subsided enough to move again.

She'd done it. The hardest part was over. She was out of the car—mostly.

The last thing to do was get her legs to rest on the snow. Then she could turn onto her stomach and begin to drag herself. Hopefully. At least, that was the plan.

What other option was there? Hop on her right leg in two-foot-deep snow?

She squirmed back and forth in an effort to move away from the car, but all she succeeded in doing was sink deeper into the soft snow.

"Shit. Now what?"

She tried again without any luck. Snow rose around her on the edges. When she turned to look at how deep it was, dried flakes of blood from her face smeared the whiteness around her head.

Using her upper body alone wouldn't work. She needed to push with her right leg and move fast because lying in the snow pierced her with a coldness much worse than lying on the front seat.

Her right leg had taken a hit when she crashed her car, but it wasn't as bad as her left. There'd be bruising, sure, but the swelling wasn't an issue. So she bent her right leg slowly until the knee was nearing her chest, placed her foot against the bottom of the car, and shoved outward, mindful of her left leg's placement.

Luckily, she slid along the top of the snow until she was completely clear of the car.

Now what? Lying on her back and staring at the sky was an accomplishment she yearned for when back in the car. But now that she was out here, every plan that got her to the road involved snow, crawling, dragging, and more snow—and it all had to be done on her stomach.

This meant her left knee would be touching the ground. Which also meant the possibility of passing out again. Unless the snow was so soft and powdery that the knee barely registered the contact.

Sarah lifted her right foot to press against the car door, then shoved it closed so it would be out of the way when she rolled over. It slammed shut harder than she expected, the sound echoing through the trees around her.

Then she rolled to her right side, holding her left leg up, and finally plopped onto her stomach. Her efforts to keep her left leg from falling too fast into the snow were in vain. The contact made was as gentle as touching a large sponge, but it still sent a bolt of pain up her thigh, through her crotch, and into her stomach.

"Stay awake, stay awake, stay awake," she mumbled to herself.

When it started to subside, she brought her jacket up and wrapped it loosely around her neck. Trying to slip it on now while lying on her stomach seemed too much of a task. She needed to crawl, and she needed to do it before she got too cold to function well.

One arm in front of the other, she dug deep and pulled.

Her body followed, but it was slow going. She tried to push with her good leg but only succeeded in shoving snow backward.

What felt like ten minutes got her to the rear of the car.

When she stopped to stare up at the hill she needed to climb, she could barely see where the car made contact after jumping off the edge of the shoulder. It had snowed so much overnight that there was a small impression about fifteen feet behind the vehicle.

Her vehicle was completely white, from the rear bumper to the roof and hood. From above, no one would be able to see that a car was parked down here against a tree. Even if they were looking for her, it would take until the spring melt to see the car.

She lowered her head and waited until she caught her breath and felt ready to continue. The tremors had intensified, and the shivering had spread to become a whole-body experience. To survive this, she had to keep moving, so she found the wherewithal from somewhere deep inside, placed her bent arms in front of her until they sank in the snow, and pushed with her uninjured leg, moving another inch.

"Shit," she said, wincing at the pain. "This'll take a year."

She tried again. And again.

The sun was moving farther west, casting her area in shadows. Thirty minutes, maybe forty-five, and she'd be crawling in the dark *if* she was still crawling.

"Come on," she said, each word a short clip to keep from expanding her ribcage. "You can do this."

Each time her arms moved in front, and she dragged herself forward, the pain in her ribs made her drop back onto the snow.

It was too much.

She wasn't a quitter, but the pain kept her down. Maybe one more night inside the car wouldn't have been too bad.

Closing her eyes, letting the pain win, and stopping—that was a death sentence. She had to fight through it. She had to for Willow.

Gritting her teeth, moaning at all the shitty luck and discomfort, she pushed up again and moved forward. Then again. Then again.

By the time the sunshine had left the area and was only touching the tops of the trees behind her, she'd gone ten feet from the car.

When she assessed the distance she still had to climb, it looked like forty or even fifty feet, not to mention it got steeper closer to the road.

She needed two more hours of daylight and three shots of morphine.

Without those, the task was like climbing a mountain.

Yet she put one numb arm in front of the other and dragged her body upward. Only once did she catch a glimpse of her left hand, and what she saw scared her. The tips of two of her fingers had turned from a dark red to something waxy and pale now. Was this an area where people didn't come back from whole? Was the next stage black? Dead tissue and amputation?

This sort of freezing maimed a body, if the person lived at all.

So she dug her arms in again and again, desperation covering her forehead in sweat, even though it made her shiver relentlessly.

When she glanced over her shoulder, she'd made even more distance. The car rested against the tree at least twenty feet away now.

The issue in front of her was the slope.

She was entering the steepest part of the hill.

So, without hesitation, with thoughts of her daughter pushing her onward, Sarah placed both arms down and rolled them under her. Then she did it again, almost like the oars of a boat, shoving the hull through resistant water.

Gaining three feet quickly, hope surged through her, and she continued the process.

Until something rolled under her arms. A rock or a piece of ice shifted beneath her, and she slid downward. The momentum picked up until her frozen body acted like a snowboard, and she slid to the bottom, her left leg barely missing the bumper of her car as she slid past it.

When she stopped, she was ten feet below her car, farther down the hill.

Every single inch she had gained out here on her stomach was lost.

It was over. At this hour, in that amount of pain, she couldn't continue.

Curling up in the car for another night, as horrible as that sounded, was her only chance.

Afraid to look, she lifted her hands and took in the darkening tips of her fingers.

How could this be happening? Why didn't Vivian warn her?

Parkman had tried to, but she didn't listen.

She rolled onto her back, and that slight movement got her sliding again.

Toward the trees.

"Oh, shit."

To avoid hitting her left leg, she bent it out of the way, then screamed with the pain.

The trunk of a tree came too fast. Thankfully, her right leg took the impact.

But then her body crumpled around it, her left knee bumped it as her ribs screamed, and Sarah lost consciousness one last time with her mouth open wide.

# Chapter 10

SOUNDLESSLY, TIPTOEING THROUGH THE mansion at three in the morning scared the hell out of her. Maria would be reported if only one person saw her, and the penalties could mean death. Only a skeleton crew worked at this hour, though, and most of them were out on the grounds, patrolling the fence and the front gate.

Sometimes they'd take a break in the large kitchen, so she hoped it was empty. She only needed five minutes in the kitchen—alone.

The kitchen was on the second floor of the Palazzo. This design was so that it could easily service the rooms above it, as well as the main dining area that was on the back of the second floor, with a large veranda that overlooked the gardens and the three pools.

This meant she needed to descend one set of stairs. The one that was out in the open. While walking down the steps, she'd be completely exposed to anyone on the second or third floor.

Yet there was no other way.

Maria moved out of the shadows, stepping up to the banister to peek over the edge. Several night lights were on, but many areas lay in shadows.

Voices came to her from somewhere below.

She froze, listening to see whether they were outside, moving closer or farther away. After a moment, the voices faded, and she breathed a soft sigh.

Unsure where the floor would creak even though she'd traversed these stairs hundreds of times, she descended them close to the wall, her back sliding along it, her head on a swivel. Her stomach was doing flips, and each limb shook, but she forced herself to ignore it. Giving in to nerves wasn't the road to freedom. She'd learned years ago that the body had a mind of its own. The central nervous system wasn't wired directly into the brain. There was no amount of rationale she could offer her adrenal glands to get them to regulate her blood pressure and chill out. They were firing on all cylinders, regardless of whether they understood her situation.

Each step got her closer to freedom, each stair increasing her hope by degrees. But she still felt sick and weakened by the acids pumping into her abdomen.

On the balls of her feet, she scurried along the corridor that led to the side of the kitchen, only pausing at the saloon-like door to listen for someone on the other side. Generally, the kitchen staff didn't report for duty until five in the morning, when they'd begin baking bread. Then it was onto preparing breakfast for the thirty staff and the few slaves, which was only one now—her—soon-to-be none.

When she heard nothing emanating from the kitchen, she opened the door and slipped inside.

The digital clock offered a red-digit display over the ovens. It was several minutes past four in the morning.

She needed five minutes, tops. Then she could leave this building for good.

With little illumination from the overhead night lights, Maria opened the drawer with the utensils but didn't find what she was looking for.

*Where could it be?*

She opened the second drawer and saw it. The meat tenderizer hammer had a square head with small dots. Now she just needed the tip of the digital food thermometer. It had a long, silver pin-like tip that she'd use to shove in the button on the GPS monitor wrapped around her ankle.

After checking three drawers and not seeing one, she glanced around the vast kitchen, wiping sweat from her brow. Time wasn't her partner here. The urge to run nearly overwhelmed her, but with the GPS locator on her person, they'd catch her within ten minutes of running.

The options were elementary. One, remove the GPS. Or two, go quietly back to her room and remain a slave until they buried her in the yard—or until the pigs ate her and became part of the humus via pig excrement.

She skirted a steel cutting table, ran by a chopping block, and stopped beside the locked fridge door. There was a large silver table where cooked dishes rested momentarily. Above it was a magnetic strip that held various knives, spatulas, and two long, needle-like food thermometers.

A door banged open behind her somewhere.

A small *yip* escaped her as she ducked below the counter and crawled under a steel table. If it were possible, her breathing doubled in speed as if she'd been running for an hour. Now, if she got caught, it would be because her own body thwarted her.

The kitchen light flickered to life.

*How come they were here this early?*

She ducked her head and closed her eyes, listening for movement. Someone was definitely in the kitchen. A pot clanged, a tray shifted, and then more lights turned on.

It was over.

She was as good as dead.

No valid explanation would excuse a slave from their room. The general staff would rat her out because they'd be killed alongside her if they didn't. She had no allies, no friends, no one to confide in except Samantha. But Sam was dead now, and Maria was as good as dead, too.

That thought seemed to calm her breathing.

She opened her eyes, resolved to the fact that it was over.

Relief washed over her as she crawled out of hiding, stepped onto the kitchen floor, and stood to her full height of five feet, eight inches. All one hundred and ten pounds of Maria Christy remained on the spot, looking at the back of the person who just sentenced her to death.

She thought his name was Reginald or Ricardo, but couldn't be sure, so she went with Ricardo. The kitchen staff weren't people slaves dealt with regularly. Sure, they made them their food, but their minders delivered it. The kitchen staff were relegated to the kitchen.

Meat tenderizer still in hand, Maria started walking toward Ricardo.

There was only one way this could end, and Maria refused to be the one who died.

If she still had a fighting chance, then she would fight.

She raised the tenderizer over her head as she approached the man, a sneer of madness forcing her lips back, her grip tight on the handle.

Then Ricardo swung around to face her, his hands up in a defensive posture.

And she swung.

# Chapter 11

WHEN PARKMAN PULLED OVER at Crooked Bay, Aaron was already there with seven of his students from the dojo. They all carried flashlights—one even had a handheld spotlight—extra gloves and hats were all stored in Aaron's trunk.

Parkman slapped him on the shoulder. "You got Willow situated well?"

Aaron nodded. "Daniel took her. All good." Aaron glanced at Alex, then moved toward him. They whispered a few words to each other, both their faces expressionless, like Medusa had turned them to stone, then Alex moved away and dropped into the passenger seat of Parkman's car.

When Aaron walked back to the group, Parkman leaned close to him. "What was that all about?"

"We're good. That's all that matters." Aaron faced his team of searchers. "Guys, listen up. All we know so far is that Sarah's cell phone pinged a tower about two to three kilometers north of us yesterday afternoon during the snowstorm. No one has heard a thing since, and her cell goes right to voicemail. So, we suspect her car went off the road." He glanced back at Parkman, then faced the students again. "If she did, then she's in a ditch somewhere, likely covered in snow. It's early evening, and I know it's already dark. That's why we brought the flashlights. Guys, listen to me. If she's out there, we have to find her. We can't let her spend another night in this cold. The temperature will be dropping well below freezing overnight, and I can't imagine what that will do to someone wounded or stuck in their vehicle." He gestured at Parkman. "This man will lead us up the highway to where her cell phone was last detected. Then we will walk from there, searching the sides of the highway."

"Walk?" a short man with long hair tied into a bun asked.

"Yes, walk. I know it's cold, so Parkman will be driving one relief vehicle, and I'll be driving the other. We will rotate. Four men are in the vehicles for half an hour while four walk on the shoulder. Then we switch out. There's plenty of donuts and coffee in thermoses for everyone until the morning, but I suspect we won't have to wait that long."

"You think we'll find her?" Parkman asked. "In this darkness?"

Aaron nodded without looking at him. "We will find her." Then he turned. "We have to."

"Then let's move. Everyone, follow me. I'll take three of you in my back seat. The rest stay with Aaron."

Parkman got back behind the wheel and waited for three of the students to drop in his back seat, then he drove out to the exit and paused until Aaron's vehicle edged in behind him.

A minute later, they were driving north on Highway 400.

"You guys spoke?" he said to Alex.

"Yeah."

"About what?"

"Later."

Parkman sat up straighter and focused on his driving. Whatever was going on between Aaron and Alex wasn't good. With Parkman's limited knowledge, he'd probably have to side with Alex because Aaron had been a dick for quite some time now. Maybe someone calling him out would change that. Maybe not.

He pulled over about a kilometer north of where Darwin told him he'd last seen Sarah's cell active, then got out. Alex got out, too. Without a word to anyone, he started walking up the road alone, flashlight aimed at the ditch.

Aaron met Parkman at the trunk. "Where's he going?" Aaron asked.

"To look for Sarah." Even though Aaron knew exactly what Alex was doing, Parkman felt the need to answer. "He's just out of sorts with this whole thing."

Aaron met his gaze. "Out of sorts? Is that what you call it?"

"You got something better?"

"Yeah, insanity. Challenging me like that on the phone." Aaron shook his head. "I don't need motivation to help find Sarah. You all know what she means to me."

"Do we?"

Aaron leaned closer. "What does that mean?"

Parkman studied him for a moment. "You want to do this now?"

Several of the students were milling about, shuffling their feet. They were either anxious to get searching or wondering where the tension toward Aaron was coming from.

"Now's not the time," Aaron said, easing back. "Find Sarah. Then we talk."

Parkman hitched up his pants, the cold already making him shiver, then turned and dropped back behind the wheel. He set his four-way flashers and waited for some of the students to join him in the warm car, but no one did.

Aaron said something outside that he couldn't pick up, and then everyone strode past Parkman and stepped into the glare of his headlights. He did a quick count. That was everyone—including Aaron —except one.

When he glanced in his mirrors, he saw the student with the man-bun drop into the driver's seat of Aaron's car.

Once the group was about twenty feet ahead, Parkman eased forward. Man Bun pulled in behind him.

They walked and rode like that for close to an hour when three of the students jumped into Parkman's back seat to warm up. They'd covered almost four kilometers so far, and no one had seen anything unusual in the ditch. Just snow, and more of it.

Ten minutes later, they switched out, and Parkman gave his wheel to one of the students so he could walk for a bit.

By three in the morning, with over fifteen kilometers covered, they stopped to talk as a group.

"We need rest," one said.

"Yeah, I'm freezing."

"How about you?"

Aaron held up a hand. "Okay, agreed. Let's find a motel. Get four or five hours' sleep, and come back out to this point tomorrow morning."

Parkman nodded, even though his gut screamed that this was a mistake. Leaving Sarah out here all night could only spell trouble. "That makes the most sense," he forced himself to say. "Also, the RCMP should be out helping us soon."

He glanced around but couldn't see Alex. "Hey, where's Alex?"

"He moved too fast," one of the students said. Then he pointed north. "Likely up there another kilometer."

Parkman turned for his car. "I'll go get him. Find a motel north of us and text me its location."

Aaron nodded, and Parkman dropped into the driver's seat. Five minutes later, he caught up to Alex and lowered the passenger window.

"Hey, get in here. We're calling it for the night."

Alex kept walking, the flashlight aimed to the right.

"Hey! Alex!"

Nothing.

Parkman hit the horn. Twice.

Alex stopped and looked at him.

"We're calling it. We sleep for four hours. Then come back with sunshine. Comprende?"

They stared at each other for several seconds, then Alex opened the door and dropped inside. His face was a mask of white from the cold, and his hands had a slight shake.

As Parkman got the vehicle going, Alex lowered his head.

"You did not fail her." Parkman glanced over, then looked back at the road. "We tried our best. And we will continue."

Alex didn't say a word for the rest of the drive. Even after they found a motel half an hour away and settled in their rooms under warm blankets, Alex didn't speak.

Sarah's disappearance had changed the man, and Parkman suspected he'd never know the depth of what this all meant to Alex.

Or how he'd likely kill Aaron in a fight if Aaron had refused to help.

What bugged him all night was seeing the men at odds with each other. And what did they whisper to one another? Was this the beginning of a rift that wouldn't heal?

Find Sarah first, then he could see about mending fences with these two.

Or did this all stem from a place of love?

Was Alex in love with Sarah, and he felt the lesser man—Aaron—wasn't appreciating her enough?

If that were the case, their fences would take much more than mending to be put back together again. Aaron had pushed too far lately, too hard.

One of Parkman's last thoughts before sleep took him was about fighting.

If Alex and Aaron got caught up in their discontent and a fight broke out, he would not be the one trying to break it up. Whoever stepped in between those two would likely receive a free ticket in an ambulance and a week-long stay in a local hospital—perhaps longer.

# Chapter 12

MARIA'S LEFT ARM DIDN'T falter when Ricardo saw her coming. She was thankful for this, as the moment he shouted, the meat tenderizer cut him off by entering his wide-open mouth. It shattered several of his bottom teeth and lodged deep in his maw, making his eyes widen in shock. In that brief second, she detected his jawbone breaking back by his ear.

Maria yanked the hammer-like device from the jowls of the head chef and then swung it again as he crumpled to the floor. It connected with the side of his head, knocking him to the floor faster than gravity's hold on him.

She stepped back to avoid his body landing on her feet, her arm already raised for another blow.

But it wouldn't be necessary. The chef's eyes rolled back in his head, and he lay motionless, his lower jaw bleeding where it sat at an odd angle.

Maria felt nothing for this man. Everyone was a co-conspirator if they worked willingly for Alonzo and Alberto Baglioni. They were all mean to the slaves and taunted them often. Ricardo had never had sex with her—she was pretty sure he had a woman at home—but he felt her up several times, spoke once about tasting her, and said his day would come when he would get a piece of her.

*It had come, all right. Didn't it, asshole?*

Even if they showed her mercy for escaping her room, even if they accepted her story of being ravenous, hence the reason for the late-night kitchen visit, and even if they'd let her live—all of those options were swiftly taken away by the attack on their head chef.

What she had just done guaranteed her a long and slow death in the madness of Alonzo's twisted brain. He would make her scream, beg, and bleed for days. She was sure of it.

If she was going to escape, it had to be now.

There was no backing out of it.

She could see much better with the kitchen light on as she ran back over to grab the temperature gauge. On the floor, she applied the tip to the release catch on the GPS monitor with her broken right hand, raised the meat tenderizer in her left—it had splotches of blood on it now—and smacked the end.

Nothing happened.

She did it again.

The GPS monitor remained intact.

She reapplied the tip of the long, silver, needle-like temperature gauge with one subtle adjustment, then smacked it harder.

Still nothing. Her left hand didn't have the coordination of her right one, but there was no way she could wield a hammer with her right hand at the moment. Maybe in two months, but escaping slaves didn't have the luxury of time on their side.

Ricardo moaned from fifteen feet away.

"Shit."

Her escape plans would end if he got up and could call someone.

She gave the temperature gauge another smack on the end, and it broke apart, shattering the end.

The GPS remained clamped to her leg.

"Shit, shit, shit."

She clambered to her feet and ran back over to the chef. He was still on the ground. His glazed eyes roamed the ceiling, likely seeing nothing as he appeared quite dazed.

Then she saw what he had in his hand.

A cell phone.

She lunged for it and smashed it against the floor with the tenderizer. He reached for her with a lazy grab, but she stomped on his hand, then jumped back.

When did she become so fast to resort to violence?

An audible crack had signaled that one of his fingers might have broken.

Something broke on the inside of Maria, too. There was a certain sense of joy in standing up for herself after being held captive for five long years. After all the injustice, the vile living conditions, and the threat of constant rape or being killed, she finally stood up for herself.

And it felt good. It felt right.

Maybe that was why she tried to stomp on the chef's hand again, but he moved it, and she lost her balance, toppling over to the floor. Luckily, she protected her broken hand from hitting anything, or she might have passed out with the pain, only to wake up bleeding all over herself with Alonzo's visage the last thing she saw.

Breathing like a mad woman through her clenched teeth, Maria stared down at the GPS clamped to her leg, then raised the tenderizer and smashed the side of it. Her leg jerked to the right, but the plastic clamp took most of the hit.

She smacked it again, then again, until small pieces chipped off.

The flashing green light blinked out, and then she whacked it again, and the device crumpled off her leg.

The skin had broken in two spots, and bits of blood bubbled to the surface. There would be a large, bruised area around the broken skin, but the damn thing was off, and she could still walk.

Maria released the tenderizer and scrambled to her feet with the remnants of the GPS tracker in her hand. She ran for the stove and flicked on the gas burners, the blue flames clicking to attention on all six of them. After setting the plastic monitor in between two burners, she grabbed a large bucket of grease from beside the fryer and hefted its weight with her left hand.

"Nooo," Ricardo mumbled through his broken jaw. "Don't."

She wondered how he could even try to speak with all his pain. Blood flowed freely from his wounded jaw. How he was conscious was beyond her.

She'd wished he'd remained unconscious.

No one deserved to be burned alive—or was that burned *awake*?

The digital clock now read 04:35 a.m.

It was later than she wanted. This had taken too long.

She needed to go. *Now!*

Maria raised the container of grease as high as she could, then tossed it onto the stove's open flames and jumped back.

The fire rose and spread rapidly, the broken GPS monitor melting at the center of the fire.

She grabbed placemats and threw them on the flames. Then baskets, and finally, another metal container of grease.

The wall beyond the stove was engulfed in flames, licking up toward the edge of the roof.

She coughed twice as she ran back over to Ricardo, who was miraculously awake.

"Crawl, crawl, if you want to live. I'm out of here."

Something clicked loudly in the room, and the sprinkler system shot water from the roof above them, soaking Maria through in seconds.

Then the fire alarm sounded.

Even though Ricardo's mouth was severely broken, Maria saw what looked like a smile play across his mouth as his upper lip pulled back in a sneer.

His eyes told her everything. She was done for. The fire wouldn't spread. He was alive—she was the one who would be dead soon.

Like a punter kicking a soccer ball, she slammed her foot into his gut, knocking him back into the metal cabinet behind him.

Ricardo, the chef, moaned deeply as the wind was knocked from his lungs.

Then she ran for the window, only stopping at the small employee fridge for a second, where she snatched two ready-made sandwiches.

The window opened with ease, and just as she suspected, it was the window that had a roof edge leading to the back of the property.

The alarm still sounded behind her as she climbed out, almost dropping the sandwiches because she only had one hand.

Allowing gravity to help, Maria slipped off the sill and dropped to the roof. Without wasting a moment, she ran the length of the roof and jumped into the open air, hugging her broken hand close to her chest.

Below that particular corner were large bundles of hay that they stored for the stables.

As suspected, the hay softened her fall, and she rolled off it quietly.

The fire alarm sounded less intense outside. What scared her out here was the shouting as men ran inside from the yard, the fence line—from all over the compound—to deal with whatever was causing the alarm.

Every single employee of Alonzo would want that alarm silenced at this early hour for fear of waking him. The reprisals would be madness.

Maria Christy waited and watched, catching her breath.

When the last man bolted inside the doors to her left, she ran for the fence, the wind in her hair.

It was her first taste of freedom because the GPS monitor wasn't jangling around on her ankle.

She reached the fence at an area where the guards often stood with Doberman Pinschers. To prepare, she unwrapped a sandwich, then bit into it, chewing madly, waiting. After several bites, not a single dog came to scare her away or bite her.

Regardless, she opened the remainder of the sandwich, dropped the ham slice on the ground, and, using her left hand in the holes of the fence, began to climb it. She supported the other sandwich close to her chest with her broken right hand.

The wires dug into the flesh of her hand, but she did her best to ignore them. Freedom had a cost, which was a minimal price to pay compared to remaining on the property.

At the top, she leaned over the edge with her stomach pressing down on the bar and the pointy pieces of wire, then wrapped her legs over carefully. It was too far to jump. An ankle would break for sure at this height. So she placed her hand inside another hole and slowly descended the other side, wincing at the strain.

Someone screamed from the house area.

That person sounded angry—*very* angry.

It raised goosebumps on her arms and neck when she touched the ground on the other side. Those screams made her turn and run like she was leaving Hades, and hounds were chasing her.

Maria ran until she couldn't and was forced to walk fast. Once she'd caught her breath, she ran again, crossing grassy fields and wading through small streams as the sun rose.

It wasn't until the sun was high that she saw a house in the distance, a small line of smoke rising from the chimney.

After one last look over her shoulder, she jogged toward the house.

She prayed they weren't in cahoots with the Baglioni family or had sworn any sort of loyalty to them.

She would hate to have to kill them or burn their house down.

# Chapter 13

INDISTINCT VOICES CAME TO her like in a delirium. They were arguing about something. A man and a woman.

Sarah remembered her name and who she was. She recalled how cold she was and that it didn't hurt so much anymore. Was she warming up? Was she dead?

Those people wouldn't stop arguing. All she wanted was to sleep.

Before long, the couple went quiet, and she drifted back to sleep.

\*\*\*

They were speaking again and not arguing this time. Why did the word *scheming* come to mind?

She tried to open her eyes.

A bed. A room with a wooden ceiling. A ceiling fan that wasn't moving.

The crackle of a fire close by came to her.

A cabin of some sort? She was much warmer.

*How did I get here?*

Sarah rolled her head sideways.

A man and a woman sat on a couch, staring at her.

"You're awake." The man got off the couch and approached her, shooting quick glances back at the woman. His body language was as tentative as his tone.

Why were they acting so weirded out? Sarah closed her eyes and rested a moment longer. Did they know who she was and were afraid of the authorities or something?

"Yeah." Sarah opened her eyes. "Looks like I have you two to thank for that."

"Oh, it's nothing." The man waved a hand and furtively looked at the woman again.

Sarah rolled her head back and stared at the ceiling, eyes half-lidded. She didn't care who they were or what their deal was—they saved her from freezing to death. That's what mattered.

Now she had a chance to get home to Willow.

"Where am I?"

The man was standing over her now. "In our cabin in the woods."

She closed her eyes, waited a heartbeat, then opened them. "I mean, where specifically?"

"You want our address?" the woman asked from the couch. "See, Mike? I knew this was trouble."

*Trouble? Saving my life?*

"It's no trouble," Mike said, with a nervous laugh.

Her fingers. How bad were they?

She moved her hand, but it didn't budge. She lifted her head and scanned the length of her body. They had her tied to a thin mattress with ropes in the living room of their cabin. She let her head flop back down.

*What the hell is this, Vivian?*

"Why am I tied down?"

"Uhm, well, we didn't want you to roll out of bed and hurt yourself."

He was lying. They were up to something else. *Scheming.*

"I'm fine now. A little tired, but fine. I won't roll. So, please, untie me."

The woman clucked her tongue from the couch. "Not going to happen, darling."

"And why not?"

Mike raised a hand at the woman. Likely his way of silencing her. "Because you were active in your sleep." Mike leaned closer. "When you fall back to sleep, we can't have you rolling out of bed. You're too close to the fireplace."

Sarah closed her eyes again. She was tired, but being tied up wasn't good for several reasons, most of which she couldn't recall at the moment.

"Am I healing?"

"Healing?"

"Yeah, will I lose any fingers or toes or anything?"

"No losses. Everything is healing. Your fingers were close to being frostbitten, and your left knee is banged up pretty badly, but it doesn't look broken. Also, you have a goose egg on your forehead, but we cleaned up the blood. You'll be as good as new in a few days, well, except for a limp until the swelling in your knee goes down." He cleared his throat. "We found you just after you slid down the hill by your car and got you to the fire to thaw out."

"How?"

"How what?"

"How did you find me?" The words were drawn out as sleep made her lethargic.

"Candace and I were snowshoeing back from the store and heard a car door slam."

Sarah recalled kicking the passenger door shut after climbing out of the car. Who knew that noise would save her life?

"So we left the trail to investigate, and when we approached your car, you were sliding down the hill farther into the ditch. And, well, here you are."

"You guys are angels." She inhaled. "Thank you."

"Don't mention it."

"Yeah, don't mention it," Candace echoed.

*What's her problem? Does she think Mike's into me?*

"I'm married," Sarah managed to say, thinking that made sense, even though she wasn't.

"Great." The woman was moving closer. "There's no ring on your finger, but it doesn't matter where you're going." She was standing over her now, so close Sarah felt warm breath on her cheek.

Just before Sarah fell back to sleep, the woman spoke again, but Sarah couldn't force herself to stay awake.

"Call him again," Candace said. "Tell him it happens tonight or not at all. We can't wait. Someone'll come looking for this bitch, and she can't be here when they do."

"All right, all right." Mike scurried away.

Then Sarah lost consciousness as that infernal woman whispered something about going to Hell into her ear.

# Chapter 14

PARKMAN DIDN'T SLEEP WELL at all. Visions of Sarah bruised, broken, and frozen to death, plagued his waking hours, while insane dreams stirred him awake each time he dozed off.

Light streamed through the thin sheers covering the cheap motel they found on the side of the highway. When he rolled over to check the time, he saw he'd missed several calls from the Parry Sound RCMP.

In under three minutes, he was dressed and outside so he could talk without waking the boys sleeping around his room.

He dialed the number and waited.

"RCMP, Parry Sound. How can I direct your call?"

"This is Parkman. Someone called me several times this morning."

"Parkman, who, sir? I'll need a second name."

"It's about Sarah Roberts. Did you guys find her?"

"Sarah Roberts?" the woman repeated. "Oh, you're looking for Sergeant Chris James. He's in the field. I'll patch you through to his cell number. Please hold." There was a click on the line. Then a phone rang in Parkman's ear.

"James here," a man answered.

"Sergeant James. This is Parkman. You got something on Sarah Roberts?" Parkman moved away from the motel room door, pivoted, walked past it, then pivoted again.

"You're the one who filed that missing persons report?"

"Yes. She's been gone for almost forty hours now."

"We got a search party of auxiliary members together and are heading south of Parry Sound now. Where are you?"

"At a motel off of Highway 400 with a bunch of searchers. We walked the highway until around four this morning."

"Where exactly is this motel?"

Parkman told him.

"Shit, we'll be passing that area in thirty minutes. Let's meet in the parking lot and discuss search patterns."

"I'll get everyone up and ready. Oh, and hey, can you bring ten coffees and several dozen donuts? Get your boys loaded up, too. I'll pay you when you get here. Just get here with everything, and let's go find her."

"I can do that."

The line died.

Parkman slipped the phone away and ripped open the door to his room to see that the guys were already stirring awake.

"I'm taking the first shower," he announced as he stormed across the room toward the bathroom at the back. "Wake everyone up in the other room, too. The cops will be here in thirty minutes with breakfast. We need to be ready. Let's go."

"You got it," one of Aaron's students said, slipping into a jacket.

The motel room door opened and closed a few times in the room as Parkman got the hot water going in the shower.

"We're coming, Sarah. We got you now."

Even spoken aloud, the words offered him little comfort.

***

At the forty-five-minute mark, all of the students, including Aaron and Alex, were outside in the motel parking lot, surrounded by three RCMP SUV vehicles and seven men in police jackets.

Sergeant James was leading the discussion, and he had everyone's attention.

"Tracks may be more visible today. The sun was out all day yesterday, causing the initial bulk from the storm to decrease. Whatever the storm covered on the day she disappeared will start to be uncovered today." He lifted his hand and pulled down a finger for each thing he said. "We are looking for tire tracks on the shoulder, tracks off the shoulder, sections of a car reflecting the sunshine, imprints in the snow past the shoulder that are larger than a deer's, and anything else out of the ordinary, meaning something that isn't animal, tree, or snow related." He lowered his hands. "Got it?"

Heads nodded all around as the boys drank coffee, inhaled donuts, and listened to Sergeant James.

Parkman noticed Alex on the fringes of the group, itching to get searching, and he hopped from one foot to the other. When he scanned everyone to find Aaron, the man was alone by his car, sipping a coffee and listening to the sergeant.

"This won't be a grid pattern search across an open field. We'll all be walking along the highway to see if she lost control in the storm and is currently staying warm in her car. So, most importantly, you're looking for odd shapes covered in snow." The sergeant glanced at Parkman. "I understand the last communication anyone had with her was late afternoon."

Parkman nodded.

"And her cell phone was picked up just north of the Crooked Bay area."

He nodded again.

"With all that information and the knowledge that Sarah was heading toward Parry Sound but didn't make it, we have to assume a high probability that she is somewhere along this highway. So, no more wasting time. Let's suit up and head south. We will drive about fifteen kilometers north of Crooked Bay and begin walking south on the northbound lane. Once we take a break, we will walk north back here by the evening. Everyone good with that?"

Heads nodded again. Parkman could tell the boys were getting restless. They wanted to start searching while the morning sun was bright.

"Let's go," James shouted.

All five vehicles—three RCMP SUVs and Parkman's and Aaron's car—handled everyone as they raced south to where James had pegged where the search would start.

Alex sat beside Parkman.

"You doing okay today?"

Alex nodded, his face forlorn.

"We'll find her, buddy."

"We have to." Alex rubbed his face. "We can't live without Sarah. The world wouldn't be the same. It wouldn't make sense."

Parkman listened to Alex's words, then stared at the road. "Amen, brother. Amen."

Up ahead, the RCMP vehicles eased off the road and onto the shoulder. Parkman and Aaron followed. Once all the vehicles were parked, most of the searchers gathered by the head SUV. Leaving his car idling with the heater on, Parkman joined them.

"This is where we start," James shouted. "When the road's clear, run to the other side and head south. Let's split into two groups. I want a smaller group on this side."

"This side?" Aaron spoke up for the first time. "She was heading north. These are the southbound lanes."

"Who are you?" James asked.

"I'm her boyfriend. She's the mother of our child." He exchanged a short glance with Alex.

"Were you on the phone with her?"

Aaron frowned and shook his head. "No."

"So you didn't talk to her while she drove north toward Parry Sound?"

Aaron pointed at Parkman. "As far as I know, Parkman was the last to speak with her."

"Well, if you weren't in direct contact with your girlfriend on the day in question, then how do you know whether she didn't see how bad the storm was and decided to head south to wait it out? My point is, she might've turned around and gone off the road on this side." Sergeant James turned to face Parkman. "Were you boys searching this side yesterday?"

Parkman shook his head.

"Okay then, four men on this side, the rest over there. Let's go. Our first break will be lunch, which happens when we get to Crooked Bay."

"Sir, that's fifteen kilometers away," one of his auxiliary members said. "About a three-hour walk or longer."

"Then I suggest you guys get moving."

Everyone dispersed quickly, with over ten people running across the highway to begin the walk heading south on the northbound lane.

Parkman headed back to his car but stopped when someone placed a hand on his shoulder.

He spun around to look Sergeant James in the face.

"Tell me about that Aaron guy." James stared into Parkman's eyes. "Is he solid? Not someone I should worry about?"

Parkman glanced over James's shoulder. Aaron had glanced back at them as he speed-walked down the highway.

"He can be a dick sometimes, but he's out here because he loves her."

"Then why wasn't he the last one to speak with her? How come he doesn't know what you know? When he said 'boyfriend,' that threw me for a loop."

"Like I said, he can be a dick sometimes. They love each other, but his attitude and ego make it tough for them to stay together. They're currently dealing with a separation."

"Is it amicable? Or should I keep a close eye on him?"

"They have a daughter." Parkman nodded once. "It's amicable. He'd never hurt her physically. If he tried, she'd probably kick his ass."

James's eyebrow raised as he released Parkman's shoulder. "How's custody working out for them?"

"Not sure yet. Sarah was served papers last Thursday. They'll deal with it in court."

James turned to watch the searchers as they moved farther away. "And you're telling me this has nothing to do with all that, right? Even though papers were served just the other day."

Parkman shook his head. "Nothing to do with it at all. Wrong tree with all that barking. I assure you."

James seemed to think about it for a moment, then nodded to himself. "Duly noted. It doesn't mean that the door is closed. You understand, right, being an ex-cop yourself?"

"I understand, but Aaron wouldn't hurt Sarah. Her heart, sure, but that's it."

"Good enough for me." He stared at Parkman a moment. "For now."

"Let's find her, and all the speculation can dissipate."

James headed back toward his SUV. "That's the plan," he shouted over his shoulder. "That's the plan."

Parkman watched Aaron as he ran ahead of the group.

For once, he saw the man alone, not part of the team, trying to handle things on his own, but all he was doing was alienating the people who cared about him.

Why did people do these things? What point was he trying to prove?

It would make sense if he didn't love Sarah, but they all knew he did. So why?

Parkman shook his head, got behind the wheel, and drove south. He'd wait for the boys to get to him at the halfway mark—about seven kilometers south—then he would switch out with the coldest of the team.

They'd find her today.

If she could be found.

# Chapter 15

MARIA APPROACHED THE HOUSE from behind a row of cypress trees. She prayed that if they had a dog, it would be safely inside the house or tied up.

From the outside, the house was a nondescript Italian villa, complete with fieldstone walls and a lovely pergola at the back. The owners had recently dug a pool in the back, but it wasn't finished. From Maria's vantage point, it appeared they were working on the deck around the pool and in the process of building a small pool house.

At the last tree in the row of cypresses, she stepped out and walked to the side of the house, where she leaned her back and scanned the fields all around the area.

There were no pursuers, no dogs chasing her, no Alonzo or Alberto.

After she caught her breath, she lowered to her knees and peeked inside a basement window.

There was nothing to see. The window was painted over in black.

Why would someone paint their window black? What were they hiding?

Back on her feet, she edged along the side of the house and slowly looked inside. This window gave her a glimpse of an empty dining room. Eight gorgeous chairs surrounded a large family table. A credenza sat on one side, and a large cabinet sat on the other.

She moved higher, more to the right, and saw a door that appeared to lead to the kitchen and another door to the right that opened into the front foyer.

Someone was home because a steady stream of smoke had exited the chimney as she approached the house.

Should she knock on the front door dressed as she was or keep prowling their property? What if they called the Italian police, the Carabinieri? How would she explain herself to them, most of whom were probably on Alonzo's payroll?

So, her decision made, she moved around to the front of the house, took one last look at the way she came, then hopped up the two steps to their veranda and knocked.

After several seconds, steps approached from the other side of the door. A shadow crossed the peephole, then moved away.

The door didn't open. If she was nervous before, she was manic now.

Getting this far only to be handed back to Alonzo couldn't happen. To be this free for a few hours, only to be taken back, would be worse than Hell itself.

A shadow crossed the eyepiece again.

Then the lock clicked, and the inside door eased open.

"Are you alone?" a woman asked, with a soft hint of an Italian accent.

"Yes." Maria heard the plea in her tone but wasn't bothered by it. "Please, I need your help."

The door closed. The deadbolt clicked into place.

Two voices sounded like they were locked in an argument behind the door.

Maria checked over her shoulder. The landscape was still clear. With each second, the reality that she escaped her captivity was setting in, and it felt good.

But she wasn't home free yet.

The lock clicked again, and this time the door swung all the way open.

"Come in," the woman said.

Maria nodded and stepped inside, taking in the fresh scents of coffee and jasmine.

The woman was in her forties and still looked young and healthy. Probably did yoga and played tennis or something. The man standing behind her had grayed early, likely in his fifties, and probably played tennis with her.

"Where did you come from?" the man asked, with even less of an Italian accent than his wife.

She studied him for a moment, then noted why he looked stilted. His hands were locked behind his back.

"I was taken from my home years ago and held by some bad people from that direction." She pointed toward the area she'd just come from.

The man's face blanched, and the woman turned to stare up at him.

"You need to leave." He opened the door all the way. "Please, you can't be in our house. Get out."

Maria couldn't stop the emotion as it gushed forth. She'd suppressed it for years, and now, like a broken spigot on the kitchen sink, tears rushed to her eyes and covered her vision. "Can't you call someone to help me? *Please.* I beg you. They've kept me prisoner, a virtual slave. I just need to get away."

The man eased his wife behind him, and Maria saw what was in his hand through her tears.

He'd been hiding a gun.

It was pointed at the floor about one foot in front of her.

She lowered to her knees. This couldn't be happening. "Oh no, oh no," she rambled. "Please, please, I can't go back there. You don't understand. What they'll do to me—"

"We know all about them and want nothing to do with them."

These people were afraid. They were literally neighbors, and as long as they minded their own business, Alonzo probably left them alone. Maybe he'd even financed that new pool out back for their silence.

"Please, no one has to know. Just drive me somewhere. I'll disappear again. Alonzo won't find me. I just can't"—her shoulders hitched, and she dropped to her elbows, keeping her broken hand bent inward—"get away on foot. They'll catch up."

When she looked up, the woman's eyes revealed concern. If the woman were home alone, Maria figured she would help. But the husband, the protector, didn't want to get involved. And by not getting involved, he felt he was protecting his family.

Maria understood all that and didn't at the same time. How could they not help a woman who just needed a ride?

"We have an arrangement with the Baglioni family. We see nothing, and they do nothing. We've lived this way for years. You being here breaks our bond." The man lowered himself to be closer to her. "I'm sorry for what you've gone through. Truly, I am. But this isn't our problem. Please don't give them a reason to hurt us, too."

Where did the tough Maria go from the kitchen back at the compound? How could she beat up the cook and escape such a facility, but then fall apart at the first house she got to?

These people weren't going to help. She could see that now. The man would use the gun to protect his family, his way of life.

She had to do this on her own.

She wiped her face and tried to kill the waterworks, but her eyes refused to stop leaking salty tears. With her left hand, she pushed up and rested on her knees. Then, using the wall beside the door, she got to her feet.

"I saw Alonzo slit a woman's throat the other day. She was the only friend I had in there, and she bled out on me. Then that Devil's son broke my hand." The woman covered her mouth. "I will leave and never come back." The man was looking impatient. "I wanted you to know that so you understood who you are protecting, whose side you're on."

"It's not our choice," the man said. "We're victims here, too."

Her tears dried up as anger swept through her as the primary emotion. These people weren't on the compound actively keeping her prisoner, but they were just as guilty for that attitude.

It was best not to involve them, but there was always another way.

"Then give me your car."

The woman gasped.

"What?" the man mumbled. "Say again."

"Give me your car and tell them when they come that a crazy woman broke in here and stole it."

"They won't believe that, and even if they did, Alonzo would torture the truth out of us and then kill us." The man shook his head. "No, just leave. This isn't our fight."

"Where are we?"

He frowned. "Lady, if you don't leave, I will be forced to throw you out the door."

She backed up to the wall. She couldn't fight him as she didn't have the energy. Well, that and he had a weapon.

"Just tell me where we are so I can walk in the right direction. Is there a town close by, a village?"

"Seven kilometers that way," the woman said, pointing toward the back of her house. "You will find Sambucetole. From there, you can take a bus to Amelia. After that, you can go to Orte or Terni. Avoid the police until you get to Orte or Terni."

"Honey," the man said, his tone clipped. "You're *helping* her. If they find out—"

"They won't," Maria cut in. "I'm dead if they catch me."

The woman extended her hand. In it were fifty euros. "This'll help you eat and take the buses. Now, please go. You were never here."

Maria took the money, folded it, and slipped it deep into her pants pocket. "I was never here." She stared into the man's eyes. "You did the right thing today."

"I didn't do anything," he said.

"You could've stopped her from giving me the money."

The man gestured at the door. "Please," was all he said.

Maria turned to leave but stopped short.

The sound of vehicles approaching forced a chill through her. They were coming fast, too. This was no tourist, no local coming home from the market.

They'd found her.

When she turned back to look at the man and the woman, their faces registered that they knew exactly who was coming.

"We're all dead now," the man said.

Maria pulled back her leg and kicked him hard in the balls, lifting him several inches off the floor. He dropped to the foyer floor as the woman gasped and stared at her fallen man.

He had dropped the gun when his hands grasped his crotch.

Maria snatched it up and slammed the door shut.

The vehicles stopped out front.

She raised the gun at the woman. "I'm not going back with them, so do as I say, or we all die."

# Chapter 16

ALEX LED THEM ALONG the northbound lanes, walking south as they trudged through the plowed snow without seeing a thing out of the ordinary. The cold didn't affect him—he did his best to ignore it. If Sarah were out there, the cold she would be enduring was far worse than anything he'd have to deal with while walking along this highway.

Aaron didn't affect him, either. The man could be annoying, sure, but he loved him like a brother. That threat of violence came from a dark place, and he meant every word of it. They'd all come too far with Sarah for over a decade to just let her fend for herself. Aaron would be part of the search party, or Alex would've had a problem with that, issues aside.

And yet, Aaron was here. If Aaron had something to say about how Alex handled that situation on the phone, he hoped Aaron would be man enough to say it to his face. The few words they'd exchanged covered the basics to ensure they could still work together until they had a heart-to-heart.

And even if they fought, it wouldn't be about hospitalizing one another. It would be two brothers exerting negative energy. Some sort of alpha male bonding shit that Alex wasn't too interested in but had no issue playing along with. If someone needed a beating to feel included, he'd oblige.

Not knowing where Sarah was was what worried him—immensely.

Could she still be alive? He was sure of it. She had to be.

After everything they've endured, this would be a shitty way to go.

So he kept the faith that they'd find her and she'd be okay.

He slowed to check their progress. A small group was on the other side of the highway, and the rest were following him about fifty meters back.

When he turned to face forward, something caught his eye.

He moved closer to the edge of the steep slope to get a better look at the rock with the odd shape—a jagged edge on the right, a perfect line on the left.

Then saw that it wasn't a rock at all, and nature didn't make perfect lines.

It was the back window of a car. The rest of the car was camouflaged by snow.

His heart doubled in speed as he took in the vehicle's position with the hood wrapped around a tree.

The perfect line on the left of what he thought was a rock was actually the roof's edge, and the jagged section on the right was where the snow had bunched up on the trunk. The dark contrast in the snowy landscape wasn't a rock but the interior of the back of the car, which was too hard to see from the highway, as everything was so white.

At night, there would have been no way they could've seen it for what it was.

Alex stepped closer and leaned over to look for tire tracks, but saw none. Either she flew into the tree from the highway, or the snow covered her tracks completely.

Even at the edge of the road, the plows had left behind a triangle of snow piled high without a single depression to indicate a car had driven off the edge here.

"Hey?" someone yelled from the other side of the road. "What are you looking at? You find something?"

Alex stepped backward off the shoulder of the highway until he was standing on the dry asphalt, then ran toward the slope, a scream emitting from his mouth as he jumped.

He controlled his body in the air for several seconds and waited for impact. Once he hit the downward slope, he spun onto his left and bent his left knee inward, his right leg stretched out straight, with both boots digging in to slow him down.

Near the bottom, he shoved them downward into the heavier snow, causing his feet to stop, the forward motion forcing his upper body to rise until he was standing.

Then he lumbered to Sarah's car through the snow, each step a challenge as his feet disappeared into the thickness up to his knees.

When he rounded the trunk area, he saw where the snow was stained red with blood, and his heart sank. There were dozens of impressions in the snow around the car.

He leaned into the vehicle. It was empty.

No Sarah.

Then he examined all the footprints to determine their direction.

Voices from the highway above were calling to him, but he ignored them. Several men were sliding down the embankment to join him now.

Alex followed the trail of blood and quickly deduced what Sarah had been trying to do.

She had climbed out of the passenger side and dragged herself toward the hill that led to the highway. He saw how far she had gotten before sliding back down to an area past the car's trunk. That's where the majority of the footprints were scattered.

Someone came and got her. Someone helped her.

Which likely meant she was alive.

But they'd called the hospitals. The police were involved. Wouldn't someone already know where she was if others had come to get her?

A sick feeling coursed through his stomach as the students from his dojo and two RCMP officers in uniform bunched up around him.

"Is this her car?" a cop asked.

Alex nodded. "It is."

"Holy shit," the cop said. "She tried to climb back up, but then—" He stared at the footprints. "This is a good sign." His voice rose in excitement. "She survived the accident, and it looks like someone saved her." He unclipped his radio and relayed the details of their find to everyone listening. Someone was calling Parkman so he could drive back to their area. Aaron was on his way, too.

Alex strolled over toward the cluster of footprints and followed them into the trees.

That's where they stopped.

He frowned.

How could they just stop?

Deep inside the trees, the canopy thick overhead, the snow was a dusting here and there, sitting amidst drifts where the wind had piled snow at the base of random trees. In many areas, pine needles covered the forest floor with such a light dusting of snow that it looked like someone had sprinkled salt everywhere.

He leaned closer and barely detected a footprint. As he moved deeper into the woods, the snow decreased, and there were no signs of prints.

Whoever took Sarah knew what they were doing. There was something nefarious about their actions because they took pains to conceal their direction. As one walks through these trees, they would leave behind evidence because the snow is piled in spots all over the pathways. To avoid leaving a trail, one must step carefully, avoiding the snow and aiming for the pine needles.

So, he deduced that someone had taken Sarah, and they didn't want to leave a trail behind.

Why not move thirty or forty meters down the road, where the slope was gone, and they could stand on the side of the highway and flag someone down? Why not get the injured female driver to a doctor?

Because whoever helped her out of the woods wanted something from her.

Who were they, and what could they possibly want with Sarah?

His mind went to dark places as he clenched his fists. It had to be someone who lived in the area.

They happened upon the accident and seized the chance to take Sarah somewhere.

But where?

Or was she shoved off the road and abducted?

Alex turned around and ran toward the cop on his radio.

They needed a list of all the residences within walking distance of this accident scene.

And they needed it yesterday.

# Chapter 17

THEY WERE ARGUING AGAIN. But something was different this time.

Sarah kept her eyes closed and listened.

The man—Mike—was on the phone with someone, and the woman —Candace—was arguing points like she was talking in his ear.

"I know, man." Mike moaned the words as if speaking them distressed him. "This'll clear up my debt, though, right?"

Sarah opened her eyes to a slit and saw Mike jerk his head in a nod. Candace snapped her fingers, then slapped her hands softly.

"What's that?" Mike asked into the phone, leaning forward as if that would make him hear better. Then he looked at Sarah. "Yeah, man, she's right here. Undamaged." He paused. "Well, maybe a bruise or something, but otherwise, she's fine."

Candace looked at Sarah. Their eyes met, and Candace's smile could be described as contemptuous. She moved closer to Sarah and leaned on her bed to be close to her face.

While Mike spoke in the background, Candace whispered, "You're our free ticket out of here, baby. You are a blessing. I can't believe we found you."

"What's happening?" Sarah asked, feeling much better now that she'd rested for so long. Warm, too. She was finally completely warm, and her fingers and toes were moving.

"Nothing's happening, darling. Some men will be here soon, and they'll take you away. Then our debt is paid."

"Your debt?"

Candace flicked the tip of Sarah's nose. "Nothing to worry your pretty little head about, cutie. Just thank us for saving your life. You'd've died out there had we not shown up."

"Those men." Sarah swallowed, her mouth dry. "Those men who are coming. Will they take me to the hospital and get me all checked out?"

Candace laughed, then stepped away without answering, her head shaking. She moved back beside Mike, who was still talking on the phone. After a minute, he hung up and faced Candace.

"Jimmy did it," he shouted. "We're in!" They high-fived each other, then Candace did a short dance, shaking her hips.

"How is this possible?" Candace asked. "How could Jimmy know those guys?"

"Well." Mike lowered his gaze. "I don't think he *knows* them. It's from a friend of a friend. A message was dropped at that bar downtown, and we got a response. They're coming now."

"Now!" Candace shrieked, her hands shooting over her head. "We have to get ready. How long before they're here?"

"About an hour. But Jimmy's coming first." Mike extended his arm, then bent it inward to stare at his watch. "He'll be here in about twenty minutes."

"Holy shit, is this really happening?"

Mike nodded exuberantly. "It is, baby. And they're forgiving our entire debt for this deal."

"All of it?"

He nodded. "Every cent."

"That's nearly a hundred grand."

Mike grabbed her by the arms. "Jimmy said they often pay fifty or a hundred thousand more, but since it's a debt they're forgiving, and they're missing out on a bunch of the interest, they'll take her for the hundred owing."

*Take her? What the fuck?*

"Guys?" Sarah said, hoping she'd be loud enough to be heard over all their excitement. "Take me where?"

They both looked at her, then looked back at each other.

"We can't tell you yet, sweetie," Candace said. "Let's just say we saved your life, and now you're saving ours."

"You owed a lot of money to somebody," Sarah said. "Drugs? Gambling? You steal it?"

Candace jumped like a rabbit and landed beside the bed Sarah was still strapped to. Pain shot up through her scalp as Candace grabbed a fistful of hair.

"Listen, bitch. Don't come into my house and disrespect us like that. You know nothing about us, you fuckin' skank. Got that!"

"Candace," Mike shouted. "No marks, no bruises. Remember? Let her go. She's theirs now. We can't hurt her."

The immediacy of the pain eased when the woman released her hair.

Their eyes met.

"Don't you fuck with me." Candace snorted and eased back a bit. "Our business ain't none of yours, skank. You should be thanking us instead of judging us. We saved your fucking life." Candace shook her head. "People these days."

"Candace," Mike said again, this time not as loud. "Go get ready. When Jimmy comes, he'll give us the lowdown. Then *they* come, and it's over. Tonight, we party. We're finally free."

Candace shot her arms over her head and hollered, eyes scrunched shut. Then she grabbed Mike's face in both hands, kissed him several times, shoved him away, and ran toward one of the rooms out of Sarah's field of vision.

A door closed hard, leaving Mike and Sarah alone.

He studied her for a long moment as her stomach twisted at whatever it was they had done.

"What's going on, Mike?" she asked. "I've got a little girl at home waiting for me. Don't tell me you sold me or something."

His face fell briefly, then he inhaled and moved closer to her. "I'm sorry. You were dead without us."

"Okay, but I'm alive now."

"Some people will come and take you somewhere and then forgive our debt. It's a win/win for everyone."

"Who are these people?"

Mike shook his head. "Even if I knew, I couldn't tell you. They'd kill me."

Her stomach dropped. "That can't be good, Mike. What do you think they'll do with me?"

"I don't know."

"Undo these ropes, Mike. I'll walk away. This could end right now."

He shook his head. "I could never do that. They'd kill me for sure. These kinds of people would paint the interior of this cabin with my blood while keeping me alive so I could watch the redecoration."

"They don't sound too friendly. What kind of trouble were you in? How'd you owe so much?"

The door behind her snapped open, making Mike look up.

"You talking to that harlot?" Candace yelled. "Don't get to know her. Don't ask her name. She's a commodity or some shit now. A piece of meat that we found in the bush and just sold. Now, get in here and help me try on a dress. I wanna look extra special for those boys who are bringing the coffin."

*Coffin? Vivian, is this why I had the accident? To get inside here and deal with this somehow?*

"What's that about a coffin, Mike?" Sarah craned her neck to watch him as he walked around her and headed toward the door where Candace was. "Mike, why do they need a coffin?" He didn't answer. "*Mike?*"

The door slammed.

"Vivian. What have you done?"

# Chapter 18

MARIA EASED BACK BEHIND the door as the man's wife helped him to his feet. The voices outside the house were getting closer.

"They're going to knock." Maria couldn't stop her hands from shaking. "You know what to say to them, right?"

The woman nodded.

"You know I'll shoot you if you hand me over to them, right?"

The man raised his hand in front of the gun. "Please, we'll do as you say. They should be gone in a few minutes."

"No signals."

The woman frowned. "Signals?"

"You know, like a quirked eyebrow, or mouthing *help* or some shit."

"Lady, this isn't a Tarantino movie. We will get rid of them. Then you leave."

"Deal."

The knock on the door made them all jump. "Open up."

"Who is it?" the man asked, his voice almost back to normal.

"Baglioni family. Your neighbors." It sounded like Alonzo, and it turned her stomach to a sour green soup of month-old yogurt.

The woman twisted the knob, took a deep breath, and then opened the door.

The second the morning sun hit them both, they lit up like they were on stage.

"What can we do for you?" the man asked, his voice cheerful.

"When we pulled up, you closed the door. Not very neighborly of you."

"Well"—they exchanged a glance, then stared back out at Alonzo—"we didn't know who was pulling up. Better to be safe."

Maria pressed her shoulder blades against the wall, trying to disappear into it. As long as the Baglionis remained outside, they'd never see her.

"Mind if we come in?"

Of course, Alonzo would want to come in.

"Uhm, well, we were about to head into town for groceries." The man emitted a nervous laugh. "You know, we weren't expecting a social call. What's this all about?"

For a few moments, there was no answer. Maria heard her heart pounding in her ears as sweat made her readjust her grip on the weapon.

"A woman did some terrible things in our home, then ran away. We came to collect our property."

"Oh, that doesn't sound good. What's she look like? If we see her, we'll let you know."

"We think she ran this way."

"Oh," the woman said, a hand rising to her chest.

They were overacting. This wouldn't end well.

"So, we want to walk through your house to make sure she didn't break in and is right this second hiding in one of your bedrooms."

"Well, ahhh—"

"It's for your own safety," Alonzo added. "She hurt someone on my staff. This woman could resort to violence." His voice lowered to something more sinister. "As neighbors, we wouldn't want anything to happen to you. You understand, right?"

"Of course. Please. Our house is your house."

The woman shot a glance at Maria, then averted her gaze down the hallway.

This couldn't end well. There was no time to run. Alonzo would not take no for an answer—he was about to enter the house.

They were all as good as dead.

"May I?" Alonzo said as he stepped into view beside the man, his gaze on the living room to the right.

As he turned toward where Maria was standing, his eyes hardened.

She saw Hell in that face and the pleasure a demon would take in the suffering of others.

So, to end the Alonzo Baglioni demon's reign on Earth, she raised the weapon in her hand from about two feet away, aimed it at the bridge of his nose, and pulled the trigger while screaming.

# Chapter 19

PARKMAN STOOD IN A semi-circle with Aaron and Alex, along with three RCMP officers, as they scanned a map of the area.

Sergeant James slapped a hand on the map, which was placed on the hood of his cruiser. "We'll spread into three teams and move through the trees in search of anything that might indicate a direction of travel. While we're doing that, I'll have officers knocking on doors."

"How many doors are we talking about?" Parkman asked.

"In the immediate area, and we're talking walking distance, no more than twenty."

"Good, so we'll be able to cover that within an hour."

"Whoa, whoa, hold your horses." James reared back and looked at Parkman. "How many men do you think I have? And do you know how far apart these houses are in the countryside?"

"No worries, Sergeant. Aaron and I will help knock on doors, too."

The sergeant glanced at Aaron and shook his head. "No offense, but this is a police matter. Search party volunteers are one thing, but I can't have the *ex*-boyfriend knocking on people's doors and possibly losing his temper."

Aaron started with the use of *ex* in his title. "I'll be fine," he said, his tone clipped.

"No." The sergeant turned to one of his men. "Distribute the addresses to Bob and Sam. Take three yourself, then get knocking." He lightly shoved the man's shoulder. "Now go."

The man bolted to the cruiser parked behind the sergeant's.

When he turned back to the crew, he hitched up his belt and

surveyed the faces staring back at him.

Parkman watched him stop at Alex. He seemed to be trying to figure Alex out, but that wouldn't happen in the time they knew each other.

"I have everyone on their way and a full-scale search underway for Miss Roberts. A tow truck is en route, and our team will be knocking on doors within the hour. Meanwhile, our office staff are checking on hospitals in Barrie, Parry Sound, and Orillia. We'll find her, boys, we'll find her."

Alex stepped away from the group, walked over to the edge of the shoulder, and stared out at the trees.

"What's up with him?" James asked.

"He's the silent type." Parkman watched Alex, then stepped over beside his friend. "What's on your mind?"

"She's out there somewhere."

"And we'll find her."

Alex shook his head. "I doubt that."

Parkman turned to look out at the trees. "You know something we don't."

"The people that dragged her away didn't leave a trail for a reason."

"Why would that be? People aren't abducted from accident scenes all too often."

"Why take her into the woods? Why not walk over there and signal passing motorists for help?" Alex pointed at a level area twenty meters away where someone could easily walk up to the shoulder of the highway.

"Maybe their house is nearby, and they needed to get her warm fast, then call for help."

"Maybe. So then she'll show up at a hospital and forget everything I'm saying. Otherwise, it's on us to find her."

"What are you guys thinking?" Aaron asked as he stepped in beside Alex.

"I'm going into the woods to find Sarah." Alex nodded at the trees. "She's in there somewhere. I don't think they'll find her at a hospital. They won't find her in some nice family's house. They would've called it in by now."

"Something doesn't add up about this." Aaron turned around to walk back to his car. "I'll get some food. We may be walking all night."

Parkman raised his hands outward, then slapped them back to his sides. "Well, I wonder what got into Aaron." He fixed his gaze on Alex. "You might have given him the verbal slap he needed."

"I gave him nothing. He already had it. All I did was remind him." Then Alex jumped, slid down the hill, landed on his feet, and walked to the edge of the trees. "I'll wait in here," he said over his shoulder loud enough for Parkman to hear.

"Where's he going?" Sergeant James asked as he stepped up beside Parkman.

"*We* are going to look for Sarah."

"Still doing the search party thing?"

"You could say that. We'll walk the forest until dark, I suppose."

James slapped Parkman on the shoulder. "Call me if you need anything. Oh, and don't get lost in there."

"We won't," Aaron said, walking by them, a bag of food in his arms.

Then Aaron jumped in the same fashion as Alex moments before, slid to the bottom, and snapped gracefully to his feet.

"Shit," Parkman mumbled.

Sergeant James gestured at the hill. "They're waiting."

"Yeah, yeah, I'm going."

Parkman stepped over the edge, his feet went out from under him, and he landed on his butt. Several of the men gasped behind him. Or did they suppress their laughter?

Before he could grab onto anything, he was sliding down the hill. At the bottom, he dug his feet in to right himself like Alex and Aaron had done before him, but he tripped over his feet and rolled onto his shoulders.

When he stopped, covered in snow, some of it shoved into the top of his pants, he rolled onto his butt to wipe it off his face. Up at the roadside, the sergeant was still watching him, hands on his hips, head slowly shaking back and forth.

"I'm okay," Parkman shouted for the sergeant's benefit. "All good," he added under his breath. "Fucking embarrassing, young fuckers."

A hand materialized to his left.

Parkman looked over to see Aaron waiting to help him up.

"Come on," he said. "We got work to do."

Parkman took the proffered hand, got to his feet, brushed himself off, then followed Aaron into the woods without looking back up at the road.

# Chapter 20

SOMEONE KNOCKED ON THE cabin door. Mike was pacing the living room in front of the sofa, and Candace was in the bathroom applying makeup.

They weren't ready, but whoever was there wasn't interested in waiting as they knocked harder the second time.

"Coming," Mike shouted loud enough for Candace to hear him.

There was a rustling from the bathroom as Candace dropped something in her rush to pack up and get to the living room.

Sarah tested her binds, but like before, they held fast. "You'll regret this, Mike. Don't do it."

He looked back at her with his hand on the knob, indecision written all over his face. When he averted his gaze to Candace, she jerked her hand in an open-the-door-already gesture.

The person knocked a third time, but it sounded like they kicked the door.

Mike ripped it open. "What the fuck, man?" he shouted at the guy who stormed inside.

"Is this her?" the stranger asked.

He strode across the room to look down at her. The guy was definitely on a meth diet with his red-dotted, pockmarked, gaunt face. He wouldn't weigh more than ninety pounds carrying a sack of potatoes, but wore large pants and a sweater like he wanted to appear bigger.

This had to be the guy named Jimmy they were talking about.

"Yeah, I'm her, skinny Jimmy."

His eyes widened so much she worried they'd pop out of his

cadaverous orbital bones. Then he spun around to face Mike. "You told her my *name*?"

"Well." Mike lifted one shoulder. "Not really. She must've heard us talking." He stole a glance at Candace as if asking for help.

"Where is she going, Jimmy?" Candace asked, moving closer to Sarah's bedside.

"Going?" Jimmy scratched at something on his neck. "How the fuck should I know? I never talk to these people. I just passed along the message."

"Okay, I'll ask a different way. Where do you think she's going?"

He raised both hands out to his side and lifted his shoulders to his earlobes. "Fucked if I know. What's with all the questions?"

Candace placed one hand on her hip and used the other when she talked. "Jimmy, let me ask you this then. Is she coming back?"

Jimmy frowned. "Back? Where? Here?"

Candace fixed her gaze on Mike. "Help me get him to understand English before I slap this excuse of a dickstain."

"Jimmy." Mike closed the door and walked over to him. "She's asking leading questions."

"Leading?" He swung his head from Candace to Mike. "What does she want to lead?"

Mike shook his head. "Listen, man. She's trying to tell you that this girl will disappear. She'll never come back. These people are powerful. Even if she escapes from them, which she can't do, they'll execute her." Mike placed a hand on Jimmy's shoulder. "So it doesn't matter that she knows our names."

Jimmy looked from Mike to Candace, then back to Mike again. "Oh, right, okay." He snapped his fingers once. "I knew that. Of course." He turned back to Sarah. "You guys told her everything?"

"No, we told her nothing. All she knows is we saved her life. She was going to freeze to death. She's warm and cozy now, and she'll do exactly—"

"Wait!" Jimmy shouted, leaning closer to Sarah. "What the fuck did you do to her forehead?"

"That was from the car accident."

Jimmy spun around, fear mixed with something else on his face—maybe anger. "You said she was flawless, untouched, unharmed. They'll be pissed about this."

"She is flawless. Just look at her. We didn't hurt her." Mike had a pleading tone to his voice. "She ran her car off the road. Of course, she'll have an injury or two. Even her knee was banged up."

Jimmy scanned Sarah's body until his eyes stopped on her left knee. "Oh. My. Fuck. Look at that swelling." He spun around so fast that Sarah wondered how he didn't break his neck. "They will kill us all."

"What?" Candace blurted. "Why? She's fine. And when they get her where she's going, she'll heal fast, no?"

*Where am I going, Vivian? Who are these people?*

"Doesn't work like that." Jimmy stared down at his fidgeting hands, shaking his head back and forth like a five-year-old child after being asked if he had eaten all the cookies in the jar. "Dude, these people are connected." Jimmy moved away from Sarah's bed and stopped at the window to peek outside. When he looked back at Mike and Candace, his face was the color of soured yogurt, and the expression communicated that he might vomit at any second. "My dealer knows two dealers who get their stuff from Big Carlo. Big Carlo knows a dealer who *might* know how to reach these people." He still fidgeted with his hands. "When you send a message through this chain, it better be real. It better be true."

"And if it isn't?" Candace dropped onto the couch. "What then?" She shot a hand up to point at Sarah. "I mean, she's fine. Seriously. They won't kill the deal because of a gash on her forehead. We even wiped up the blood, for fuck's sake. We cleaned her up for them. Look at that white towel that's stained now." She pointed at the ruined towel on the kitchen counter.

"The plan is falling apart already, eh?" Sarah asked.

In unison, Mike and Candace yelled, "Shut up!"

Sarah smiled at them. "Your fuckup, not mine."

Candace glared at Sarah. "If we weren't waiting for these people, I'd kill you myself."

"Hey," Jimmy shouted. "Focus. Don't let her draw you in. We can't touch her now. As far as they"—he used finger quotes for that word—"are concerned, she's already their property." Jimmy checked his watch. "We've got fifteen minutes until they arrive. Hurry, tell me everything. We have to make this go smoothly, or we could find ourselves six feet deep."

"It won't go smoothly, fuckface." Sarah looked from one to the other. "You're all dead unless you untie me and leave now."

"And how would you know that, skank?" Candace had both hands on her hips now.

"Did you google me?"

"Google you? Why would I do that? You were in a car accident. You're a nobody. And guess what? You just disappeared."

"Oh, my fuck. You guys are so dead." Sarah rolled her head back to stare at the ceiling. "Untie me. We all run. We all live. That's it. Leaving me here for them means you three die, and I live."

"Yeah, right," Mike said, his voice cracking. "Like we'd google you. What are you, the prime minister's daughter?"

"I'm not saying it because of my ego. This isn't about how *important* I am, far from it. But, you know what, don't worry about it. Too late now. I can't save everybody. Haven't been able to for a long time. Some people are beyond saving."

"Save everybody from what?" Jimmy asked.

She angled her head to stare at him. "Themselves."

When Jimmy spun toward Mike, his hand shot out, palm up. "Give me her ID."

Mike scanned the cabin, then ran over to the kitchen table and grabbed a small red folder. Her insurance documents from the glove box of the car were in it. He handed them to Jimmy, who rifled through the papers.

Then he looked up. "Sarah Roberts. Can't say I know the name."

Sarah rolled her head to look at the three of them as they stared back at her. "Hence the googling comment."

It was Candace who reacted first. Her face turned from concern to quizzical.

"Wait a damn minute. Are you saying you're that psychic woman?"

Mike gaped at his girlfriend. "You know her?"

Sarah turned to look at her, too. "I'm not saying shit until I'm untied."

Candace lunged for her phone on the coffee table, tapped on the screen quickly, then jerked up to stare at Sarah.

"What?" Mike asked.

Candace handed him her phone.

Mike took it and stared, his eyes slowly widening, while Jimmy looked over his shoulder, scratching at something on his face now.

"Holy fuck." They looked up in unison. "You're Sarah Roberts."

"And when you guys untie me and call the cops to tell them you found me, everyone gets a pat on the back. But if you leave me here to deal with Big Carlo's boys, everyone will get a bullet in the back."

Mike stared at Jimmy, then Candace, having lost all color. "Shit, we should listen to her."

Jimmy reared back like he'd been punched. "Are you fuckin' kidding me, man?" His words came out so fast that his tongue stumbled over the curse word. "There's no going back on this now. We're all dead for sure if we tried something like that." He turned to Sarah. "Besides, if this twat is so psychic, why is she tied up on that bed in your cabin? Why didn't she see it coming?"

"Because, fuckhead," Candace said, still staring at her phone. "Every time she uses her psychic ability shit, it's to stop some bad dudes." She looked up. "People like us."

"You mean"—Mike swallowed—"this was her plan all along?"

"My sister's plan," Sarah said, making sure they heard the dejection in her voice. Maybe it would be enough for them to buy her story and release her. She had no interest in Big Carlo's friends, who were willing to forgive a hundred grand for her.

"Wait, wait." Candace raised her right hand, index finger extended. "Current Google updates say that the police are looking for her. They've got a search party out on the highway right now." She placed a hand on Mike's shoulder, stricken by something she just read. "I might need to sit down." She dropped onto the couch, a hand on her forehead.

"What?" Mike shouted. "Tell us."

"They found her car and are going to canvass the area." Her voice took on a hollow tone. "This means cops could be at our door any minute."

"Oh shit, oh shit," Jimmy mumbled. "They better not be in the area when the other guys show up to get her."

"See? Your plan is going to shit," Sarah said. "Untie me. I'll run out and tell everyone how you guys saved my life. Then we'll deal with *the other guys* when they arrive and stop whatever they're doing. That's the safest bet for everyone."

"Wait." Jimmy moved to the door, peeked outside, then closed and locked it. "Don't you guys see what she's trying to do?"

"Yeah." Mike nodded. "I do. She's trying to help us."

"No, you fuckin' idiot. She's trying to get us to let her go."

"What's the alternative?"

"The alternative?" Jimmy shook his head. "Dude, if we let her go and she's not here in like thirty minutes when those boys get here, we are dead. Even if we run, these are the kinds of people who find you, whether you went to Nepal or Peru."

"So, okay." Candace got back to her feet and slipped her phone into her pocket. "We're committed, so we have to be committed all the way. But …"

"But what?" Mike asked.

"People know her to be psychic. What if she's right?"

"Right about what?"

Candace frowned at Mike, then turned to Jimmy to ask him. "What if everything she's said is right?"

"Then we're dead. Letting her go guarantees we die in some terrible way. Giving her to them gives us a chance."

"What if we kill them when they walk in the door?"

"Don't be stupid. Not tonight of all nights. Please, don't be stupid." Jimmy started pacing. "Besides, this is a good development."

"How so?" Mike asked.

"Once they learn she's some psychic bitch, she'll be worth more."

"Worth more?" Mike's voice rose. "How so?"

"You owe them a hundred grand, right?"

Mike nodded. "Thereabouts."

"Well, then, when they show up, we explain that we want fifty grand in cash for this new development."

"Ohh, I like that," Mike said, nodding.

Candace raised her head to stare at the ceiling. "You guys are so fucked it's unbelievable. I'd have better luck working with Bozo the Clown and Pee Wee Herman, although he just died, rest his soul." She slammed a hand on the coffee table. "Nothing changes. We know nothing. They come and get her, and we're done. That's it." Candace glared at Sarah. "This is all her doing. See how she's trying to divide us. Psychic? Yeah right. Psychic, my ass." She moved over to the base of the bed. "Help me lift her into the bedroom."

Mike tilted his head and frowned. "The bedroom?"

"What if that search party knocks on our door before Carlo's boys get here? We can't let them see her."

"Oh, right." Mike ran over and grabbed one end of the thin mattress, and Candace grabbed the other.

"A little help here," Candace said, lowering her end to the floor.

Jimmy stopped scratching his face long enough to lift Sarah into the bedroom, where they dropped her onto Mike's and Candace's unmade bed.

"I need a fix," Jimmy said. "This is too stressful."

"I got some stuff." Mike started for the door. "Follow me."

A pounding on the front door resonated throughout the small cabin.

Candace jerked the bedroom door closed. "Go answer it," she whispered. "And if it's the search party idiots, get rid of them."

Then she shut the bedroom door, grabbed something off the floor out of Sarah's line of sight, and jumped back up to shove it into Sarah's mouth.

It tasted of locker room socks and smelled of month-old sweat.

Sarah suppressed the urge to vomit as her gag reflex made her choke several times.

Out in the living room of the small cabin, she thought she heard the sound of Parkman's voice.

Candace leaned down to her ear. "If they hear you"—she left that sentence unfinished as she flicked open a butterfly knife and placed it against Sarah's cheek—"that seeing into the future bullshit will be all the seeing you'll be doing as I'll gouge out your eyes, you fucking skank piece of shit."

Sarah gagged again as she inhaled Candace's sour breath.

# Chapter 21

THE GUN SPAT AND jerked in her hand.

Maria had never fired a weapon in her life, but her aim was true from this distance.

Alonzo's head snapped back with the impact, then his body followed. On the wall behind where his head had been was a smear of blood, chunks of bone, and brain matter. It reminded her of looking at blood in someone's vomit, which she'd seen all too often back at the villa.

She darted around the door and caught sight of the man who'd come to the door with Alonzo.

He had jumped off the porch and was hightailing it back to the SUVs. Her aim would suck on a moving target from this range while using her left hand, so she jumped out the door and bolted after the man.

At the SUV, instead of hopping inside and trying to drive away, he opened the door, grabbed something out of sight, then stepped away from the door.

Then Maria saw what he had grabbed.

A long-barreled weapon.

Even as she jumped to the side to hide behind the residents' small Fiat, the report from the weapon sounded like a cannon going off.

Someone was screaming from the house now.

*How did they get hit?*

Maria rolled when she hit the ground, keeping her broken hand close to her chest, but she'd lost her grip on the gun.

Scrambling through the thick grass, she scurried over and snatched it up.

Heavy footsteps pounded closer.

She raised the weapon, slipped her finger inside the trigger guard, then fired as the man rounded the corner of the Fiat.

She missed.

He leveled his giant gun—what she thought was a shotgun—at her face, but she was already pulling the trigger again.

This time, it hit him in the chest, knocking his aim off.

His weapon boomed near her face, but the bullets entered the earth one foot to her right.

Without realizing the gun was empty, she clicked the trigger three more times as the man dropped to his knees, then tilted sideways and fell to the grass. He gurgled something, but then she realized he was just trying to breathe.

Maria relieved him of the shotgun, turned it around to train on him, and pulled back on the trigger.

The top of the man's head separated, staining the green grass a dark red that resembled spilled wine.

She was pretty sure his name was Gio, short for Giovanni. He was one of the muscle who guarded the front of the villa.

The screaming in the house continued, but Maria, being hyper-vigilant to make sure no one else would pop up and shoot her, ran to the SUVs to ensure they were empty.

Two vehicles, two men. That was it.

A weight lifted from her as she strode back toward the house.

Alonzo was dead.

The torturer was gone.

It was over.

Even if she didn't make it, even if she didn't get back to her husband in America, she got to kill that bastard, and that felt good—no, it felt *great*.

Should she be worried, though? How could murder *feel* good? Was she empty inside? Had they taken *everything* from her?

She kicked open the front door. Alonzo still lay in the foyer, eyes impossibly wide and staring at nothing; the entry wound a small dark hole with bubbled edges in his brow.

Crying and intermittent whispering came from what Maria guessed was the house's living room.

She moved that way, the gun still in her hand.

The woman sat on an antique-looking sofa, and the man was on the floor, his arms wrapped around his wife's legs. They wept together, with the man whispering platitudes to her.

When he saw Maria, he faced her and released his wife's legs. "Are they dead?"

She nodded. "Both of them."

He looked away and rubbed his wife's knee.

They didn't deserve this, but neither did she. No one deserved what Alonzo had been doing for far too long.

"You know," she said, taking in the scene and seeing it as pathetic, "not wanting to help is a version of compliance."

The woman wiped her face with a handkerchief and looked up, her eyes a mask of redness. "What?"

"You're in league with them, condoning what they do by refusing to help me earlier."

"I gave you money, told you how to take the bus."

"I'll give you that, but you did it reluctantly. And if you weren't home, I doubt this guy would've helped." She pointed the tip of the weapon at him.

When the man recoiled from the gun, she quickly slipped it behind her legs.

"Sorry, I was just pointing. I won't use this thing on you." Then she thought about it and added, "I'll only use it if more of Alonzo's men come through that doo—"

"Please leave," the man said.

"I can't take one of their SUVs. Too easy for them to track me. Where are your car keys?"

"You're a thief now, too?"

"I'm a woman who was abducted over five years ago," she shouted. "I was made to be a slave at the villa up the road." Her voice rose with each word. "They beat me, fucked me, and worked me for sixteen hours per day without regard for my humanity. So if stealing your car gets me home, then I'd steal one hundred cars. Now, fuck off with your judgment and give me the car keys." The gun came out from behind her leg. She wouldn't shoot either one of them, but they didn't know that.

The man pointed. "They're in the kitchen on a keyholder on the wall. The Fiat is out front."

"I saw it." She stormed away toward the kitchen.

"You won't get very far, though. Might as well stick around with us."

She stopped at the kitchen door and turned back to them. That's when she noticed the cell phone on the coffee table behind him.

"What did you do?" A chill coursed through her at how cold her voice sounded. "Who did you call?"

"People are dead, lady. Shot on our property—our neighbors, no less. They are powerful people. What you just did also sentenced my wife and me to death."

"Who did you call?" she shouted, frantic that they'd called Alberto to tell him where she was, and at this very moment, fifty men were pulling up out front.

"We called the state police. At that level, there will be less corruption. They'll place us in some witness protection program and get you to safety before the Baglioni family can get to either of us."

She stared at them for a long moment.

"Or you can take our car and make a run for it."

She kept staring at them, her mind running through the options. The first sounds of police sirens could now be heard in the distance.

There'd be no more running today.

She turned from them, strode to the front door, stepped over Alonzo's body in the foyer, then walked outside, where she strode up to the other man—Giovanni. She set the gun down beside him, then moved to the middle of the lawn and dropped to her knees to wait for the authorities.

Eight Italian police cruisers rushed up to the house seconds later.

Maria Christy was taken into police custody without a fight.

# Chapter 22

THEY HAD ALREADY KNOCKED on a dozen houses, with only one having occupants. The others were summer homes, they were told. The older couple in the occupied house had been very kind, offering them hot chocolate and cookies.

Alex was eager to keep searching while they still had daylight, so he quickly got them out of there.

They'd found a paved road half a kilometer into the trees, and Parkman moved along behind them now, listening to the sounds of the highway to their left.

Another house came up on the right, set back from the road.

"Let's check this one," he said, angling toward it.

He couldn't help but feel discouraged. This was a long road, and there were dozens like it. Sarah could be anywhere by now.

The temperature was dropping by the hour, too, which was easy enough to manage. The arctic cold front between Aaron and Alex was a harder iceberg to climb, and neither one had done anything to thaw it.

He'd shout at them to stop being so childish if they didn't talk soon. Or rather, shout at Aaron because he was the one who spurred this on, and get him to make it right.

Alex hopped onto the porch of the small cabin-like shack and knocked on the door.

"Looks like someone's home," Parkman said. "Light's on inside. Two vehicles out here tell a story." He moved closer to the carport and glimpsed the usual stuff: cross-country skis suspended from the roof, a canoe on the wall at the back, sports equipment tacked to the side walls, some tools lying haphazardly around, and oil stains on the ground.

He nudged Aaron. "There must not be a lot of theft in this area to leave such pricey stuff out like that."

Aaron nodded, staring at the open carport as Alex knocked again.

Someone hollered something from the inside when Parkman noticed the snowshoes.

They were wet like they'd been used recently, dripping onto the concrete floor.

Then the door swung open, and a man stuck his skeletal face out. "What do you want? Looking to sell something? If so, we're not interested." He scratched at his neck. A tiny smear of blood the size of a Remembrance Day poppy formed where he'd been scratching.

"Sell something?" Alex shook his head. "No, we're looking for a girl."

"Not that kinda place, hoss." The guy stepped back. "Try downtown, where the hookers walk the streets."

The door swung closed, but Alex was faster. An inch before it latched, Alex had stopped it.

Aaron moved up the porch steps to stand beside Alex when the door was ripped open again.

"What the hell, man? You come looking for the wrong shit, dude, got it? This ain't the place to be fuckin' around."

"You didn't let us show you her photo." Aaron extended his cell phone to show what was presumably a photo of Sarah.

The guy looked for all of a second, then turned toward them, now scratching at his cheek. "Never seen her, but she's a looker."

Aaron moved an inch, but Alex stuck out his arm to stop him, which Parkman was thankful for. Flared tempers and broken bones wouldn't help find Sarah. It gets his boys in lockup for the night.

"You sure?" Aaron asked. "Take another look."

"What, she missing or something?" The junkie leaned out farther to look at Parkman. "You guys cops or something?"

"Yes," Alex said. "She's missing, and we've volunteered to help find her. This is a joint effort with the RCMP. Her car went off the highway, and someone dragged her from the accident scene."

"Whoa, dude. I ain't got nothing to do with shit like that."

They stared at each other for a long moment. Then Parkman broke the silence.

"Where'd you go today?"

Aaron and Alex looked over their shoulders.

The man at the door shook his head and flitted one hand up, then down. "I didn't go nowhere, man."

Parkman pointed at the carport. "Those snowshoes were used recently."

Aaron turned back to the man. "Who else lives here with you?"

"Wait, I don't live here. I'm just visiting."

"Then who lives here?"

"I do." A man stepped out past the junkie. This guy looked halfway decent but was as white as the snow surrounding his house. "And my girlfriend and I go snowshoeing on the trails around here every day." He snapped his finger twice. "Let me see that picture you showed Jimmy."

The junkie smacked his arm and muttered through partially closed lips, "No names."

Aaron showed the new guy Sarah's photo.

The guy seemed interested, but then shook his head. "Nope, haven't seen her."

They stared at each other for another uncomfortable moment. What was wrong here? Sarah would outsmart, outwit, and outfight a couple of junkies. These guys couldn't be involved.

"Hey," Parkman said, pulling his collar higher. "Getting cold. We should keep moving."

Aaron slipped his phone away and stepped back.

Alex didn't move.

"Good luck," the junkie said, then disappeared inside.

"Yeah, hope you find her," the other guy said, then went to close the door.

Alex jerked as if he saw something, then shoved his shoulder into the door before it closed all the way.

It smacked open so fast the guy on the inside lost his grip, and the door banged against the interior wall.

"What the fuck, man?" the guy shouted.

Parkman ran for the porch as Aaron followed Alex inside. Alex was standing by the kitchen sink in the open-concept cabin when he reached the open door. It was basically one large room with two doors along the rear wall, likely for the bedroom and the bathroom.

"Where'd this blood come from?" Alex asked, all friendliness gone from his tone as he lifted a small white towel stained with blood.

The men exchanged a glance, then looked back at Alex. The junkie —Jimmy—stuttered something, but the other guy spoke in complete sentences.

"That's so embarrassing, man. I wish you hadn't done that."

"Explain," Alex said, the rag still held high. "Now."

"Jimmy here takes too many drugs—"

"We can tell," Aaron cut in.

"—because he hasn't got long to live."

Alex set the rag down slowly.

"Jimmy has cancer. These open sores on his neck and face that he's scratching at are Kaposi sarcoma. He can't handle them, so he scratches them, and they bleed. Sometimes they bleed a lot. We were using that rag to clean them up."

Alex moved to the sink and rinsed his hands.

Jimmy started scratching again.

Aaron just watched.

"You live alone?" Parkman asked.

"No, it's me and my girlfriend, Candace. She's in the bedroom changing."

"She's taking a long time to change."

The guy shrugged. "You know women."

Parkman scanned the rest of the cabin. The fireplace had embers, but no one had put on more wood. The coffee table was out of place— pushed up against the sofa—leaving a rectangular space in front of the fireplace, and the dining table seemed to have been moved against the outer wall. Moving furniture wasn't a crime, but the problem with guys like this is that officials stereotyped them, thinking they must be up to something nefarious.

"Apologies for barging in on you guys tonight." Parkman jerked his head toward the door. Aaron and Alex moved that way.

"Good luck on your search," Jimmy said, still scratching his face.

Parkman nodded and turned to leave.

"Honey?" A woman's voice stopped him. He turned back around.

The woman had just stepped out of one of the back doors.

"What's going on, Mike? Who are these guys?"

"They're looking for a missing woman. There was some sort of car accident."

Aaron marched across the living room to show the woman the photo on his phone.

"Have you seen her?" he asked.

The woman took a good, long look, then shook her head. "Can't say I have." She turned to Jimmy. "You're bleeding again." On her way to the sink, she waved at the other man. "Close the door when they leave. You're letting all the heat out."

Aaron and Alex moved toward the door. Then all three stepped out onto the porch.

"Good luck, guys," the man—Mike—said as he closed the door.

"Something's off here," Alex said. "I can smell it."

"You saw the furniture in disarray?" Aaron asked.

Parkman nodded as Alex stared off into the distance.

"Look, guys." Parkman waved them along. "We got inside, looked around, saw nothing but used snowshoes, moved furniture, and a bloody rag. None of that points directly at Sarah, and none of that makes them liars."

"But it *could* fit the narrative," Aaron added. "Somehow."

"Sure, but with nothing further to go on, we have to keep going. These guys are junkies. Who knows what's going on inside that cabin?"

Parkman got to the end of the driveway and turned around. Aaron was right behind him, but Alex stood by the carport, his eyes on the house.

"You coming?"

After several moments, Alex started toward them. "There's something about those guys that's bothering me. Something's off."

"Well, now's the time to figure that out because if you think Sarah's in there, we need to know."

Alex stared back at the house once more, then shook his head. "She would've called out, left a signal, or something. These guys are no match for her."

Parkman watched him walk away, his shoulders slumped.

Aaron followed, head low, likely dejected. They were no closer to finding Sarah.

Parkman took up the rear, only looking back once.

The living room curtains were shut now, but there was a dark shadow at the seam.

Someone was watching them leave.

When Parkman stopped and stared, the shadow ducked back, leaving the curtains billowing softly for a moment.

*What the fuck is that all about?*

# Chapter 23

"WHAT THE HELL WERE you thinking, letting them inside our house?" Candace shouted at Mike as she jumped back from the front curtains.

"What were you doing at the curtains?" Mike twisted his hands up and jerked his head twice in a gesture of surprise. "Were you watching them? What if they saw you? And for your information, I didn't *let them in*. They barged inside."

"Barged?" she said in a high-pitched tone, mocking him. "Yeah, sure, because volunteer searcher dudes just randomly suspect everyone and smash in front doors." She shook her head. "This is serious business. If Big Carlo's boys had shown up with those guys in here—" She cut herself off. "I don't even want to think about it."

"Hey," Jimmy said, slapping Mike's arm. "You covered up that bloody rag pretty good, though, man."

"Yeah, I heard you boys going on out here." Candace opened the bathroom door. "You guys had it all under control. No wonder I had to come out of hiding to get them to leave."

"We were doing just fine," Mike hollered back, shaking his head at her. He'd gotten their debt forgiven with Carlo's guys. Why couldn't she show some gratitude?

The bathroom door was about to close, but it stopped, and Candace stared across the room at him. She opened her mouth, closed it, then slammed the door.

"She seems upset," Jimmy said.

"Yeah. She'll get over it. We're partying tonight once that Sarah girl is taken out of here. In a few hours, Candy will be liquored up and will have forgotten all about this shit."

"What's she doing in the bathroom?" Jimmy moved onto his other foot. "I gotta take a piss. Nervous shit like what just happened always makes me need to pee." He bounced from one foot to the other, then back again.

"Go piss outside then. Make some yellow snow."

"Dude, I'm not going outside to take a fucking pee. It's too cold—" His phone rang, making him jump. He yanked it from his pocket. "Shit, it's blocked."

"Answer it, dumbass."

Jimmy tapped the button and put the phone to his ear. All Mike could hear was the tinny voice of a man asking a question.

"Yeah," Jimmy said, nodding as if the caller could see him. "He's right here with me." He paused. "Yeah, okay." He pulled the phone away, ended the call, and slipped it back into his pocket. "Shit, now I really gotta pee."

"You gonna tell me who that was?"

"That was Big Carlo."

When Jimmy didn't offer more, Mike said, "He called you directly? Well, what the hell did he say?"

"Okay, fuck it." Jimmy ran for the door. "I'm going outside to pee."

"Are you going to tell me why Big Carlo called you or not?"

"After my piss, man." Jimmy ripped open the door and bumped into a man dressed in black.

He was shoved inside the cabin so hard that he staggered backward several steps, then hit the rear of the couch and flipped over it.

Three large men entered the cabin, each armed with weapons protruding from under their jackets.

A fourth man moved inside, lit a cigarette, took a long pull on it, then stared at Mike through the smoke wafting up in front of his face.

Jimmy scrambled to get back to his feet but lost his balance again and fell sideways, rolled onto the couch, then dropped to the other side and hit the floor. Crawling backward, he edged away from the couch and got his feet while everyone waited.

When he stood up, his pants were wet around the crotch.

"Fuck me," Jimmy whispered, looking down. "I pissed meself."

Under any other circumstances, Mike would have rolled on the floor, slapping his legs and laughing. But not now. Jimmy may have pissed himself, but Mike was about ready to shit himself. These four men were part of the syndicate he owed a hundred grand to, and they were here to take that psychic woman to a place she'd never return from. These were dangerous men of the likes he'd never met before or dealt with. All his dealings were with men like Jimmy. Addicts who sold him his shit and sometimes set up poker tournaments at a rave party— that's how he lost eighty grand he didn't have—betting to pay off the twenty thousand he owed.

"Who's Jimmy?" the fourth man—the smoker—asked.

The man's stern voice matched his chiseled face, sending a shiver of fear through Mike's gut.

"I'm him." Jimmy raised a hand like they were in school, and the teacher was checking to see who was present.

"Carlo just called you, right?"

Jimmy nodded.

There was silence for a moment. The three giant men moved a few steps away from the smoker, fanning out in the cabin.

The smoker shut the cabin door slowly, then turned the bolt, locking them all inside.

"Did. Carlo. Call?" the smoker repeated, glaring at Jimmy.

"Yeah, man." Jimmy's voice cracked. "He called."

"You're the contact? Is that correct?" The smoker walked toward the kitchen, scanned the counters, glanced at the bloody rag, then turned back to face Jimmy, waiting for an answer.

Jimmy nodded frantically. "Yeah, I called my guys who got in touch with Big Carlo about this deal."

The bathroom door swung open, and Candace stared at everyone. "What the—"

Two of the gorillas had reached for their weapons but then lowered their empty hands to their sides.

"And you are?"

"His girlfriend." Candace pointed at Mike.

The smoker sighed, then extended his arm to look at his watch. When he adjusted his sleeve back into place, he studied Mike's face.

"Are you going to give us trouble?"

Mike tapped his chest. "Me?" He swung his head back and forth. "Never. Why would I do that?"

"These two seem eager to fuck with me."

"Hey, wait a sec—"

"No!" The smoker shouted, cutting off Candace. "I asked who you were, and you gave me a non-answer." He gestured at Jimmy. "He answers with head gestures, which I find disrespectful during a proper business meeting." Now he pointed at Mike. "So far, this man is the only one who answered with respect."

"But I didn't—"

"Stop." Smoker raised a hand and looked at the floor, cutting off Jimmy. "This is a business meeting. We are performing a transaction that is worth a hundred grand." Smoker looked up, a vein throbbing on his forehead. "Since we've *already* invested the money, where is the product?"

"In that room," Mike pointed at the bedroom door.

"Then I'd suggest you go get her and bring her out so we can inspect what we're buying."

Mike stepped toward the door but stopped when Smoker spoke again.

"Buyer beware," he said in that same hard tone—the dangerous one. "She had better be in the state quoted by Big Carlo, which was communicated by Jimmy here, through you, Mike, the man who already got paid a hundred large." Smoker shook his head. "We don't play games. If she's some junkie you're trying to pawn off on us, or she's—"

"You'll like this one," Jimmy cut in. "She comes with an added bonus."

Smoker nodded at one of his men.

That man pulled his weapon, aimed it at Jimmy, and fired.

Jimmy took the bullet in his left arm. It spun him around violently until he smashed into the couch again and dropped to the floor, moaning and grunting.

Candace shrieked at the report of the weapon, her hands raised to cover her mouth.

Mike jumped on the spot, his head swiveling from the smoker to the shooter.

"What?" he mumbled. "What, what …"

"No one interrupts me."

Mike was nodding so fast he had to stop to stave off a dizzy spell.

"Get me the girl," Smoker said, sucking on his cigarette. "Or don't. We have lots of bullets. Do not make me ask twice to see what we bought for one hundred big ones."

Mike ran for the bedroom door as a pool of blood formed on his living room floor, where Jimmy writhed and squealed, clinging to his arm.

They were fucked. They made a deal with the devil, and now he came to collect.

If they lived through this, he'd start going to church again. He'd find a way to read the Bible.

If he lived through this, he'd be reborn. There was no doubt in his mind.

But first, he had to live through this, and the odds weren't looking so good.

# Chapter 24

MARIA SAT IN A dank holding cell, a bullet-resistant vest wrapped around her chest and abdomen. They had brought in an interpreter to interview her with members of the state police.

She'd spent several hours telling them who she was and what had happened that led to her being in their custody. An hour wasn't enough to cover five years of the sordid tale, but she gave them the basics and glossed over each beating and every violation.

Then they fed her, gave her a large bottle of water, and left her locked in the holding cell with two armed officers standing guard outside her door.

Could she finally hope this was all over?

The door clicked. Someone was coming inside.

It opened slowly, and the interpreter stepped inside with a female officer from the state police.

"We have good news," the interpreter said. "You are being transferred over to the Antimafia Investigative Directorate (DIA) division. They're coming to take you into protective custody until their investigation is concluded."

"How long should that take?" Maria asked, her fatigue evident in her voice. "I just want to go home."

Her interpreter—she forgot the woman's name—smiled at her. "Of course, but they need every bit of information you might have to close down the Baglioni human trafficking operation."

"Human trafficking," Maria repeated the words, looking off to the side. "I hadn't thought of it that way. I always thought human trafficking was sex workers locked up in hotel rooms and forced to perform."

The interpreter gestured at the chair in front of Maria's thin mattress. "May I?"

Maria nodded, and the woman sat. The officer remained near the door.

"There are nearly forty million slaves around the world today, all held for a variety of reasons. Yes, there are sex slaves. But forced labor is the most common. I was just looking at the numbers online, and it stated that modern slavery is increasing across the globe."

She'd been a slave. But she survived. Samantha hadn't, like all the others before her. Alonzo was dead. He couldn't torture, maim, or kill anyone anymore.

"When can I go home?"

"Unfortunately, I'm not at liberty to say. That's something only the DIA can determine. Their goal, though, as I understand it, is to make this as painless as possible for you."

Maria nodded.

"Maria, having been inside the Baglioni villa and lived to tell about it, is a miracle. Not only that, I translated your statement. I know you killed your abuser, Alonzo Baglioni, and one of his enforcers. You're a survivor. Get through the coming days or weeks, and then go back to your family. The hard part is over."

Hearing those words filled her eyes with tears. It may be over, but she was damaged goods. She'd been violated by over a hundred men hundreds of times since they'd abducted her from the woods where she used to jog in the mornings back in her home state of Vermont. She got up at five that morning, was on the trail by five-thirty, and was bound and gagged in the back of a van by six, never to be seen again.

"Has anyone called my husband?"

The interpreter nodded. "He's been informed, and last I heard, he has booked a flight to Rome to come get you."

Now she did cry. Could it be truly over? Was she really going home?

Her sobs made her shoulders hitch, and she flinched when the woman touched her shoulder.

The interpreter's hand pulled away.

Then someone knocked on the door. The interpreter got to her feet as the door clicked open, and five men filed inside. They spoke in rapid Italian, agreed on something, and then the interpreter turned to Maria.

"These men are with the Antimafia Investigative Unit. They're here to take you into protective custody. I've been informed that once they have all they need from you, they will bring in your husband and, with the help of the United States embassy, arrange for you two to travel safely back home." Her eyes kind, her words soft, she asked, "How does that sound?"

Everyone in the room stared at her, waiting for a reply.

"Like I received a ticket out of Hell, and now I'm heading to Heaven."

"Well then, without delay, let's get a move on."

The men came closer until she saw what they were carrying.

"What's this?" Maria asked, easing back from the man with an arm full of items.

"Extra protection during transport. You're to wear the hood so no one can identify you."

"They think someone will try to kill me?"

"Maria," the interpreter said gently, like the patience her mother had when she tried to explain how to tie her shoelaces. "The Baglioni family isn't interested in having you take the stand in a case against them. You'll be safe with these men, but please understand something. You executed their eldest son, Alonzo. They won't rest until you're not breathing."

"What about when I go back to the States? That's where they nabbed me in the first place."

"Of course. And that's why we've been in contact with your embassy. You'll be entering witness protection in the States. Effectively, you'll disappear again. I'm sorry, but there's no other choice."

The complete understanding of what she was saying came over her.

Maria nodded at the men and allowed them to wrap her in more Kevlar. Once she was on her feet, trying not to recoil at the gentle touch of these men—they were friendly and helping her, but men had touched her against her will for too many years not to flinch away from them—they produced a black hood.

"Is that really necessary?"

"I'm afraid it is. We transport prisoners in such a way. The media has picked up this story. The Baglionis know where you are. That's why we have to transport you immediately. We can't wait. These men won't take the risk of losing you. The Baglionis may have a man in a neighboring building just waiting for you to stick your head out. With this hood covering your appearance, they can't be sure and won't fire randomly."

"The media?"

Her interpreter nodded. "Yes, you're all over Italy's papers at the moment. All the more reason for you to disappear again."

Exhausted, her broken hand aching, Maria offered a slight nod to the men, and they slipped the hood over her head.

Then they placed something cold over her wrist, easing her broken hand closer to the center at the front of her abdomen.

"What are they doing?" she asked, a frantic edge to her voice.

"Handcuffing you."

"But *why*?"

"They're trying to make it look like you're a prisoner. The vehicle they brought is a prisoner transport. This way, it'll throw off anyone looking for you because, for obvious reasons, you're not a prisoner."

Without resisting further, she allowed them to cuff her other hand.

"Okay. I understand."

She could breathe through the hood quite easily and even glimpse a little of the floor in front of her.

"Are you coming with me?" she asked.

"No, the DIA has its own interpreters, I'm afraid. This is the last we'll talk."

After all that had happened to her, Maria was no longer a hugger. Maybe that would come back in time, but for now, all human contact seemed to bother her. So she touched the interpreter's arm as she passed her in the holding cell.

"Thank you," she whispered.

Then they were out of the holding cell and walking through the building, a man on either side. Once out back, men gripped her upper arms and quickly loaded her into the back of an armored vehicle, where she took a seat with her back to the wall.

She tilted her head back to see everyone's shoes. Men sat on either side of her, with two across from her.

The doors were slammed shut, and the vehicle took off as if in a hurry.

She just wanted this to be over. She'd survived Alonzo. Now she wanted her life back, her husband, her family.

But it would appear they stole more than five years from her by abducting her all those years ago.

They also stole a large portion of her future.

Inside the hood, she wept for everything she'd lost, hoping her husband hadn't found a new woman in her absence, hoping he'd take her back and disappear with her to some new life constructed by a government he didn't trust. Her husband had never trusted the government, and because they never found her, he'd trust the authorities much less.

Even though she'd escaped Alonzo and killed him to secure her future, that future wasn't looking too bright at the moment.

# Chapter 25

SARAH FIDGETED ON THE thin mattress as much as she could to get one of her limbs loose, but nothing worked. They'd found a way to secure the ropes to the mattress handles on the side. Until someone released her, she wasn't going anywhere.

Her bladder would explode if she didn't get out soon. That bitch Candace had jammed a dirty sock in her mouth so she couldn't call out for help. And since she'd woken up hours ago, there'd been no bathroom break.

Earlier, she'd been too cold to know if she'd gone or not. In her delirium upon waking in their cabin, she thought she wasn't wearing pants once, but when she woke again, they were on her.

Candace told her they'd laundered them because they were soiled.

*Soiled.* That's what she'd called it.

Well, her pants were about to be *soiled* again if they didn't return soon.

More voices were in the other room now. She focused on them and was able to hear one new male voice. He was talking about someone named Carlo.

*Vivian, you got something for me here? Because I'd really like to get back to Willow, you know.*

Someone else spoke. Silence followed.

When a gun fired, she jerked on the mattress, her body filling with adrenaline. She had to clench to keep from pissing herself.

Something fell on the floor. Someone was moaning loudly while someone else was talking.

What the hell was going on out there?

Footsteps smacked the wooden floor. They sounded like they were moving closer. The bedroom door flew open, and Mike ran inside, followed by Candace. They maneuvered her mattress, then dragged it along the floor through the bedroom door and out into the main room.

Sarah saw the man by the kitchen sink, then took in the men spaced out evenly throughout the cabin.

"Here she is," Mike said.

The man by the sink raised a cigarette to his mouth, drew on it, then let the smoke cover his face like he was being filmed in some movie. His cool act came off as overacting.

"Check the windows," the smoker said.

Two of the three men moved to the curtains and peeked behind them.

"Clear," they both said.

"Take that thing out of her mouth."

Mike yanked the sock with one hard pull.

Sarah gasped for fresh breath from her mouth. "You fuckers," she said between breaths. "That was a shitty rag. And you left it in too long. I have to fucking take a piss."

The smoker was the only one who nodded.

Two of the men who seemed to be with him ran over and began to untie her.

*Finally.*

"You won't fight." The smoker didn't ask it—he stated it. "You won't try to run. You won't get far."

"Yeah, sure. Got it. I'll walk to the toilet, not run."

His lips twitched like he wanted to smile, but he didn't because he had to keep up the act of being some tough shithead.

She tried to stand once they got the ropes off, but it seemed like a huge struggle.

"What the hell is wrong with my legs?"

"They atrophied."

"Yeah. Sure."

"How long have you been lying there?"

"Fucked if I know. A couple of days."

"Your legs are fine. Just get moving, and they'll be normal in no time."

"A little help, please."

Mike and Candace moved in on either side and helped her up, leading her to the bathroom door on wobbly legs while she favored the left knee that was still sore.

"You go in with her," the smoker said to Candace. "You stay out."

Mike released her when Sarah could use the wall for support.

"I can piss on my own." Sarah shot a glance back at the mobster tough guy.

"Chattel doesn't work alone."

Sarah paused to stare at him. "If my legs were stronger ..."

He nodded once to her. "I get that. I respect that. Hurry, though. Piss, and we'll talk."

Mike had gone completely white beside her while Candace nudged her forward into the bathroom.

Once she was done, she flushed, and Candace helped her up.

"Do what he says," she whispered into Sarah's ear. "He means business. He just shot Jimmy." Candace turned on the sink. "He could kill us all."

"Not my problem. I warned you guys, didn't I?"

Candace's eyes widened as she likely remembered Sarah's warning about being psychic and how letting her go kept them alive.

The door opened. One of the mobster's men stood there. They must have heard the toilet flush and didn't want them alone too long.

"Out," was all he said.

Candace bolted past him for the living room.

Sarah finished washing her hands, then dried them, watching him.

He waited.

Then she stepped past him and moved back into the living room with only a slight limp now.

The mobster guy nodded at another man who moved closer with zip ties.

"What the fuck is this now?"

"For your safety," the mobster said.

"*My* safety? How's that?"

Another man walked over to stand by Jimmy, a weapon in his hand.

"My guy will put them on you," the mobster said, "and you'll let him."

"And if I don't?"

The report of the gun made her jump, then stumble. She grabbed the wall to remain standing.

When she looked over, Jimmy's head was a mess of flesh and bone. The man was no longer in pain because he was no longer of this world.

The shooter moved toward Mike, who raised his hands and backed away until he bumped into the wall. Then he squeezed his eyes shut and lowered to his butt, pleading for the man not to shoot.

The mobster dragged on his cigarette again, then said, "Put them on." Each word was accentuated with a burst of smoke coming out of his breath.

He didn't have to say *or else*. That was clearly implied.

Candace was whimpering in the corner by the TV stand as if moving farther from these men could save her from a bullet.

Sarah extended her arms, wrists up for the man to apply the zip ties.

"You going to tell me what this is all about?" she asked.

"I have business with this couple first. Then you and I will take a ride, and I'll explain everything."

The man holding the gun on Mike slipped his weapon away and moved several feet from Mike, who was a complete mess now.

Once the zip ties were applied, the man led her to a chair, where he pushed her down and rested a hand on her shoulder. She jerked hard to have the hand fall off, but he replaced it. She bent forward, but he yanked her back and shoved his hand down harder, tightening his grip.

The mobster wannabe looked over at her. "I like you. I really do. In a situation like this, people only show fear." He ran a hand through his hair, his eyes never leaving her face. "Only fear. But not you. I wonder, what have you seen in your life that shooting a man in the face doesn't fuck you up." He nodded toward the body on Mike's floor. When Sarah glared back at him without speaking, he added, "Don't test me, is all

I'm asking. You seem like a prize. I'd hate to disfigure that pretty face of yours."

He turned to Mike and kicked him in the side. "Get up."

Mike struggled to his feet.

"One hundred large is a lot of money." Mobster puffed on his smoke. "We had a deal, and I see that you lied to us."

"What, what?" Mike stammered through his shaking lips. The guy's entire body was shaking so much that Sarah wondered how he remained upright.

"You said she was unharmed, but her forehead has a nasty cut."

"Yeah, that." Mike swallowed. "That'll heal, though. Right?"

"It might leave a scar." Mobster turned to stare at her.

"Are you guys talking about *buying* me?" Sarah shook her head. "This'll be interesting because I'm not for sale."

Mobster didn't respond to her. He looked over at Candace. "Explain how you came upon her. Give me the details."

Candace was shaken, but not as severely as Mike. She summarized finding Sarah in the snow and how they brought her here to warm her up. Mike recalled something about a few missing girls in the area, and how Jimmy said they weren't missing. They asked questions and dug deeper until Jimmy told them about Big Carlo and how they could sell the girl.

"So we asked Jimmy to negotiate the deal."

Mobster pointed at the dead man on the floor. "You got a junkie to make you a deal?"

Candace nodded. "We were in for a hundred and were told it would be taken care of."

"Did you know the cops are looking for this woman?"

Candace nodded again. "Searchers came knocking about ten minutes before you guys showed up."

Mobster pointed at the living room window. One of his men moved there, where he remained, his eyes glued to the road.

"She's worth more than a hundred grand, though." It looked like Candace said those words before she could take them back as she slapped a hand over her mouth.

Maybe she'd seen Sarah's defiance and recognized it for what it was. The mobster respected someone who stood up for themselves. But she didn't know that he had a limit, and Sarah was someone he wanted alive, so Sarah could push him further, whereas Candace didn't matter. She had no leverage. That's how psychopaths work. To him, Candace was a nuisance. Moving her to the side and stepping past her, or killing her and moving her body to the side, was the same thing for him—she was simply an obstacle.

The mobster sauntered toward her, his face blank. In this scenario, there was a plus side—he didn't order any of his men to kill her.

"No," Mike said, his voice weak. "Please don't."

"Hey," Sarah said. "She's right. I am worth more."

Neither one of them broke the mobster's concentration on Candace.

He stopped in front of her, his eyes roaming her face. Then he touched her cheek with his left hand, and she recoiled slightly. He eased her hair behind her ear.

What was his right hand doing in his front pocket?

Something was on his fingers when his hand came out of his pocket.

"Hey," Sarah shouted, but it was too late.

The man's hand came up so fast that Candace barely reacted as he punched her in the forehead.

Candace dropped to the floor, her legs crumpling under her.

Sarah went to stand, but the man's hand on her shoulder dug in so tight that she cried out in pain.

"Fuck off," she yelled at the guy. "You're going to break my fuckin' collarbone."

He released her and placed a hand on her other shoulder.

Bolstered by someone hitting his girl, Mike scrambled to get off the floor. Once on his feet, a gun was placed to his face.

"I am not messing around," the wannabe mobster said as he pulled the miniature version of brass knuckles off his fingers. "This is serious money, serious business."

Candace moaned on the floor as blood seeped through his fingers. He'd hit her with the brass knuckles so hard he split her skin, and her forehead bled badly. She'd be covered in no time.

"So, here's what we're going to do." Mobster moved into the middle of the living room. "The cops need a body."

"What?" Mike gasped the word. "No, please."

"Shut up," Mobster shouted. "The cops'll want a body. Here's my proposal." He stopped to see who would interrupt him, but no one did. "Candace has a forehead wound in the same spot as hers." He pointed at Sarah. "Candace will walk to the car accident scene without a jacket."

"What? Why?" Mike was so nervous he could barely stand on his own. Finally, gravity won, and he plopped onto the edge of the couch.

These two were in way over their heads and had no play here, but they thought they could talk their way out. They'd be executed if they didn't get with the program quickly.

"We need to give the cops something to chew on while we take her" —he pointed at Sarah without looking at her—"where she's going. Do you understand?"

Mike stared at Candace, who was watching them through her blood-covered face.

"She will say," Mobster continued, "that she stole the car. The driver left it running. She has no idea who or where the driver is." He raised a finger. "But this plan only works if those volunteers who came knocking didn't see her." He looked from Candace to Mike, then back to Candace. "Did they see her when they came to the door?"

Mike jerked his head back and forth. "No, she stayed in the bedroom with her." He nodded at Sarah.

That wasn't what happened, but Sarah wasn't about to correct him.

"Last issue to deal with."

Everyone waited as Mobster dropped his cigarette to the floor and ground it under his polished dress shoe. Then he lit another one and puffed on it twice.

"What did Candace mean about this girl being worth more?"

"She meant nothing by it. We're happy with the deal." Mike was done. He had a dead friend on his living room floor, and his woman's forehead wouldn't clot. "Please," he begged.

Mobster nodded at one of his men, who walked toward Mike, a gun coming up.

"Wait," Mike screamed. "She meant that Sarah is psychic." The words came out like a stream of consciousness, something similar to an auctioneer.

The mobster guy waved a hand, and his minion slipped the weapon away.

"Tell me more."

"We looked her up on Google. She's Sarah Roberts, some psychic who has helped the authorities in the past. We were talking"—he inhaled like he was running out of breath or hyperventilating—"and felt she was a prize."

The mobster turned to look at Sarah. "Is this true? You can tell the future?"

"Well, not exactly."

"Don't lie to him," Mike shouted. "You don't know who you're dealing with."

"If he speaks again, break some of his teeth." Mobster walked toward Sarah. "Tell me about you, something I won't find on Google."

"There's nothing to tell other than my dead sister tells me things about the future, and I try to correct imbalances."

"Is she talking to you right now? Has she told you about us?"

"No, she's oddly silent about this situation, which is starting to piss me off."

The mobster smiled one of those ear-to-ear grins. "I like you. I think I'll keep you around for a while." He turned back to Mike. "So, do we have a deal? Candace takes the fall for your fuckups? She goes outside, gets cold, nearly freezes to death, and explains that she was driving the car when they ask. Suddenly, the cops have to look far and wide for Sarah because they'll have no idea where she stopped to leave the car running. And all that time, Candace here can claim she doesn't remember much after hitting her head. End of story." He ran a hand through his hair again. "Everyone agrees?"

"Well, if there's another way to handle it," Mike said, "I'd rather not put her through that."

"There is another way." Mobster moved closer to Mike. "There's always another way."

"Yeah." Mike's voice cracked. "True. I agree."

"I could kill her and dump her body by the car. That's another way. Would you prefer that?"

Mike swung his head back and forth. "No, no, that's not what I was thinking. Please don't."

"How about I walk out of here, and everyone goes home?" Sarah waited until Mobster turned to look at her. "Problem solved."

Mobster shook his head. "No, this piece of shit would still owe us a hundred grand. I think I'll take you in lieu of payment."

"But I'm not for sale."

"And Copernicus thought the Earth was flat. He was wrong, too." He turned back to Mike but spoke to Candace. "Candace, are you agreeable?"

"Yes," she said.

"Are you agreeable, Mike?"

"The deal was a hundred grand for her." He pointed at Sarah. "Can we get a little something for the work and time Candace is adding to this arrangement?"

Why was he trying to be strong now? They were in the homestretch. Just shut up and agree, and it could all go away.

Mobster glanced around the room, a cocky smile on his face. "What would you like?" he asked, his tone hard.

The man seemed out of patience, and stupid Mike couldn't tell.

"He doesn't know what he's asking for," Sarah said, trying to save his skin. "Just leave it alone, Mike."

"Hey, who are you to do my negotiating here?" Mike leaned forward, bolstered by his own stupidity. He glanced up at Mobster and rubbed his nose like something tickled his face. "I want twenty grand more for Candace's help. That way, I can cover legal expenses when they pick her up and charge her with stealing the car and some shit like that—"

"No!" Sarah shouted, interrupting Mike.

He'd been so wrapped up in his own bullshit that he didn't see Mobster nod ever so slightly at one of his men.

Even Candace didn't see it as she was wiping fresh blood from her face.

One of Mobster's men stepped in behind Mike, placed the gun by the man's left ear, and pulled the trigger.

The exit wound was massive, removing a large portion of the right side of Mike's face as if he'd been chewing on a firecracker, and it blew out his cheek. The man's mouth dangled to the side, his jaw shattered, broken, and mostly missing, and his right eye swung with the muscles it remained attached to grotesquely.

Sarah looked away from the mutilated image as Mike rolled forward and dropped to the floor with a heavy thump of finality.

And Candace screamed as madness seeped in around the corners of her sanity.

# Chapter 26

THEY RODE IN THE back of the state police vehicle for close to a half-hour, by Maria's estimation, before they'd finally slowed and were backing up to something.

One of the men grabbed her hood and removed it.

"Is that safe?" she asked.

No one answered. No one looked at her.

The pit of her stomach twisted. She couldn't grasp the concept that all of these men could be in league with Baglioni. There was no way. He couldn't be that powerful. Could he?

The back door opened, and sunlight filtered inside. Her eyes slitted to avoid the brightness after being covered in the hood.

They lifted her by her arms and guided her to exit the rear of the vehicle. When she blinked rapidly to see again, she caught a glimpse of roughly a dozen men standing in a semi-circle around the back of the police van.

When her eyes stopped at Alberto Baglioni's face, she moaned and tried to back away, her stomach turning sour.

The men roughly handed her off to Alberto's men, who shoved her to her knees and forcefully held her there. She gagged, trying to hold down the meal the police had given her at the station.

"Grazie," Alberto said. He switched to English when he added, "You will be rewarded handsomely for this. All of you will receive three years' pay in cash. Leave us now. You were never here."

The officers piled into the state police van, the doors closed, and the tires kicked up dirt as Alberto turned to face her.

Hope left her body through her tears, one by one, dropping off her cheeks as she stared at the ground. She would die here, and she could do nothing about that now.

"The bitch is back," Alberto whispered.

She glanced up at him and grimaced at the hatred on his face.

"You murdered my brother." Each word was clipped, forced. It was as if he was whispering, the words hard to speak, straining to come out. "You will be dead by the end of the week. I'd kill you now, but listening to you scream will help me grieve Alonzo." He jerked his hand, and Maria was lifted to her feet. "This will be a week from Hell for you, make no mistake. You'll be begging me to kill you within days." He stepped back. "Tie her up in the cellar. Take off her clothes and burn them. Cut off her hair. Then bring me my tools. When I'm back from retrieving my brother's body from the morgue, I have to prepare for the funeral."

They dragged her away as he was talking.

"I'll see you tonight," he called after her. "Your last week on Earth begins now."

Maria hung her head. She'd been so close.

At least now, it would be over. Just one more week to go.

She wasn't sure how she'd last that long, though. There had to be a way to end it more quickly.

Then an idea came to her. It was the only way.

Knowing this was the absolute end, she would have the courage to do it.

At least, she hoped so.

# Chapter 27

"I'M THINKING WE GO back to that house," Aaron said.

They'd knocked on twenty more doors and got nowhere over the past hour. Not a single person they spoke to had seen Sarah anywhere.

"What house?" Parkman asked. "That one with the junkies?"

Aaron checked his watch. "Yeah, it's getting late in the day. We've been at this for over an hour, maybe longer." He looked up at Alex and Parkman. "The sun has set, and we've found nothing. The only place where they were acting weird was that house." He waved a hand, gesturing all around them. "We're far enough from the accident that it's unlikely she's gone this far."

"They were acting weird because they're junkies, Aaron."

Aaron nodded once, glanced at Alex for input, and when nothing was forthcoming, he said, "Probably. But still, we're far from the area where it's likely someone took her."

"Meaning?" Parkman shivered with the cold.

"Meaning, if they carried her out of the woods, they put her in a car and drove off."

"Is that what you think?"

"Look, maybe the cold is getting to me. I'll be clearer. She's stuck in one of the houses we encountered when we found this road at the end of the path we followed. Or, she's gone somewhere else because the people who have her had a vehicle." He waved a hand at the houses around them. "This is a few kilometers from where we came out of the woods. The odds are decreasing with each house we hit."

Parkman looked at Alex. They both watched him as he stared down the road.

"Alex," Aaron said. "Thoughts?"

Alex turned to him and nodded once. "I'd agree. Continuing farther from the woods has a lower probability of success."

"And the junkie house?"

"Revisit them."

They started walking again.

"They'd used snowshoes recently, too," Parkman added.

"And that rag on the counter." Aaron shook his head. "There was more blood on it than what that guy could've scratched out of his face, no?"

Parkman and Alex turned to him.

"Maybe we aren't trained investigators like cops or you, Parkman, but something seemed off there," Aaron added.

Alex picked up his speed.

"Hey," Parkman said. "I won't be able to match that pace for long."

Aaron moved quickly to stay with Alex. "We don't have to arrive as a team. If Sarah is there and needs us, Alex can take care of himself."

Then Alex was jogging with Aaron right beside him.

If Sarah were there, and they had walked away, he'd never forgive himself if something happened to her.

What would they tell Willow? How could he face her if they missed Sarah by mere inches and then something happened?

Now, Aaron was running faster than Alex.

Something told him they had to get there—now.

Or were they just working themselves up needlessly?

# Chapter 28

"SHUT HER UP," MOBSTER said, pointing at Candace.

His man stepped over, reared back his right leg, and kicked Candace in the face. Her head snapped sideways, bounced off the wall behind her, and her eyes rolled up as she slumped to the floor.

"You didn't have to do that." Sarah glared at Mobster.

"Fuck me, now I've got this bitch telling me how to do my job." He shook his head as if exasperated with a co-worker. "Get the coffin out of the truck."

Two of his men disappeared out the front door, closing it behind them.

Candace moaned as she slowly came to. When she pushed herself up into a sitting position, her eyes roamed the faces staring back at her.

"Still with us?" Mobster asked.

She stared at him as if trying to comprehend who he was.

"Don't scream again." He raised a finger as if chastising a child. "You hear me? I don't want to have to kill you. You're worth slightly more alive." He shrugged, then said as an afterthought. "Well, at the moment."

Candace rubbed her eyes, then blinked as she studied the room while taking shaky breaths. Her head shook back and forth slightly as if in denial. Her body swayed, and she placed a hand over her stomach. Then she squeezed her eyes shut as if that would block out the world—or, perhaps, block out the madness. When her eyes opened again, they weren't just widened. They were bulging from their sockets.

Sarah watched Candace, but her thoughts returned to the coffin.

Why would they be driving around with a coffin?

Then it came to her, and she turned to face the mob guy as he was lighting another cigarette.

"You came here to kill Mike, didn't you? There was no deal to be had."

He swung his arm to kill the flame at the tip of the match, then took a drag on his smoke, watching her the whole time.

"Mike had to die. His debt was too high. Drugs and gambling dens don't mix."

"A den of iniquity."

"Cute."

They stared at each other for a long moment.

"And Jimmy?"

The mobster shrugged. "This transaction can't have any leaks. No one walks away from here, but people I've personally vetted and trust. Jimmy was a junkie. You do the math."

Sarah took a quick look at Candace to see if she understood what the guy just said, but she was rocking back and forth now, eyes on the floor, mumbling something to herself as blood dripped from her mouth. When the guy kicked her, he must've knocked a tooth loose or torn the inside of her cheek.

"This was a *dead* deal from the beginning." The man certainly loved to smoke. He punctuated his sentences with a drag. Then he spoke again, his words accompanied by smoke that exited his mouth like cloudy breath. "How did Jimmy even know to contact Big Carlo about what I do? That's a leak I'll have to fix once you're on your way."

"On my way? Where am I going?"

"You'll find out when you get there."

"Such a mystery," she said, her voice raised as if this were all fun and games.

"You can approach tension and fear with humor, Miss Roberts. I don't mind. Although, I think where you're going will take all that away from you." He walked closer to her. "Where you're going, there is no humor. It's like a cancer that will eat at your soul until you give in, give up—until you're broken. Then you die."

"Looking forward to it." Sarah grinned at him. "Of course, my sister would set this up as that sounds like my kind of place."

Mobster blinked twice while staring at her. "Are you utterly mad?"

"Baby, I was born this way."

The door banged open, making them both turn to watch as Mobster's men carried a large coffin into Mike and Candace's living room.

"Can you fit both bodies in there?" Sarah asked, hoping he wouldn't say all three while Candace was still alive and sobbing in the corner.

"That's not for them."

That sentence sank in hard. She didn't expect it. Frowning, she wondered if he planned on killing her, too. Wasn't he executing everyone and plugging holes to keep his organization protected, and didn't that mean that he came to take her with him—

"No fucking way," she whispered when it fully hit her. "I'm not getting inside that thing."

"I'm afraid you don't have a choice, darling."

She struggled to stand, but the man behind her had to have concrete in his hands and shoulders because when he pressed downward, she remained immobilized.

"How about this?" The smoker walked closer to Candace while talking to Sarah. "I need Candace alive for my story to work. Candace returns to the accident scene and claims she stole your car; that's the end of the story. She tells them she didn't see you and has no idea where you are—"

"As long as I get inside that thing," Sarah finished for him.

Candace was nodding as she listened to him, essentially pleading for her life.

"Sort of."

"Meaning?"

"Well, there's another option."

"Which is?"

"They find Candace's body close to the accident scene and discover that she stole the car and ran it off the road."

Candace was shaking her head now, crying.

"So, what will it be?" Sarah asked. "She's alive and tells them, or she's dead, and they figure it all out?"

"See? That's the part that's up to you. Get in the coffin. Candace lives. Refuse, and Candace dies." The smoker stuck the cigarette between his lips, then produced a weapon and racked the slide. "I don't care either way." He held up a finger. "Wait, actually, I do care. I'd prefer if you refused." He gave her an evil grin, more of a sneer. "Please refuse." Then he pointed the weapon at Candace.

The woman stared at Sarah from across the living room. Her world had turned to hell over the past half an hour, and Sarah saw regret all over her face. If only they could turn back the clock.

"I'll go."

The mobster didn't move. The gun didn't waver. "Are you sure?"

"I said, I'll go. There's nothing to decipher in a statement like that. It's pretty absolute, meaning you have a deal. Now lower the weapon and coach her on what to say."

The gun went back in his pants, and he stepped away from Candace. "Listen to her, boys." He laughed. "Telling me how to do my job."

Several of his men laughed as if they were paid robots.

"Get her inside that thing."

She was lifted from under the arms and carried over to the coffin on the living room floor as the other man opened the lid.

The inside was not what she expected. A plush interior with a few cables in the center and what looked like an air filter built in above the head area. There were four large, sealed gas containers inside.

"Burning down the house?" she asked.

"Fire, the great purifier." Mobster tapped his gun. "Of course, I'm not leaving evidence behind."

She hoped Candace could run fast. "How long will I be inside?"

"Until you get there."

"Where am I going?"

"When that lid opens, you will have arrived. You will learn all about your new home then."

"What are these cables for?" she asked.

They were taking the gas containers out. Once that was done, they lifted her and eased her inside the coffin, her guts twisting at the thought of being inside one of these things. Will she ever escape this death trap? Will she ever see her daughter again?

"The cables allow you to pee while lying down." He moved closer and pointed at one of his men. "Show her."

The man lifted a curved bedpan and rested it on the bottom of the coffin in a way that would catch her urine when she was lying down.

"There's an air filter at the top that gives you fresh oxygen throughout your trip, and a water tube connected to a one-liter jug installed in the side. Be warned, though, when that liter runs out, there's no more water."

"Food?"

"When you arrive."

"Then tell me how long you expect me to be in here."

"It'll be about twelve hours, maybe more."

She stared at him. "You're kidding, right?"

"I don't have much of a sense of humor, I'm afraid. Using a coffin gets you on a plane and through customs as a dead body. No one will open it to inspect the body. We have someone who handles the paperwork for us. The walls are soundproofed, so you won't hear the outside, and no one will hear anything if you're screaming. Once that lid closes, it's bolted shut until you arrive. So don't lose your mind in there."

"Wait." She raised a hand to stop the lid from closing. "Is this really necessary? I mean, I can travel easily right beside you."

"As much as I'd like that, you no longer have intrinsic value as a human being. You're chattel, a piece of farm equipment that's used until it breaks, then discarded. You have no feelings, no concerns, and I don't care if you suffocate in there or live through this ordeal, whether you're frightened or delighted." He moved closer. "In other words, you mean absolutely nothing to us except for the value you'll create as a slave." He placed the gun so close to her face that she had to ease back to avoid being touched by it. "If I kill you now, then I'd have to kill Candace.

And then, I'd have to go snatch some woman off the street to take your place. This selfless act of lying down and enduring the ride will save countless women from unnecessary trauma."

"How sick are you?" Sarah stared up at him, rapidly going through options on how to change the current dynamic and coming up empty. "I mean, are you even on the spectrum, or haven't they made one big enough for you?"

"Cute." He pulled the gun away. "Lock her in place."

All three of his men got to work securing her ankles to the base of the coffin, ensuring her feet were flat against the bottom. Then her wrists were secured, and finally, a strong strap was wrapped over her shoulders.

"Locked in as you are, there's enough play on your right wrist to maneuver that bedpan device to piss."

"What about my pants?"

"Piss through them. You'll get new clothes where you're going."

"Not very effective then, is it?"

They closed the lid on the bottom half and locked it in place. It gave her the shivers because if people attended her open-casket funeral, this was precisely what they'd see.

There was no escaping this contraption—she was no Houdini.

Before closing the top section, the mobster got to his feet and faced the whimpering Candace, still sitting on the floor, her back against the wall. The blood coming out of her mouth had stopped, but the right side of her face was red and swollen.

"On second thought." The smoker raised his weapon. "I'll just use your body."

He fired multiple times, each bullet tearing into Candace, with more than half of them ripping apart her face. Her body jerked against the wall until his gun went silent, and she slumped forward.

Sarah screamed through clenched teeth, grunting like an animal as she fought the restraints holding her in place.

"Toot-a-loo," he said, waving his fingers as his men slammed the lid down, dropping her into darkness.

She wailed against the darkness and tried to ram her head against the lid, but it didn't do a thing with all the soft pillow-like cushioning.

Something clicked above her head, and fresh air began streaming inside. Then soft piano music fluttered in, likely designed to comfort the unsettled traveler.

She rocked in place as they lifted her and carried her outside like pallbearers.

She called to her sister, begged for an audience, and swore she'd kill her when she got to the other side if she didn't get to see Willow again.

But Vivian didn't answer.

After a short period of time, she felt the gentle rocking of a vehicle.

Her journey had begun.

How it would end was anybody's guess.

But one thing was certain—she'd have to deal with the mobster somehow. Men like that couldn't be allowed to roam free. They were taking random women off the streets at will. And for what? To make them slaves?

Some people should die.

It made for a better world.

# Chapter 29

PARKMAN'S PHONE RANG AS he watched Aaron and Alex run away from him. He wasn't going to run to catch up. They'd get to the junkie's house and deal with whatever they found without him. He'd get there when he got there.

He stopped for a moment to grab his phone and saw that the number was blocked.

After stabbing the answer button, he said, "Yeah, Parkman here."

"It's Darwin. Any luck on Sarah?"

Parkman updated him on their search, the episode at the junkie house, and how they had nothing to prove for their day so far.

"We're heading back to the junkie house now to rule out that their weird behavior was nothing more than that." Parkman got walking again.

"Okay, let me know what you find, but when you do, call and leave a message. I won't be available for a couple of days."

"Are you flying over here to help look for Sarah?"

"I can't at the moment. I have a problem in my own backyard."

"What sort of problem?"

"There's an American woman who entered police custody with an outrageous story about being a slave for years. The papers picked it up before the story was killed."

"A slave?" Parkman moved to the side of the road to let a couple of pickups roll by. One of them had a coffin in the back. He nodded at the driver, who waved at him. "I had no idea the Italians bought and sold people."

"Well, technically, the Italians don't. But certain rich people do. From my underground sources, the Baglioni family, who live in the Amelia and Terni area, which is over an hour south of us, are involved."

"You know these people?"

"Not personally, but I know of them. Bad dudes who made their money years ago in tobacco farming and now distribute a different kind of tobacco. Anyway, they found Alonzo Baglioni and one of his henchmen dead in their neighbor's house. You want to know what happened to those neighbors?"

"Executed?"

"And dismembered. Their house burned down, too."

"So you're going after the Baglioni family?"

"Not necessarily. I'm going to look for the woman named Maria Christy."

Parkman rounded a corner in the road and stared down the length of it, but couldn't see Aaron and Alex. "Who is she?"

"She's the American woman who was in police custody."

"Was? I thought you said she entered custody a moment ago."

"I did, but they can't find her now."

"How does that happen?"

"A back door left open. A Baglioni man standing by the door."

"No way. That still goes on there?"

"In more ways than you know. Anyway, I've assembled a small team to offer surveillance. We'll be in their area in twenty minutes, so I wanted to call and let you know that I'll be out of contact for a few days."

"Okay, do your thing, and if you need us, you know we'll hop on a plane in a second."

"Just find Sarah. She's the priority."

A bright orange flickering light by the woods was coming up on the right. Then his phone buzzed as another call was coming in.

"Hey, Darwin, I have another call coming in."

"Go, deal with your stuff and get Sarah. I'll be here if you need me in a few days."

"On it, talk soon."

He clicked over to the other call as he picked up his pace. "Parkman."

"This is Sergeant James. We found something."

Parkman slowed down, then stopped and stared at nothing for a moment. "Something? What's that mean?"

"We found a body."

His heart sank. No way. It couldn't be. He refused to believe it.

"I'm assuming it's a blond female."

"Yes," James said. "Same height, same hair. Also, she has a forehead wound consistent with hitting a windshield, but the rest of her face is a mess."

His mouth went parched, and he had trouble forming the words. "A mess?"

"At this point, we have to assume someone forced her off the road, dragged her from the car, kept her for a couple of days, then killed her."

"What?" Parkman leaned on a car. "I don't understand."

"She's not frozen. If she'd been outside all this time, she'd be colder."

"Why is her face a mess?"

"Someone shot her multiple times."

"Oh," squeaked out of his mouth in a pitch he didn't recognize.

That orange glow was bigger now. Was something on fire up ahead?

"Can you come back to the highway? I'll drive you guys to the morgue for a positive ID."

"Yeah. Give us a half hour."

"I'll wait."

Parkman ended the call and put one foot in front of the other until he rounded the last corner and saw a house on fire.

He sprinted the length of the road until Aaron and Alex came into view.

It was the junkie's house. Even the carport was engulfed in flames now.

A firefighter's siren wailed in the distance as all three men stepped back farther, as the heat coming off the house was getting intense.

He had no idea how to tell them about his call with Sergeant James.

Maybe he wouldn't. Maybe he'd just walk them to the highway.

But they'd need to know where they were going. They'd ask, and it was better coming from him than the sergeant.

"Fuckin' junkies burned their house down." Aaron shook his head as he stared at the flames.

Red lights flashed across neighboring houses as the fire trucks arrived.

"We need to step back, guys," Parkman said, hoping they'd follow him to the side so he could explain why he'd gone numb all over after the sergeant's call.

It was Alex who noticed his facial expression first.

He placed a hand on Parkman's shoulder to help steady him. "You don't look so good."

"I heard from Sergeant James."

Aaron turned to look at them. Now he had their undivided attention.

"They found a body."

Aaron shook his head. "No, it can't be."

"They think it's her."

Alex's hand squeezed Parkman's shoulder, but he didn't move away. "They *think*?"

Parkman nodded, hoping he wouldn't throw up. "Same height, same hair, but they can't tell. They need us for a positive ID."

"Why can't they tell?" Alex asked, but Aaron stepped back and still shook his head.

"Because—" Emotion closed his vocal cords. He inhaled and looked skyward in the hopes of keeping his eyes dry. "Because someone shot her in the face multiple times."

Aaron made a moaning sound as he bounced on his feet now. The moans sounded like he was chanting *no* under his breath.

"The sergeant suspects someone forced her off the road, took her somewhere, then shot her and tossed her body in the woods."

"Oh, Sarah." Aaron groaned the words. "No, no, no, no ..."

Alex released Parkman's shoulder to wipe a tear from his eye.

"Where are they now?"

"Waiting for us on the highway to take us to the morgue for that positive ID."

Alex moved away from them and started toward the woods.

"Come on," Parkman said, taking Aaron by the arm and forcing him to follow Alex.

"It's not her," Alex said over his shoulder. "It can't be *her*."

His voice cracked on the last word.

Had they failed Sarah in some way? What would life be like without her?

Clearly, Aaron was distraught. Even after all they had gone through, he still loved her. Of this, Parkman had no doubt.

They all loved her.

They wouldn't survive her death.

If that were Sarah at the morgue, they'd never be the same again.

# Chapter 30

MARIA THOUGHT SHE HAD a relationship with pain, understood it, and could endure it. But the last twelve hours had been torture indescribable.

They'd brought her back down to the cellar—the cages were gone, as well as Samantha's body—and tied her to the wall at the seven-foot mark. Her hands were bound above her head because she stood less than six feet tall. The pins and needles had come and gone, and now her arms were numb. Yet, the pain in her neck and shoulders was aflame. There was no movement, no position she could find comfort in.

Her legs were holding her up, but she couldn't walk or take a seat. Falling asleep would be madness in this position. If she did that, all her weight would drag her downward, and her wrists would suffer. Could the blood be cut off from her hands altogether? Would she lose her hands?

With the plans Alberto had for her, did any of that matter in the long run? She was dead anyway. It was the road to death that made her think she had to walk through Hell to get there. Usually, people had to die first before Hell became an option.

The door opened, filling the room with light.

At that moment, she was reminded of something from Bible study when she was a teenager. The light is on in the hallway, but the room is dark. When the door opens, the darkness doesn't spill into the hallway. No, the light spills into the room. In other words, darkness can't win. Light will always conquer.

Bolstered with the thought that God was with her, she struggled to stand upright, even though it was challenging to have any dignity while tied to a wall completely naked.

Three men materialized from the corridor, with Alberto leading them.

Was this going to be the first gang rape? Maybe one of them will have a knife she could grab. She prayed one of them would be careless. Please, just once.

"Whore cow," Alberto said as he stopped in front of her. "I'm trying on different names for the last week of your life. Something like murderer is too bland, even though you killed my brother. Oh, and you killed those neighbors."

She stared at him, her eyes narrowed. Maybe she could rile him up, piss him off, find his triggers so he'll lose his mind, and stab or shoot her.

"You killed them, asshole."

He smiled with half his mouth. "Okay, you're right there. But still, if you hadn't stopped at their house, they'd be alive today." He shrugged. "So, technically, you killed them and burned down their house."

The three men stood like sentries behind him, their eyes roaming her body. At least none of them were disrobing yet.

She focused her attention back on Alberto's face. "You came all the way down here to tell me that so I'd be tortured with remorse? Is that it?"

He glanced over his shoulder at his men, then back to her, his smile wider. "Wow, you're saucy now. Where did this attitude come from? That small taste of freedom did you no favors."

"They're looking for me. They know I was in police custody. Even the media wrote about it. They'll come, and when they do, we'll see who's crying." She leaned forward and grimaced with the pain.

"Sure, whatever you say. But I should tell you that the police closed the case. The file said the American woman who cried wolf has gone home to her husband. The media dropped the story. You're all mine until I decide otherwise. There will be no escape for you this time, well, unless you can cut your hands off and slip out of those things."

"Provide me with a sharp knife, and you'll see what I'd do to escape."

He chortled for a few seconds, then his face turned serious. He stepped closer, looking down at her breasts. "Maria, haven't you wondered why we left you alone for the past twelve hours?"

"I have no idea. If I'm dead anyway, just end it."

"There's plenty of time for that." Alberto grabbed her right breast and squeezed, then her left one.

She tried to angle away but only succeeded in moaning as the pain in her shoulders flared like knives sliced through her joints.

"Oh, you like that," Alberto said. He moved closer and cupped her vagina with his hand, pushing his fingers through her labia. "How about this? I bet you want lots of this before you die."

Ignoring the pain and not caring what he'd do to her, she spat in his face, then tried to headbutt him but missed.

When her saliva landed on his cheek, he'd reared back just out of reach for the headbutt.

"Wow, you're much spicier than I remember." He lifted the bottom of his shirt to dab at the spit, wiping his cheek clean. "Guys, she likes it in the face. Once the cook is through with her, fuck every hole and unload on her face. Make sure to get it in her eyes and mouth."

"The cook?" she said.

"That's what I came to tell you. He should be out of the hospital by tomorrow. You know, they had to wire his jaw. He'll be eating with a straw for many, many months because of you. So, I've ordered you to be left alone until he gets here. As a special request to our chef, he wants the first crack at you, and what he has planned isn't going to be tasty. Well, at least not for you."

"Fuck you."

"Yeah, I figured. Anger and names won't save your ass." He stepped back and smelled his finger. "Whoa, guys. Unhook her and bathe her. Make sure she's clean for when the cook gets back tomorrow."

"Sure thing, boss."

They moved forward as a group. When the cuffs came off and her arms dropped, Maria wondered if she'd pass out with the pain.

They carried her out of the cellar without a care in the world, where their hands went.

She'd find a way out of this. Hope was in short supply, but there had to be some as long as her heart was still beating.

Or at least there was a glimmer of hope before the cook came back.

She had no idea what he had planned, but the man was good with knives, and it was evident he'd violate her in a hundred different ways because he was always creepy and inappropriate when they'd been in the kitchen together over the years.

Her time was coming. She could feel it.

And when it came, she'd jump at the chance to escape this place—through death.

# Chapter 31

EVERYONE REMAINED SILENT AS the sergeant drove them to the morgue, each man lost in their own thoughts. To get their minds off the fact that they were heading to positively ID Sarah's body, Parkman asked, "Have we considered why there was a fire at the junkie house?"

Neither man moved at first, then Aaron looked over at him from the back seat. "You think it's connected somehow?"

"What I think is when we positively ID this woman, who I don't think is Sarah, we head back to that house and find out everything we can."

"Won't the fire marshal launch an investigation in the coming days *after* the fire is extinguished?"

"Sure, but we might get preliminary findings. They can probably tell how many bodies were in there, too."

"Bodies?" Aaron adjusted himself to face Parkman. "Are you suggesting the fire is to cover something up?"

"All I'm saying is, something was weird about that place. We all felt it and decided to investigate further. By the time we get back there, it's engulfed in flames, and now the authorities have a body in a morgue. Things are being wrapped up too quickly, which leads me to conclude someone is behind it all. As soon as we identify the bodies, assuming there are some, we can begin to connect known associates and move from there."

"Did you guys see that truck with the coffin?" Alex asked from the front passenger seat.

"What coffin?" Sergeant James averted his eyes from the road for a brief moment. "You guys saw a coffin?"

Alex nodded.

"Yeah," Parkman said. "Two trucks drove by us as we ran for the junkie house on fire. An SUV and a large pickup with a coffin in the back."

The sergeant met his gaze in the rearview mirror. "A pickup and not a hearse?"

Parkman nodded. "A pickup."

"That's weird." The sergeant shook his head slowly. "Look, we'll be at the morgue in a few minutes. Tell me where the house is, and I'll run the address to see who lives there."

"I didn't catch the street name or the number. Did you guys?"

Aaron and Alex shook their heads.

"I can show you on Google Maps, though. And, once we're done at the morgue, we're going back there anyway. We want to speak to the fire investigator on site."

"I'll join you," James said. "I'm invested now. We need to get to the bottom of this because if the woman lying in the morgue is not Sarah, then I've got a murder *and* a possible abduction on my hands."

"Maybe you'll know them by name," Parkman said. "We saw three people in the house. A woman named Candace, who came out just as we were leaving, and a junkie named Jimmy. I didn't get the other guy's name—"

"Jimmy?" the sergeant said. "Jimmy 'Five Finger' Gower? No way. I've known Jimmy for about a decade. No one knows how he's still alive."

"'Five Finger'?" Parkman repeated.

"Yeah, if it's the same guy, he used to work for Big Carlo years ago. He's an old gang banger out of Orillia. Well, I should change that because I'm giving him too much credit. A low-life criminal out of Orillia who runs rave parties, illegal gambling, girls, and drugs. Anything that can make him money, he peddles it. We've arrested him several times, but he's Teflon—nothing sticks to Big Carlo." The sergeant signaled and made a right turn. "Jimmy ran things for a while for Carlo, but he skimmed off the top and got caught. They hospitalized him several times, and now he sells drugs for Carlo to make back what he stole with interest. We've been trying to nail Big Carlo for years." The sergeant shook his head. "If they're involved, that's good and bad."

"Why good and bad?" Aaron asked.

"Good, because we might get him on something and close him down finally." He paused. "I'm not sure you guys want to hear the bad."

Alex turned to him. "We can take it. Tell us."

"If Sarah is with these guys, they'll have her in a motel room somewhere for a month. The rotating door will have twenty to thirty men coming and going while she's tied to a bed. We rescued one girl two months ago. She counted over fifty men per day but wouldn't point at her abusers. She remained silent. Which means Big Carlo gets to keep doing what he wants." The sergeant paused. "That seventeen-year-old girl hung herself three days after we rescued her."

Parkman clenched his hands into fists. "That's why murder shouldn't be illegal for people like Big Carlo."

"I hear that," the sergeant said, glancing at Parkman in the mirror. "If he has her, and it's all speculation because the house that burned might have had Jimmy in it, she'll be discarded somewhere when they're done with her. Sometimes with a pulse, sometimes not. Nothing ever gets traced back to Big Carlo."

"Something tells me we need to pay a visit to Big Carlo," Aaron said, clenching his fists, too.

"Guys, one step at a time," the sergeant said. "Let's find out if it's Mike and Candace's house, which, as far as I can remember, is walking distance from that accident scene. Then we'll look for Jimmy—due process and shit. Big Carlo has a house on Rama Road near the casino. Armed men guard it well. You can't just walk in there and intimidate him. You'll all end up in a hospital, and how will that help Sarah?"

Parkman and Aaron exchanged a glance, which Parkman understood right away.

There was no due process for them, especially where Sarah was involved.

If Big Carlo had anything to do with her disappearance, they'll make him regret everything that led him to a life of crime.

Effectively, they'd do Sergeant James's job for him—on their terms.

The car eased to a stop.

"We're here." The sergeant opened his door. "Let's go see who we have under the sheet."

# Chapter 32

DARWIN KOSTAS AND HIS team of four men entered the Santa Maria Hospital in Terni, each wearing Kevlar hidden under collared shirts and suit jackets, each packing a concealed sidearm.

While driving south, Darwin read every article on the Baglioni case he could find, the woman who escaped and then disappeared again, and the death of Alonzo Baglioni. He found one article that spoke of how she put a man in the hospital before escaping Alonzo's property.

The Baglioni chef.

Since that man was being discharged later today, Darwin felt a visit with him before he went back to the Baglioni family house was the natural first step.

Darwin leaned in close to his men as they waited for the elevator. "Guys, my wife was able to get his room number."

"Did she hack their system?" Seven asked.

When asked what their names would be out in the field, Darwin told them to pick a number between one and ten. Seven went with Seven because he was always lucky. Four was chosen because it was his lucky number. Ten went with his number because of his vanity, and Zero got his number because of Ground Zero—he was the bomb expert. Darwin had no trouble using Zero, even though it wasn't a number between one and ten.

"No, she didn't hack their system. She called the hospital and asked."

"Oh." Seven stared at the closed elevator door for a moment. "Smart."

"We have to expect Baglioni security will be here."

"Want me to take them out?" Zero asked. "I got some neat stuff that'll do the trick."

Darwin shook his head. "No explosives in the hospital."

"Dammit."

"Besides, this is not that type of job. All I want to do is talk to him."

The elevator doors opened, and they piled inside.

"How will you do that, boss?" Four asked.

"By watching the room and waiting for his security detail to leave their post."

"That sounds like it'll take too long. And what if he comes back?"

"I'll claim to be his long-lost brother who heard what happened in the media."

Four's eyebrows raised as he lowered his head. "And the chef will just agree that he's got a brother?"

Darwin stared at Four. "If he wants to live through the night, he'll agree to anything."

Four nodded. "Got it."

"You good, Ten?" Darwin patted his arm. "You seem quiet."

"I hate hospitals."

"You're not the only one." Those three words made him think of Sarah. He hoped she was fine wherever she was, knowing Vivian was taking care of her. She had to be.

The elevator dinged on the fourth floor, one below the chef's. When the door slid open, three of them exited.

"See you on the fifth floor," Darwin said.

Seven, who had become something of Darwin's right-hand man, remained with him as per their plan.

When the door opened on the fifth floor, they exited and began looking for room 505. According to Rosina, the chef had his jaw wired shut during a four-hour procedure and was out of surgery. He had stayed overnight but could leave later in the day once the doctor revisited him. The wires, screws, and plastic bands would remain in place for six weeks. Until then, he'd be on a liquid diet.

Darwin led the way past a nurses' station until he saw rooms 508 and 507. Two doors up, they stared at a large man on a chair outside the door to 505, tapping on his phone.

Darwin slowed and directed Seven into room 506.

An older woman lay on the bed to their left. "Are you bringing my meds?" the woman asked.

"Yes, of course. One second." Darwin moved close to Seven. "We need to get him out of his chair. There's no point in waiting for him to take a bathroom break or something. I need inside that room without that idiot knowing."

Seven nodded. "I can do that."

"How?"

"Leave it to me." Seven tapped Darwin's shoulder.

"That's what scares me. We can't hurt him. That would make it obvious."

"I get it. No need to worry."

"Then do your thing."

Seven led the way out the door, with the woman in the bed behind them saying, "My meds, don't forget my meds," before the door shut.

Darwin held back and pretended to look at his phone while watching Seven.

The man strode past the Baglioni guard at the door, walked over to a mostly empty trolley, and began wheeling it down the hall, back toward the guard, nodding at two nurses and a doctor. He strode confidently, making it look like he belonged there, so no one asked him what he was doing.

He nodded once at Darwin as he approached the man.

*Get ready.*

Darwin slipped his phone away and moved along the wall closer to room 505.

When Seven was about to pass the Baglioni guard, he pretended to trip and shoved the trolley ahead so hard and fast that it smacked into the guard's hand, knocking the man's phone from his grasp.

The cell phone hit the tiled hospital floor and slid past Darwin almost to room 507's door.

The guard was instantly on his feet, shoving the trolley away from him with one hand while shaking the hand that had been hit. The trolley clattered to the hospital floor in a cacophony of clanging metal.

"I'm so sorry," Seven apologized profusely while backing away. "I didn't see you. I tripped. Won't happen again." He righted the trolley, then hustled down the corridor. No one said a thing or attempted to stop Seven.

The moment the Baglioni man had regained control of his temper and realized his phone was several doors away, a doctor was picking it up.

Darwin made his move while he still had a window.

They passed each other in the hall, Darwin's gaze at the floor. When he got to room 505, he turned and entered with only a short glance back at Baglioni's man.

He was taking the cell phone from the doctor and inspecting it for damage, his back to Darwin.

Then the door to room 505 closed.

It was a private room with one bed. There were no flowers.

The chef was awake, watching the small TV suspended on the wall. The swelling in his face indicated that the man had likely broken something under the fleshy part of his cheek. The man's jaw was wired shut, and a heavy purple coloring was just coming in strong.

*When a woman wants to escape captivity, men need to just get out of the way.*

The chef's eyes moved to Darwin. Then they took on a look of fear.

Without knowing how much time he had, Darwin pulled out his weapon and showed it to the chef while approaching the bed.

The man's head pushed backward into the pillow as he moaned something.

"You will die if you don't do as I say." Darwin tapped the man's temple with the gun's tip.

The chef moaned something close to *yes, yes.*

"I'm your long-lost brother. I've come to visit you in the hospital. Understand?"

The chef moaned twice.

"We lost touch over the years, but when I saw your name in the news, I just had to come. Understand?"

He nodded, then his eyes closed briefly with the pain.

"Stick to that story, and you will live to see tomorrow. I have no personal beef with you. I just want information." Darwin slipped the gun away, hiding it under his vest. Then he grabbed a thick pad of paper and a pen from the small table beside the bed and handed them to the chef.

"Tell me your name. Quickly."

The chef wrote it down.

"You wouldn't lie, would you?"

He tried to shake his head, then stopped and grunted something.

Darwin stared at the pad of paper. The name Ricardo Luca was written on the page.

"Okay, since I'm your brother from America, I will call you Richie."

The door opened behind Darwin. He tore off the top sheet with the chef's name on it and scrunched it up, slipping the paper into his pocket as footsteps stormed up behind him.

Ricardo moaned loudly as the guard's hand slammed down on Darwin's shoulder and spun him around.

"Who the fuck are you?" The man tried to growl the words.

"I'd ask you the same thing"—Darwin smacked the man's hand off his shoulder—"storming in like that to my brother's hospital room. What if you startled him? Made him jump?" Darwin gestured at Ricardo. "Have you seen Richie's face?"

The guard seemed ready to grab Darwin for smacking his arm away, but stopped when he heard the word "brother." His face contorted into a frown.

"He ain't got no brother."

"If you're his friend, you sure have a weird way of greeting family." Darwin stuck out his hand. "Frank Luca, United States Army."

*Shit, where did the Army bit come from?*

He hadn't thought that part through well enough, but if Ricardo's guard had any sense about him, he'd recognize the Kevlar vest and ask questions. Since Darwin's accent was North American, perhaps working with the US Military gave him an out.

The Baglioni man glanced past Darwin's shoulder. "Is he your brother?"

Without looking at what the chef would say, Darwin stared at the guard, waiting for his face to calm, as the chef's response would determine whether he would be allowed to proceed. If the guard went for his weapon, Darwin would kill him silently before he touched it.

When the guard looked back at Darwin, he let his hands drop to the side.

"Don't stay too long. You'll tire him out, and he's going home today."

"I won't be long. We ship out tonight, anyway, so I must get back."

The guard walked backward toward the door, then slipped out into the corridor. The door slowly closed behind him.

That was easier than expected.

Darwin spun back around and handed the pad to the chef. Then he flicked the switch on the side of the hospital bed to move it into a raised position.

The chef's eyes roamed Darwin's face, likely wondering if he was an American operative of some sort.

"Tell me where Maria is. Leave nothing out. I want to know everything. How long she's been with the Baglionis, what they've done to her, and where she is now."

The chef gestured for the pad. Once it was in his hand, he wrote, "That'll take too long." He looked up, then added, "She's at the compound. In the cellar. If I write more, they'll kill me."

"Where is the cellar? And if you *don't* tell me, *I'll* kill you."

The chef stared at him for a long moment, then wrote, "You can't get her. They have many men. You need 100. To get inside is a death wish."

The chef shook his pen hand like it was starting to cramp.

An idea formed, so Darwin pulled out his phone and texted his wife an emergency message:

"Find anyone and everyone connected to the chef—family preferred —Ricardo Luca. Then send me their identities, photos, and locations."

He slipped his phone away and leaned closer to the man. "How many women has Alonzo taken over the years? Who's in charge now that Alonzo is dead? Where are they getting their women? How are they brought to Italy without being detected?" He stood back up to his full height and tapped the area where his gun was stashed. "Write fast, then rip off the sheets and give them to me."

The chef wrote furiously.

And Darwin knew exactly how he was going to get Maria to safety.

# Chapter 33

THEY LET AARON MOVE through the morgue first, directly behind the sergeant. If Sarah was on that table in the room up ahead of them, the job fell to the man she loved for so many years, the father of their child.

When Parkman stared at Aaron's slumped shoulders, he could see the emotional weight on them dragging him down. He considered what Sarah and Aaron had been going through as a couple over the past few years and couldn't imagine what Aaron must be thinking or dealing with. His emotions had to be spiking.

Alex too. The poor guy looked like he wanted to cry, while at the same time, he appeared ready to fight someone to let off some steam.

Parkman just wanted this to end. In his heart, he didn't believe Sarah was in the morgue. But they weren't sure, so they needed to get through this official positive ID business.

"We're waiting on the fingerprints," the sergeant said as they walked the length of a sterile hallway. He slowed, then turned around to address them. "I pulled everyone to come search for Sarah, so we were vastly understaffed. I will have a positive ID on the victim at any moment, but thought since we found a body in the vicinity, and you guys were close by, not to mention she's the same body type and weight"—he shrugged—"figured we could use a visual for a positive ID."

Aaron gestured for the sergeant to lead the way.

"Through this door." The sergeant moved in front of Alex and Parkman. "I only need one in the room. This may be hard for some people to see."

"If it's Sarah, Alex, and Parkman need to be in there with me," Aaron said. "I'm not sure anyone will be able to keep them out, anyway, so it's better to avoid a fight."

The sergeant stepped out of the way, his hands raised. "Suit yourself."

He swiped a card along a reader bolted to the wall. A click sounded, then he pushed open the door and led them into a room with metal drawers along one wall. A steel bed on wheels sat in the center of the room. On it was a body covered in a white sheet.

"Showing you the face won't help, as there's little left of that area. So, in a moment, I'll pull back the sheet to uncover her upper half. If you're unsure if it's Sarah, I can reveal her entire body."

They nodded.

"Are you sure you can handle this?"

Aaron grabbed the sheet and pulled it back without waiting for the sergeant.

No sound could be heard except for the clock ticking on the wall. No one gasped at the state of the woman's face—which was pulverized by massive force, shoving it inward upon itself. Only her forehead remained intact, a large slash across it.

The hair was wrong, the shoulders didn't match, and the proportions differed from Sarah's. Parkman had never seen Sarah's breasts, but he was pretty sure these weren't it.

He released a sigh of relief—they had confirmation.

It wasn't Sarah lying on that slab.

Was it wrong to be staring at a murder victim and feel elated?

Aaron was feeling it, too. His head snapped up. "It's not Sarah." He backed away, bumped into Alex, then turned around and stormed into the hallway.

Alex moved closer, leaning into the woman to inspect something on her neck.

"We saw this woman earlier tonight. Alive."

Parkman frowned and moved closer. "Where?" he asked, staring at her features and trying to figure out what Alex was seeing.

"Yeah, where?" Sergeant James asked.

Then his phone rang. He grabbed it and stared at the screen. "Oh, wait, they might have the ID for me. One second." He touched his phone's screen. "Yeah?" After a moment, he said, "You got a name?"

He looked at Parkman, then Alex.

"Okay, send everything to my email." Then he ended the call and slipped his phone away.

"Candace," Alex said.

The sergeant nodded. "How did you know?"

"We were at the junkie's house. Before we left, she came out of the bathroom. I remember this mole on her neck, the color of her hair."

"Damn, brother." Parkman shook his head. "You'd make a good detective."

"Not interested in that line of work." Alex glanced at him. "Only interested in working with Sarah."

Sergeant James gave Parkman a funny look, then shook his head as he covered the body with the sheet again. "Okay, so Mike's girlfriend is dead. You guys saw Jimmy, Mike, and Candace at their house tonight, acting weird. You head back, and their house is on fire, and Candace is now in here, getting colder by the minute. Have I got that right?"

"Sounds about right to me," Parkman said. "But how could this all be connected to Sarah's disappearance? And if they are connected and are all dead now ..." He let that thought go unfinished.

"We don't know if Mike and Jimmy are dead. We also don't know who did this. It could be an enemy because last we heard, Mike was into some powerful people for a lot of money."

Parkman whistled. "You seem to hear a lot. How could you know so much without making arrests?"

"We're using confidential informants to bring in the big fish."

Parkman rubbed his chin in thought. "That's a lot of scratch for a junkie."

"Rave parties, drinking, drugs. Places where Mike and Candace hang out. He was into one of Jimmy's boys for twenty grand. Then everyone started gambling. Next thing you know, Mike owes one of Big Carlo's boys a hundred large."

"Wait, for you to know that much, one of Big Carlo's boys must be on the payroll."

The sergeant nodded. "It's Jimmy. He's my confidential informant. I've been using him as a CI for about six months. Big Carlo almost had him killed several times. Jimmy figures if Carlo goes down, he'll be safer on the streets. We've been trying to nab Big Carlo for years. As I mentioned, nothing sticks."

Alex started for the door.

"Where are you going?" Parkman asked.

Alex stopped, his hand on the knob. "To check on Aaron." He looked up, his eyes wet. "He may be a dick most of the time, but he's still my brother." Then Alex stepped out into the corridor.

"They're brothers?" James asked, sounding surprised.

Parkman shook his head. "Brotherly love, not biological."

James walked around the body and headed for the door. "No reason to stay in here. Let's head over to the fire scene."

"Works for me."

The sergeant's phone rang again. He snatched it up and answered it. "Sergeant James here." He'd entered the hallway but stopped walking to turn to Parkman. "You're sure?" He lowered his gaze and rubbed the bridge of his nose. "Shit. Okay. Seal it off. I'll be there inside twenty minutes." He ended the call and stashed his phone.

Parkman's gut twisted. "Did they find another body?"

James nodded. "Two bodies."

"Where?"

"Inside the house that burned down."

"Female?"

James shook his head. "They appear to be male."

Again, Parkman blew out an air of relief—neither body was Sarah. "Shit, that's sad."

"It's probably Mike and Jimmy, which sucks. All the work we put into Jimmy. Why was he there? Selling something? Or witnessing a deal? Or did Big Carlo find out he was my CI and decide to take him out in such a display that no one will ever talk to us?"

"Whatever it is, we need to get there, talk to neighbors, and find out how the fire started."

They got walking along the corridor. "It was arson. Gasoline poured throughout the interior."

"Then I think it's time to pay a visit to Big Carlo."

"We can't. Not without a warrant."

"Alex, Aaron, and I don't need warrants."

Sergeant James slowed his step and looked sideways at him. "True. Very true. But he'll never talk to you guys. And if you push, you might end up in that room where Candace is now."

"Let us worry about that."

Then they ran for the sergeant's car.

# Chapter 34

SARAH ROBERTS FOUGHT TO stave off claustrophobia. After feeling them lifting her and walking with her—eerily like they were her pallbearers —the coffin lay flat. Then it was moving again with the gentle susurrations of a vehicle.

During that time, panic had set in, and even though she tried to talk herself down from the edge of hysteria, it didn't seem to be working. Her thoughts remained rational and coherent, but her body had a mind of its own.

Even though she knew they'd bolted it on the outside, she tried multiple times to open the lid, but it didn't budge.

Not knowing the exact amount of time she'd be in the coffin, she only sipped the water twice to ration it. Oxygen didn't seem to be a problem, and the thing either had heaters or was insulated quite well because she was warm.

Whatever happened to that woman in Parry Sound she was driving to meet? Was that a ruse perpetrated by Vivian to get her onto the highway so this—whatever *this* was—could happen?

The frustrating thing was that Vivian never explained anything before Sarah needed to know it. When whatever happened was over, Sarah often looked back and saw how it all came together and how Vivian played it well for everyone involved.

But right now, stuck inside a coffin, her heart rate increased. If she knew what the hell was coming and what would happen, it would go a long way to easing her nerves.

But still, her sister was quiet.

*I thought those days were over.* Sarah waited for an answer. When none came, she said, *You were supposed to be more involved in my life, more chatty.*

Still no answer.

*So what, I disappear from Willow, and you disappear from me? Is this supposed to be some sort of lesson?*

At some point, while focusing on other things, she was able to fall asleep. When she woke, the urge to turn over made her try, but that was impossible.

The movement outside the coffin was different now, though. It wasn't a vehicle anymore, yet it still moved. Nothing like footsteps, either.

A plane.

That guy had said she'd be on a plane, and no one would check a coffin through customs.

Where the hell were they taking her? South America? Europe?

He spoke of her being a slave, but wasn't that figurative?

Where was Willow at the moment? It had been a few days since the accident. Would Parkman and the boys be looking for her? Sadly, she suspected Aaron would stay back with Willow while everyone else searched for her.

What had happened to them as a couple? Could that ever be fixed?

She was dozing off again in the dark interior, thinking about Aaron and all they'd shared and lost together. She yearned for a time when it was them against the world, just the two of them fighting for what was right.

But it was never just the two of them. Parkman had been there from the beginning. His support had been unwavering since day one. Alex, too—what would she ever do without him?

And Darwin. He'd been their rock for so many years. What about everyone they'd lost, too? Benjamin and Bruno's loss still hurt her heart.

Maybe the people around her would always support her way of life more than the person she shared a bed with. That's not how it was supposed to be, but perhaps that's how it is and always will be.

Did they spike the water in her coffin? Was there a sleeping agent in it? Or maybe it was the oxygen machine thing malfunctioning.

Either way, she needed to sleep again.

She fell into a meditative sleep, the subtle movements of the coffin gently rocking her to sleep, with thoughts of Willow smiling and laughing on her mind.

When would she get to see her daughter again?

# Chapter 35

DARWIN HAD SPENT TOO much time in the hospital room with Ricardo Luca. That Baglioni guard outside the door might get suspicious and want more information. For Darwin's plan to work, he couldn't be found out.

Still waiting for Rosina to get back to him, he moved to the window and looked outside. A small ledge ran the length of the outside of the building, a few feet below the window. The corner of the building appeared to have several windows to the left.

Falling from this height would kill or hospitalize him. But walking out that door might get him stopped by the guard.

His phone vibrated. When he looked at the text, he knew he had the chef in his pocket. Then Rosina sent Facebook photos.

There could be no denying the chef's compliance now.

Darwin ran back over to the bed and told Ricardo what he wanted him to do and how he expected him to do it because two of his men were over at Carla's house.

Ricardo's eyes widened, and he wrote furiously. "Don't hurt her. She has nothing to do with this."

"Get Maria out of that cellar and out in the open, preferably near the front gate, and we'll take care of the rest."

Instead of nodding, Ricardo wrote, "I'll do it."

"Carla will have an accident if you don't. And we will still attack the compound. You know what that means for you, right?"

"I'll die."

Darwin shrugged, hating to have to hoodwink the guy but wanting the man's unwavering compliance. "It is likely you will die."

He wrote something as Darwin checked the time.

"I want out" was on the paper. "I'll help with Maria. You help me."

Darwin stared at the man for a long moment, then nodded. "If you're sincere, then that can also be arranged." Darwin collected all the papers Ricardo had been writing on and scrunched them up. "I'm leaving now."

He ran for the window, unclipped the latch, then eased through it with his right leg first. After bending his upper body through, he pulled his left leg out. When the window dropped back into place, the latch snapped to the locked position on the inside.

Grasping the upper lip of the window, he shimmied along the ledge, moving toward the corner of the building.

\*\*\*

Ricardo Luca had fought to suppress the acid in his stomach the entire time that man was in his room. Vomiting with his jaw wired shut would not only be extremely painful, but he'd probably die. He hadn't thought to ask the doctor what to do during a regurgitation event.

Then the man had shown him that picture of Carla when she was pregnant with the baby they'd lost. It had been two years, and they were trying again. He promised her he'd leave the Baglioni job, but had no idea how he could quit something like that. They offered severance pay, but it was a different sort of severance.

Usually, he'd never trust a man like the kind of man who was just in his room, but what option did he have now? Letting Maria get away wouldn't be too hard. He could say she smacked his face, and the pain knocked him unconscious. If that were all he needed to do to avoid being killed or having harm come to Carla, then he'd do it.

Even though he was angry at Maria for what she'd done to him—a meat tenderizer to the face? *Really?*—he understood why she attacked him.

When he returned to the villa, he'd demand to see her. No one would suspect he'd be kind and just let her go, which was a plus.

The hospital room door opened, and the Baglioni man stepped

inside, his eyes roving the room.

"Where is he?"

Ricardo frowned as if to say, *Who?*

"Your brother."

Ricardo pointed at the door.

"He went this way?"

The chef nodded softly to avoid causing himself any pain.

"No." The guard shook his head. He ran over to the window and looked out. "This is too high to jump." Then he touched the latch. It was locked from the inside. He turned back to Ricardo, shaking his head. "I would have seen him if he went out that door."

Ricardo waved a hand around the room as if to say, *well, he ain't here.*

"Shit," the guard said, then ran from the room, the door closing slowly behind him.

If they did any sort of background check on him and looked deep enough, they'd see that he didn't have a brother. That could cause him some trouble because he already covered for the guy, especially at a time when his guard could've taken care of the intruder.

Why he did it, he had no idea.

What he was going to do now was noble but frightening.

Even more so with his face in such a mess.

# Chapter 36

THE FIRE AT THE junkie house had been extinguished before it spread to neighboring homes or the trees. The fire marshal was on site and talking to Sergeant James about the two male bodies inside.

Parkman waved for Aaron and Alex to move in closer.

"What's going on?" Aaron asked.

Parkman gestured at the sergeant and the fire marshal. "They're talking about the two men inside the house. Their bodies will be brought out as soon as it is safe to do so."

"So we're waiting?" Alex said. "Not sure this is a good idea. Sarah's still out there somewhere."

"That's why we *aren't* waiting."

Aaron waved a hand once. "Go on, then. What's our next play?"

Parkman crossed his arms over his chest. "You guys have any weapons?"

Both men shook their heads.

"Just these." Alex held up his hands. "And they're itching to get some work done."

"We need to visit Big Carlo and see how he's connected to this."

"Okay," Aaron said. "Where's Big Carlo?"

"Orillia."

"You think Sarah's in Orillia?"

Parkman shook his head. "I have no idea where Sarah is. I couldn't even speculate. But James and I think Big Carlo knows."

Aaron moved closer. "Update us on how he's involved."

Parkman told them about his conversation with the sergeant, how

Jimmy was a CI, and gave the sergeant intel on Big Carlo and the debt Mike owed.

"Because we saw Jimmy and Mike together here"—Parkman pointed at the husk of a house—"as well as Candace, and now they're all dead—likely dead—the sergeant figures Big Carlo is involved."

Aaron looked from Alex to Parkman. "But how does that link up with Sarah?"

"There's nothing definitive, but if Sarah were here and they're all dead, the only one who would know anything is Big Carlo."

"Are they going after Big Carlo? Using a warrant?" Alex asked.

Parkman shook his head. "Not enough of anything for a judge to sign one."

"Meaning," Aaron said, "we're going in." He voiced it as a statement and not a question.

Parkman nodded.

"Do you know where in Orillia?"

Parkman nodded again. "Rama Road. Only a couple of miles from the casino. A fenced-off property with a few buildings out front, then a main house at the back."

Aaron rubbed his chin as if thinking. "Access will be tough, right?"

It was Parkman's smile that made them both stare at him. "If he's involved in whatever happened to Sarah, it won't be tough at all."

"How's that?" Aaron asked.

"We show up and tell him we know the identity of a confidential informant. We know about Mike, and we know they're dead. We bluff our way in."

"And get killed?" Aaron shook his head. "That's the plan?"

Parkman shrugged. "I figured as long as we get in to see Big Carlo, we'd improvise from there."

"Improvise?"

Alex clucked his tongue once. "Just get me inside, get me close to *Big* Carlo. He'll tell us what he knows."

Aaron stepped back. "If we don't get killed."

Alex faced him. "Look, man, if he knows *anything*, we need that information. What if he has her stashed somewhere? Sure, this is the lion's den and shit, but how many times have we been there and walked away?"

Aaron stared at Alex for a long moment. "You're right. Let's do this."

"For Sarah," Parkman said.

"For Sarah," the boys repeated in unison.

They moved toward the sergeant as a unit.

"Sergeant?" Parkman called. "We need a car."

Sergeant James turned toward them. "Where are you three going?"

"Rama Road."

He quirked an eyebrow. "Why there?"

"To do a little gambling."

The sergeant stared at them for a long moment. "I'll get you a car."

# Chapter 37

MANY OF THE SUBTLE movements had ceased, and it was now quiet. Waking in complete darkness had gotten irritating when it should have been comforting, perhaps even relaxing. A thousand questions ran through her mind—where was she? What time was it? How long had she been inside the coffin? Four hours? Fifteen hours?

She could only wait until someone came along and opened the lid to let her out—*if* they let her out.

Was gravity off somehow? It felt like she was in a standing position. Could that be right, though? Why would the coffin be angled upward?

Disoriented, she adjusted her body, clenched her hands, and rolled her feet. Sure enough, her feet were tough to roll because they pressed against the end—now the bottom—of the coffin.

Something smacked the outside hard enough to make her jump.

*What the hell was that?*

The lid moved. It wasn't her imagination. Someone was opening the lid.

She squinted her eyes in case it was bright out. The contrast would blind her if it were too sudden.

Sure enough, the lid lifted an inch.

"You alive in there?" a man asked.

European accent? Maybe Italian.

"Yes," she said.

"I will open the top slowly. Keep your eyes closed if you have to."

She closed her eyes briefly, then slit them to peek through her lids.

They'd brought her inside what looked like a grand house. The ceiling was gorgeous, with crown molding along the edges. Her vision lowered to the far wall. It was covered in modern art, with small marble and bronze statues resting on little pedestals and stands. Most importantly, the lights were dim, and the window to the left was dark—nighttime or early morning.

"Where am I?" she asked, somewhat surprised at the affluence of the building.

"You're in your new home."

She turned to the man, focusing on his face. "Oh, how nice. You bought me a home?"

He laughed, but it sounded forced. That was either a sarcastic laugh, or the man was a psychopath and didn't know how to act his humor too well.

"This is my family's villa, but you'll be staying with us for the foreseeable future."

"I doubt it."

The laugh was gone, replaced by a quizzical look and raised eyebrows. "You might take some time to break." He tilted his head to the side. "This could be fun."

She glared at him. "I won't break."

"A challenge? Well, then, let's get the introductions over so we can get down to business."

"You're wasting your time. Unhook me from this deathbed, bring me new clothes, and I'll be on my way. All other decisions are like good intentions—they'll lead you to Hell." Her eyes didn't waver.

He stared at her for a long moment, then burst into laughter, slapping his leg. This guy really was playing it up.

"We'll see who gets the last laugh, dickshit."

"Name-calling?" He slapped his leg again. "I love this. We haven't had one like you since I was a kid, and my dad taught me how to break her."

A knot of fear locked up her stomach.

*What the hell is this, Vivian? You will answer me, or I'll be seriously pissed.*

*Hang in there,* Vivian whispered.

"Oh, there you are!" Sarah shouted out loud, startling the guy. "About fucking time!"

"What?" the man said, leaning closer. "You seeing something?"

"My sister just decided to show up—finally, for fuck's sake."

The man glanced over each shoulder, then looked back at Sarah. "What?"

"Oh, nothing. I'm pissed at her, though."

"Right, okay." He nodded, staring down at her. "You schizo or something?"

"Schizo, bipolar, manic, and a few others. What's it to ya?"

"Shit, when you break, you'll break hard. I'll have to have a suicide watch on your ass."

"Oh, don't worry. I'm a megalomaniac, too. There's enormous self-love going on inside me. I could never hurt myself."

His mouth formed into a straight line on the blank face canvas, and then he lost it. The man laughed so hard he had to sit down.

"Boss, boss, everything okay?" another man asked from somewhere to Sarah's left.

"Yeah," the man said, wiping at his face. "This one is the absolute best. We've never had anyone like her. She's tough with a sense of humor I could get used to."

"Want me to bring in the boys?"

The man nodded, looking at the other man out of Sarah's field of vision. "Let's introduce her to everyone, give her the house rules, and then get her set up."

"What the fuck is this?" she asked. "House rules? I don't need any rules because I won't be staying long."

The man wiped his face again, collecting himself. Then he stood over her and studied her face.

"This, my dear, is your new home. You're replacing Samantha, and you'll be staying here until the day you die. Next week, I'll receive another coffin with someone who will replace Maria. But first, so you get an idea of how things work around here, you will witness Maria's execution." He leaned in closer. "My name is Alberto Baglioni. I'm your new owner."

# Chapter 38

EVER SINCE HIS "BROTHER" had visited and then disappeared, the guard from the hospital room watched him suspiciously. The doctor cleared him to leave, and the guard guided him toward the exit, where another Baglioni man waited in the SUV to drive them back to the villa.

Tonight, Ricardo Luca would either be killed or be successful, and that sucked. How could those options make him happy?

The hospital's exit doors swung open, and a man standing off to the side by a trimmed hedge came into view. Ricardo stared at the man who had claimed to be his brother.

He winked at him. The game was on, and this man would be watching.

Clara, his beloved, would pay for any indecision on his part, any inaction.

He looked away and fixed his gaze on the SUV. Once inside, he glanced back at the trimmed hedge, but the man was gone.

The guard from his hospital room sat in the passenger side, watching him from the corner of his eye.

"That *brother* of yours is concerning," the man said.

Alberto had so many guards that he couldn't keep track of them all. Usually, he kept his head down and just worked in the kitchen. The servers were in contact with the guards, but him, not so much.

The man turned in his seat further. "I didn't like the look of him. U.S. Military? You know, Alberto may want to know you're related to an American. Did you ever think to tell him?"

Ricardo shook his head, then gestured for paper. He could tell the man was a step-brother, not a biological one. Having different mothers would make more sense.

"I haven't got anything to write on. You can tell Alberto all about it when we get back." He turned around in his seat to face forward.

He had half an hour to come up with a believable story, or he would be in trouble.

And so would Carla.

# Chapter 39

THEY KNEW WHERE THE Baglioni villa was located, so Darwin followed at a distance.

"We go in tonight," he said.

His men nodded.

"We wait for the chef to get settled. He will request to see the woman who broke his face, then figure out how to get her to the front gate area without getting killed."

"And we'll breach the front," Four said, "grab the woman, kill as many as we can, and run?"

"Something like that." Darwin thought about it a moment more. "Or we go deeper."

"Deeper?" Zero asked. "How deep?"

Darwin glanced over at him, then back at the road. "If resistance is low, all the way."

"And if we're facing off with an army?" Four asked.

"We retreat and come back another day."

They fell into silence for a bit.

"Is this just about a woman?" Zero asked.

Darwin shook his head. "No, it's more about what she said than what happened to her."

"What'd she say?" Seven, who'd been quiet for a bit, asked.

"That she'd been abducted five years ago and was a slave to the Baglionis. The article was pulled from the paper, and then, while in police custody, she disappeared." Darwin made a lane change to pass a slow-moving car, then got back in his lane. "When I met with the chef, the man she beat up to escape, he confirmed she's back at the Baglioni villa."

"How many cops do the Baglionis have in their pocket to arrange that?" Four asked, surprise evident in his voice.

"None if he's dead." Darwin tightened his hands on the wheel. "It'll likely launch a huge investigation into the family, too."

"What's your beef with them? Why go after one of the families that might be associated with Cosa Nostra?"

"I have so many answers for that, but I'll keep it to one." He cleared his throat. "Many years ago, they came after my family, and they almost got us. I'm permanently scarred, and my wife took a few years to decompress the psychological damage they caused. We went into hiding several hours north of Rome, so I could track and kill them when the opportunity presented itself."

"So, you're, like, a mafia serial killer?"

His shoulders hitched as he laughed softly. "I've never really thought of it that way, but yeah. I can't count how many we've taken out. Here in Italy and abroad."

"You're not afraid of the families pooling their resources and coming after you?"

Darwin shook his head. "No, they're always at war with each other. They'd never make peace long enough to take out one man. Maybe another family that was encroaching on their territory, but not me."

Up ahead, the SUV's taillights carrying the chef flared as the brakes were applied.

"This is it," Darwin said. "We'll drive right past the entrance, then hide this car and make our way to the front through the trees."

The SUV turned onto a private road, and Darwin drove right past it. He carried on for a few hundred meters, then pulled deep onto the shoulder while scouting in the dark for a place to park, with Seven holding a flashlight out the window to give Darwin a better view.

About another twenty meters went by until there was a flat area that led to several trees.

He eased to the right and drove over the grass until the bumper touched the trunk of a tree.

"Okay, we need to cover the lights so headlights on the road don't reflect off them and pick up the vehicle's location." Doors were opening on either side. "Grab as many weapons and ammo as you can carry, and let's go."

The men went to work and were ready within minutes.

"We get as close to the front as possible, then climb trees to see inside the walls. The moment the chef brings Maria out in the open, we blow the front gate, grab them, and retreat back here. Everyone on board?"

They all nodded.

"The only change to the plan would be if there's little to no resistance. Then I want to take the house to see if they've got anyone else like Maria."

More nods all around.

"Let's go hunt some assholes."

Zero seemed quite happy. "I love blowing shit up," he said, a bounce in his step as they got moving.

"Asshole hunting," Seven repeated, ignoring Zero. "I like that."

The five men split up and moved about ten meters apart through the forest.

Darwin felt good about today, tonight. He had an inside man—the chef—and a noble plan—to save a woman.

It wouldn't feel like cold-blooded murder when he executed the Baglionis because they gave him a solid reason to execute them.

That left him with no choice but to kill as many as he could.

Even if his men retreated to the vehicle, Darwin would stay on the property to clear the family of every last member of its name.

Tonight, if Darwin had anything to say on the matter, the Baglioni family would become extinct.

# Chapter 40

ABOUT AN HOUR AFTER Sergeant James got them a car, Parkman pulled onto Rama Road.

"This is it, guys. We'll be there in about five minutes."

Aaron leaned forward between the two seats, his head swiveling to Alex, then Parkman. "And our tactic for getting inside the gate is to tell them we have inside information on a narc?"

"If you've got something else that'll work, please share."

Parkman watched the GPS on his phone. When Aaron didn't speak up with new ideas, he said, "One minute out."

Aaron sat back. "How about one of us remains hidden somewhere? If there's trouble, then we have backup they don't know about."

Parkman looked over at Alex. "That work for you?"

Alex nodded. "We can do that. I'll hang back. No one will see me until I let them."

Parkman stared at Aaron in the rearview mirror. "You good with that?"

"Yeah, he's the best at blending in."

"Stop the car." Alex was already opening the door.

Parkman jerked it to the side of the road, and Alex slipped out, the door shutting softly behind him.

"Decision made, and he's off," Parkman said. "That was fast."

"No time to waste," Aaron said as Parkman got the car rolling again.

Three more houses passed on the right, and then he pulled onto the shoulder again, cut the lights, stopped, and killed the engine.

"You ready?"

"Should we go over the story again?"

Parkman watched him in the mirror. "Been out of the game for a bit, eh?"

Aaron nodded. "We can't say things that conflict."

Parkman ran down the details in under a minute. "You good with that?"

Aaron stared across the street at the house. "Yeah, I'm good."

"Now, remember. This guy probably knows where Sarah is. If he doesn't, he knows someone who does. You know what that means?"

"What?"

"We don't leave until we get answers or Big Carlo is hospitalized." He paused. "Or dead."

"Got it."

"That also means some of Carlo's men may be collateral damage if they get in the way. Some may be killed."

Aaron nodded in the back seat.

"Just be clear because you have Willow to think about. You can stay in the car if you want. This isn't your fight."

Aaron locked eyes with him. "Isn't my fight? I know I've been a shithead with Sarah for a while, but if she needs help, then it *is* my fight. I love that woman, dammit. That's why I take the stance I've been taking. So she doesn't do this shit anymore."

"And how's that going for you?" Parkman shot a hand up in the air. "No, wait. I'll tell you. It's going shitty because Sarah will never stop doing what she does, and all this time, she's lost her partner, and you've lost her. This way of thinking doesn't create a win/win. You're giving her an ultimatum. Do what I say, or I'm leaving, and Sarah's the last person in the world who will respond well to an ultimatum. People who give her ultimatums usually end up in the hospital, and the only reason you're not in a hospital is because she loves you." He spun around in his seat to face Aaron. "All you've done is hurt her and weaken her defenses."

Aaron's lower lip quivered like he was suppressing tears. "Are you saying this is my fault?"

"No, I'm saying she's weaker without you by her side."

"Then I'll stand by her. I'll stand with her. Because the truth is, this is way worse. I mean, if she'll have me."

"Why the sudden about-face?"

Aaron looked down at his lap while fiddling with his fingers. "If the alternative is I'm still on the sidelines helping when she's in trouble, I'd rather have a front-row ticket." He raised his head. "That, and I've missed her. It's been hard on both of us. I just truly thought she'd turn off her sister and give us a chance."

Parkman watched him for a long moment, then patted his leg. "Let's find out what Big Carlo knows, and then get Sarah and bring her home to Willow."

Aaron exited the car before Parkman, energized at the prospect of finding Sarah.

They approached the front gate together. Five steps before they reached it, a man moved out from behind a tree.

"What you want?" he asked, his words curt like he was upset someone was approaching the gate.

"Big Carlo," Parkman said.

"Never heard of him."

"Yeah, okay. Sure." Aaron shook his head and blew air out of his mouth. "Don't waste our time. Go get your parents, you know, like one of the adults on the property."

"Fuck you." The man tilted his head back and eased his jacket open to reveal a gun sticking out of his pants.

Aaron lifted his jacket and spun in a circle. "Look, no weapons. So, you got me beat. You're the bigger man than me. Now, we still have to speak with Carlo. If you can't set that up, get someone who will."

"Ain't going to happen."

"Why? Is he dead?"

The man leaned his head down and spoke into a microphone clipped onto the inside of his jacket, but he was too far away for Parkman to decipher the whispered words.

Parkman touched the gate and shook it. "Tell Big Carlo we come with a message."

The guard lifted his head. "Leave the message at the gate and run along home before it's too late."

Aaron laughed. "Cute."

"Not going to happen." Parkman shook the gate again. "Personal delivery."

The man spoke into his jacket once more.

"Tell him it concerns Jimmy, Mike, and Mike's girlfriend, Candace."

The man's eyes gave him up. He knew those names and likely knew what happened to them tonight.

"Tell him we know the whole story, and if he wants to remain living outside prison walls, he'd better hear what we have to say."

The man spoke furiously into his jacket now, his eyes not wavering as he stared at Parkman.

A light came on at the house about a hundred meters down the laneway. The front door opened, and several men piled out.

Parkman and Aaron exchanged a glance. This was it.

"Just hold up. These men will escort you inside and see if we can find someone named Carlo somewhere."

"I'm sure you will," Aaron said, then added under his breath, "Fuckin' idiot."

The man snapped his head to Aaron. "What was that?"

"Open the gate without your backup. Let's see who's the better man."

"You know, that mouth will get you in trouble."

"Wouldn't be the first time."

"Then you're stupid, *and* you don't learn."

Parkman wondered why Aaron was pushing the guy so hard, but didn't attempt to stop him. Maybe he wanted a fight—*needed* a fight—some excuse to hurt someone. Or, perhaps, he felt so bad for whatever Sarah was going through that he took the blame, was angry with himself, and felt he deserved a beat down for his bad behavior.

"There'll be no need to fight." Parkman took his hands off the gate. "We just want to talk to Carlo. Then we'll be on our way."

The gate clicked open, and Parkman pushed it all the way.

The backup had arrived. They were all carrying pistols in their hands. The largest of the men nodded toward the house.

"Carlo will see you now. Follow me."

Parkman moved in behind the guy.

"Not this one."

He stopped and looked back. Two men, including the gate guard, held weapons on Aaron.

"He stays with us until you come back. You know, insurance against any funny stuff."

"You good with that?" Parkman looked directly at Aaron.

He nodded. "Golden."

Parkman turned and followed the other men to the front of the house. They frisked him for weapons and any listening devices, then opened the front door.

Without hesitation, Parkman stepped inside Big Carlo's house.

As soon as he cleared the foyer, something smashed into the back of his head. He shuffled forward, lost his balance, hit the tile floor, and slid a few feet.

The lights dimmed, wavered, then went out.

# Chapter 41

STILL IN RESTRAINTS INSIDE the coffin, her bladder raging for release, Sarah stared at the man who had identified himself as Alberto Baglioni, her "new owner." Then it was her turn to burst out laughing, trying to curl her body inward to avoid pissing herself.

"Oh shit, that's a good one. Hurry, untie me so I can piss."

"You won't be laughing for long, slave, but we have a protocol here. I will introduce you to the others, give you the rules, and then untie you. Because one of the rules is that insubordination won't be tolerated, you can spend the first night in the cellar. Your attitude just cost you a decent sleep in a bed."

"Good." She spat at the man, but he dodged left, and she missed. "Beats spending the night in this fuckin' thing."

He sneered at her. "You will wish to be back inside the plush-lined coffin once hooked up to the cellar walls. I guarantee that."

Everything came together quickly for her as she considered where she was and what was happening. They'd executed everyone involved in the transaction back at Mike's and Candace's house to remove any security leaks, then burned the house down with those gas cans that had come in the coffin.

These people were stealing women and shipping them to Europe, then binding them to slavery until they died. The only way to stop them was to become a slave, to eat away at the poison from the inside.

So Vivian set it up that Sarah would be taken, and here she was— without backup, and no one knew where she had gone. These men weren't the kind who would leave her unattended or near weapons.

*Hey, Vivian, how do you expect me to break out of here and save the day?*

A door opened to the left. Sarah glanced that way as over a dozen hardened men filed in, one by one. They reminded her of a group of men she'd seen in the movie *The Expendables*. There was a tall Dolph Lundgren lookalike, a Jason Statham, Sylvester, Arnold, Bruce Willis, and even a longer-haired Mickey Rourke among them, along with five or six others.

They all wore angry faces and sneers. Two were smiling, and several just had creepy faces.

The Dolph lookalike first moved in front of the coffin to stare down at her. "Fresh meat," he said, his voice deep and creepy at the same time.

Some of the guys behind him laughed, and one cheered. That cheer left her with goosebumps—this place had a disturbing vibe that she hated.

Immobilized in the coffin, unable to move or defend herself, she was subject to their whims.

And sure enough, Dolph extended his hand and cupped her breast.

"Hands off, animal. Or I'll slice them off."

He chuckled under his breath as he squeezed until it hurt. He moved closer when he released her breast and cupped her between her legs.

"Hmm, still wet from when she pissed herself." He released her and wiped his hand on her thigh. "We'll get you cleaned up so all of us can take turns on that pussy of yours and get you dirty again. Gotta work you in before you work those fields."

"Fuck you," came out of her mouth, forced through her teeth, a seething rage building from inside her chest.

Dolph laughed and moved aside as Rourke came into view. He slapped her face once, watched her expression, frowned, then slapped her again.

"Wow, you're an angry bitch." He glanced back at Alberto. "I'll enjoy breaking this one."

Alberto nodded at him, a wide grin pasted on his face. "She comes with a lot of attitude. You'll have to ride her hard."

Rourke spun back around so fast she didn't see his hand. He whacked her a third time, knocking her head sideways. Blood pooled in her mouth, where her teeth cut the inside of her cheek.

She waited a moment, her cheek on fire, allowing the blood to pool, then smiled at Rourke.

His brow knitted close together like he was confounded that she didn't cry out or whimper, which was likely something he was used to.

When he leaned close, she horked a gob of blood-filled saliva at his face, connecting with his cheek and upper neck.

A shout erupted from him as he wiped it away with the bottom of his shirt. "This one is a keeper," he yelled. "Damn, brother. I think I'm in love."

"Okay, guys," Alberto shouted. "This is Sarah. She'll be living with us until she isn't. She's off limits tonight as she'll spend the night in the cellar."

There were whines all around.

"Why?" Dolph asked. "I want to break that little thing in tonight."

"And when he's done, I yearn to hurt her real good."

Alberto tapped Rourke on the back. "Guys, she'll be here for years. You'll have plenty of time to work her over. And we have another new girl coming next week."

Dolph slapped his hands together and rubbed them vigorously. "Gotta love fresh meat."

Alberto eyed her. "This one was talking back. She was insubordinate. I'm about to go over the rules with her. Then, Dolph, you can take her and tie her up with Maria."

The men paraded past her, some grabbing her breasts, some just watching her, and one rubbing her between the legs, whispering something about golden showers, then they were gone, and it was only Dolph and Alberto.

"To survive here, you will follow our rules or starve and eventually die. Our punishments are brutal." He raised a finger. "We need you to work the fields, but we don't *need* you. If you die next week, we'll just grab another one. Many women are out there waiting to be snatched from their lives."

Sarah glared at him, fury raging inside her with thoughts of what she would do to these men.

"Rule number one. You are never permitted to leave the property unless you're being taken to a doctor's appointment, but then you will be escorted. Because of this, we track your every movement." He moved out of sight, then stepped back in front of her with a small black clamp in his hand. "This is your GPS tracker." He leaned down and clipped it in place on her right ankle. Still secured to the coffin's interior offered her little chance to fight him off. "Your presence will be monitored every hour of every day. If you move close to the property's exterior, alarms will sound. If you escape, you will be shot on sight or recaptured, then returned here to be tortured and killed. The punishment for breaking this rule is always death."

He stepped away from her and took a seat. Dolph moved to lean against a wall.

"Rule number two concerns working hours. You will work twelve- to sixteen-hour days and take food when we give it to you. The only place you will eat is in your room. Stealing or sneaking food is a violation and will result in a whipping. Whether you're in pain, bleeding, or crying, you're working the fields. We don't care, so avoid breaking this rule."

He leaned back and crossed his legs.

"Rule number three concerns you."

Dolph seemed impressed with rule number three because he grunted something under his breath while grinning like an idiot.

"As a woman, you are required to service my men whenever they want. I don't care how often or when. If you're out in the field and two or three men need to fuck you, you will bend over, let them borrow you, and keep working. It's your job at night to ensure they're all taken care of, but no picking favorites. Part of this rule is that you're not allowed to have or express feelings for any of the men. Just use what God gave you to pleasure them, and they'll leave you alone for the most part. After a few months, the men get bored with the new girl anyway and move on to the next one. So this rule won't matter in the months to come."

"That rule—" Sarah choked up, suppressing her rage. "That rule won't ever apply to me or any other woman."

The men exchanged a glance. After a two-second delay, they burst out laughing, with Alberto slapping his thigh.

"You were right about this one," Dolph said between gasps for air while laughing. "She will take a bit longer to break."

"Oh, I do love the challenging ones." Alberto shook his head. "Too bad Alonzo wasn't here to see this. He'd break her knees, so she was always lying down. Then he'd break her elbows so she could never push a man away. Finally, he'd break her jaw so she couldn't talk back." Alberto spun around to Dolph. "Speaking of broken jaws, when will Ricardo be here?"

Dolph produced a phone. "I'll call them and find out."

Alberto nodded as Dolph stepped away. "I'll summarize the rest of the rules while we wait for him to return." He lifted his fingers, then pulled one down. "There is to be no gathering with other slaves. You'll be whipped if we catch you chatting with other chattel." He pulled another finger down. "You're prohibited from speaking or learning Italian. We require a layer of security while talking in your presence."

Sarah only half-listened. The man spouted madness. She couldn't believe this place was real, that these people did this sort of thing unhindered.

*Vivian, what have you done? Out here alone, with no one to help?*

Another finger dropped. "We don't tolerate insubordination. Since this was your first time, one night in the cellar should fix that." His eyes narrowed. "On second thought, I don't think the cellar will adjust your attitude, which is fine by me. It will just make the punishments more juicy for us."

He stepped up until he was directly in front of her. "Listen carefully. Violate these rules, and your punishment will be meted out. It can be anything from whipping, mutilation, burning your flesh, branding you, a simple beating, shackling—which is what's already coming to you— rape. You don't want that one because it usually involves half a dozen men, and they tend to cause a lot of damage. Most women can't walk for a week after, so we carry them out to the fields to work and carry them back."

Sarah wouldn't be surprised if he grew horns in front of her. This horror of a place couldn't be real.

"I think the worst is being hoisted up by your thumbs, then whipped until you die." He clucked his tongue. "What you have to get is that you have zero value to us except for what you can do in the fields." He gestured at her crotch. "Well, except for that. We prefer it when the slave is alive. So, you're still without value, but we'll use you until we're through. Got it?"

"I'll kill you first," Sarah whispered.

He blinked, then moved a few inches closer. "What was that?"

She glared at him. "Tonight, you die. I will kill you first."

The surprise on his face gave him a dazed look as his mouth fell open a few millimeters. There was a split second where his breathing was suspended, then a short bark of laughter.

"Holy shit." He took a step back. "I've never met one like you before. You have zero appreciation for where you are and your predicament."

"Actually, I do."

He shook his head violently, then glared at her. "*No*, you don't. This is soul murder, baby. Soul murder, and we're the best at it. When we're done with you, and you're a walking husk of your former self, only then do we kill the body. You will die over and over on this land, but remain breathing until we say so."

"Boss," Dolph shouted, running through a side door.

Sarah inhaled deeply. She'd been holding her breath, listening for Vivian, but all she got was static.

"They're pulling up to the gate."

Alberto clapped his hands. "Perfect. Take this one down to the cellar and shackle her beside Maria. When the chef gets here, I want her"—he pointed at Sarah—"to watch while he destroys Maria's body, then executes her."

"You'll do no such thing," Sarah said loudly enough for both of them to hear.

Dolph's body went rigid, then relaxed. "Oh, boss, where did you get this one?"

"Long story and no time. Shackle her up. No food. Get it done because I want to meet Ricardo and get him settled over Maria."

Alberto walked out of view as Dolph moved to stand in front of her.

"When I untie you from this thing, will you give me any trouble?"

She shook her head. "Not at all. I'll be an angel."

He kicked his head back. "Yeah, right. And I believe that." His meaty fist came from the side so fast she barely had time to close her eyes. Before opening them, he struck her again. Then again.

On the edge of blacking out from the force and the pain, her restraints were removed, and she dropped from her position onto something pressing into her stomach.

Then they were moving.

Her senses dulled, she understood that he was carrying her, and the pressure on her stomach was his shoulder.

She moved her jaw to check if it was broken—it wasn't. But the pain in her face and head was too much to fight back.

Blood dripped from her nose and mouth.

The only voice she had was on the inside, and she was using it to shout Vivian's name—along with a dozen curse words.

She warned her sister that she had better work out a way to end this and break up their slave trade business, or there would be a "soul murder" when Sarah got to the other side because Vivian's soul wouldn't be worth much by then.

# Chapter 42

PARKMAN CAME TO AND shook his head. His breath moved dust around on the floor as he pushed up and rubbed the back of his neck. He got up to his hands and knees, then looked back as the door opened behind him.

"What the fuck, man?"

Just as he caught sight of men leading Aaron inside, two men grabbed him from under the arms and dragged him into a living room, where they dropped him roughly onto the carpet.

He grunted and rolled over. "Fuck's sake."

They plopped Aaron into a chair, blood leaking from his mouth and a large red mound forming on his cheek.

"They fucking tased me," he mumbled. "Then kicked me in the face." He lifted one shoulder. "Had no ability. To use. My hands."

"Shut the fuck up," one of the men shouted. "This isn't the time to speak."

A door popped open on the side, and all the men in the room jerked to attention.

Parkman swung around as a large man, he had to be seven feet tall, with a watermelon gut and thick rhino legs, moved into the room. He didn't walk as much as plod into the room.

The man stopped to take in the scene, then eased his bulk onto the loveseat, placing himself squarely in the middle.

"What message you got for me?" the man asked.

Parkman had to assume this was Big Carlo based on his size alone. He sat up until his back rested against the base of a couch.

"We came to tell you something we learned." Parkman stopped to look at Carlo's men, then back to him. "But these assholes knocked me out and tased my friend."

"Last time. What message you got for me?"

One of Carlo's men withdrew a pistol and cocked it.

"Hey, none of that is necessary." Parkman's stomach twisted. They were unprepared for a meeting like this. Perhaps they should've come in covertly.

The man with the gun moved closer to Aaron and raised the weapon to Aaron's head.

"Hey, hey," Parkman shouted. "What the fuck?"

"Talk," Carlo ordered.

"It's about Jimmy."

The gun lowered. All eyes were on Parkman.

"What about Jimmy?" Carlo asked.

"He was a CI, a confidential informant."

Carlo jolted on the couch like he burped. "We know. What else you got?"

*Shit, this isn't going over well.*

"He's dead."

Big Carlo glanced up and moved his gaze along his men. "Where's Mark?"

One of the men stepped forward. "I think he went back to the front gate."

"Get him."

The men bolted for the door and ran outside.

"I have to ask him why he allowed these bitches to come in here with information I already know."

"You know Jimmy is dead?"

Carlo didn't respond, his eyes on Parkman.

"What about Mike and Candace?" Parkman was sure he was digging himself into a bigger hole while hoping Alex was figuring out a way to get in here.

"Mike owed me a lot of money. There was no way he could pay me." Carlo leaned back on the couch and crossed his thick sausage arms. "I've known Jimmy was talking to the cops for months. They set their own trap."

Carlo was staring at his men now, as if he wanted them to know this information. It certainly didn't feel like it was for Parkman's benefit.

"When Mike came up with a way to repay the dough, I called Jimmy to make sure he went to Mike's house to oversee the transaction." He burped again. "Everything went very well. And now they're all gone. It could never be traced back to me because the people involved are ghosts."

"You mean the men driving the pickup with the coffin in the back."

That got Carlo's attention. He uncrossed his arms and sat up, placing a hand on each leg. "You saw them?"

Parkman nodded.

Carlo glanced at Aaron, who also nodded.

"Motherfucker, that's a first." His eyes roamed the men again. "Fuckin' idiots. Where's Mark, and where's Johnny?"

"He didn't come back from going to get Mark."

Carlo pointed at two men. "You and you, go find out what the fuck is holding them up."

Both men ran from the room, and a second later, the door banged shut behind them.

Now, Parkman had a man standing over him, and Aaron still had the man with the gun in his hand standing over him. Their odds were increasing.

"What else you see?" Carlo asked.

"Enough to know someone else was in that house before it burned." Assuming this was about Sarah somehow, he added that line as a fishing expedition.

Carlo's eyes were on the move again as if he was thinking and couldn't concentrate on anything. "Why come and tell me all this? You looking for money or something?" He paused, then stared at his men. "Tell me you guys checked for wires."

They both nodded. "They're clean."

"We're clean," Parkman said. "We came to chat about that other person. We want to know where she is."

Carlo shrugged. "That's not going to happen."

Parkman wanted to look at Aaron, but resisted. Carlo didn't deny it. That had to mean Sarah was the other person, and she *was* in that house.

"Why not?"

"Because I have no idea where she is. All I can tell you is that she's not in the country anymore, and you'll never find her. Gone to the wind. Wait, like that old Kansas song; she's dust in the wind."

Parkman frowned, feeling sick at the thought that Sarah was so far away that they couldn't just drive over and pick her up.

From the corner of his eye, he detected Aaron leaning forward, holding his gut. This was harder on him than Parkman thought it would be.

"Not in the country?" Aaron repeated Carlo's words. "How is that possible?"

"Nothing to do with me. I will be paid well. That little issue is a faded memory now. It's as if it didn't happen, and I've got no problem with that." He shuffled his rear end forward until he was sitting on the edge of the loveseat. "But what I do have a particular problem with is how much you two know about my business. I mean, who the fuck are you? What made you think you could walk in here and say all this shit to me and even for a second imagine that you could waltz back out as if nothing ever happened?"

Parkman shot a glance at Aaron, hoping he wouldn't lose his cool. That Taser changed him from the guy who wanted a fight at the front gate to a quiet listener in the chair. But Parkman detected the want-to-fight side of Aaron was rising to the surface again.

The man with the gun raised it a notch. He must've also detected Aaron's agitation, but Parkman guessed it was all for show to keep them from trying anything because they wouldn't shoot them inside Carlo's living room—too messy. They'd take them somewhere else to do it.

"We're just looking for Sarah," Aaron said. "And we're hurting anyone who gets in our way."

Carlo glared at him. "You be threatening me? In my own home?" The man's words held a warning that Parkman hoped Aaron would heed —at least until Alex surfaced. Alex had to be responsible for Carlo's men going missing at the gate.

"Not unless you're in the way," Aaron said.

Big Carlo looked at his man, then back to Aaron. "In the way of what?"

"Finding my Sarah."

"I ain't in the way of nuthin', but you won't find no Sarah here." Carlo fixed his gaze on the man beside Parkman. "Where the fuck is everybody? Get their asses in here. I'm done talking to these wannabe assholes."

When the man moved toward the door, Carlo slipped a hand between the cushions, then brought up a gun. "I still got you covered," he said to Parkman. "I shoot your face"—he jerked his head at the other guy—"he kills your friend, the conversation dies, too." When he grinned in the dim light of the living room, he revealed the stained teeth of a heavy smoker. "See how that works?"

The door from the outside opened, and a man stepped in. Something made a spitting sound, and the man standing over Aaron grunted, dropped his weapon, then fell to the floor.

Carlo swung his gun up, but that spitting sound came again, and Carlo's shoulder burst in a red mist.

Big Carlo's gun kept coming, but the tip lowered until it was aimed downward.

After one more spitting sound, Carlo dropped the weapon in front of Parkman, who scrambled forward and snatched it up off the floor to aim it at the large man.

Carlo fell back on the small couch, moaning something unintelligible as Alex entered the living room.

He marched across the room and stood over Big Carlo, a large gun in his hand with a sound suppressor attached to the end of it.

"Where have they taken her?" Alex asked as Parkman and Aaron stepped in beside him.

"Fuck you," Carlo said. "You're all fucking dead."

"You're wrong. All of your men are dead."

Parkman shot a glance at Alex, then Aaron.

Carlo's eyes widened, and for the first time, Parkman saw fear in them, which was likely something Big Carlo rarely felt.

Alex jerked the gun in Carlo's face. "Last chance before we do more real damage. Where is she?"

"I don't know."

Alex lowered the weapon and shot Carlo's foot.

The man's body jerked, and he screamed in pain. Gasping for air, he said, "What, man? I can't tell you what I don't know."

Alex shot him in the other foot. Amid the man's screams, Parkman wanted to talk Alex down but was afraid to stop the interrogation.

"I'm almost out of bullets." Alex was emotionless, like a robot offering answers. "The last one goes between your eyes. Tell us everything we want to know."

He raised the weapon and aimed it at Carlo's thigh.

"Okay, okay," he said, rocking back and forth in pain, his hand trying to stem the blood seeping from his shoulder wound. "I'll tell you everything. Just call an ambulance first."

Alex shook his head. "Talk first."

"It all started when you walked in that door. I knew you were assholes the second I saw you—" Carlo cut himself off as he laughed like a madman.

Alex shot him in the thigh.

# Chapter 43

THE PHONE RANG, AND the guard in the passenger seat picked it up. "Yes?" He paused, glanced over his shoulder at Ricardo, then faced forward. "Yes, I've got him right here." The man nodded. "Sure, open the gate. We're pulling up now." He ended the call.

"That was Alberto's right-hand man wanting to know when you'll be coming." He paused for a moment. "Are you ready to take out your pain and anger on Maria for what she did to you?"

Up ahead, the double gates were sliding open to admit them. Guards on either side stepped out, their automatic weapons gripped tightly as they surveyed the exterior property.

The driver eased inside, then stopped.

Ricardo glanced back as the gates closed, wondering how that guy's team would get through there and save them.

He soothingly talked to himself, trying to remain calm. He could do this—he had to do this.

"What are you waiting for?" the driver asked.

Ricardo glanced outside. The house was still a hundred meters away.

Then he saw what the man was referring to. The door to the cellar was sitting open off to the right, about thirty meters away. Men with flashlights stood around the opening, with Alberto waving for him to join them.

Ricardo eased out of the car. The second the door closed, it sped away.

*Here goes nothing.*

He started toward the men and the cellar. Was this the end for him? Were they going to toss him in the cellar?

Whatever they did, he just hoped they didn't slap his face.

"Whoa, she really did a number on you," Alberto said, flashing the light on Ricardo's face. "If you're not up to it tonight, I'll understand."

Ricardo nodded, then withdrew his cell phone and typed, "I need to see her."

"Of course." Alberto slapped him gently on the back. "Men, move aside and let the chef go down to assess the meat."

They cleared a path, and Ricardo slowly descended the stairs. At the bottom, he lowered his head and surveyed the two rooms built underground that he'd never seen. He knew of their existence but never had a reason to come down here.

This cellar held a dual purpose. To house the slaves during raids and to punish them for rule violations.

Along the side wall were steel hooks and built-in clamps suspended by chains. To his right were several tables that had all sorts of torture implements on them.

He moved toward the next room, where a steel beam supported the roof. From this beam, Maria Christy, the woman who savagely beat him to escape, was suspended by her wrists, completely naked.

She appeared otherwise unharmed.

Ricardo turned back to see Alberto behind him.

"Go on, take a look at the woman who did that nastiness to your face."

Ricardo moved in front of Maria.

She opened her eyes to look at him and saw a resolve there like she knew this wouldn't be good, whatever this was. She'd endure it because, in the end, it would be over. It would finally be over.

"Ricardo, you have twenty-four hours to take your revenge out on Maria. Do as you please." Alberto pointed. "Over there are the ankle restraints if she puts up a fight, but I don't think she will. This one knows it's over."

Maria's eyes closed as she drew inward.

"Here." Alberto handed Ricardo the keys to the shackles. "Be careful with this one if you release her. She can be feisty."

There was a commotion by the door.

Ricardo and Alberto both glanced back that way.

"And here comes our new girl."

Alberto's right-hand man dragged a blond woman in who could barely walk.

"Sorry, boss, I had to subdue her with a few punches. She struggled too much."

"No matter. Get her shackled to the wall. I want her to watch the end of Maria's life. That'll knock her attitude loose."

Two men went to work locking up the new girl. Once she was bound to the wall, her arms over her head, they walked past Alberto and headed for the stairs.

Alberto pulled something from his pants. "Here, take this." He held out a gun for Ricardo. "There's one in the chamber and several more inside. If you untie her for some reason and she runs, shoot the bitch like this." He raised the weapon and fired into the dirt wall about a foot from the new blond girl's hips. He laughed. "Damn, she barely flinched. I wonder how many times she got punched."

Ricardo took the offered weapon, felt its weight, and wondered if he should shoot Alberto and run for it. He couldn't miss from this distance.

Several of Alberto's men lingered by the open door of the cellar, though. He wouldn't get very far because these men were trained criminals, and he was just a cook.

Alberto grabbed his shoulder and nodded at the woman tied to the back wall. "I hope you don't mind an audience. I want the new girl to see what's in store for her."

Ricardo shook his head and slipped the gun into his pants, hoping he didn't accidentally discharge the damn thing. With his phone in his hand, he typed, "It's better this way. We need the new girl to learn so this"—he stopped to point at his face—"doesn't happen again."

Alberto tapped his shoulder a few times. "My thoughts exactly." He stepped away. "I'll leave the cellar door unlocked. Come up to the house when you're done. I'll have some consommé soup made for you and wine, each with its very own straws."

Then Alberto moved to the other room and climbed the stairs. He waited for the sound of the cellar door closing, but didn't hear it.

How could this be happening? This was too good to be true.

They literally left him with the keys and a gun.

The blond girl was quiet, her eyes closed. She swung softly from her shackles, her feet barely touching the dirt floor.

Ricardo started typing. "Maria, I won't harm you. I am breaking us out of here. This is no way to live. They gave me a gun. I will release you and take you to the front gate. If I have to, I'll shoot the guards at the front, and we will leave the property as I have people waiting just outside the gate who are heavily armed and prepared to help. Do you understand?"

Then he touched her shoulder gently, trying to rouse her. He lifted her chin and brushed her hair out of her eyes until they fluttered open.

With the cell phone in his hand, he lifted it so she could read what he'd typed.

Suspicion clouded her eyes when she finished reading and looked at him.

He typed quickly. "It's true. I'm not lying. Here, I'll untie you."

After she read his new message, he slipped the phone away and used the keys to unhook her arms.

They dropped out of the shackles, and now that nothing was supporting her, she fell to her knees.

Ricardo typed, "Please, get to your feet. We need to leave," then shoved the phone in her face.

He hadn't thought of bringing her food or clothes, but that would've been an odd request. She was naked and likely hungry. She was probably wondering what kind of trick he was playing, given that she had used a meat tenderizer on his face, and now he was helping her escape. It didn't make sense.

As they stood on the other side of the gate, heading to freedom, it didn't need to make sense. They'd be free of this place.

He wrapped her arm around his shoulder, winced when her hand brushed his cheek, then lifted and half-dragged her toward the stairs, where he set her down. If one of the men stood guard above, he had to deal with him before bringing her up.

At the top of the stairs, he peeked outside.

The entire area around him was bathed in darkness. The only lights were coming from the house, with one on each side of the gate, which sat roughly thirty meters away.

He ran back down and grabbed Maria, lifting her onto his shoulders again. There was no time to think or to be nervous. This was the perfect time to run. Everything was as if it was meant to be.

He whispered a silent prayer for the new blond girl they'd brought in, hoping she'd be okay. If all went well, they'd be off the property in ten minutes and riding to safety, and maybe they could send someone back for her.

With some difficulty, he coaxed Maria to the top of the stairs. He took one last look around to confirm no one was close by watching them.

He kept Maria on his left side so he could hold the gun in his right hand. He wasn't experienced with weapons, but if he was going to shoot someone, his odds were better in that hand as he was right-handed.

They shuffled toward the gates, still not seeing anyone.

Where did the guards usually stand? Did they do perimeter patrols? Is that why they weren't visible?

Since he'd been at the villa, he was either in the kitchen or his room so often that he never paid attention to security routines.

Yet, something in his gut told him this wasn't right.

Maria was more awake now, mostly standing on her own.

"Where are the guards?" she asked, her voice barely above a whisper.

Ricardo shrugged as he couldn't answer her without typing into his phone, and he couldn't stop to do that now.

They pressed on and came to the keypad that opened the gate. None of the employees were ever given the codes to open or close the gates. Only the gate guards knew what buttons to press.

But didn't that *brother* of his at the hospital say all he had to do was get her out in the open, and they'd handle the rest?

If so, where were they?

More frantic by the second, supporting Maria's weight, he tapped a few buttons on the keypad, but nothing happened.

*Shit!*

He wanted to scream at the injustice, but couldn't open his mouth. To be so close to freedom, and there was nothing he could do—

The gate clicked and slowly began opening.

Ricardo ducked and glanced around. Who had done that?

Still, no one was in sight.

What was going on? His nerves were bad before. Now he was shaking so much he didn't think he could support Maria for much longer.

Pulling her along with him, he scrambled through the opening and almost bumped into one of the guards.

"What the fuck is this?" the guard said.

Without a moment of hesitation, Ricardo raised his weapon, aimed at the man's face from less than a foot away, and pulled the trigger.

# Chapter 44

DARWIN WATCHED EVERYTHING FROM his perch in a tree about fifty meters from the Baglioni gate using a strong monocular. His four men were scattered among the trees doing the same.

The car had entered, then stopped just inside the gate. Ricardo exited the vehicle and walked toward a hole in the ground where several armed men had gathered around. Then he disappeared inside.

Another large man approached the hole in the ground, carrying a blond woman who reminded him of Sarah. She looked eerily close in size and shape, but he couldn't see her face in the dark.

They disappeared into the hole.

Finally, after a few minutes, everyone came up to ground level and headed toward the house.

Except for Ricardo and that blond woman.

They'd left him down there. That was either a good thing or a bad thing.

Focusing back on the gate guards, he saw two men chatting with their heads close together. Then they parted and walked along the fence in opposite directions, likely beginning a perimeter check.

Too bad he couldn't spend a week watching the place to get familiar with their routines and schedules. Going in under these conditions was risky, making it more probable that people would be killed, but he couldn't wait. A woman's life hung in the balance.

From his vantage point, the Baglioni villa and gate appeared abandoned. This in itself wasn't an odd development. The gate was solid concrete and was probably built to withstand direct hits from vehicles. But it wouldn't be able to withstand Zero's explosives.

They all waited in the trees, watching.

And were rewarded as Ricardo showed his face again—supporting a naked woman up the stairs.

"Holy shit," Darwin whispered. "He's got her."

He climbed down, whistled softly, and moved closer to the gate. His four men had climbed down from their trees and fell in behind him. This meant they couldn't see inside the gates anymore, but as soon as it opened, they'd have Ricardo and the woman.

"Any minute now," Darwin whispered.

The sound of a metallic click made him turn.

Cold steel pressed against his neck.

"One move, and I'll blow your head off."

At least twenty armed Baglioni men surrounded his men. No wonder the gate had been deserted. They needed Ricardo to feel safe and for Darwin's team to advance.

How did he miss the signs? How could he fuck up this badly?

Zero moved away from them all. "Sorry, Darwin." He shrugged. "Alberto paid me double what you were offering."

Darwin didn't respond as his mind raced through possible scenarios. He missed the days of working with Bruno. This wouldn't have happened with a man like Bruno. That man's loyalty was like none other.

The men frisked Darwin and the others, removing all their weapons, and then the front gates began to open.

"Move," the man holding the gun on Darwin ordered.

As a group, they walked through the trees toward the road that led to the gate, his loyal men at his side. Zero held back, chatting about his payment and how many explosive devices he could experiment with when he got paid.

Darwin wanted to scream a warning when he saw Ricardo and the woman stumble through the gates, but it was too late. One of Baglioni's guards was already there.

Then Ricardo raised his hand. He had a weapon in it.

And he pulled the trigger in front of the guard's face.

# Chapter 45

WHIMPERING ON THE FLOOR as he slid off the loveseat once the bullet went through his thigh, Carlo sounded like he was crying now.

"Don't shoot me again. Wrap my leg. Call an ambulance. Do something."

"Tell us what we want to know," Aaron shouted, a foot from Carlo's face.

"There's nothing to tell," Carlo yelled back. "Mike owed me a hundred large." He scrunched up his face and grimaced. "Then Jimmy called and said he found a girl."

Parkman and Aaron exchanged a glance.

"Go to the kitchen," Alex said, his eyes not wavering from Big Carlo. "Get me a large knife."

"No, no." Carlo raised a bloody hand. "I'll tell you what you want to know." He coughed.

Aaron exited the room as Alex handed the gun to Parkman.

"Everything," Parkman said, pushing the weapon's tip into the flesh on top of Carlo's other uninjured thigh.

"Okay, okay, seriously, guys."

Aaron returned with a long serrated knife ideal for cutting thick bread—or flesh.

Alex snatched it from him and whacked at Carlo's arm once, drawing blood.

Carlo wailed.

Again, Parkman wanted to reel Alex in but thought better of it. Aaron seemed to be enjoying it all too much.

There was a point of no return, where Carlo would bleed too much to come back from, and he was nearing that point now.

"I'm not feeling too good, fellas." He lowered his head to the carpet.

"You want to live?" Parkman shouted.

The man moaned a *yes*.

"Then tell us quickly what happened to the girl."

"They took her."

"Who are *they*?"

"The Italians."

They all exchanged a glance, with thoughts of Darwin on Parkman's mind.

"How can we find the Italians?" Aaron yelled.

"My phone."

Parkman quickly surveyed the living room but saw nothing.

"Beside my bed."

Aaron bolted from the living room and returned seconds later with an iPhone. "This?" He held it up.

Carlo's eyes had shut, and his breathing moved in and out in rapid spurts.

Parkman kicked the man's legs. "Guys, we're losing him."

Aaron dropped to his knees and pulled up Carlo's eyelids. "This your phone?"

The big man startled awake and glanced around. "Yeah. Their number is the last number dialed."

Aaron swiped to open the phone, then held it in front of Carlo's face.

It opened. He tapped the buttons to go to caller history, then held it in front of Carlo's face again.

"This one?"

Carlo looked at it and barely nodded. "They won't talk to you, though. They only know me. This only works if I'm alive."

"What did they buy?"

Carlo's half-lidded eyes tried to focus on Aaron.

Parkman stared at the shoulder wound that oozed blood with each heartbeat and the thigh and feet wounds. The man's blood stained the carpet below him as his skin took on a sickly pallor.

"They only traffick in women who can't be found. They transport them in coffins ..." his voice faded, and it looked like he had stopped breathing.

Aaron slapped the man's face. "Hey, wake up. You're not done." He backhanded the man across the cheek.

Carlo jolted and opened his eyes.

"You were telling us about coffins."

Carlo moaned in pain. "Is the ambulance coming?"

"Yeah, to take you to Hell." Aaron leaned closer. "The coffin?"

"They take the girls who go missing and are never found again in a coffin. It signifies death, as their old life is over, and when they get to Italy, they are reborn as slaves. You can ask them yourselves when they get here."

"Get here?" Parkman stared at Alex. No one was watching the gate. He faced Carlo. "When are you expecting them?"

"Within a half hour. They have my payment."

Parkman fought to hold his trigger finger. Who could do this to a woman? Sell her into slavery? Who could do something like this to Sarah? It was unthinkable.

"Where did they take her in Italy?"

"No idea. The Baglionis never gave me their address."

*Baglionis?* Darwin would know that name. They had to call Darwin, then buy tickets to Italy.

"Guys," Carlo's voice had grown very weak. "Wake me when the ambulance gets here. I think I'm going to sleep for a while. I'm exhausted ..."

Carlo closed his eyes. Within a minute, the blood seeping from his wounds slowed to a stop.

The man's heart had ceased activity.

Without waiting for any preamble or scripted speech, Aaron hit the number on Carlo's phone, then tapped for speaker. On the second ring, he held it up for Parkman and Alex to listen in.

"What?" a man answered.

"We have another girl."

"We said we don't need another for a week."

They looked at each other. If there were any qualms about executing Big Carlo and his men, they were decreasing by the second.

"You want me to lock this one up for a week?"

There was a pause on the other end. Someone whispered something to someone else.

"Where is she?"

"Here. My home on Rama Road."

"I have men en route with tonight's payment. Show them. If she passes, we will talk about picking her up sooner."

"When can I expect your men? Shouldn't they be here by now?"

"They're pulling up to your gate." The line died.

"Shit," Parkman whispered as he turned to Alex. "Where did you put the bodies?"

"Piled up inside the edge of the trees. Not visible from the road."

"Okay, guys. These men who are coming know everything about where Sarah is at the moment." He looked down at Big Carlo, then back up. "Meet them at the gate. Bring them in here. Once they're inside the house, we end this. We find Sarah."

Aaron and Alex bolted outside, and Parkman got ready for company by dragging Carlo's corpse out of sight.

# Chapter 46

DARWIN WATCHED AS RICARDO'S gun didn't spit out a bullet. Dumbfounded, he stared at it, then pulled the trigger again.

Nothing.

The Baglioni guard wasn't waiting for a third time. He raised his weapon and shouted in Italian for Ricardo to drop the gun.

Ricardo did what he was told, then used his other hand to support Maria further.

Another man stepped out from behind the open gate.

"Ricardo?" the new man said. "How could you?" He shook his head. "What are you doing here?" The man placed his hands on his hips.

Darwin watched from fifteen feet away. It seemed this man and his conversation held everyone rapt.

The man glanced over at Darwin and pointed. "You must be the *brother*." He lowered his arm and laughed. "When my man called and said Ricardo's brother was in his hospital room, I must say I was surprised." The man shook his head. "I didn't know Ricardo had a brother."

He moved closer to Darwin. "Allow me to introduce myself, Darwin Kostas. I'm Alberto Baglioni."

When the man said Darwin's name, it felt like a gut punch. "How do you know who I am?"

He laughed for his men, all of this a show of bravado. "Hospital cameras." He glanced around. "A wonderful thing, yeah?"

His men laughed softly, then fell silent.

"We ran your face and learned the mafia killer was planning an attack in town. How noble of you to save the woman first." He turned and looked at the naked woman still clinging to Ricardo.

"Yes." Zero stepped forward. "The mafia *serial* killer was the name used earlier."

Alberto frowned. "Who are you?"

"I'm the one you offered double what Darwin was paying me to tell you where we were."

"Oh, the Judas."

Zero laughed, a nervous edge to his tone. "Well, I wouldn't go that far—"

"Kill him."

The shock on Zero's face lasted a second before bullets turned him into a red Swiss cheese. His body dropped on the grass beside the road.

None of Darwin's men flinched. Betrayal in this business usually meant big bucks or death. They all knew the score.

"Feed for my pigs." Alberto glanced back at Ricardo. "Take them all to the cellar and shackle them. It's getting late, and we have a big day tomorrow."

"Uh, boss?" A tall blond man with a pronounced jawline stepped forward. "We're keeping them alive?"

"The pigs can only eat so much. We'll execute one per day until we get to Ricardo and Darwin. Ricardo must go last so he can watch what's coming all week. But Darwin"—he pointed at him—"this one's a prize. I have a few families to call. They'll want to know I have him locked away. They will want his wife, too. I'm sure Darwin here will tell us where his wife is located. Perhaps they have a dog. A cat. Maybe children. We have to find others associated with Darwin so they can suffer for his misdeeds as well." He moved closer to Darwin until he stood close enough for Darwin to smell his breath. "Eventually, you and everyone you know, plus people who have a memory of you, will be erased from this planet, never to be thought of again. How's that sound?"

"Amateur and unprofessional. Not killing me now is too risky."

Besides a cricket off in the distance, no sound came from any of the nearly thirty men standing around them in a semi-circle.

Then Alberto laughed—cackled—and clapped his hands above his head. His men joined in until Alberto calmed enough to catch his breath.

"I like you. The balls on this one." He pointed again. "Fuck, I'm going to hate to have to kill you. I mean, if only you'd worked *for* us instead of *against* us." He shook his head, appraising Darwin. "Nothing can change the inevitable." He swung his hand in the air. "Lock them up." Then pointed at Zero. "And chop him up."

Men shoved Ricardo back toward the hole in the ground. He supported Maria as they moved across the lawn toward the hole.

Darwin saw no play here, no move. There was nothing he could do but walk forward and retain a measure of hope that an opportunity would arise soon.

Ricardo helped Maria into the hole, then Four and Seven headed down, followed by Ten.

Across the lawn, Alberto was reentering his house with the tall blond guy. Who the hell was Alberto going to call? What kind of torture would they make him endure?

If he ran and they shot him, things would end much quicker.

Someone shoved him from behind, and he nearly fell down the stairs. A quick arm on the edge of the doorframe stopped his fall.

Then he got his feet under him and moved down the stairs. When he entered the cellar, one of Alberto's men pointed a weapon and gestured for him to move into the other room.

He did as he was told.

Inside the second room, that blond woman he'd seen them bring in here from his perch in the trees—the one who reminded him of Sarah—was suspended by shackles along the back wall. He couldn't see her face because her head was bowed forward, and her hair covered all her features.

They pushed him in beside her, and while one man shoved a weapon into his cheekbone, two other men bound his wrists to iron cuffs attached to the wall.

Within five minutes, the men had locked everyone up in different areas of the cellar and then left.

The underground room fell into darkness. Darwin heard nothing but groans of pain and heavy breathing.

Then the woman to his right woke and whispered something.

"What's that?" Darwin asked.

"They'll all be dead soon," she whispered. "Every last fucking one of them."

Darwin's eyes widened in the dark as he looked in her general direction. "Sarah?" he asked.

There was no answer. The woman was back asleep.

# Chapter 47

EXHAUSTED AFTER DRAGGING CARLO'S huge body into the back bedroom, Parkman moved to the kitchen window. From there, he could see the front gates.

Aaron and Alex had taken up positions on either side of the gate as if they were sentries working for Carlo.

They didn't have to wait long.

A pickup truck, similar to the one they saw with a coffin in it, slowed at the entrance and flashed its lights. Aaron walked to the center of the gate, unlatched something, then pulled it open.

When he looked for Alex, he couldn't find him. Where the hell had he gone now?

The pickup truck eased through the gate and drove toward the house.

"Shit, I'm on my own." He stared at the bloodstains on the carpet and wondered if that would throw them off. It was a considerable effort to drag Carlo's body around the corner, but he'd done it with only a few minutes to spare.

Car doors slammed outside. Heavy footsteps clomped up the front stairs, the door was opened, and three men stepped inside the front foyer.

"In here," Parkman called.

He stood near the hallway, his mind racing on what to say, with it all coming together in pieces.

The three men entered the living room and fanned out. The man in the center held a black briefcase.

"Where's Big Carlo?"

"He isn't here."

The men glanced at each other, then back at Parkman. "Well, that's unfortunate."

"How so?"

The frontman tapped the black case. "This is for him, and I have instructions to only give it to him. Also, he called about another girl."

"There's no other girl. And that"—he gestured at the case—"I don't want it."

"Who *are* you?"

Parkman eyed them, knowing the kind of men they were and wanting to delay as long as possible. "Who I am doesn't matter."

The men didn't waver. They offered no response.

The lead man glanced around the room until his eyes stopped on the blood stains in front of the loveseat.

"Someone have an accident?"

Parkman nodded once slowly. "In a manner of speaking. That's why Carlo isn't here. Otherwise, he would've been."

"You're aware we can't leave this with you."

He nodded once again. "We've covered that. I'd prefer you didn't."

They stared at each other for several heartbeats. Parkman forced himself not to blink.

The other man looked away first. "Then I guess we'll be leaving."

He needed to say something, like ask them about Sarah. But what did Aaron and Alex have planned?

Before he could act, the leader stopped in the alcove of the opening that led to the living room, then slowly turned to face Parkman.

"I thought I recognized you."

The pit in his stomach dropped further. "I doubt it."

The man wore a knowing smile as he nodded ever so slightly. "When we left Mike's place earlier today." He glanced at his men, their hands crossed in front of their belts. "You were on the street. I saw your face. We drove past you."

Parkman waited to respond. He didn't want to appear too eager to confirm the man's memory.

"Mike was into Big Carlo for a hundred large." He paused as the men watched him, appearing eager to hear more. "This exchange was important to him. So, of course, Carlo would send someone to ensure everything went smoothly."

The man squinted his eyes. "So he sent men to watch us?"

Parkman nodded, then saw Aaron and Alex standing behind the threesome. "He sent all of us to make sure you did the right thing. We wouldn't want anyone left alive to whisper the name *Baglioni*, now would we?"

Those narrowed eyes widened. "You know a lot for one of his security. Have I got that right? You work for him? As some sort of security guard?"

"Actually, no." When he paused this time, the two men—who hadn't noticed Aaron and Alex behind them yet—slipped their hands onto the butts of their weapons. "I'm an independent contractor."

"He must trust you to have you meet us."

"Implicitly."

Again, they eyed each other for what felt like minutes but was only seconds. Then the leader grunted something.

"Tell him we'll call."

Something clicked from behind the trio. Then the two men dropped like stone statues as the Tasers Aaron and Alex held sent fifty thousand volts through them.

Parkman sprang into action to cover the ten feet separating him from the man with the briefcase, but didn't need to, as Alex had already fired a weapon into the man's leg.

He dropped to the floor, shouting curses.

Parkman would have to talk to Alex about shooting people too fast. They lose blood and die. Not a solid negotiation tactic.

Quickly, before anyone could recover, they relieved the men on the floor of all their weapons while tasing them once more.

"You're all dead," the man with the bullet in his leg shouted at them. "Do you know who we are?"

Aaron jumped down and grabbed the man's lapels, dragging his face up to meet Aaron's. "Yes, we know who you are, and we're coming after all of you." He slapped the man several times, back and forth. "Wake up. It's time to die, asshole." Then he shoved him to the floor so hard the man's head bounced once.

"It doesn't matter *who* you are." Parkman moved in front of the man as Alex pressed the Tasers again. "You are only men: flesh and blood. You will die like the rest of them. Your connections are just some twisted tribal mentality security blanket that allowed you to get sloppy. Because you're so *connected*, you came in here unprepared. Now, to keep breathing, we require all the details on the woman you stole and placed in that coffin of yours."

"Fuck you." He spat at him, the gob falling short. "Kill me. You'll get nothing out of me."

Parkman shrugged, then looked at Alex and Aaron. "We're short on time, and these assholes are trafficking women. They've got Sarah. After what happened to Carlo, it's your call on how we deal with these guys."

"Save the expensive trial." Aaron glared at the men. "Send a message. I'm tired of these above-the-law assholes destroying lives for profit."

He lifted a weapon and fired.

One of the men with Taser prongs still in him jerked when the bullet hit his thigh. Then he screamed.

The other guy raised his hands. "I'll tell you everything."

The leader snapped his head to the left. "Shut your mouth. We die with honor."

Aaron aimed his weapon at the leader with the briefcase. "One warning only. Shut up, or take a bullet."

"Fuck you—"

Aaron fired into the man's side. The bullet entered the area where the appendix would likely be. He grunted and pulled inward.

"I don't bluff. Don't speak again."

Parkman turned to the man who was still free of bullet holes. "You were saying?"

"They put her in the coffin and drove her to the airport. She arrived in Italy a few hours ago."

Their suspicions confirmed by the name Baglioni, Parkman waved at the man to continue.

"I don't know much more other than there's no money in that case."

Parkman frowned. "What?"

"We don't leave witnesses. Our job tonight was to execute Carlo and his men."

"Which is why Jimmy, Mike, and Candace are dead?"

The man nodded.

"Hey," the leader shouted. "I need help here. I'm bleeding too much."

Aaron stared down at the man, his gun hand shaking with rage. "How many women have you taken? How many lives have you stolen?"

"Bleeding heart cocksuckers—fuck you. Here's how it works. I live, you live. I die. They hunt and kill you."

As if what the man said went unheard, Aaron continued, "You took my woman. She doesn't just mean a lot to me. She means a lot to hundreds, if not thousands, of people. You stole that from everyone." He brought the weapon higher. "I hope they come." Parkman saw a tear on Aaron's cheek. "I hope one thousand men from your tribe come. And when they do, I'll kill them all, and the world will be a better place."

Aaron fired. The man's head snapped back. Then he lay still.

They all turned to the other men.

"Where is Sarah now?"

"Italy."

"You said that. Where in Italy?"

"We don't know. They don't tell us, but we all work for the Baglioni family."

Parkman turned to Aaron and Alex. "These guys can never go back because he's dead now." He pointed at their dead leader. "They'll be watching over their shoulders forever. Which means we leave them and just go. They'll be dead by the end of the week anyway."

For a moment, Parkman was worried Aaron had flipped a switch and had become a murderer, through and through. It was one thing to kill a man in defense. But subdued on the floor like they were at the moment was murder.

Or would it be Alex who did it?

Whatever happened in the next few minutes, Parkman realized he wouldn't stop them if they tried. What did that say about him, then?

Alex jumped forward and grabbed the uninjured man. "You're coming with us."

"What? Why?"

"We're going to see a man named Sergeant James, and you'll tell him everything you know. Or we shoot you in the feet and leave you here for when his bosses send more men." He gestured at the dead man with the black case.

"I'll go. I'll talk. But will he offer me protection?"

"Ask him. Let's go."

Alex shoved the man forward.

"Hey," the other guy said from the floor. "What about me?"

"Your pickup is out front." Aaron moved toward the door. "Crawl to it and drive somewhere safe."

"There is nowhere safe with these guys."

"Not our problem."

The three men led their captive to their car out on the road, then placed him in the back with Alex.

"We should've burned the place down," Aaron said, getting in the passenger side.

"Better to leave it like that." Parkman gestured behind him at the new guy. "With his boss's body, they can rule it a territory hit or something. No one will look too deeply into this one. Everyone knows who Big Carlo is and won't care that he's gone."

As soon as they got heading north again, he called Sergeant James.

Before he let the man speak, he said, "We've got news for you. Do you have any contacts with the Italian authorities?"

"Is this Parkman?"

"Yes, and we know where Sarah is."

"Did you say Italian authorities?"

"I did."

"Wait, you're saying she went off the road, was dragged from her car, and then someone flew her to Italy?"

"The Baglioni family did it. They're human traffickers. Call someone high up in the Italian police. Call their state police. Call someone. Sarah's in trouble and needs us."

"What proof do you have?"

"One of the people Sarah was sold to is in the car with us. We're bringing him to you. He's agreed to spell it out, but he wants protection."

James was silent for a moment. "You're not fucking with me, are you?"

"No." Parkman watched the road, his hand tightening on the wheel. "Make some calls, James. Make something happen. The Baglioni family. They're in Italy, and they have Sarah."

"Okay, okay. Get that man here. I'll start making calls."

The line died.

Parkman hit the gas harder, and the car sped into the night.

They'd crossed over to a darker place today. Back at Big Carlo's place were more lives than they'd ever taken at once, all piled up like trash.

What had happened to them? Weren't they better than that?

Or had this triggered something in them that said *I've had enough*?

He looked in the mirror and saw the same resolute stare on Alex's face that was always there.

Maybe he did make the right choice. Any of those men back there would have killed him in a heartbeat if given the chance. If he simply tied them up, there's the chance that one would get untied. Loose ends got people killed. And an enemy of this caliber could never be underestimated.

He'd make peace with what happened tonight when Sarah was safe and everything was over.

Or he wouldn't.

One thing was for sure, though. A new understanding had dawned: they were all murderers deep down inside.

Cold-blooded and all.

Fuck with Sarah and take your chances.

Why did that have sex appeal? Why did it feel so right?

# Chapter 48

A LIGHT TURNED ON in the cellar. Darwin blinked to get his eyes adjusted.

Someone was coming down the stairs. Before they entered the room, he glanced at the woman beside him.

She was awake and looking back at him in disbelief.

Darwin stared into Sarah's eyes in surprise, a part of him convinced this was a joke, that she was a perfect doppelgänger.

"Sarah?" he whispered. "How—"

A man entered the room. "Everyone, get up. We are taking you all to the main house."

Three more men stepped into view. They unlocked Ricardo's shackles, then zip-tied his wrist to Maria. Once she was unshackled from the wall, they allowed Ricardo to lead Maria—still naked—toward the stairs.

Then they unlocked Darwin's men. Ten, Four, and Seven were led upstairs, their hands zip-tied at the back.

Only Darwin and Sarah remained.

Darwin leaned as close as he could to her. "You were missing. The guys are looking for you."

She nodded. "Happy you found me."

"Sarah, you're missing in Ontario, Canada. What are you doing here?"

"They shipped me here in a coffin."

"In a what—?"

The men entered the room and unlocked one of Darwin's shackles, then the other. A third man held an automatic weapon aimed at him.

"Don't do anything stupid," the man said. "Let them tie your hands together."

"Why are we all going to the house? Is there a grand ball this evening?"

"Who writes your material?" The man shook his head as the other guys zip-tied his arm. "You'll have to work on your humor."

Then they undid Sarah's restraints. Once they weren't holding her up any longer, she dropped to her knees. They pulled her closer and zip-tied her to Darwin, who helped her stay on her feet.

"Take her," the man said. "Help her up the stairs."

Darwin did as instructed. He couldn't believe he had Sarah in his hands. What were the odds? Did Vivian set this all up? If so, how? Because he certainly wasn't an instrument of hers.

At the top of the stairs, he stepped out onto the grass. He held Sarah, but she was standing on her own now, only favoring her left leg with a slight limp.

Over by the road to the house, about twenty feet from them, his three men sat on their knees, their heads bowed. Behind them was a single soldier, a gun in his hand.

"What's this?" he asked as the Baglioni men came up the stairs behind him.

"We don't need them after all, and we certainly aren't going to feed them."

"Wait, what? Don't do this. You don't have to."

The man moved around to stand in front of him. "And why not? You guys were about to break in here and kill us. We got the upper hand, and here we are." The smirk on his face revealed his contempt. "Don't deny it. You'd do the same to us. This is war, or at least today's version of war, when the world is at peace. Kill or be killed."

"Then take me."

The man chortled. "You? Never. My boss would slice *my* throat if we killed you. We can hurt you, but can't kill you—yet. The women are slaves, and you and Ricardo will die, that's for sure. But while we wait for that, we won't babysit your mercenaries whose only goal is to kill us." He shook his head. "Too risky."

No one else was outside. This wasn't a show to teach anyone a lesson. This wasn't a public execution. They were taking out the trash, and all those men did, their only crime was to help him get to Sarah.

His heart went out to them, but he could do nothing. Their job always came with risks. Ultimately, this was one of them.

Seven looked up, and their eyes locked. He smiled at Darwin, resigned to his fate, and likely not wanting Darwin to feel bad.

"What are we waiting for?" Alberto yelled from the front steps of the house.

Everyone looked his way.

Alberto waved a hand. "Kill those mercs, and get that bitch and the mafia killer in here before the troops arrive."

*Troops? Who was coming?*

The man holding the gun slid one into the chamber, held the gun to the back of Four's head, and pulled the trigger.

Four slumped to the ground.

Alberto clapped from the front porch.

The man placed the weapon at the back of Ten's head and pulled the trigger. He slumped to the ground.

Alberto's clapping grew louder.

The clapping stopped when the man held the weapon to the back of Seven's head.

Everyone looked at the front of the house.

Alberto's head was aimed downward as he stared at his chest. It was covered in roving red lights. When he looked up, his face was a mask of surprise.

"Fuck," he got out before an artillery of weapons fire struck him so hard he shot backward and smacked into the outside wall of the house, leaving a red stain on the siding when he dropped to the porch.

The man who held a gun on Seven hadn't fired yet. Darwin followed his gaze when he spun around to look at the gate.

Small round objects littered the top. In the dark, it took all of one full second for Darwin to discern they were the heads of men covered in helmets and wearing goggles.

More weapons fired, and the man standing over Seven jerked and spasmed before falling dead.

Seven shot sideways and lay facedown to make himself less of a target.

Then the gate was opening, and like a thousand ants filing out of their home in the ground, the Italian army rushed inside the Baglioni compound, their weapons butted up on their shoulders.

The two men standing beside Darwin and Sarah raised their weapons, and Darwin had no choice but to shove Sarah backward down the stairs they'd just ascended.

He was able to keep her from dropping to the bottom of the stairs because their hands were zip-tied together, but both their wrists were yanked hard.

A cacophony of automatic fire sounded above them, followed by the sound of men dropping and grunting.

Darwin pushed Sarah deeper until they were up against a wall, then covered her with his body and waited.

He didn't have to wait long.

Italian military men surrounded them within seconds, barking orders in Italian.

"English," Darwin shouted. "We speak English."

"Are you prisoners?"

Darwin held up their zip-tied wrists.

"Come with us."

The men helped them to their feet, did a cursory feel to ensure they had no weapons, then led them outside.

The Italians had led Ricardo back outside the house, too. Maria was draped in a blanket beside Ricardo, crying. Seven was helping to hold her up as she whispered repeatedly, "Is it over? Is it over?"

Gunfire erupted sporadically from inside the house.

Sarah wrapped an arm around Darwin. "Hold me," she whispered.

And Darwin held her. And she wept.

# Chapter 49

AFTER TWO WEEKS OF statements, interrogations, and medical attention, Sarah and Darwin were booked on a flight to Toronto. Upon arrival, the authorities escorted them in private vehicles, taking all security measures necessary. After two weeks back on Canadian soil, once the authorities took their entire statement of accounts, including what happened to Sarah on the northbound lanes heading to Parry Sound that fateful day, they were released and driven to the dojo where everyone awaited them.

Maria Christy had been released and escorted back to her family stateside. After Samantha's family was notified, they properly buried her remains.

The investigation into trafficking became an international case as authorities exercised search warrants at dozens of known locations of Baglioni associates. Over another dozen women were freed within ten days of the raid on the Baglioni villa from various other Baglioni enterprises across Italy, America, and Canada.

Parkman, Aaron, and Alex were waiting for them when they arrived at the dojo. Sarah had easily gained her strength back during her two-week stay in Rome and the subsequent time in Ontario. She hugged each man with enthusiasm, squeezing them out of breath.

Each of them had played a pivotal role in getting her home safe.

"I can't believe I'm here." She eyed them all. "I'm still standing because of you guys. I love you all." Her eyes fell on Aaron.

He wiped his face, seemingly overwhelmed with emotion. "We thought we'd lost you this time. Like, for good."

She punched his shoulder lightly. "I lost faith in Vivian on this one, but someone was looking out for us."

Parkman cleared his throat. "Could it be she knew the news of Maria's escape would inspire Darwin into action? So she put you in harm's way to bring us all together?"

Sarah took a seat and shook her head. "I can't wrap my mind around it because if that's the case, then aren't we all just puppets on a stage? If so, for whose benefit? Vivian's?"

"This conversation harkens back to our purpose here on Earth and why we're here to evolve our souls."

"Yeah, too deep for me at the moment."

Aaron sat next to Sarah. Alex sat on the other side. Parkman and Darwin grabbed water bottles and distributed them.

"What did you guys do while I was gone?" Sarah twisted the cap off her bottle and took a swig.

"Well, it all started with our search for you," Parkman began.

"And Alex threatened my life," Aaron added.

Alex grinned. "Motivation comes in many colors. Sometimes black and blue."

Sarah stared at them for a moment, then glanced at Darwin. "Any idea what they're talking about?"

He shook his head. "I'm sure they'll explain, though."

Sarah listened as they recounted everything they did, including their visit to Mike's place, where they saw the bloody rag, unaware that she was in the back room. How they passed the truck with the coffin, and what happened to Big Carlo and Baglioni's men.

"Holy shit." She stared at them again with newfound awe. "That's a lot of dead men. How did you walk away from it?"

"We called Sergeant James with all the information we had. When the authorities showed up at Big Carlo's place, it was labeled a turf war and connected to the murders of Mike, Jimmy, and Candace. After the pickup was seen at Mike's place and then burned down, they found the same pickup at Carlo's place. They added it up and found the sum matched the scene."

Darwin shook his head. "I'm afraid at my end, there was mistake after mistake."

Parkman turned to him. "Tell us."

Darwin covered how he recruited his men, how Zero double-crossed him, and how they got sloppy—or cocky, whatever works—and were captured. When they tied him up beside Sarah in the cellar, he understood his purpose. It was her the whole time.

They spoke about how Sergeant James called in the information. It traveled fast, prompting the Italian authorities to raid the place with a highly trained contingent of the Italian army.

"Even though there was a tight lid on secrecy around the Baglioni villa raid," Darwin said, "someone warned Alberto Baglioni about half an hour before the raid occurred. So, he wanted everyone brought up to the house to conceal us, and he ordered the execution of my men as they weren't needed. But he was too late by minutes. They shot Alberto on sight because the Italians witnessed them executing prisoners on the front lawn. They had to make that call because they saw Sarah standing there bound to me by the wrist." Darwin shrugged and glanced at Sarah. "They thought we were next, and the entire raid was predicated on the notion that Baglioni was a human trafficker and had female slaves."

Parkman nodded. "We were lucky with the information we got for the sergeant. How he got it up the channels so quickly is mystifying, but we were told the Italians were already investigating how Maria went missing once she was in custody. To see her on Baglioni's property again, they were ordered to take the building at all costs."

Aaron turned to Sarah. "How much of this did Vivian tell you, Sarah?"

Sarah looked at him. "Nothing. I was in the dark, literally."

He blew air through his teeth. "Ouch."

"Yeah, I was pissed at her, but we've talked since, and I understand some of her reasoning." She raised a finger before anyone could say anything. "I didn't say I like it, but I *understand* it."

"That about sums it up," Parkman said, rising to his feet. "Happy to have you back in one piece. We've got a lot to discuss in the coming week. Your car insurance rep wants to meet with you. And what about that woman in Parry Sound you were heading to meet? There are loose ends to tie up."

Sarah nodded and offered him a smile. "All in due time. We'll sort everything out." She glanced around the room. "I'm just happy to be back with my family. And just in time, too. Vivian says there's something to be done about a liar. Something she called, *The Whole Truth.*"

Alex got up, his chair scraping the floor. He moved over and wrapped his arms around her. "So happy to see you." He kissed her cheek. "Keep me closer. I'll watch your back."

She placed her hands on his forearm. "Of course. I wouldn't have it any other way."

When Alex released her, he walked by Aaron, tapped his shoulder twice, and exited through the dojo's back door.

"I'll take my leave," Parkman said. "Darwin? Can I interest you in a drink?"

Darwin pushed away from the table. "You're on. I could use a few."

"Well, hey, I'll buy the first one."

Darwin wrapped an arm around Parkman's shoulders. "And I'll buy the next one."

They moved toward the back door, whispering and laughing about something.

Sarah fixed her gaze on Aaron. "Now that that's out of the way and everyone left us alone on purpose, speak your piece. Tell me how wrong I was. Judge me, and tell me I should stop listening to Vivian." She glanced down at her lap so he wouldn't see the pain in her eyes. "Even though I *wasn't* listening to her on this one."

"Sarah." His voice cracked, but she didn't look up. "I love you."

She frowned, waited a moment, then raised her head. His eyes had glazed over.

"I'm sorry. For everything."

She wanted to hug him, hold him, her man, the father of their child, but she waited. This was his moment. Whatever was coming, she wanted—needed—to hear it.

He wiped at a tear before it hit his cheek. "I was wrong—I *am* wrong. I've always been wrong about you." Now he looked away, his head shaking. "I thought you would listen to me, listen to what I was saying."

"And what were you saying?"

He faced her. "That my love for you was so strong that I can't imagine losing you. That the dangerous life we live—you live—has shown me time and again how narrow the margin between life and death can be. We've come too close on too many occasions, and we've lost Benjamin, Bruno, and so many more." He gulped for air. "I can't lose you."

"This mental push and shove you were doing *was* losing me, though."

He nodded, glancing at his lap. "I know. That was me reliving my trauma of losing my sister. I loved her, too, and life got dangerous. Now she's gone. I love you, and life is dangerous. I just can't lose you."

"Then stand beside me, dumbass. We're stronger together."

"I see that now more than ever. This disappearance thing wasn't your doing. It fell into your lap, and you needed your circle to unite and rally around you. You needed us to bring this to a close, and we all stepped up when needed. I shudder to think of what would've happened had I not joined this effort."

"But you did join."

"Yeah, after Alex threatened to hospitalize me if I didn't."

"He said that?"

Aaron nodded, the corner of his mouth lifting in a half-grin. "He said he'd kick my ass for real."

"Could he?"

Aaron looked up. His face had turned serious. "Bloody hell, I think he could. I'd put up a good fight for all of a minute, but that fucker knows shit that I never taught him. He's wiry and fast." He tapped his fingers on the table. "I've never heard words like that from him. I've never seen the rage inside Alex like I saw at Big Carlo's house before. Alex just executed everyone when he heard Carlo sold you for a hundred grand. He was that furious."

Sarah's smile widened. "Gonna have to give that guy a big hug soon."

"That's the support I needed to see. In life and in death, we stick with each other. I've been wrong, and I want to take it all back if it's not too late. People are tilted, their reasoning twisted."

"How do you mean?"

"Someone once said, we ignore those who adore us, adore those who ignore us, love those who hurt us, and hurt those who love us." He took her hand. "I don't want to ignore or hurt you ever again."

Sarah looked away for a moment, but she didn't take her hand away. "What are you saying? Go back to the way things were? You, me, and Willow? Living together? No more separation orders, motions filed, and court dates?" She waited a moment, then turned around to face him.

"If you'll have me, that's exactly what I'm saying. But there's one more thing."

"What's that?"

Aaron pushed back his chair and dropped to one knee. "We need to make it official." He produced a small box, popped it open, and made a vow to remain at her side, to protect her with his life, never to waver, always to be there, the two of them against the world, to love and cherish her, to devote his life to her, to care and understand even when that gets challenging, to respect and offer reassurance when needed, but most of all to love her until his heart stopped beating.

Then he asked her a life-changing question.

And Sarah answered it honestly.

# Afterword

This was a tough novel to write because I'm used to Sarah instigating the violence, the heroic act, and the call to duty. The inciting incident began when she was injured after going off the road and getting stuck in the snow and freezing temperatures. She's abducted and placed in a coffin—which was to signify her death and rebirth at the Baglioni villa —and delivered to her slave future.

Sarah isn't a Marvel character. She doesn't have superpowers. If she's tied down effectively, she cannot escape unless someone unties her. So, as long as her captors are smart and do a good job, Sarah will be a victim, just like anyone else.

That made this novel difficult because it had to be other people who were strong, fighting for what was right, doing everything they could to find her, and in so doing, they uncovered a human trafficking giant.

People go missing every day, many of them women, and they're never heard from again. I've always wondered, with the high numbers of human trafficking, if some of those "missing" people were simply relocated into new lives.

Not only that, I wanted a novel where the focus was on the people around Sarah. I wanted them to feel her loss in their core and bring out some kind of animal ferocity to find her.

Finally, I wanted Aaron to *feel* something. It's been a long time coming. That was a side goal here since that man infuriated me time and again. His *need* to be protective after what happened to his sister, well over fifteen years ago (available in the novel, The Specter), drove a wedge between them. He reached a point where he felt compelled to prove a point. Aaron went on a mission to *force* Sarah to see his side of the facts, which wasn't working. He was alienating his close friends as well.

Although Sarah, being Sarah, still had feelings for him, she accepted that if that were what he wanted, then she'd let him go. There'd be no negotiating, no begging.

But with her missing, lost, and freezing somewhere, Aaron *felt* the weight of that loss and the responsibility. It became a mission to locate her and ensure she was okay. Well, not to mention Alex's determination to find Sarah. Parkman was there, too, but Alex was more verbal about the punishment if Aaron didn't step up to the plate on this one.

For Aaron to hear and see their level of dedication to Sarah, and they weren't even lovers or Willow's dad, something clicked, and he understood where he stood—or at least where he should be standing. It certainly wasn't in a courtroom, fighting her for custody.

Overall, I wanted to show that Sarah needs everyone around her, and they need her. They've been through so much together for dozens of books, and staying together will bring them to book fifty—well, most of them. I'm sure we'll lose one or two along the way, but you never know, and that's certainly not a topic I can discuss here—it would be a spoiler in every sense of the word.

Those freezing scenes brought up nasty memories for me as I lost my brother in such a way after he got lost skiing on Sunshine Mountain in Alberta, Canada. He went missing, and ultimately, a group of snowshoers found his frozen body leaning up against a tree two weeks later.

All of that is in the past, though, and as much as Sarah and Aaron have to move on from their messy separation, I must write about characters who are struggling to move on from their past as well.

Talking about the past, I've focused the last few books on increasing the divide between Sarah and Aaron, making things worse for them. All of that was to prepare for this novel. Even if you're arguing with someone, when they go missing and could be dead or dying, all the pettiness goes out the window. When Aaron was able to look past all the pettiness, he saw how he felt about her, and that's what mattered.

And here we are.

Now, what did Sarah say to Aaron when he proposed?

We shall see in the next Sarah novel, *The Whole Truth*, but I suspect most of you already know.

Until then, we'll see you soon.

Take care of yourself and each other.

I love you all,

Jonas Saul

The Whole Truth

Book Thirty-Five

Part One

# Chapter 1

"WHAT ARE WE DOING here, Sarah?" Aaron lowered his window and inhaled the cool breeze, his gaze on the highway in the distance.

Sarah watched him, still unsure if his heart was in it or not. Either way, it didn't matter. This trip would be the test—there was no two ways about it. He claimed he was all in. She'd see soon enough. Her proposal for him was dangerous, but he'd go for it if he were truly all in.

She glanced away to stare out the car window. "I'll know him when I see him."

"Who?" Aaron snapped his head her way. "Who are we waiting for?"

Sarah kept her gaze fixed on the people coming and going from the clubhouse, then leaned back and watched another man on the putting green to her right.

"Soon," she whispered. "The bastard will be here soon."

Aaron huffed out a breath.

That made her look at him. "If you don't want to be here, you can leave."

His eyes narrowed. "Don't misread me. I sighed because I hate the not knowing, the waiting. Not because I don't want to be here." He took a breath and sighed again. "If I didn't want to be here, I would leave."

She stared at the clubhouse door again. "That wasn't a sigh. It was a heavy huff, sometimes called a scoff." She adjusted herself in her seat. "So, operating with limited knowledge bothers you? How do you suppose I feel? You think Vivian is always so forthcoming?" She shook her head, then whispered, "In a perfect world."

Aaron's head lowered. "You're right." Then, after a moment, he added, "I'm sorry."

"The elevator is out of order. We must take the stairs to this, whatever *this* is, one step at a time." She cracked her door open, then stopped. "And we have to have faith in Vivian." Her eyes lowered to the glove box, where a Glock was stored. Then she rubbed her face once and turned to Aaron. "But you know all this, so maybe what we're doing isn't for you."

"Sarah, wait." He touched her forearm before she could exit the car. "I'm here, aren't I? Whatever we're doing here will be dangerous, right? Can I be blamed for wanting to be at home, fixing dinner, sipping wine with you?" He took his hand away. "Instead, we're parked out here at a golf course in fucking North Bay, about four hours from home, and our life—"

"Because we need the *truth*."

"Right, the *whole truth*, like you said. I get it. I truly do. But didn't you say this person is influential in the community?"

Sarah leaned on the open door and kept her eyes glued on the clubhouse. "Not just that."

"There's more?"

"Vivian said it involved kids."

"*Kids?* How so?"

She lifted one shoulder. "Not sure yet. Although, I'm thinking we'll know more soon."

"Kids," Aaron whispered as if talking to himself. "What the fuck are we walking into?"

Sarah pushed the door open and got out, the light breeze cooling her forehead. Wherever there was movement, she focused her attention on it, scanning for the man she was supposed to meet. The *influential* man in this community. Was he the guy loading his clubs into the trunk of his BMW? The guy on the putting green? One of the threesomes heading toward their balls on the eighteenth green?

Vivian said she'd know him on sight.

*That helps.*

Her phone vibrated in her pocket. She slipped it out and saw a text from Alex. Instead of responding, she hit his number.

"I'm here," he said. "Parkman and I are in position."

"Don't get arrested, but do everything you can to stop the police from entering the premises when they come."

"We have a plan."

"Good. This shouldn't take long." She clicked off and turned around.

Aaron was out of the car now. "Don't get arrested? Holy shit! How serious is this?"

Sarah faced him. "We are here to have a chat with a man who may be dangerous."

"*Dangerous?* I thought he was *influential?*"

"Both."

"Fuck me," Aaron said to himself as he shut his car door and moved to sit on the hood.

The sun cast an eerie glow on the golf course as the final groups played out the last five holes. The parking lot had been slowly emptying since they'd arrived half an hour before.

After a moment, Aaron said, "I'm whining, aren't I?"

Sarah moved toward him. "Yes, you're whining. It's unbecoming."

He glanced sideways at her, then winced when he saw her smile. "You know, maybe it's because I asked you a serious question a few weeks ago, and you haven't committed either way, yet you expect my commitment."

She frowned, then raised a finger and waved it back and forth. "That's not the case. I answered that question with a proposal of my own."

"Right, instead of *speaking* of commitments, we must *show* our commitments."

"Actions have a way of informing the world." Sarah stopped wagging her finger and then raised her lips into a half-smile. "I'm stable. I'm always *all in*. I'll never waver. You used to be that way. Bring back the old Aaron, and we're golden. This new Aaron has doubt and fear, and he whines—"

"Okay, okay, I get it. I'll shut up until this is over." He crossed his arms over his chest. "Then you'll give me your answer?"

Sarah peered at an overweight man as he moved toward the clubhouse.

"Sarah, we deal with this *truth* thing and the *kids* thing, then I get your answer, right? Because waiting around can belittle a man's confiden—"

"That's him," she cut in.

She brought out her cell phone and tapped a message to Alex.

*We're a go!*

# Chapter 2

SARAH HEADED TOWARD THE clubhouse without hesitation, barely registering Aaron's footfalls behind her.

Vivian told her some of what this man was made of, but certainly not enough. Everything would come together with or without Vivian's information, or lack thereof. At least, she hoped so because listening to Aaron had stirred doubt in her belly.

She entered the clubhouse and scanned the faces of the golfers.

The man she'd followed inside was gone—he'd disappeared from sight.

Aaron entered behind her and leaned closer to her ear. "Where is he?" he whispered.

Sarah moved forward and took a seat at an empty table. A moment later, Aaron sat opposite her.

Their eyes met briefly. It was enough for her to see his nerves on the surface. Was it the kids' thing that bothered him? Since their daughter was born, he always claimed he was worried Willow could lose her mother, which was one of the reasons he wanted her to calm down with Vivian.

Could it be that he changed as a man after Willow was born, and his fears came from having Willow grow up without a father? What if Aaron's fear of the unknown, his fear of what they've been doing for over a decade, wasn't about her after all? What if it was all about him and his mortality?

She forced her eyes away from his face when a door banged near the back of the clubhouse.

The man she'd come to meet had just exited the men's room and was making his way to a table in the far corner where another man sat waiting.

Pushing all thoughts about Aaron's doubts out of her head, knowing that Vivian would warn her if something that serious was coming their way, Sarah got to her feet and headed across the restaurant toward the table with the two men.

She caught the wait staff's eye and waved them off.

As she approached, the men at the table said something to each other, their menus held up. Without preamble, Sarah eased back a chair and sat down.

The men lowered their menus, stared at her, and then looked at each other.

"Can we help you?" the dark-haired man to her left asked.

Sarah kept her gaze on the heavier man, the one with the white goatee and the thin glasses—the one Vivian showed her in a vision. She estimated him to be in his late fifties, but his eyes suggested he might be in his early sixties. He cast a stern, fixed stare as he scrutinized her, determining whether he knew her.

His companion, the dark-haired one, leaned forward. "I think you've got the wrong table, lady."

Sarah glanced at him briefly, then back at her target. "No, I'm exactly where I'm supposed to be."

Her target set his menu down and offered her a smile without a trace of joy. "What's this all about? Do I know you?" A burp of a laugh escaped his lips. "Seems a bit rude to just invite yourself to our table and stare at me."

"I'm summing you up, trying to figure out what you did that's so bad."

A chortle rumbled from his chest. "What I did? That's funny." He placed his elbows on the table and tilted his head back to stare at her through his glasses. "Look, little girl, get up from our table and wander back to the kitchen where you belong. Or better yet, get off the property before I have you thrown out."

Her eyes narrowed. "What have you done?" she asked as if

speaking to herself.

Her target glanced at his companion, then back to Sarah. "A lot of things, but nothing that concerns you. Now, fuck off, little gnat." He waved a hand. "Get lost before we get serious."

"Serious?" She shook her head slightly, eyes not leaving his face. "We haven't even begun to get serious."

"Excuse me," he said, twisting in his chair, arm raised to attract the wait staff's attention. "Can we get the manager?"

One of the wait staff nodded. "Of course, Mr. Griffin. Right away."

"Warner, do something with this rude woman. I'm tired of her eyes on me."

His companion got to his feet and moved toward Sarah.

Aaron stepped in the way, his chest bumping Warner's shoulder.

"Hey, what the fuck is this?" Warner asked. "Step aside, or I'll have you arrested."

"You could try," Aaron said without emotion.

Her Aaron was back. Either that, or he was shitting himself and acting tough.

Warner raised his hands, but Aaron was one step ahead of him. He locked the man's wrist in a hold, spun him around, and forced him back to his chair, his arm bent at an odd angle. It happened in the second it took for the surprised man to plop back into his chair.

Then Aaron moved behind him, still holding the man's wrist. "Once she's done talking, we'll leave. Not before."

Warner grunted in pain, then glanced sideways at the waiter, who gawked at them open-mouthed. "Help." Warner forced the word out. "Call the police."

"You are the police," Griffin said. "Fucking do something."

Sarah slapped the table hard to get everyone's attention. Even Aaron jumped and almost let go of Warner's wrist.

"My sister told me about you."

"Like I fucking care." Griffin turned in his seat. "Where's the manager?"

"She sent me with a message."

Griffin angled back to look at her. "What's that? Come on, tell me."

Is it some kind of threat?"

"She told me to tell you to stop what you're doing."

He clapped his hands together. "Great. Message delivered. Now fuck off."

Aaron jerked his head toward the door. *Time to go.*

"What you're up to must stop, or the consequences will involve your daughter."

Griffin's face morphed into something representing fury. His jaw clenched, veins rose on his neck and forehead, and his skin reddened to the point that Sarah thought he was holding his breath.

"Are you threatening my family?" His tone reflected the anger as he spoke through his teeth.

Sarah shook her head. "I'm merely educating you on what I was told. Continue whatever the hell it is you're doing, and your daughter will suffer."

"That sounds like a threat to me."

"Sarah," Aaron grunted, jerking his head toward the kitchen. "We need to go."

She looked that way and saw two people filming the exchange with their cell phones while a man was on the kitchen phone, speaking loudly. From what she could gather, it sounded like he was talking with the police.

Vivian told her they'd come. This was all part of it.

Griffin gestured with his thumb at his companion. "Do you know who this man is?"

"No, but I'm sure you'll tell me."

"Let me introduce you to North Bay's Chief of Police, Bill Warner. You can't get much higher than that."

Her stomach dropped, and her chest tightened. *Fuck, Vivian, what did you make me walk into?*

Evidenced by the yogurt-white look on Aaron's face, he was thinking the same thing as he still had his hands on the chief of police, locking him in place on the chair.

"And even though I'm retiring next year," Griffin went on, "I'm still the regional senior justice, otherwise known as Judge Griffin.

Criminal court. North Bay. So, tell me"—he leaned forward—"did this sister of yours run afoul of the law and end up in my court? Is that why you're here, threatening me and my family?"

Sarah fought the urge to glance at Aaron, knowing his eyes would tell her to run as fast as they could, hoping none of this returned to haunt them.

All Sarah could think to say were four words. "My sister is dead."

Griffin blinked once, then sat back. "How long?"

"She was murdered when I was very young."

He frowned. "You're late twenties or early thirties. Judging by that age gap, I would've been a fresh lawyer back then. My daughter wasn't even born yet. How could your sister possibly have a message for me now?"

Sarah tilted her head slightly. "My sister still speaks to me. She told me your marriage dissolved five years ago. Your daughter is estranged, but you keep trying to win her back." Sarah averted her gaze to the chief of police. The color on his face had returned somewhat as he stopped fighting Aaron. "She also told me the police would attend this meeting, but I thought it was because someone would call them. Interesting that the police are already here."

"We've called the police," a staff member added from several tables over.

Sarah didn't look their way. She kept her eyes on Warner, Griffin's companion. "You're involved, aren't you?"

"This is ridiculous," Warner said. "You'll both be arrested shortly and can explain yourself during your arraignment tomorrow morning."

"My message stands." Sarah moved her eyes from Warner to Griffin, then back to Warner. "Stop whatever it is you're doing, or his daughter pays for it."

Griffin laughed. "What? Stop being a judge? Stop being the chief of police? You're insane, you fucking twat." He pointed at the door. "Best leave now before the cavalry comes."

She glared back at him. "No one's coming. I've blocked the entrance."

Griffin laughed again, but this time with less confidence.

Then Vivian added another detail.

Sarah jerked back at the words—more like *recoiled* at them. When she set her eyes on Griffin again, hatred oozed from her.

"You've done some terrible things for personal profit. It'll all come out now." She pushed up to her feet, then faced Chief Warner. "And you've colluded. You're both fucked. I think it's too late for you two."

Griffin seemed genuinely shocked by her statement. His mouth moved, but nothing came out.

"I'm only here for your daughter's sake now. I don't care what happens to you two." She took a step toward the door, then stopped and turned back. "Wait, scratch that. I do care what happens to you two. I'll be around. I won't leave the city. I'm here until you're both dealt with." She leaned in close to Judge Griffin, who edged back from her. "You will pay for what you've done."

Then she spun on her heels and headed for the door as Aaron released the police chief's wrist. When she smashed open the door to exit the clubhouse, Aaron's heavy footfalls came running up behind her.

"We've got to get out of here."

They bolted for the car and dropped inside. Aaron fired up the engine, jammed it into gear, and skidded toward the exit.

Parkman's car was blocking the only way in, his hood up.

Aaron smacked the horn.

Parkman's head came up over the hood. Then he slammed it down and walked to the driver's side.

Behind his car, on the road, three cruisers waited with their lights flashing.

Parkman moved his vehicle aside, and Aaron edged past him as the cruisers gunned it up the golf course road toward the clubhouse.

Then they were on the road, off the golf course property, and headed toward the open highway, Parkman following close behind.

Sarah pulled out her phone and tapped Alex's number.

"Alex here."

"We good?"

"Yeah, Parkman was able to stall them at the entrance. They just ran inside the clubhouse." He paused. "Wait, the cops are coming back out."

"We'll be on the highway in one minute."
"Don't worry. I'll stall them for at least two."
The line died.

# Chapter 3

ALEX MOVED TOWARD THE cruiser closest to the exit and stood in front of it.

Two uniformed men gestured at him to move as they ripped open their doors. The driver paused to stare at him.

"Hey!" the cop shouted. "Get the fuck out of the way."

"Aren't you guys looking for that blond girl and the guy she was with?"

"Yeah, why? You know where they went?"

Alex shook his head. "I sure wish I did, but they were driving that brown Jeep that headed south."

The cop frowned. "Jeep? I didn't see any Jeep when we arrived."

Alex moved to the side as one of the cruisers lined up behind the front one and hit his horn. "They parked over there"—he pointed at a corner of the lot—"until you guys ran inside. Then they bolted. Brown Jeep, license plate was something like 256-AEO."

The cop in the passenger seat wrote that number down.

"Hey, thanks, kid. Now get out of the way." The driver dropped into the front seat, and the three cruisers took off as a unit.

Alex nonchalantly headed toward the clubhouse restaurant and slipped inside.

"Sorry," one of the staff said. "We're closed."

"Oh, it's okay." Alex waved at him. "I just need a Coke. Then I'll be gone." He moved closer to the table where five people milled around two older men. These two had to be the men Sarah had just spoken to.

"Did you get a good look at them?" one person asked.

289

A waiter held up his phone. "I got most of it on video."

"We will need that video," the older man with a white goatee said.

His dark-haired companion nodded. "I'm confiscating that as evidence."

"Wait," the employee said. "Can't I just email the video to you?"

Goatee man snatched the phone from the man's hand. "What's your passcode?"

The waiter told him. Once the video was on screen, the man with the goatee raised the volume and angled it so the dark-haired man could see it.

Alex heard Sarah's voice loud and clear. She was angry about something. And she told them she wouldn't leave until they were both dealt with, warning them they would pay for what they'd done.

*What the hell happened in here? What could these men have done that pissed off Sarah so much?*

"Here you go," a waiter said, dropping a can of Coke in front of him.

"How much?"

"Five bucks."

Alex stared at him. "Seriously?"

"Yeah. It's a golf course. Everything's more pricey here."

"Fuck it," Alex said and walked away, leaving the Coke on the table.

Before he hit the door, he heard something that chilled him.

"Hey, I recognize that girl," a woman said.

Alex slowed and glanced back.

One of the female staff was hunched over the men, staring at the camera. "I was sure it was her. Here, look." She produced her own phone, tapped something onto it, and then turned it for the men to see. "Her name is Sarah Roberts. She's like a local hero or something in the Toronto area. Some psychic vigilante shit."

The older men exchanged a glance.

"Find her and that asshole she was with." The man with the goatee rose to his feet. "I want them arrested tonight and in my courtroom by the morning. These are serious charges. Threatening a senior justice of the peace and assaulting the chief of police. I'll make sure they do time for this."

Alex exited the clubhouse and pulled out his cell phone.

Sarah needed to know that she may have disturbed a hornet's nest.

The kind there's no coming back from.

# Chapter 4

"Fuck, Sarah." Aaron smacked the steering wheel. "Did you know those guys were a judge and a police chief?"

Sarah leaned forward to stare into the side mirror. Parkman was right behind them. "No. My sister didn't tell me that part."

"So Vivian just sent you into a golf course clubhouse to warn—oh, wait—*threaten* a judge and a high-ranking cop?"

"Looks that way."

He stared at her, then gazed out at the road. "What else is she withholding?"

"Tricky question. Because, if I knew that, then it wouldn't be withheld, now would it?"

"Sarah!" He snapped her name. "This is serious."

"Aaron, calm the fuck down or get out and walk. I'll drive."

"I'm not walking, and neither are you. We're going to figure this shit out together, then make amends somehow and leave this city behind us."

"Make amends? How do you propose we do that? Walk into the police station and apologize? Are you serious?" She shook her head. "Listen to yourself. That doesn't make any sense."

"I just manhandled the chief of police. I'll be lucky if I get two years in jail for that. And all because Vivian wanted them to stop what they're doing, while you still don't know *what* they're doing."

"I know some of it now."

He switched hands on the wheel as they made it to the highway. "Pray tell."

"They're making illegal arrests and *creating* evidence so people they target are taken off the streets."

"Great. Likely, they're targeting assholes who keep breaking the law and constantly getting away with it. All the better." His voice rose. "So why would Vivian want that stopped?"

Sarah shook her head. "They're targeting people they don't like."

"What? Like in non-criminals?"

She nodded. "People who don't deserve to be in the courtroom or behind bars."

There was a moment of silence, broken only by Aaron's heavy exhalation. "Vivian told you all that?"

"And more."

"Like?"

"They're high school friends. Grew up here. Formed a pact when Judge Griffin was a lawyer. Sent him clients, sometimes on bogus charges, so Griffin could get them off, look good, and rise to the top. Drug busts that had cash were split between them, and any mention of the missing money was shut down in Griffin's court."

"Huh," Aaron said. "All of a sudden, Vivian's quite talkative."

"That's not how it works. The information is sent to me *through* her. I receive it in a quantity sometimes, and I just know stuff."

"Anything about Griffin's daughter? How is she involved?"

Sarah shook her head. "All that I know is she's in her twenties and estranged from him."

"Estranged? Then how could she pay for his crimes?"

"I have no idea. Vivian said so, and that's it."

They sat in silence for a few minutes as Aaron drove south along the highway. Sarah watched Parkman behind them.

There was no sign of police cruisers.

"Where are we staying tonight?" Aaron asked.

"Continue south to an area called Ferris. There's a motel down that way where we can pay cash."

Sarah's phone rang. It was Alex.

"Yeah?"

"We may have trouble."

"Tell me about it." That came out sounding facetious. "Sorry, I meant that literally. Tell me about it, as in, explain what you mean."

"You threatened a judge and the police chief of North Bay."

"I know. Anything else?"

Alex didn't speak for a moment. "Okay, three cruisers responded to the call and left the golf course in pursuit of a Jeep."

"That should buy us some time."

"But Sarah."

"What?"

"They know who you are."

That pit in her stomach grew to a chunk of lead, weighing her down in the seat. "Shit, that increases our timetable."

"Yeah. They'll come looking for you. Nowhere is safe now."

"Call Daniel. He has to take Willow to a friend's house and stay hidden until we call and tell him it's safe to return."

"I can do that."

"Anything else?" she asked.

"These guys won't stop until they get what they want."

Sarah caught Aaron staring at her sideways. "Vivian did say they were influential men in the community. We'll handle the fallout. I just can't be detained until I deal with the other stuff we came here for."

"So, we're still on for tonight?"

Sarah nodded, even though Alex couldn't see her. "Yeah, nothing changes."

"I'll be there."

"Bring coffee for all of us."

The line died—Alex's new way to say goodbye.

"What's up?"

There was no point in hiding what Alex told her. "They know who I am."

"Fuckin' great. Your name, and mine, too, will be blasted all over the media by tonight. Everyone and their dog will be looking for us now." He glanced at her. "Is that why Daniel has to take Willow and hide? Cops will be showing up at the dojo? His apartment?"

Sarah nodded.

"We're fucked, Sarah. You know that, right?"
She kept nodding, thinking about his attitude. "It would seem so."

# Chapter 5

"THE HOTEL OPTION IS gone," Sarah said. "Let's find a desolate road off Highway 654 to turn down, one without buildings. We'll park in the bushes and decide what to do next."

Ten minutes later, after not speaking to each other again, Aaron eased the car to the side near the southern tip of Lake Nipissing. He killed the engine and cut the lights.

Parkman pulled in behind them and killed his lights.

The area fell into almost complete darkness, only slightly illuminated by the stars and the small fingernail moon.

Sarah got out on shaky legs and moved to the car's trunk. After a moment, Aaron and Parkman joined her.

"How did everything go?" Parkman asked. "By the look on your face, I'm guessing not so well."

Sarah and Aaron filled him in on everything, from their conversation in the clubhouse to the call with Alex.

"Shit." Parkman popped a toothpick in his mouth. "So they know who you are and will have every cop from here to Toronto hunting for you within hours. Great. What's next? Vivian instructing us on how to evade capture and leave the country?"

Sarah glared at Parkman momentarily, then realized he had to be joking. It was dark, but her eyes were adjusting, allowing her to see him better.

"We have to see this through. We can still achieve our goals here." Sarah leaned against the trunk.

"How's that?" Aaron said. "This is a classic case of our cover being blown."

Parkman raised a hand. "Let's hear what she has to say." He lowered his hand. "And don't forget that Vivian always has some sort of plan, or fate drags us through with Vivian playing a role. Either way, we act smart and work this right, whatever *this* is, and we walk away in the end."

Aaron grunted. "Glad someone's still got the faith."

Parkman stared at him. "Are you saying you don't?"

Aaron didn't answer right away.

"Because if you don't, and I hate to come off rude, but …" Parkman paused. "Why are you here?"

"Whoa, man. Step off my back. I just assaulted the chief of police, and Sarah threatened a judge. We're fucked here, man. There's no way out of this."

"True, for a defeatist. But I'm confident Sarah will figure it out."

"Guys." Sarah raised her hands and moved between them. "You're both right. We are fucked, but we'll find a way out of this. We have to, and it doesn't involve us ending up in jail for any length of time."

"Damn right, it doesn't." Aaron stepped to the side, hands on his hips, looking skyward.

"Parkman, you and Alex aren't identified yet—"

"Yet?" Parkman moved the toothpick to the other side of his mouth. "You think that's coming?"

She nodded. "Labeled under known associates."

Parkman spun halfway to the side, his hands flopping upward. "Of course."

"Your ability to move around North Bay will be severely limited by tomorrow. So, here's what I need you to do."

She told him everything, and Parkman took it all in, then simply nodded.

"Consider it done. I'll leave now, pick up Alex, and bring you everything you need."

Sarah turned toward Aaron. "In the meantime, Aaron and I will wait here."

"Are you sure that's a good idea?" Parkman looked at Aaron, who had moved about a dozen feet to the side. He was bent over, his hands on his thighs, as if he wanted to vomit.

"Yeah, he'll be fine. Just the usual whining."

"How's your tolerance, your temper, with all that?" Parkman touched her shoulder like a father would. "You okay?"

Sarah lowered her cheek onto his hand, held it there a moment, and then righted herself. "Yeah. I'm cutting him some slack. He's dealing with Benjamin still. He's a father, and he's trying to keep us all together. His veneer has cracks, but I think things'll smooth out soon enough." She shrugged, her eyes on Aaron. "And if they don't, we'll move on." She faced Parkman. "There are only two ways for this to go. With or without him."

"That sounded like U2." Parkman flipped his toothpick, making it look like it swam to the other side of his mouth this time.

"What?"

"You know, the song, 'With Or Without You.'"

"I'm sure I heard it, but it was before my time."

"Anyway, gotta run. You want us to meet you back here?"

"We may leave this area. I'm not sure, but I'll call you on my burner if things change, and then we can meet in town. They don't know this car, so we can possibly get to where we're going without too much trouble."

Parkman headed to his car. "I'll watch for your call." He dropped into the driver's seat, fired it up, and almost blinded her with his headlights. After a three-point turn, his taillights disappeared in the darkness.

"Aaron?" Sarah said. "We should probably talk."

"About what?"

"About where we're going tonight. It's not going to be pretty."

"Oh, another judge? More cops to fuck with?"

Sarah moved closer. "No, worse."

"What could be worse?"

"You remember that comment I made about kids?"

He stared at her in the dark. "What about kids?"

"That's the next stop. Once we meet with Parkman in a few hours, we will go there. You're free to sit that one out if you want to."

He squared his shoulders and watched her with watery eyes. "You're too important to me. I can't claim to like any of this, but I'm all in. I said it before, and I'll say it again. I'm *all* in."

"Okay, here's what we're going to do."

He plopped down onto the dirt when she finished telling him everything. "I think I'm going to be sick."

"You and me both."

# Chapter 6

SARAH PUSHED THE BASEBALL cap lower, her hair tucked up inside, as she entered the truck stop washroom with a bag of stuff Parkman had successfully gotten for her.

She'd called him, and they'd arranged to meet at this truck stop on Lakeshore so she could apply the makeup and the wig. He even bought her a cardigan to add to the image of an older woman.

The boys went inside the truck stop to order takeout. They'd eat in their cars and wait for her.

As suspected, the news had announced that the authorities were now looking for Sarah Roberts and her boyfriend, Aaron Stevens, for charges ranging from assault to unlawful confinement and robbery. They had no idea where the robbery charge cropped up from, as neither one of them stole anything, but that made sense with what Judge Griffin and the chief of police had been up to for years—creating charges to secure someone's fate—especially someone they didn't like.

How many people were incarcerated for things they didn't do because they had the misfortune of crossing paths with Judge Griffin?

It didn't take her long to apply the foundation, create soft shadows under her eyes, and add some dark eyeliner to the folds in her skin below her nostrils. Then she added liquid latex to age her flesh around the eyes and finally placed small dabs of glue on her forehead. While it dried, she scrunched up the skin in that area.

The effect was perfect. With the gray-haired wig, the cardigan, and the makeup on her face adding twenty years—or more—to her age, it would be virtually impossible for anyone to recognize her as Sarah.

After what felt like over an hour but was only thirty minutes, she vacated the ladies' washroom and sauntered back to the car, the makeup bag under her arm. Miraculously, no one tried the bathroom door the entire time.

Once back in the car, the smell of greasy burgers caused her stomach to flare in hunger. "Tell me you got something for me to eat."

They were all staring at her.

"Sarah," Parkman gasped. "You've changed."

"You think?" She extended a hand. "Burger, please."

Aaron reached over the seat and handed her one. "It might be a bit cold."

"That's fine. I haven't eaten since Webers on the highway coming north this morning. I'm famished." She unwrapped the burger and dove in, chewing ravenously. Slowly, her mastication came to a stop. All eyes were still on her. "Really?" she said around a mouthful of beef and bun.

They all turned away but Alex. He was in the back seat beside her. "You did amazing. Easy, twenty to thirty years on you."

Parkman watched her in the mirror. "When you approached the car, if I didn't know your usual gait, I would've wondered who the hell the old lady was trying to get in."

She was halfway through the burger when she checked the time on the dashboard. "We should get going." She took another bite, swallowed, and added, "Once we're done at the next place, I can check us into a motel somewhere, and then you guys can join me. That way, no one sees your faces."

"Works for me." Parkman turned on the car and flicked the lights. "Where to?"

Sarah gave him the address. Aaron typed it into the maps app on his phone with the plan to help navigate to the location as Parkman pulled out of the truck stop parking lot.

"Four Mile Lake Road." Aaron held the phone close to his face, zooming in with his fingers. "Out of town. Lots of privacy."

Sarah scrunched up the burger's wrapper, then set it on the seat beside her. "Did you get me the Bible I requested?"

"Right here." Aaron handed it back to her.

She held its weight, then opened it to a random page.

"Will this work?" Aaron asked.

Sarah shrugged. "If it doesn't, we go in by force. I'm not leaving those kids behind."

A silence fell over them as each one anticipated what was coming.

Sarah stared at the pages of the Bible, trying to keep her mind off what Vivian told her she'd find on Four Mile Lake Road, but it wasn't working.

# Chapter 7

JUDGE MARK GRIFFIN SET his whisky glass down. His eyes focused on the middle distance, the fingers of his other hand drumming the desktop.

"What are you thinking?" The Chief of Police, Bill Warner, grabbed the decanter and topped up both their glasses.

Griffin blinked and turned to look at Warner. "Stop what?"

Warner frowned. "Huh?"

"That bitch said we have to stop what we're doing, or Melody will pay for it." Griffin stopped tapping on the desk and raised his hand. "What am I doing that's connected to my daughter? Absolutely nothing. Melody is in Europe, last I heard, and has been for several months. She doesn't take my calls. I saw her at Christmas, and that was because she was visiting her brother before she took off on some other grand tour vacation thing."

Warner leaned his head back and stared at the ceiling of his palatial home. "How is Bruce, anyway? Is your son keeping his nose clean?"

Griffin scoffed. "Who knows with that boy? If it isn't the drugs, it's the whores. Why do I even try?" He emptied his glass. "I need more, and then I'm staying in your guest room tonight."

Warner grabbed the bottle off the table and poured three fingers into the judge's glass.

"No court tomorrow?"

Griffin huffed. "Tonight, I drink. Tomorrow, I sleep. Then you bring that Sarah bitch into my court for an arraignment."

A short guffaw escaped Warner. "When we arrest her and her

boyfriend, they won't go in front of you. No one would allow that. Conflict of interest, and all that."

Griffin glared at him. "Then I'll give everyone the day off when her arraignment is up. She stands before me, and that's it." His voice rose on the final words, his tone too harsh. "Look, I'm tired, I'm tipsy, and I'm angry." Griffin swished the whisky in his glass. "Tell me they arrested them already."

"I wish I could." Warner was back to staring at the ceiling. "They can't hide forever. If it ends up that we catch them in Toronto, they'll escort them back here for the charges. That witch isn't above the law. She'll stand trial for her threats to your family, and her boyfriend will do time for what he did to me." The chief raised a finger. "Of this, I'm quite certain."

Griffin sipped his drink, scanning the large living room. "You enjoy living here alone? I mean, this is a large house. How many bedrooms again?"

"A dozen. But it's not about the size. It's what you do with it. Each room has a purpose now."

"I'm too tired to hear all that. Just tell me." Griffin glanced at his old friend. "Are you happy?"

Warner's forehead scrunched together. "Are you?"

"Sure, relatively. I mean, I wish Melody were closer and Bruce had finished law school, but I can't control my kids. I'm happy the ex-wife is out of my life. She wasn't just a financial burden. She was a vacuum when it came to money."

"Where is this going?" Warner leaned forward. "You know I'm not your therapist, right?" He stared at Griffin a moment. "Wait a second. Are you thinking there's something to that witch's warning? That there's something you're involved in that'll actually hurt Melody?"

"Don't be ridiculous." Griffin scoffed again but knew it wasn't convincing. "Just that, what if she was right? She's been right before."

"You looked her up." Warner ran a hand through his hair. "You researched her." His tone suggested surprise.

"Of course, I looked her up. If she's an enemy, I need to learn more about my opponent."

"And you found out she's a truth-teller instead of a charlatan?"

"Something like that."

Warner set his glass down, rose from his chair, and walked to the large floor-to-ceiling window where he stared out at the gardens. After a moment, he spun back to face Griffin.

"Everything we're involved in is solid. The deal we made with Mackenzie is locked in. No one could possibly know that your guilty verdict on Michael Sommers was bought and paid for. And Sommers is in no way connected to your daughter."

Griffin glanced around the room, his whisky slipping over the edge of his glass. "Are you mad? What if one of your staffers heard that?"

"Relax, Judge, we're alone. Besides, if someone did hear me and repeated a single word of what I'd just said, they'd end up in a ditch somewhere. All my staff know that."

"Not the point." Griffin glared at him. "I don't want anyone knowing anything. The less, the better."

"No. One. Is. Here." Warner waved a hand around at the vast living room. "We're alone." He grabbed his glass off the table and drank it back in one shot, slamming the glass back down. After wiping his lips, he said, "So, tell me, if there's still doubt, how could a guilty verdict for a piece of shit repeat offender like Mike Sommers ever affect your daughter? Is there a connection?"

"I have no idea," Griffin said through clenched teeth. "I just know that Mackenzie paid us a fortune to guarantee that verdict when I would likely find him guilty anyway. We didn't ask why. We just took the cash."

Warner lifted both hands in frustration. "Do we ever ask why?" He shook his head. "C'mon, Griffin. We've been doing this for years, and no one has ever been able to suspect a thing. This is the truth, the whole truth, and nothing but the truth—"

"Really? Courtroom speak? Now?"

Warner stared at him a moment longer, then took his seat. "Wrack your brain all you want, but there's no connection to your daughter other than an emotional one."

"What's that supposed to mean?"

"Well, if you fuck up, get caught, get fired, disbarred, and humiliated, then maybe Melody would be saddened. So, there's that."

"How could we ever get caught? I preside over a case. I issue a ruling, end of story."

"My point exactly." Warner clapped his hands once. "See, nothing to worry about."

"Yet, I'm still worried."

"How about this?" Warner sat up on the edge of his seat. "When my guys arrest Sarah, we'll have a long chat with her, find out what she meant. How about that?"

Griffin nodded. "Find her first. Get her in our holding cells. Then call me." He got to his feet. "I'm heading to the guest room. I'm done."

"Go. Leave it to me. I'm sure we'll have her in custody by the morning."

Griffin headed for the darkened corridor. "I sure hope so because if you don't, I want to research Mackenzie further."

"What?" Warner's tone brooked no negotiation. "Why would you do that? Are you mad?"

Griffin stopped at the alcove in the hallway. "What if he's connected to Melody in some way? I need to know that issuing a guilty verdict on Sommers won't hurt my daughter before I do it."

Warner shot to his feet. "Don't be insane," he shouted. "Even if you find the slightest connection, Mackenzie isn't the type of person you piss off."

"Oh, fuck you." Griffin roared. "Is that some sort of passive threat? I couldn't care less about Mackenzie. All he means to me is cash."

"Yeah, half a million in cash."

"Maybe you must ask yourself why he's so desperate to have Mike Sommers doing time."

"Maybe you have to ask yourself why you can be bought?" Warner glared at him from across the room. "You can't take money from these people for decades, then cut off the pipeline like some nervous Nellie. We're in this together, and I won't end up in a shallow grave because you got skittish."

Griffin's response raced to the tip of his tongue, but he held it back in time. They'd been drinking. The conversation needed to end, or they'd say things they couldn't come back from.

Almost forty years together could be upturned in five minutes of accusations and old resentments. Griffin was tired, too tired.

He nodded once at Warner, then turned and made his way to the guest room.

When this was over—whatever *this* was—he'd find a way to stop. How much money did one man need anyway?

And if Warner weren't on board, he'd find a way to get the chief of police transferred, fired, or taken out.

It didn't matter one way or the other.

There was no honor among thieves, especially when millions were at stake.

No honor at all.

If the man he had done business with for decades got itchy feet, then Judge Griffin would deal with it—with extreme prejudice.

# Chapter 8

SARAH DIRECTED PARKMAN TO drive by the residence first, then park down the road. Once he flicked off the headlights, they dropped into an almost absolute darkness. The streetlights were spaced far enough apart on this road, which allowed them to see silhouettes of their heads but not their facial expressions.

This area north of the city offered an expanse of heavy forest and a house every half a kilometer or so.

"You guys know what to do." Sarah clutched the Bible close to her midriff. "Make sure there's no dogs first, though. No alarms, either. Then circle the house and wait for my signal to enter."

All three men nodded.

"And you're sure this isn't dangerous for you?" Aaron asked. "All alone on their doorstep?"

"Not according to Vivian."

"How so? She actually said that?"

Sarah lifted the Bible. "She told me this will get me inside."

"Just holding a Bible will be enough?" Parkman asked.

"Vivian directed me to several passages. Don't worry about me, guys. Just be ready for my signal. Then get inside that house fast. I was told that when I signal you, it'll be serious."

Aaron turned in the front seat to face her. "When will that be so we're more prepared? And how will you signal us?"

"No idea yet, but you'll know it when it comes. Just don't try to break in or anything until you hear from me. Let me gain access, then come fast when I call you."

"Not sure I like this," Aaron said.

"Guys." Sarah used the plural but was only speaking to Aaron. "I'm knocking on their front door. As far as they can tell, I have a Bible in my arms, and I'm an older lady. Nobody is going to shoot me, stab me, or attempt anything stupid." She paused. "At least not right away."

"Yeah, but they have a secret to protect. They'll be on edge."

"And that's where you guys come in." She pointed over the seat toward the dashboard. "Parkman, turn off that interior light switch so it stays dark when I open the door."

"Already done."

"Okay, let's do this. Then we drive to a motel and get a good night's sleep. I've got lots to do tomorrow before we leave this area and head home."

She cracked open her door, exited, then closed it quietly. A moment later, Alex did the same.

*** 

Parkman tried to see them in the rearview mirror, but it was too dark. "They're gone. Disappeared into the night."

"With Alex, that makes sense. You wouldn't see him if the sun were up."

Parkman glanced over at him. "You doing okay?"

"Yeah, it's just. I was taking a break from this stuff for a bit, and now I'm back full-time."

"And? The break wasn't long enough?"

Aaron adjusted himself in the seat to face forward. "I'm back because I'm with Sarah, and either I'm with her or not. We talked about it after she disappeared on that highway several months ago. I committed to be all in."

Parkman slapped his shoulder. "Well, I, for one, am glad to hear that. She needs you. We're all better off *with* you as opposed to *without* you." Parkman jerked. "Shit, that's that U2 song again."

"What?"

"Oh, nothing. It's just the second time I quoted U2 tonight."

"Why are you doing that?"

"No idea." He waved a hand. "Anyway, let's go. We need to be in position when Sarah signals us." He opened his door and made to exit when Aaron dropped a hand onto Parkman's forearm.

"Did Sarah tell you what's inside this house?"

Parkman stared across the front seat at him. "No."

"So, tonight, you do this blindly?"

"Aaron, if you're having second thoughts—"

"I'm not. It's just she told me what to expect."

"Great, then you've got a leg up on the rest of us."

"Parkman, when this is all over, can you impart some of that trust, or whatever it is, that allows you to follow Sarah without question?"

Parkman kept his eyes on Aaron as the man's hand fell away from his forearm. "See, that's the issue you've always had."

"And what's this issue you speak of?" Aaron tried to inject humor into his voice, but it didn't work.

"It's not trust in Sarah, of which I've got an abundance. It's trust in the team, in the process. It's about Vivian and what she stands for, the assholes we go up against, the darkness that Sarah and her sister shed light on. Most importantly, it's the wrongs we right. This isn't just Sarah. This is a team, and I'm happy I've gotten to play on this team for over a decade." He shrugged without thinking that Aaron couldn't see his shoulder in the dark. "As a team, we all take our hits. We even take penalty shots to the head. But at the end of the day, we're helping people who often can't help themselves. I sleep at night knowing we saved someone. And one day"—he raised his finger to punctuate this part—"when it's my time to go home, and I'm asked, 'what have you done with the life I've given you?' I want to say that I served well, that I protected His children"—he pointed upward, whether Aaron could see his finger or not—"and that I stepped in when a woman needed someone to do that for her. I want to do the right thing when it counts, not when it serves me or my interests. It's what's best for the team, not what's best for me. This isn't an individual thing."

"Hey, man, sorry." Aaron leaned back against the door. "I didn't mean to pull a speech from you. Just wanted to feel what you're feeling regarding what we're doing here."

"Well, that's what I'm feeling, and that's why when Sarah calls and says we have shit to do, I'm there. Every damn time. It's not just trust in that woman. It's trust in her side, her people. But also, her heart is one thousand percent always in the right place. I've never, ever seen her heart darken. The only thing that hurts Sarah, I mean *really* hurts her, is when she encounters evil—pure evil. And you know what happens then?"

"What?"

"She cries. It tears her up inside when she sees evil. And we're back to my point about shedding light on it. That's what eradicates the cockroaches in this world: light, and lots of it. Vivian's team and Sarah's team represent light to me. So I show up. Every damn time."

Aaron opened his door. "Thanks, man. Let's continue this later."

Parkman jumped out and closed his door softly. "Anytime, brother. Anytime."

Then, they dropped into the ditch and ran along the line of trees toward the house in question.

# Chapter 9

SARAH MOVED OFF THE road's pavement and onto the gravel driveway and stopped to take in the dilapidated house before her. A single light shone through the living room window, where what looked like a bedsheet was suspended in place of a curtain. The grass was sparse and uncared for, and there was no garden to speak of. The lack of kids' toys saddened her. A boy and a girl lived here, but there was no evidence of that from the front of the house.

According to Vivian, the boy was ten, and his sister was fourteen. Although the Children's Aid Society was involved in the past, no action was being taken currently.

Alcohol was forbidden in the home. Hair samples from the father were supposed to be taken, but that hadn't happened in months. The final point Vivian made was that they were fervently religious people and that they lived by the letter of the law according to the Bible.

Sarah inhaled deeply, put one foot in front of the other, and moved to the front porch. The Bible clutched close to her chest.

She raised her hand to knock, but stopped when she heard voices emanating from inside the house.

The TV was on.

She listened a moment longer, then checked behind her and only saw trees and darkness, as it was around nine at night. She turned back and knocked.

The volume of the TV died. Somewhere inside, there was movement.

She waited.

No one came to the door.

It was hard to tell, but it sounded like someone was whispering behind the door.

A shadow crept over the peephole.

Sarah knocked lightly again. "I'm with the local Bible Study Group. We're in the area tonight spreading the Good Word." She held up the Bible and smiled at whoever was watching.

The shadow behind the peephole disappeared.

She waited—one second, two, then about half a minute.

*Shit, they aren't going to open the door.*

"Hello?" she called.

Nothing.

She flipped through the pages of the Bible, then read the passage Vivian had told her to read. "'My son, do not regard the discipline of the Lord lightly, nor be weary when reproved by him. For the Lord disciplines the ones he loves and chastises every son whom he receives.'"

She waited.

Still nothing.

Her heart raced, and sweat cooled her forehead and back. She didn't want to do this the hard way. It would upset the kids.

She flipped through more pages of the Bible, then ran her finger down to the middle of the page where she'd left a mark, opened her mouth, and—

—and screamed. A short clip of a scream.

A man had appeared from beside the house, startling her.

"Oh, hello." She clutched at her chest after having almost dropped the Bible. "I'm sorry. You surprised me."

"Whatchu doing out here all alone?" the man asked.

The man's checkered lumberjack shirt bulged over the beige toolbelt strapped about his waist. It looked like he was using the toolbelt to hold up his stained pants.

"Well, sir, I'm spreading the Lord's Good Word, is all."

The man turned to the road, then back to Sarah. "All alone?"

Sarah followed his gaze, then faced him head-on. There was

something in his eyes, something that made her shudder. It was like staring at a predator.

"Is there a need for company when I've got the Lord by my side? We've got others a few blocks over." She stepped off the porch and then moved closer. "Have you ever read the allegorical Christian poem called *Footprints In The Sand*?"

"Yessum, I sure have. What's it to you?"

"Well"—she raised the Bible—"I'm hoping I could speak with you and the missus about the Lord our Savior for a few moments, and then I'll be on my way." She let out a brief chuckle to diffuse the tension. "I say, five minutes in one house has saved a soul or two in my time."

"What makes you thinking we need asavin'?"

"Oh no, sir, many don't. You may well be on your way to salvation as we speak, but without spending even a few minutes with you, how would one know such a thing? I mean, we're not psychic." She hiccupped a laugh, shrugged, then raised the Bible again. "If you're well on your way, if you've been shown the light, then my talents would be wasted on folks such as yourself. I'd be better served moving on to your neighbors."

He placed his hands on his hips and tilted his head. "You were gonna quote somethin' on the porch a moment ago. What was it?"

Sarah flipped open the Bible again, felt her fingers go numb, and watched as Vivian stopped the book on a certain page. Then her hand shot forward on its own accord, her finger locking on the beginning of a passage.

*Really now?*

"I wanted to read this from Proverbs 29:17. It states, 'Discipline your child, and he/she will give you rest; he/she will give you delight to your heart.' And a scripture from Proverbs 13:24. 'He who spares the rod hates his son, but he who loves him is careful to discipline him.'" She looked up to examine the man's response.

Movement caught her eye behind him.

Alex had come out of hiding and stood five feet behind the man.

Sarah stared over the man's shoulder for a brief moment, then spoke up. "I don't think so. Now is not a good time. Not yet."

Alex eased back into the shadows.

"Not a good time for what?" the man asked.

She refocused on the man with the toolbelt. "For my visit. Perhaps I've come too late in the evening. Disturbed your quiet Sunday night."

"Nonsense." The man pointed at the house. "Edna," he shouted. "Open the door. We have a guest from the church." He gestured toward the door. "Now, what kinda Christian would I be if I didn't offer you a place to sit to rest your feet, a cup of tea to warm you on the inside, and a little conversation on the Lord?"

The door opened, then the screen door. Edna had to be waiting just behind the door this whole time. When Sarah took in the bruises on her face and arms, the hallowed, deep-set eyes, the missing teeth, and the open sores on her face, she knew this to be the right house.

Something had to be done. Tonight, they'd do it, whatever that was.

The man moved in behind her. "Come inside and spread your Good Word."

Why did that sound wrong? What was this guy's deal?

Sarah moved toward the open door with one quick glance back to where Alex had been.

The area was empty. No one was there.

When the door closed behind her, the smell hit her first. The man was close enough that she could smell the booze now—or was it the house?

Inside their tiny hovel—that's what she had to call it—the air seemed toxic. Clothes were strewn everywhere. Dirty dishes were left on any surface where they could be balanced. Years of smoking with the windows closed left a yellow film on everything. The stench of an old locker room, an overused toilet, and something rancid caused a thickness in the air that came off as humidity.

When she turned around, the man was bolting the door.

There were four bolts.

*Four? Why four up here in no-crime land?*

Sarah studied the immediate room and saw no signs of children. How could Vivian be wrong about that part? They were supposed to have a fourteen-year-old and a ten-year-old.

"Put on tea, Edna." The man issued it like an order. "Wouldn't want our guest to feel unwelcome, now would we?" He swung his hand out to point at the furniture. "Please, take a seat and tell us all about the word you're spreading in our community."

"Oh," she said, her voice cracking on purpose. If this charade didn't end soon, she'd drive her hand into the guy's nose and her foot into his crotch, then find the kids on her own. "Where would you like me to sit?"

Papers, garbage, and apple cores covered the two-seater couch. A solitary kitchen chair was set up by the entrance to the kitchen, and a torn recliner, at least twenty years old, sat by the window. It was the only chair without debris of any sort.

"This one's mine," he said, patting the recliner. It moved like a rocking chair, squeaking. "No one sits here but Daddy." He nodded at the two-seater. "I'll clean a spot for your tired legs, ma'am. All that walking, from house to house." He glanced over his shoulder at the kitchen. "They paying you for this?"

"Oh, no, sir. I do this from the goodness of my heart."

"They oughta be paying you. Dangerous work, knocking on people's houses in the dark." He looked at Edna again. "Hey, maybe you could get Edna out spreading the Good Word. It'll do her some good to exercise, and she could make us some money." He grabbed the edges of his toolbelt and hiked it upward.

"Well," she shook her head, an awkward smile playing on her lips, "our church doesn't pay us because it's our mission. Bringing people out of the dark and into the light brings more souls back into the fold."

The man watched her sidelong, one brow raised. "If you say so."

The kettle brewing in the kitchen made a whistling sound.

Once a spot was cleared for her, Sarah sat gingerly on the edge of the couch. The man dropped into the recliner, adjusting his toolbelt for comfort. Other than the wooden handle of the hammer dangling from his side, she caught a glimpse of a yellow tool secreted in a pocket like a holster.

"Working on a shed out back? A renovating job?" she asked, nodding toward his waist.

The man looked down, then back up to her. An awkward moment of silence fell over the living room. Then Edna slipped past that solitary kitchen chair separating the kitchen from the living room, a mug of tea in her hand.

"I didn't know if you wanted sugar or cream." Her voice was soft, feminine. She set the mug on a small pile of paper. "It's herbal."

"That's fine," Sarah said, waving her off. "I drink herbal just like that. Thank you."

Edna offered her a thin smile, backed away, and strode down the hallway. A door opened, then closed. Edna was gone.

The man was still staring at her.

None of this was right. What the hell had she walked into? Where did Edna go?

"Who are you with?"

Sarah adjusted herself in her seat. "I'm sorry?"

"Who do you work for?"

"Oh, uhm, the Calvary Baptist Church."

"Which one?"

Damn it. She hadn't thought that far ahead.

*Vivian? A street name, please!*

"Well, I don't limit myself to a specific church." She rubbed the top of the Bible, glancing down at it. "Even though it's the house of God." She looked up to meet his eyes. "We must move from church to church, meet people, and be there for each other."

When something on the muted TV caught his eye, Sarah glanced at the door. Four deadbolts? All in line with the peephole above the knob. What the hell for? To keep bad guys out? Or to keep something *in*?

Without looking her way, he said, "What street is it on?"

Two words popped into her head, but they made no sense. How could that be?

"Ski club." Why the hell did she just say that *ski club*? *Vivian, help!*

The man fixed his gaze back on her, the edges of a smile playing at his lips. "I've visited the Baptist church on Ski Club Road several times. Can't say I've ever seen you there."

She sighed in relief that the *ski club* was the road's name, but the sigh came out more like a huff. "That can happen." She glanced down the hall. "Won't Edna join us?"

He pushed off the floor with his feet, sending the recliner into a rocking motion, then pointed at the table. "Drink your tea. Be polite. Edna will join us soon enough."

Everything in her being told her something was wrong, but she couldn't place it. Could they just be so weird that nothing they did made sense? Was Edna prepping the kids for a visitor? Or, was she taking them out back to whatever he was building with that toolbelt of his, making it harder for Sarah to get them somewhere safe?

It was time to end the shenanigans.

She opened the Bible to the passage Vivian said would be the final one, left it open across her thighs, and then wrapped her hands around the tea mug to feel the warmth from the hot water.

"More reading?" he asked.

"At least one more passage," Sarah said, raising the mug to her lips. She sniffed the concoction and then got a warning from Vivian. Without responding in alarm, she placed the tea back on the table.

The man watched it descend. "Something wrong?"

"Oh, just too hot for me. I'll get to it in a few minutes."

He nodded, turning back to the mute TV. "Let me hear this passage of yours."

Sarah placed her finger on the spot and read. "'If someone has a stubborn and rebellious son who does not obey his father and mother and will not listen to them when they discipline him, his father and mother shall take hold of him and bring him to the elders at the gate of his town. They shall say to the elders, 'This son of ours is stubborn and rebellious. He will not obey us.' Then, all the men of his town are to stone him to death. You must purge the evil from among you.'" She looked up. "Isn't that interesting? Right here in the Good Book." She tapped the page with her finger. "I mean, in today's world, who would sacrifice their own child?"

A vein throbbed on the man's neck, and she caught sight of his right fist clenching. Without moving his lips, he asked, "Who sent you?"

"Excuse me?"

The man pushed up to his feet, adjusted his toolbelt, and glared down at her. "Who sent you to my *house*?" He snarled the last word.

"Sir, if something I've said has upset you, then I apologize."

"Allow me to explain the situation." His hand slipped into the toolbelt. When it emerged, he was carrying a Taser.

*A Taser? That was the yellow tool! Fuck!*

His other hand yanked the hammer from the belt.

"I got me a good thing going here." He lowered his voice and bent forward slightly, the Taser still aimed at the floor.

Sarah clutched the Bible in her lap, wondering if she could use it as a weapon to knock some sense into the guy.

"I got a wife who obeys," he went on, "a son who needs routine discipline, and a daughter who is being taught what it means to be a woman."

She'd heard enough. That part pushed her past wanting to hurt the man to wanting to kill the man.

The charade was over.

"What does that mean?" she asked. "What does it mean to be a woman?"

"Then you come in here," he continued as if she hadn't said a word, "on a Sunday night talking about *spreading the Good Word*," he mocked a woman's voice on those four words. "And yet, all you preach is how to discipline a child. Why the focus on my kids? Why read to me the passages that I already live by?"

Sarah pushed upward to stand, but the Taser shot forward, making her stop.

"These prongs will enter your flesh if you get up. You're not leaving that fast. You will stay on the couch until you tell me who that other guy is hiding in the bushes to the right of my house."

By *other guy*, he must've seen Alex. Had he seen Parkman and Aaron yet? They still had the advantage, but things weren't looking too good with a Taser in her face. How was she supposed to send a signal? And how would they bypass those four bolts on the door?

"You saw my friend?"

"My cameras saw you and him. I've got the property surrounded."

Why all the security for this rundown shack of a house? To protect a drug business? Or were his kids being used for something worse?

Then everything came to her immediately, and she placed a hand over her stomach. The man had clients. That much was for sure. But they weren't trafficking in drugs. This man's commodity was flesh—young flesh.

He was teaching his daughter what it meant to be a woman, one John at a time.

How could the mother allow that? What was the boy's role? And why hadn't CAS closed this down?

"Please," Sarah said, a hand on her chest, feigning fear. "I mean you no harm. I merely read those passages because I wanted to ask if you hate your child."

The Taser lowered back to his side. "Hate my child? What's it to you?"

"Well, if you do hate your child, then you don't discipline them. But if you *love* your child, a parent's job is to teach them through discipline, just as it states in the Bible." She forced her face to be expressionless, to keep the anger seething inside her off of it. "I try to find passages that relate to the situation I'm walking into."

He blinked as if dumbfounded at what she was saying. "But how did you know we have kids, though?"

"Because I know all about you." It was time to hurt the man.

His eyes narrowed, and his lips thinned. "Then tell me, Miss Smartypants, what do you know about me?" He jerked his head back once in anger, looking down his nose at her. "And tell me who you work for? Are you with those children's aid people? The CAS?"

Sarah shook her head. "Nothing like that."

"Then who?"

"I'm with something much more scarier."

He jerked again, his grip on the hammer tightening as it swung in a soft arc beside his thigh.

"Why does that sound like a threat?"

"Allow me this tea, and we'll discuss it." She leaned forward and grabbed the cup. Because he'd had Edna drug the tea, he would have no issue with her drinking it. She'd be more compliant and sleepy soon enough, he'd assume. No need for violence. Yet.

She brought the tea to her lips, then jerked forward and upward, shoving the cup of hot liquid at his face.

He jerked away from the stream, but not fast enough. The heavy hammer in his hand restricted his upper body from full movement.

As he spun back around, his red face glistening with liquid, a deep moan emanating from him, Sarah was already lunging for the hammer. She snatched it from his grip and dove to the right, landing on her shoulder and rolling away from him.

A door opened somewhere.

A woman shrieked.

And Sarah pushed up to her feet.

She raised the hammer.

The man raised the Taser.

She threw the hammer, and even though she aimed for the large living room window beside the man, he ducked.

Glass shattered as the hammer exited the house.

"Get in here *now!*" she shouted.

# Chapter 10

PARKMAN STAYED CLOSE TO Aaron as they moved through the trees to the right of the house. He kept an eye out for Alex but didn't expect to see him.

With the house about twenty meters away, they moved slowly from tree to tree while listening for any signal from Sarah.

Near the rear of the house, Aaron came to a sudden stop. Parkman was able to avoid a collision by leaning his shoulder into a tree.

"What's up?" Parkman whispered.

Aaron leaned back, his finger raised to point at something. "Look."

Parkman narrowed his eyes and followed Aaron's finger. In the distance, a small shack, slightly larger than a shed, sat by itself in the center of a group of trees.

Then Aaron was moving again.

As they neared the front of the shed, it was evident that this building was well cared for. The grass out front was well-maintained, the door featured a welcome mat, and the single window was adorned with curtains. What seemed odd was the aluminum foil covering the bottom half of the window. That and the lock attached to the door—it was the push-button kind real estate agents often left outside so other agents could show the listing.

Why not use a padlock on the shed? Why have a code lock? Did more than one person need to gain access at different times, and exchanging a key was too much of a challenge?

With one solid door and one mostly blocked window, they couldn't be sure if the lights were on inside or not.

Parkman moved closer, then slowly placed an ear to the door. He waited several moments, holding his breath, until he was rewarded with the sound of movement.

He met Aaron's gaze and nodded once. *Someone's inside*, he mouthed.

Aaron moved away to circle the small shack while Parkman glanced back at the house. He wondered what was going on inside, then considered how far back they were. If Sarah needed immediate help, they'd take too long to return to the house.

Aaron came around behind him, having circled the whole place. He shook his head: *nothing*.

Parkman pointed at the coded lock on the door handle, then nodded toward the main house. Aaron understood—they weren't getting inside any time soon, and it was time to move back into position.

They strolled up the walkway, no longer moving among the trees, when something caught Parkman's eye. He tapped Aaron's shoulder and pointed.

The basement window on the left was open.

They both understood. Alex had gained entry through the basement of the house.

Parkman leaned in close to Aaron's ear. "Did Sarah send a signal? Did we miss it?"

"No idea."

They picked up the pace, then jumped when the glass broke at the front of the house.

Even though they were behind the building, they heard the distinctive yell as Sarah bellowed, "Get in here *now*!"

The sound of a woman screeching from somewhere in the house sent chills through Parkman as both men broke into a run.

# Chapter 11

THE MAN RIGHTED HIMSELF, aimed the Taser, and clenched his hand.

At that exact moment, Edna lunged at Sarah. She'd made it down the hall, shrieking the entire way, her hands in the shape of claws, scratching for Sarah's flesh.

The barbs shot forth and into Edna's back as Sarah defended herself for all of one second—then Edna went rigid and dropped to the floor at Sarah's feet.

"What have you done?" the man roared, leaning forward in a rage, his eyes bulging from his still-wet face as he dropped the Taser onto the floor. "I'll slaughter you like the lamb of God you are, whoremonger, Jezebel."

He dove straight at her.

Sarah dodged to the left, undid one deadbolt on the front door, then moved aside as the man regained his balance and dove at her again.

This time, his arms widened as he tried to clothesline her. She was able to duck below his arm and move toward the kitchen.

But she didn't see Edna's hand thrust out, grabbing at her. The electrical current had ended when the man dropped the Taser, and now Edna had regained control of her muscles.

She swiped at Sarah's ankle, got a firm hold, and as Sarah lunged under the man's embrace, her foot didn't advance, causing her to lose her balance. She tumbled to the dirty floor of the small house, her shoulder connecting painfully with the cupboards.

"Fuck," escaped her lips as she shuffled to the side to get to her feet.

A heavy weight, like a wall, collapsed onto her back, knocking the wind clear of her chest.

She couldn't breathe. One of her arms was locked behind her. Something slipped between her legs, making her try to close them. Even in the horror of not breathing, mouth open, no air coming in, the man's weight oppressive on her back, he had his hand down there, rubbing her. Like a large boulder, his mass secured her to the floor while his hand moved up and down.

"You'll be tied up," he grunted near her ear. "I'll fuck you until you die and bury your used-up body in the woods, you harlot."

Glass was breaking somewhere in the house. She thought she heard her name. Unable to breathe, blackness clouded her vision as her head lowered to the floor.

That hand wouldn't stop. It angered her and made her want to hurt the man, but she was still unable to move.

More glass broke. Someone grunted.

A woman shrieked somewhere. Was that Edna again?

Then the man's weight disappeared, and air rushed back into her lungs. The blackness in her vision dissipated, and the room came back into focus.

Edna was screaming a high-pitched wail as her man was being hauled away from Sarah by Alex.

How the hell could such a small man haul that sort of weight?

Then Parkman hopped in through the living room window, the hammer she'd thrown through it in his hand. It all came clear to her. Parkman had used the hammer to clear a spot on the window to gain access. That was the broken glass she'd heard. As Aaron jumped in behind Parkman, Sarah pushed up to her feet, still gasping for breath.

The man struggled under Alex's grip, but then Alex took his wrist, bent it at an odd angle, applied pressure to a certain point, and the man went limp, whimpering.

"Okay, okay, okay," he said. "Mercy. We was just playing, is all."

Sarah could barely hear him over Edna's shouting, so she dropped to one knee to be in front of the woman, then slapped her face twice—hard and fast.

Edna turned off like someone pulled the plug. Eyes wide, she stared up at Sarah.

"It's over," Sarah said. "This, whatever this is, ends today."

"Fuck you," the man said, his words strained with effort.

Sarah looked at Alex, then Parkman, and finally Aaron. "I had this, but the fuckin' guy wears a toolbelt with a Taser and a hammer. Didn't expect that."

"We're good," Parkman said. "What's next?"

"The kids." Sarah held out her hand for the hammer.

Parkman looked down at the hammer, then back to Sarah. After a brief hesitation, he handed it over.

"Keep her away from this," she said, pointing at Edna.

Parkman and Aaron moved to stand over the woman who was sniveling and wiping her nose.

Sarah stood in front of the man on the floor, his back up against the couch, arm still twisted at an odd angle.

"You said some terrible things a moment ago."

"Yeah. Just playing." He gave her a half-smile. "No harm, no foul."

"Sticks and stones and all." Sarah tapped his knee with the business end of the hammer.

"Hey, you don't wanna do anything stupid, now, do ya?"

Alex tightened his grip, and the man moaned from deep within his chest.

"But you touched me inappropriately." Sarah shook her head. "You shouldn't have done that."

She pulled the hammer back, then brought it down on the man's kneecap. There was an audible crack, followed by the man's mouth and eyes widening.

Edna gasped from behind Parkman.

Alex released his hand. There was no need to secure the man anymore. He wasn't going anywhere anytime soon.

Then the wailing came, long and hard, as he grasped at his shattered knee. The redness in his face quickly turned to white, then a shade of pale green.

"Where are the kids?" Sarah asked.

His eyes found her, then moved back to his knee. She kicked the foot of the uninjured leg.

He shouted.

"Focus," she yelled at him. "Where are the kids?"

"Hey, Sarah." Aaron stepped in beside her. "Is this really necessary?" He stared at the man's knee, rubbing his chin.

She breathed through her teeth, the rage at what this man had done filling her through Vivian. "Aaron, I'm going to break the other knee before we leave. I can't have him walking for a few months. There's a reason."

Aaron glanced at her with a look of disbelief on his face. "You're kidding, right?"

"Alex." Sarah focused on Alex's face. "If anyone tries to stop me, step in."

Alex nodded without hesitation, his body position changing slightly, balance adjusting from one foot to the other.

Aaron raised his hands, palms out, and stepped back. "Okay, have it your way."

"Now, talk." Sarah jammed the hammer toward the man.

"I see what you did there," the man said, spittle shooting from his mouth. "That sympathy thing. It makes me think someone in the room cares. The indirect threat about breaking my other knee." He shook his head. "And if I talk, you all just wander off, and it's over, am I right?"

Sarah lowered to her haunches. "We weren't playing any games. My friend is actually concerned about how far I'm willing to go. Knee number one was for what you did to me. Knee number two will be for what you did to those kids and to Edna."

"Fuck you. I'll get new knees with the money from the lawsuit. You can't break into my house and assault me." The man glanced around at all of them. "And try to kidnap my kids."

"Have at her," Sarah said, "if that's what you think this is. Sue our asses when this is over. All we want is to see the kids."

Parkman snapped his fingers. "Hey, with all this commotion, I forgot to mention the shack behind the house."

The man's head snapped to Parkman, a look of fear washing over his face.

"There's a lock on the door." Parkman moved to stand beside her now. "We need the code. When I put my ear to the door, I was pretty sure I heard movement."

The man shook his head. "Break my knees, break my arms, break whatever the hell you want. I'll *never* give you that code."

"I will." Edna's voice was weak and squeaky.

They all turned to her.

"You'll do no such thing," the man declared like it was an order. "You know what'll happen if you do."

"I can't anymore." Edna lowered her head and stared at the floor, tears falling to make small pools by her leg. "It's gone on long enough."

"What has?" Sarah asked in a soft tone.

"The abuse."

"Abuse?"

"What he makes our daughter do—" Edna's voice caught with a hiccup.

"What's he make her do?"

Edna looked over at the man she shared the house with, her eyes filled with something that made Sarah think of dread. Or maybe it was resolve. The look of someone who knows it's over.

"He holds the kids over my head. Threatens to take them from me —"

"Stop talking, bitch."

"—and says I'll lose this house, which my mother gave me."

"There are laws against what he's telling you." Sarah needed it all to come out. "Family law. Equalization." They had nowhere else to go until the morning. Edna was unburdening herself, which was something Sarah didn't want to stop, but they needed to get to the kids.

"To fight him, I'd need money." Edna wiped her face and looked up at Sarah with bloodshot eyes. "He keeps all the money we make from our kids. I could never afford a lawyer."

A sharp pain cut through her gut when she heard *money we make off our kids*. Vivian said *Abuse unchecked*. Vivian said CAS missed things. Vivian said the man would respond to scripture about disciplining a child. She didn't say anything about them profiting from their children.

"Do you mean you're foster parents?" Parkman asked.

Sarah was grateful he spoke up as she hadn't found her voice yet.

Edna shook her head. "No, they're our kids. Our flesh and blood."

"Then how do you make money off them?" Parkman placed a comforting hand on Sarah's shoulder as they waited for the answer.

The air in the room thickened. Sarah held her breath.

"Five-five-four-four-three." Edna looked up at Sarah. "Don't let that one back there." She pointed at Aaron. "He won't be able to stomach it. He's too soft." She stared at Sarah. "You won't like it, and I'm sorry I couldn't stop it. I pray God will have mercy on my soul." She wiped her eyes, then stared at the floor. "The kids are in that shed; the code is five-five-four-four-three."

Sarah tightened the grip on the hammer. "Why won't we like it?" She was stalling, debating whether they should call in the authorities now or go look for themselves.

"For years now, our daughter has been servicing men. They pay online, and then they're given the access code. We change it when they leave. No one comes to this house. No cash is ever handled in person."

"How?" Sarah gulped, her voice locking up. "Wait, are you serious —what?" Sarah steadied herself with Parkman's help.

Edna went on as if Sarah hadn't said a word. "Sometimes it's our son, too. He beats me when I protest. Beats the kids, too, but not enough that they can't work. And the worst is what he does to them when business slows down—"

"I'll murder you ten times over for what you just said," the man whispered. "You're a dead woman talking. I'll murder those brats of yours, find me a woman, and get more kids. Fuck this, fuck them, and fuck you all."

Alex wrapped his arms around the man's neck and squeezed to shut him up. Choking for air, the man fumbled at Alex's forearm, but to no avail.

Then, the hammer was yanked from Sarah's hand.

She reacted by her hands jerking up in a defensive posture.

It was Aaron, though.

He walked over to the man, a tear streaming down his face, and drove the hammer's business end into the man's other knee.

Alex let go of his throat so he could take in the much-needed air to scream.

Aaron met Sarah's stare, their eyes glazed over. He nodded and handed the hammer back as the man's scream filled the small room.

Then Aaron stepped forward and hugged Sarah. She hugged him back.

"I'm sorry," he whispered into her ear. "I'm here and always will be."

When they pulled away, she faced Parkman. "Call in the proper authorities. Tell them what we have here. Tell them to bring child psychologists. Then give them the code for that lock." She glanced around the room. "None of us is qualified to go back there. When they pull in, we watch from the trees, then leave. Agreed?"

All heads nodded, but Alex, who was staring down at the man with murderous intent on his face.

"Alex?" Sarah raised her voice. "Agreed?"

After a few heartbeats, he looked up, then nodded. "I won't kill him tonight." He glanced back at the man wailing and shaking on the floor. "We have plenty of time for that another day."

"Secure her, call this in. We need to get out of here."

The men went to work, and Parkman got on their house phone.

"Done," he said, hanging up. "We've only got a few minutes."

Sarah moved to stand over Edna, who was now duct-taped to the fridge's door handle. "We hope you get the help you need, but understand, people will blame you for some of this, claiming you could've stopped it."

Edna was nodding. "I know." She sounded so defeated, dejected.

"That you were complicit."

Her shoulders hitched, and more tears fell, but she couldn't wipe them now as Aaron had secured her hands to the fridge door.

A siren came to them from somewhere in the distance.

"Sarah?" Parkman said. "Time's up."

The man lay on his side, staring at nothing on the floor, breathing in and out rapidly, likely trying to manage the pain.

"Let's go out the front door. Leave it wide open."

They were in the trees near the road several minutes later, watching as police cruisers arrived.

More cars were coming, flashing lights filling the night like an eighties disco.

Now, men were walking to the shed in the back, the flashlights in their hands casting eerie shadows.

The door back there opened. They shone flashlights inside. One of the men gasped—audible from where they were hiding—turned and vomited into the bushes. The other man took one step back, covering his mouth.

He pulled out his phone, tapped on it, and then placed it to his ear. Nothing he said could be heard from where they were hidden.

Sarah turned away. She wanted to run and never stop.

She moved toward their car without a care in the world about how much noise she made.

They needed to get as far away from this place as possible.

Then, she needed to find somewhere to be alone and cry.

And think of her daughter.

And go home and shower her with love.

Then cry some more …

The world was disgusting. The world was evil.

For all that they do, there was no saving this sick world from itself. Yet, she'd continue doing what she did because every bit counted.

"Every bit counts," she muttered as she dropped into the back seat of the car. "Every bit counts."

The boys got in, and Parkman drove them away.

No one said a word.

There was no point.

# Chapter 12

THE NIGHT WENT BY slowly, with sleep being elusive. Sarah kept waking to the sound of the police officer vomiting at the sight of whatever was inside that shed.

She slipped out of bed and sauntered to the bathroom. When she was done, she checked the clock and saw it was just after seven in the morning. She had some time before their last stop in North Bay. Then, they could head home and be done with this crazy place.

"How'd you sleep?" Aaron asked.

She lowered herself into the chair by the motel window, rubbed her face, then stared at him. "Not so good."

"Me neither." He sat up in bed, adjusted the covers evenly, and then ran a hand through his hair. "What's left to do here?"

"One coffee shop chat. Simple and fast. Then we're gone."

"Good. Not sure if we could handle a repeat of last night."

They stared at each other a moment, then Sarah looked away and peered out past the curtain. The parking lot was empty.

Aaron's footsteps were soft on the carpeted floor as he moved to the bathroom. Sarah was still watching the parking lot when he exited the bathroom. A moment later, his hands were on her shoulders, rubbing.

She closed her eyes and let him massage out some of the stress.

"How much time have we got?"

Sarah opened her eyes and tilted her head back to look up at him. "About an hour."

"Good, because I want to go get coffee and breakfast for everyone."

"Go and hurry back. I'll shower and get ready. Then we check out, hit that last stop, and head home to Willow." She pushed up out of the chair, Aaron's hands falling away. "We're fucking done with this town."

"I second that." Aaron headed for his clothes draped over the chair on his side of the bed.

Sarah grabbed a new towel and entered the bathroom to turn on the shower.

Twenty minutes later, clean and ready for their last few hours in North Bay, she ate the McMuffin Aaron had brought her, then sipped her coffee while applying makeup and glue. The wig was the final step.

Finished, she moved into the room and sat at the window with her phone. She wanted one more look at the local news before leaving, in case that couple from last night described them to the authorities, and now they were looking for the old lady Sarah had been portraying. On close inspection, anyone could likely tell her disguise was fake, but they'd have to stand up close and scrutinize every detail. Her face and hair may appear older, but they didn't match her physique, which was still tight and lithe.

As suspected, the *North Bay Nugget* newspaper had a piece about the raid last night at a house on Four Mile Lake Road. Sarah went to scroll past, but stopped when she read the mother of the children was found dead, likely by suicide.

She leaned forward over the phone and tapped to read the article.

The man was found incapacitated, but the woman was found dead in their kitchen with self-inflicted wounds. The authorities had not been able to save her in time.

There were two children found on the property. They were now in protective custody.

Below that was a small article from the Children's Aid Society on previous visits to the home. The newspaper reported on court proceedings of the prior year to further substantiate the article above.

"Why is this public knowledge?" she whispered to the empty room.

During previous CAS visits, when the children were seized from the property, the boy had missed several weeks of school. The father was a drinker, and until they could prove he'd stopped drinking, the kids wouldn't be returned to the home.

"They should've never been returned."

She scrolled further through the article. The boy had an undiagnosed kidney infection, a bowel impaction—which she looked up to see precisely what that meant and learned it was totally preventable —and was malnourished, likely anemic. He was also twenty pounds underweight for his age. They kept their kids in a bug-infested room in the house on a urine-soaked mattress.

Nothing in the court proceedings mentioned the daughter.

That was almost two years ago.

Likely, their father renovated that shed in the back and cleaned it up, stopped drinking long enough to get the kids back, and voila—they were in his custody again.

All CAS did was let those kids go back to another version of Hell.

This was the second time Sarah had dealt with Children's Aid mistakes in this area. She lowered her phone and wondered how CAS workers were trained. Couldn't they see the obvious signs of abuse and neglect? Why would they send kids back to abusers, time and again?

The motel room door opened, and Aaron stepped in.

"Oh," he said. "It's my old lady."

"Don't call me that."

"Men call their girlfriends old lady all the time, but now it's even more appropriate. I mean, look at you."

His humor didn't translate. She looked away and stared at nothing.

Aaron moved closer, his eyes on her phone. "Reading that *Nugget* article?"

Sarah nodded slightly.

"We read it, too. No idea how Edna got out of that duct tape or how she killed herself."

They both stared out the window.

"How could she live with herself after everything that happened?" Sarah glanced up at him. "Their life was about to become quite public. There'll be considerable attention placed on the mother. She probably thought death was easier than facing her future."

Aaron nodded. "Imagine so."

"Did you see anything about me?" she asked. "My disguise? If they're looking for us?" She watched a car drive by on Lakeshore Boulevard. "That man had to've told them about us. No way he'd break his own kneecaps."

"Yeah, but there's nothing in any of the local papers. Well, except for that police chief and Judge Griffin bit. They're still looking for you. Your photo was relegated to page three, though."

"We'll have to deal with that soon enough."

"How? They have a list of charges published in the paper." Aaron moved to sit on the edge of the bed. "What are you going to do? Turn yourself in and hire a lawyer?"

Sarah glanced down at her phone and then turned it off. "It's all bullshit. All I said was stop what you're doing, or the consequences will cause a ripple effect and hurt your daughter. A message, not a threat."

"Yeah, and I assaulted the chief of police."

"Well, there's that." Sarah met his gaze. "You won't do time for it, though. We'll work it out."

"Hope so." Aaron bounced on the side of the bed for a moment. "I've been thinking."

When he said nothing more, she asked, "About what?"

"When we're done today, you three head home."

Her brows turned inward. "And what? Leave you here?"

He nodded once. "Yeah, to end this threat, I'll get bail and come home in a few days. We'll get a lawyer and come back up in a year for the court date." He cleared his throat. "The important thing is to get this target off our backs. How can you do what you do while every cop in the province is looking for you?"

Sarah waved a hand in his direction. "First things first. We do this final visit in an hour, then decide what's next. Maybe Vivian will give us an answer."

Aaron's expression hardened. Evidently, he didn't like her idea. Did he want to be a martyr? Sacrifice himself for her? He didn't have to prove anything by spending time in jail. If it came to that, they'd deal with it, but the crimes the police chief and that judge had committed were far worse, and Sarah had to find a way to expose that.

Even though hope was scarce, she held onto a small glimmer of hope that the solution lay in holding the judge and his friend accountable for their actions.

But how? They were too powerful.

Then, the entire idea came to her. Everything was spelled out by her sister and filled her conscious thoughts.

She smiled as she checked the time on her phone. "We need to get going. I can't miss this meeting."

Aaron got to his feet. "Alex and Parkman are ready. I'll bring the car around."

Sarah stood and nodded. "Let's do this. But before we get to the meeting, we have one stop to make first."

"Where are we going?"

Sarah told him, then stepped outside, leaving him standing there with his mouth open wide.

# Chapter 13

JUDGE GRIFFIN PACED HIS chambers and waited for Police Chief Warner to join him. He'd called Warner's cell ten minutes before when he'd heard what happened on Four Mile Lake Road last night, and Warner told him that the Joseph and Edna Nate incident involved Sarah and that he was on his way up.

Griffin stared at his bottle of scotch on the side table, then changed his mind. It was only a matter of time before they had that witch in custody, and he didn't want to be out of sorts. He was still dealing with a hangover from last night.

He placed a hand over his stomach and walked around his desk to take a seat. The coffee that morning must've had sour milk, as it felt like it was curdling in his stomach.

Focusing on his docket today would be a task, but he'd get through it. A mishmash of cases in the morning, and then the Mike Sommers's case in the afternoon, and the guilty verdict he'd give. The money Mackenzie was paying to ensure Sommers did time—twenty years minimum—was enough to carry him to retirement. It was dumb of Sommers to be driving around, speeding no less, with all those weapons and drugs in his trunk. The man had had enough guns to arm a small militia. This was all his fault. There was no way a judge could be blamed for locking up someone like Michael Sommers.

If there were any validity to what that psychic witch said, then fine, he'd stop after the Sommers trial. Stopping now was absolutely out of the question. Not today. Not having already taken Mackenzie's money.

Sommers's attorney had argued that his client had stolen the car, and the guns weren't his. This case should be reduced to charging him for stealing a car. He'd pay a fine, the guns and drugs could be disposed of at the government's discretion, and that would be the end of it.

Even though the car was registered to a company that had nothing to do with Sommers, and Sommers's attorney was effective, sowing doubt throughout the trial, Judge Griffin would find him guilty on all counts and remand him into the custody of the penal system within hours.

That's what half a million dollars of Mackenzie's money will get with Judge Griffin.

He smiled to himself, knowing he never asked Mackenzie *why* Sommers in jail was worth so much—that wasn't the sort of question you asked a man like Mackenzie. You either took the deal or you didn't.

Judge Griffin and Police Chief Warner took the deal.

The knock on his office door made him jump.

"Come," he called.

The heavy wooden door opened, and Warner slipped inside, then closed it behind him.

"What have you got?" Griffin asked, glancing at his watch. "My first case is in ten minutes. Speak with brevity."

Warner's wide smile as he moved to stand on the other side of Griffin's desk was unexpected. Griffin couldn't tell if it was a cocky smile or a self-assured one.

"Well?" Griffin glanced at his Rolex. "Time waits for no asshole with a smile."

"We've got her."

Griffin smacked both hands on the top of his desk and resisted the urge to stand. "Where? In the holding cells?"

Warner shook his head. "She was at the Nate house last night."

Griffin jerked back as if stung, his chair squeaking. Then he leaned back and steepled his fingers in front of his mouth.

"What the hell was she doing there? You said it *involved* her when we spoke on the phone. You didn't say she was there. Why was she there?" He was rambling but didn't care.

"We don't know why she was there yet, but Joseph Nate is in the hospital and quite willing to talk."

"About what? How he abused those kids? Is he willing to sign a confession?"

"Investigating officers are handling that. CAS has the kids. They're safe now and meeting with child psychologists later today."

"Then what did Joseph Nate want to talk about?"

"About a woman and three men terrorizing his family in their own home last night."

Griffin stopped breathing briefly. He gasped for breath, then said, "Go on."

"Apparently, this woman pretended to be an older lady representing a church, but she wasn't from any church, and she wasn't old."

"And the three men?"

Warner clapped his hands. "Descriptions from Joseph sound just like Sarah's usual suspects: Aaron, Parkman, and Alex."

"How's that possible?" Griffin pulled back, his face scrunched up. "Why would they go to Joseph Nate's house? What I mean is, how would they know to target him?"

Warner shrugged. "Does it matter? We got her." He snapped his fingers. "How about we ask her when she's arrested for over a dozen charges, starting with aggravated assault with a deadly weapon, personation, break and enter, and … *murder*."

Griffin gasped. "Murder?" he repeated the word. "What did she do?" he asked under his breath. "What the hell are you talking about?"

"She broke Joseph's knees with a hammer."

Griffin scoffed. "*What? Really?*"

Warner tipped his head back, then lowered it to his chin, nodding exaggeratedly. "And that's not all."

Griffin checked the time. "What else happened? Tell me what you meant about murder." He fiddled with his watch. "Hurry."

"Edna Nate is dead."

"Yeah, I read that. Self-inflicted wounds. Suicide. It was in the paper this morning."

Warner shook his head. "She was duct taped to the fridge door."

"And?"

"Sarah, or one of her cronies, took a butcher knife to her thighs, particularly her inner thighs, and savagely cut her femoral artery while she was bound and couldn't defend herself. She bled out on the kitchen floor before medical could arrive. Sarah must've been pissed that a mother left her children in such a sorry state and decided she didn't deserve to live."

"Holy shit." Griffin shook his head, staring at Warner. "The paper said suicide," he added as if talking to himself.

"That was all me."

"Yet there was no mention of a home invasion."

"Me again." Warner looked genuinely proud of himself. "I spoke with the *Nugget* to ensure the whole truth wasn't published until we apprehended the people responsible. Then I said I would give them an exclusive."

"Good." Griffin rose from his chair. "I've got court and that Sommers thing this afternoon. Keep working on this and bring me that witch. This just got worse for her—much worse."

"Well, arresting her shouldn't be too hard now."

Griffin was moving toward the chamber door that led to his court. He glanced back over his shoulder. "How's that?"

"Joseph Nate gave expert descriptions of all four of them, including Sarah in her gray old-lady wig."

When Griffin placed his hand on the door, he stopped and turned around. "Gray wig?"

Warner nodded. "She dressed like an older woman, wore a wig, and did something with her makeup to add years to her face. But by the time she was done in the Nate house, he could tell she was in her late twenties, early thirties."

"How did she convince him to let her and the boys inside?"

"She came to the front door alone, carrying a Bible."

"A Bible?" Griffin lowered his face but kept his eyes on Warner.

"Yup." Warner nodded. "She was talking about spreading the Good Word. She even read passages to him about disciplining a child. Once inside, she attacked him and his wife, broke out their living room window, and let her three friends in to terrorize them further and kill

Edna. When they left, Joseph crawled to the kitchen to call the police. Unfortunate for him that officers discovered his shed in the back, but better for the kids."

"Yeah, happy I don't practice family law. That's worse than criminal court." Griffin opened the door that led to his courtroom, then stopped. "So you've got a description of Sarah in the wig?"

Warner fished a folded piece of paper from his jacket pocket and opened it. "Every officer in a hundred-mile radius has this."

Griffin stared at the visage of Sarah as an older woman. "Good, things are looking up. We'll have her today, I'm sure."

"I can almost guarantee that."

Judge Griffin stepped through the door and into his court.

"All rise," the court clerk shouted. "The Honorable Senior Justice Griffin is presiding."

His stomach was already feeling better as he took his seat. Things were looking up. That meddling bitch would be arrested for murder before the day ended.

He was sure of it.

He'd request the case, too. That way, he could guarantee that no one except prison guards would ever have to see her face again. The maximum time allowable by law would be handed down without the chance for parole, as he'd claim the home invasion was targeted and that Nate woman's death was premeditated.

He thought he had read somewhere that Sarah was a mother, so of course, she'd execute a mother who allowed her children to be abused to the extent those Nate kids were.

When he was done with Sarah, she'd be an old woman after all.

Griffin allowed a grin to crease his lips.

She should've never tried to fuck with him or his family. He was the king of his castle, and his castle was the North Bay district.

That witch had no idea of the consequences he could dish out.

None whatsoever.

# Chapter 14

AARON DROVE THEM TO the coffee shop on Algonquin Avenue, then parked near the back, close to the exit.

Sarah studied the parking lot for the car of her target, a Mustang, but couldn't see it. They were fifteen minutes early as their first stop went rather quickly. Parkman and Alex waited outside during that stop. They had questions, but hadn't asked any yet.

"We're on the south side of North Bay," Aaron said. "The moment you get in the car, we can be out of this town within minutes."

"That's the plan, providing the judge takes our advice. If not, we may be stuck here another day or so." Sarah checked her face and wig in the passenger sun visor mirror. "Wait here for me. I shouldn't be long."

"Sarah? Wait." Aaron stared at her. "What if the judge didn't take our advice? How long will we be here?"

"I've already told Alex and Parkman what to do."

Aaron frowned. "How will you know?"

"We'll all know within the hour."

The car's back doors opened behind her.

Sarah stopped to glance over her shoulder. "Where are you guys going?"

Alex was already out of the car and closing the door, but Parkman leaned back inside.

"We'll be watching over everything. Aaron can stay with the car in case we need to get out of here quickly. If things go south, we know where and when to find you."

"Okay, but it's just some guy in his twenties. He's being blackmailed, and I've got some answers for him. A simple in and out, so don't go far."

"I'm sure we'll be done and gone in no time. But until then, Alex and I talked about it in the room this morning before Aaron brought breakfast. We'll watch over everything, and that's that. And ... if we aren't leaving town right away, we'll take off and do what you asked us to do."

Parkman exited the car, closing the door behind him. As usual, Alex was already gone somewhere—she couldn't see where.

"Time to send your message." Aaron gestured toward the coffee shop. "Then let's get out of here."

"Hope so." Sarah pushed the visor back into place, checked the time on the dashboard, then got out and walked toward the building. Once inside, she waited in line until her order was taken, grabbed her coffee, and then took a seat with her back to the outside wall.

She didn't have to wait long. Right on schedule, or perhaps a few minutes late, the rumble of his Mustang as he backed it into a parking spot could be heard throughout the coffee shop.

Unexpectedly, though, two male friends exited the Mustang with the driver and started toward the entrance.

She raised the coffee cup to her lips and whispered behind it, "Shit, friends pose a problem." *You didn't tell me there'd be friends, Vivian.*

The trio came in laughing. One of them told a joke, with the others responding boisterously. Parkman entered and stood right behind them, glancing her way once.

They stood in line, slowly moving to the counter to place their orders, and then stood to the side to wait for their food to be prepared.

"So, I told the guy," her target said, "to get lost."

"Yeah." One of his friends nodded.

"I mean, what was he thinking?"

"Exactly," the other guy said, animatedly shaking his head.

The Mustang driver was clean-cut, with one earring in his left ear. His neck boasted a blotch of ink behind the right ear—she was too far away to see what the design could be. Of medium build, she was confident he could take care of himself. The two friends were hanging on his every word, meaning he liked his ego stroked by hanging around with these groupies, or whatever they called them.

Their food was ready—they had ordered the chili deal, donut, and coffee each. All three men meandered through the tables and sat at a table just one away from Sarah.

Parkman only ordered a coffee and was already seated by the window, no doubt in a position where Alex could watch him in case he was needed.

After last night, they were nervous that this could escalate into something much worse than it was, which she could understand. Everyone was on edge, especially with the authorities looking for them after what happened at the golf course.

Sarah waited while the men ate, listening to them talk about a football game, who scored this goal or that, and then about a woman one of them recently met. They did their usual teasing, and then the chilis were finished.

Mustang Driver placed the trays on the empty table beside theirs, then dug into his donut. The other two were already finished and were just sipping their coffees.

She figured this was the best time to interrupt their otherwise calm morning.

Sarah got up from her table and moved slowly to stand beside Mustang Driver, remembering that she looked like an old woman. Would it be like this when she was still working Vivian's magic in her seventies? Would she be a version of Esmerelda, her dear friend from almost a decade ago? Thinking of Esmerelda made her feel nostalgic. That life was ages ago.

*If you could see me now*, she'd say to her if she could.

Sarah moved into his line of vision and addressed her target. "I need to speak with you for a moment." She glanced at the other two guys. "Alone." She kept her tone soft so it didn't sound like an order.

One of them laughed. "What's this old hag have to say to you, Bruce?" He slapped his friend's arm, and they released a short laugh together.

Bruce set down his donut—an apple fritter, one of Sarah's favorites —and eyed her up and down.

"Whatever you got to say to me, old lady," he flicked his fingers toward his boys, "they can hear this, too."

Sarah stared at the center of the table for a moment, then at Bruce. "I don't think so."

Now, all three laughed.

"It's about Heather," she added.

Bruce's laugh died, and his face fell. He glared up at Sarah, his jaw clenching, his hand tightening into a fist.

His friends grew quiet until one asked, "Hey, man, who's Heather? You never told us about any Heather."

"Shut up," Bruce said.

"Boys," Parkman stood behind the friends. They strained their necks to look up at him. "Time to step outside and let the lady chat with Bruce for a moment."

"He's right," Bruce said, motioning for his friends to leave. "I'll be out in a few minutes."

They pushed their chairs back, mumbling something under their breath.

"Hey, man," one of them said, staring at Bruce, "we got no idea what this is about, but if you need us, we'll be right outside that door."

"I got this," Bruce said. "I'll be out in a minute. Wait by the car."

Sarah waited until they were halfway to the door, followed by Parkman, before she took a seat opposite Bruce. She focused on him, her hands clasped together on the table.

"Speak." He kicked his head back once. "What's this about Heather? She wants more money or something? I already gave her twenty grand. How much more does she want?"

"You need to stop."

He blinked, shook his head, then leaned in closer. "Excuse me? Stop what?"

"Don't give her any more money."

"So, you're *not* with her, come here to send me some kinda message?"

Sarah shook her head. "No, I'm not with her, although I do have a message."

"Then speak your piece."

"It's blackmail, extortion, whatever you want to call it, and she's working others, too. It isn't just you. She's fleecing money from other men as well."

He dropped back in his chair so hard he bounced once. Mouth open, he gawked at her. "What are you saying?"

"Bruce, you need to listen to me. I know what Heather does, who she is, and what she's been doing—"

"If you know so much, why don't you tell me what she does?"

Sarah exhaled loudly. "If that's how you want this to go, then I will, but I haven't got much time."

"Hurry up then."

"Heather is a high-priced call girl. You meet at her condo for a few hours, drop the cash, and off you go. I get it. Oldest profession and all, but what she does with the condom afterward, specifically the semen, is why you're in the position you're in. That DNA proof she has on you? It's fake."

He leaned forward again, glancing around the coffee shop conspiratorially. "What does that mean? What does she do with my come?"

"She freezes it, bags it, and hands it to her new boyfriend."

"New boyfriend?" He shook his head.

Sarah nodded.

"And what's he do to it?" Bruce asked.

"He works at the DNA lab here in town ..." she petered off when she saw the realization kick in.

He slapped the side of his head. "So she's not really pregnant with my baby?"

Sarah shook her head.

"Even though I saw the DNA test telling me it was mine?" Bruce had lost some of the color in his face.

"She's pregnant all right, but it's her boyfriend's baby. They've decided she'll leave the call girl business for good when they hit the seventh or eighth month. In the meantime, they're fleecing as many of her past clients as possible along the way. This has been in the works for over a year. They handpicked men who could afford the ten, twenty, or thirty grand to make her go away. I understand a few men paid more, a lot more."

He stared at his lap, forehead resting on the palm of his hand, his head slowly shaking back and forth.

"The question is," Sarah continued, "what can you do? Get your money back? No, that's gone. Remember, she's got a DNA test that matches your DNA, even though it's not your baby. How about calling the authorities and making it public? You'd humiliate yourself, but maybe when the baby is born, you could get another test done by some independent firm." She glanced around the room. No one was watching them, yet she felt the strong urge that someone had been. She fixed her gaze back on Bruce. "They're in a fortified position at the moment. I just wanted you to know so you'll stop giving her money now."

He looked up at her, his eyes welling with tears and already bloodshot. "I thought I was having a baby. That's what I was paying for —a baby. Even though it was *her*, I would have a child."

Sarah offered him a sympathetic look. "I understand, but so did ten other men in the community and over twenty in the province. They're all thinking the same thing."

*Ten, twenty?* He mouthed the words, emotion stealing his ability to speak.

Sarah unclasped her hands and wiped at her forehead. Some of the glue came off on the back of her hand. She flicked it aside, but not before it caught his attention.

"I figure by telling you," she went on, "Heather would stop what she was doing. I mean, who would complain to the authorities? She chose men who had something to lose by going to the police. Which makes sense because didn't she threaten you with exposure?"

He was staring at her forehead now.

*Shit, what did I do?*

"What?" she asked. "Something wrong?"

"Who are you?" His eyes lowered to meet hers. "How do you know all this?"

"That's not important."

His eyes roamed her face, her neck, then he leaned sideways and took in her body from the side. When he looked back at her a moment later, she thought she detected anger in his eyes.

"Why are you wearing a disguise? You're easily twenty or thirty years younger than you're trying to look."

Once in the car, they'd be gone, out of North Bay. This conversation had gone on too long. Therefore, the disguise was of no use now.

She felt someone's eyes on her again, but resisted the urge to look around.

She grabbed the wig and eased it off her head. After setting it on the table, she unclasped her hair and let it fall over her shoulders. While he studied her in surprise, she rubbed her forehead, cheeks, and lips to remove as much of the glue as possible.

"What I look like doesn't matter anymore. I'm leaving." She pushed her chair back. "Just stop paying Heather. Call her, tell her you're done. Tell her whatever you want, just save the money. There—message delivered."

"What about the other guys she's lied to?"

"They're not your concern." She shrugged. "Maybe when you cut her off, and she has no recourse but to accept it, she'll wonder how you figured it out, and she'll end it on her own with the others. I don't know. All I do know is that I was supposed to give you this message. So, consider it delivered."

Sarah got to her feet.

"Wait, please." Bruce extended a hand.

She stared down at him, then looked around briefly before sitting back down. "I'll stay another moment. What is it?"

"How are you connected?"

"Not important."

"Are you Heather's sister or something?"

Sarah shook her head. "No need to search for a connection. You won't find one."

"Then how do you know all this?"

"Too long a story to get into now."

"Okay." He rubbed his face and stared upward, then refocused on her. "Then why should I listen to you? I mean, what if you're wrong, and it is my child?"

"It isn't."

"Okay, but what if it is? And I listened to you. Then what?"

"Your decision, but if you follow that path of reasoning, you'll see eventually that I was right and wish you'd listen to me."

Bruce pulled out his phone. "How about I call her right now?"

"Do whatever you want. I'm leaving." Sarah got to her feet again.

He held up the phone and snapped a picture. He hadn't been preparing to dial a number. He had opened the camera app.

"Hey, delete that."

"Fuck no. When I meet Heather and explain why I'm not paying her another red cent, I want to show her your photo so she knows who ratted her out. I'm grateful and all, but what are you hiding from? What's your story?"

Sarah retook her seat one more time. "Delete that photo, or I'll take your phone, smash it, and feed it to the donut fryer in the back, where it'll melt into nothingness in seconds."

He slipped it into his jacket pocket, zipped it up, and gave her a cocky smile.

Sarah pulled out her phone and dialed Aaron's number. He answered right away.

"The target's name is Bruce."

"Okay."

"He's got a phone in the inside pocket of his jacket. Tell the others. I need that phone." She stared at Bruce from across the table. "He doesn't leave the premises with that phone."

"Got it. Calling them now."

Sarah slipped her phone away. "We done here?"

"What was that? Some ploy to intimidate me? What are you, a spy or something? Because now you're making me angry."

"Anger is a good emotion. I've felt it from time to time."

Bruce stared out the window. Sarah followed his gaze to the parking lot. His friends stood by the Mustang, with Parkman walking back toward the entrance, a phone pushed to his ear.

"You think that old man is going to take this phone from me?" Bruce laughed. "Or is he in disguise, too?"

"It doesn't matter who takes the phone. You won't leave with it."

He jumped to his feet. "You know what? Fuck this and fuck you." He raised his voice, calling attention to their table. "I didn't ask for this and don't want it."

He started toward the exit, then stopped. "Do you even know who I am?"

That hadn't crossed her mind, and Vivian hadn't mentioned it. "Does it matter?"

"Soon enough, you'll learn how much it matters." He backed away, bumped a table, then spun around and slammed into the door at the entrance.

She watched the door close and waited for Parkman to stop him, but she couldn't see Parkman now.

Where did he go?

Leaving the wig on the table with her coffee cup, she got to her feet and followed Bruce's path to the exit. Before she got there, a flash of movement caught her eye.

"Sarah Roberts," a man to her left said. "Don't resist. You're under arrest." She was shoved into the brick wall beside the exit door, her arms wrenched behind her back.

How did they not see this coming? Why didn't her sister warn her?

They wrenched her arms back, had her wrists cuffed, and were leading her outside in seconds. Four police cruisers, no lights flashing, sat to the left of the door in a spot she would never have seen from the inside.

From where Aaron parked and Parkman stood, they wouldn't have seen these cruisers either.

As she turned to the right, men surrounded their car and pulled Aaron out by his arms. The sounds of grunts and scuffling came to her from fifteen vehicles away.

Blessedly, there was no sign of Parkman or Alex.

They'd seen the threat and disappeared in time, which she'd instructed them to do. If this went south, they had to escape at all costs to prepare for later.

Bruce made it to his car without anyone challenging him for his phone. When he rejoined his friends, they were all watching as the officers marched Sarah to the back of a cruiser.

Before going inside, she caught Bruce laughing and pointing at her.

So much for wanting to help a guy.

Once inside the car, two officers jumped in the front and hit the gas.

The passenger turned in his seat. "Do you know what you're being charged with?"

"No idea." She stared out the side window, unwilling to say anything that might further incriminate her.

"There are almost twenty charges, but the big one is murder in the first degree."

Her head snapped forward to stare at the cop. "What? Wait, who did I *allegedly* kill?"

"You're under arrest for the murder of Edna Nate of Four Mile Lake Road."

"I didn't kill Edna," she said, her voice raised. "She was alive when we left. The papers said it was a suicide."

The cops laughed as the passenger turned back to face the front.

"*She was alive when we left*," the man said in a high-pitched female voice, mocking her plea. "Tell that to the judge. You'll be processed and sit before Judge Griffin soon enough. Give him your not-guilty plea. See how that goes for you."

They laughed again.

*Vivian, what have you done now?*

# Chapter 15

AFTER GETTING RID OF Scott and Jay Jay with the excuse that he had things to do, Bruce called Heather's private number, but she didn't pick up. He hung up when it went to voicemail.

He was no one's play toy. If what that girl said was true, Heather couldn't just use him, steal his money, and then ride off into the proverbial sunset with some other asshole.

Or, everything that girl said at the coffee shop could be a lie.

Whatever the case, he was determined to learn the truth and needed to know it now. Not tomorrow, not yesterday—*now.*

He drove too fast but didn't care. If they pulled him over, he'd tell them who his father was, and the cops in town usually let him off with a warning.

The ten-minute drive to Heather's condo took him six minutes. He found a spot in the visitor's parking, killed the engine, then opened the glove box.

He withdrew the Smith & Wesson, checked that it was loaded and that there was one in the chamber, and then slipped it into his jacket pocket.

It was around noon on a Monday, so the parking lot was half empty. With no one around, he waited. It wasn't long until an old station wagon pulled in. A woman got out, gathered her grocery bags, locked her car, and headed for the building entrance. He hopped out and ran for the door. He stepped closer as she inserted her key, her arms laden with bags.

"Here, let me get that for you."

Jonas Saul

"Thank you," she muttered, then stepped in under his extended arm.

He jogged ahead and pushed the button for the elevator, then waited beside the woman.

"Decent weather for this time of year, eh?"

She nodded. "Bit of a chilly spring, but it's okay."

He smiled and glanced up at the number above the elevator doors. It was on the second floor, then the first.

The doors opened, and three teenagers exited.

He waved for her to enter.

"Floor?"

"Two."

He pushed two and four, then rode the elevator, already thinking about what he'd say. The woman exited on the second floor, and he ascended to the fourth, breaking out into a slight sweat.

He decided Heather had to come clean. He'd ask her, *cajole* her to spill the beans. He'd be kind in exchange for her honesty by offering her and her baby a gift. He'd already given her twenty grand. Simply repay fifteen thousand, and she could keep the five thousand as a gift.

Then he'd leave her apartment and her life and keep his mouth shut.

There was a condition, though. She had to pay him the fifteen thousand *before* he left, or he wouldn't go. As if she would call the cops on him—a call girl, a lady of the night, a prostitute, calling the cops— what a joke. It wouldn't happen.

He got to her condo door and placed an ear against it. No noise emanated from the inside.

After looking both ways along the hallway, he knocked, then moved to the side in case she used the peephole.

A soft thump came from the other side of the door. Someone had rested against it to look into the hallway.

"Hello?" Heather's voice came through, weakened by the thick door.

Bruce moved in front of the peephole.

The deadbolt clicked, then the knob turned. "Bruce, baby, I didn't expect you today."

He couldn't help glancing down at her belly. At five months, she was barely starting to show.

"Can I come in? I need to talk to you."

She didn't open the door further as she eyed him up and down. "Are you okay?"

"Yeah, we just need to talk."

When she didn't move aside, he pushed the door open and barged into her condo.

"Bruce," Heather said, her tone sounding impatient. "I have a client coming soon."

"Cancel it."

"What?" Now, her tone was cold.

He spun around and glared at her. "Close the door."

"I don't like how you barged in here. Please come back when you've cooled off, and call ahead next time. I'm often busy."

"Yeah, right. Fucking clients while you're pregnant, are you?" He allowed his eyes to drop to her belly again. "*Supposedly*, with our child."

She placed her hands on her hips, the door resting open against her shoulder. "I'm not sure I like your tone."

"Oh, you don't like my tone, but you like my money, is that it?"

After a brief moment, Heather eased to the side and let the door close, then leaned her back against it, crossing her arms over her chest. "What's this all about?"

He pulled out his cell phone, brought up the picture of the woman in the coffee shop, and then showed it to Heather.

"Who is this?" he asked.

Heather leaned in, then moved back against the door. "I have no idea."

Bruce slipped his phone away. "Well, she knows you, and she knows about your boyfriend."

Heather glanced toward the bedroom door, then back to Bruce.

"Wait, is someone here?"

"I told you. I have a client."

"No. You didn't." He looked toward the bedroom. "You said you have a client coming soon." Bruce placed his hands on either side of his mouth and shouted, "Come on out. I don't bite."

"Bruce," she snapped. "That's so unprofessional. Please don't yell. I can't have my neighbors complaining."

The door opened, and a man stepped out of the bedroom dressed in shorts and a white tank top. The guy had to be a walking advertisement for bodybuilding magazines. He had to be at least three hundred pounds of solid muscle.

"This him?"

"Him who?" Heather asked, exasperated now.

"The DNA expert who fixed the results for me and about a dozen or more other guys?"

They exchanged a look, and then both of them stared at Bruce.

The boyfriend moved closer. "Hey, man, listen. Let's all remain calm and discuss this. Do you want a drink? Take a seat, and then we'll —"

"I don't want to take a seat," Bruce cut in. "I want the truth."

Heather moved away from the door to stand closer to her boyfriend. "Where did you hear about Sam?"

"I told you." Bruce pointed at his phone. "That woman told me."

They looked at each other again.

"May I see the photo?" Sam asked, moving closer to Bruce.

He pulled out his cell phone, brought up the picture, and held it out for Sam to see.

The man shook his head and stepped back. "I have no idea who that is."

"Well, she knows all about you two."

The boyfriend gestured toward the sofa beside Bruce, then led Heather to the loveseat.

Bruce watched them without making a move to sit.

Once they were seated, bodybuilder Sam said, "Tell us what this woman told you."

"She told me everything you've been doing."

"Like what?" Heather asked. "What have we been doing?"

Bruce placed his hands on the back of the couch, leaned forward, and told them all of it. Starting with the wig and makeup, all the way to her arrest in the parking lot.

"This woman sounds like trouble from the get-go," Heather said. "It's obvious she made it all up. We'd never do that. We don't know her, and she was arrested right there, at the coffee shop. How could you possibly believe her over me?"

Bruce took in her words, wished they were true, and then moved around the couch to stand in front of it.

He placed his hand inside his jacket pocket, gripped the gun's handle, then eased it out and lowered it to sit on the couch, placing the weapon on his thigh.

Sam's eyes widened, and Heather pushed back to lean into Sam.

"Hey, man, what's that for?" Sam asked. "There's no need for a gun. Heather's pregnant, man." His voice cracked on the last word.

"All I want is the truth. Be honest with me, and I'll walk away." He couldn't control the shake in his arms, his hands. There was too much adrenaline in his system. "I'll sweeten the pot. I'll pay you five thousand bucks for the truth, the whole truth, and nothing but the truth."

Heather gripped Sam's arm and leaned further into him, her eyes beseeching him to do something.

"How do we convince you we're telling the truth?" Sam asked.

"That's your job to figure out."

"Okay, we'll tell you the truth. You serious about that five grand offer?"

"I'm so serious, I'd put it in writing. I only want the truth."

"You got that sort of cash on you?"

Bruce frowned, lifted the gun to wave it back and forth, and shook his head. "That's not how this works. You extorted twenty big ones out of me. So, tell me the truth and pay me fifteen grand of my stolen money, and I'll leave. No one gets hurt. We never see each other again. Your secret will remain safe with me. Sayonara, hasta la vista, and all that crap." Bruce leaned forward, the gun resting over his knees now, aimed toward their feet. "So, the question that should be asked is, do you have that sort of cash on you?" He waited a moment, then sat back on the couch, easing the weapon to aim at Sam. "Because I'm not leaving until I get the truth and at least fifteen thousand in cash." He waved the gun once more to aim it between the two of them. "And neither are you two. So, spill it. Tell me everything. Start at the beginning. And make sure you're not lying. I'll know, Mr. DNA specialist. I'll know."

Heather opened her mouth and spoke what sounded like the truth.

# Chapter 16

DURING A SHORT RECESS, Judge Griffin headed to his chambers. He hung his robe on the coat rack, dropped the case files on his desk, and then moved to the side cabinet to pour that finger of scotch he'd been yearning for all day.

He glanced around his office, glass in hand, and pondered what that witch had warned him about. Other questions floated around, like what could she possibly be doing at the Nate residence last night? Why show up there in disguise, cripple the man, and kill the wife? From what he read online about Sarah, outright murder wasn't her thing. She wasn't averse to violence, but murder didn't fit.

He kicked back the scotch with one swig, then poured another—this time two fingers. He'd need to be fortified for the rest of the day.

Drink in hand, he moved to his desk, opened the files, and began the arduous task of poring over the case files he'd be presiding over before lunch.

When his phone rang, he jerked slightly, then glanced over to see Warner's name on call display.

He set his scotch down and snatched it up. "Tell me you've got good news."

"I've got good news."

"Explain."

"Sarah Roberts and Aaron Stevens are in custody."

"Well," Judge Griffin sat back in his chair and stared up at the ceiling, "done!"

"They're being processed as we speak."

"And the charges?"

"First-degree murder to start. About twenty or thirty more will be added. They'll be in our system for a long time to come."

Griffin shot forward and placed his elbows on the case files. "I want to see her."

Warner had a sharp intake of breath. "What?" After a moment, he said, "Why?"

"The Sommers's thing this afternoon is just a formality. We both know I'm sending him to prison. Process that witch and bring her to my chambers. But Warner, *you* bring her."

"Are you sure that's a good idea?"

Griffin remained silent for a moment, debating how to answer. "She came at us on the golf course yesterday. She knows something, and I want to know what that is. Aaron assaulted you. Think about it—"

"I have, and it was stupid of them to do it that way. They could have given you a handwritten note and walked away. They could've set up a meeting with me in my office. Said she knew some psychic shit and wanted to pass on a message. But no, they chose to come at us the way they did. So now we come at them, but even harder."

"I know, I know." Griffin grabbed his scotch glass with his free hand. "What I'm saying is, think about her message. What could she know? But what's more important is how it would ever affect my daughter. Melody is in Europe. Last I heard from her was when she and her new boyfriend were in Rome."

"Rome?"

"Yeah, she sent me a photo of them standing in front of the Coliseum."

Warner was quiet for a second, so Griffin drank from his glass.

"Why me?" Warner asked.

"Why me what?"

"Why should I bring her to your chambers?"

"Because, imbecile, I want you to hear her excuses, her bullshit whining, and pleading. I want you to hear who put her up to it. You'll get the recognition for making the arrest and obtaining her confession, too."

"Fine, but her lawyer will have a field day with that."

"Fuck due process on this. She threatened my daughter yesterday, then attacked the Nate family and murdered the mother. Everyone will understand my motivation to question her myself."

"We'll be there inside thirty minutes."

"Don't bring that boyfriend, Stevens guy—just her. Put him in a holding cell with whoever else you have down there. He can sweat it out with some of Sommers's gang members."

"Way ahead of you. I'm transferring several tough guys to the large cell, and I've spread the word that Aaron hates tattoos."

"Tell the guards that no one dies, well, not yet anyway. A few weeks in the infirmary never hurt anybody, though." Griffin emptied his glass in one swig, then placed it on his desk, knocking over the picture of his wife. She may have left him, but he still pined for her.

"My thinking exactly. After what Aaron did to my wrist yesterday, I'll be off my golf game for a few weeks—"

"Excuses!" Griffin jumped in, laughing.

"I'll enjoy chatting with him in the infirmary, listing all his charges to him—"

"Warner, just get it done. I'm waiting in my chambers."

"Be there shortly."

Griffin hung up and poured one more shot, then called the court clerk and canceled the rest of the docket for the day. He'd still see the Sommers case, but that was it.

It was the milk he consumed, he claimed. Something upset his stomach.

He'd be back to a hundred percent tomorrow. He was sure of it.

He just needed that Sarah bitch arraigned and remanded into custody until her court date in a year.

Yeah, he'd feel a whole lot better by tomorrow.

# Chapter 17

WHEN HEATHER WAS DONE talking, Bruce felt sorry for her.

"You're pathetic, you know that." He shook his head. "I should shoot you both on principle, just because."

"Hey, now." Sam raised a hand for calm.

"Don't *hey now* me." Bruce brought the weapon up to point at Sam's face.

When Sam recoiled and turned away, Bruce slowly lowered the gun.

"Did you even hear yourself?" Bruce asked Heather. "You blamed everyone but yourself. You owned none of your actions. It was your mom's fault, your dad's fault, the abuse you received as a child, and you even blamed your first boyfriend, who took your virginity when you were twelve."

Bruce pushed up off the couch and moved to the balcony doors, keeping them in his peripheral vision.

"Okay," Heather whispered. "You're right. I have to own this."

He averted his gaze to look at them. They were holding hands now, and something about that cut through him.

"Sam had nothing to do with this," Heather continued. "I came up with the plan to give him the DNA of my wealthiest clients and set it up to appear like they were a match for my baby." Heather placed a hand on her belly.

"Are you even pregnant?" Bruce asked.

They both looked up at him, then nodded.

"Call girls have boyfriends." She wiped a tear. "We're still human.

We still want love. Clients don't understand that, nor do I tell them. Seeing someone like me is a fantasy. If they thought that I sucked ten other dicks that day, they wouldn't want to see me."

"You're right." Bruce turned away again. "When we were seeing each other, I knew you saw other men, but I didn't think about it. The way you made me feel, though ..." he drifted off. "You must've made all your clients feel the same way."

"It's part of the fantasy. But then Sam and I were getting serious." They were staring at each other again when Bruce faced them. "We talked about the future, marriage, and kids. Then we talked about money." Heather wiped her face to rid herself of the wetness on her cheeks. "I was clearing over ten grand a month working part-time. We couldn't just walk away from that sort of cash, but we'd decided I had to quit."

"So you came up with the extortion plan?" Bruce's tone had hardened, and he didn't mind—the anger had to go somewhere.

"That's too harsh a word, but okay." Heather glanced down at the couch, picked something off the cushion, and then flicked it aside. "We devised a plan to bring in three or more years' worth of income before the baby was born. That way, we'd start with a leg up."

"However illegal and immoral that was."

Heather nodded, not looking up. "And we regret that now."

"Bullshit," Bruce shouted. "If you regretted it, you'd have called, apologized, and returned my money. You're only saying *regret* because I'm the one holding the gun."

Sam appealed for calm with his hands again, raising and lowering them. "Please, she's pregnant. Let's all try to be civil."

"Civil?" Bruce spat the word. "You want civil after what you did to me, to others?" He fixed his glare on Heather. "I don't even know you anymore."

She met his gaze. "To be fair, you never really *knew* me. You knew the call girl, me."

"Oh, right. Of course." Bruce threw up his hands.

"Heather," Sam said, a pleading tone to his voice. "I've worked with guys like him before. Remember my dad? Please, don't further upset him."

"Upset me? Oh, boy, you two! I'm way past upset, you fucker. I'm royally pissed off. I think if Heather weren't pregnant, I'd shoot you both and be done with it. And what's this about your dad?"

Sam's color drained, which made Bruce feel marginally better.

"Do you know who my dad is?" Sam asked.

Bruce waved him off. "I don't care who your dad is. Fuck that. Last question, then you can go get me my fifteen thousand." He rubbed his face. "No idea why I'm still willing to leave five grand on the table. Maybe I'm a nice guy after all."

"What's the question?" Heather asked, her tone soft and caring, like back when they were in bed together, and she'd ask what position he preferred.

"How many men have you done this to?"

Heather glanced at Sam.

"Don't look at him," Bruce snapped. "Look at me. Tell me the number."

Heather refocused on Bruce. "I mostly chose men who could afford to cover the abortion, which I never intended to get. I went after men who could afford to pay for my pain and suffering, too."

"Right. I get that." He swallowed, his mouth gone dry. "How many?"

"Twenty."

Bruce raised his hands to rub at his temples, the Smith & Wesson bumping his cheek hard. "Shit," he mumbled. "Twenty."

Heather and Sam sat on their couch, smug and scared but likely laughing on the inside. They'd move on to have their baby, and the DNA specialist would build a career and provide for them. They were set. They were ready for their life to begin. They were in love, something he always wanted but never found. Women were always too bitchy for him.

Now he was single, and he'd lost his favorite call girl.

But that wasn't just it, was it?

He'd lost twenty thousand bucks, too.

"How much did the others pay you?"

"Now, now," Sam said. "What does that matter?"

"How? Much?" Bruce spoke low, rumbling the words through his teeth, his gut roiling at the thought of what they'd done to so many unsuspecting men.

"About the same as you—"

"How *much*?" he roared, leaning forward to shout at Sam.

"A couple of hundred thousand in total."

That was a sobering thought. Bruce leaned against the glass door to his right and took in that number, whistling once.

"If it makes you feel any better, you paid the least amount," Heather said.

"Who paid the most?" Like on autopilot, Bruce asked the question in a daze.

Sam looked at Heather, but she kept her eyes on Bruce.

"A wealthy man from Toronto. Owns towers, buildings, or something."

"A man with a family?"

Heather nodded. "Three kids. He paid without question. The kind of man who would never *not* pay. Too much risk, too much to lose."

"He could never have this scheme made public, could he?"

Heather shook her head.

"And that's just one of what? Twenty?"

Heather's head stopped moving. "More than twenty."

"Heather," Sam whispered, caution in his voice.

"What?" she snapped at him, pulling her hand away. "What did Bruce ever do to us? He was one of my best customers, and we've hurt him. The least we can do is offer him the truth he's asking for."

"And my twenty grand," Bruce whispered.

Sam looked up. "You said fifteen. You said Heather could keep five of it."

"I changed my mind. I want nothing to do with the two of you. I want to erase the memories, and I don't want to leave anything behind. Not a single thing, not a single dollar. You've got hundreds of thousands. You don't need my measly five grand."

"Okay," Heather said. "I understand. Just give us a few days to withdraw that amount from the bank—"

"Fuck that. I'm not leaving until you hand it all over in cash."

They exchanged a look between them, then they both stared at him. "Bruce, we don't carry more than a few hundred dollars on us at any given time."

Bruce waved the gun in Sam's direction. "You know what you're in for, don't you? Hooking up with this one?"

"What, what—"

"A lifetime of bullshit and payments."

"Payments?"

Bruce nodded as he grabbed a dining room chair, spun it around to sit on, and rested his arms on the top.

"I learned years ago that every piece of ass has a price. It's never free. Have a girlfriend, and pay emotionally as she tears you down here and there. Get married, pay for it with each check, and then get divorced"—he whistled—"pay for it by leaving everything in her name." He shook his head. "All pussy comes with a price. So, armed with that knowledge, I pay for it by the hour and move on. Tell them to catch a taxi home. Better that way." He shook his head. "Tell me something. What benefits do men get from marriage? Huh?"

Sam and Heather stared at him from ten feet away, Heather's legs shaking back and forth like she had to pee.

"Nothing," Bruce continued. "Women, conversely, get several things like security, protection, money, whatever. But men get nothing from marriage—actually, less than nothing." He chuckled at his own wisdom. "Once a woman is married, sex drops off; she needs money, and she's out with her girlfriends all the time." He spun to look at them; his reverie ended. "You," he pointed the gun at Sam again, jerking it back and forth like a finger, "you will pay for it for the rest of your life, my friend."

Bruce pushed upward and got back to his feet. "But not me, and not with her." He pointed at Heather now, and Sam leaned over to block her from the gun's aim. "Aww, isn't that special? What if the gun was fired by accident? Look at that, Heather. He'd be willing to take a bullet for you." Bruce lowered his gun hand so it aimed at the floor. "Don't worry, and don't insult me. My finger is on the trigger guard. I would never discharge my pistol by accident. I'm hurt, devastated at what you two did to me, but I'd never hurt Heather."

Bruce shook his head in disgust.

"You know, you people really piss me off. I don't even want to be around you. I need out of here. But I'm not leaving until I have twenty grand in my hand, so conjure it up from thin air. I don't care." He moved closer, then glared at Heather. "I paid for my sessions. You got tipped, too. I refuse to leave any more money in your filthy palms. You don't get to name any price and hoodwink me"—he slapped his chest—"*me* into handing it over. We're done here. Get me my money, or I'll start shooting people. Up to you."

"Bruce," Sam said, his hand raised, palm out. "Please, we'll get you the money. Maybe we can PayPal it or wire it. But please, taking twenty large out at the bank teller window will raise questions."

Bruce raised the weapon, slipped his finger inside the trigger guard, and pulled it back, aiming precisely where he wanted.

The weapon fired, hitting his target like a dart to a bullseye.

Heather screamed.

# Chapter 18

JUDGE GRIFFIN WAS ON his fourth scotch and thinking about one more for the road when he considered slowing down. Once Warner brought that witch to his chambers, he would nap in his office to take the edge off. His colleagues thought he wasn't feeling well, so that would make sense. Tomorrow was another day, one he'd face knowing this Sarah Roberts business was concluded.

They were powerful men. What made her think she could waltz into their town, threaten them, and kill a mother of two children?

"Who do you think you are?" he muttered to himself, hearing the slight slur in his voice.

They'd be there at any moment. He needed water. His mouth had gone pasty.

He wandered over to the office fridge under the side shelves, snatched a water bottle from the interior, and drank from it thirstily.

A knock on the door startled him, making him gasp and choke on the water. He coughed with vigor to clear his throat as the door opened.

Warner hustled across the judge's chamber floor and patted his back.

Griffin waved him off, holding up the water bottle. "Wrong"—he coughed, but it sounded more like a hack—"tube."

When he righted himself, he was staring at Sarah Roberts, flanked by two officers at his open door. He thought he recognized one of the men, but it didn't matter. His attention was on the witch.

Her hands were cuffed, and a chain was connected to two thick clasps around her ankles. She hadn't been processed yet, as she was still in civilian clothes.

"Leave us," Griffin said.

The officers frowned until the one on the right said, "But, sir—"

"You heard what Judge Griffin said," Warner shouted. "I've got the prisoner. Wait outside in the hall until I return her to you."

The men in uniform glanced at one another, then backed away and stepped outside the office. The door closed softly behind Sarah.

She hadn't taken her eyes off them. "You have nothing on me," she said. "This mistake," she raised the cuffs, making them rattle loudly in the office, "will be the end of you two."

"More threats," Griffin said, a smile playing on his lips. He moved to his desk chair. Better to be sitting for this. "You're in no position." He plopped down in his chair.

Warner watched him for a moment, his gaze wary, then faced Sarah. "What the judge means is you're in no position to be issuing threats to a criminal justice of the peace or the chief of police. You're the one in a lot of trouble, young lady."

Her smirk irritated Griffin. He wanted to smack it off her face.

"Funny, I see it completely differently," she said.

Griffin listened to them and watched them, holding his tongue. He drank heartily from the rest of the water bottle, coughed once more, then set the empty bottle in front of him.

"How do you see it, witch?" Griffin asked, the booze affecting his tongue.

Sarah gestured toward the two-seater couch on her right. "May I?"

Griffin waved in the direction of the sofa and nodded. "By all means."

Sarah shuffled toward it, the chains clinking, adjusted herself so the restraints were lined up in front of her, then eased downward.

Warner spun one of Griffin's visitor chairs around and took a seat. "Now that we're all comfy, tell us—how do you see your predicament?"

"We met at the golf course." Sarah eyed them both, her gaze roaming back and forth. When neither spoke, she continued. "I told you to stop what you were doing as it would have a ripple effect and hurt your daughter."

"And?" Warner tapped his fingers on his thigh.

Griffin saw the man's hand moving, but kept his eyes on the witch.

"And you tried to place your hands on Aaron, so he defended himself."

Warner laughed. "Is that what you'll tell the court? Aaron restraining me was self-defense?"

"The Nate family situation will play itself out," Sarah said. "Once those kids are processed, and everyone learns what their parents were doing and allowing to be done to them, no jury would worry that we put a stop to it."

Now Warner was shaking his head. He turned back to Griffin.

Griffin couldn't shake the grin Sarah's words were causing in him.

"Are you hearing this?" Warner asked Griffin.

The judge nodded. "Every damn word."

There was a glint of something in Sarah's eyes for a brief moment. Was that fear? Or anger? Did anything scare this woman?

Warner turned back around, and Griffin waited. This was Warner's beast to slay.

"You put a stop to the abuse of the Nate children, all right. I mean, what were you thinking?"

Sarah frowned, tilting her head slightly. "Would you have us do something different? Like, call in an anonymous tip?" Sarah shook her head. "They'd have covered it up again. CAS is a waste of time up here in Northern Ontario. They're uneducated and untrained. In most cases, they're complete assholes. Not all, I'll admit, but most."

"And you know this how?"

It was Sarah's turn to smile. "Sometimes, I just know stuff."

Griffin cleared his throat. "Like how you just happen to know something about us?"

"Yeah. Like that."

"What do you know?"

She lifted her shoulders, then dropped them. "It's not *what* I know. It's more *that* I know you're taking money for verdicts. Even one person knowing is enough for you to stop. By stopping, I go home, and your family is safe. No one will need to know anything else. Just stop, retire, whatever, and we all move on." Sarah paused, clasping her cuffed hands together. "Or don't stop, and Melody—I think that's your daughter's name—has to deal with the consequences."

Griffin slapped the top of his desk. "Don't speak my daughter's name again."

"Melody is a nice name," Sarah said, looking genuinely confused. "Why don't you like the sound of it?"

Griffin shoved his chair back but stopped when Warner jumped to his feet and raised a cautionary arm.

"Everyone, calm down," Warner said, moving in front of Griffin's desk to momentarily block his view of Sarah. "Remember, this woman is here on a murder charge. She'll be in our system until she's as old as the wig she used, so there's lots of time to hear everything—"

Sarah laughed loudly and with enthusiasm. If her hands weren't cuffed, Griffin thought she'd be slapping her leg, too.

"What's so funny?" Warner asked, his neck reddening by his collar.

"You guys," Sarah gasped. "Murder?" She chuckled again, but quieter. "Who's dead? Hmm? Who did I kill?"

"Edna Nate, the mother of those kids last night."

Sarah's laugh died as she stared at them. "The paper said it was suicide. How could you possibly spin that to be murder?"

Warner was shaking his head, and Griffin studied Sarah's face, watching for the reaction when Warner told her.

"That suicide story was fake. She was murdered."

"What? How?"

"A kitchen knife to the femoral artery. She bled to death in minutes, still duct-taped to the fridge door. She didn't do it to herself."

Sarah stared at nothing for a moment, likely working out the details. Then she blinked and glanced back at them.

"We tied her up so she wouldn't run until the authorities got there."

"Tied her up and cut her. Who did it? You?"

"No one cut her."

"We have Joseph's statement. He described you and your wig, Parkman, Aaron, and Alex. You're all facing life without parole for the murder of Edna Nate."

Sarah gaped at them for a moment. "Of course, you'd believe that monster over us. Glad it doesn't matter what you believe. We have a right to a fair trial, although it'll never get to that." She shook her head and seemed to be thinking something over. "How did Joseph make it to her? He had to have crawled."

"What's that?" Warner asked. "Speak up."

"His knees."

Warner nodded. "We know. A hammer to his kneecaps. They'll both need replacing."

"We left him at the base of the couch in so much pain, I don't know how he didn't pass out. How did he get to Edna? Where'd he get the knife from?"

"Nice story, Sarah, but that's not how the crown attorney will see it. Especially when we pull your prints from the knife."

Her eyes snapped to attention. "I didn't touch any knives."

"You left the Bible behind."

"And?"

"Your prints are on the Bible."

"Your point?"

"When we lift those prints, it'll be labeled as coming off the knife handle."

They stared at each other for a long moment.

Warner continued. "Edna and Joseph's prints are expected on that knife. It was from their kitchen. But yours? Well, that's painting a picture."

"One that's untrue."

"We'll see how the jury takes it."

Griffin raised a finger. "Unless you opt for a judge during the trial. The choice will be yours."

"Don't you see what's happening here?" Sarah asked.

Neither man spoke.

"Joseph had to kill Edna," Sarah went on. "He couldn't have her testifying against him or leaving anything damaging in a statement."

"Then why would he call the police himself?" Warner asked.

"For a police chief, I'd expect more. You're such a fucking idiot."

Sarah rattled her chains by lifting her hands and then setting them back down. "What else was he to do? How else could he cover up the murder of his wife? She was already talking. She's the one who gave us the code to the shed."

"Code to the shed?"

Sarah told them about the shed behind the house, where they had watched from the trees as the authorities arrived and returned.

"Parkman called the police and gave them the code over the phone. If Edna lived, she'd tell the authorities everything. Joseph couldn't have that."

Warner glanced over his shoulder at Griffin. "Are you listening to this?"

Griffin nodded, and his world spun for a moment—too much scotch —way too much.

"Parkman will testify he called it in," Sarah added. "They record those calls. The court will hear his voice. No matter how you spin this, it all comes up smelling roses."

Griffin heard her words, but there was a slight tinge of doubt in her tone. She dug a hole too deep to climb out of, and she knew it.

"Your posse was at the Nate house last night," Griffin said, speaking slowly, making sure the scotch didn't manipulate his tongue. "Within minutes of you lot leaving, the father is found on the kitchen floor beside his dead wife. He was in so much pain that emergency personnel didn't know how he hadn't passed out. You broke his knees and killed his wife, then left." Griffin shrugged. "Perhaps the kids were safe from your horrific home invasion because they were found in a shed at the back. Or maybe you don't hurt kids." He stopped to study her face. "If hurting kids isn't your thing, then why come after mine?"

Sarah didn't respond, but her body language spoke volumes. She slouched down onto the sofa, her face expressionless, her eyes not leaving Griffin.

"Why the long face?" Warner asked.

No response.

"That 'you have the right to remain silent' jargon is an American thing. They called it the Miranda Warning. We don't have that in

Canada. You don't have to *remain* silent, Sarah. Feel free to speak up."

Still, Sarah said nothing.

Warner pulled a yellow envelope from inside his jacket pocket, unfolded it, and withdrew photos from inside.

"Well, maybe this'll jar your mouth to start talking." He walked over to the table at her knees and placed photo after photo on the table. Then he pointed at the first of six. "These were taken this morning of the crime scene you left behind. This one is from the kitchen. See the blood?"

Sarah leaned forward and followed Warner's finger.

"See here," he said, "this is where you left the knife. And here," he pointed at another, "is where we found Joseph. You can tell by the marks his pants left in the blood when he dragged himself to the phone."

Sarah lifted her chin in a short nod toward that photo. "And see where there's evidence of Joseph sliding through the blood. We left him by the couch. He dragged himself over and killed his wife."

"We agree that he dragged himself over. But it was to call us."

She sat back and stared at Griffin. "We'll see about that."

Griffin rose to his feet. "What's that supposed to mean?"

"Where's Aaron right now?"

Warner collected the photos, slipped them back inside the envelope, and then moved to place them on Griffin's desk.

"In custody," he said. "He's the least of your concerns."

"Parkman and Alex?"

"In the wind, but we'll get them. It's only a matter of time."

She shook her head and looked off to the right. "Then tell me," she said, staring at the floor.

"Tell you what? Who are you talking to?"

"Shut up." Sarah closed her eyes. "I'm listening to something."

Goosebumps rose on Griffin's arms as he leaned forward at his desk and watched Sarah jerking her head back and forth, her hair falling in her face.

Then she stopped and looked up, peeking through the hair that covered her face, creepy as that was. Hands bound, she was unable to brush it out of the way.

"I've had enough of this." Warner moved toward the door.

"Wait," Sarah shouted.

Warner stopped halfway and glanced back at Griffin, who nodded.

"Let's hear what she has to say before she rots in prison for a hundred years."

Sarah's eyes were filled with something like hatred now. Or was it madness? Something had changed in her.

Griffin adjusted himself in his chair, unsettled by her intensity.

"You've set Aaron up," she said.

"What?" Warner looked at Griffin again, then back to Sarah. "What could you possibly be talking about?"

"Gang members. Holding cell. I see it all."

"Sure, a holding cell often contains gang members." Warner shrugged. "What's it to you?"

"No. You set it up."

There was a moment of silence. Then Warner moved toward the door again. "More wasted time. As I said, I've had enough of this."

Before he reached the door, Sarah said, "If anything happens to Aaron, I won't help with Bruce. And Melody is on her own."

"Wait!" Griffin shouted as Warner's hand was on the doorknob.

Warner eased back from the door.

Griffin got to his feet. "What about Bruce?"

"You've got some sway in this courthouse." Her bottom lip extended outward as she blew upward to remove the hair from her face. All it did was lift it momentarily before it dropped back into the same spot. "Bring Aaron here."

Griffin walked around his desk and marched across his office floor, suddenly feeling quite sober.

Warner stepped in front of him before he got to Sarah. "We can't harm her while she's in a judge's chambers."

Griffin let Warner hold him back as he glared at her. "What are you not telling me?"

"How fucked you are."

Griffin pushed off Warner, then stepped back. "Get her out of here before I strangle her, and you're looking for a place to dump the body."

Warner jumped at the door, ripped it open, and ordered the officers to take Sarah back to the holding cell to be processed.

Griffin only faintly heard Warner and the officers behind him as he ran back to his desk, snatched up his cell phone, and dialed Bruce's number.

It rang five times and went to voicemail.

He dialed again.

There was no answer.

He waited a moment, then tried once more.

Nothing.

# Chapter 19

TWELVE MEN SHARED THE same large holding cell, each claiming a spot to sit or lie down. No one seemed to care about anyone else in there, each man keeping to himself.

Except for the four men who seemed to be together. They all wore the same black T-shirt, and they all had tattoos in one place or another; two of them had leather vests on.

Without being obvious, Aaron watched them to determine who their leader was in case they became an issue. They gave themselves away like any pack animal, lounging around their alpha, laughing when he told a joke, grunting or groaning to impress him.

Aaron closed his eyes and listened to the room. It gave him time to think about their situation and how they could extricate themselves from it. Overall, what was the worst they'd done? He assaulted the police chicf, and they broke into that house last night. If anything were to stick, it would be an assault charge on the police chief.

Last night wasn't exactly a *break-in*. Sarah was invited inside, then she called for help as that man came after her. It was third-party self-defense. Ask any jury to convict them on anything after they found out what was happening at the house, and they'd be sent home with an apology and a thank you.

Even wounding the father was a version of third-party self-defense. It had to be. They were defending children who couldn't stand up for themselves.

The coffee shop meeting today went off without an issue.

So file the charges, they'll sign a promise to appear, or whatever they call it nowadays, and come back to North Bay in a year. What could be the big deal?

Something bumped his feet.

He jerked, eyes opening, hands up. He must've been drifting off because he hadn't noticed how quiet the holding cell had become.

Officers weren't roaming the hallways either.

All twelve men were alone in the cell, seven of them up against the bars, far from him.

And the four gang members were now staring down at him.

"What's up?" he asked, lowering his hands. "You startled me awake. Find another spot to sit."

They laughed in response, but the leader didn't move. "Get up."

"You got a key?"

The leader frowned, and his bushy eyebrows knitted together when he did.

"A key?" Unibrow asked.

"If you don't have the key to that door, and we aren't leaving this shitty cell, then I'm sleeping until you do." Aaron adjusted himself on the bench, placed a hand behind his head, and wondered how this would play out—a likely scenario already coming together in his mind. "Wake me when you have a key."

Unibrow reared back and drove his fist forward, but Aaron caught the movement and slipped sideways just in time.

Unibrow's knuckles grazed off the wall, then hit the bench where Aaron's head had been a moment before.

Someone wrapped their arms around his legs, but he was able to kick his way out of that as Unibrow came in for him again.

Aaron rolled off the bench, missing several punches aimed at him, then kicked the backs of a man's knees, sending him headlong into the wall.

He shoved Unibrow's feet one way with his right foot and yanked the man's knees forward with a kick from his left foot.

The man crashed onto the bench as Aaron squirmed to the side and got to his feet, still untouched by their blows.

The two men who were still standing ran at him.

He jabbed the throat of the one closest, then clotheslined the other.

Both men dropped hard, the throat guy clutching at his neck, choking.

Unibrow was the first back to his feet, blood now dripping from the torn skin over his knuckles.

"You're a dead man," Unibrow muttered.

"If I had a dollar …" Aaron drifted off.

Unibrow ran at him like a rugby player, ready to tackle him to the concrete floor.

It was easy to spin on his heels and let the man run right by him. What wasn't as easy was seeing one of his men come up behind him with a shot to the lower back—he'd missed that.

Aaron grunted, arching his back, and turned to see a fist inches from his jaw—too late. He couldn't avoid it, either.

It felt like a rock collided with his cheek. It'd been a long time since he'd taken a shot to the face, and the intensity of the pain surprised him.

He heard Unibrow grunting, footsteps pounding behind him, so he sidestepped, still holding his jaw.

The leader missed him, running into the man who had just punched his jaw. They were able to stay on their feet, but barely.

Then, the leader raised his fists and gestured for Aaron to fight him.

"C'mon," he said. "One on one."

Aaron lifted his hands and got into his fighting stance.

This was going to be too easy. The pain in his jaw woke him—an equivalent of several energy drinks—and angered him to a comfortable level.

They moved in circles, each man taking a swing at the other.

After waiting until the right time, Aaron stepped in, extended his left hand to shove the man's fists downward while bringing his right hand up and smacking the man's face. Then he jumped back. As soon as his opponent drove forward again, he kicked into the man's stomach area, and as the stomach blow made the man lean forward, collapsing over the gut shot, Aaron elbowed one side of the man's face, then extended his arm to punch the other side.

Everyone else in the holding cell had given them ample room, but now, someone was yelling for them to stop.

Bars rattled.

The cavalry was here.

Arms grabbed Aaron and yanked him backward as uniformed officers pulled the leader away.

"Enough," a man shouted. "Step off."

Another man stepped in front of Aaron and pointed at him. "Take him upstairs to his own holding cell."

Aaron was dragged from the area, but not before he looked back and caught a glimpse of the officers releasing the gang members.

They were whispering to each other.

Like they knew each other.

# Chapter 20

BRUCE HAD GRABBED TEA towels from a drawer in the kitchen and wrapped Sam's hand with two of them. They'd have to change them soon, as blood was already soaking through.

"Why'd you shoot me in the hand?" Sam's voice was weakened by pain. "I need a hospital."

"Bruce, please." Heather was shaking as she tried wrapping another towel around Sam's hand. "We're in an apartment building. Someone was bound to hear that gunshot."

"You think I fucking care?" Bruce got up to pace in front of them. "Press charges. Have me arrested. My dad's the fucking judge in these parts. Besides, wait until *everyone* hears why I'm here. How you embezzled money out of me and another twenty guys at least. You'll be in much more shit than me."

"Okay, okay, we won't say anything." Heather exhaled as the towel dropped out of Sam's hand. She tried again with a new one. "The bleeding isn't stopping. This can't be good." She spun to face Bruce. "Listen, you have to let us take him to a hospital. If he bleeds out ..."

"Yeah, right. A hospital. Where the law states they have to call the police for bullet wounds. No fucking way. Stop the bleeding or die. See if I care."

"That's not the Bruce I know talking," Heather said. "What happened to you?"

He stopped pacing and glared at her. "*You don't know me*," he shouted.

"Why the hand, man?" Sam said, his head back on the couch, face aimed upward. "Do you know who my dad is?" The man had gone as white as fresh snow, and Bruce suspected he was about to pass out.

"Your dad? The fuck I care who your dad is? You kept waving your hands around like an idiot." Bruce shook his head. "It was annoying. And you're some DNA guy, right? I mean, you work in a lab or something. So, you have to use your hands." He shrugged. "Now, the scars I gave you will always remind you of the guy you tried to fuck. Hey," they both looked at him, "next time, kiss me when you fuck me."

Bruce cocked his head at the sound of a siren.

He ran over to the balcony door, unlocked it, slid it aside, and hopped out onto the balcony. Four stories below, he saw two cruisers screech into the parking lot, their lights rotating but their sirens off. The sirens he was hearing were three more cruisers coming up Lakeshore— he could see them from the elevated perch of the balcony.

A breeze picked up, cooling his forehead and reminding him how much he'd sweat into his shirt.

"Shit," he muttered. His father would be pissed.

Then his cell phone rang in his jacket pocket. He grabbed it and saw it was his dad calling.

*What the fuck? Could he already know?*

Bruce turned back to go inside Heather's apartment, then glanced over and saw the empty couch.

"Motherfucker," he shouted.

The apartment door was open.

He bolted for it, his gun still in his hand.

His money was running away. How could they do that? Steal from him, and when he caught them, they ran—even though they had ample resources to pay him back.

In the hallway, he caught the stairwell door just closing.

His phone rang again as he took off running. He shouldered into the stairwell door, then stopped to listen. Below, the sound of footsteps descending and voices whispering emanated up to him.

"Where's my money?" he shouted, taking the stairs two at a time, jumping down at each level.

By the time he reached the second floor, he saw them halfway to the first, Heather keeping Sam upright.

"Stop," he shouted, then aimed and fired into the concrete wall.

Heather ducked as chips of concrete debris fell behind them.

But they didn't stop.

Then, they were through the door on the first floor.

And his phone was ringing again.

"*Fuck!*" he shouted in pure frustration, then dropped down to the first-floor door as it was still closing. He ripped it open and jumped through—only to be greeted by four officers, their hands up, each aiming a gun at him.

"Drop it!" one of them shouted.

Behind the uniformed men, he caught sight of Heather's hair as she turned the corner and pushed Sam ahead of her into the main lobby by the mailbox room.

Then they were gone from sight.

It was over.

For now.

Bruce opened his hand and released the gun. It dropped harmlessly to the carpeted floor beside him.

"Take it easy, guys. Do you know who my dad is—?"

"Lie down," the officer shouted. "On your stomach. Hands on your head."

He did as he was told.

Heather and Sam would pay for this. When his dad got him out of jail, they'd pay, which wouldn't just be money now. He'd get his pound of flesh, too, because he'd tell everyone everything about their little extortion scheme.

No one would press charges on Bruce Griffin. He'd get his twenty thousand bucks back, and his dad would pat him on the back for standing up for himself.

His damn phone was ringing in his pocket again as they slapped the cuffs on too tightly.

"Hey, man," he protested. "Take it easy."

They yanked him to his feet by his arms and slammed him into the wall. The pain was immediate, making him moan. It felt like his shoulders had been ripped off.

"Apologies," the officer said, his tone anything but sorry. "Lost my balance there. Let's hope I don't lose my balance again, asshole."

They half-carried him, half-dragged him out to the cruisers.

"You know you were chasing a pregnant woman, right?" the cop asked.

"How would you know she was pregnant? She's not showing yet."

The cop opened the back door to the cruiser and turned Bruce into position to frisk him.

"You got anything sharp in your pockets that'll prick me? Anything I should know about?"

"Tell me how you knew, asshole. You were a client of that whore, weren't you? You fucked her, too. I can tell. A pig fucking a whore."

The man frisked him roughly, then shoved him inside the cruiser.

"Your dad won't be able to get you out of this one. You'll probably be the reason for his early retirement, dickstain."

The cop slammed the door and sauntered away.

That cop would pay for speaking to him like that. He'd get his badge number and name, and then see about getting a nice new desk job somewhere.

Nobody pushed Bruce Griffin around.

Nobody.

# Chapter 21

THE MEETING WITH SARAH enraged him. He had been on the bench for a long time. In his court, he would've declared her in contempt. He would've easily given her thirty days and a fine for that level of disrespect.

*How fucked you are*—her last words to him.

He eyed the bottle of scotch, then went to the fridge for another water. After drinking half of it back, he opened Messenger on his phone and hit the call button for Melody.

It rang and rang until he disconnected the call.

"Where the fuck are my kids?" he mumbled to himself.

Someone knocked on the door.

"Enter," he shouted.

Police Chief Warner stepped inside, waited for the door to close, then leaned against the wall.

"What's up now? You look defeated. It doesn't suit you."

"You're not going to believe this."

"Lay it on me." Griffin picked up a pen and idly tapped the tip on his desk calendar.

"Aaron Stevens got into a fight with four gang members in the large holding cell."

"And? Is he in the infirmary? Please tell me they broke a few bones."

Warner shook his head. "Other than one punch to the face, he hasn't got a scratch on him. The other four guys didn't fare so well."

Griffin stopped tapping the pen. "What?"

"What, as in you didn't hear me? Or what, as in, you can't believe it?"

Griffin dropped the pen. "How is that possible? What kind of gang members were they? With a Teletubbies gang, or maybe a purple Barney club or something?"

"We might have underestimated Sarah's group. We can't find Parkman or Alex. They've gone to ground. And anything we throw at Aaron, it's deflected."

"Then throw more."

Warner moved farther inside the office. "There's only so much we can do without drawing attention to ourselves."

Griffin lowered his head and rubbed his eyes. "You're right. And if they're going to be in the system for decades, we have plenty of time to ruin their lives."

"Exactly."

"Where are they now?"

"They're in their own individual holding cells at the moment. On this floor."

"Good. Leave them there until tomorrow. Oh, and Warner, I get their cases. They sit before me."

"That's not going to happen since it was you, Sarah, who threatened."

"Then charge them for the Nate murder and home invasion only. Leave my name out of it."

"You'd be willing to forget what happened at the golf course?" Warner sounded surprised.

"Of course." Griffin gave him a stern look. "Wouldn't you if it meant I'm presiding over their case?"

Warner seemed to contemplate that a moment. "I suppose so."

"Oh, come on. Don't let your bruised ego get in the way of true justice. The years I can give him for murder are way better than what's allowable by law for hurting your little wrist."

Warner bristled at that comment. Color rose above his collar, and he crossed his arms.

"I'll get it all done, but they will lawyer up soon. Their story will come out, and the others'll substantiate it."

"In my courtroom, what I say goes, and what I say is that Sarah's lawyer didn't instill any reasonable doubt. She's guilty, Aaron's guilty, and there's no two ways about it."

Warner nodded and turned to leave, but stopped when his cell phone rang.

He took the call at the door.

"Hello." He paused and stared at Griffin. "Yeah, I'm right here with him." Another pause. "I see. Okay, I'll tell him." He hung up.

Warner's redness around the collar dissipated quickly and was replaced by a sickly white as he moved to stand on the other side of Judge Griffin's large desk.

"What? Tell me, what is it now?"

"That was Officer Hanover. He wanted to let me know that they have your son, Bruce, in custody downstairs."

Griffin shot forward in his chair so fast he bumped his knee on the desk and winced.

"What the hell for?"

"He shot a man. Officers found Bruce with the gun in his hand, still chasing the guy he shot as a pregnant woman helped him escape."

"This is a joke." Griffin shot his hands up in the air. "This is a fucking joke! You gotta be bloody well kidding me." His voice cracked. "Take me to him. *Now!*"

# Chapter 22

IT TOOK ANOTHER HALF hour before anyone came for Sarah again. In that time, Vivian gave her a brief version of what was happening and what was coming.

It was not appealing, like bad weather, but they'd endure somehow.

"Sarah Roberts," a woman officer said. "Please come with us."

Two male officers flanked her while the female cop led them back to the judge's chambers. Of course, they were headed back there. Judge Griffin was confused about what Sarah knew and didn't know, and couldn't have her out there with information potentially damaging him.

There was that, plus his son would've been arrested by now.

After a short walk through the police station attached to the courthouse, the female officer knocked on the judge's door.

A distinctive "Enter!" could be heard through the door, and then it was opened from the inside.

The female officer waved for Sarah to go inside, so she shuffled in, the chains rattling with each step.

The judge was behind his desk, the chief of police was in the office chair, and the judge's son, Bruce Griffin, was handcuffed in the other chair.

"It's been a while," Sarah said as the door closed behind her, and she sat on the two-seater sofa at the back.

"Cut the bullshit," Griffin said. "Just tell us what you want."

She offered them all a wide grin. "Justice," she said in a breathy voice. "We're all on the same team. We all want justice, don't we?"

"Don't flatter yourself." Warner got to his feet and walked around behind his chair. "A lot has happened since we met at the golf course yesterday."

Sarah nodded once. "A lot indeed."

"Seems like you rolled into town, and the shit came with you."

She lifted one shoulder. "You could say that, but it wouldn't be true." She nodded at each one of them. "The shit was already here."

"You are one sassy lady," Judge Griffin said. "A mouth like yours never lasts in a courtroom."

She fixed him with a cocky smirk. "That's why I don't talk much in courtrooms." She rested her back on the couch. "What I meant was you were already doing your dealings with Warner here, which is shit. And Bruce was being extorted, which is also shit. So, the *shit* was already here. Generally speaking, people are shitty at being decent human beings. I just came to help, then leave. I'm innocent in all this ... shit."

Griffin was tapping a pen on his desk now, his lips in a firm line. "Bruce showed me the photo of you on his phone. He took it at the coffee shop a few hours ago. That and an off-duty cop recognized you. So, you were arrested at that coffee shop, which places you with my son. Without that photo, all we had was an arrest location. Tying you to Bruce could explain why he went temporarily insane and chased his ex-girlfriend."

Sarah scoffed so violently that her lips fluttered. "Is that what he told you? Ex-girlfriend?" She stared at Bruce.

"Well," Bruce looked at Sarah, then back to his dad. "They do call it a GFE."

Griffin frowned. "As in girlfriend experience?"

Bruce lowered his eyes. "It'll come out eventually."

"You were seeing a *hooker*?" Griffin's voice rose with each word. "And you got her pregnant?"

"No!" Bruce's voice shot up. "She's pregnant, but it's not mine."

"Oh, right." Griffin threw the pen he was tapping across the room. "That extortion shit Sarah told you about."

"She was right, too. Heather was extorting me, along with a bunch of other men." Bruce grunted with indignation. "At least I was stepping up, doing the right thing."

"C'mon, guys," Warner jumped in. "Deal with this at home. There are bigger fish to fry here."

They all eyed each other for a long moment, the silence becoming palpable.

"So." The judge clasped his hands together on his desk and scrutinized Sarah's face. "What is it you want?"

"I've got what I want."

"And that is?"

"Everyone where they're supposed to be."

"For what?"

"You'll see."

"Oh," he sneered down his nose at her, "drop the psychic bitch stuff."

Warner pushed off the chair he was leaning on and moved to the window. Bruce followed him with his gaze until the judge got up from his chair.

He moved over to Warner and whispered something to him, and then they both looked at Sarah.

"It seems you don't respond well to threats."

Sarah shook her head in the negative.

"So, let's move in another direction."

"Sure." Sarah gave them a brief toothy smile, then a long face.

"We'll drop all charges, but you leave town."

"Hmmm." Sarah tilted her head upward as if thinking about it.

"But you remain silent. Speak of these antics to no one. If we hear one word, the Edna Nate case reopens, and you're our candidate for murder."

"So you believe we left Edna alive when we exited that house?"

The judge waved his hands as if an annoying fly was buzzing around near his chest.

"Stop with the theatrics. We know Parkman's voice will be matched to the recording at 9-1-1. We know Edna's husband had a motive to silence her. We aren't stupid." Now, he jabbed his forefinger to punctuate his following words. "But we control the law in this town. If we want you to go down for murder, then you go down for murder."

Bruce spun from Sarah to his father. "What are you saying, Dad?"

"Oh, shut up." Griffin looked positively upset with his son, as if he were twelve years old again and in trouble for a neighborhood slight. "I've been running North Bay since before you were born, and nothing is going to change now."

"And that's the issue," Sarah added.

"What?" Griffin shouted. "Say it again."

"I said," Sarah raised her voice, "and that's the issue."

"Oh yeah, little girl, how so?"

"The people you're fucking with are powerful." She let that sink in. When no one responded immediately, she added, "More powerful than you."

Warner stepped away from the window and scoffed. "I'm the chief of police, and this is a senior judge." He shook his head. "No one's more powerful than us around here."

Sarah pursed her lips and waited. They had time—thirty minutes at least before all hell broke loose.

"Dad, what's this all about?" Bruce had spun completely around on his chair to stare up at his father.

"This witch is saying that your sister is in trouble if I let a certain verdict swing one way or the other."

Bruce fixed his gaze on Sarah. "Then listen to her. She knew everything about Heather." He glanced at her, then back to his dad. "If she *knows* shit like that, then you have to listen to her. She may be trying to save you."

"And why is that, hmm?" Griffin's voice rose a notch. "Why bother?"

"Because this might affect Melody."

Judge Griffin moved closer to his son, leaning toward him while pointing at Sarah. "You think she knows *shit* because she told you about that extortion bid? How do you not know that she isn't in on it? How do you not know that it wasn't her idea, and this Heather whore stopped paying her the fifteen percent cut they agreed on, so Sarah's going after her?" Griffin jerked back so hard that he almost bumped into Warner. "C'mon, son, they're all in it together." He looked at Sarah. "You're a scammer, aren't you? A fucking scammer coming off as a psychic. That's what you do, don't you? Set it all up, then tell people what they want to hear while stealing from them."

The judge returned to his chair, where he dropped into it hard. "Warner, when you draft up the charges, add everything in the criminal code around embezzlement and extortion. Make sure her legal team will take years to come out from under what we're preparing."

"That can and will be done." Warner placed his hands on his hips. "But I still don't get it. Why not warn Bruce, then leave? Why go to the Nate house? And why, oh why, come at us?" He was shaking his head now. "Something doesn't add up. I don't see the financial gain."

"You'll all see what's going on soon enough."

"More cryptic talk." The judge huffed out a heavy sigh. "Take her out of my chambers. Write it up. Process her. All she had to do was agree to stay quiet, and she could go home to her daughter. But no, she had to sit there with that smug look on her face like she won. Well, little girl, we'll see who wins here."

Warner didn't move.

"Warner?" The judge looked over at him. "Did you hear me? Get her out of here."

Warner stared at Sarah a moment longer. "I'm not convinced this is over."

"Well, I am," Griffin's voice thundered. "I want her out of here now, and if you won't do it, I'll call it in." Griffin lifted his phone.

"Set the phone down," Warner said without looking at the judge.

Griffin hesitated for a few seconds, then replaced the receiver.

"Tell us, Sarah," Warner said. "What do you mean by *soon enough*?"

Sarah stared at the three men as they all watched her.

"Your case this afternoon," she said. "Michael Sommers."

The judge frowned. "What about it?"

"Don't skip it."

Warner and Griffin exchanged a glance.

"How did you know about …?" Griffin's words drifted off.

Sarah ignored the question. "And don't do what Mackenzie has paid you to do."

Judge Griffin gasped so loud his son jumped.

Warner's eyes hardened as he stumbled on his feet, then took three large steps back to his chair, where he plopped down.

"How do you know about that?" Griffin said, barely audible.

"The money Mackenzie paid you can be replaced. All the people who will die because of it cannot be replaced. Starting with your daughter."

No one said a word for another entire minute as they let Sarah's words sink in.

"That's impossible," Griffin said finally. "Everything you're saying is impossible. My daughter isn't connected to Mackenzie in any way. This I know."

Sarah nodded. "You're right. Not connected to Mackenzie."

He narrowed his eyes, glaring at her. "Who are you? Who do you work for? How could you know anything about these names, this deal?"

Sarah checked the clock on the wall, then met Judge Griffin's searing stare.

"Bring me Aaron, and I'll tell you."

"Fuck no, fuck that, and fuck you!" Griffin shouted, slamming his hands on the top of his desk. "Tell me who you are!"

Bruce jumped again under the onslaught of his father's rage, but Warner just leaned forward, eager to hear her answer.

"You've heard my terms. Until you meet them, you're the one in danger. Not me."

"I've had enough of this." Griffin shot to his feet. "*Get her out of here!*"

Warner got to his feet and faced the judge. "Shut up," he shouted. "Stop yelling. You're only drawing attention to us." He pointed back at Sarah while still facing Griffin. "Don't you see that she knows *every*thing? We can't send her back. One call to the authorities, the RCMP, her lawyer, and a full investigation would be launched. Just shut up and let me think."

The judge's face screwed up in a seething rage. "When this is all over, we're done, Warner. You don't get to talk to me that way."

"Good, because I can't handle that ego of yours. But one thing is for sure—I'm not going down because you were an asshole. So shut up and think."

"Hurry." Sarah winked at the judge. "Bring me Aaron because we've only got about twenty minutes."

"Twenty minutes for what?"

"Before your world implodes." She waggled a finger between Warner and Griffin. "Both of you."

# Chapter 23

JUDGE GRIFFIN MADE THE call, and Police Chief Warner went to assist in the escort. Just over ten minutes later, Aaron Stevens entered the judge's chambers with Warner.

He nodded at Sarah, then took a seat beside her.

Warner retook his chair.

Everyone was where they were supposed to be, and she hoped Alex and Parkman were where they were supposed to be—not in police custody.

"You managed well." Sarah leaned closer, examining the discoloration on his cheek. "Only one shot to the face."

"There were four of them."

Sarah nodded, then looked at Warner. "You know, that's not a smart play with what we're doing here."

"And what is that? Just what are we doing here?" Griffin asked before Warner could respond.

"We'll get to that."

"I want to know *now*."

"Well, sometimes we don't get what we want, do we?"

"Listen here, young lady—"

"Would you shut up!" Warner spun on Griffin. "Just shut up and let Sarah talk."

Griffin's mouth remained open for a moment, then he closed it and reclined in his chair. Sarah could only imagine the revenge he was plotting on Warner when this was over, but that didn't matter to her. What mattered was that it was coming, whether they liked it or not.

"Bruce." Sarah faced him. "You must remain in custody for a few days."

"Out of the question," Judge Griffin said. "I won't have my son held like a common prisoner because some harlot tried to extort money from him, and all he did was go to get it back. The gun went off by accident. It was self-defense. I don't care how the picture is painted, but my son is at home, in his own bed tonight. Non-negotiable."

Sarah sighed. "If I had known how thick-headed you would be, I might've told my sister I wasn't interested."

"Where's your sister?" Bruce asked. "How does she fit into all this?"

"My sister is dead."

Bruce frowned. "Wait, what did you mean about telling your sister you weren't interested?"

Sarah and Aaron exchanged a glance. Then she stared at each of the men in turn. "Whether any of you believe it or not, I don't care, but it's my sister who tells me everything."

"And you just do her bidding?" Griffin asked. "Without question."

"Pretty much."

"Please." Warner waved a hand. "Do go on. I'm beginning to find this fascinating."

Sarah cleared her throat once, then faced Bruce. "Everything up to this moment was set up for the final act."

"Like in a play?" Bruce asked.

Sarah nodded. "Like in a play. I needed you in custody so you'll be safe." She turned to Warner. "I'm thinking you can manage that for two days?"

Warner nodded. "That can be arranged."

"I don't agree," Griffin said, "nor do I like this one bit, but I'm willing to listen."

"In about five minutes, you'll have no problem keeping Bruce behind bars for a few days."

"Why?" the judge leaned forward. "What's happening in five minutes?"

"Well, now, that would ruin the surprise."

The Sarah Roberts Series Vol. 34-36

"Oh, pray tell, my crystal ball mystic," Griffin said, mocking her with a high-pitched voice. "Please ruin us with your wisdom."

Warner spun and opened his mouth to rebuke Griffin, but Sarah cut him off.

"Wait!" she shouted. Warner closed his mouth and turned to Sarah. "In a few minutes, the judge will be humbled into silence, and we'll all witness it. Just wait."

"Whatever's coming, I'll hold you responsible, Miss Roberts." The judge steepled his fingers. "No one is psychic. If so, you wouldn't waste your time helping us in any way. You'd win lotteries, buy stocks you knew would increase in value, and invest in sure things. You'd be enjoying life on a tropical beach, not handcuffed on a couch in a judge's chambers." He looked at his son while pointing at Sarah. "See, Bruce? If she was *really* psychic, why didn't she see this coming?" He scoffed. "Crystal ball, my ass."

There was enough play in Aaron's cuffs for him to place a hand on her leg. She glanced down at it and remained calm. The judge's phone would ring any minute now. He'd know soon enough what was coming.

"Cat got your tongue?" the judge asked.

Warner clucked his tongue—a signal that he was losing his patience with the judge.

"Warner," Sarah said. "After the judge takes a call in a few minutes, he'll be inconsolable. You'll need to take these cuffs off and drop all charges against us so Aaron and I are free to help."

Warner stared at her while the judge shook his head.

"Oh, I get it," Griffin said. "You're going to have Alex or Parkman call with some sort of leverage against me. Is that it? Some ploy to release you so you can all return to Toronto?"

"No, that's not it. But without our help, no one wins."

The judge scowled at her with something close to hatred in his eyes.

"Lastly, Judge Griffin, even though you'll have to deal with something quite unpleasant soon, you will still need to attend court this afternoon."

"Oh, yeah? And why's that?"

"You'll see."

"Cryptic again, eh?" The judge got back to his feet. "I've had about enough of this." He stormed across the length of his office, opened the door to the main hallway, and called for officers.

Three men and the woman who escorted Sarah earlier stepped inside.

"I want these two prisoners to be taken back to holding until they're processed, and I want those cuffs off my son. He'll sign a promise to appear if needed, but he's leaving with me."

Warner got to his feet, his hands up. "Wait." The officers by the door stopped moving. "Step outside," he said to them. "We'll call you back in a few moments."

Confused about who to listen to, the officers stared at Warner, then the judge.

The judge's phone ringing broke the silence.

"Wait here," he said, hustling back to his desk.

"This is it," Sarah said.

Warner understood immediately as he ran over to the office door and whispered to the officers to get out—*now!*

"Oh," the judge said, staring at his phone as the office door closed, and they were all alone again. "It's a Messenger call from my daughter." He tapped the button to answer and then held the phone out as it was a video call. "Hello? Melody? Are you still in Europe?"

A man's voice came on the line. "In a few minutes, you'll receive a package."

The man's voice was heavily accented and muffled.

Sarah placed her hand over Aaron's and squeezed. "This is it," she whispered to him.

"What you do with that package is up to you."

"Who's this?" the judge asked. "Where's Melody?"

"Who I am isn't important. For now, Melody is alive. Whether she stays that way is up to you."

The judge's face fell, and he struggled to stay on his feet. He glanced at Warner, then back to his phone.

"What, what are you saying?"

"The package is coming. Once you do what is required, Melody will be released without further harm."

"*Further* harm?" A vein pulsed on the judge's forehead. "What have you done to her?"

Someone knocked hard on the office door.

Then, there was a clicking sound as the call disconnected.

The judge slowly set the phone down while staring at his office door.

Warner moved to the door and opened it halfway. "What?" he said.

Someone spoke to him, but the words were unintelligible from inside the office.

"Who is it?" Griffin called from behind his desk, his voice cracking once.

Warner turned around and closed the door. "A package for you, sir."

He walked over to the desk and set the box, slightly smaller than a shoe box, on the judge's desk.

Judge Griffin looked around uncertainly as if debating what he was supposed to do next.

He slowly ripped off the tape, used a pen to puncture the stronger pieces, and eventually pulled it back.

Then he opened the lid and exhaled in relief.

"A note," he said, pulling the note out.

As he read it, his face whitened. Then he stared at Sarah.

"How could you know?"

"What does it say?" Warner asked, already stalking to the desk and snatching the letter from the judge's hands. He read aloud, "Michael Sommers is not guilty of the crimes he's been charged with. Find him not guilty and let him walk this afternoon, or your daughter will never walk again. The finger is pointed at you. The proof is in the pudding."

Warner lowered the note and stared down at the box. "Is there any pudding in there?"

Griffin leaned forward to look inside. "Yeah. This." He held up a small container of chocolate pudding, then peeled back the top—and promptly dropped it to his desk, shoving backward and gasping so loud that Bruce jumped again.

Warner lunged forward and snatched up the pudding container.

He eased back the top while the judge whispered *no, no, no,* over and over.

Warner angled the package for Sarah and Aaron to see, but Vivian had already told her what to expect.

"You'll see that the finger tattoo matches Melody's." Sarah nodded. "It's real. As real as the threat." She held up the cuffs. "Warner, please do the honors and release us, or the judge's daughter, Melody Griffin, will die tonight. We are the only people who can stop this chain of events."

Warner faced the judge.

He waved a hand at him. "Release them immediately. Save my baby girl."

Part Two

# Chapter 24

SARAH AND AARON WALKED out of the police station with only the marks on their wrists where the cuffs had been to remind them of their short-lived ordeal inside the North Bay police station and courthouse.

Judge Griffin, in his heightened state of grief and sorrow, agreed to free Michael Sommers within the hour to secure his daughter's safety. He would hear the final arguments from either side, and in a short summation, he would find the accused not guilty. The stolen car issue would be buried, and nothing other than an arrest record would have Michael Sommers's name on it.

When Sarah asked what they'd tell Mackenzie, Griffin was indignant. He'd say to the bastard, a real estate tycoon in these parts—who also ran with some undesirables and was linked to several missing people, corrupt dealings, and more—where he could shove his bribe money. They'd give every penny back to him, and all would be well in their world.

Because of Sarah's involvement and her *knowing* what was coming, Griffin and Warner both agreed that it would be best for Griffin's son to remain in custody for a few days.

Then they dropped all charges against them, disregarded Joseph Nate's entire statement about a violent home invasion—claiming he lied and killed his wife to keep her quiet, then they charged him with her murder—and let Sarah and Aaron walk out the front door of the courthouse.

An hour later, Police Chief Bill Warner waved at them once, then turned to reenter the building at the exact moment Judge Griffin was issuing his not-guilty verdict in courtroom one.

Michael Sommers was free to go and would leave the building in half an hour or less.

Outside at the curb, Parkman and Alex were waiting as instructed, the car idling.

"So good to see you two," Parkman said through his open window before they even got inside the car.

"You brought coffee?" Sarah asked, dropping into the back seat with Aaron.

"As you requested." Parkman handed them back one by one. "This is my preferred Vivian."

Everyone looked at him as he rested his arm on the top of the steering wheel.

"What? All I'm saying is, Sarah was given two scenarios." He turned to look at her. "One, we finish in the coffee shop after warning Bruce Griffin and head home, or two, you were arrested. In that case, you told us to bring coffee and park out here by three in the afternoon. And here we are."

Alex had turned in his seat to stare at Aaron's face. He gestured at the bruised cheek.

Aaron touched it gingerly. "Got into a fight inside the holding cell."

"How many?" Alex asked.

"Four."

Alex nodded once and then turned back around to stare out the windshield. He'd grown slightly quiet again after Sarah had gone missing the past winter. Darwin found her in Italy. It might have to do with how he felt about her, but she suspected it had more to do with how many men he killed in anger during his search for her.

He was the best sort of person in this life, but maybe this life wasn't the best for him. She'd have to consider that going forward. Maybe once they got back home, she'd talk with him.

Alex should take a break and do something personal for himself.

Sarah sipped her coffee—blessed coffee—thinking about Alex while nodding at Parkman. "Take us to the motel on Lakeshore Road."

He turned in his seat and got the car rolling. "What's there? A place for dinner and a night's sleep before heading home?"

"I think Melody Griffin is in one of the rooms."

Aaron shot a look at her, resting his coffee on his thigh. "Isn't she in Europe? I thought Griffin said something about Rome."

Sarah shook her head. "Someone has her here. Vivian said she never made it to Europe. She's been in North Bay the whole time."

"Someone?" Parkman pulled out into traffic, then looked at her in the rearview mirror.

Sarah pulled the coffee cup from her mouth. "Vivian just gave me this feeling about the situation being tenuous."

"When is it *not* tenuous?"

"True, but we have to get Melody, and we have to be careful."

Aaron gripped his coffee with both hands. "Why are we getting Melody? Why can't we tell the judge his daughter is here and she's safe?"

After a moment, Sarah narrowed her eyes and turned to stare at him. "What?"

"Why us? I mean, isn't she safe now? That guy Sommers got what he wanted. He's been found not guilty."

Sarah continued staring at him.

"Okay, okay." Aaron raised his hands, the coffee still tight in his palms. "Just asking in case Vivian told you some specific reason. Otherwise, if you knew where she was, and it's dangerous—oh, wait, *tenuous*—wouldn't it be better to have Chief Warner involved? Have his men surround the motel, extract her with some S.W.A.T. team or some shit?"

Sarah relaxed her facial muscles. "We need her because she'll be safe with us. According to my sister, she has less than an hour to live. Warner wouldn't be ready in time. They require considerable convincing to mobilize any sort of response. We're her only hope."

"See? That's what I'm talking about." Aaron scratched his head.

"What?" Parkman asked.

"Vivian told her something specific about Melody. So, let's go get her and save the girl's life."

"That's what—" Parkman started.

"—we're doing," Sarah finished for him.

"Great." Aaron was now rubbing the bruise on his cheek, staring out the window.

Sarah wondered if he was asking for the sake of clarity or if he was back to his old ways already. He seemed all in with the home invasion and hammer-to-knee business, but this question about Melody didn't sit well with her.

His apprehension had always been there, but after they lost Benjamin, it had increased. Maybe he needed a break, too. But even if she wanted to give him a break, he ended up getting pulled back in anyway.

Things to ponder for another day, she thought as Parkman drove them to the motel Vivian told her about.

Even though it was edging closer to four in the afternoon, the sun this far north was moving closer to the horizon. It would be dark within the hour. They had to have Melody with them by that time.

"Drive by when you get there."

"Drive by what?" Parkman asked.

"The motel. There has to be someone watching the door, the parking lot."

"You know her room number?"

"No."

There was a moment of silence. "Oh," Parkman uttered. "But you're sure this is the place?"

"Yeah."

"So, how do we get to her without a room number?"

"Whoever is watching the place knows which room."

"And they'll just tell us?"

"Oh, yeah," Sarah said. "I'm sure of it." She kept her eyes on the Park Motel as it eased by on the left. "Pull into the church parking lot over there."

"Why are people watching the room?" Aaron asked. "If they're after Melody, why not just get her?"

"They're staking the place out for Sommers, I think."

Aaron nodded as Parkman pulled into the church.

It was a large brown-brick building with an empty parking lot situated right beside the Park Motel. They were separated by a copse of thick trees that were part of a dense forest behind both buildings. Back in the woods, the shadows were long and deep already as the sun kept dropping.

Parkman drove through the lot and stopped on the far side. Anyone inside or outside watching the Park Motel couldn't see them now.

Sarah twisted in her seat. "Look over there." She pointed across the street to the Wayland Inn. "Parkman, I need you and Aaron to get us a room for the night at that place. Make sure the window faces the Park Motel."

"We can do that," Parkman said. "Where will you and Alex be?"

"Getting Melody."

Aaron spun toward her. "Just the two of you? I thought it was dangerous or tenuous."

"It is, but I think we'll be okay."

"Wait." Aaron raised a hand toward Alex in the front seat. "Why him? Why don't we do this, and they get a room?"

"Aaron, honey, there's a reason for everything." Sarah rubbed the top of his hand to console him, but it came off as patronizing. To recover quickly, she added, "The truth?"

Aaron nodded, his ego bruised.

"To get the information we need, Alex will do as I ask instantly. Break a finger, Alex." Sarah clapped her hands. "Finger's broken. Break a nose." She clapped. "Break a wrist." She clapped. "Pull a few teeth." She lowered her hands. "Understand now? I need information from an asshole over there," she pointed in the general direction of the Park Motel, "and Alex never, and I mean never, hesitates. Nor does he ask questions."

Aaron lowered his gaze. "Okay, okay. I get it. You need a minion."

"No, not a minion. I have his trust. Vivian has his trust. But most of all, we have his loyalty."

Aaron lifted his gaze. "You have mine as well."

"Great, but Alex comes with me. You go with Parkman. And no more questions. When we're dealing with something from Vivian, unless it strikes you as morally corrupt, no questions. They slow the process, and sometimes we don't have time to discuss it."

"Sarah." Aaron chuckled once. "Everything we do is morally corrupt."

She looked away, thought about it a moment, then turned back. "I'll give you that one because that's been your struggle ever since we met. Get over that, and you'll do just fine." She patted his shoulder. Now, she was patronizing, and it didn't bother her one bit.

If he wanted her answer regarding marriage, he needed to come to terms with whom he was marrying. There was nothing more to discuss because she wouldn't marry him simply to give Willow her parents under one roof.

She'd read somewhere that children of separated—but happy—parents did far better than children of married, unhappy parents.

She opened her door. "Alex," she said. "You're up."

After both doors closed, Parkman pulled away.

Sarah ran for the woods with Alex on her heels.

Neither one said a word as the trees enveloped them.

There was nothing that needed to be said.

# Chapter 25

PARKMAN USED HIS CREDIT card to secure two rooms, each with two double beds. One room could be for Sarah, Aaron, and Melody. The other could be for him and Alex.

Once they got the room keys, both men marched along the outside walkway until they got to the rooms, neither one looking toward the Park Motel across the street.

Then he followed Aaron into his room, where they both took a spot on either side of the room's large square window that gazed out into the parking lot and farther to the Park Motel across the street.

"See anything unusual?" Parkman asked.

"Other than that dressing down in front of you all?" Aaron sounded defeated, beaten.

Parkman snuck a glance at Aaron. "C'mon, man. Sarah loves you. She *chose* you. It's been you and her since she walked into your dojo when those Rapturites were chasing her."

"She has a funny way of showing it."

"Aaron, Sarah has a funny way of showing anything. That's why we all love her." Parkman counted the cars in the lot across the street. "I see seven cars over there. With two of them, I can't tell if anyone is sitting inside. The windows are too dark."

"I can't tell either." Aaron eased the curtain away from his face. "Is Alex in love with Sarah?"

Parkman stepped back to stare at Aaron. "What?"

"You heard me."

"Dude, of course, Alex loves Sarah. So much so that he'd give his life to protect her—as I would. It's rare to find someone like her. That whole thing about fighting fire with fire is Sarah. She fights for those who can't, and as much as bad guys swear, they can get violent. So, we have to get violent." He pulled the curtain back and peeked out at the street again. "The law plays it differently. They have procedures to follow, a rule book. We don't, which is why we always get into trouble. That's it in a nutshell."

When he glanced at Aaron, he backed away and sat on the corner of the bed.

"Now, I will offer another answer to your question. Does Alex *love* Sarah in any intimate way? No, not that I'm aware of. I've never seen that. But he certainly idolizes her, focuses his every fiber on where she is and what she's doing." He moved closer to Aaron. "That's why when she went missing last winter, and yet she was so close when that coffin drove by us in the back of that truck, Alex was upset with himself for feeling like he failed her. When that happens, he will stray from the path at times."

Aaron nodded, his eyes on the ugly motel room's shag carpet.

Parkman continued. "That's why Alex killed those people involved. He could've hurt them badly, but he lost himself a bit. He calmed down once he heard she was safe and with Darwin in Italy."

"I'm struggling here, Parkman." He shrugged, his gaze far away. "Not sure why."

"Maybe you've been out of practice for too long."

"Maybe."

"Or maybe this stuff isn't for you. It's not for everybody."

"But I want it to be for me because I want Sarah."

"Then make it so, but if you're forcing it …" His voice trailed off. "That round peg in the square hole bit."

Aaron nodded. "I know."

"How about this? Examine how you feel about Sarah."

He looked up at Parkman. "What do you mean?"

"Well, for one," Parkman slipped a hand in his pocket, produced a toothpick, and popped it into his mouth, "do you love her?"

"Of course I do."

"And wouldn't you do anything to protect the ones you love?"

"Without a doubt."

"So, here we are, doing what we can to care for Sarah."

Aaron raised a finger. "There's a difference here, though."

"How so?"

"What if my girlfriend walked into a biker bar every Friday night, accepted drinks from them, called them a bunch of patsy names, slapped a few around, walked outside, and kicked over their bikes? Basically, she was looking for a fight, instigating them to attack her. Would I protect her? Would I fight for her?" He pushed up off the bed and walked to the window to ease the curtain back. "Sure. Once. Maybe twice. But every Friday night?" Aaron shook his head. "That's just asking for trouble. I'd leave a girl like that."

"Hmm, I never thought about it that way."

"All I'm saying is, Sarah intentionally puts herself in these positions. On purpose, she involves herself with the filth of society, pisses them off, and irritates them. We all fight to take care of each other, then ..."

"Then what?"

"Then Benjamin died. Bruno died. Drake and Spencer are dead."

Parkman stared at him for a long moment. "That's what this is about, isn't it? You blame Sarah for their deaths. Somewhere, deep inside, you've made it her fault."

Aaron stopped hiding behind the curtain and looked at Parkman. "I don't *blame* her, but she is partly responsible."

"Allow me to disavow you of that notion." Parkman approached the curtain and stared across the street at the Park Motel. "We all volunteer. We can walk away at any time. We don't have to be here. But we *are* here. And if something happens, then it's on us. We have to own it. Benjamin knew the risks. Hell, he got shot more than most and survived. And he kept showing up." Parkman stopped to collect himself. It was the most he'd spoken about Benjamin in some time. "We all know the risks going in, and we've all stopped a lot of bad guys over the years. The odds were tipped in our favor for quite some time."

"So the scale adjusted, and Benjamin died?" Aaron's voice was flat, void of emotion.

"If that'll help you sleep at night, then sure. I see it as something to do with fate."

"Fate?"

"Sure." Parkman nodded to himself as Aaron stared across the street now. "Eventually, fate will catch up with all of us. Age is creeping up on me. I don't mind that Sarah has me driving the cars and securing motel rooms. I can easily extract information from the bad guys—I know how to hurt people. But it's so much better that Alex does the more physical jobs. My feelings aren't hurt."

"Well, that makes sense."

"And she's cautious with you because she wants you here, with us, but she doesn't want to overload you with violence or violent tasks. Where Alex will do anything she needs instantly. It's all about track record."

"Track record?"

"Yeah, examine your track record résumé versus Alex's since Benjamin died. Who will she pick for a dirty job? It would be a thousand percent, Alex. It has nothing to do with loving you less or wanting to hurt your feelings. To Alex's hundred percent, you're an eighty. You may even be a ninety, but you're not one hundred. We all know that. And that's why she wasn't *dressing you down* back there in the car. She was informing you of something we all know, and we thought you did, too."

They fell silent for a moment, both watching nothing but random cars passing by on Lakeshore Boulevard.

"Then I need to officially leave this all behind and walk away, or commit to Sarah at Alex's level or higher, without hovering in the middle somewhere. Is that it?"

Parkman stole a glance at Aaron. "I couldn't have said it better. Those are the two options. One leads to separation and visitation agreements for Willow, with no say regarding Sarah's life or choices because she refuses to stop working with Vivian. And the other should lead toward marriage and a unified family."

More silence.

"Although, you're missing something," Parkman said.

"What's that?" Aaron asked.

"That analogy about the biker bar doesn't work."

"How so?"

"Sarah isn't stirring up a hornet's nest and hoping not to get stung, then waiting for her men to save her. She's doing something righteous, backed by the other side. As we discussed in the car yesterday, this is the closest to being on a mission from God himself."

"Hey, wasn't there a movie with that line?"

Parkman nodded. *"The Blues Brothers."*

Aaron snapped his fingers. "Right, that's it."

They both stared out the window again.

"So, you're thinking of picking a side?" Parkman asked.

"A side?"

"Yeah, all in or separation."

"Already have."

Parkman waited for more, but then he saw Sarah materialize from the side of the Park Motel.

"There's Sarah."

"I see her."

"Shit, who's this guy?"

A man exited a car in the parking lot in front of them on their side of the road.

"I didn't see him," Aaron said.

"Me neither. I was watching cars on the other side of the road."

"Shit, he's armed."

Parkman studied the man's waist but saw no bulge. Then he lowered his gaze to the man's ankles. Sure enough, there was a bulge on his right foot.

Across the busy Lakeshore Boulevard, Sarah slowed in front of a motel room door and then looked around.

The man on their side of the street pretended to be locking his car. He turned toward their window, and both of them let the curtain fall back into place.

"What now?" Aaron whispered.

"If he's a danger to Sarah, we neutralize him."

"On it." Aaron headed to the door.

"Wait."

Aaron stopped and looked back, his hand on the doorknob.

"You sure you're up to this?"

Aaron stared at him for a long moment, then nodded. "I'm all in, Parkman. Always have been. I just don't want to lose anyone else, especially Sarah."

"Then fight for her. Step up and *make sure* we never lose anyone else."

"I can do that."

Aaron opened the door and slipped outside, closing it firmly behind him.

# Chapter 26

S ARAH LED THE WAY through the trees quietly, with Alex following close behind her, making even less sound. When they were directly behind the Park Motel, she stopped and lowered to her knees, scanning the area. After seeing no one around and no movement, she glanced over her shoulder to see what Alex was doing.

He was also lowered to his knees, shoulder resting against a tree, eyes roving the back of the motel.

Then, without a word, he pushed up to his feet, stepped between two trees, and was gone.

Wondering what caught his eye, she got up and followed slowly. After ten meters, fifteen, then twenty, the rear parking lot of the Park Motel came into view. Eight cars were parked back there. Some snuggled up close to the building, while others were covered in road dust, making them appear to belong to long-term guests.

Sarah caught a glimpse of Alex's gray shirt and loose jeans as he moved to the right, putting him in front of her.

In full view now, about twenty meters ahead, just short of the parking lot, Alex stopped and said something.

But it wasn't for Sarah.

Then she caught on to what Alex was doing.

A tall man, over six feet tall and several feet wide, wearing a black leather jacket, stood by a tree and lit a cigarette. As he exhaled, a cloudy fug hovered around his face while he stared at Alex. The difference in weight between the two men was an easy two hundred pounds—Alex at one hundred and fifty, the man watching the back of the motel at three hundred and fifty.

The other difference was that the large man had to own shares in a gym because from where Sarah was standing, he seemed bigger than the "Rock," Dwayne Johnson.

"What?" the man grunted.

Sarah moved closer, then placed herself directly behind a tree, entirely out of view. Now, she was close enough to listen without being observed if that man happened to look her way.

"Spare a smoke?" Alex asked.

Sarah frowned. What was he up to?

Without the benefit of eyes on the situation, she had to rely on noise, but all she detected was a rustling of fabric.

"What are you doing out here?" the man asked.

"Lighter?" Alex again—avoiding the guy's question.

The distinctive sound of a lighter flicking into a flame could be heard, then an exhale.

"I asked you a question." The man's tone seemed complicated, less patient.

"Looking for a girl."

"A girl?" The man's tone changed and became more suspicious. "What girl?"

A silence followed. Something stirred in Sarah's gut as she waited to hear what came next.

"What are *you* doing out here?" Alex asked.

"Having a smoke like it was any of your business." The man sounded quite impatient now. "Now, what girl are you looking for in these woods?"

"Your woman kicked you out of the room?" Alex was winding the guy up, pissing him off.

"I'll ask you one more time, and you *will* answer me."

Sarah detected footsteps. She eased around the edge of the thick tree and saw the man facing Alex, staring him down.

The man leaned even closer. "What *girl?*"

With the lit cigarette in his fingers, held in front of his face, Alex shrugged.

"Just a girl."

Then he flicked the smoke at the man's face, making him jerk back and close his eyes.

In that brief second, Alex struck.

Three quick blows to the man's throat and face, and his knees buckled as he grunted and dropped to the pine-needle-covered ground.

Sarah was close enough to feel him make contact with the earth as much as see it.

Alex jammed his hands into the man's midsection, withdrew a gun, and the knife clipped to his belt, then tossed the gun to Sarah as she ran up to them.

Sarah caught the weapon and slipped it into the back of her pants as Alex threw the knife into the trees.

The man on the ground clutched at his throat, eyes wide, in a desperate bid to find air.

"He'll live?" she asked.

Alex moved behind him and yanked the man's head back by the hair. "It wasn't a fatal blow. I restrained myself."

Sarah nodded once at Alex, then dropped to her knees and watched the man for a moment. "Which room is Melody Griffin in?"

The man watched her, still gasping, blinking rapidly. Bits of air were getting through now, and even though his face had gone gray, color had started to return. The sun's light was diminishing quickly, but the back parking lot of the Park Motel was well-lit, with large orange lights illuminating the area. One of those lights streamed in to wash the man with a Halloween-like glow.

"Which room?" she asked again, then glanced around to see if they had drawn any attention to themselves, but as far as she could tell, they were still alone.

The man grunted something, but it was unintelligible.

"Hold him."

Alex secured one of the man's arms up over his head, then twisted his wrist back and painfully jabbed his thumb into a nerve.

The large bodybuilder cried out in pain, his abdomen arching upward in an attempt to alleviate the pressure Alex was applying.

Alex slapped a hand over the man's mouth and leaned close to his ear. "Shhh," he said.

Sarah patted the man's pockets, then rifled through them until she located a wallet. After yanking it out, she opened the front and examined his driver's license.

"John Bishop." She glanced over the top of the license. "Didn't peg you for a Bishop, but I guess you never know someone's name by looking at them." She stared at the license again, then slipped it into her pocket. "We've got your home address, Mr. Bishop. We need information. You're going to give it to us, or the people at this address will."

Bishop jerked forward, and his strength, after years of gym discipline, almost dislodged Alex. But Alex held on and dug in, redoubling the pressure.

The large man fell back and cried out again, but the sound was muffled behind Alex's other hand. Then Alex repositioned and locked onto something on the man's neck behind his ear. Bishop's eyes widened as far as they could, and he froze, immobilized by Alex's grip.

"My friend can damage you, Bishop." Sarah made a tsking sound. "I wouldn't try to resist again." She snatched a card from his wallet and then tossed the wallet aside. "Here we go. Mackenzie Construction." She glanced at Alex, then at Bishop's bulging eyes, which were on her. "You work for Mackenzie, yet you're out here watching Melody's motel room." Sarah frowned in mock concern. "I wonder why that is, hmmm. Do you want to tell us? Or do you want my friend here to do damage you won't walk away from?"

The man grunted, and Alex relieved the pressure enough that Bishop drew a deep breath.

Sarah waited for him to try to escape Alex again, but he seemed compliant for the moment.

"We are waiting for someone else. Not the girl. Mackenzie doesn't care about the girl."

"Who are you waiting for?"

Bishop stared at Sarah without answering her.

Alex tightened his grip until Bishop moaned, then eased off.

"Who?" Sarah asked again.

"Sommers."

Sarah nodded. "Now that makes sense." Sarah leaned in close, and Alex wrapped one arm around Bishop's neck, with the other still on the sensitive pressure point behind his ear.

"Don't be stupid," Alex whispered in the man's ear. "Remain compliant, or I might accidentally paralyze you."

"What room is Melody in?" Sarah said. "It's my last question."

The man tried to shake his head, but Alex's grip tightened, and he seized up.

"Answer her." Alex released some of the pressure.

"I'm a dead man already. No way."

"What room?" Sarah asked again.

The man stared at her. "I can't," he muttered, his lower lip quivering with the pain he must be enduring under Alex's grip.

Sarah looked at Alex. "I need a room number. He's no good to us without that. Get it for me, please."

"Of course."

Alex spun around to secure the man's hand, and in one fluid motion, he had the wrist twisted back, and then the man's middle finger was in his grip. He held it to the breaking point as Bishop writhed underneath him.

"The room number," Sarah said.

"Fuck you," the man exhaled the words between breaths as he attempted to manage the pain.

Alex pulled back like breaking a pencil in half.

The bone snapped back, the man's fingertip now touching the top of his wrist.

When the pain came seconds later, the man screamed in a high pitch, but not before Alex wrapped his hand over the man's mouth. Volume was still evident, but it wasn't something a guest in one of the motel rooms would likely hear.

Sarah leaned in close so he could hear her. "You've got a bunch of fingers." Sarah pointed at his other hand. "Then my friend will break your knees, elbows, wrists, and finally, the femurs in both legs. Those are nasty and painful. My friend knows how to do so much damage that it'll take years to recover from if you don't tell us what we want to—"

"One ten," the man grunted through the pain.

"What was that?" Sarah leaned forward again.

"Room one ten. Please, tell him to stop."

Sarah looked at Alex. "Sleepy time."

Alex released Bishop's hand, wrapped his arms around the man's thick neck, and then applied pressure in the correct spot. When Bishop was asleep, Alex got to his feet, grabbed the knife he'd tossed into the bushes, and then wiped the forest debris off his jeans.

"He'll wake soon." He held the knife as if ready to strike. "We haven't much time."

They started toward the back of the motel.

"Keep an eye peeled for others," Sarah said. "They may be sitting in any of these cars."

Alex moved off to the left.

In the parking lot now, Sarah took the time to stare into each vehicle as she made her way around the building toward the front.

The traffic noise from the road in front of the motel increased in volume once she was out of the trees. When she glanced over her shoulder, Alex was following at a distance.

Sarah turned to look at the motel across the street, but couldn't see Parkman or Aaron—just their empty car.

She passed room 101, then 102, and picked up her pace.

The man in the trees could be waking now. She kicked herself for not locating his cell phone.

"That was dumb," she mumbled as she passed 107.

Coming up to room 110, she slowed, took one more look around, saw Alex back around room 104, and raised her hand to knock.

She waited, her back to the door.

Across the road, at the other motel, she caught sight of Aaron moving through the parking lot now.

A man had gotten out of his car and appeared to be watching her, his cell phone up as if he might be recording.

Alex moved closer to her side, his eyes fixed on Aaron.

So Sarah knocked again.

"Mike?" came the voice on the other side of the door.

She leaned in closer. "My name is Sarah. Mike Sommers told me to come get you. He was found not guilty and wants to celebrate."

There was no response.

"Melody? It's okay. Seriously, Mike sent me." She looked over at the other parking lot. The man by the car was talking on his cell phone, staring at Sarah. She was sure of it now. He held it up again.

When she narrowed her eyes, it looked like he had a gun in his other hand.

Then Aaron was behind him.

He smacked the phone out of the man's hand, and when he spun toward Aaron, he locked the man's gun arm up, drove several shots to his face, then kneed him hard in the midsection.

The man dropped from view as Aaron retrieved something off the pavement at his feet. When he stood, he offered Sarah a thumbs-up.

Sarah knocked again. "Melody, I'm going to need you to trust me. I just spoke to your father, Judge Griffin, and your brother, Bruce. They were all very concerned about you—"

The door clicked open, and Melody peeked out behind the chain. She had reddish hair, pretty eyes, and pouty lips. About Sarah's height, she leaned forward and asked, "Did Michael really send you?"

Sarah nodded at her with as much feeling on her face as she could muster because this woman was innocent in all this carnage. "He said we have to meet him elsewhere. It's not safe for you here anymore."

The door closed, and the lock engaged. "I don't believe you." Her muffled reply came through the door. "Go away."

Sarah leaned up against the door, her gaze across the street now as Aaron dragged the unconscious man from the parking lot toward their room. Parkman had exited the room to help him carry the guy.

"I'm afraid I can't go anywhere without you."

"I'm calling Michael now. He'll tell me what's up."

"Have you ever heard of a man named Mackenzie?"

Melody didn't respond. Sarah turned and looked back at Alex, who was watching Parkman and Aaron carry the man into their room. Their door closed. They were inside now.

"Yes," Melody said. "Why?"

"He sent men to watch this room."

"What?"

"But they aren't watching it anymore."

"Why aren't they watching it anymore?"

"Because we took care of them. But more will come. Soon, very soon. So we must get you to safety."

Sarah leaned back and whispered to Alex, "We may need to go in by force."

Alex nodded. "Just tell me when."

The lock clicked again.

They looked at each other. Then the door opened wide.

Melody stared at Sarah. "Where are we going?"

Sarah pointed across the street. "Just over there until Michael arrives. Then everything will be fine."

"Seriously? Just over there?"

Sarah nodded. "He didn't want to take you far. Just somewhere so Mackenzie's people couldn't get to you."

Melody nodded once. "Let me get my purse."

When she walked away from the door, Sarah saw the large white bandage wrapped around Melody's missing finger.

The poor girl. How much did she suffer?

A minute later, they were crossing the street on foot.

Alex got to the room door first.

Aaron opened it, and they all slipped inside.

Step one was complete.

# Chapter 27

AARON HAD RIPPED THE curtains off the bathroom window and was tying the man's hands together when Sarah entered the room, followed by Alex and Melody.

"Who are you people?" Melody asked, easing back toward the door.

"Friends of Michael Sommers," Sarah said, loud enough for everyone else to hear.

One by one, they all nodded confirmation.

Parkman stared at Aaron for a long moment, a toothpick flicking from one side of his mouth to the other. "Hey, you know I booked this room on my credit card, right? Those curtains are likely only worth fifty bucks, but they'll bill me a few hundred for them."

Aaron glanced up at him. "Find me something else to secure this man with, and I'll put them back up."

"You can't. They're ripped and torn now."

"My bad."

Sarah watched as Aaron took a small piece he'd ripped from the edge of the curtains, wadded it up, and jammed it in the man's mouth.

The man moaned as Alex started going through his pockets. He fished out his wallet and went through his cards.

"He had a weapon?" Sarah asked.

Aaron lifted his shirt to show the gun.

The judge's daughter grabbed for the door to leave.

"Melody." Sarah placed a hand on Melody's shoulder. "You're safe with us. This man works for someone named Mackenzie."

"Greg Callum," Parkman said, holding up the ID that Alex had just handed to him. "Works for Mackenzie Construction."

"See?" Sarah said.

Melody nodded, a fearful expression on her face, her cheeks blossoming red. "Mike said the plan would work. That Mackenzie would pay for what he did to him."

"What plan?" Sarah asked. "What did Mackenzie do?" Sarah spun around to face Parkman. "You got two rooms, right?"

Parkman nodded.

Sarah extended her hand. "I need the key. Melody and I will chat in the other room."

Parkman tossed it over. Sarah caught it easily, then opened the door, peeked into the parking area, and led Melody outside.

"One second," she said to Melody, then turned back to the boys. "Find out everything he knows, then one of you come join us."

Alex and Parkman nodded and moved closer to the man as Aaron finished securing their prisoner's hands.

Sarah led Melody to the room next door, opened the door, and gestured for her to step inside. When she glanced over at the Park Motel, she slipped behind the door to watch.

The man Alex hurt, John Bishop, was standing in the corner, slightly hunched over, holding his wounded hand close to his stomach. She glanced to the right as an ambulance entered the parking lot across the street and sped over to him.

Then she closed the door.

"Please, take a seat and tell me about this plan of yours. We don't have much time before Michael gets here."

Melody appeared to be fighting back tears. She sat in the corner on the one chair that was used for the little desk area.

"Mackenzie and Mike don't see eye to eye."

"I figured as much."

"And I know my father—"

"Judge Griffin." Sarah wasn't asking, but Melody nodded.

"I always fell for the bad boys, my dad would say. Listening to grunge rock, partying late. Dating men with tattoos influenced me to get my own tattoos, he claims."

"I'm sure he loves you." Sarah took a seat on the edge of the bed closest to her.

"My father and I became estranged when my mom left him."

"Your father makes his own trouble."

"How so?" Melody crossed, then uncrossed her legs.

"Before I get into that, can you tell me if you're interested in helping him?"

Melody averted her gaze momentarily, blinked a few times, then looked back up at Sarah.

"Yes. I still love him. He's just so thick-headed sometimes."

Sarah sighed. "I get that."

Sarah went on to tell the judge's daughter what he'd been up to and why they were there.

"I, uhm, wow, I kinda knew he did what he wanted in court, but I had no idea how serious it had gotten." Her tone was softened by incredulity.

"Now, knowing all that," Sarah leaned forward, "is there anything you want to tell me?"

"Like what?"

"Your dad seems to think you're in Europe."

Melody hiked one shoulder. "I tell him stuff like that, so he'll leave me alone. I even sent him doctored photos of me in front of monuments, so it's believable."

"You've been trying to piss him off for quite some time, haven't you?"

"Well, I wouldn't say that was my primary goal, even though it may have looked like that."

"The bad boys, the partying, the tattoos."

A scowl scrunched up her eyebrows. "It's my life, right? My goal isn't to anger my dad. That just happens."

Sarah stared down at the gauze wrapped around her hand. "Take that off."

Melody stirred uncomfortably, adjusting herself in her seat. "I don't know. What if it gets infected?"

"Melody, this won't work if we aren't honest with each other. All you and Sommers did was piss off Mackenzie, and he will go after your father now. He'll stop at nothing to get to Sommers, too, knowing he's on the streets." Sarah nodded at the bandage. "Take that off, and stop with the games."

Melody stared down at her hand so long that Sarah got up and went to the front window. She eased back the curtain.

Across the street, the ambulance was gone, and so was Bishop and his broken finger.

When Sarah turned back around, Melody was unwrapping the bandage. She watched her a moment, then looked back outside.

A short scream came from the room beside them—the boys extracting whatever information they could get.

When Sarah looked back at Melody, the bandage was off.

"See? That's better."

Melody's fingers were all intact. Not a single one was missing.

"None of your fingers had been chopped off. It was all a ruse to get your boyfriend free because he really did just steal a car—a bait car that Mackenzie fed him so he'd get arrested. Then Sommers heard about Mackenzie's plan to have him put away for decades and, while out on bail, befriended you to get to the judge."

Melody shook her head, her mouth dropping open. "No, that's not true. Michael and I are in love. We're going to get married. He said so himself."

"Okay, Melody. How about we ask him in a few minutes when he shows up."

Melody got to her feet so fast that her hair bounced and obscured her face. She brushed it aside. "I don't want to be here anymore."

Before Sarah could respond, someone knocked on the door.

"Hold that thought." She opened the door without looking, already knowing it was Aaron.

He stepped inside, and Sarah closed the door, then peeked back outside.

"What did he tell you?" Sarah asked, turning to face Aaron.

"In front of her?" He gestured to Melody.

Sarah nodded. "She needs to hear this."

"Mackenzie placed two of his men to watch Melody's room."

The judge's daughter retook her seat, both hands nervously rubbing the tops of her thighs.

Aaron continued. "There was a guy in the back. He called the guy we caught"—Aaron jabbed a thumb in the direction of the other room—"to tell him a skinny guy and a woman had attacked him. They broke his finger and knocked him out. He called an ambulance, too."

"That's why he was watching us as we made our way to Melody's room."

"So, Greg Callum, the guy we're talking to, exited his car and called Mackenzie to update him. We snatched him mid-sentence."

"How much did he tell Mackenzie?"

"That you and Alex were at Melody's door, and it looked like you were trying to gain access. A gun was already in his hand."

Sarah glanced over at Melody, who was now staring at a painting on the wall, listening to everything Aaron was saying.

"And why was he armed? Did he tell you why he had his gun out?"

Aaron nodded. "Their instructions were to kill Michael Sommers when he arrived and whoever else was in the room."

Melody drew a sudden intake of air and then whimpered. "How could people do that?" she asked, not directing her question to either of them as she stared at nothing with a look of dread.

"So, stake out the place, wait for Sommers, then get inside the room and execute everyone present?" Sarah repeated it that way for Melody's benefit. She needed to understand the gravity of it all.

"When you and Alex were knocking, coupled with the call he'd gotten from Bishop, they thought Sommers was already there and launching some sort of attack on Mackenzie's men."

"Fair enough." Sarah shook her head. "But if it were Sommers's people, Mackenzie's men would have been killed. Knocking out Bishop allowed him to wake up and warn the others."

Sarah patted Aaron on the shoulder, then stepped around him.

Melody was shaking her head. "There's no way," she whispered.

"No way, what?" Sarah asked, sitting across from her again.

"No way Michael would kill anyone."

Sarah and Aaron exchanged a glance.

"I'm sorry, Melody, but you're the victim here. At least it's just your heart that got broken and not your face."

"Sarah," Aaron snapped. "Not sure how consoling *that* is."

"Right." She slapped her leg. "Sorry."

"Now what?" Aaron asked.

"Now we end this charade."

"How?"

"In five minutes or less, Michael Sommers will arrive. Then we head to the next stage."

"Which is?"

"We go to Mackenzie's house for a chat."

"Whoa," Aaron raised his hands. "That doesn't sound like a good thing to do." He shook his head. "I don't know about that."

"Bring me Greg's cell phone."

"What?"

She waved a hand impatiently. "Greg's phone. Make sure you use his face to open it first. It's locked to facial recognition."

Aaron slipped outside and closed the door behind him.

Melody buried her face in her hands and quietly sobbed.

Less than a minute later, there was a soft knock on the door again. Sarah opened it, and Aaron walked in, the cell phone in hand.

Sarah opened it to the Photos app and brought up the pictures the man had taken. There was even a video.

"See?" Sarah said, playing the video. "He recorded Alex and me at Melody's motel room door."

Melody wiped her eyes and looked up as Sarah showed Aaron the video.

"Why would he do that?" Aaron asked.

"Well, for several reasons. If we got away from them, they would know what we look like."

"And?"

Sarah met Aaron's gaze. "He sent these photos and video to his employer before you attacked him."

"Shit. No way."

Sarah nodded, then opened Messenger. She clicked on the Mackenzie Construction page and then showed the outgoing messages to Aaron.

Below the photos and the single video, there was a response.

Sarah angled the phone so Melody could see it.

The response read:

*Remove that blond woman and her skinny friend quietly. Then, take care of Melody. Make it look like an accident. We will deal with MS when he arrives.*

Sarah faced Aaron. "And that's why we must go to Mackenzie's house tonight. We'll bring along our new friends and see how everything turns out."

"See how everything turns out?" Aaron asked, his voice rising in doubt.

"Yeah, I'm just hoping no one gets killed."

# Chapter 28

JUDGE GRIFFIN ENTERED HIS chambers, happy his day in court had ended. His gut still roiled at the fact that his daughter was missing a finger, but with Sommers free, he held onto a sliver of hope that she'd be released unharmed.

What drove him insane the entire time he sat on the bench staring down at Sommers and his attorney was that he couldn't berate the man for being involved in his daughter's missing finger.

This was a dangerous game. Going after his daughter would ensure the outcome they wanted. Money was a close second.

He hung his robe on the coat rack, then moved to the whisky on the side table. If he ever needed a drink, today was the day.

Halfway through pouring, his chamber door burst open, startling him and making him spill some of the whisky on the cabinet's surface.

"Don't *ever* enter my chambers without knocking," he said, raising his voice at Chief Warner, the stress of the day oozing through the cracks.

Warner stomped up to him, a cell phone in his hand. "We haven't got time for niceties," he blurted. "We fucked up, and now we've got trouble."

Griffin's stomach flipped, hoping the news wasn't about Melody. He wouldn't be able to handle that. Remaining calm on the outside, he sipped from his glass, then moved to his desk chair, praying his shaking legs would deliver him to it without stumbling.

"What trouble?" he asked, taking his seat.

"We should never have let that Sarah witch go."

He didn't expect that comment. "What could you possibly be talking about?"

"Look." Warner tapped his cell phone, then swung it around for Griffin to watch.

He leaned forward and narrowed his eyes as Sarah and a male were videoed knocking on a motel room door.

"Who's that with her?"

"I'm pretty sure that's Alex, one of her men. We never did apprehend him."

"What are they doing?" Griffin asked, still watching as they knocked.

Warner pulled the phone away, slipped it into his pocket, and stormed over to the whisky.

"Hey." Griffin raised his voice. "You going to tell me what's going on?"

"Sarah has Melody."

Griffin inhaled so fast that he swallowed and choked on the air briefly. He coughed, then collected himself.

In a deep voice, he said, "Excuse me."

"You heard me." Warner shot back his first pour, then poured another and turned around. "Mackenzie is angry. He wants his money back yesterday."

"Understandable, but what's this about Melody? Isn't she in Europe? Why would Sarah have her—scratch that," he lowered his head and waved a hand, "how did Sarah know where she was? And if she knew, why didn't she tell us?"

"Are you senile? Got dementia?" Warner drank from his glass, half emptying it.

"I'm warning you. Watch your fucking mouth."

"We're fucked."

Griffin didn't know if he wanted to drive a fist into Warner's smug mouth for his blatant disrespect or yank on his collar to get him to talk faster.

"Tell me what's going on," Griffin shouted. "I demand to know."

"Oh, you *demand*, do you?" Warner shook his head and pushed off the cabinet, walking into the middle of the large office. "A judge, a simple man. Leverage. Could happen to anyone."

"What are you on about?" Griffin was getting closer to throttling the man.

Warner spun around with a death stare, his eyes projecting fury. "We let her go. More specifically, *you* let her go."

"And? What's that matter now? So she went to a motel? Who cares?"

"The motel where Melody is staying!" Warner shouted at him from five feet away. "Don't you see? Sarah Roberts played us all."

Griffin slumped in the chair, thinking it through. "Why?" he whispered.

"Who knows," Warner said, then emptied his glass and strode over to the side cabinet. "To fuck with you would be my guess."

"How did you get that video?"

"Mackenzie's people sent it to me."

Griffin frowned. "Why would they send it to you?"

"Loyalty? Honor? Fealty? Who the fuck knows now? All of that is lost because you let Sommers go. Mackenzie is pissed. He sent the video to show us our choice was in error."

"What?" Griffin said, almost to himself. "Wait. What does that mean?"

"It means," Warner spun around to face him, "you bet on the wrong racehorse."

"Can you explain things less eloquently, you horse's ass? What the *fuck* does that mean?"

"You let Sommers go with a not-guilty plea and let Sarah leave without any charges."

"And?"

"Then Sarah raced to the motel where your daughter was staying and abducted her."

"*Abducted* her? What the hell for?"

"No idea, but I'm sure we'll hear from her soon enough."

"I thought Melody was in Europe."

"You thought wrong." Warner raised his glass. "You thought a lot of things wrong, Your Honor."

"Do not patronize me, you pigdick. We're in this together."

"Yeah, but I don't have your power. All these years, all the people we put away who didn't deserve it, all the people around town who cut us off on the road, pissed us off, or upset us in any way, we made sure they paid for fucking with us. We planted drugs, we set them up, and you *judged* them. But now that's all crashing down because they have your daughter." Warner raised his hands in defeat, almost spilling the little drink he had left in his glass. "I should've known you were weak when we got into this together."

"Fuck you. I'm not weak."

"Then what do you call letting Sarah walk out of this building to kidnap your own daughter? Do you know how many people Sarah and her group of *vigilantes* have killed over the years? All without repercussions, too. But, hey, that's the least of our worries. Mackenzie is gunning for us."

"How so?"

"He wants his money back today, with interest."

"Not going to happen."

"What?" Warner's voice rose to something close to hysterical. "Why?"

"Transferring half a million dollars isn't something you send through PayPal. Call him. Tell him it'll take time, but it's coming. Then tell him we're done. No more deals. I'll put in for my early retirement."

Warner set his glass down, crossed his arms, and stared at Griffin. "You want my advice?"

"No, but I'm sure you'll give it to me anyway."

"Find a plot, order a casket, and get ready to die. Mackenzie is coming, and nobody stops that man."

Griffin clucked his tongue and showed a strong face, even though he felt sick to his stomach. "C'mon, now you're talking ridiculous. Nobody kills a judge. And no one will come for you. Mackenzie is a businessman. He bought a deal that didn't go through. He'll invest elsewhere and move on."

"He invited us to his house tonight."

"Tell him I can't make it." Griffin emptied his glass.

"He invited us to his house to discuss the problem of Michael Sommers."

"Then you go."

Warner scoffed. "Asshole. I'm not going like a lamb to be slaughtered. We go together. You did this. You have to own it."

"Fine. Tell him I'll come. But in the meantime, send every available unit to that motel and get Sarah back into custody. I want to hear from her what she's up to before we meet with Mackenzie."

"I'll do you one better."

"How?"

"I'll call her."

"You have her cell number?"

Warner nodded.

"Track it."

"What?" Warner stared at him, his eyes swimming.

"Call her and tell me where the hell she is." Griffin jumped to his feet. "And if that doesn't work, and you can't locate Sarah, send officers in Toronto to pick up her daughter. This leverage business has to end, and when it does, I'll end up on top."

"Just listen to yourself," Warner said. "You're talking about abducting Sarah's daughter, who is like six or seven years old now, just to get Sarah to do what you ask of her. Sound familiar?"

Griffin spun around so fast he lost his balance and had to clutch the desk to stay upright. "I'll do whatever it takes to save my family. Even if I have to kill her."

"It may come to that."

Griffin nodded. "Tell Mackenzie we'll be there tonight. Tell him I want my daughter back and that meddling bitch Sarah Roberts dead. Make it a car accident. Have her fall off a cliff. I don't fucking care, but there are dozens of ways to have someone killed where reasonable doubt won't even play into it. Actually, have her disappear. No body, no case. Then he can have whatever he wants."

Warner set his glass down and headed for the door. He stopped with his hand on the knob. "Are you sure you want Mackenzie to know that you want Sarah Roberts dead? A kill order like that is tough to reverse." He leaned his back against the door. "Maybe you're just angry. Maybe it's the booze talking. How much have you had to drink?"

"Don't be so condescending. It's beneath you and, frankly, unbecoming."

"Then be absolutely clear. What is it you want?"

Griffin shook his head in a short spurt, waving a hand in front of him as if swatting at a fly. "I'm done with all this bullshit. I'm retiring. I want my family back. If I'm to believe that video Mackenzie sent you, then Sarah walked out of here to snatch Melody, which means she knew where she was the whole time. Why didn't Sarah tell us my daughter wasn't in Europe? Why hide shit like that?" He raised a finger. "I'll tell you why. To take her and use her against me. Well, fuck Sarah, and fuck everyone else. I want Sarah dead, and Melody returned to me. And if Mackenzie is involved in any way or hurts my daughter, he'll pay for it, too. End of story. After this business is concluded, we all go our severed ways."

"Severed ways? Don't you mean *separate* ways?"

Griffin paid his attitude no attention. "And release my son on a promise to appear. I know he did nothing wrong, and now that this business is concluded, he doesn't need to be locked up like a common criminal."

Warner nodded and opened the door. "I'll send the message and release Bruce." He stepped out and turned around, holding the door open. "Be ready for tonight. And don't be drunk."

"Oh, fuck off."

The door closed, and Chief Warner was gone.

Judge Griffin stared up at the ceiling, rubbed his face, then walked over to the side cabinet and poured himself another drink.

It was going to be a long day, after all.

# Chapter 29

SARAH PULLED BACK THE curtain just in time.

Michael Sommers had arrived in a black SUV with four other men at the Park Motel across the street.

"Looks like your boyfriend has arrived," Sarah said.

Melody got up and ran for the door.

Sarah moved in front of it. "Not this way."

Melody's forehead filled with lines as it scrunched up. "Why? I don't understand."

"Peek through the curtains first. If you like what you see, you're free to go."

Melody looked from Sarah to Aaron to the curtains. "What are you talking about? What am I supposed to see?" Nerves affected her voice, making it shaky.

Aaron lifted the edge of the curtains. "Take a look for yourself."

From across the street, which wasn't as busy as earlier, they could hear a man calling Melody's name.

She moved to the curtain, pulled it back slightly, and looked out. Sarah moved in beside her, with Aaron on the other side.

Sommers strolled to the motel door of room 110, his shoulders back, arms swinging with his strut like he was angry. To the right, the SUV was still running, the front passenger door open wide—Sommers left it that way. As far as Sarah could tell, there were at least three others inside the SUV.

"Doesn't look like he planned on staying," Sarah said. "He left his car door open."

"That's weird." Melody's voice was soft. "We set it up to persuade my dad into releasing him. After that, he was supposed to come stay with me in the room. Alone." She paused as they watched Sommers pound on the motel room door and holler her name. "I didn't know he was bringing people with him."

When the room door didn't open, Sommers moved to the window and tried to peek inside, but it didn't look like the curtains were open as he leaned near the corners.

Then he spun around, raised his arms in an I-don't-know gesture, and moved back to the motel room door to pound on it again.

"Maybe I should let him know where I am." Melody eased back from the window.

"Keep watching," Sarah said. "Then decide. Less than a minute left."

Melody retook her position at the window.

Sommers shouted her name and banged on the door once more. When it didn't open, he grabbed something from his waist and pointed his hand at the doorknob.

Melody sucked in air. "Is that a—"

The weapon's report was muffled by distance, but the firecracker sound of the gun discharging was unmistakable.

"A gun?" Sarah finished for her.

Melody raised her hands to her mouth. "What if I were on the other side of the door?"

Sommers fired once more, then stepped back and kicked at the knob. After three hits, the knob gave way, and the door swung open.

He stopped to look around him, the weapon concealed behind his thigh. Then he raised the weapon, shoved the door all the way open, and fired randomly into the room at least three times.

Now Melody gasped. "Wait. What's he doing? I was supposed to be in there. What if I was sleeping?"

"That's what we wanted you to see." Sarah touched her shoulder gingerly, glancing across at Aaron, who seemed as shocked as Melody.

Sommers reappeared, looking flustered. He ran for the SUV, jumped inside, and it screeched out of the parking lot.

Someone exited the motel office and half ran, half walked to room 110. When they pushed open the door, they spun around and dialed out on a cell phone.

"He's calling the police now. We'd better step back."

Melody wiped her eyes. "I'm sorry." She hiccupped. "I shouldn't waste one tear on that man, but I agreed to his scheme. I thought he was one of the good guys. I thought he loved me."

"Have a seat, Melody." Sarah gestured to the side of the bed. Sarah sat across from her once she was seated, and Aaron got her the tissue box. "I don't know everything, but as far as I understand it, this Mackenzie is quite the businessman."

Melody sobbed into her tissue, blew her nose, and then nodded. "He's a friend of my dad's. They golf together sometimes."

Sarah glanced at Aaron, then back to Melody. "Well, Sommers used to work for him."

Melody nodded again. "He told me that."

"What else did he tell you?"

"That Mackenzie screwed him on a deal. Something about percentages. All I know is that when the math was done, Mackenzie owed Michael lots of money and never paid up."

"So what did Michael do?" Sarah asked, but suspected she already knew the answer.

"He took what was his."

Sarah figured as much.

"How?" Aaron asked. "Like a robbery?"

Melody shook her head. "He said he was in charge of something called a bill of lading for shipments."

Aaron frowned. "What sort of things did Mackenzie ship? I thought he was in the construction business."

Melody did a final wipe of her face, her short spat of tears drying up now. "I don't know what it was exactly, but they ship a lot of stuff." She glanced at the curtains. "I can't believe he had a gun." She looked down at her lap, where her fingers fiddled with a piece of tissue. "He fired it into the room. Why would he do that? He could've hit me."

Sarah stared at Aaron for a moment, then adjusted herself and moved closer to Melody. "Would you like the yoga pants version?"

Melody frowned and looked up at Sarah, her eyes bloodshot with tears now. "What's a yoga pants version mean?"

"Well, yoga pants always tell the truth. You can't hide in those."

"Oh." She looked back down. Then, a short laugh shook her shoulders. "Not funny."

"Evidently." Sarah touched her knee. "I'm just trying to lighten the mood before I tell you something that'll be hard to hear."

"Go ahead." She lifted her gaze again. "Lay it on me."

"The whole truth—"

"And nothing but," Melody cut in.

"Is that Michael knew about Mackenzie wanting him to go down for a lot of years."

"For a lot of years? What do you mean?"

Sarah explained Mackenzie's deal with her father and how Michael was supposed to get twenty years. "He learned about it five months ago while out on bail."

"Wait, we met five months ago …" Her voice trailed off as the realization hit her. "Are you saying he played me to get to my—"

"I am."

She stared at Sarah for a long moment, then said slightly above a whisper. "He used me to get to my father."

Sarah nodded. "I'm sorry."

"He took me to so many fancy dinners, bought me things, and promised a lifetime of bliss. Then committed to marriage, as long as I tricked my dad this once. He couldn't bear being without me, stuck in jail." She glanced down at her fidgeting fingers. "All he'd done was steal a car, so I agreed." She met Sarah's gaze. "That bastard."

It was good to see her pain morphing into anger and not more sadness.

"He told me the car he stole was full of weapons and that he could be gone for five to ten years. Maybe more."

"Twenty," Aaron added.

Melody nodded. "So I agreed to help, knowing my dad was pliable. I suspected he'd done unsavory deals in the past."

"Well, it worked. Michael Sommers was released. Your father found him not guilty."

They stared at each other for a long moment, a police siren wailing somewhere in the distance.

"And now Michael doesn't need me anymore."

Sarah shook her head. "He doesn't."

"But why try to hurt me, or," she paused, "kill me?" Her eyes bugged out on the last two words.

"You know too much and are close to the authorities, the law. Your dad is the judge. He couldn't leave you to chance while he goes after Mackenzie."

Melody blinked several times in disbelief. "Goes after Mackenzie? What does that mean?"

The sirens seemed quite close outside. Sarah raised a finger, signaling for Melody to wait a moment, then moved to the curtain.

"Shit."

"What is it?" Aaron asked as he moved to the curtain.

Five cruisers had pulled into the Park Motel, and the officers were standing around the open door of room 110. Two police cruisers were turning into their motel parking lot now.

"We can't be here." Sarah turned around. "We need to leave. Parkman put these rooms in his name. If they're looking for us, they'll be at our doors very soon." She gestured at Melody. "Your father will want to see you and get you into protective custody."

Melody shook her head. "I don't want to see him. Not now, anyway. This has become too chaotic. I need to think first. Figure things out."

Sarah looked back outside. More cruisers were pulling in.

Someone knocked on the door, making her jump.

She clutched at her chest. "Holy shit," she said, gasping for breath. "That knock scared the crank out of me."

"The crank?" Aaron asked, moving to check who was at the door. "It's Parkman." He opened it, and Parkman stepped inside.

"We should probably get moving," Parkman said, a sense of urgency to his voice.

"Agreed." Sarah edged sideways to stand beside Melody. "Give me the car keys, then grab Alex. We'll walk her out, get in, and pull the car up to get you guys. Then we'll get out of here."

Parkman fished the keys out of his pocket and tossed them to her, turned to leave, then stopped. "And Mackenzie's guy?"

"He's alive, right?"

Parkman frowned. "Ahh, yeah. He's in pain but alive."

"Okay, leave him. Someone will come and pick him up."

"But he's in a motel room with my name on it?"

Sarah pocketed the car keys. "None of that will matter by the end of the night. I've been told it all ends tonight."

He stared at her for a long moment.

"Parkman, if we get separated, meet us at the coffee shop where we met Bruce. Got it?"

He nodded, turned, and exited the room, closing the door behind him.

Sarah faced Melody. "We want you to come with us so we can keep you safe."

Melody nodded. "As long as I don't have to go to my dad. I can't face him yet."

"I understand."

Someone knocked on the door.

Sarah frowned and looked at Aaron, who moved toward the peephole.

He spun around. "Shit, it's the police."

"Open up," a man shouted on the other side of the door. "North Bay Police Department."

# Chapter 30

BRUCE GRIFFIN HAD NO tolerance for waiting. Yet his father made him wait all day to be released. And even then, they made him sign several documents that he would show up for court at a later date. When that day came, would Heather's lying about being pregnant come up? Would her fleecing him be spoken about in open court? What about the other men she screwed over?

Probably not.

All they'd want to hear was why he had a gun that wasn't registered to him and why he shot Sam in the hand. Where was the justice in that? Was Bruce a bad guy running around shooting people in the hand for sport? No, he'd never done it in his life. He wasn't a danger to the general public.

But when provoked by such a despicable and criminal activity as Heather and Sam had done, maybe he could lose his temper.

"A threat to society?" he asked himself as he walked through the police parking lot. "Never. But fuck with me, and you'll see the threat materialize."

His Mustang had been brought to the station, and his keys returned to him ten minutes ago.

But they kept his gun.

"Assholes."

He got to his car, unlocked it, and dropped inside. Everything looked the same. None of Dad's asshole cop buddies took her for a spin, as far as he could tell.

Key in the ignition, he fired up the engine and listened to it purr, trying hard to keep his mind off Heather. Where did she find that asshole, *Sam*, anyway? What a dick he was and so vain. All those muscles, all that time in the gym. And for what? To get laid? To stare in the mirror and pose? All ego.

"Complete dick," he mumbled, turning on the stereo. "The *ego* has landed," he sang. "Fly like an ego."

He flipped the stereo to Bluetooth, then opened iTunes on his phone and brought up his favorite band, Ice Nine Kills. Once "Funeral Derangements" was playing, he cranked the volume, lowered his window—should piss off someone—then backed out of the spot.

To cool off, he'd go for a drive out by Trout Lake or maybe up the highway to the lookout over Lake Nipissing. He just needed the wind in his hair and the accompaniment of loud music.

He drove up Algonquin Avenue toward the highway, music blaring from his speakers, screaming along with the lead vocalist, Spencer Charnas. After cruising through several streetlights, he stopped at the highway bypass and decided to continue going straight. A drive up into the countryside past the truck stop north of North Bay would do him good.

Then he'd call his dad, chat about Heather and *Sam*, and find out what they would do with them. There had to be something, some charges or threat of charges, that would get them to pay him his money back.

Heather's boyfriend Sam had alluded to having an important dad, someone influential. Once they learned who he was, Chief Warner could pay them all a visit.

Instead of the twenty grand he spent on Heather, they could pay him back fifty or a hundred grand and drop all the charges. The story could be that he found the gun and showed it to them. It was discharged by accident.

His dad could speak to the judge presiding over his case in the months to come and get him community service or some shit—which he wouldn't do anyway. This just needed to go away, and Heather, Warner, and his dad would take care of it.

Otherwise, everyone would know what Heather had been doing to those johns, those men she'd been fucking—literally and figuratively.

Someone honked at him from behind. He checked his mirror as they flashed their high beams at him. He stuck his finger out the window and hit the gas.

The light had changed, but lost in thought, he'd missed it.

Wind in his hair, the Mustang's engine revving to his soft touch, Bruce hit the bottom of Thibeault Hill and gunned it.

The vehicle with the high beams remained close to his ass.

"Lower the lights, dickhead." No one could hear him shout from within his own vehicle, but it felt good to be angry.

He smacked his brakes once, then again.

There were multiple lanes up Thibeault Hill so that cars could easily pass slow-moving trucks, but the guy behind him wasn't interested in passing. He just wanted to tailgate the Mustang.

"Get off my ass, you piece of shit!"

As he reached the top of the hill, Bruce approached Cedar Heights Road by the gas station and slowed quickly to take a right-hand turn.

Fear spiked through his gut as the vehicle behind him almost rear-ended the Mustang, but at the last second, he was able to avoid colliding with his bumper.

"Holy shit!" Bruce roared in the front seat of his Mustang. "You fucker! That was *way* too close."

He wrenched the wheel to the right, keeping his eyes on the high beams in his mirror.

Why was he turning, too?

When he looked forward, it was too late—much too late.

A pickup truck came off the shoulder of the road and hit his Mustang head-on.

Bruce shot forward into the steering wheel as the airbag drove into his chest, and the loud metal song on his car stereo cut off mid-scream.

Then, something hit the Mustang from behind, whipping his head back into the seat.

Something clicked in his neck, causing intense pain to flare in his head.

Bruce screamed between gasps of breath as the car came to rest at the side of the road. The airbag almost knocked him out cold, but the hit from behind kept him cognizant and in pain.

Panting like a stressed-out cat along for a car ride, tongue out, mouth wide, he stared outside his smashed windshield at the darkness as men ran toward him.

His wits about him, everything coming back in a rush through the pain in his neck, he realized his precious Mustang was totaled. The tailgating asshole did it.

Someone wrenched on the door beside him, but it wouldn't open.

Men outside the car were trying to pry it from the side of the Mustang, but the impact must've dented it, and now it was stuck.

Someone smacked the window with a hard object, such as metal.

Bruce turned to look, then scrunched his eyes shut as searing white hot pain erupted from below his ears.

A burst of sound made him jump, and then the driver's side window burst inward, showering him with glass.

Someone shot the glass out with a bullet.

*Motherfucker.* He would kill them all.

Hands rushed inside his vehicle. Someone undid his seatbelt. Men were hauling him from his seat, their hands roughly under his arms.

His lower leg caught on the bottom of the steering wheel, stopping his withdrawal from the car's window and making him scream.

More men reached inside.

His leg was adjusted, and then he was freed.

Three men carried him. One behind his head, two holding a leg each.

"What the fuck, man?" he said in a daze of pain. "You're all dead."

They lifted him high, then let go.

Nausea filled his gut in a burst as he dropped into the back of the pickup.

When he banged his head on the steel bed in the back of the vehicle, consciousness left him—blessedly.

# Chapter 31

SARAH SPUN AROUND AND ran for the bathroom at the back of the motel room. "Go with them," she told Aaron and Melody over her shoulder.

"What about you?" Aaron asked.

The knock came again. "Police! Open up!"

"I can't go with them."

Aaron seemed torn, watching her with a scowl on his face when she looked back. Melody just looked lost, wondering what was happening.

Then Sarah was in the bathroom, turning on the shower. She slipped behind the bathroom door and listened to their protest at the front of the room.

"What's this all about?" Aaron asked.

"Exit the room, sir. Both of you, please."

"My wife is in the shower. I'll wait inside for her."

*Wife?* Why did he use that term? It sounded pleasant, but she hadn't committed to marriage yet. She was waiting for him to commit to her—in all ways.

The sound of a scuffle could be heard over the running water.

"Hey," Aaron shouted. "What are you doing?"

Sarah fought the urge to come around the corner and stop whatever was happening, but she couldn't. According to Vivian, that wouldn't work.

She couldn't go with the authorities.

Not now.

It wouldn't end well.

"Get him in the cruiser," a man shouted.

Then there was silence.

She was supposed to be in the shower. The door was slightly ajar. There was no way a cop would walk down and peek inside. Or would he? The man would call from around the corner, somewhere beyond the open bathroom door.

That theory went out the window when an officer marched into the bathroom and yanked back the shower curtain.

*What an asshole!*

She shot out from behind the door and shoved him into the steaming hot water.

His shins smacked the side of the porcelain bathtub, and with a small yelp, the cop collapsed forward, his upper chest and face hitting the wall first before he crumpled into the tub, the shower curtain ripping off several rings along the way.

Sarah dove forward as the officer was pushing up to get out of the tub, his balance forward, his upper body covered in water, unclipped his holster, and snatched the officer's gun before he had a chance to protect it.

Then she kicked his ass—literally—and the cop fell back into the tub, getting completely soaked through his uniform, steam rising all around him.

He shouted and scrambled to get out of the water flow, then got smart and jammed the spigot to the off position.

The water stopped.

He wiped his face and blinked up at her.

"Cuff yourself. Hurry."

"Fuck you."

She made a show of clicking off the safety, then aimed the pistol at him and slipped her finger over the trigger.

"A bullet to the foot stops you from chasing me. Or handcuffs. You've got three seconds to make up your mind."

She waited a moment as he stared at her, and then she placed the gun against his right shoe.

"Okay, okay!" he shouted, ripping the cuffs off his utility belt. "You're fucking insane. I'm a cop, you know."

"Yeah, sure." She leaned back and peeked into the room. It was empty, but the door was still wide open. When she looked back at him, he had one cuff on and had stopped before placing the other on.

"Is this really necessary? Can't you tell I'm a police officer?"

"I was supposed to be in the shower, which people generally do in the nude. Yet you waltzed in here and ripped back the shower curtain. You're a fucking pig, is what you are. Now that's a fitting name, isn't it? Now cuff that other wrist before I shoot you just because."

"You'll rot in prison for this." His grimace had turned to a death stare.

"When all this comes out, I don't think I'll be the one in prison, asshole. You might want to get used to those cuffs."

Something flashed in his eyes. Was that a shade of fear behind his tough-guy stance?

Sarah backed away. "Wait a few minutes before making any noise. If I don't clear this room, I'll shoot you. If you shout too early, I'll shoot you. If they catch me, I'll shoot you. Are we clear?"

He nodded, looking up at her, his face registering his predicament. What would he tell his colleagues now? A woman bested him, cuffed, and had his gun stolen.

"Yeah, we're clear. Whatever I do, you'll shoot me."

"That about sums it up. Don't move. Don't get shot." Sarah closed the door, then slipped the cop's gun in the back of her pants—she had Bishop's gun still, too—and ran for the open door.

She leaned back against the wall and peeked outside.

Four cruisers were in the parking lot outside her door, with six at the motel on the other side of the road.

What prompted such a response?

Then Vivian told her.

Judge Griffin had Chief Warner send officers after seeing the cell phone footage from Mackenzie's men.

They all knew about Sarah knocking on Melody's door. And now they were after Sarah because the judge's daughter was found in a motel room with Aaron.

And the judge's daughter had all her fingers.

Griffin would want to know why Sarah wasn't more forthcoming in his presence. Why had she withheld information from him? So they sent an army of cops to pick them all up.

"Shit," she whispered as she exited the room and walked toward their car.

Aaron and Melody were nowhere to be seen. Parkman and Alex's motel room door was wide open, the lights on, but she couldn't see anyone inside—not even Mackenzie's man.

She pulled the keys from her pocket, opened the car door, and dropped behind the driver's seat.

Within seconds, she backed out of the spot, got to the end of the parking area, then hopped out onto Lakeshore Boulevard and shoved the pedal downward.

She needed as much distance from Chief Warner's men as possible.

Then she'd head back to where they were all meeting.

Tonight, she was the surprise guest.

# Chapter 32

CHIEF WARNER REFUSED TO go to Mackenzie's house in the exact vehicle, and Griffin couldn't understand why. He was probably upset with how everything turned out today. That, and he had to give his portion of Mackenzie's money back now that Sommers was a free man.

Griffin had drunk too much to drive there alone, so he took a taxi. During the ride to the construction magnate's property, he couldn't shake the feeling that he was in trouble, like when he was a child and had to wait until his father got home.

Mackenzie was by no means his father. They were businessmen, equals on many levels. They'd done several huge deals together and worked closely for years. A man like Mackenzie had to be *friendly* with city staff if he wanted things to go his way, like special permits. An enemy city official could ruin someone like Mackenzie or at least limit their potential.

As a senior judge, Griffin would be the highest-ranking official in the room tonight.

So there would be no dressing down, no delinquent child in front of Daddy.

They had a deal that fell through. That was it. When Mackenzie learned why it fell through—Griffin's daughter's life depended on it— he'd understand, and that would be it.

They'd eat their food, drink their drinks, alleviate the tension throughout the night, and be off.

Judge Griffin would file his resignation papers later in the week and retire by the end of the summer. Mackenzie could wiggle his way into the back pocket of some other judge by Christmas, and all would be well in the world.

As for Chief Warner, Griffin would have to think about what he would do with that man. He knew too much—everything, to be exact. If he went off the rails, Griffin would go down with him, and prison was no place for a chief of police or a judge.

That was their pact from the beginning when they did their first "favor" almost thirty years ago.

The taxi pulled into the long, winding driveway of Mackenzie Estates. It meandered up to the front entrance, where the wraparound drive circled a large fountain with the warrior goddess Athena standing with her bow and arrow. It was supposed to be the goddess Venus in the scallop shell, but Mackenzie had Athena brought in, and now she stood in the shell.

To the uneducated, the depiction was impressive. To those who adored Venus, it was disrespectful.

But when you had the money Mackenzie had, there were no limits to poor taste.

The taxi came around the fountain and stopped behind two police cars.

Judge Griffin frowned at them. What were the police doing here? Arresting the man of the house? Or were they here for some other nefarious reason?

He paid the driver and exited the cab. As it pulled away, Griffin inhaled a deep breath of fresh air and noticed three more cars parked in the shadows ahead of the cruisers.

Two SUVs, a pickup truck, and Warner's car.

So, everyone was already here.

He had to admit before turning and entering the building that he did fear the unknown. Perhaps it was something else, like an ominous premonition that something was wrong. No matter how he examined it, his stomach was upset, and he was already looking forward to going home tonight. That drink before bed would go down smoothly and signal this horrible day's end.

When he turned to face the front of the house, two men stood on either side of the doors. Both were large, thick men who had to be over six feet tall. Each man's hands were empty, but their weapons would be close. They were carrying, that was for sure, but he couldn't detect a bulge in their clothing.

"This way, sir," the man on the left said as he opened the door. "He's expecting you."

The judge nodded and, without saying a word, mounted the three steps to the top of the concrete porch, then entered Mackenzie's domain.

For a foyer, Griffin was always impressed. A staircase ascended to the second floor on the right. It was wide enough for five people to walk side by side. The art was something Griffin didn't understand, though. Abstract paintings, marble and bronze statues in various poses, standing in lit alcoves, with the particular lighting focused on specific areas. Did the man live here? Or was this a gallery where interested parties would attend for a viewing?

Heavy footsteps approached from behind as he observed a knight holding a spear, neatly secluded under the staircase.

"Mr. Griffin, sir."

The judge turned to see another of Mackenzie's security detail, just like the FBI—same suit, same shoes. They probably all wore the same sunglasses during the daytime, too.

"They're waiting for you in the main lounge."

Griffin nodded. "I'll follow you."

The man pivoted on his heels and headed along the wide corridor. Griffin stayed close to him, observing the décor as he sauntered along. This would likely be the last time he was in this house, and he wanted to savor the moment. Once he returned Mackenzie's money for not finding Sommers guilty and locking him up, and he retired, there'd be no reason to ever set foot in Mackenzie's mansion again. They were done. Tonight concluded their business.

The beefy security man in a tailored Hugo Boss suit—at least he thought it was a Hugo Boss, although he wasn't a suit expert—slowed at the opening to a vast room with a fireplace already rising in full swing.

"Please, sir," the security man said, his head bowed, arm extended.

Griffin nodded at him and moved into the vast living room, reminding him of something from a movie. Like *Glass Onion*, that *Knives Out* movie where the large room was decorated with valuable art pieces and various spots to sit.

After a sweeping glance, he took in all the faces staring back at him. Some he expected to see, some he didn't.

Chief Warner sat on a long four-seater couch with his back to the wall. Two men in police uniforms sat on a smaller sofa, facing the fireplace, with one of the officers looking as though he had gotten wet for some reason. To the right, he saw a man he knew, who had departed his office earlier that day—Sarah's boyfriend, Aaron Stevens.

*What the hell is he doing here?*

And finally, a young couple sat on a loveseat all by themselves, holding hands. He'd never seen them before, but the man didn't look so good. His eyes were bloodshot, and his face was so white it was as if sunshine had never graced his skin. He was a thick man—bodybuilder by the looks of it—and one of his hands boasted a bulging white gauze that made it look like his arm ended with the white bulb of a large Q-Tip.

Griffin nodded at the couple, stared at Aaron a moment, gave the officers a passing glance, and then moved to sit beside Warner.

"What's all this?" he said under his breath to Warner.

"No idea. Mackenzie wanted us all here, so we're here."

"You make it sound like when he calls, we just do as he says."

Warner turned to look at him. "We went back on our deal with him today. Understandably, he'll be upset about that. When he calls, we *don't* just do as he says. But today, we're making an exception."

Griffin nodded and leaned back to take in the room. Everyone had a drink in front of them. Water for Aaron, water for the cops, orange juice and some kind of dark pop for the couple, and an amber-colored drink for Warner.

"How did you score a drink around here? Is there a waiter, or did you get it yourself?"

"They'll bring you what you want."

Griffin leaned forward, caught the eye of one of the security detail, and waved a hand. "I'll need a scotch," he said. "Single malt Islay, if you have it. The peatier, the better."

The man listened to something in his ear, tilting his head slightly, a hand covering the earpiece. He nodded once, then faced Griffin.

"Right away, sir."

The man moved out of view, his footfalls echoing along the corridor.

Griffin glanced over at the two officers and then turned to Aaron. "What are you doing here?"

Aaron pointed at the cops. "Those assholes snatched me."

One of the cops got to his feet, the wet one, and started toward Aaron. "I'm done with the name-calling, you little prick—"

"*Hey!*" a man shouted.

From out of nowhere, three thick men in suits materialized from the hallway.

The officer stopped four feet in front of Aaron.

"Take your seat," one of Mackenzie's security detail said, his tone commanding, making it clear that it wasn't open for discussion.

The cop stared at Aaron a moment longer.

"Now," the man said, moving toward the cop.

The officer raised his hands and stepped backward. "Okay, okay, *fuck*. We're the police, you know. You'd do well to remember that."

"You're a guest in Mr. Mackenzie's home. You will do well to remember your manners." His tone suggested that someone would be happy to teach them manners if they forgot them.

"Sit down." Warner spoke it as a command. "You got beaten up, she took your service revolver, and now you want to play tough guy. Just sit the fuck down."

The officer kept his eyes off Warner, turned to glare at Aaron, then moved to his seat and plopped back down beside the other cop. They whispered something to one another, eyes on Aaron.

The security detail eased back out of sight.

They were hovering, listening, and they wanted everyone to know that. But what were they waiting for? The food to be ready? Wasn't this a dinner meeting? And why were they all meeting like this, with so much tension in the air?

"Who took that cop's gun?" Griffin asked.

Warner leaned closer. "Sarah did."

"Oh. Shit."

He watched the cop for a moment, wondering if he'd have a job by the end of the week.

Footsteps echoed down the corridor again, and then the man who spoke to Griffin moments before was back, a glass in hand.

He strode over to the side table beside Griffin and set the glass down.

"Your Islay scotch, sir."

Griffin nodded once, took the glass, sniffed it, then drank a sip and inhaled the aroma.

The couple sitting alone whispered something to each other, and then the woman pointed at Griffin. The man with the Q-Tip hand glanced his way, his eyes narrowing as if Griffin had slighted him somehow.

"Do we know each other?" he asked them.

"You're Judge Griffin, right?" the woman asked.

"I am. And you are?"

The woman ignored the question. "That's Bruce's dad," she said to the man beside her.

"You know my son?" Griffin leaned forward in his seat.

The man held up his Q-Tip hand. "He shot me today."

That stirring in Griffin's stomach worsened. He glanced at Warner, then back to the couple. "So you're the call girl and her boyfriend. The ones extorting money from my son." His tone hardened with irritation. "Why are you here? Shouldn't you be at the hospital or something? Or maybe the bank, getting my son's money for him?"

"We're here because this is my father's home." The man shook his head. "We've met before, but you wouldn't remember me. I don't mingle in my father's *elite* circles that often."

This was his father's home? Bruce Griffin shot Mackenzie's son in the hand on the day Judge Griffin killed the Sommers deal?

Mackenzie will have questions that Griffin won't have answers for.

That was too coincidental to be by chance, even though it was entirely by chance.

That last part Q-Tip said about elite circles was spoken with a high level of disdain, but how could he respond? What would he say now? Griffin was lost for words.

"I understand you guys released Bruce today," Q-Tip man said, contempt dripping off his every word.

That was the icing on the cake. Mackenzie would want his pound of flesh, meaning Griffin didn't want to be here anymore.

Warner and Griffin exchanged a worried glance, but Griffin couldn't find any words at the moment.

"He was released on a promise to appear," Warner said. "Standard procedure. He'll have his day in court."

Q-Tip shook his head. "Whatever suits the judge, eh? Is that how it goes with you people?"

"You people?" Griffin muttered, finding his voice.

"Your son has your ego. The apple and tree bit works here."

Heat rose to his collar. What was Mackenzie's plan? Put them all in a room and make them sweat while he watched on a camera feed or something? Allow them to argue among themselves while his security detail waits in the wings to break it up if it comes to fisticuffs?

Judge Griffin drank the rest of the scotch in one swig, set his glass down, and got to his feet.

"Well, it's been great." He stepped around a large coffee table. "Say hello to Mackenzie for me, Warner. Tell him I'll call." He glanced at the extortion couple as he strode by them. "I won't sit here and be talked down to by passive-aggressive little people who have a beef with my son *after* robbing *him* of twenty thousand dollars."

Q-Tip donned a cocky smile as Griffin passed, then he looked away.

At the entrance to the corridor, four huge men in suits formed a line, their hands clasped in front of them near their belts.

The man who brought him his drink eyed him up and down. "Take your seat, sir. Mr. Mackenzie will be here shortly."

"Step aside, gentlemen. I'll be leaving now."

No one moved.

"Griffin," Warner called to him. "Come sit down. We can't leave yet."

"Sir," the man said, his arm extended toward the couch. "Please."

Griffin crossed his arms over his chest. "Are you saying you will not *allow* me to leave?"

"That's correct, sir. No one leaves until Mr. Mackenzie gets here. So, please, retake your seat."

Griffin scoffed, shot a backward glance over his shoulder at Warner, then spun back to the line of men. "I'm Judge Griffin. That there is the chief of police." He pointed at Warner without looking at him. "Do you know who you're fucking with?"

There was a pause, then the man spoke again.

"Sir. Your seat."

"Well," Griffin said, gasping the word. "When this little meeting is over, I want your names. These officers will file charges. You are forcibly confining me to this house against my will—"

"Sir, we will *take* you back to your seat if you cannot make it on your own."

The men moved closer to him.

"Fine, fine. I'll sit down. But please, bring me more scotch."

"As you wish, sir."

Griffin strode back to his seat beside Warner, shaking his head and avoiding eye contact with anyone else in the room.

Dejected and feeling like he'd been humiliated in front of everyone, he sat beside Warner and leaned in close.

"What's going on here?"

"I suspect more than we know."

What sounded like wheels echoed from somewhere in the house. It got closer until everyone was staring at the hallway opening where Griffin had tried to leave through a moment before.

A moment later, a wheelchair came into view.

The man sitting in the wheelchair had a black hood placed over his head. Splotches of what looked like blood were smeared all over the man's clothes. His shirt was streaked with it, and his pants were torn in several places.

"What the hell?" Griffin muttered.

"Gentlemen." Mackenzie's voice boomed throughout the living room.

He materialized from a side cabinet, which had to double as a hidden door because he wasn't there one moment, and the next, he was.

The man of the house moved behind the wheelchair, taking the place of his security detail, who had been pushing it.

"The man of the hour," Mackenzie said, lifting the black hood off the wheelchair-bound man.

There were a few gasps around the room at the bloody ruin of the man's face. Griffin could tell the man's nose was broken from where he sat. One eye was swollen shut, and the other was nearly as swollen. Several teeth were missing, and his lips were swollen and split, blood still trickling from half a dozen spots on his face.

A flutter of recognition came to Griffin. He leaned forward, his mouth open.

It couldn't be, could it?

"No ..." he muttered.

"Yes," Mackenzie said, his voice echoing off the walls. "Your son, Judge Griffin, had a terrible car accident this evening. If it weren't for my men pulling him out of his car when they did, he'd likely be dead." Mackenzie animated an explosion with his hands. "Boom," he shouted. "The Mustang blew up seconds after we extracted him. You should be thanking me."

Griffin pushed up to his feet, but someone grabbed him and yanked him back down.

"Sir," a security brute said from behind him. "Remain seated."

Those two words came out as an order.

"What have you done to my son?" Griffin asked, uttering the words from a place of shock and pain. "Why have you done this?" He met Mackenzie's eyes.

"I might ask you the same thing." Mackenzie pointed at Q-Tip man. "What have you done to *my* son? Why would you kill the Sommers deal and have Bruce here"—he smacked Bruce's shoulder twice, making him wince—"drive to Heather's apartment to shoot Sam, my only son?"

Mackenzie tapped the side of his head with one finger near his temple. "What were you thinking, *Judge* Griffin?"

Like a landed fish, Griffin opened and closed his mouth without saying a word, his eyes on his son.

Then, a name popped into his head.

*Sarah Roberts.*

"Sarah did this," he muttered.

"What?" Mackenzie said. "Speak up. I can't hear you."

Griffin averted his gaze to Aaron. "Sarah Roberts did all of this. She sent my son to Heather's apartment today. He went there fueled with the need for vengeance." He averted his gaze to Mackenzie. "She warned me not to do the deal with you by saying my daughter would be in trouble if I did. You have to understand. Sommers had my daughter. He delivered her severed finger to my office with a message to let him go, or Melody would be dead."

Mackenzie was shaking his head. "Judge, judge, judge. You've been played by a master, then."

"What?" Griffin said, his stomach churning so bad he thought he'd vomit.

Mackenzie whispered to one of his men, and the man hustled away.

He raised a finger for everyone to remain quiet, to wait.

Griffin touched his stomach, hoping he didn't lose the contents. From where he sat, his son looked near death. He'd have a long road to recovery.

Half a minute later, footsteps pounded closer.

Then Melody, his daughter, stepped around the corner. She looked radiant in her pretty dress, with her hair well-groomed.

Her eyes darted left and right, her movements quick, giving off a fearful expression.

"Melody—" Griffin said, trying to get up. "You're here. You're alive." He glanced at her hand, his breath catching in his throat. "Your finger—"

"Remain seated," Mackenzie said as Griffin was shoved down again from behind.

Mackenzie grabbed Melody's hands and raised them, displaying each finger. "Which finger is it that Sommers removed? Huh?" He glared at Griffin. "It was all a hoax perpetrated by your daughter to free that bastard."

Griffin fell back on the couch. He stared at his daughter's intact hands and was grateful Sommers hadn't mutilated her. But none of it made sense now. Why would she be involved with Sommers?

"What is going on?" Griffin turned to Warner, then Aaron, and back to Melody. "I don't understand any of this. Whose finger came to my office today?"

"These kind officers found your daughter in a motel room with him." Mackenzie ignored his question, then pointed at Aaron. He shoved Melody to sit beside him.

"What have you done?" Griffin asked Aaron. "You and Sarah did this. All of it is on your head. This is my family you fucked with. How could you?"

"Yeah?" Aaron stared at him intently. "Well, fuck you."

Griffin shot from his seat, but rough hands drove him back down once more.

"Remain seated was *not* a request," the man said from behind him. "Stand again, and I have orders to cause you pain."

Mackenzie grinned at him. "Don't worry, Judge Griffin. Before the night is over, you'll have your pound of flesh, and I'll have mine."

"What the hell does that mean?" Griffin shouted. "This is preposterous!"

"It means you owe me. And you are not leaving until you pay me everything you owe. If you can't, then you never leave. At least not in one piece."

"How dare you?" Griffin said through his teeth.

"Stand again." Mackenzie taunted him. "Go ahead. Try me." He shook his head. "Pathetic, that's what you are. Fucking pathetic." He moved toward the corridor. "Once we have Sarah, Michael Sommers, and the others all here, we'll sort everything out. Then we will bury the bodies of those responsible in the back and return to work in the morning."

Mackenzie moved down the corridor, his footfalls echoing away from them.

"It's a lovely evening to collect on my debts and to make right several wrongs, Judge Griffin. Get comfortable. Have another drink. You'll be here for some time."

A door closed somewhere, then silence followed.

Griffin picked up his empty glass and shook it, knowing his fate may be sealed. He felt sorrow for his son and pity for his daughter. So many unanswered questions. Why would she lie to him to help Sommers? Or was she forced to help?

He glanced down at his empty glass in thought.

"I could sure use another one of these. Hell, bring me the bottle."

# Chapter 33

SARAH PULLED INTO THE parking lot of the coffee shop where she'd met with Bruce about ten hours ago, killed the engine, and sank lower in her seat to wait. Cars were sparse at this late hour. Even though it was a twenty-four-hour stop, she counted only eight vehicles, as opposed to earlier in the day when there were fewer than three or four spots to park.

They were far enough away from the motels that Parkman and Alex, if they got away, would have to take a taxi. Otherwise, it was a three-hour walk at least, and she couldn't wait that long.

It was all ending tonight, according to Vivian. And it would only be successful with ice and nine kills. Sarah pleaded with her, asking why nine people had to die, but Vivian had left her consciousness.

Sarah didn't have to wait long—fifteen minutes max—before Parkman stepped out from behind a car and started toward her.

Then someone knocked on her window, startling the shit out of her. She did a short scream and bumped her thighs on the bottom of the steering wheel.

"What the fuck?" she said, unlocking the door for Alex.

He slipped in the back and closed the door, then Parkman jumped in beside her.

"You scared the bejesus out of me."

"We need to leave," Parkman said.

Sarah started the car and got them rolling, her heart still in her throat.

"What happened to Aaron?" Parkman asked.

"He got taken in the raid on the motel." He looked at her, asking with his eyes how she didn't get taken. "I hid in the bathroom, then pushed a cop into the shower and made him handcuff himself."

"And when you came out of the bathroom?"

"The other cops had moved down the length of the rooms. I slipped into the car, and here I am." She glanced back at Alex. "You guys?"

"When I left your room, Alex was already outside. He saw what they were doing, and we bolted for the road. Not a single cop looked at us as we walked down the sidewalk like two citizens."

"Why raid the motels?" Alex asked.

"Because," Sarah said. "The guy you were chatting with in the room had already sent the video of me knocking on Melody's door at the Park Motel. Mackenzie had it and forwarded it to the judge and the police chief. Then they sent cops to each room." Sarah took a left to follow the bypass around the city. "And they got Melody and Aaron."

"Something tells me they aren't at the police station." Parkman stared back at Alex, then Sarah.

"They aren't." She slowed with traffic, then got moving again as they passed a large Walmart on the right. "As far as I can tell, they're all at Mackenzie's house. We've got one quick stop to make, then we'll head up there."

"And what? Knock on the door? Ask for Aaron back?"

"Close."

"Seriously?"

Sarah looked at both of them. "Vivian said it's important that we use ice, and there are nine kills. Apparently, that'll draw them out."

Parkman frowned. "What? That doesn't sound good."

"The music?" Alex said from the back seat. "As in Ice Nine Kills?"

"*What?*" Sarah and Parkman said at the same time.

"Ice Nine Kills is the name of a metal band."

They waited for more, and he continued.

"I think I know what Vivian means," Alex said. "Let me explain."

As Sarah took a right on Algonquin and another right on Shirreff Avenue, Alex guessed what Sarah's sister was trying to tell them.

"That could make sense," Sarah said. "But why that band? Why not just tell me to play metal?"

Alex shrugged. "Maybe they're loud enough to upset someone. What if Mackenzie hates metal? Or that band means something to someone inside the house?"

She pulled into the parking area of the building they were coming to visit, stopped the car, killed the engine, and got out. Before several seconds passed, men in uniform approached them.

Parkman swished his toothpick from one side of his mouth to the other as Alex took up a fighting stance.

"Guys, it's fine. They're with us. We haven't got much time." Sarah moved toward the approaching uniforms. "Let's do this quickly, then go play some metal."

# Chapter 34

JUDGE GRIFFIN WAS ON his third glass of scotch—they'd brought him the bottle—and thought he might want to slow down.

Other than a few whispers coming from the Q-Tip couple, no one had spoken in the ten minutes since Mackenzie had walked away.

The waiting was driving Griffin insane. What were they waiting for? *Who* were they waiting for? Did Mackenzie think Sommers would show up at his house unannounced with all the security men he had floating around?

Griffin set his glass down and twisted around in his seat. Warner eyed him warily. Griffin twisted farther until he was staring up at the beefy man behind him.

"I need to console my son."

The man nodded once without looking down. "Console him from here."

"Now, you listen to me—"

The man's face contorted with anger as he adjusted his gaze to glare down at the judge.

"One day, I'll be on the bench, and you'll be in my courtroom."

"I don't think so, sir." The man's voice was animal-like, husky, and filled with violence.

"And on that day, I'll sentence you to the maximum allowable by law and then some."

Warner placed a hand on Griffin's shoulder, gently coaxing him to turn back around.

"Easy now," Warner whispered. "Don't threaten Mackenzie's staff there, tiger."

Griffin jerked his shoulder away from Warner's hand. "Don't patronize me."

Warner leaned close to him. "Then don't get drunk, asshole. Not at a time like this." Warner waved his hand toward Melody, who sat quietly sobbing now and then, and pointed at Bruce, who needed a hospital. "Consider the needs of your children here."

Melody raised her head and looked at him from ten feet away. "When has he ever done that?"

"Oh, come on," Griffin said, drawing out the words. "I've always been there for you."

She smirked, tilted her head, then looked away. "Yeah, right. Daddy of the year right there."

Aaron, Sarah's man, sat there watching him, his head slowly shaking back and forth.

"What's your problem?" Griffin asked him.

Aaron didn't respond.

"Just as I thought. Nothing to say after setting this all up with Sarah? You're the reason we're all here."

"Funny," Aaron muttered.

"Funny? How so?"

"How I see it is you're the reason we're all here."

Griffin stared at him for a long moment, wondering how he came to that conclusion, then brushed it off as nonsense.

"You don't know shit about me, and if even for a second you got a glimpse into my life, the things I've done for my family, then you would—"

A speaker system clicked on overhead. The whistle of feedback was loud, grating on Griffin's nerves. He grimaced while glancing around the room at everyone else who was doing the same.

"What the fuck?" he said.

Then Warner was on his feet and walking over to sit on a single chair by the opening of the hallway.

"Hey," Griffin shouted, twisting around to stare up at the brute behind him. "He's allowed to get up, but I'm not?"

"That is correct, sir."

"Oh, cut the *sir* crap. You don't respect me as much as I don't respect you."

The man stared forward at nothing.

Griffin spun around, his empty whisky glass slipping from his grip. It hit the carpet and rolled to the side.

"What's this all about, Warner? You with Mackenzie now?"

"*With* Mackenzie?" Warner seemed to chew on those words, contemplating them. "I thought we both were—until several hours ago."

"What's that supposed to mean?"

Then, loud and clear voices came through the loudspeaker. A voice Griffin recognized as his own, the same one he had spoken with fanaticism to Warner earlier that day.

"*Mackenzie is gunning for us.*" Warner's voice issued loud and clear from the speakers above everyone's head.

"*How so?*" Griffin's voice.

He narrowed his eyes at Warner. "You bastard," he shouted from across Mackenzie's living room.

"*He wants his money back today, with interest.*"

"*Not going to happen.*"

"*What?*" Warner's voice rose on the speakers. "*Why?*"

"*Transferring half a million dollars isn't something you send through PayPal. Call him. Tell him it'll take time, but it's coming. Then tell him we're done. No more deals. I'll put in for my early retirement.*"

The judge tried to get up again, but this time, the man didn't just push him down. He punched the side of Griffin's head, knocking him down so hard that Griffin fell sideways and lay sprawled out on the couch.

"*You want my advice?*" Warner's voice.

The judge held the side of his head, gawking up at the security man whose hand was ready to strike again.

"Stay down, asshole."

"*No, but I'm sure you'll give it to me anyway.*"

The *sir* was gone now. Their respect was depleted.

"*Find a plot, order a casket, and get ready to die. Mackenzie is coming, and nobody stops that man."*

*"C'mon, now you're talking ridiculous. Nobody kills a judge. And no one will come for you. Mackenzie is a businessman. He bought a deal that didn't go through. He'll invest elsewhere and move on."*

*"He invited us to his house tonight."*

Griffin pushed up to sit but didn't try to stand as he stared around the room.

*"Tell him I can't make it."* Griffin's voice boomed through the speakers. He knew what was coming and regretted every word spoken in front of the traitor, Chief Warner.

*"He invited us to his house to discuss the problem of Michael Sommers."*

*"Then you go."*

Warner scoffed over the speakers. *"Asshole. I'm not going like a lamb to be slaughtered. We go together. You did this. You have to own it."*

"Stop the recording," Mackenzie bellowed from the hallway.

Silence filled the room as everyone's eyes were on Mackenzie as he moved into the light. He focused on Griffin.

"You know," he said. "I've worked with a lot of people in my time." He paused. "All I ask is that you do what you say you'll do. That's it." He clapped his hands once, then splayed them open, palms facing upward. "If you do what you say you'll do, I can trust you. Based on a track record, my trust thickens. And, if I can trust you, I can pay you upfront, knowing you'll do what we discussed." He lowered his hands and shook his head once. "But you didn't, Judge Griffin."

"I thought Sommers had my daughter," Griffin said, his voice pathetically close to a whine. He looked at Melody. "I was led to believe her life was in jeopardy."

"Evidently, he didn't have her." Mackenzie pointed at Melody. "Sarah knew where she was the whole time. As soon as they left your courthouse, Sarah and this man"—he pointed at Aaron—"drove right to her. Two of my men were watching Sommers's motel room. Sarah's boys attacked both, one mutilated in a motel room that was rented to a man named Parkman." He fixed his gaze on Aaron. "We'll round up all those boys in due time."

Aaron adjusted himself in his seat, obviously uncomfortable with what Mackenzie was saying.

"But that has nothing to do with me." Griffin was pleading again, and he knew it. The side of his head throbbed where the man hit him.

"My son was shot today," Mackenzie said, walking around to stand behind Q-Tip man. "Can you imagine the day I've had, Judge?"

Griffin's stomach roiled. He didn't know how much more he could take. His son was watching him through the one eye that still had a thin slit before it was swollen shut, too. His injuries weren't consistent with a car accident. Anyone could tell just by looking at him that Mackenzie's men had beaten him, and Griffin feared more was coming —for everyone.

"Before I show you what I do to disloyal people, allow me to show you what I do when someone is loyal."

A security man stepped forward and handed Mackenzie two thick envelopes.

Mackenzie nodded at the uniformed officers. "Gentlemen, please stand."

Both men in uniform—one wet, one not—got to their feet.

Mackenzie extended his arms, handing each man an envelope. "Here's fifty thousand each for risking your lives and jobs to bring me Melody and Aaron."

They took the envelopes.

Mackenzie shrugged. "It would be double if you brought me Sarah, but I understand. She can be difficult to contain."

"If you only knew," Aaron mumbled.

Everyone glanced his way.

"Just saying." He sat back, sighing hard enough to flutter his lips.

"Comedy aside," Mackenzie went on. "Thank you for your service. You're no longer needed this evening. Go home, get a drink, get cleaned up, and get some rest. My men will be in touch when we need something else in the future."

Both officers rubbed the envelopes like they were filled with gold, glanced at each other, then headed for the corridor, steeling one glance at Warner, who nodded at them before the security detail spread apart to let them by.

Mackenzie slapped his hands together as he had been handling something like bread or cookies and was now ridding them of crumbs. "Chief Warner," he said, turning to face the man. "To thank you for this recording, I have decided there will be no interest owing from you. In fact, I will declare your debt paid. You are free to leave, but since you'll remain the chief of police for several more years, we will be in touch."

Warner got to his feet, adjusted his suit jacket, pulled up his pants a notch, nodded with respect to Mackenzie, and then headed for the corridor without a look back at the judge.

"Bastard," Griffin called after him.

Warner didn't miss a beat. He just kept walking as the security detail spread to allow him access to the corridor. Then, like the sea after jumping into it, they moved back into place, sealing off the corridor.

"Sam, Heather." Mackenzie turned to his son. "Please stay for the last bit so you don't see me as a monster."

They exchanged a glance, then sat back. "Carry on," Sam said, his gaze moving to land on Griffin.

"Play the recording," Mackenzie shouted.

*"Call her and tell me where the hell she is. And if that doesn't work, and you can't locate Sarah, then send officers to Toronto to pick up her daughter. This leverage business has to end, and when it does, I'll end up on top."*

Aaron spun around so fast to glare at Griffin that two security men hopped closer to him, then stopped when he remained seated.

*"Just listen to yourself. You're talking about abducting Sarah's daughter, who is like six or seven years old now, just to get Sarah to do what you ask of her. Sound familiar?"*

"You're the bastard," Aaron said. "I'd kill you for that."

*"I'll do whatever it takes to save my family. Even if I have to kill her."*

*"It may come to that."*

Judge Griffin pointed at the ceiling speakers as if to enunciate that point, then sent a soft gaze toward Melody. "Anything for my family," he said.

"*Tell Mackenzie we'll be there tonight. Tell him I want my daughter back and that meddling bitch Sarah Roberts dead. Make it a car accident. Have her fall off a cliff. I don't fucking care, but there are dozens of ways to have someone killed where reasonable doubt won't even play into it. Actually, have her disappear. No body, no case. Then he can have whatever he wants.*"

Aaron's face had darkened to a deep red. Mackenzie's security men moved close enough to grab him if he tried to lunge at Griffin.

"*Are you sure you want Mackenzie to know that you want Sarah Roberts dead? A kill order like that is tough to reverse. Maybe you're just angry. Maybe it's the booze talking. How much have you had to drink—*"

"*Don't be so condescending. It's beneath you and, frankly, unbecoming.*"

"*Then be absolutely clear. What is it you want?*"

"Stop!" Mackenzie yelled. Silence filled the room. "Yeah, Judge Griffin. Pray tell. What *exactly* do you want?" After a brief few seconds, Mackenzie shouted, "Again!"

"*I'm done with all this bullshit. I'm retiring. I want my family back. If I'm to believe that video Mackenzie sent you, then Sarah walked out of here to snatch Melody, which means she knew where she was the whole time. Why didn't Sarah tell us my daughter wasn't in Europe? Why hide shit like that? I'll tell you why. To take her and use her against me. Well, fuck Sarah, and fuck everyone else. I want Sarah dead, and Melody returned to me. And if Mackenzie is involved in any way or hurts my daughter, he'll pay for it, too. End of story. After this business is concluded, we all go our severed ways.*"

"*Severed ways? Don't you mean* separate *ways?*"

"*And release my son on a promise to appear. I know he did nothing wrong, and now that this business is concluded, he doesn't need to be locked up like a common criminal.*"

"*I'll send the message and release Bruce. Be ready for tonight. And don't be drunk.*"

"*Oh, fuck off.*"

"Stop!" Mackenzie ordered.

The recording ceased, and the speakers clicked twice as whoever controlled them turned something off.

Mackenzie raised the fingers of one hand, then pulled down his index finger. "One, you ordered Sarah's death." He pulled down his middle finger. "Then you ordered *my* death." The third finger went down. "Then you claim your son did nothing wrong and released him because he isn't, and I quote, a 'common criminal.'" Mackenzie lowered his hands. "Who the fuck do you think you are, Judge Griffin? The Godfather himself?" He advanced on the judge, his security detail falling in behind him. "You think what Bruce did to my son was *nothing*!"

"No, I, uhh." Griffin scrambled for words as he pushed backward onto the couch. "I was angry. There's no excuse for what I said—"

"You were angry." Mackenzie laughed, tilting his head back and placing his hands over his stomach. It died off quickly until he was staring at Griffin again. "You have to understand that I can't have people out there wanting me dead. When you threaten someone, you become a threat to that person. And you know what I do to threats?"

Griffin shook his head.

"I neutralize them." Mackenzie brought out a weapon, aimed it at Griffin, and then stopped when Melody screamed.

"Are you going to shoot the judge?" Aaron asked.

Then, someone fired a weapon outside the building.

Twice.

# Chapter 35

THEY HAD DONE A quick job of getting prepared for the evening, and within thirty minutes, they had left the downtown area and were now one kilometer from Mackenzie Estates, setting up under the cover of darkness.

All exits from Mackenzie's property were barricaded.

Those in charge elected to move closer to the house, using the woods for cover. They gave Sarah, Alex, and Parkman a pair of goggles each, enabling them to see in the dark. Even though she thought it was called infrared, the area was cast in a greenish hue as she moved through the trees.

When they got within sight of the house, everyone took their places for the next performance.

Sarah removed her goggles and then glanced around for Alex. She edged closer to Parkman. "Where's Alex?" she whispered.

She detected his shrug in the dark. "No idea. He was right beside me, then he wasn't."

"Likely patrolling somewhere nearby."

She moved to the man with the stereo equipment. "You ready?"

He nodded. "Whenever you are. Just give me a few more seconds."

"You've got the band Ice Nine Kills queued?"

"Yes, with songs like 'The American Nightmare,' 'A Grave Mistake,' and 'Assault & Batteries' all ready." The man stopped moving. "You're sure this is going to help?"

"I've been told it will, even though I have no idea why it's necessary. Just hit them with it—"

The sound of a car, then another, starting up made her spin around. "Who's leaving?"

The man touched his ear. "My boss is saying Mackenzie let two cops go, and Chief Warner."

"Your people will handle them?"

The man spoke into his mouthpiece, then waited a moment. "Copy that." He glanced up at Sarah. "They will stop them when they attempt to exit the property. They'll do it far enough away that those still inside the house won't know."

"Good. Let's wait until that's dealt with, then."

Sarah moved closer to Parkman. "You doing okay?"

He leaned toward her and wrapped an arm over her shoulders. "How about you? Aaron's inside. That's gotta concern you."

"Yeah, but he wanted this. I had to let him do it. He'll be fine."

Two police cars exited slowly, followed by the chief of police's vehicle. Sarah barely detected noise coming from the house. It was as if someone was speaking into a microphone, with the voice coming from a speaker.

She could barely see flashing lights in the distance through the trees behind them as the cop cars pulled over.

Then someone came running through the trees. Her stereo man jerked upright.

Before she could ask what was going on, the man running pushed past her, a gun in his hand. He raised it, aimed skyward, then fired the weapon.

Twice.

# Chapter 36

BRUCE GRIFFIN SAT, LURCHED over in the wheelchair, hoping not to draw any attention to himself. Other than being upset with Heather over the money she'd extorted from him, he had done nothing to deserve the beating he took at the hands of Mackenzie's men. What did he ever do to Mackenzie? Sure, he shot Sam in the hand, but how was he to know that the man fucking Heather was Mackenzie's son?

His dad had always been on the wrong side of the law, but no one questioned it over the years, and everyone got along. Now that his father had pissed off Mackenzie on the same day that he shot his son— well, things weren't turning out too well for the Griffin family.

Anger brimmed at the surface for what they did to his beloved Mustang. They didn't have to destroy his baby.

He burped a laugh at the thought that he was more upset with them for what they did to his Mustang than for what they did to his face.

And to sit and listen to what his father said on that recording had to be humiliating for Dad. What an idiot to allow himself to be recorded, though. Although, he couldn't deny that his heart swelled when he heard how he felt about family. That he did it all for Melody—fucked Mackenzie out of the deal and said that his son wasn't a "common criminal."

Bruce wished his father had said those things to his face years ago. Maybe everything would have turned out differently for them.

He watched Mackenzie work himself into a rage. Watched the gun lift, aimed at his father, and nearly jumped from the chair to attack Mackenzie.

But the sound of gunfire outside kept him rooted in his seat.

Mackenzie lowered his weapon without firing as he stared at the large window, beyond which nothing could be seen—the window was as black as night.

"Go," Mackenzie ordered. "Find out what that was, then report back. We will wait inside."

Four men jogged down the corridor. When their footfalls stopped echoing, a door slammed, and a bolt locked into place.

Then silence.

Bruce moved his one good eye to watch that Aaron guy. He seemed calm, studying the room. Aaron's eyes were on Mackenzie as the man slipped the gun away. Then Aaron's eyes moved to the security men standing around the room. Without craning his neck, Bruce counted at least six men, with some likely in reserve around the property.

They all had to work out at the same gym. Either that or Mackenzie's prerequisite to getting hired was that you had to bench press at least three hundred.

His father cowered on the couch, curled into himself, his face turned away from Melody. The man drank too much tonight and then got humiliated in front of everybody. No one wanted to go through that, especially not in front of your kids.

Anyone would feel sorry for the judge, and there was a soft spot in Bruce that couldn't deal with his dad turning into a blubbering ball of tears. But his dad was a shit and had done shitty things to influential people. Perhaps everyone in life gets their comeuppance eventually.

Mackenzie stood at the window, his hands cupped on either side of his face, staring out into the night.

"John," he said. "They just ran into the woods on the left of the driveway. Something must've caught their eye. Radio them for an update."

The man behind the couch—the one where his dad was sniveling—stepped away and tapped something in his ear.

"Dave," he said. "What's out there? Do we have an intruder?"

He kept his eyes on Mackenzie, who was still staring out into the night.

"Dave?" John said louder, his hand still over his ear. "Who fired that weapon?"

Mackenzie spun around, glaring at John. "Is he responding?"

John shook his head. "I'm sorry, sir. It's like his earpiece is turned off."

Bruce detected a current of worry cross Mackenzie's otherwise stern face.

When he glanced over at Aaron, the hint of a smile could be seen lifting the edge of his lips. What did he know?

"How many men do you have in the house?" Mackenzie asked.

John seemed to be doing the mental math as he counted on his fingers. "Eight, sir."

"Including you?"

John nodded. "Including me."

"You stay, weapon drawn. Send the rest out to see what the fuck is going on out there—"

Music boomed from somewhere outside. It was like someone cranked their car stereo.

Mackenzie spun around to the window and smacked his forehead against it as he cupped his hands and tried to see something.

"Find out what's going on," Mackenzie shouted, his voice weirdly reverberating off the glass. "Send everyone. I want that music shut down. *Now!*"

John turned away, speaking into his mic, ordering the entire security force on the property to converge on the location of the music.

Footsteps echoed from several spots in the house. Two different doors slammed shut somewhere.

What interested Bruce the most was Aaron's response. As Mackenzie got more agitated, Aaron seemed happier.

Then it came to him.

The music.

He listened more intently while staring at the floor with one good eye, focusing.

Someone was playing his favorite band, Ice Nine Kills. This was from their *Welcome To Horrorwood, The Silver Scream* album.

He glanced up to stare at the dark window. Who would be playing *that* in the woods by Mackenzie's estate house?

Then, like an epiphany, it hit him.

It was that girl. Sarah Roberts.

She *knew* things. She knew about Heather. She knew about Melody. She saved his sister, and she was trying to save them from Mackenzie.

But how?

And how could she know what music Bruce liked?

Another thought struck him: Sarah was sending him a signal.

That had to be it.

But what was she trying to tell him?

The song "A Grave Mistake" was playing. If they played it song after song, the next would be "Assault & Batteries."

He blinked his one eye rapidly, the pain fading with the realization of what Sarah was asking of him.

Mackenzie had made a *grave mistake*, and it was Bruce's job to *assault* the man. No one would expect it from him. He was the cripple in the wheelchair.

"Tell me you have something," Mackenzie shouted at his security man.

Bruce glanced their way. The security man had a weapon in his hand. Sam had an arm around Heather. What good would that do if a bullet came your way?

Aaron seemed to be whispering something to Melody, even though Melody didn't seem to be paying attention.

And now his father, the judge, had sat up to see what was going on while wiping his face.

John, the security man, shook his head. "Every single man we sent out is unaccounted for. No one is responding, sir."

"That's impossible!" Mackenzie shot his hands in the air. "It's ridiculous, now isn't it?" He spun in a circle, losing all the composure he'd maintained throughout the night.

He spun his head on a swivel to stare at Bruce and then his dad. "You." He breathed the word. "You did this."

Judge Griffin raised his hands. "I swear, I have no idea who's out there or what's going on."

Mackenzie yanked out his weapon and aimed it at the judge. "Tell me the truth, *Judge*! I want the whole truth now."

"I swear," Griffin shouted, his hands up.

The gun aimed at Bruce. He didn't flinch as Ice Nine Kills screamed the chorus, bolstering him to be strong and tough.

"Is this your doing?"

Bruce stared at the tip of the weapon, the black hole where the bullet would exit if Mackenzie pulled the trigger.

"How?" Bruce mumbled through his mashed lips, his tongue touching the holes where several of his teeth used to be. "I left the courthouse, drove up the hill, and had a car accident. Your men brought me here. How and when could I organize anything? I didn't even know I'd be here tonight."

Mackenzie's gaze moved in Aaron and Melody's direction. "Is this your girl, that Sarah bitch? She's out there, isn't she?"

Aaron lifted his hands when the gun's focus was on him. "Hey, man, lower the gun. We got nabbed by those asshole cops at the motel. I have no idea where Sarah is or what she's up to, and she has no idea where I am."

"Isn't she psychic or something?" Mackenzie walked around the couch the judge sat on to stand in front of Aaron, the gun loosely aimed at his gut.

"Yeah, sure. But I'm not."

Mackenzie spun back to his security man. "Anything yet?"

John shook his head. "They all ran into those trees and disappeared, sir. We have to assume it's just you and me."

"Fuck!" Mackenzie yelled.

He paced in front of Aaron and Melody until he slowed when the song changed. Now "Assault & Batteries" was playing.

Bruce was convinced that the psychic girl knew something was coming. She'd set this up to remove Mackenzie's men—no idea how she did that, but she did. And now Mackenzie was impotent without all his muscle standing around him—a gang of twenty men, down to a gang of two.

"I'll kill you all," Mackenzie said, looking around at everyone. "Sam," he said, facing them. "Get Heather out of here. I'll call you guys later. You don't need to see what comes next."

"But, sir. Shouldn't we stay in here with you if there's something dangerous outside?"

Mackenzie seemed to think about it for a moment, then nodded. "Fine, then take her up to your old bedroom at the back of the house. Go now, and don't come out until John or I come for you."

Sam and Heather got to their feet and disappeared around the corner.

"Now, do I get answers? Or do I start killing people?"

He pointed his pistol at Aaron, then Melody. After a moment, he aimed it at Bruce.

The judge moaned. "Just shoot me," Griffin said. "Leave my kids out of this."

"Oh, how noble of you. In your dying breath, that's how you want to go out? As a nobleman and not the pig-fucker that you are?"

Mackenzie, in all his fury and rage, aimed his weapon at Judge Griffin and fired.

Everyone jumped at the report of the weapon. What struck Bruce as odd was that Aaron's mouth was moving, like he was whispering something.

What the hell was wrong with that guy?

The bullet had entered the couch one foot to Griffin's left.

"Oops, I missed." Mackenzie stepped back, closed one eye, and set up his weapon, staring down the barrel. "Let's see how my aim is now."

Bruce had seen enough.

Ice Nine Kills was calling.

He shoved himself up and out of the chair, ignoring the pain that flared through his leg, and dove at Mackenzie before anyone could stop him.

"*Sir!*" his security man called, raising his weapon.

At the exact second Mackenzie fired his second bullet, Bruce hit him, and they sprawled onto the hard tile floor in front of the couch.

Then someone pounced on his back, and Bruce elbowed upward,

connecting with the man's jaw.

In his peripheral vision, he caught sight of Aaron's face and felt like shit instantly.

Aaron rolled off him, and John, Mackenzie's security man, roughly shoved Bruce off his boss.

Mackenzie roared like a caged animal from the floor as he clambered to his knees and hands, then pushed to his feet.

"I'll kill him. I'll kill them all." Mackenzie's hands opened and closed, but they were empty.

His gun was gone.

A weapon fired, and everyone jumped again. Melody released a short yelp.

John, the last security man, slipped sideways and dropped, blood spurting from a head wound.

Bruce slowly turned to see who had fired the shot.

Aaron was now holding Mackenzie's gun. That's what he was doing on Bruce's back—he had dove for the gun.

"Motherfucker," Bruce whispered in respect while Melody sobbed on the couch, curled into herself, hiding her head.

Then Aaron fired a bullet into the top corner of the large glass window, shattering it into a million pieces.

The music outside died a moment later.

"Situation under control," Aaron said as if talking to himself. "I have a gun on Mackenzie. No one else is armed. Room secure."

Bruce stared up at Aaron from the floor, pain flaring all over his body. All that time, he hadn't been talking to himself or Melody. He was whispering to someone outside.

"Who are you talking to?" he asked, moving into a sitting position, the pain from his swollen lips making him wince.

"I'm wired." Aaron's eyes didn't leave Mackenzie, who was standing back against the wall now, looking sorely defeated. "The Royal Canadian Mounted Police heard everything, Mackenzie." Aaron glanced to his right briefly, then back to Mackenzie. "We need medics." He raised his voice. "Judge Griffin has been hit."

Melody moaned in her seat, then started saying *Daddy, Daddy,*

*Daddy* over and over.

"Repeat, Mackenzie fired his weapon twice. The first bullet missed. The second bullet appears to have entered the judge's lower abdomen. Hurry, he's bleeding badly."

Bruce pulled himself up from the floor, wincing and moaning with the pain, then grabbed a throw pillow and gently applied pressure to his father's wound as his dad stared up at the ceiling and his sister cried behind him.

In under a minute, Mackenzie's living room was swarming with uniforms and men in suits.

# Chapter 37

SARAH NURSED A COKE while Parkman drove beside her.

"You know," Parkman said. "This trip cost me the most."

Sarah glanced over at him. "How do you figure?"

He glanced at her quickly with one eyebrow raised, his toothpick tilting dangerously close to the edge of his open mouth.

"How about almost three weeks in North Bay?" He averted his gaze back to the highway. "All the motel rooms, the towel replacements"—he glanced in the rearview mirror at Aaron—"the eating out in restaurants." He shook his head. "You'd think the government would pitch in after all we did for them."

Sarah turned in her seat to stare back at Aaron and Alex. "You guys did great." She focused on Aaron. "Remember that first morning? When I told you we needed to make a stop before going to meet Bruce at the coffee shop?"

Aaron nodded.

"I told you we were going to the RCMP office and what I wanted to do there, and you stood gaping at me as I walked out of the room."

Aaron smiled at her. "I had no idea how much of a role they'd play, and feared what would've happened if the RCMP hadn't wired me."

"Luckily, they agreed to help after an hour of convincing them, not to mention that they were already investigating Mackenzie and the judge. They just didn't have anything concrete on them until we showed up. They had a file two inches thick, but nothing could stick until Aaron went into Mackenzie's house wired. When you questioned him, they also recorded everything that guy said in the motel room. Not that they could use much of it, but they were listening."

Parkman looked over at her. "Alex and I wondered what you were up to by going there first that morning, but didn't ask, figuring if we needed to know, you'd be forthcoming." He paused, then added, "And because the RCMP were listening in, they knew to fire that weapon to distract Mackenzie from shooting the judge that first time. It was brilliant."

"Well, there's that, but Aaron was whispering updates the whole time he was in that living room."

"I wanted them to *see* everything I saw," Aaron added.

"What made you play that music?" Parkman asked Sarah.

"Vivian told me to, and we later learned that it inspired Bruce into action. That bullet that went through the judge's stomach was aimed at his heart, according to Vivian. He wasn't meant to die yet." She shrugged. "The judge is still in the hospital, but he'll live. He's expected to be discharged this week. The authorities are waiting for him with a slew of charges."

"I saw Bruce dive on Mackenzie when he was prepared to shoot his father," Aaron added. "So I dove for the gun and got an elbow in the jaw for my efforts. When Mackenzie's security man raised his weapon, there was no doubt in my mind that he would just shoot me. There'd be no warning. So I shot him."

"Didn't Bruce apologize a dozen times for that elbow shot?" Sarah asked.

Aaron nodded. "He felt bad about it, thinking it was Mackenzie's man on his back."

Sarah clucked her tongue once. "Well, they got Mackenzie on everything from bribing a judge to attempted murder, to murder, and a bunch of other charges. They're still digging up sections of his property. I heard they found four skeletons in his backyard yesterday. My guess is the charges against Mackenzie will keep him locked away until he dies."

"Anything happening with the judge on the legal side of things? Like his caseload?" Parkman asked. "You guys were inside giving statements for two weeks. Alex and I haven't been given any updates on that."

"Every single case Judge Griffin presided over for the past twenty years is being reopened. He's willing to confess to certain ones where he was paid for a specific result."

"And Chief Warner?"

"He was terminated and arrested and is being held without bail until they determine how involved he was with Judge Griffin. With him, they're following the money. Just like those two cops who left Mackenzie's property with envelopes of cash—they'll be spending a lot of time in prison with the people they sent there over the years."

Parkman shook his head. "It's never good when cops are in jail. They don't fare well."

Aaron leaned against the door. "At least this didn't trickle down too hard on the judge's kids. Melody walked away with a broken heart, and Bruce still has that aggravated assault with a weapon charge to deal with, but they might go easy on him, considering."

"They arrested Heather and Sam, too." Sarah turned back in her seat to stare forward. "All the money they extorted was seized, and once the investigation is concluded, I heard the money will be sent back to its rightful owners, Bruce Griffin included."

"And I hope they will consider that when he stands before a judge later this year," Parkman added.

"We'll see. Who knows."

Silence descended upon them for a few moments, then Sarah turned around again and stared at Alex. "Are you okay? You're awfully quiet."

He looked at her briefly, then resumed staring out the window. "I'm good."

"Tell me something."

He looked back at her.

"Where did you go when we set up in the woods that night?"

Alex glanced at Aaron for a moment, then back to Sarah. "To find a way inside the house."

"And did you?"

He shook his head. "It ended quickly."

She stared at him. "What's bothering you?"

He didn't respond for so long that everyone was staring at him—even Parkman in the rearview mirror.

"I can't help but think about what happened at the Nate house. How can someone like Joseph Nate exist?"

Alex was right. In a world created by a loving God, why were the Joseph Nates of the world allowed to exist?

"And," Alex continued, "I can't deal with Michael Sommers still being out there somewhere. Melody Griffin might still be in danger." Alex met Sarah's gaze. "We have to find him."

She nodded. "I'll speak with Vivian. She should know where he will turn up."

Alex looked out the window again. Something else was bothering him, but she couldn't put her finger on it.

Over the past week, all she heard from her sister was Alex's name. Why did she keep calling his name? Since they'd been dealing with the aftermath of the RCMP investigation into the Mackenzie case, she hadn't given a lot of time to Alex.

When they got home and settled, she would check on him. See how he's doing.

*Alex* … Vivian whispered. *He needs you … or he'll die before his time.*

# Afterword

Another Sarah Roberts novel has ended, and as always, a few items in this novel have meaning for me—little nuggets that I drop to keep me zoned into the material. It reminds me how severe or traumatizing life can be and how fiction is closely related because a novel has tension and conflict on every page—like life often does.

Allow me to focus on those key points so you can also be aware of them. I'll list them in the order they appeared in the novel. Since this book is called *The Whole Truth*, in the interest of leaving some truths on the page, continue reading …

\*\*\*

After Sarah and Aaron left the property at the golf course, Alex told the police they were looking for a couple driving a Jeep, license plate 256-AEO, to throw the officers off their trail.

I'll never forget that plate number—it's the actual one from 1987 when I was an eighteen-year-old security guard in my final year of high school. On weekends, I worked the night shift, patrolling the parking lots of several adjacent apartment buildings.

Around three in the morning one night, as I did my rounds, the headlights of a Jetta pulled into the lot I was walking through. After seeing little movement that evening, I ducked out of view to watch what this vehicle would do.

The driver found a spot, cut the engine and the lights, then sat in his car for several minutes. What could he be doing?

In an apartment building parking lot at three in the morning, an individual had one of two purposes: one, to be moving toward the building, or two, to move toward a car. Anything other than that I deemed suspicious.

So, hunched down behind the hood of other cars, I made my way closer for a better look. When I was three vehicles away, the driver exited his Jetta. He glanced around suspiciously as he slipped on black gloves.

It was then that I knew he was up to something that wasn't any good.

The man bent over low and ran toward another vehicle, placed something on it, then hustled back to his car, started the engine, backed out of the parking spot, and drove away with his lights off. He flicked them on when he got to the street.

I called it in, complete with the plate number. The police arrived, examined the evidence left on the other car, and then drove to the address associated with his license plate number to pick him up.

It turns out he had been terrorizing a woman who had rebuffed his advances. Calling and hanging up on her, following her, threatening her.

The man was a stalker.

The present he left on her car was a used condom.

Based on what I witnessed, the man was arrested and pleaded guilty to all charges—I wasn't required to testify as a witness.

I'll never forget that night, nor the plate number.

Things like that stay with you.

***

The next nugget was Joseph Nate. Well, to be more specific, the name "Joseph" itself.

That was my grandfather's name—my mom's dad.

I only met him once when I was about five or six years old, and he left me with a terrible feeling. I have never forgotten his voice to this day. He spoke to me once, maybe twice, and had me in tears because he said he would break my neck if I made any noise.

He was watching a baseball game on TV at the time.

But that's not all.

The name "Joseph" was not allowed to be spoken in the family house. The word was banned.

My mom couldn't bear to hear it.

He had been an abusive man, to the lengths that I'll never know. My mother passed away in 2017, and all the abuse she endured at her father's hands died with her. She never told anybody the whole story, not even my dad.

But I did hear a few things over the years—snippets of truth. Like the time she spent weeks in the hospital healing from being run over by the tractor at the age of ten or twelve.

My mother was raised on a farm with crops and animals. She was never run over by a tractor. The broken bones she endured, the split lip, the bruising, the bleeding—all done by her father's hands for some minor slight.

There are hundreds of stories like this from my mother's childhood. Like the time her father tried to drown her brother—he almost succeeded.

The law? What did they do back in 1950 in rural Ontario?

Nothing. A man could do as he pleased with his kids. To some degree, abusers still can do as they please as long as no one speaks up. As long as the story of them falling down the stairs or being run over by the tractor stays in place. No complainant, no case.

My mother did go to his funeral, though.

I was there, too.

When we arrived, my mother had not shed a single tear. She walked up to the open casket, and after a moment of staring down at his body, she smacked the face of the corpse of her father, spit on his embalmed flesh, and said, "I only came to see for myself that the evil is finally dead," and walked out of the funeral parlor.

I will never know what he did; I don't think I want to know. But when I envisioned Joseph Nate's actions in the novel's fictional story, I needed a character name and thought it fit to represent an evil man.

So, I named him after my evil grandfather. The man who tortured my mother and made her into the pain-filled woman she turned out to be.

Once, my father told my mother that she should speak to a therapist to get some of the past out, to let some of it go. Holding onto it was doing her no good.

She responded by saying that she would feel worse.

"How's that?" my dad asked.

"I'd give the therapist nightmares, beyond which they'd never be able to reconcile. Speaking of what happened would only serve to traumatize others. I'll never do it."

The past, those secrets, the pain—all of it—died on August 22, 2017, when my mother had a stroke at the age of seventy-five.

God rest her soul.

And that's how the father of the Nate house got his name. In my mother's honor, I still refuse to speak that particular name. (Apologies to all the Josephs out there. This has nothing to do with you.)

Note: Some of that cycle was broken, but not everything. Perhaps one day, I'll dig deeper and reveal some of the things we (my brothers and sister, of which I have three) had to endure growing up with a woman (my mom) who had developed bipolar disorder, among other things. To hear what she endured inspired compassion. But to live with her from childhood was another story. My mother was evil on her bad days. In the better days, she was hard to handle and made us all feel like we were going insane.

\*\*\*

One more item, and I've discussed this before, is the Children's Aid Society in Northern Ontario. I won't go into it at length here, but they dropped the ball on the Nate family and made HUGE mistakes with other families I know—one *very* close to me.

I discussed this at length in the afterword of another Sarah book about ten books ago. Sometimes, assholes in real life find their way back into a Sarah book.

Bear in mind that what the CAS stands for and what they do is helping the majority of the time. But when they screw up, it's children who pay the price.

And that hurts the most.

It's a pain people carry forever.

Do better, CAS. Please strive to do better.

\*\*\*

Lastly, I have to mention the band Ice Nine Kills. They are featured in this novel because they are one hell of a fantastic band. If you enjoy hard rock and metal, give them a listen. They have dozens of songs written about famous books. Like the song "Funeral Derrangements" based on Stephen King's *Pet Sematary*. And how about "The American Nightmare." It's based on *Nightmare on Elm Street*. Their song "Enjoy Your Slay" comes from *The Shining* by Stephen King.

There are so many amazing, artistic songs based on books and movies that I've enjoyed over the years with this band. I love everything they do.

Take a listen on YouTube.

I hope you'll enjoy them, too.

Well, that's it for this segment. I hope you've enjoyed *The Whole Truth* and are eagerly anticipating the next Sarah book, simply called *Alex*.

Some crazy stuff is coming for sure! (Poor Alex).

Please don't say the name Joseph too often, listen to Ice Nine Kills, and watch out for condom-toting stalkers.

Until then, let's meet again in a little while on the pages of a Sarah novel.

Be kind to each other, take care of yourself, and we'll chat again soon.

All my love,

Jonas

Alex

Book Thirty-Six

# Chapter 1

*MISSING* WAS A WORD she hated. *Lost* was worse.

Yet, after exhausting all efforts to locate Alex, the anxiety Sarah Roberts had been suppressing rose from her gut to her throat.

She dialed Aaron, staring through her balcony door, looking at nothing.

He answered on the first ring. "Hey, what's up?"

"Have you heard from Alex?" All business.

He paused, then said, "No," his voice hesitant. "Should I be worried?"

Sarah turned around to pace her living room floor, clutching the phone tight to her ear. "I've called his cell several times since yesterday."

"You need him for something? Maybe I can help."

"It's not that." She made it to the kitchen, spun around, and headed back toward the balcony door. "He's been distant for some time. Like, I don't know, like he's dealing with something. I just thought he needed a friend. Someone to talk to—"

"Sarah, Alex doesn't *talk*."

"I know, and that's the problem." She was working her way back to the kitchen now. "I just thought he'd talk to me if I pushed him hard enough."

"Have you tried calling Parkman?"

"He's my next call. I just thought I'd check with you because I called the dojo, and Daniel said Alex has missed a few days of work."

Aaron was silent for a moment. "Yeah, about that."

"What?"

"He called in sick, but it's not like him."

"What do you mean? He doesn't get sick?"

"No, no, it's just, unless he's got something nasty or contagious, he still shows up. Nothing puts him down short of a hospital visit."

Sarah stopped walking and stared at her apartment door. "Tell me you checked on him."

Another pause. "Why would I do that? It's *Alex*."

"I'm going to his place."

"Why? What's the big deal? You'll likely find him in bed watching TV or something. Maybe even sleeping."

"At eleven in the morning?"

"Sarah, let me call around. I'll find out what's up and call you back. Daniel will know something—"

"You're not listening. I spoke with Daniel. He's been covering for Alex at the dojo. He knows nothing."

"And you left a message on Alex's cell phone?"

Sarah glanced up at the stuccoed ceiling, releasing a pent-up breath. "I left four messages over the last few days. And now it says his voicemail is full."

"Okay, that's concerning and not like Alex at all."

She started pacing again, switching ears to relieve the pressure as she'd been pressing the phone too hard.

"Where's Willow?" Aaron asked.

"In school until three. That gives me four hours. Plenty of time to swing by Alex's place and check on him."

"Okay, there's no need to panic yet. I'll call around, then if I come up with nothing, I'll meet you at Alex's apartment. I think I have a key lying around somewhere."

"*Somewhere?* Seriously? With all the shit we've dealt with in the past, all the assholes we've sent to prison, the cops who still don't like us—Alex leaves you a key, and you don't know where it is?"

"Hey." Aaron's voice raised a notch. "I'll find it, okay?"

"I'm calling Darwin. Maybe he can do something at his end."

"Wait, you really think we're at that stage already?"

Sarah stopped pacing in front of her couch, then dropped into it sideways, placing her free hand on her forehead to massage her temples.

"I'm worried."

"Sarah? Is there something else on your mind?"

"Like what?"

"Did Vivian say something to you?"

Sarah released her temples and let her hand fall to the side, resting her head on the couch. "She did."

"Is that why you were hanging around the dojo last week?"

"It wasn't the only reason."

"What are you not telling me?"

After losing Benjamin, Sarah couldn't contemplate losing anyone else—especially Alex. He'd been the backbone of their group for so many years. He'd been there for Aaron when he lost his sister, Joanne, even before they came into Sarah's life. The man loved his friends and fought for them like they were all blood, all related.

But now he was missing. Gone from the dojo for days, his voicemail full.

"Sarah? What did Vivian tell you?" Aaron's voice took on a note of caution. He was worried—more worried than moments before.

"After we left North Bay—"

"Yeah, that corrupt judge thing. What about it?"

"Alex was bothered by something."

"And?"

"I asked him what was bothering him, but didn't get an answer right away. Then he said something like, 'I can't stop thinking about what happened at that house.' Then Alex asked how someone like Joseph Nate could exist." She stopped to glance at the window and the gray skies beyond.

"After what that man did to his kids, I understand the question. It doesn't mean Alex would disappear, though."

"Then he commented on how Michael Sommers was still out there somewhere, saying we have to find him."

"So you think Alex took off to find that Sommers guy?"

"Not exactly."

"Then I'm not following your logic."

Should she tell him what Vivian said? Would that start a fight? Maybe she should have called Parkman instead. He'd listen to Vivian's warning with more sincerity.

"Sarah?"

"Recently, my sister has been whispering Alex's name."

Sarah could almost see Aaron's brow knitting up, causing lines to form across his forehead. "Why would she do that?"

"Now that we're settled and that North Bay thing is over, I told Vivian I would keep an eye on him. I said I'd check on him, and that's what I'm doing."

"Okay, let's stick with what we said. I'll call around, check on a few places, and if I get nowhere, I'll text you, and we can meet at his place in an hour."

"I'll call Darwin and Parkman, though."

"Fine—wait. What time is it in Italy?"

Sarah pulled the phone away from her ear. It was slightly after eleven in the morning in Toronto. "It's only five in the afternoon over there."

"Sarah, just remember. This is Alex we're talking about. Not much can take that guy down."

At first, she didn't respond. Then, "Yeah, you're right."

Aaron didn't hang up. Neither one spoke for a moment.

"Did Vivian say anything else?" Aaron asked. "Anything specific?"

This was what Sarah dreaded. If she told him the truth, he'd respond in several ways, none of them good.

But she didn't lie—wouldn't lie—so she said it word for word.

"Vivian said, 'He needs you, or he'll die before his time.' She told me it was something I do for Alex. Something specific, but I have no idea what that is."

"What the hell does that mean?" Aaron shouted in her ear. "Holy shit, why didn't you say so from the beginning?"

"Make your calls, Aaron. I'm hanging up now."

"Let's find Alex. Before it's too late."

The line died.

Sarah stared at the phone for a moment. "Oh, so now you're interested in what my sister has to say? Now it means something important, eh?"

She shook her head and called Darwin using WhatsApp, a knot forming in her stomach.

Darwin answered almost as fast as Aaron had.

"Sarah." He singsonged her name. "How's everything? Oh, wait, Rosina says hello."

"Darwin?"

"Yeah?"

"We think Alex might be missing and in trouble."

# Chapter 2

DARWIN SAID THEY'D FIND Alex quickly. By the time they hung up, Rosina was already putting away their dinner plates and logging on to their computer system to begin tracking his phone and last movements as best they could.

Sarah called Parkman next, but he hadn't heard a thing from Alex since last week.

Then she texted Aaron on the way out the door. They'd meet at Alex's place—Parkman, too, as he was the detective of the bunch— which was two blocks from the dojo on Queen Street.

Half an hour later, Sarah eased into a parking space, killed the engine, and then checked her phone.

Nothing from Alex.

"Vivian?" She spoke out loud. "You got something you can tell me?"

Vivian came when she had a message. Calling her was often useless nowadays, but trying didn't hurt. She seemed always to be around, hovering wherever she hovered.

After waiting for a response and not getting one, Sarah exited the vehicle, pocketed her keys, and strode down Queen Street until she reached Alex's corner. Up ahead, Aaron and Parkman were chatting, their heads close together. When they looked her way, she nodded, and they waved.

Picking up her pace, she reached them moments later.

"Have you guys gone up yet?"

They shook their heads.

"We were waiting for you," Parkman said, opening his arms and hugging her.

She hugged Aaron, too, and noted his tense muscles and stoic expression.

"Then let's go," she said, already worried about what they'd find in Alex's apartment. "You got the key?" she asked Aaron as they hurried along the sidewalk.

He shook his head. "No, but Daniel had one." He held it up. "We're good to go."

She stared ahead, tightening her lips at a nasty retort that formed on her tongue. How could he misplace something as important as a key entrusted to him from one of their inner circle?

That was an argument for another day.

They turned into a back alley. Alex's apartment was on the second floor over a garage, accessible only from the alley.

With Aaron in the lead, they ascended the metal stairs and stopped at Alex's door, where Aaron pounded on it hard.

"Hey, Alex," he called, "you in there?" He placed his ear to the door, staring at Sarah, then Parkman. After a moment, he smacked the door with his fist again. "Hey, Alex, open up."

Nothing.

"We need to go in," Sarah said.

Parkman nodded. "Open it up."

Aaron inserted the key, twisted it until the lock disengaged, then, with one more uncertain look at Sarah, swung the door open.

Parkman inhaled deeply, making Sarah wonder why he did that.

"Nothing stinks," Parkman said. "That's a good sign."

What he meant was Alex wasn't dead and bloating inside his apartment.

*Comforting thought.*

They stepped inside. It had been ages since Sarah had been there when he first moved in. Nothing had changed much. He remained the minimalist he had always been. A yoga mat with blocks was laid out where a coffee table usually went in the center of the small living room of the studio apartment.

The kitchenette was spotless. Not a single pot was out, and no dish was dirty in the sink.

"This place looks like a team of maids went over it twice," she said.

"That's Alex." Aaron started for the two doors on the far side of the small rental. "He was always super hygienic where he lived and breathed."

When Aaron entered Alex's bedroom, Sarah stuck her head in the bathroom. The ammonia smell made her think it had been cleaned that morning, but that could be false. If he always kept it this way, then perhaps it just hadn't been used in days.

When she exited the bathroom, Parkman stood by the yoga mat, cell phone in hand.

"Who are you calling?"

"Alex's phone." He placed it to his ear.

A phone rang in the apartment, causing Sarah to spin toward the bedroom as Aaron emerged holding a phone.

"Well," Aaron said, looking at Sarah, then Parkman. "We now know why he's not picking up. Wherever he went, he didn't take his phone with him."

"Which meant he didn't want to be tracked," Sarah added.

Parkman killed the call and pocketed his phone. "What the hell, guys? Where could he be?"

Sarah's phone dinged with an incoming WhatsApp. She yanked it out of her pocket and read the message.

"Darwin said he tracked Alex's phone to his apartment." She looked up at Aaron as he shook the phone in his hand.

"We got that."

Sarah shook her head. "There's been no other activity on Alex for days." She tapped the call button, and Darwin's voice came through the speaker a second later.

"Hi, Sarah." Darwin's voice came through the phone's speaker.

"Hey, I'm with Aaron and Parkman. We're standing in Alex's living room."

"Did you find his phone?"

"We did."

"Anything else?"

"Nothing," Parkman said. "At least nothing suspicious."

"What else can you track?" Sarah asked.

"Rosina is working on something. We had his banking information about a year ago. She's trying to see if we can sign in and check for transactions. Maybe he's taking a few days off—"

"Off what?" Sarah cut in. "Off the dojo? Nothing's been going on. It's been quiet around here."

They all looked at each other, waiting for Darwin to say something.

"Look, leave it with me." They heard the rapid clicking on a keyboard through Sarah's phone speaker. "I'll dig up something eventually."

"Okay," Aaron said. "We'll leave a note here in case he returns, then head to the dojo. Call Sarah the second you know something."

"Will do." The line died.

Sarah slipped the phone into her pocket.

Aaron pulled drawers open in the kitchenette. "Doesn't he have anything to write on?"

"I'll help," Parkman said.

Sarah moved toward the bedroom and peeked inside. The bed was made immaculately as if he had prepared it for a five-star hotel. The closet door was open, likely a sign that Aaron had been in there, and inside, all of Alex's button-up shirts were neatly hung on matching hangers.

*Where are you, my friend?*

"Sarah?" Parkman called. "You coming?"

She blinked once, hoping to dispel the simmering dread building in her gut, then followed them outside and up the few blocks to the dojo.

If she lost Alex—if *they* lost Alex—nothing would be the same.

Ever again.

# Chapter 3

Susan Nelson grabbed her purse and headed for the garage. "You coming?" she called. "This party won't wait for you."

"Yes, Mom," her daughter shouted from her room. "Almost ready!"

Susan stopped near the front door at the side table under a large mirror, lifted the pile of envelopes her husband had pulled from the mailbox, and riffled through them. Bills, bills, and more bills. She shuffled them into a neat bundle, set them back on the side table, and turned to look at the staircase.

"I'll be in the car," she shouted up the stairs, but didn't wait for a reply.

At twelve years old, Tracy took longer and longer to get ready. Makeup was her new thing, thanks to her father, who allowed her to wear it last Christmas when she received several gifts of eyeshadow and lipstick. As long as she didn't wear it to school, she could wear it when hanging out with her friends.

Tonight qualified, as tonight was Corey's birthday party.

Everyone was attending, according to Tracy. *Everyone* wasn't literal. It meant the *cool* kids.

Corey was the new kid at school, arriving a few weeks before the school let out for the summer, and he was already quite popular.

Corey's family lived several blocks away on Weir Street, but Susan was driving her daughter because she wanted to meet the parents. Letting her twelve-year-old go to a party at a house she'd never been to before to hang out with parents she'd never met wasn't going to happen. Meeting the parents was a prerequisite.

Although, she wasn't paranoid. If she were paranoid, she'd have her husband run Corey's family name through the system—her husband was the chief investigator for the Vice and Drugs Unit at the Hamilton Police Service.

This made her think of how troubled he'd been lately. A case was currently moving through the court system—two of his Vice cops were on trial for murder—some undercover deal that went bad at the park not far from their house.

Blair wasn't getting much sleep lately. She found him awake before dawn each morning, then off to court to watch the proceedings. It was expected to last a few more days as a star witness—the prosecution's *mystery* witness—was yet to take the stand. Blair told her this witness was the prosecution's ace in the hole a few days ago.

Without that witness, they had no case. Rumor had it that the witness would turn the case upside down.

With her husband's mind elsewhere, she figured she'd rely on her daughter's assessment of this newfound friend, Corey, and eyeball the parents before dropping her off, and all would be well.

She hit the button inside the garage to raise the door, then walked around the front of the car to get in.

It was nearing four in the afternoon, and they were supposed to be there by now, but she wasn't going to push Tracy. At twelve, she was showing signs of talking back and expressing her feelings in a staunch manner that edged into disrespect, which Susan had expected at sixteen or further on.

She tossed her purse in the back seat, jumped in, and waited in the quiet of the garage.

Movement caught her eye in the rearview mirror.

She leaned over to look out at the street and saw a man leaning against a tree, arms crossed. He appeared to be staring at her house, his face a mask of red.

At least it looked like he was watching her house.

She twisted around in her seat to get a better look at the guy.

It wasn't the house he was eyeballing.

He was staring directly at her.

He must have seen her moving in the front seat because when she turned to look at him, he pushed off the tree, uncrossed his arms, moved a few steps closer, and then turned away. After a moment, he looked back over his shoulder.

Why was he glaring at her like that?

"What the hell?" she muttered to herself as she opened the car door and stepped onto the garage floor.

When she got to the open garage door and stared down the street in the direction the man had gone, he was nowhere in sight.

A door banged behind her, making her jump and raise a hand to her chest.

"Mom," Tracy yelled. "What are you doing? Let's go. We're going to be late."

Tracy piled into the passenger side while Susan leaned out farther, but couldn't see where that man had gone.

An eerie feeling coursed through her. That was odd and unusual.

She'd drop off her daughter and come right back home. Or maybe she'd circle the block first, and if she saw him again, she'd call her husband. He could send a few cruisers around the neighborhood. They could chat with the guy and find out what he's up to. That is, if Blair would pick up the phone. He might have it off while the court was in session.

"*Mom!*" Tracy called, her voice muffled from the interior of the Nissan.

Susan jogged back, dropped into her seat, and fired up the engine. "Hold your horses. We're going, we're going."

"I just didn't want to be late," Tracy said. "They might eat without me."

Susan put it into reverse. "We'll be there in two minutes. They're literally around the block."

"*Three* blocks, Mom." Tracy rolled her eyes.

That was something Susan couldn't get used to—that eye-roll thing. In her day, it was so disrespectful.

"Watch those eyes, young lady."

Tracy stared out her window without replying.

Susan backed out of the garage and waited in the driveway until the garage door lowered all the way, then eased out onto Maple Avenue, where she checked all her mirrors.

No strange man in sight.

Maybe it was nothing. Perhaps she imagined him *watching* the house. People always look at houses when they're out for a walk.

She hit the gas, hoping she'd made a mistake in assessing the stranger. Yet, there was something about that man's face. Something familiar, like she'd seen him before. Or maybe it was his expression she recognized.

It was one of anguish, sorrow, and pain. Anger too.

Something was bothering that man in the street, and she wanted no part of it.

# Chapter 4

SARAH SAT ON HER balcony, steam rising from the coffee beside her on the table. She stared at her phone, waiting—*willing*—it to ring.

After meeting with Daniel at the dojo and discussing every possible scenario, none of them had come up with anything that would make sense.

As far as they were concerned, Alex had vanished.

Sarah drove home with that pit in her stomach, increasing in size by the minute. She welcomed Willow home when she got off the school bus, got her something to eat, left her to do her homework, and made a coffee. Now, she sat on the balcony, wondering who to call next.

"Where are you, Alex?"

If she was needed for anything, Daniel told her he'd take care of Willow, which she was thankful for. Even though Daniel didn't live near Willow's school, he always drove her in and picked her up while babysitting. And Willow loved hanging out with Uncle Daniel.

Finally, unable to handle the waiting, she texted Darwin for an update.

The phone rang in her hand.

She smacked the button to answer it. "Tell me you got something."

"I wish I did."

Sarah exhaled deeply and leaned forward, resting her elbows on her knees. "Darwin, I'm doing my best not to worry, but we know nothing, and Vivian is silent."

"She hasn't spoken about this at all?"

"Well, when we were finishing with that thing in North Bay, she

mentioned something, but it seemed off the cuff, like a generalization."
She went on to tell him what Vivian said.

"Sarah, I don't see that as a generalization. Alex needs you, or *he could die before his time*. Those are serious words."

"I'm always here for him. We all are. And what can't Alex handle that will kill him?"

"How about bullets, for starters? Freight trains. Plane crashes. He's tough, but he's not made of steel."

Sarah got up and stared out over her balcony, her eyes fixed on random cars as they drove through the apartment parking lot. "Which means we have to find him fast."

"Exactly."

"There's something else, Darwin."

"What's that? Tell me everything so I can be more effective in tracking him."

Sarah hesitated, unsure how she wanted to proceed. "Alex changed after Benjamin died."

"To some degree, we all did."

"Not like this, though. He turned more ruthless."

"How so?"

"Remember when you found me in that basement in Italy after I'd disappeared in a snowstorm over here?"

"Yeah."

"Well, when Parkman, Aaron, and Alex discovered the link to those junkies who took me and connected them to a guy over here named Big Carlo, it was Alex who did all the damage. I mean, he executed Big Carlo's men like they were goats being sacrificed for an Easter celebration. He didn't have to get that crazy. Break a few bones, leave them for the authorities or something. Lucky for him, the cops blamed it on a rival gang thing. Otherwise, he'd be doing time for murder."

"Maybe this vigilante stuff is weighing on him. Could he be getting desensitized to it?"

"I don't know, but I doubt it. He's disciplined enough to know where the line is and avoid crossing it."

"Yet, he's crossing it more often? Is that what you're saying?"

Sarah shifted the phone to her other ear. "When we were working the corrupt judge thing in North Bay, and we dealt with a man named Joseph Nate and those poor kids, it disturbed Alex immensely. He went inward, became less talkative, and even asked me how it was possible that there could be people like Joseph in this world."

"Maybe it triggered something in him. How well do we know his past?"

Sarah tightened her grip on the phone. "What, like he was molested or something?"

"Who knows? Or maybe he knew someone who was, someone close to him."

"Close to him? Ever since I've known Aaron and the boys, we're the ones who are close to him. Other than some of his students at the dojo, I couldn't imagine who that could be."

They waited for a moment, neither one speaking.

Then Darwin said, "I'll keep digging, but I'll go deeper. I'll look at the last known addresses. I'll look into his past as well. Maybe there's something to this *trigger* business you're contemplating."

"I'm just worried about him."

"Me too—oh, Sarah, did I tell you what Rosina found?"

Hopeful, she spun around and sat back in her chair. "No. What did she find?"

"She was able to access his bank account. His statement had no irregularities. The dojo's paychecks and GST credit from the Canadian government are going in, and his rent is coming out. He withdrew a hundred bucks two weeks ago. That's it."

"He wanted to disappear on purpose, then."

"How so?"

"Well, he left no trail, didn't take his bank card, as evidenced by his bank statement, and left his cell phone in his apartment so no one could track him. I'd say he planned this from the beginning, whatever *this* is."

"And he wanted to do *this* alone," Darwin added. "Otherwise, he would've told one of us."

A moment of silence hit them again.

Sarah broke it. "What the hell could he be up to?"

"I have no idea, but I will do my best to find out so we can step in and help him—*if* he wants help. In the meantime, I'll search deep into his past and see what I can come up with."

"Okay. Thank you. Call me the second you learn something of value, day or night. I'm leaving my phone on."

"Got it."

The line died.

Sarah set the phone on the small balcony table beside her and leaned back, staring at the vast sky.

"Where are you, Alex? What have you gotten yourself into?"

After ten minutes, she went inside to check on her daughter, her phone in her pocket, and a plea on her lips to Vivian to offer her something.

Anything.

Anything at all.

# Chapter 5

ON WEIR STREET, A minute later, Susan turned to her daughter. "What's the house number again?"

"It's forty-four."

"Got it. That's an easy number to remember." As she drove up Weir, it became clear that she didn't need the house number after all. Six cars were parked in front of a house, two on the street disgorging teenage occupants with large presents in their hands. "I think we've found it."

Susan eased the car to the side and stopped in front of 42 Weir Street. "Where's your present for Corey?"

Tracy tapped her pocket as she reached for the door. "It's in here."

Susan grabbed her arm, stopping her from leaving the car. "Hold on, missy. We're going up together. I have to meet Corey's parents."

Tracy turned back. "Ahh, Mom. Why? You're not going to embarrass me, are you?"

"Of course not." She turned off the engine. "I've only seen Corey once. Your father and I haven't met his parents. I have to at least say hello." She released her daughter's arm. "Now, let's go."

"Mom, seriously. How can you tell if they're bad people by meeting them once?"

Susan stared at her daughter for a long moment. Raising a child with a Hamilton Police Service officer for a dad shouldn't be as challenging as it was.

"Tracy, not fifty meters from us is Montgomery Park." She pointed at the houses at the end of Maple Ave. "When you use that path, you're beside the baseball diamond—"

"I know where the baseball diamond is," Tracy cut in. "C'mon, let's just go."

"No, wait." Susan's voice brokered no argument. Tracy crossed her arms and stared out the windshield. "Do you know where your dad is this week?"

"At work." Her tone was disrespectful, but Susan let that slide.

"He's in court because a year ago, a man was murdered in Montgomery Park, which is in this neighborhood. Two of his fellow officers are up on murder charges. This has been a stressful week for your father as he's convinced they didn't *murder* anyone. Now, all that is happening around you"—*and a strange man was watching us as we left our house five minutes ago*—"and you're wondering why I want to meet Corey's parents?"

"Fine." She uncrossed her arms and faced her mom. "Can we go now? I'm going to be late."

"What time is this supposed to be over?"

"I don't know. Eight, I think."

"Okay, I've made you late. I'll come late. Deal?"

Tracy nodded quickly, then reached for the door.

This time, Susan let her get out.

They exited the car together and started toward Corey's house. Every window at the front was lit up with flashing lights. This was definitely the party house—no doubt about that.

"What's in your pocket?"

Tracy snapped a quick look at her. "What?"

"You said Corey's present was in your pocket. What is it?"

"Oh, a gift card for Walmart. I don't know what to get boys." Tracy shook her head.

Susan imagined seeing that stupid eye-roll thing if she looked at her daughter's face.

"I didn't know what to get boys at your age, either. Although, I wasn't allowed to go to boys' birthday parties at your age. My dad was too strict."

"Oh, Mom. *Please* don't start with a lecture about how different things are now."

She raised her hands. "I'm not, I'm not. Just saying." She lowered her hands, then patted Tracy on the head. "Things *are* different now."

They started up the walkway as the two cars that were parked on the street were easing away from the curb.

"Hello?" A woman waved from the open door. "You must be Tracy."

Could Corey's mom recognize Tracy on sight?

"Have you been here before?" Susan asked her daughter.

"Once or twice. You know, after school."

They stepped onto the porch, and Susan extended her hand. "I'm Susan, Tracy's mom."

The woman's grip was firm.

"Very nice to meet you. I'm Helen Baker, and my husband"—she turned to peek into the house—"Scott is somewhere in the house." She turned back, gesturing for Tracy to enter. "Please, go and see your friends. Snacks are already out, and pizza is coming in an hour."

Tracy raced off without a word of goodbye.

"It's nice to finally meet you," Helen said. "I understand you live close by."

Susan pointed toward Maple Ave. "Yes, just a few minutes away on Maple." She cleared her throat. "So, you've met Tracy before, I see."

"She walked home after school with Corey a couple of times, as we had just moved here in the weeks before school ended for the summer. You know how kids are. They make friends so easily."

Susan nodded, thinking how kids make enemies easily, too.

"Listen, I think I got Tracy here a bit late—"

"Oh, no, the party is just starting."

"What time should I pick her up?"

"Well, we're thinking of ending it around seven-thirty or eight. Does that work?"

Susan nodded. "Tracy said eight, and since she was worried about being late, I told her I'd pick her up later. Like, say, around eight-ten or eight-fifteen?"

"Of course," Helen said, her voice soft and understanding. "Eight-thirty even works." She stepped backward into the house. "Now, I must be going as I have to order the pizzas soon."

"I wouldn't want to keep you." Susan tried to see inside but couldn't catch a glimpse of Tracy among the eight to ten rambunctious young teenagers milling about the snacks on the coffee table.

She turned to go but stopped when something caught her eye just as the door was shutting.

"Helen," she called.

The door stopped, then opened again slowly. Helen's friendly façade faltered, replaced with a more serious countenance.

"Your door knocker is gorgeous. One of a kind." Susan touched it, lifting the lion's head to examine its weight. "Where did you get this?"

"Pier One Imports has these. They're fantastic, aren't they?"

"*Mom!*" a boy shouted.

"Coming!" Helen yelled over her shoulder. "I really must be going."

"Of course." Susan stepped off the porch. "I'll be back in about four hours."

"We'll be here," she said in a cheery voice.

The door closed.

Susan took in the neatly trimmed grass and the garden and wondered what Scott did for a living.

That creepy man who had been watching her when she left her garage came to mind, making her want to call her husband. Maybe he could send an officer to drive around the neighborhood. But the court was still in session. His phone would either be on silent or in airplane mode.

She stopped in front of her car and looked the length of the street in either direction. Her eyes studied each tree for any indication someone might be hiding behind one—an elbow stuck out, a shoulder exposed.

But she saw nothing. As far as she could tell, no one was watching her like that creepy guy from ten minutes ago, out front of her house.

Across the street, about three houses away, was a four-door sedan with what looked like two men in the front seat. Cars weren't usually parked on the street in this area unless it was temporary.

She walked around to the driver's side and got into her car, wondering what those men were doing. Could they be waiting for someone from the house they were parked in front of?

Even though it was none of her business, it bothered her to have two men sitting in a car that resembled one of her husband's unmarked cruisers several houses down from where she left her daughter.

Itching to call her husband for advice, she grabbed her phone but didn't dial. He was going through too much this week. Two officers under him, two men he was directly responsible for in the Vice and Drug Unit, were on trial for their lives. She couldn't bother him with phone calls about men sitting in cars on a street a few blocks from where they lived.

And what about that guy watching her house?

Maybe she'd text Blair instead. He could respond when he was ready.

After texting him, she stared at her phone for a full minute. Her text went unread.

"No surprise there," she whispered as she turned up the air conditioning a notch.

When she looked up, that car with the two men had moved one house closer.

"What the hell are they doing?"

Plate number. She should get their plate number. Blair could run it when he had time. If they're with Hamilton police, he would know, and everything would be fine. If they weren't, then he could look into it from there.

Instead of trying to remember what the men looked like, she decided a photo of them would work best.

Susan opened the camera app on her phone, lowered her car window, put the car in gear, and rolled toward the unmarked cruiser.

When she was close enough, she raised the phone slightly above the dashboard and snapped a photo of the plate number. As she passed the car, she held the phone by her left elbow, just about the window ledge, and snapped a shot of the men inside the vehicle.

Then she turned at the next corner, hit the gas hard, turned again, and watched her rearview mirror to see if they were coming after her.

They weren't.

She turned two more corners, drove to Main Street, parked in a strip mall, and opened her photos app.

The license plate shot was grainy but legible. The interior shot of the car picked up only the driver's profile.

It would have to do.

Now what? She had roughly four hours to kill before she picked up her daughter, and she didn't want to go home. She didn't want to cruise her street looking for Mr. Creepy.

She texted the photos to her husband with an explanation and then drove to the mall on Upper James, where she had been shopping since she was a teenager.

Clothes and books were her favorites.

That would lighten her mood.

# Chapter 6

SARAH SAT ON THE couch for three hours and read the new Freida McFadden novel, *The Teacher*. Focusing on it proved difficult, but she managed not to guess the twist, attributing her failure to lack of focus.

When WhatsApp dinged, she dove across the couch to grab it. Darwin had sent a message asking if he could call. She messaged him back, asking him to call her.

Her phone lit up a second later.

"Darwin," she breathed into the phone. "Tell me you got something." She could not suppress the desperation in her voice and didn't care.

"Are you sitting down?"

She frowned. "Spill it. I can take it."

"We located high school pictures and an old address for Alex."

"High school pictures? Old address? You think that's relevant?"

"I may be grasping at straws here, but if something triggered Alex with what went down in North Bay with that Joseph guy, maybe it's something rooted in the past. So we headed there."

"Okay, fair enough. Tell me, why did I need to be sitting down?"

"Because Alex wasn't an only child."

Sarah sat for a moment with her mouth open. "What?"

"He had a brother. And guess what? You know him." Darwin cleared his throat. "I mean, *knew* him."

Darwin explained everything he'd found out about Alex, and Sarah listened.

Then she formed a plan.

She now knew what to do.

\*\*\*

She called Aaron on Messenger using a three-way call with Parkman. Once they were all settled, she began.

"Aaron, did you know who Alex's brother was?"

"His brother? Sure, I know who it was."

Parkman's face on the camera revealed he was as in the dark as Sarah was when Darwin told her. "You gonna tell us?"

"Benjamin."

Sarah and Parkman stared at each other on the little screen.

Aaron continued. "They're both Alex and Benjamin Russell. Daniel and I've known that since before time. It was Daniel who knew them first. Then I met them, and we've all been brothers since."

"Brothers as in friends or blood?" Parkman asked.

"The only blood brothers are Alex and Benjamin. Same parents."

"How come I'm just learning this now?" Sarah said. "How did no one ever mention it?"

Aaron shrugged. "Didn't think of it since we're all so tight. We see ourselves as family. We've always taken care of each other and watched over one another like brothers, so it wasn't something that came up." They all looked at each other for a long moment. "Look, when my sister went missing, they saved my life—all three of them. Back in those days, they were employees at the dojo. Men who stepped up and took on some danger to see me through something rather difficult. I guess we bonded over that and became *brothers* several years before we met you two." Aaron glanced down, then back up. "It just never came up."

"Darwin did some digging and discovered this, and now it makes sense."

"How so?" Parkman asked.

"Alex changed after Benjamin died."

"Sarah, we all changed," Aaron said.

"No argument there, but Alex changed in a different way. I mean, he just lost his brother, the one piece of family he had left."

Parkman asked, "Did Darwin find anything out about their

parents?"

Sarah nodded. "They grew up in Hamilton, Ontario, which is just over an hour's drive out of Toronto."

Aaron snapped his fingers. "Hey, I knew that. I mean, I've heard them speak of it once or twice. But they were always tight-lipped about their past. I think it was because something bad happened to their parents. Something bad enough to bury and forget about."

"The question is," Sarah said, "could there be something in Hamilton that would draw Alex back? Maybe he went to their cemetery to pay his respects now that Benjamin is gone. Is that it?"

They were quiet for a moment, and then Aaron leaned closer to the screen. "Sarah, a moment before, you mentioned Alex changed after Benjamin died. How so? How was it different than the rest of us?"

Sarah shared her thoughts on the old Alex and the new, more brutal one.

"When you say it like that, you're right," Parkman said. His eyes adjusted onscreen. "We saw it firsthand, Aaron. I remember when we had subdued Big Carlo, and Alex said, 'Bring me a knife.' It wasn't his usual style. He's harder now, more ruthless."

"Which makes him more dangerous," Aaron concluded.

"That's not it," Sarah said, unsure how much she wanted to share while knowing they deserved to hear everything.

"Go on," Parkman said.

She had their attention, but unsure where to start, she just dove in. "Alex's parents are dead. It was in the papers back when Alex was a teenager."

"In the papers?" Parkman said. "Why would their parents' deaths reach the media?"

"Okay," Aaron mumbled on camera as he leaned back, his hands raising in a shrug. "That's news to me."

They both looked at him, a glum expression on Sarah's face.

"Oh, sorry. I wasn't trying to make a pun. Seriously, all I meant was that I didn't know about this one."

Sarah nodded, then continued. "Their father was murdered, and within a year, their mother committed suicide."

Aaron's eyes focused on nothing as he took in the information. Parkman glanced to the side, his mouth open slightly.

No one spoke for some time.

Sarah broke the silence. "There's more."

They both blinked, coming back into the room as if hypnosis had lifted, and then zeroed in on Sarah's visage.

"More?" Parkman whispered.

She nodded. "It was rumored that Alex killed his dad when he was barely fifteen."

Aaron expelled a pent-up breath while Parkman's mouth fell open. He leaned his head back to stare at his apartment ceiling, a hand on his forehead.

"What a terrible thing to carry your entire life," Sarah said as they processed her words. "Apparently, their father's murder was the catalyst that prompted their mother to leave this world early by her own hand."

Sarah wiped at the single tear that formed and slipped from her eyelid.

"So." Aaron stared at her through the small screen. "What you're saying is that whoever killed their father *actually* killed their parents? I mean, if the father's murder was the catalyst, it's a foregone conclusion."

Sarah nodded. "Poor Alex. The weight on his shoulders must be enormous. With Benjamin gone, he feels he's carrying it alone now."

"We have to find him," Parkman said. "He needs us, and he needs a hug."

"How could we not know all this about one of our own?" Sarah asked, suddenly wondering what secrets the others might possess. "He's out there alone, likely feeling more alone than ever. And he's always been there for us without complaint or regard for personal safety."

"Do you think that's why?" Aaron asked.

"Why what?" Parkman said, leaning closer.

"Alex's history." Aaron shook his head, likely still reeling from what he heard. "The loss of his parents. Murder. Suicide. Do you think that's why he's so invested in everything Sarah does? Figuring he'll right some wrongs?"

Sarah nodded. "There could be something to that—a call to justice. We'd have to know more of his story to determine something like that for sure. I mean, why was his father killed? Who did it? Was it the wrong place at the wrong time? Or a targeted murder? And why did people think Alex was involved? Once we learn more, that might help us see what Alex sees."

"The best is to talk to him directly." Parkman ran a hand through his hair. "I'll say it again: we have to find him. Sooner rather than later."

"Before you ask, I haven't heard from Vivian." They all stared at each other for a moment. Sarah added, "But I have a guess as to where Alex may be."

"Where?" the men said in unison.

"Hamilton."

"Why would he go there?" Aaron asked. "Isn't he reeling from Benjamin's loss? Dealing with the Joseph Nates of the world? Why take off to the source of the pain, the loss?"

Sarah lifted one shoulder. "Unfinished business of some sort? Maybe visit his parents' graves in private. Why would he need to tell us if he just wants to disappear for a few days and then return? Especially on such a private matter—something he never discusses with us."

"So you think he'll be back tonight? Tomorrow?"

Sarah stared at Aaron. "I don't know, but if he isn't back by tomorrow, like Parkman said, we have to go to him."

Aaron nodded. "I'll talk to Daniel. He can teach tomorrow's classes at the dojo and then pick up Willow after school. When do her classes stop anyway?"

"At three-fifteen."

"Okay," Parkman jumped in. "So, it's settled. I'll drive. The three of us go to Hamilton and check things out. Daniel will stay here with Willow."

Sarah and Aaron nodded.

"Where will we start in Hamilton?" Parkman asked.

"On the mountain."

Aaron stared at Sarah. "Mountain? Hamilton's got a mountain? Why haven't I heard of this?"

Sarah shook her head. "They don't have a mountain, per se. They have a large hill called Hamilton Mountain. It's an escarpment cutting through the middle of the city, creating an upper and lower Hamilton. When Benjamin and Alex were younger, they lived on Garth Street, off Fennell Avenue, on the mountain."

"He might do some sightseeing, but wouldn't that leave it to pure luck that we bump into him?"

"Darwin's still digging," Sarah said. "He's likely to come up with something else by the time we get there tomorrow morning. If not, Vivian will have to come through for us. We can't leave him out there all alone."

"Or he'll come home," Aaron said.

"Right." Parkman pointed at the screen. "Exactly. He may come home, and we will hear all about his trip down memory lane." He paused. "Providing that's where he went."

"True." Sarah nodded. "We still don't know if he's in Hamilton or not. This is all speculation."

"Well," Aaron said. "Let's drive out and see. If he isn't in Hamilton, we tried. But there's something to the way he left as well."

"Meaning?"

"Well, he didn't want us to know where he was going, so maybe he doesn't want to be found. This could be going against his wishes."

"Then we'll ask him that when we find him," Sarah said. "Until then, I'm going after him. He's too important to be out there all alone, hurting."

"Agreed," Parkman said.

After a moment, Aaron added, "Agreed."

Sarah killed the call and sat back, wondering how she'd sleep that night.

"Oh, Alex, where are you? What could you be doing?"

# Chapter 7

AT SEVEN-THIRTY, AFTER shopping for a blouse, having a too-long coffee with a friend she happened to bump into, buying half a dozen books, and checking her phone repeatedly to see if her husband had seen her messages—he hadn't—Susan Nelson headed toward her car laden down with bags.

Once everything was stowed in her trunk, she hopped behind the wheel and checked the time. It was ten after eight, leaving her twenty minutes to pick up her daughter, which meant she'd likely get there past eight-thirty. Sometimes, at this hour, traffic could be horrendous.

Although, being late probably wouldn't be an issue. Didn't Corey's mom, Heather, or Helen—whatever her name was—say she could come late if she wanted to?

And where was Blair? Her husband would've finished in court by now. He should be home by seven or eight, unless he went out for a drink with his boys from Vice. Couldn't he at least check his phone?

She pulled out of the mall parking area and headed for the Sherman Access to descend the mountain. This took her to Kenilworth Avenue, where she could turn onto her street. She wanted to drive by her house before picking up Tracy in case that guy was still watching her house. If he were, she'd call the police directly before she tried to go home because her cop-husband—Blair—wasn't checking his phone.

Traffic was lighter than expected, getting her onto Maple Avenue several minutes past eight-thirty. She slowed to a crawl a few houses away, then stopped in front of a neighbor's lawn, scanning every tree and both sidewalks.

When she saw nothing unusual, she eased forward again, driving by her own house—Blair's car wasn't in the driveway. At least he wasn't home and just avoiding her—and continued toward Weir Street.

At the corner, satisfied that the creepy guy was gone, she turned up toward Corey's place.

Even that four-door sedan from earlier, with the two men in the front seat, was gone.

This made her feel much better.

"Things are looking up."

She parked in front of 44 Weir Street as no other cars were in the area, which made sense as the party had ended at eight. Everyone would've come and gone, leaving her daughter, Tracy, as Corey's sole guest.

Susan turned off the engine and exited the car.

The street seemed quiet—too quiet.

When she faced Corey's house, the windows were dark, and the curtains were pulled. She frowned, a knot forming in her stomach. All outward appearances dictated that no one was home. But that couldn't be right. Her daughter was there. Corey and Tracy were likely in his room or the basement watching TV after a loud party, while Corey's parents were in another room reading or relaxing.

She stared at the number of the house, the small garden, the clean-cut grass, even the lion's head doorknocker. This was definitely the right house—she had zero doubt about that.

Without wasting another second contemplating why it looked like no one was home, she walked up the concrete path, stepped onto the porch, and rang the doorbell.

While waiting for Heather—Helen—to come to the door, Susan glanced over her shoulder. She spun her head both ways but saw no one in the increasing gloom before the streetlights turned on, even though it felt like someone was watching her.

She turned her attention back to the house, rang the bell again, and then rapped on the door.

"Hello? Heather? Are you home?" Wait, wasn't her name Helen? "Helen? Anyone?" She knocked again. Harder this time.

Anxiety rose through her abdomen. She stepped off the porch to examine the house, the neighbor's house, and the street. This was definitely the house where she dropped Tracy off about four hours ago. She recalled several minor details about the front of the house, the lawn, and the gorgeous lion's head door knocker.

Then where are they? She didn't come that late. She'd even told Corey's mom she'd come after eight. Corey's mom was the one who said eight-thirty was fine.

She could understand they wouldn't leave the twelve-year-olds alone if they went out for an errand, but what about a heads-up? A call, a text? Otherwise, this could look bad for Corey's parents.

Suspecting it would do no good, she pounded on the door with her fist and then rang the bell repeatedly until her finger hurt.

Her heart raced like palpitations on speed. This wasn't good.

"Where's my baby?" she said aloud.

After another look up and down the street, she jumped off the porch and headed around the side of the house. Halfway up the side, she bent over, then dropped to her knees to peer inside the rectangular basement window.

Beyond the small window was an unfinished basement. Three empty boxes lay on their side in the little light left by the fading sun.

She stood to her full height and continued to the back of the house, where she flicked the latch to a wooden fence and stepped into their backyard.

The wooden deck had two chairs and a table, but was otherwise void of life. There was nothing personal, no potted plants, no summer items like a barbecue, and no shed for bikes or summer sports items.

It looked like no one lived here. Or they just moved in and hadn't bought a single item for the back except those two chairs and a small table.

She launched up onto the patio and ran for the sliding door, where she pounded with her fist, balled up.

"Hello, is anyone home?"

She tried to peek through the sheers but barely caught a glimpse into the dining area and living room beyond, near the front bay window.

They must have gone out.

That was the only explanation.

"But why go out with someone else's daughter?" she asked out loud. "That's craziness."

She headed back toward the front of the house, pulling her phone from her pocket and bringing up her husband's number. He hadn't seen her texts yet, but he would answer a phone call now. There was no way he was still busy with court after eight-thirty in the evening.

It took until the fourth ring for him to pick up, which freaked her out even more. *My daughter is gone. Now, my husband is gone, too.* For the briefest of moments, she wondered if she was being pranked or if she'd entered the *Twilight Zone.*

"Hey, what's up?" Blair asked. "Kinda busy at the moment."

"Someone took our daughter." She blurted it out because no matter how busy he was, this was important, too. His family was important.

There was a gasp on the other end of the line. "Can you repeat that?"

At least she got his attention.

"I dropped her off at Corey's birthday party, and when I came to pick her up, the house was empty. No one's here."

Blair blew out a breath. "Okay, there has to be a rational explanation. Where is this house?"

"On Weir Street. It's number forty-four, and before you ask, I know it's the same house."

There was another gasp on the other end of the line. Then, a long pause.

"Blair? Are you still there?" Susan made it out to the sidewalk. The house felt eerie now.

"Yeah, just thinking about something. Look, maybe they all went to the park. I'm sure she'll turn up." He paused. "I gotta go."

"Wait!" she nearly shouted. "You're with Hamilton police. Can't you send someone to check it out?"

"Honey, are you sure you want to call the cops because your daughter went to the park, or they went to the store and got held up by traffic? How will she feel with two or three cruisers parked out front when they saunter home from wherever they went?"

She didn't think they'd gone on any *fucking* walk. Something was wrong—she could feel it. Her husband was occupied, so he wasn't interested in helping.

"Honey, I gotta go." From the sounds coming through the phone, it sounded like Blair was walking. Or maybe he was in the car. "I'll be home in an hour. I'll look into it personally if Tracy is still not home by then."

"She's not here now. Waiting an hour will be a mistake."

"Who did you drop her off with?" Blair's tone changed as if he were talking down to her.

"Corey and his parents, Heather and Scott Baker." She was sure the woman's name was Heather now.

"Why did you leave Tracy there?"

"What?" She pulled the phone away to stare at it and then returned it to her ear. "A birthday party was arranged for Corey, who is turning twelve. Over half a dozen kids had shown up by the time I dropped off Tracy."

"Exactly."

He could be so infuriating at times. "Exactly *what*?" She didn't hide her exasperation.

"You dropped your daughter off at a birthday party with a bunch of other twelve-year-olds. She'll turn up. Relax. That house isn't known to Vice, meaning it's not a drug haven or a criminal lab. Just wait it out. See you in an hour."

The line died.

In frustration, she raised the phone over her head to throw it against the concrete, but was able to stop herself at the last second.

How could he be so indifferent? His daughter was missing.

"You're a cop, for fuck's sake. Act like one."

She marched back to her car and dropped into the driver's seat. She would drive around the park with high beams on, then return here. If they were late coming home from wherever they went, then fine. She'd deal with that.

But if something had happened to Tracy, then her husband would have to live with that guilt for the rest of his life.

She turned on her car and sat there. Maybe he didn't care enough because Tracy wasn't his daughter. He'd always treated her like his own, but when she met Blair, Tracy was five. They'd been together for seven years.

When things were good, he was a super dad.

So, when things go bad, he becomes indifferent? Is that how it would be?

Did it take her seven years to realize she picked another asshole man?

The streetlights flickered to life along Weir Street.

Something in her mirror caught her eye. She leaned closer and stared at someone walking toward the car. She squinted to see if it was Heather or Scott—or Helen! What the hell was her name?

The man walked under a street lamp and stopped.

He seemed to be staring right at her, hands in his pockets.

When she realized it was the man from earlier, the one watching her house when they left to go to the birthday party, her breath caught in her open mouth.

The man started walking again. Then he was jogging.

He was three streetlights away.

Now, he was running in a full sprint.

Two streetlights. One.

She fumbled with the shifter, slammed the car into drive, and smashed the gas pedal down as the man made it as close as her trunk—he slammed a hand onto it and yelled something, but it was unintelligible over the roar of her engine.

In that second, when the man reached the car, she screamed, her eyes closed. The car veered right, then left, but she got it under control and was soon doing eighty kilometers an hour.

She jammed on the brakes, yanked the steering wheel hard to take a right turn, overcompensated, and arced across someone's lawn.

Back on the road, she slowed to a comfortable speed. Her hands shook on the wheel, and her breath was ragged, flowing past her clenched teeth in fits and starts.

"What was that …?" She gasped the words in a breathy voice.

Before she hit Kenilworth, she pulled over to the side of the road.

The shakes overtook her, and she cried, her forehead resting against the top of the steering wheel.

"What the hell is happening?" she muttered. "Where's my daughter?"

A minute later, the short panic attack was ending. She checked her mirror, saw no one chasing her, and then grabbed her phone.

If her cop husband didn't do something about it, she'd call the real cops—the Hamilton Police Service.

# Chapter 8

BLAIR NELSON PULLED INTO the abandoned factory parking lot off Parkdale and stopped his unmarked cruiser to await the text. He checked the clock on the dashboard.

They were supposed to reach out by eight-thirty.

They were late.

He glanced over his shoulder at a darkened corner by a wall made of corrugated steel—a great spot to sit and wait.

He reversed into concealment, killing the engine and lights. In total darkness now, he dimmed his phone, made sure he had a good signal, and waited.

They'd text. There was no way his boys wouldn't get back to him.

His thoughts returned to the conversation he'd just had with his wife. How the hell was Tracy, his stepdaughter, missing from a birthday party? He shook his head. That was rich. A birthday party. Of all the things.

His phone vibrated with an incoming text.

*Five minutes out*, it said.

He sent a thumbs-up.

While he waited, he called Tracy's cell phone. It went directly to voicemail. Was her phone turned off? Why would she freak out her mother like that?

His phone vibrated in his hand. Captain Mike Simmons.

What the hell was he calling for at this hour?

Blair answered the call while glancing at the time on the dashboard.

"Hey, Cap, what's up?" He fixed his gaze on the entrance to the factory.

"I wanted to let you know that your wife called in—"

"She called *you*?"

"No, and don't cut me off."

"Sorry, Cap."

"She called for cruisers to attend."

*For fuck's sake, Susan! Really!*

He adjusted himself in his seat, sitting straighter as if the captain were looking at him, which was something he always did in the captain's office.

"Yeah, it's nothing, though. She already called me about it."

"What's going on, Nelson? If it's nothing, why is she requesting our presence?"

He didn't have time for this. *Shit!*

"Susan dropped off her daughter at a birthday party. When she went to pick her up, Tracy wasn't there. They're probably out at the park or something. It's nothing. I'm heading home within the hour. I can deal with it."

"That wasn't why she called."

Blair stared straight ahead at nothing. "Then why did she call?"

"A man was chasing her. Unidentified perp. Almost caught her, too. Hit her car with his fist as she raced away. She admitted to driving over someone's lawn and tearing up the grass when escaping this lunatic."

"What the hell?" Blair muttered. "She didn't tell me any of that when she called."

Headlights lit up the entrance. They were here. He needed to go. *Now!*

"The front desk informed me when they caught the name and home address. Cruisers should be in the vicinity now. I'm not calling them off. Where are you?"

How should he answer that question? Out protecting his crew? Taking care of business?

"Just picking up a few groceries, then heading home."

"Hurry. I listened to the recorded 911 call. Susan sounds distressed. Genuinely. Your shift ended hours ago. Get home. Now. That's an order."

"Yes, sir. On it." He started the car so the captain would hear the engine as two unmarked cruisers entered the lot and drove toward the factory building.

"Anything else, sir?"

There was no response. His captain had hung up.

He tossed the phone onto the seat beside him, cursed Susan under his breath for overreacting, and drove toward the other vehicles.

When he pulled up and parked, leaving his nose aimed toward the exit so he could leave in a hurry, his guys were already shuffling inside the complex.

Were they dragging someone with them? Who the fuck was that?

He exited his car and followed them inside, where they'd already turned on a portable construction lamp the demolition crew was using this week. The factory was scheduled to be torn down over the summer.

Hamilton has long been known as Steeltown. It got its name from the large factories that dotted the area from Burlington Street East along the east side to Sherman Avenue North. The former Deering Harvester, Dofasco, and Stelco plants employed thousands of Hamiltonians over the years.

Those factories stank, too. People driving over the Burlington Skyway en route to Niagara Falls from Toronto could easily smell the city as the stench entered their vehicles like radiation passing through their vehicle's skin. It wasn't until getting to Stoney Creek that travelers could escape Steeltown's stench.

"What's this?" Blair asked, walking past his men to stand over what looked like a vagrant.

Murphy, his former partner, was there with his hooked nose, along with Pruitt and Morgan. Pruitt's thick glasses reflected the construction lamp, making Blair wonder, as he often did, how the man could see through those lenses. Morgan rarely wore a jacket, but he wore one tonight. He'd have to ask the man if he ate more than once a day. He was that skinny. Or was cancer eating him piece by piece, and he was ignoring the pain? That would be just like Morgan. Letting shit go until it was too late.

And then there was the unknown man who looked like they dragged him in off the street. He looked more like a vagrant than a confidential informant.

Pruitt and Morgan held the man up, as he clearly couldn't stand on his own.

Murphy pointed at Blair. "Tell him what you told us," Murphy said.

"I ain't seen nothing, man," the vagrant said, his eyes rolling around in his head.

"Fuck, guys." Blair stepped back to grab a metal chair behind him. He placed it beside the vagrant. "Sit the guy down and tell me what the hell is going on."

The chair scraped on the factory floor when the man plopped onto it.

It was hard to suppress his nerves as he felt antsy after getting the captain's call.

Pruitt and Morgan had dropped the perp onto the chair and were brushing their hands together as if to rid themselves of his stench.

Murphy turned to Blair. "We did what you told us, partner. We ran that plate number, and it came up blocked."

Blair jerked his head back, not correcting Murphy—they weren't partners anymore. "Blocked? What do you mean, blocked?"

"Like classified or some shit. It wasn't one of ours, that's for sure."

"Is that why you called, saying you had a tip on where they were keeping the witnesses?"

Murphy nodded. "That license prefix belongs to the RCMP, the fucking Royal Canadian Mounted Police themselves—"

"Who handles all witness protection cases ..." Blair finished for him.

Murphy nodded. "The exact ones."

It all clicked for Blair. "Are you saying the witnesses were on *Weir Street*?" Right by Tracy's birthday party? Did they snatch the wrong people?

He lunged forward and grabbed Murphy by the lapels, yanking him briefly off his feet. "What have you done with them?"

"Hey, take it easy," Morgan said in his left ear as hands grabbed his arms to release Murphy.

Pruitt grabbed him on the other side and applied pressure on his elbow to make him release Murphy's jacket as the man struggled under his grip.

"What the fuck, man?" Murphy shouted. He moved backward as Blair's hands came off him. "Don't put your hands on me again, asshole. We go way back, but that doesn't give you the right—"

"Where are they?" Blair lunged at him again, but Pruitt stepped in the way, making his arms flail over Pruitt's shoulder.

"We don't know, dickhead."

Gasping for breath, the rage boiling inside him, Blair eased back at those words.

Pruitt pushed his glasses up his nose.

Blair glared at all of them. "Talk fast. Tell me what's happening here."

"Like you deserve the story," Murphy said, walking around behind the perp. "What the fuck was that for? I should kick your ass."

"Susan called the cops." Blair's voice was monotone.

Everyone stared at him, the only sound coming from a distant truck's airbrakes on the highway somewhere.

"*Cops?*" Murphy said. "What are you talking about? What the hell for?"

"Tracy is missing." Blair had gotten his breathing back under control. He adjusted his shirt and jacket, then huffed out a sigh. "She was at a birthday party on Weir Street. Remember? C'mon guys! It was Susan who sent me those photos. I took a screenshot of them but left the messages unread. When Susan went to pick up Tracy, she wasn't there. Then, some random guy chased her. Apparently, she drove over someone's lawn, tearing it up, to escape." He turned sideways, felt the weight of his weapon in its holster, then glared at his crew. "Captain Simmons just called to tell me all that. Then, he ordered me off the job. Told me my shift had ended and to go home and handle my wife. So, I'll ask again. Where have you taken them?"

"Nowhere, man." Murphy looked down his crooked nose at Blair. "We haven't taken anyone anywhere."

Blair blinked. "Then why are they missing?"

"You've always been impatient. If you'd let us explain, you wouldn't have lost your shit. And for the record, we have no idea *why they're missing*. How do you even know one thing has anything to do with the other?"

Blair glanced at his watch, then back to Murphy. "Cruisers are in my neighborhood right now, chatting it up with my wife. I just got off the phone with the captain. Impatient? Well, maybe I have a *fucking reason*." He shouted the last two words.

Murphy nodded at him. Pruitt and Morgan stared at Murphy while Morgan moved behind the vagrant now.

"Tell him," Morgan said, his jaw clenching in his chiseled face. "Spill it so the boss can get to his family."

Murphy sighed heavily. "We were up on the mountain when you called and sent those pictures. Once the plates came back tagged as RCMP, we raced down to Weir Street, but the car with the two men was gone."

"How long?"

"What?"

"How long did it take for you to get there from when I sent the photo?"

"An hour, maybe more."

Blair scoffed and shook his head, staring at the wall behind Murphy.

"Look, man." Murphy raised his hands. "We ran the plates, made a few calls, and then decided to attend. With rush hour at five this afternoon, it took some time."

"And the car was gone when you got there?"

Murphy nodded. "There was no indication of an RCMP presence anywhere. No safe house. No sign of Albert Wagner and his *lovely* family of witnesses."

Everyone caught the sarcasm on *lovely*.

The Wagners had been in Montgomery Park one year ago, filming their son, Patrick Wagner, on the swings. When Albert and Rebecca filmed him walking to the slide, they caught two men on film. Then, minutes later, after two shots rang out in the night, there were two more

—a total of four bullets were fired. Albert dragged his wife and child to the ground and swung his camera toward the fleeing suspects.

The same suspects were on trial for their lives—the same suspects who are cops and school friends of Inspector Blair Nelson.

And he's convinced they aren't murderers.

The Wagner family went into hiding, protected by the RCMP. This week, they were back in Hamilton for the murder trial. They were supposed to take the witness stand tomorrow.

It wasn't murder, though, in Blair's esteemed opinion. He felt he could prove it, but he was not taking part in the trial.

This was a simple case of the system crucifying the police in search of a better public opinion. The public wanted the police defunded. They wanted them to pay for crimes they didn't commit. So, when a drug dealer in Montgomery Park, four blocks from his house, was shot by fellow undercover officers, who swore up and down that the dealer fired first and were on trial for their lives, Blair's team decided they wanted to have a chat with the witnesses—something less professional than a court of law, and something deemed highly illegal.

If the prosecution or the defense wouldn't let them be a part of the downfall of members of their unit, then they would find another way.

They had no intention of intimidating the witnesses or tampering with evidence, far from it. Blair was responsible for a crew. If his men showed up and murdered that dealer, robbed him, and thought they could get away with it, then he wanted them out of his unit.

But he'd known those boys since elementary school.

And he didn't believe they were murderers.

Not one bit.

"So, I sent you a lead because I was in court supporting our men, and you got there late and missed the RCMP."

"People always have a choice on how they want to look at shit. If that's how you want to see it, then fine, fuck you. But that's *not* how it went down."

"Then talk faster."

"We got the tip. Checked it out. Then responded to the address. End of story. We did nothing wrong."

Blair nodded. "Yeah, but you did nothing right, either. Our boys will be killed in prison, and all because the Wagners allegedly have them on video in the park at the time of the murder. The prosecution claims they have enough evidence to convict. The video will be played tomorrow in court. That leaves tonight to find them."

"Which is unlikely," Murphy said, "without him."

"Tell me how he plays into it."

"He saw them."

"What's with the half-answers? Saw *who*?" Heat rose to his collar.

Murphy stepped in front of the vagrant/perp and snapped his fingers.

"Hey, wake up. Your turn to talk." When the man grunted a reply, Murphy slapped him. "Wake up, asshole."

"What?" the man said, his head lolling to the side.

"Tell the bossman what you saw."

"People coming and going. This way and that …" It appeared the vagrant was ready to doze off again.

"How high is he?" Blair asked.

Murphy didn't respond. He leaned closer and drove a fist into the perp's cheek, knocking him from the chair.

"Owww," the man said from the floor, curling into the fetal position, a hand over his face. "Why hit me, man? I'm cool."

Murphy bent over the man and shouted, "Tell him what you saw."

"People. Running with suitcases. Into three cars. Then, driving toward Kenilworth. That's it, man. That's all."

Murphy turned back to Blair. "From the time Susan sent you that text, and we arrived on scene an hour later, they were gone. We think it's them, though." He pointed at the vagrant on the floor who was massaging his cheek, his eyes wide now. "He said it was men in suits."

"Except for the people not in suits," the vagrant added.

"How many were not in suits?" Blair asked.

"Not sure. Two. Maybe three. Could be four or five."

"What house number?"

The man's eyes found Blair. Then he blinked rapidly. "You serious, dude? You think I got an address book on me?"

"What street then? Describe the area."

"I already told them. Weir Street by Maple. That's all I know. I was in Montgomery Park, minding my own business, when I heard a bunch of engines revving. I stepped onto Weir to take a look, and that's what I saw."

They all turned to Blair.

It was Morgan who spoke first. "Do you think it was where Susan's daughter was visiting?"

Blair shook his head. "No, she went to a birthday party for a school friend who is turning twelve. I checked them out—Scott and Helen Baker and their kid, Corey. If the Wagner family were here for the trial, they wouldn't be five blocks from my house and having their kid attend the local school. Besides, Montgomery Park is right beside them. That'd be like returning the witnesses to the crime scene." He shook his head. "The RCMP don't work like that."

"What if they did this time?" Murphy asked. "I mean, that was an unmarked RCMP cruiser. And this dickhead said he saw people being rushed away. They could have seen Susan snap their picture and thought their cover was blown. Or maybe they monitor our systems and detected us checking their plate number."

"Okay, fine. It could be them, but still, it wasn't the *Baker* family."

"The Wagners could be disguised as the Bakers."

"I *said* I checked the Bakers—they've got history. They moved from Bowmanville and bought that house. You might recall their kid, Patrick Wagner, was ten. He wouldn't be turning twelve for another eighteen months yet." Blair checked the time again. "It's not them. But they might have been neighbors, and the activity on the street spooked the kids at Corey's birthday party. So it would make sense to relocate those kids for a bit." He stepped backward. "I gotta go. I need to check in with Susan and find Tracy. You guys have until court is in session tomorrow morning to find the Wagners. Get it done. All I want to do is talk to them."

When he turned to hurry to his cruiser, he detected a few sighs and one scoff behind him. Maybe they weren't as invested in protecting their fellow officers as Blair was.

Rumor had it the Wagners were liars. Their camera footage had been edited. They were there on another night. All kinds of information about that night had come up so far in court. But the one damning piece of evidence hadn't been delivered yet—the actual footage, with Albert Wagner's commentary.

Apparently, according to the prosecution in their opening statement, there would be no doubt as to who shot whom and when.

But if the Wagners were painting an unpleasant and unfair picture for his men, he was committed to stopping it.

Even if it costs him his job.

Two men were fighting for their lives here.

The least he could do was fight alongside them.

# Chapter 9

When Blair pulled onto Weir Street, the red and blue strobing lights atop two cruisers were visible from the end of the road. He gunned the engine, then braked beside his wife's car, slamming it into park as he opened his car door.

One of the uniformed officers turned to him and then started his way.

"What's going on here?" Blair asked, flipping out his inspector badge.

"Got a prowler call." The cop checked his notebook. "A stalker, the woman called it." He shook his head. "And a missing girl, but she's not a missing persons case yet."

"Blair," Susan called from one house away. She ran toward him, and even in the streetlights, he could see her tear-stained red face.

"She knows you, Inspector?" the cop asked.

"Susan Nelson is my wife."

The cop stood straighter. "Uhm, sorry, sir. I didn't know that."

Susan threw her arms around him with such force that he had to step back once to maintain his balance.

"There, there," he whispered in her ear as she sobbed.

Susan pulled away, her eyes frantic. "Tracy's gone."

"Honey, there's got to be a good explanation for this. We'll figure it out."

Susan shook her head. "Nope, they took her."

"They? Who's they?"

"Heather and Scott Baker." She pointed at the house. "I dropped

Tracy off there, and when I returned, no one was home—they're still not home!"

"It's okay, honey. We'll find them. *Helen* and Scott haven't—"

Susan jerked backward out of his arms. "Helen? Why did you say that?"

"Her name isn't Heather. It's Helen."

"How would you know something like that?"

He tilted his head and smirked at her. "You think I'd let Tracy go to a birthday party without vetting the parents first? I ran their names yesterday. They moved from Bowmanville in June. They bought this house and set up their son Corey in Tracy's school. Everything checked out."

Susan blew out an exasperated breath. It was like she was at an oncologist's and just got the cancer-free news.

"Oh, Blair, thank you, thank you, thank you." She dropped back into his arms, her last words of gratitude muffled by his suit jacket.

"Honey," he said, easing her out of his arms. "What's this about a stalker?"

The uniformed officer had eased away to give them a moment.

Susan explained how she saw the strange man as she backed out of their driveway, then again after banging on the Bakers' doors and windows.

"He *ran* at the car?" Blair asked, looking down into her eyes. "And smacked the trunk?"

She nodded, wiping moisture from her cheeks. "It was more like he punched the trunk."

"And you didn't recognize him?"

She shook her head.

"Sir?" The cop was back.

"We've got descriptions—everything we need for now. We'll drive around the area to look for that stalker guy. But until tomorrow, there's not much we can do."

He waved them away. "Go, I've got this."

The cop walked over to join three others standing by the second cruiser. They spoke in hushed tones as Blair looked down the length of

Weir Street, wondering if the Wagners might be hiding out in one of these houses.

"Did the officers check with the neighbors?" he asked.

Susan nodded. "They knocked on the doors of four houses each way from this one"—she pointed at 44 Weir Street—"where I dropped Tracy off around four this afternoon."

"Anyone home? Anyone see anything?"

She shook her head. "Nothing. Out of the eight houses on this side and four on the other side, only two people were home when the birthday party was happening. They claim to have seen nothing."

He studied the façade of the house. "And you're sure it was this place?"

Susan put her hands on her hips and jerked her head toward the four officers still standing by their cruisers. "They asked me the same thing. Of course, I'm sure. I remember commenting to Heather—"

"Helen."

"*Whatever*," she blurted under her breath. "I remember talking about the lion's head door knocker. This is the place."

"Okay, let's go home for now." He put his arm around her. "I'll make some calls and see what I can do from home. I can send out a current picture of her and have every cop in the city looking for Helen and Scott Baker."

She lumbered along, leaning into him. "Where were you all this time? Didn't court finish hours ago?"

"Honey, I'm in court all day. Work still calls. I had things to do with active cases." He hated lying to her, but protecting his officers wasn't her business.

Even if he found the Wagner family in time, he only wanted to see the proof for himself. The court system can have its opinion, but these men worked with him. They risked their lives every day, and each man —and woman—had their back.

If the proof were sketchy, they would ensure the Wagner family never saw the inside of the courtroom. The prosecution would rest, and his men would be found not guilty.

He wasn't a kidnapper or a murderer. He just wanted them to see the value of destroying the evidence and carrying on with their lives.

Unless, of course, his men did as the prosecution suggested—cold-blooded murder of a drug dealer in Montgomery Park. If so, he'd escort the Wagner family to court tomorrow morning if that's what he saw on Albert Wagner's camera.

Most of this was just a pipe dream, though. Getting to the witnesses while the RCMP was protecting them would be impossible. It was just something that occupied their thoughts and time.

But if he saw Albert Wagner at a donut shop, he wouldn't hesitate to approach the man.

They reached Susan's car, where he released her and stared into her eyes. "Are you okay to drive home?"

She nodded. "I feel sick. I can't handle the waiting. Where could they have taken my baby?" She started crying again, and it tore at his heart.

"Maybe I'll get one of these uniforms to drive you home."

Something moved at the corner of his eye, near the edge of his vision. He lifted his head slowly to see someone staring at them from behind a bush between two houses.

Someone was hiding back there, and when they stuck their head out to look down the street, the side of their face was caught in the streetlight.

Keeping his head down as if he were looking at Susan, he stared at the opening between the houses but saw nothing now.

"Honey, I need you to get inside your car and lock your door. I'll go get a uniform to drive you home."

She nodded, slipped into the car, and then edged over to the passenger side.

He leaned down to look at her. "One more thing. You said there was a stalker, someone watching you. Can you describe this person?"

She hiccupped and wiped at her face. From the glove box, she pulled a tissue and blew her nose.

"It was a male, Caucasian. Slim build but fast like a gazelle. He had very short hair, and it seemed like he had a perpetual grimace. I thought I recognized him at first, but now I don't think so."

"Recognized him?" That was surprising. "Like from a mall, coffee shop, or the grocery store? Something like that?"

"Oh, I don't know. He just had one of those faces, you know. Common or something."

"Okay, okay. Give me a minute."

Blair shut the door, and without looking between the houses, he walked quickly back to the four officers who were separating and heading to their cruisers.

"Hey, guys, wait up." He jogged the rest of the way. "Listen, I think we've got a problem."

The officer he spoke to earlier stepped closer. "What seems to be the problem, Inspector?"

"Someone is hiding in the bushes back where my wife parked her car. They're right between houses number forty and thirty-eight. I need you guys to circle around to the street behind those houses, access the alleyway, and flush him out toward me. If we go right at him, we could lose him in the dark of someone's backyard."

The officer chanced a look that way.

"*Don't* let him see you do that. He'll know we're onto him. Now, let's go. I'll move back to my wife's car." He pointed at the cop beside him. "You're with me. You have your Taser?"

The cop nodded. "Yes, sir."

"Good, be ready to use it." He turned to the other officers. "Go now. Flush him out."

They all nodded and headed toward their cruisers.

"Good night, guys," Blair said, loud enough so the lurker could hear him.

The two cruisers pulled out, and their lights clicked off as they drove up Weir away from where the man was hiding.

"What's your name, Officer?" Blair asked as they trudged slowly toward Susan's car.

"Hart. Just H-A-R-T. Officer Hart."

"Okay, Officer Hart, follow my lead and be ready."

"Yes, sir."

They neared the car. Blair glanced around but saw nothing. The man was too well hidden.

"So, your partner will meet you at my house?" Blair said loud enough for the lurker to hear.

"Yes, sir," Hart said.

"I really appreciate you doing this. My wife is too distraught to drive herself. We don't live far."

"It's no problem, sir. Really."

"But wait." Blair moved to the car's passenger side so they were standing on the sidewalk.

Officer Hart followed.

He tapped on the window, and Susan lowered it. "This officer will drive you home, honey."

She nodded and sniffled into a tissue without looking up.

"But we have to wait for a few minutes."

Now she looked up. Her eyes were bloodshot and glazed over. "Why?" She sobbed the word if that was possible.

Blair leaned in closer to whisper. "Because I sent those other three officers on an errand. They won't be long now."

"What are they doing?"

"Honey." Blair used his soft voice. "In a few moments, I will need you to identify the man who ran after you and hit the car."

Her eyes widened. "You got him?" Her shoulders hitched.

"I suspect we'll have him soon." Blair stood back up to his full height. "Now, honey, raise the window and lock the doors." He'd told her to lock the doors before he walked to the uniforms moments ago, but she hadn't yet.

Now she did.

Then the window went up. She glanced up the street, then leaned down to check her mirrors.

A man yelled something from a street over. A thumping sound followed that.

"Hey, what the hell?" someone else shouted.

"That's our cue," Blair said. "Follow me. Have your Taser ready."

Blair bolted toward the bushes where he'd seen the face.

He was less than two meters from the bushes when the man bolted out into the open—more like he *sprang* from the bushes because he launched over five feet in the air to clear them.

Blair dove, but the wiry man had landed and rolled away.

The man bumped into the wall of the house, then shoved off it and scrambled to his feet.

All that, and he just wasn't fast enough.

Officer Hart's Taser fired its prongs into the man's chest. As he shoved forward, his muscles stopped working, and he flopped to the ground, arms and legs rigid.

Then Blair was on him, working the cuffs onto the punk's wrists.

Two other officers ran around the house to join them.

"He was trying to run. We bumped into him. Officer Darrow is back there nursing a sore wrist. This asshole might have broken it when Darrow pointed his Taser at him."

"Fucker." Blair yanked on the cuffs, tightening them as far as they would go.

To his credit, the man didn't let out a peep.

They got him to his feet and marched him toward the road. He seemed subdued, the fight gone out of him.

"Go get your cruiser," Blair said. "This young man has some explaining to do."

When he saw the look of recognition on his wife's face in the car, he turned the man around to study him.

"Holy shit." Blair leaned back farther. "You're that guy, Alex, a crime-fighter dude with Sarah Roberts's crew. I know *exactly* who you are." He shook his head. "Nothing but a vigilante punk stalking my wife. You made a mistake today, my friend. A terrible mistake." He glanced around the street. "Where's Sarah? The rest of your crew?" When he looked back into Alex's face, a horrific idea struck him, and he jerked Alex toward him. The boy must weigh all of one hundred pounds. "You and Sarah are behind all this shit. So, tell me, where are they? Where did you stash the Bakers and Susan's daughter?" He leaned closer to Alex's ear. "Where are the Wagners?"

When he pulled back, their eyes met. Blair thought he caught something dark in Alex's gaze, like hatred or rage.

He shoved him toward Officer Hart. "You'll pay for this. All of you will! Take him to holding. We've got all night to find out what you know."

# Chapter 10

Sarah had lain awake for hours, tossing and turning, worried about Alex. The last time she remembered checking the clock was 02:45 a.m.

But now her phone was ringing, and the clock said it was 04:14 a.m.

Who would call at such an early hour? Her mind wandered between sleep and answering the phone.

Then, everything hit her at once.

*Alex is missing.* It could be him. Or Aaron telling her they found him.

She leaned over and snatched up her phone, instantly awake.

"Hello? Hello?"

"Where are you right now?" a man asked.

"What? Who's this?" What a time for a pervert to call. She'd answered so fast she didn't check the number on the screen.

"Just tell me where you are. What city?"

"I'm hanging up now, asshole."

"Wait!"

She resisted pushing the button to end the call.

"We have Alex."

If she wasn't fully awake a moment ago, she was now.

"Where? Who's we?"

"He's in holding here at the Hamilton police station—"

"Hamilton?" Her mind reeled. Alex went home. Something drew him back home. "Why is he in holding? What's he charged with?"

"He's been arrested for assaulting one of my officers."

"And he gave you my number to call?"

"No."

Fully awake or not, she was confused. "Why am I not following?"

"Just tell me what part of Hamilton you're in, and we'll meet. Let's have coffee. We can figure everything out."

She turned on the small lamp beside the bed and sat up. "Figure what out?"

"Sarah, do me a favor and stop playing dumb. Please. You're testing my patience."

She was too sleepy for a smartass retort. "Sure, just tell me what's going on."

"Why are you avoiding the question?"

"What question?" She rubbed her forehead. "Wait, who am I speaking with?"

"Like you don't know." The man scoffed in her ear. "You're supposed to be psychic."

She shook her head and blinked sleep out of her eyes. *What an asshole.*

"Are you going to be straight with me?" he asked.

"Sure. That would be a fun game. You go first."

"Shit, you're so annoying."

"I've been told that." After a moment, she said, "Are you going to tell me what this is all about?"

"Your boy was stalking my wife."

*Alex? A stalker?* "Yeah, right. Tell me another one."

"Believe what you want, but the charges against your boy are growing by the hour, and it's only going to get worse for him."

"In other words, *cop*, we'll have him out on a promise to appear in the morning, right?" It was her turn to scoff. "Egos make threats to scare and intimidate. But it doesn't work on people who aren't scared easily. Got something else for me? Or are we done here? I need to call our lawyer."

"A family is missing. My stepdaughter is with them wherever they are, and Alex had something to do with it. Since you people don't work alone, I know this is all your doing. So, tell me where they are. Release the family to me, and we'll go our separate ways. I'll even get the charges against Alex dropped. If you need that in writing, I'll do it. All we want is that family back."

Sarah was rarely stunned into silence, but she had no idea what to say next. A family? Missing? And the Hamilton authorities were convinced she had something to do with it? *How fucked up is that?*

"Cat got your tongue?" the man asked. "Okay, play hardball. Let's see how this plays out—"

"I genuinely have no idea what you're talking about."

"Really now? Are you saying Alex showed up in Hamilton and orchestrated this all on his own? And you expect the Hamilton Police Service to believe that?"

"Hey, whoever you are, I'm in Toronto right now, in my apartment. I have been here all day and night. For several days, actually. And that alibi can be corroborated by my friends and daughter, whom I saw after school. Whatever Alex was up to, we're all unaware of it. He disappeared a few days ago. We were looking for him."

"Disappeared to Hamilton? To do whatever the hell you sent him to do? And you expect me to believe that?" She could envision the man shaking his head. "No, Sarah, he has done some terrible things here, and now he's not talking. Not a single peep. He hasn't even asked for a lawyer in over six hours of sitting in our interview room, taking question after question. The guy's tough. I'll give him that. But tough won't make it in Hamilton. We'll break him."

"I'm calling my lawyer. Then I'm coming to Hamilton—"

"Stay away. You've been warned. I don't have any patience left." He raised his voice. "Sorry, all used up. Working on my last nerve now. Don't come to Hamilton, Sarah. Don't push me. You *will* regret it."

The line died.

Sarah gasped, inhaling deeply.

"What the hell is going on?" she muttered to herself as she jumped off the bed. "I will regret it? Hell, that only makes me want to come more."

Before getting showered and dressed, she called Aaron, woke him, and then filled him in.

They were leaving for Hamilton by seven as soon as she could drop Willow off with Daniel.

Aaron would drive.

He'd had more sleep.

# Chapter 11

SUNSHINE FOUND ITS WAY through the crack in her bedroom curtains, waking Susan Nelson to a splitting headache. She'd slept terribly, wondering all night where her daughter was and if she was okay.

Tossing and turning throughout the darkest hours caused her sheets to pile at the foot of the bed.

When she looked to her right, Blair's side of the bed was empty. A dozen questions raced through her mind. Where was Blair? Why wasn't he home? Had they found Tracy?

She sat up slowly and took a moment to linger on the edge of the bed. After a moment, she found a headache tablet in the medicine cabinet in the bathroom. Then she got dressed and went to make coffee.

While it brewed, she called Blair's number, but his phone must've been turned off as it went to voicemail. Once the coffee was ready, she took her cup to Tracy's room and stared at her untouched bed.

"Where are you, my baby?"

Waiting would drive her insane, and Blair wasn't picking up when she tried him again, so she dumped her coffee in the sink, put on her shoes, and headed out for a walk.

Her stalker was in custody. She could only imagine what he was telling them.

That being said, she wasn't afraid to walk the streets with him at the police station.

She turned right at the corner of Maple and Weir and started toward house number forty-four.

Nearing the house, she could tell something was different. The curtains had been moved. Someone was there!

Hope surged through her. They'd come home through the night. Maybe it was so late due to a flat tire or something that they didn't want to call and wake her.

She jogged up their walkway, mounted the porch, and rang the doorbell, the lion's head knocker level with her nose.

Noises emanated from behind the door.

Someone was home!

"Hello? Heather?" She shook her head. "I mean, Helen? Are you in there?"

The lock clicked, the knob turned, and the door opened to a man she didn't recognize. This wasn't Scott Baker. Though she only caught a brief side view of him, she was sure this wasn't Mr. Baker.

This man was clean-cut, had recently shaved, and had no facial hair. He was built, too, like he spent time in the gym.

"Is Helen Baker home?" she asked, trying to peek over the man's shoulders.

"I'm sorry, you must have the wrong house." The man moved to close the door.

"Who is it, darling?" a woman asked from somewhere behind the man.

Susan shook her head. "Oh no, this is the house, all right." She glanced at the lion's head knocker on the door, then back to the man. "Just send Tracy out here, or I'll call the police."

The man frowned and raised a hand. "Now, hold on, lady. Who's Tracy?"

"My daughter." Susan said those words so fast that it was accompanied by spittle. Frustration at this man blocking the door was making her mad. She moved closer, then rose onto the balls of her feet. The living room resembled the one from yesterday. This was the house. If she ever had a percent of doubt, an iota, it was gone now.

"Look, lady, we don't know any Tracy."

A woman in her thirties moved into view behind the man. "Are you okay, ma'am? Would you like us to call someone for you?"

"Of course I'm okay," she shouted. "I just want my daughter back."

Sirens wailed in the distance, making Susan step back and look down the length of Weir Street. Two marked police cars raced by and entered the access to Montgomery Park.

*What the hell is going on in the park now?*

When she looked back at the man and woman blocking her from Tracy, they had leaned out to look at the police cars, too.

"Well." Susan crossed her arms. "Will you give me back my daughter, or am I coming in there to get her?"

The man's hand came up again. "I'm sorry, but you most certainly have the wrong house. My wife and I have lived here since June. I'm sorry you've lost your daughter, I truly am, but I assure you we don't have her."

He tried to close the door, but Susan rammed her shoulder into it. She pushed and screamed, but was no match for the man's strength. The door closed with finality, the deadbolt snapping into place.

Susan shouted obscenities and banged on the door several more times until her fists hurt. When the curtains in the window moved, she glanced that way.

The woman was watching her, slowly shaking her head.

She jabbed a finger at her. "You watch," Susan shouted. "I'll get my husband and a hundred cops, and we'll break in there and get my Tracy."

Susan jumped off the porch and ran to the side of the house. The daylight made it hard to see inside the basement window, but when she dropped to her knees and leaned closer, cupping her hands on either side of her face, the basement's interior came into view.

It was just like last night. Three empty boxes were on the floor of the unfinished basement.

She pushed up to her feet and ran for the fence, where she unlatched the gate and darted into their backyard. She pulled the balcony door on their back deck, which still held a small table and two chairs, but it didn't budge. She pounded on the glass, but that only served to hurt her hands.

"We're calling the police, ma'am." The woman's voice came through the glass. A moment later, while she tried to catch her breath, she overheard the woman's voice again. "Yes, Officer? Yes, that's right. We have a crazy woman claiming we have her daughter. She's outside the house right now." A pause. "That's right, in our backyard. She's trying to break into our house." Another pause. "No, we're safe for now. She's still outside. My husband is home. Yes, we'll wait for the police to get here."

Susan pushed off the door and headed back through the open gate. Blair would be furious with her, but she didn't care. Something fishy was going on, and her daughter was still missing. She had dropped her off here last night, and now some other couple was living in this house. She hadn't lost her mind—*had she?*—someone was playing with her family.

The door popped open as she passed the front of the house. "Aren't you going to stay and wait for the police?" the woman asked. Her tone had turned snarky.

"Bitch," Susan said, loud enough for the woman to hear as she ran into the street and headed back toward her house.

She would call her husband. He'd get to the bottom of this.

More police sirens screamed on neighboring streets.

What the hell is going on at Montgomery Park? She marched toward the entrance to the park, turned near the baseball diamond, and stopped there.

Yellow tape was being strung up by the bushes on the side. Centered beyond the yellow tape was a black tarp on the ground, covering what appeared to be a body.

"Ma'am," someone said behind her. "You're going to have to leave this area. It's a crime scene now."

She turned to look at the policeman as he sauntered toward her, his belly obliterating any chance of seeing his belt.

"Another murder?" When she spoke, it was like someone else was talking. Her voice sounded distant. "More murder," she whispered.

The body was too big to be Tracy's.

She turned and ran toward her house. Halfway there, she slowed to a fast walk, already winded.

That, and she couldn't see where she was going through the tears.

# Chapter 12

SARAH WENT OVER THE call in her head repeatedly, then recited as much as she could to Aaron and Parkman on the ride to Hamilton.

"He said Alex wasn't talking?" Parkman asked.

Sarah nodded from the front seat. "I wish we knew why Alex went to Hamilton, how he's mixed up in this missing family thing, and why he assaulted a cop."

"That's so weird." Aaron changed lanes on the 403 highway, then glanced at Sarah. "He doesn't do this sort of thing without us. What prompted him to go to Hamilton is what I want to know."

Sarah clutched her phone in her hand, tossing it back and forth. "What pisses me off is that cop telling us *not* to come to Hamilton." She turned in her seat to look at Parkman. "I mean, why wouldn't we? It's not illegal to go help a friend in need."

"Unless the man you spoke to is up to something nefarious."

"Nefarious?" Aaron said, glancing in the rearview mirror. "Really?"

Sarah raised her phone and shook it. "Maybe that's why he didn't give me his name, and when I checked my call history, his phone number was blocked."

"Could be." Parkman nodded at her.

Her phone dinged in her hand. "Guys, it's Darwin. I'll put it on speaker." She answered the call and then hit the speaker button. "Darwin, I've got Aaron and Parkman in the car."

"Okay, good. Where are you guys heading?"

"Hamilton." Sarah looked at Aaron.

"Oh, how did you know? Did Vivian send you there?"

"Know what?" Sarah stared at Aaron.

"I'm calling to tell you that Alex was arrested. They're holding him at the Hamilton police station. His name came up in one of my searches."

"What else can you tell us?"

"They're holding him on assault charges. Apparently, he hit a cop. There might be more, but I couldn't learn more without calling."

"Did you call?"

Darwin laughed. "Of course, I called. I pretended to be his lawyer, but they gave me nothing and then hung up on me. Why are you guys going there? How did you hear?"

Sarah told him about the man calling her sometime after four in the morning.

"And he told you *not* to come to Hamilton?" Darwin sounded surprised.

"Yeah, that was our reaction, too," Parkman said, leaning forward and raising his voice to be heard better.

"Something's wrong in Hamilton, that's for sure." Darwin paused. "I learned more, but I don't think it'll help."

Sarah turned in her seat to face forward. "Tell us anyway."

"Alex used to work at a Taco Bell. It's still there, too, on Upper James by a shopping mall."

Aaron snapped his fingers. "That's right. I seem to recall Benjamin talking about that once. Alex eventually wanted to buy the franchise name and open his own Taco Bell. Some dream he had when they were teenagers."

"Geez, that's so not like the Alex we know." Sarah shook her head.

"Now for the juicy stuff," Darwin said.

Sarah checked that the volume was high and held the phone higher for Parkman and Aaron to hear better.

"I can't find anything on Alex's parents."

"You mean there are no records?"

"No, I mean whatever records there are, they're sealed."

Sarah frowned. "Sealed? What the hell for? Were they military or something?"

"I have no idea. I searched records for birth notices and several microfiche archives for his parents' names going back to when Alex was born, and I think I located them, but when Alex was around fifteen, his parents ceased to exist."

"What were their names?"

"Allen and Cathy Russell. But remember, I'm speculating here because that couple is the closest match."

"What do you mean, *match*?"

"I mean, most probable. Let me explain. When I checked the dates for Alex's birth and cross-referenced them with Benjamin's birth, there were half a dozen couples that could fit in the Hamilton area. Through the process of elimination, I went down the proverbial rabbit hole with each couple, searching them up to today. Two had pictures on Facebook with their kids and grandkids, so they were taken off the list. Others had more kids, whom I found online. Finally, I came down to Allen and Cathy Russell. Who pretty match vanished when Alex was fifteen."

"You said 'most probable.' What's stopping you from being certain?"

"Because Allen and Cathy Russell had three kids."

They all looked at each other.

Sarah spoke first. "What if Alex went to Hamilton searching for his other brother?"

"Or sister," Parkman added.

Sarah twisted around to look at him.

"But even so," Darwin continued, "if that were the case, why am I not seeing that in my searches? Sealed files aren't that common. Top secret government projects, undercover officers, witness protection programs, and court-ordered files, to name a few, can be sealed this tight. If this Allen and Cathy are Alex and Benjamin's parents, what happened to them, and why is there no mention of their third child?"

"Is there something else that makes them the most probable?" Sarah asked.

"All the other cases we encountered led to a result of some kind. I saw death certificates and the places their kids moved to. Rosina even called a friend in the DMV to confirm that a certain someone now lives in the States. The only thing stopping us from confirming that Allen and Cathy Russell are Alex's parents is further information, which we can't get because it's just not there. And trust me, we've looked."

"That's so strange," Sarah whispered.

"So, you guys are probably wondering why Alex went to Hamilton on his own and left without a word to anyone, right?"

Sarah nodded, even though they weren't on camera. "Yes, we are, and we're hoping to ask him soon. We'll be there shortly."

"Well, I suspect he had some unfinished business in Hamilton. Some unfinished *family* business. Presuming Allen and Cathy are his parents, and their files are sealed everywhere, then Alex *had* to go on his own. Sarah suspected that Benjamin's passing was the catalyst. My guess is you are correct. Guys, be ready to be shocked when you get to the bottom of this. Something dark is lurking in Alex's past. Dark enough to warrant wiping his parents off the government computer system. Even the Freedom of Information Act won't work here. I have nothing more. My hands are tied. Only Alex can help further."

"Aaron is pulling off the highway now. We'll be at the police station in ten minutes or so."

"Keep me updated."

"You got it. Thanks for giving us this much." They said their goodbyes, and Sarah ended the call.

"Holy shit," she whispered, setting the phone on her lap.

"I second that," Parkman said.

"Something dark lurking in Alex's past," Aaron echoed Darwin's words. "No wonder that boy is who he is. Whatever happened all those years ago that got his family's files sealed was traumatic enough to create a monster."

"A monster with a heart," Sarah added. "He cares way too much sometimes."

Sarah dropped her phone to the passenger seat footwell when her hands numbed. She shot a glance at Aaron.

"Sarah? You okay?"

"Vivian—"

Her sister cut her off with a short piece of information, and then she was gone.

"We're not going to the police station." Sarah spoke with a monotone voice.

Aaron frowned.

Parkman leaned forward in the back seat. "Where are we going?"

Sarah told them where they were going and about the Kevlar vest, which made zero sense to her.

# Chapter 13

INSPECTOR BLAIR NELSON BARELY caught two hours' sleep at the station after a grueling night of questioning the mute suspect, Alex Russell. Nothing broke that boy. Withholding bathroom breaks, giving him tons of coffee and soda, then withholding all drinks and food—it was like he was willing to torture himself. One word, one sound would have gotten him a bathroom break. A few sentences would have earned him a sandwich. But nothing issued forth from him.

Captain Simmons put an end to it when he got called in this morning on another matter.

Blair drove calmly, conscious of his lack of sleep. When he got home, he would have to deal with a distraught wife. Console her that everything would work out, and then try to get some sleep.

His cell rang through the car speakers. He tapped the button on the steering wheel.

"Inspector Nelson."

"Nelson, it's Morgan."

"What's up?"

"We need you in Montgomery Park."

He frowned. "Why do you need me?"

"We got a body."

"I don't work Homicide."

"Dude, one second." Morgan sounded like he was walking somewhere. "It's one of our CIs. A small-time dealer. Homicide is going to have questions."

Blair smacked the steering wheel. "Why? How does everyone know who our CIs are?"

"There was a note."

"Suicide note?"

"Another kind of note."

"Morgan, stop being so cryptic."

"Look, Blair, just come down here, okay? There's the weapon thing, too."

"See, you're being cryptic again. What weapon thing?"

There was some sort of interference on the line. Morgan had placed a hand over the mouthpiece. Blair heard him talking to someone else.

Then he was back.

"Okay, I just confirmed it. They want to talk to you. They found a police-issued sidearm beside the body and a note saying, *This is for Inspector Nelson.*"

His stomach dropped as a cold sweat broke out on his forehead and lower back. "What the hell, man? Who would write such a thing?"

"Nelson." Morgan's voice lowered. "It was the CI from the warehouse last night."

"*What?*" Blair sucked air in past his clenched teeth. "Didn't you guys take him home?"

"No, he wanted to come to the park. Score something, and get high. Pruitt and I left him by the basketball courts. He was fine at eleven last night. They're saying someone shot him in his sleep sometime after midnight."

"This is bad, man. Did anyone see you guys dropping him off?"

"The right answer is no, but how can I tell who might have been hiding in the bushes? There may be witnesses connecting us to him last night."

"Oh, no …" An idea hit Blair, one he didn't want to contemplate.

"How far out are you?" Morgan asked.

"Five minutes."

"I'll wait here. Just hurry."

He tapped the button on the steering wheel to end the call.

Could Alex have done this before they apprehended him? Is that why he wasn't talking last night? Did he watch their house to break in and steal one of Blair's police guns, only to use it in the park and dedicate the kill to him? Of course, Alex didn't want to say anything to incriminate himself. Or was he waiting to spill the beans once Blair left the police station because it had to do with him?

"That prick will get his." Blair slammed his hand on the steering wheel again as he ran a yellow light on Main Street.

His phone rang. He tapped the answer button without looking to see who it was.

"*What?*" he shouted over the sound of his revving engine.

"Honey, it's me."

"Oh, sorry. What's up, Susan? I got work stuff."

"There's someone in the house—"

"*What!*" His head spun at the possibilities. No way. Alex was downtown, locked away. Sarah was in Toronto—apparently—when he called her. Susan continued before he could tell her to get out of the house.

"They're different than the people who answered last night."

He grimaced as his tired mind raced to catch up with her. "Oh, you mean on Weir Street? The house you dropped Tracy at last night?"

"Yeah, and they were rude to me, too. When I said I wanted my daughter back, they called the police on me." Susan sobbed into the phone.

"Where are you now?"

"I'm back home."

"Okay, stay there. I'll join you soon. I just have something I have to attend to."

"Are you talking about the body in the park?"

Stupefied. That was the word he would use at that moment. Stumped, he wondered how everyone knew about the body in the park but him. "Did someone call you looking for me?"

"No."

"Then how do you know about the body?"

"After I left that Weir house, I saw all the cruisers entering the park, so I wandered over. They were putting up yellow police tape around a body that was covered in a black tarp."

"Oh, honey, you shouldn't've seen that."

"That's what they told me. The overweight cop at the *crime scene* told me I had to leave. My daughter is missing, and when I see police cars entering the park, of course, I want to see why. The tarp was too big to cover Tracy's body, though."

"Oh, honey, don't even think like that. Tracy will come home. Today, if I have anything to do with it." He hit the brakes at a red light, waited until it was clear, smashed the pedal down, and raced through on the red. "Hey, that's where I'm heading right now. I'll find out what's going on and come home to explain everything very soon."

He was feeling more nauseous by the second. How could life fall apart so fast? And what could Alex have done? The better question was, *Why did he do it?*

"Blair, honey, don't forget that house that has Tracy. Someone's home now. They know something. I can feel it."

"Right. I'm on it. I'll go there next. See you within the hour."

"Okay. I love you." She was crying again.

"I love you, too. We'll find Tracy. Just stay home. Do not go back outside. It's too dangerous right now. At least until I get a grip on things."

"I'll wait here for you."

"Good. Stay by the phone in case the Bakers call about Tracy, too."

"They won't be calling."

He was coming up to Weir Street now. He'd be at the park in seconds and needed off the phone.

"What makes you say that?"

"Because those people at the house know where she is. Mother's intuition."

"Okay, I'll talk to them." He turned onto Weir. "Gotta go, honey."

"Oh, one more thing."

"What?" Blair tried to keep his frustration out of that word but failed.

"That stalker guy."

"What about him?"

"Did he talk last night? Tell you anything important, like why he was after me?"

"Nothing. The guy didn't say two words to me. I pressured him, too. Got me nowhere. Now, honey, I really have to go."

He killed the call without waiting for her response.

Five seconds later, he turned into the Montgomery Park access and saw Morgan.

The man started toward him, his thick shoulders swaying as he walked.

Blair jumped from the car and jogged over.

"Where were you last night?" Morgan asked.

Blair stopped walking to look at him. "Why? Is that you asking, or what Homicide's asking?" He clenched his fists at his sides. "Are they seriously going to try to put this on me? The big problem with that is, why leave a note dedicating the kill to me if I had anything to do with it?" He shook his head. "Assholes."

"No, no." Morgan waved him off the ledge. "This murder points at you, though. Your name is on the note. The gun's serial number has been removed with some factory precision shit. But it's a Glock, the police-issue kind. There are going to be some tough questions in the days to come. Knowing you were nowhere near this will help you immensely."

"I was at the station all night. Interview room four, with Alex, the suspect, who I think had something to do with this, but he's not talking. I made a phone call from the station sometime after four in the morning, then fell asleep on the couch in my office. Janitors woke me. There are cameras all over the place." He leaned close to Morgan. "No one can pin this on me. I'm solid."

"Hey," Morgan said, his hands raised. "I'm not the enemy here, man. I'm just here to walk you through—"

"Inspector Nelson," a man said, cutting Morgan off. "A word, please."

The well-dressed man stood several feet away, hands clasped in front of his crotch.

*What a smug asshole.* Blair offered him a slight grin. "I heard there's been a murder. One of my CIs got hit." He moved closer to the man. "I was hoping you'd fill me in on what you got."

"Gladly." The man grinned back. "If you'll just follow me this way."

Blair moved forward on autopilot, his eyes heavy. He wondered how long this would take.

His wife was waiting for him. His stepdaughter was still missing.

What the hell had happened to their life?

And while contemplating that question, one word kept moving through his mind.

*Alex ... Alex ... Alex ...*

# Chapter 14

SARAH STARED AT THE map on her phone, offering directions to Aaron. Both men were still upset that they weren't going to fetch Alex first.

Vivian said this was their only chance to get to this specific person. If they wanted to talk to her, it had to be today.

"Reminder," Sarah said. "Vivian gave me the impression that we get to Alex *through* this woman."

Aaron turned to her. "But he's in lockup, right?"

Sarah nodded. "According to the cop who called me last night. But until they release him, showing up at the police station probably won't do us any good."

"So, who is this woman again?" Parkman asked.

"I'm not entirely sure." Sarah pointed at the next street. "Take a right here." She glanced back at Parkman. "I just know that this woman is important. We're supposed to go to 38 Maple Avenue." She turned back in her seat to stare at the map.

"And this'll lead us to Alex?" Aaron asked, the doubt obvious in his tone.

Sarah nodded, deflecting any attitude he might have. "Alex isn't going anywhere. This woman is." She wouldn't let Aaron get to her. He was here. That was what was important.

"We're on Maple now." Sarah looked down at her map, glanced back up, and pointed. "That house there."

Aaron slowed the car.

"Stop here. We can't spook her."

Aaron hit the brakes. "Spook her? What are you talking about?"

She turned around in her seat. "Parkman, do you still carry your private investigator license on you?"

He nodded.

"She will know Aaron and me on sight. Your face isn't as readily recognizable to her. Go to the door and tell her you'll help with her case. You've been hired by someone who wants to remain confidential."

He frowned, the toothpick he'd placed in his mouth drooping at an angle. "What case?"

"Yeah," Aaron chimed in. "And how would this woman recognize us?"

"Guys, I don't know. Vivian told me it had to be Parkman. It was the only way inside."

"So she needs help with a case," Parkman said, "and we don't know anything about the case?"

Sarah stared at them a moment longer, then nodded slowly.

"Is she a detective? Like, working on a case?"

"I have no idea. Just make shit up. Just get inside. When we knock a minute later, you let us in."

"Then what?" Aaron asked.

"We take her."

"*What?*" Aaron jerked back. "Take her? Where?"

"For a ride. I have no idea. But she can't stay in that house. And I have to find a Kevlar vest."

"What's the vest for?"

"A drug dealer."

Aaron gave a short jerk of his head. "Why the hell would you give a vest to a dealer? Are we saving a coke peddler's life now?"

Sarah rubbed the back of her neck. "Look, all I know is giving this dealer a vest breaks some cases wide open." She raised a finger. "Don't ask what *cases* because I have no idea."

"Okay, who's the dealer? Where is he?"

"Wouldn't that be great if my sister were more forthcoming?"

"We've worked on limited information before." Parkman tapped Sarah's shoulder. "If getting into this house will get Alex back, and that's what Vivian told you, then let's get a move on."

He opened the side door, hopped out, and closed it gently.

"Another kidnapping," Aaron mumbled to himself. "Working with drug dealers." He shook his head.

"Honey, don't look at it like that." Sarah watched Parkman approach the front door of the woman's house. "These people are mixed up in the trouble Alex is in, and Vivian said doing this will *un*mix it. Once we secure her, we can talk, meet Alex, and go from there to locate this dealer guy."

He stared at her, but she didn't turn to him.

Parkman had knocked on the door. He stepped back, his ID wallet in his hand.

The door opened, and the side profile of a woman came into view.

Sarah lowered in her seat, and Aaron followed suit.

Parkman said a few things, showed his ID, nodded once, stepped inside the house, and closed the door.

"You said, 'Meet Alex.'" Aaron's voice was monotone. "Meaning, Vivian told you he would be released?"

Sarah shrugged. "I can't tell the future. I can only tell you what Vivian says." She opened her door to get out, but stopped. "And that's what she said—meet Alex. Now, come on. Let's go introduce ourselves to this mystery woman."

She exited the car and reached the sidewalk before Aaron got out.

Half a minute later, they knocked, the door opened, Parkman let them inside the woman's house, closed the door, and the woman screamed, her hands over her mouth.

"*You!*" the woman shouted. "What have you done?"

# Chapter 15

INSPECTOR BLAIR NELSON COULD not believe what he was hearing.

"Can you repeat that?"

"Sir, it appears you're taking this personally. I might ask why that is."

Nelson glared at the Homicide detective, exhaled slowly, and then unclenched his hands at his side.

"This man, this vagrant, was a solid informant. We spent two years working with him on Vice. One of the biggest cases that he had key information on was the murder of the dealer in this park last year." He gulped in air as his heart raced. "I'll remind you that two officers are on trial for their lives this week. I've been in court all week in support of my men."

"I'm aware of the trial."

The smirk, that smug look, was back. Anywhere else, Blair would squash the man's lip against his teeth with his knuckles. But here, near a dead body that the detective was investigating, he forced himself to remain in control.

"So, to answer your questions, yes, I knew the man. Yes, my team worked with him. No, I wasn't here last night, and no, that wasn't my gun." Even if it were, he wouldn't admit that here.

"Yet, we have a witness who places Morgan and another inspector" —the man glanced at his notepad, then looked back up—"Pruitt in the park with this man within hours of him being killed."

Blair nodded once. "We had a chat with him last night. When I say *we*, I mean Vice."

"About what?"

"None of your business."

The man quirked an eyebrow high, his eyes widening. "And if it relates to his murder?"

"I guess we'll never know. My investigation has nothing to do with yours."

The Homicide man—Blair forgot his name and didn't care—smiled and turned sideways to ease closer. "Inspector Nelson. We're all on the same side here. I'm going to need you to work with me. Morgan has already told me he was with the deceased last night. You're not willing to talk about your case"—he raised his hands—"and I get that, I truly do, but it likely ties into this." He pointed at the body the coroner was now carrying to a white van. "Whoever he was ratting out or spilling the beans on wanted him shut down—permanently."

Blair would never tell this man about Alex, how his stepdaughter was missing, or his suspicions that it was Sarah's people. No way. This was his case, and he would see it to the end.

"Are we finished here?" Blair stepped back, intimating that he was leaving.

The Homicide guy removed a card from his wallet and extended his hand. "Take this and call me to set up an appointment. Once we gather more details, we'll want to speak with you again."

"I've told you everything I know."

"Sure you have, and I believe you, but take it anyway. We *will* be talking again. Your name is on the note. You're involved, Inspector Nelson, whether you like it or not." He extended his arm farther.

Blair slipped the card into his back pocket, then spun on his heels and started back to his car with a hundred questions clouding his weary thoughts.

Why kill their CI? What did he know that had to be silenced? Was it related to the trial or something else?

He slammed the door in his unmarked cruiser, reversed out of the park, and then gunned the engine toward Weir Street.

It was time to deal with the people at the house where Tracy was dropped off.

Something had to go right for him today, or he'd start shooting people.

# Chapter 16

"WHAT—" THE WOMAN GASPED, "are you doing here?"

"We were hoping you'd tell us that," Sarah said. "How are you connected to Alex Russell?"

"That's what this is about? The man my husband arrested?"

Sarah glanced at Parkman, then Aaron. "Your husband?"

The woman took them all in, then stepped to the side to enter the living room, where she sat on the sofa.

"My husband is an inspector with Hamilton police. He arrested Alex last night after I caught him watching the house. Then he chased me—"

"Your husband chased you?" Aaron asked.

Sarah frowned at him as the woman continued.

"No, Alex chased me a few blocks over when I was in my car. Scared me something awful when he almost caught me. They found him hiding in a bush."

"Hiding in a bush?" Sarah repeated, watching the woman's face for signs she was lying. "That doesn't sound like our Alex at all. I'm sorry, I believe you, but it's just so strange."

"Well, he won't get out of holding for some time, likely until his court date. They'll remand him into custody after what he did."

Sarah wasn't sure they had the whole story. "He scared you in your car. How is that a flight risk?"

"It's what he did when they arrested him."

They stood in a semi-circle, staring down at the woman on the couch.

"What did Alex do when they arrested him?" Parkman asked.

"He hurt one of the cops. The list of charges is long, but assaulting an officer and resisting arrest are serious ones. Judges don't look too kindly on suspects when they attack cops who were just trying to do their jobs."

Sarah caught Parkman and Aaron staring at her from each side, but she kept her eyes on the woman.

"What's your name?"

The woman crossed her arms defiantly. "What's it to you? And how dare you barge in here under the pretenses of wanting to help me find my daughter?" She lunged for the cordless phone on the side table, but Sarah beat her to it, knocking it off the table where it hit the wall and fell to the floor, the battery pack snapping off.

"How dare you?" The woman scoffed, a scowl tightening her face.

"Don't tell us your name, then." Sarah towered over her. "Don't help us at all. But what my friend over there said about finding your daughter was true. We will help. But first, you have to help us."

"Oh, yeah, and how's that?"

Sarah understood that attitude for someone in her predicament—she wouldn't fault her for it. Her daughter was missing, which meant she likely had a rough night. What she couldn't understand was Alex's connection to all this.

"We need you to come with us."

"I'm not going anywhere with you," she shouted, pushing off the couch to get to her feet.

Sarah shoved the woman's shoulder, forcing her to drop back onto the couch.

"Who do you think you are?" she screamed. "Get *out*! Get out of my house!"

Sarah leaned down to eye level. "Listen, lady, you can scream all you want, but our friend is in trouble, and I have it on good authority that you are in a position to help us, so you're coming with us whether you like it or not." She stood back up to her full height. "We mean you no harm. Once Alex is returned to us, we will help you find your daughter."

Aaron and Parkman edged closer until the three of them stood over the woman.

A tear slipped from her eye, and she wiped it with a trembling hand.

"You're supposed to be psychic, right?" She stared up at Sarah, her gaze unwavering.

Sarah nodded. "I hear things sometimes."

"And it helps you save people or catch bad guys where the police fail."

Sarah kept nodding.

"I've read about you in the papers over the years."

*That was why Parkman came to your door and not me*, Sarah thought.

"I can't help you with your friend. That's out of my control. The police have him."

"We'll see about that." Sarah fought the urge to check the time. They needed to get out of this house before her husband came home.

"You have a little girl, right, Sarah?"

Her eyes narrowed. Anytime someone asked about Willow, her mommy hackles rose. "How is that relevant?"

"My twelve-year-old daughter is missing. If I have your word you'll help me, I'll go with you willingly to wherever you want to take me." She edged forward on the sofa until she sat on the edge of the cushion. Aaron and Parkman stepped back, and the woman got to her feet. She stared into Sarah's eyes. "You wouldn't leave a twelve-year-old to suffer out there all alone, would you? You care too much for strangers to let that happen."

Vivian hadn't said anything about this woman's daughter. Sarah wouldn't make any promises she couldn't keep, but if it were in her power to help, of course, she would.

The woman extended her hand in a formal gesture. "My name is Susan Nelson."

They shook hands as each said their name in turn.

Sarah held the woman's hand for a beat longer. "I promise you we'll do our best to help you."

Susan nodded. "That's good enough for me. Shall we go?" Susan pointed toward the door. "Just let me get my purse." She headed toward the kitchen.

Sarah nodded at Parkman, who jumped into action, walking behind the woman in case she ran for the back door.

"You sure about this?" Aaron asked.

"As sure as the earth is flat."

He frowned. "But it's not flat."

"Exactly."

# Chapter 17

INSPECTOR BLAIR NELSON SQUEALED to a halt in front of 44 Weir Street, jumped from his car, and ran up the walkway to the front door.

His shadow preceded him as the sun was at his back. It reflected off the bay window, shining in his eyes and making it impossible for him to see if anyone watched his approach.

He banged on the door hard enough to leave a mark on the wood. "Open up," he shouted. "Hamilton police. I know you're in there." He stepped back, eyed the door, waited another second, then banged on it again. "Hamilton police."

The lock clicked, then the door opened a few inches, stopping at the extent of the chain attached to the inside.

"We need to see ID," the man said.

Fidgeting on their small porch, Blair nodded wildly, like a man urgently needing to pee.

"Sure thing." He snatched his ID wallet from the inside breast pocket of his jacket, flipped it open, and showed it briefly to the man.

The door closed, followed by the sound of the chain dislodging. The door opened again, but wider this time.

"Can we help you, Officer?" The man stood in front of the door, his hand still holding it like he might slam it shut at any moment.

A woman moved in behind the man. Now, they were both staring at him as he shifted his weight from one foot to the other.

What was it that Susan had told him on the phone? *When I said I wanted my daughter back, they called the police on me.*

Blair glanced over his shoulder at the road, then back to the couple.

"How many officers responded when you called them?"

The man frowned. "I'm sorry?"

The woman remained expressionless.

"My wife was just here, say, about a half hour ago. She was looking for her daughter. Her words were, 'They called the police on me.' So, as I'm Inspector Nelson with Hamilton Police Service, I'd like to know how many officers responded to your call."

The couple exchanged a glance. When the man looked back at Blair, his expression had softened.

"We only said that to get the woman off our property. We didn't *actually* call anyone. It was a fake call."

Blair was nodding again like he was in on the joke. "Hilarious. And how did my wife take that?"

"Look, Inspector. She came banging on our door. We tried to be polite, but she accused us of having something to do with her daughter's disappearance. Then, she broke into our backyard and tried to gain access to our house. We have a right to call the authorities, but because we saw she was hurting badly, we didn't call them for real. We just wanted her off our property."

Blair pushed up onto the balls of his feet and peeked over the man's shoulder, saw nothing irregular in the living room, then dropped back and fixed his gaze on the man.

"Look, the game is up. Whatever it is you're doing, we don't want any part of it. Just return Tracy to us, and you can go on playing your games. I've got other fish to fry today—bigger fish."

"He's the same," the man said to the woman, shaking his head slightly.

"The same?" Blair asked. "What does that mean?"

"Showing up here and banging on our door, hoping we'll magically hand you back this mysterious missing daughter. Newsflash: *we don't have your daughter*. We're the only people in this house and have been since we bought it in June. Now, leave us alone."

The man went to slam the door, but Blair jammed his foot in the way. When the door hit his foot, he suppressed the scream of pain and held on. If he'd been tired before, he was wide awake now. The pain woke him up.

"Hey," the man shouted.

Before the man could take another swing at closing the door, Blair lunged forward like a hockey player going in for a low body check, his shoulder leading the way.

Ripped from the man's hand, the door shot inward and smacked the interior wall.

"*Hey!*" the man shouted again as Blair shoved past him.

"Where is she? Huh?" He spun around, took in the room, and ran for the stairs.

"You can't go up there," the woman shouted. "I'm calling the *real* police now."

Blair wasn't listening to their antics anymore. He mounted the stairs two at a time. In the second-floor hallway, he entered the master bedroom first. The closet was full of clothes, but no Tracy. The next bedroom was for a teenager. A poster of Taylor Swift and one of Star Wars characters took up the space between shelves that held the small boxes of Funko Pop figures. The single bed had a small pile of clothes on it. He checked the closet—nothing.

Back in the hall, he ran into a smaller room that appeared to be for a guest, then checked the upstairs bathroom.

Where else could they be keeping Tracy?

*The basement!*

He ran down the stairs, jumped onto the landing, and headed for the basement door.

"Hold on there, Inspector Nelson." A new man in a suit stepped from the kitchen ahead of him, his hand raised. Then he spun his hand around to reveal an ID—an RCMP badge.

"What's this?" Blair yelled, twisting to look behind him.

Five men surrounded him now, two with hands on their weapons.

"We're going to need you to calm down. You're trained to de-escalate the situation."

"Calm down, eh?" He brushed loose hair from his face that had draped in front of his eyes. "How about you give me Tracy, then we'll talk about de-escalating?"

"Read the room, Inspector."

"Read the *what*?" The last word came out with spittle.

"If you do not calm down and leave this house, you will be arrested for obstruction. You are impeding an active investigation."

He laughed in a short burst. "That's a joke. What investigation?" His head was on a swivel, glaring at the row of armed men behind him, then addressing the man who was speaking in front of him.

"Just tell me where Tracy is, and I'll walk away. No harm, no foul."

The men exchanged a glance.

"What?" Blair asked. "What are you not telling me?"

"We don't know where Tracy is, nor do we know where the family who were living here yesterday is."

The name *Alex* filtered through his mind again. "What the hell does that mean?"

"It means they disappeared before we got here."

Puzzle pieces tried to fit together in his brain, but something was still wrong. "So the Bakers weren't really the Bakers? Is that what you're telling me?"

"We can't speak further on an *active* investigation."

"Bullshit." His breathing was calming, but his heart still pounded hard. "Then tell me if the people who were living here were the Wagners. Were they here for court this week? Is that who it was? And when they saw your boys sitting in that car out front yesterday, they panicked and ran for it?"

"We will not be discussing this further, Inspector. Leave this house and don't come back. As it is, you've already jeopardized our investigation. Go home to your wife. Do this, and keep your job. *Don't* do this, and we'll arrest you. How will Captain Simmons respond when you're brought up on federal charges?"

They knew his boss? Had they investigated him after Susan tried to get Tracy?

He scanned the faces of the men and one woman in the room.

"Fuck." He punched the wall beside him as he made for the front door.

The men parted to let him pass.

Outside, the door closed behind him. Before he made it to the car, his phone rang. He retrieved it from his pocket, clicked the answer button, and jumped in the driver's seat, confusion and rage his competing emotions.

"Nelson."

"Hey, Nelson, it's Pruitt."

He had his hand on the car keys, ready to turn the vehicle on, but hesitated.

"What's up?"

"Did you hear about that guy you brought in last night?"

"No, what guy?" He shook his head. "Wait, you mean Alex Russell?"

"That's the one."

"What about him?"

"Captain Simmons let him go."

Blair stared out his windshield at nothing. He could not have heard Pruitt correctly. There was no way Alex was free to walk the streets after stalking his wife—a *cop's* wife, assaulting that cop, and resisting arrest.

"Can you repeat that? I don't think I heard you."

"Simmons released that Russell kid. And get this—the captain apologized to him first."

"Are you *fucking* serious?"

"As serious as cancer."

Blair released the car keys and sat back, staring at the roof of the car. "What the hell is going on? I think I need sleep, man, because nothing is making sense today."

"And you know about that CI from last night—" Pruitt kept talking, but Blair was only half listening.

"Pruitt, did Simmons say why he released the guy?"

"Dude, were you even listening?"

"Yes, I was listening."

"I was telling you about the CI from last—"

"I know," Blair cut in. "He's dead. What did Captain Simmons say about Alex Russell?"

"Holy shit, dude. Don't bite my head off. I was calling to warn you."

His eyes widened, and he glanced over at the house filled with those RCMP dicks. "Warn me? What the hell are you *warning* me about?"

"Simmons wants to talk to you. He seems pissed."

"About what?"

"Procedural shit with the Russell arrest."

Blair scrunched up his face. "*Procedural* shit? I must be on Planet Oz because I have no idea what you're talking about. The fucking stalker dickhead was arrested in the act of hiding in bushes between two houses while watching Susan. He fought back, spraining or breaking Officer Darrow's wrist, and was taken into custody. As clean and tight as it comes."

"Not according to the captain. As soon as you left this morning, a few boys went in to talk to Russell, and that boy whistled."

The RCMP dickheads had opened the front door, and now three of them were watching from the front porch, their arms crossed. Parked out front might still be construed as obstruction.

Blair turned on the car, put it in gear, and hit the gas.

"Wait, are you saying Alex Russell talked to other officers?" *I couldn't get him to even look at me, let alone talk.*

"He told them everything, whatever that means. They took it to the captain, then Simmons sat with the kid. After that, word is the captain apologized to Russell and let the guy go without charges."

"Well, I'll be a motherfucker." He took a right turn, shaking his head.

"With that CI murder and Homicide wanting a statement from all of us now, and Simmons wanting to talk to you about that Russell arrest, I'd say don't come to the station for a few hours. Let things simmer down."

"No one has called me—" His phone chimed. He had an incoming call. "Hold on." He pulled it away and saw Captain Simmons calling. "Shit, it's Simmons."

"Yeah, let it go to voicemail. Tell him you were sleeping. Ten minutes ago, I heard him shouting your name as he went through your desk."

"He went through my *desk*? What the hell for?" He couldn't remember when he'd eaten last. His stomach had filled with the acidity of nerves, making him feel queasy. How could someone's life turn so upside down in less than a day?

"I got no clue what he was looking for in your desk. Just be cool. You'll get through this."

The phone chimed in his ear again. He glanced at the number but didn't recognize it.

"Another call?" Pruitt asked.

"Yeah."

"Probably Homicide. They have more questions. They're convinced you're connected to the CI's murder. Not that you did it—your alibi is solid—but that note, man. Raises questions."

"Questions? What am I supposed to tell them?" He could give them Alex Russell's name. That kid was somehow connected to all this.

"Word around the department is—they have an *eye*witness."

"To last night's murder?"

"Yeah."

"Great. I was with Alex Russell all night. This has nothing to do with me. Homicide should go arrest the guy who murdered the CI and leave me alone."

"Okay, then talk to them. Put this to rest. You got nothing to fear."

"I will. But first, I need sleep." He turned onto Maple Avenue. "I'll be home in less than a minute. My wife's upset. I have to go."

"Okay, just don't say I didn't warn you. Stay away from Captain Simmons for a spell."

"Will do." He ended the call and slipped the phone into his jacket pocket.

He parked in the driveway behind Susan's car, got out, and went in the front door—which was unlocked.

*That's strange ...*

"Susan?" he called, stepping inside. When he got no response, he called again, but much louder. "*Susan!*"

He frowned. Is this more *Twilight Zone* stuff happening? He just got off the phone with her about half an hour ago. He specifically told her to stay home, and she agreed not to move. Her car was out front.

He scratched his head and yawned. She had to be home.

Maybe she was in the bathtub or her home office with headphones on. Even the front door was unlocked, so she had to be in the house.

"Honey?" he called several times, walking throughout the first floor.

The bathrooms were empty. Her office was empty. He peeked into the backyard, but she wasn't there, either.

After checking the second floor, he concluded that Susan Nelson had disappeared, just like her daughter.

"I'm losing my mind." He grabbed a handful of hair on either side of his head. "I'm absolutely losing my fucking mind."

His phone rang in his pocket. He yanked it out and checked the screen.

It said unknown number.

Would the captain block his number? If it were Homicide, he had nothing to fear. Those boys had zilch on him.

So he answered it. "Hello?"

"Let's barter, Inspector." A woman's deep voice. Unrecognizable.

"Who's this?"

"Who I am isn't important. What I want is what's important."

"Listen here," he said, pushing the phone against his lips as he ran for the front door. "I ain't got time for games, bitch."

"Would you like to see Susan again? How about that, *Inspector*? Is your wife a game?"

He stopped in his tracks and stared at the back of the front door.

"What did you just say?"

"Barter, Inspector. I'd like to bring Susan home. But there's something I want in return. How about a trade?"

"What kind of trade? You want money?"

"No, I don't want money. I said *trade*. But that's fine. You're not listening or interested. Good day."

"Wait, *wait*!"

There was a moment's pause, and Blair wondered if the caller had hung up.

"What sort of trade?" he asked.

"Release Alex Russell, and we'll bring Susan home. It's as simple as eating key lime pie. I'll be in touch with a location."

"Wait, is this Sarah Roberts?" he asked, but he was talking to a dead line.

"Key lime pie? What the hell is that?"

He didn't have Alex. The captain released him. For all he knew, Alex Russell could be halfway to America by now.

His head spun. What was he going to do with everything so fucked up and nothing making sense?

Blair Nelson grabbed his hair again, pulled hard, and screamed inside his empty house.

# Chapter 18

Aaron drove, with Parkman turned in the passenger seat to face Sarah and Susan Nelson in the back.

Sarah had just gotten back in the car after calling Blair. Earlier, when she'd asked about Susan's husband, she gave Inspector Blair Nelson's business card with his contact information and told her he'd been responsible for Alex's arrest.

The call Sarah received after four that morning was likely from Susan's husband. It was all coming together—slowly, but it was coming together.

They were now driving along Main Street, heading toward Highway 403, which would take them toward Burlington. Most importantly, they wanted to leave Hamilton, where the risk of someone recognizing Susan was higher.

Sarah turned to her. "Why would Alex come after you? He would've had to know you in some way unless you called him for help. Did you call him?"

Susan stared out the window. "I don't know how much I want to tell you." She narrowed her eyes as if dealing with some difficult thoughts, then turned to Sarah. "It would be better if Alex were present. There are things I know that should come from him."

"I'm so confused." Sarah looked at Parkman, who raised an eyebrow and then popped a new toothpick in his mouth. After a moment, he spun around to face forward.

"I am, too." Susan let her attention be drawn to the window again. "I have no idea why Alex did what he did."

"What do you mean?"

"Why did he come here?" Susan said it so low that Sarah almost didn't catch her words.

They drove in silence until they reached the highway.

"Anyone hungry?" Sarah asked.

Parkman and Aaron shook their heads. Susan didn't respond.

"Coffee then?"

More head shaking.

"Aaron?"

"Yeah?" He glanced at her in the rearview mirror.

"Take us somewhere to talk."

"Sure. How about a motel room? It'll be private. It'll have a bathroom, and we can order food in later. I'd imagine we'll be staying a few days until we figure out what Alex has been up to."

"That works."

Aaron had successfully gotten them out of Hamilton and into the Burlington area. He pulled off the 403 at Guelph Line to access the south service road after seeing a Best Western Hotel, but ended up pulling into a Comfort Inn.

"I'll grab two rooms," Parkman said, hopping out. "Wait here for me."

"I'm so curious as to how you and Alex are connected." Sarah studied the woman sitting beside her. "Not just that. I want to ask him why he was stalking you."

Susan adjusted herself in her seat until she was facing Sarah. "I suspect I know why, and it has to do with Benjamin, his brother."

Another surprise reveal. Even Aaron turned in his seat. They both gawked at the stranger in their car.

"You knew Benjamin?" Sarah asked. "And that they were brothers?"

Susan glanced down at her hands as she fidgeted with a nail on her index finger. When she looked up, her eyes had glazed over.

"I loved Benjamin." She hiccupped a sob from deep within. "Broke my heart to hear he died." Her head moved back and forth before she looked down at her nail again. "Just another person who knew Alex.

Another person who was now dead." When Susan raised her head, her face seemed more determined and braver. "Alex killed my parents many years ago, and I wonder if he came looking for me to finish the job."

# Chapter 19

BLAIR'S PHONE RANG IN his hand. He had just pulled it out to call Morgan, and now Morgan's name popped up on his screen.

"Speak of the Devil," he said to himself, then hit the answer button. "I was just going to call you." Blair walked over to sit on his sofa and stare out at the street. His life was unraveling faster than he could rein it in.

"You weren't sleeping?" Morgan asked. "After the night you had?"

"No. Something came up, and now I need your help."

"Well, let me fill you in on why I'm calling first. It's twofold."

"Shoot."

"One, the trial was adjourned until Monday. The prosecution's star witness is missing."

"Not surprised to hear that." The Baker/Wagner house was vacated quickly. So fast they took Tracy with them. The RCMP is now staking out the place. It's the site of an active investigation. Where had Alex and his friends stashed them? Once he found the Bakers/Wagners, he'd find his stepdaughter. He was sure of that.

"Two," Morgan continued. "Homicide just finished with me."

"With you? What did they want?"

"Every single detail about last night."

"Fill me in. What did you tell them?"

"That we picked up the CI, drove him to a warehouse where none of his buddies would see him talking to us, and returned him to the park by the basketball courts around midnight. That was it. He was alive when we left him."

"Why are they so fucked up about this dealer getting popped? Geez, lay off my crew. Like a cop would kill him."

"Word on the street is that this particular CI was talking to Homicide. They were building a case."

"What case?"

"There have been several dealers murdered around the city. They now think they're connected."

"You mean one killer?"

"Yup. A serial."

"So, how's that our problem? We're Vice. Nothing to do with us."

There was a pause on the line. It lasted so long that Blair wondered if they got cut off.

"Morgan? You still there?"

"Yeah." He cleared his throat. "You asked how it's our problem."

"Is it something we should be worried about?" Blair ran a hand through his hair, waiting for another revelation to further upset his sense of balance in the world.

"It's our problem because the CI claimed to see the shooter on the night that the other dealer was executed in Montgomery Park—the one currently in the court system. This would mean our boys sitting in the prisoner box in court all week didn't do it."

Blair didn't expect Morgan to say that. "But now the CI is dead." He clucked his tongue. "Hey, finally, some good news. I went to school with those boys. They couldn't pull the trigger unless it were a righteous kill. I knew it." He slapped his leg. Maybe things were turning around for the better.

"Well, that's another reason the case was adjourned. Both sides are reexamining the evidence and will reconvene on Monday to decide their next step. And now, yes, the CI is dead. No one is saying shit about whether or not they have enough to let our boys hunt down the actual murderer."

"Do they have a person of interest?"

Another pause. "They do, and he works in the department. But they're keeping the man's name close to their chest at the moment in case he bolts."

"Oh, shit. Your voice just deepened. I'm not going to like this, am I?"

"I don't think so."

"Who is it?"

"An inspector on Vice. Right here, in our department. They may call us all in on Monday."

That was completely unexpected. "But there are only six of us. How's that possible? We're all solid."

"Dude, they're investigating Pruitt, me, and you, among others, but suspicion is mounting on you, dickhead."

"*Me!* Why?"

"Because they think you're avoiding them."

"I *am* avoiding them. I'm tired, and I was nowhere near the park all night."

"They checked. They know that."

"Then tell them to talk to someone else. I'm busy. And my stepdaughter is missing."

"They want to talk to you because they suspect you know the shooter."

"And how would I know that? Besides, if I did know the shooter, wouldn't I arrest them myself?"

"They came to this conclusion because of that note. The shooter clearly knows you."

"And if the CI told them their suspect from last year's murder is one of my crew, then, of course, the shooter would know me. Doesn't automatically mean I know *who* the shooter is, though." He shook his head at the insanity of it all. "What assholes. How does an inspector in Homicide get promoted if they don't know how to inspect?"

If what Morgan was saying was true, and one of his inspectors was guilty of murdering drug dealers in the park several blocks from his house, then how were Alex and his friends from Toronto involved? Why was Alex watching his wife? Could all that be completely unrelated?

And where the fuck was his stepdaughter? Something else was going on. He could feel it.

"You said you wanted my help with something," Morgan said.

"Yeah, I have a problem." Blair went on to tell him about Tracy, the RCMP officers in the house on Weir Street, and how he told Susan to wait in the house for him. He finished with the phone call from a woman with a deep voice.

"You're not serious," Morgan said when Blair was finished. "She said, *trade*? Who kidnaps a cop's wife to get someone out of holding?"

"The captain released Alex Russell, so I don't even have Alex to barter with."

"Is that why you need my help?"

"I want to arrange a trade. We have to figure this out somehow. Find a way to outsmart them. I need to get Susan back safely and make some arrests."

"Count me in. You want Pruitt, too?"

"Sure. More is better in this scenario. We won't be able to rely on backup. It'll just be us."

"When and where?"

"Come to my house. One hour."

"No. Won't work."

Blair frowned. "Why's that?"

"Because Homicide is en route to your place as we speak. A team of those boys should be pulling up out front in about"—he paused, likely to check his watch—"five minutes."

"Holy shit. Why didn't you say so earlier?" Blair jumped from the sofa and ran for the front door.

"Because you still have time."

He opened it an inch, then stopped. Out front, two vehicles came to a halt, their engines revving. He leaned in to check the peephole. The Homicide boys he'd met in Montgomery Park at the crime scene emerged from their vehicles.

"Shit, they're here!"

"Oh," Morgan mumbled. "Faster than I thought. Sorry, bro. Uhm, surrender to them or run."

Blair spun around and ran through the house. He fumbled with the lock at the back door, got it open, and then closed it softly behind him. All the while, Morgan was still talking on the phone.

"I gotta go, man." Blair ran for the back fence. "Come pick me up. Grab Pruitt, and then we solve this shit."

He reached the back fence, tossed his phone into his jacket pocket, then mounted the fence. When he got to the top, he swung over and let go, landing on his feet in the alley. The fence at the back of his property completely concealed him from the rear of his house. They wouldn't see him walk away if they stood at his kitchen window.

Morgan was asking him something when he retrieved his phone and stuck it back to his ear.

"What's that?" Blair asked, jogging toward Weir Street.

"Where do you want a pick-up?"

Blair thought about it a moment, then came up with a place. "You know Normandy Road connects with Weir, right?"

"Yeah."

"One street over on Normandy is Tragina Avenue South."

"I know it."

"At the top of Tragina, it dead ends into a church."

"Yeah, the Holy Cross Parish or something."

"The Holy Cross *Croatian* Parish. That's the one. Where Tragina ends, their back parking area begins. I'll stay out of sight until you and Pruitt show up."

"Got it. I know exactly where that is."

"How far out are you?"

"Fifteen minutes."

"Make it five."

Morgan scoffed. "Impossible."

"Yeah, because you're still talking to me." Blair ended the call.

When he got to Weir, he turned right toward Normandy. He must not be thinking too clearly. Lack of sleep would have to take the blame. Walking this way would take him right past 44 Weir Street—the house filled with RCMP dickheads.

Sure enough, two of them watched him as he strode by the house.

"Fuckers," he mumbled under his breath. "Stick to your own cases and stay out of my city."

The scowls on their faces didn't reassure him that they were on the same team and working toward a common goal, as all law enforcement would have the public believe.

The phone in the man's hand, the rapid tapping of buttons, and then the frantic shove to the side of his head made Blair wonder if they were calling his captain.

By the time he got to Normandy Road, his phone rang.

It was the captain again. The fucking Mounties probably did call him.

He didn't answer it.

Everyone would have to wait, at least until he could get Susan back.

It was the captain's fault that he was in this mess in the first place. Blair couldn't think of what possessed his boss to release the one man responsible for turning his life completely upside down—Alex Russell.

But, once again, it was left to him to right everyone else's wrongs.

Something else struck him as funny as he turned onto Tragina Avenue. He'd been looking for the Wagners to examine their *evidence* against his two cops sitting on trial for their lives when he should have been looking right in his own backyard.

According to the dead CI, the shooter was one of his men. However, was that solid information? He could've lied because he didn't want to work with them anymore.

The note made sense now. A Vice cop was being framed as a serial drug dealer killer. Everything would eventually point to Inspector Blair Nelson.

All that did was paint a bullseye on his back.

So, of course, he had to run.

# Chapter 20

PARKMAN JOGGED BACK TO the car, and Aaron lowered the passenger window. "Rooms 112 and 114." Parkman pointed. "Around the side."

"You want in?" Aaron asked.

"I'll walk it."

Aaron pulled the car around to where Parkman was pointing. Once parked, Parkman opened Susan's door and gestured for her to exit.

Sarah detected a subtle change in Parkman's expression when Susan exited the car and got to her feet. It was probably nothing more than empathy, given the woman's tears, but there seemed to be something else. Something she'd never seen on his face before.

Desire.

Sarah was sure Parkman *had* desire, but when they were together, dealing with whatever they were dealing with, he put the primary goal first. What Parkman did in his free time, she never knew all the details.

"Are you okay?" he asked Susan, pulling a tissue from his pocket.

She took it and dabbed at her cheeks, then closed her eyes and touched the tissue to her eyelids.

They entered the hotel through a side door, found their rooms, and then stepped inside room 112.

"Who's hungry?" Aaron asked. "Let's get that out of the way, then we can talk, sort out all this murder business."

Sarah shot him a nasty look. This wasn't the time to be sarcastic.

Susan's comments came from a place of hurt, and Aaron may not like Susan's comments, but in her case, sarcasm would shut her down.

Susan shook her head, indicating she didn't want anything to eat.

Parkman waved him off, then glared at Sarah. "What's this about murder business?" he asked, keeping his voice soft.

Sarah told him what Susan had said when he was securing their rooms.

He turned to Susan. "In love with Benjamin?" His mouth opened so far in surprise that his toothpick teetered on the edge of his lower lip, hanging precariously. The consummate toothpick expert didn't drop it, though. The second gravity won, and the toothpick headed off his lip, his mouth snapped closed, locking it back in place.

Parkman went to say something else, but stopped when Sarah's phone vibrated. She checked the screen and didn't recognize the number.

"Hello?" She stared at Parkman.

"Can we meet?"

Sarah's eyes widened as she straightened up. "Alex? Holy shit. Where are you?"

Susan snapped her head toward Sarah.

"In Montgomery Park, near Susan's house."

Sarah frowned and stared at Aaron. "We thought you were at the police station."

"They released me. Look, I need to get out of this area. Where are you guys?"

"How did you know we were here?" Could Alex have some sort of psychic ability, too?

"When they released me, I headed back to speak with Susan. I saw you guys taking her to your car. I shouted, but then you all drove away."

"That was over half an hour ago."

"I know, but not a minute after you left, cop cars roamed the streets. I didn't know if they had changed their minds about me, so I went for a walk. Anyway, I'm ready to meet and explain everything."

"We're at the Comfort Inn on the South Service Road in Burlington, just off the Guelph Line exit."

"I'll take a taxi. Be there in twenty. Oh, and Sarah?"

"Yeah?"

"I came alone for a reason. You guys were never meant to be

involved. This was something I needed to do on my own. So, for that, I'm sorry. I should have forewarned you. But things got out of control. Anyway, I'll explain when I get there."

He ended the call. Sarah stared at her phone. "Alex will be here in twenty minutes."

"No." Susan shook her head. "That won't work."

Everyone looked at her. "What?" Aaron asked.

"After what he did? Nope"—her head kept shaking—"I can't be in the same room as him."

"Well, I think that's not an option now. Alex won't hurt you. We'll be here."

"That's not what I'm worried about."

"Then what is it?"

Susan looked from one of them to the other, then said, "I'm afraid that if given the chance, *I'll* kill him after what he did to my family."

# Chapter 21

BLAIR NELSON STEPPED OUT from the shade of a line of small bushes at the back of the church when he saw Morgan and Pruitt pull up twelve minutes later.

He ran over and jumped in the back seat. Morgan got the car moving immediately.

"What the hell, man," Pruitt said, turning to look at him. "For a guy who did nothing wrong, you're in a heap of trouble."

"Tell me about it." Blair scoffed. "Someone killed the CI and added my name to a note. And the arrest of Alex Russell last night was done by uniformed officers, not me. Of course, I was *personally* interested in why he was going after my wife, but the asshole wouldn't talk to me."

"Oh, he talked, all right. He just waited until you left. The captain spent an hour with him. Even gave him a hug when he left."

Blair stared at Pruitt. "No way. Now I know you're fucking with me."

"It's true," Morgan said, looking at him in the rearview mirror.

"What? Why? What could Russell say to elicit that sort of response?"

"No one knows." Pruitt pushed up his glasses. "The captain isn't telling. But he's hot for you, though."

"What, you think he wants my gun and badge? You think it's that serious?"

"Another mystery. The captain isn't saying what he wants with you. Although, he sent out a message to everyone to bring you in."

"*Bring me in?*" Blair rubbed the tops of his thighs. "What the hell did I do, man?" This gave him the same feeling when the teacher in school sent him to the principal's office. However, being expelled was far less painful than losing his job or, worse, going to prison. "Look, guys. I have a problem to figure out first. Someone took Susan."

"What do you mean, *took* Susan?" Morgan asked. "Explain it to Pruitt. Tell him what you told me."

"Abducted her?" Pruitt jumped in. "Seriously?"

Blair nodded, still rubbing his thighs. "I got a call from a woman with a deep voice saying they wanted to do a trade. Alex Russell for my wife."

Morgan and Pruitt exchanged a glance.

"Now you're the one fucking with us," Pruitt said. "Those sorts of things don't happen in real life. This ain't the movies."

Blair ignored his response. "Here's the thing—I don't have Alex. The captain released him. So, I will have to *pretend* to have Alex and set up a meeting. Then we devise a plan to end this and get Susan back."

Pruitt took off his glasses and wiped the lenses on his shirt. "Shouldn't we bring the department in on this?"

"Guys, I can't risk it. The captain wants me. Homicide wants me. I can face the music, get some sleep, and deal with the wife thing tomorrow, but I'm thinking that's not a good idea. When that woman calls back, I need to be ready."

No one said a word for several city blocks.

"Guys?" Blair leaned forward in his seat. "Are you in? Will you help me?"

Pruitt shook his head. "I don't know, man. Sounds like it's crossing a line."

"What line? We get a call from kidnappers. We agree to meet. We show up and arrest them. No line crossed."

Pruitt shot a glance at Morgan, who lifted a shoulder, indicating they weren't convinced.

"Look," Morgan said. "We should deal with the other thing first. I mean, I got a call from one of the Homicide guys before I picked up Pruitt."

"What'd he say?" Blair asked.

"That they found evidence in your house."

Blair sat back, his shoulders slumped. He placed a hand on his forehead. This wasn't happening. It couldn't be true.

Pruitt twisted in the front seat to look at him. "We know you didn't pull the trigger, man. Okay?"

"What, what did they find in my house?"

"The guy said your front door was open—"

"Bullshit," Blair interrupted. "Unlocked, maybe. But not open." He thought about going to the door and checking the peephole. "Wait. Shit. I think I did open it. I was going to run to my car to leave when they pulled up. Maybe I didn't close the door firmly."

"According to them," Morgan went on. "When they got to your house, you had just been there. Your car is still there. They think you ran out the back to avoid them."

"I *did* run out the back to avoid them. You're the one who told me they were coming."

"Yeah, I know. But I was hoping it wouldn't make you look guilty of something. Some of the Homicide guys are back at the station reviewing last night's camera footage of you being in the building all night to ensure it wasn't doctored."

"What the hell are they looking for?"

"To verify your alibi is solid. They *need* to know you were actually there all night."

Blair stared out the side window, the scenery racing by like the life he once had. "What was this evidence they supposedly found in my house?"

"The CI's cell phone was found inside a shoebox in an upstairs closet."

Blair's mouth dropped open. "No." He shook his head in disbelief. "No way. Impossible."

Morgan met his gaze in the mirror. "Sorry, man. Someone's trying to paint this picture that you're an accessory after the fact or something. And they know you were looking for the Wagners. Someone on our crew leaked your obsession with seeing their evidence."

"Holy shit, my life is in ruins."

"And that's not it," Pruitt jumped in.

"Really?" Blair felt like his own men were in on his downfall. "Tell me. What else could there possibly be?"

"Two RCMP officials visited the captain ten minutes before Morgan called me to come pick you up."

His heart sank. Things had gotten bad. Now, it was worse.

But how could they fault him for looking for Tracy? She was a twelve-year-old girl who happened to be missing.

Pruitt continued. "The RCMP boys threatened charges. A whole slew of issues were raised regarding your conduct—"

"And this was public knowledge?" Blair couldn't contain his anger. "How do you know all this?"

"After the Mounties left, I was putting on my jacket to meet Morgan when the captain stuck his head out and shouted that you were to be found *now*." He emphasized the last word.

His eyes moved between Morgan and Pruitt and back to Morgan. "So, where are you taking me? Into custody?"

The men in the front seat exchanged a glance.

"No," Morgan said. "We're taking you to get your wife. Then into custody."

# Chapter 22

THERE WAS LITTLE TALK between them while they waited for Alex to arrive. Susan sat on the corner of the bed closest to the window, staring out at the passing vehicles on Highway 403. She whispered her daughter's name a few times while Aaron and Sarah huddled close on the other bed.

Parkman was on his phone at the small desk, chatting with Darwin about something, while the hotel TV was on an all-news channel, the volume loud enough to talk under.

"You think we can find her daughter?" Aaron asked in a hushed voice.

Sarah nodded. "We will. Vivian gave me the impression that once Alex gets here, we can move forward."

Aaron's eyebrows drew close. "Move forward? That's what she said? She wasn't more specific?"

"She knows what we want." Sarah snuck a glance at Susan. "My sister wouldn't leave me with the impression of moving forward if that didn't mean helping Susan reunite with her daughter. Otherwise, what are we doing here?" She refocused on Aaron. "If Vivian meant something else and we don't help Susan, my sister knows that will *really* piss me off." Sarah brushed a piece of lint off her jeans absentmindedly. "I don't even want to think about that." She leaned back on her elbows. "We'll help this woman. But first, we find out what's going on with Alex and what their connection is."

Aaron rolled onto his back and stared at the ceiling, his hands laced together behind his head. "Yeah, what the hell is Alex up to in

Hamilton?"

A soft rap on the door made Sarah snap sideways.

Parkman jerked up from his chair and got to the door first. Without saying a word, he opened it and stepped aside.

Alex entered the room.

His eyes roved between Parkman, Sarah, and Aaron until they found Susan.

Then he stopped moving and just stared at her.

Sarah wondered how they knew each other. What would have prompted Alex to kill her parents so long ago? Was that even true? And how could she love Benjamin, and yet none of them knew about this mysterious woman in Hamilton?

All those questions and more raced through Sarah's mind as she watched the tension grow between Alex and Susan.

"Excuse me," Alex said, gently touching Parkman's sleeve. He unlocked eyes with Susan, nodded at Aaron, then moved closer and extended his hand to Sarah. She took it, and he squeezed her gently. "Please, give us a few moments."

Aaron shook his head. "No, we can't leave you alone with her."

Alex turned and gave him a sidelong glance. "Not alone. I'll speak with Susan first. Listen to what we talk about. Then I'll have less to explain when it's your turn. Cool?"

Aaron and Sarah nodded.

Parkman retook his seat at the desk and popped a new toothpick in the corner of his mouth.

Alex released Sarah's hand, his eyes back on Susan. "Just give us some time to chat, and then I'll explain everything." He ambled over to stand in front of Susan.

"I'm so sorry," he whispered.

Susan's head lowered as tears dripped from her eyes. After a moment's pause, she opened her arms, and Alex stepped into them.

*Hugging? The man who murdered your parents?* Confused, Sarah stared at Aaron, who shrugged. She leaned in close to whisper. "Didn't she say she might kill him?"

Aaron gave a short shake of his head as if to say, *don't worry about that.*

They hugged for a long moment, both of them silently weeping.

Sarah couldn't suppress her own tears now. She rubbed her eyes twice as they stood by the window, embracing. Obviously, this woman meant something to Alex in a deep, profound way, but it was still a mystery to the rest of them.

Susan took some tissues from her pocket when they separated and dabbed at her face.

"Why did you come to Hamilton?" she asked. "That can of worms needs to remain closed."

"I had to see you."

"Why? After all these years, why?"

"Because." Alex swallowed, got himself under control, then added, "Because of Benjamin."

"I heard."

"So you know?"

Susan nodded. "I saw it on the news."

"You follow us? What we do?"

"I wouldn't say *follow*, but when something comes up, I read about it."

This woman was connected to Alex and Benjamin. It made sense how Alex had been acting recently, how he'd withdrawn after Benjamin, his brother, died, and how he'd gotten more ruthless. It wasn't that he lacked a heart. It was that his heart was broken, injured.

"Why watch my house, though? My husband is a cop. How else did you think this would end?"

"I didn't want to intrude on your life. I was waiting until you were alone. I didn't get that opportunity during my brief stay. I stepped out from behind that tree when I thought you were leaving your garage on your own yesterday afternoon. But then, at the last second, I saw your daughter enter the garage and jump in the passenger seat. I couldn't approach you with her or your husband present. I just couldn't do it."

Susan nodded as if this was normal behavior. Sarah turned to Aaron, who was held rapt at what he was hearing. Parkman was frowning, the toothpick in his mouth flicking in circles, his eyes fixed on Alex.

It almost sounded like Alex had had an affair with this woman and would always be the other guy or something.

"Okay, then, why run after my car when I was parked on Weir Street later that evening? I mean, that freaked me out."

Alex nodded, looking down at his hands. When he looked up, his eyes had glistened over again. "I saw you drive by your house moments before, glancing in all directions. I figured you were looking for me, so I stayed out of sight, even though you were alone this time." Susan nodded, watching him. "When you turned onto Weir, I ran down the street to see where you were going."

"And you saw my car parked in front of that house? You probably saw me get back in my car—alone."

Alex moved over to lean against the wall beside the window. "When I saw you were alone, and only about ten houses away, I broke into a run. I'd finally got an opportunity that I couldn't let pass. We needed to talk about Benjamin, among other things."

"And when I pulled away, you smacked the trunk."

He glanced out the window. "Yeah. I was frustrated. Trying to catch you alone for days can do that."

"I remember your thin patience, your frustration."

*Remember?* Sarah thought. *How long have they known each other?*

"How much did you screw up my life this time?" Susan asked. "What did you tell my husband when they had you at the station?"

Alex faced her and stood straighter. "I didn't utter a word in his presence. I told him nothing. He will know about us when *you're* ready to tell him *if* you ever tell him."

*About us?* Sarah felt Aaron's eyes on her. When she turned to him, he was frowning deeply, his brow lined and creased. This sounded more and more like an affair, but she hoped not. Her respect for Alex would plummet if that were the case.

"So Blair doesn't know a thing about us?"

Alex shook his head, and Sarah suppressed a gasp by placing a hand over her mouth.

Normally, this would be awkward. But Alex was like family to them. It was better to listen to this reunion as it happened than to have

Alex recite everything to them later.

"Tell me one thing before we continue this, whatever it is we're doing."

Alex nodded.

Susan's face hardened. "Do you have anything to do with my daughter's disappearance?"

The tension in the room thickened as they all stared at Alex. He stepped closer to her, his eyes unblinking. "I had nothing to do with that. I only came to speak with you about Benjamin and to check that you were doing okay. I've ..." His voice locked up for a moment. "I've missed you. I've missed us."

Sarah stared at Susan and noticed her movements and features for the first time. She scrutinized her in a new light, watched her nod once, and then move her shoulders back like she was determined to handle something difficult.

It reminded her of Alex. He did that.

Wait—are they *related*?

Darwin's words resonated through her head. *Because Alex wasn't an only child. He had a brother.*

Susan had said that Alex had killed *her* parents. Could it be that they had the same parents? Was she referring to what they'd learned before coming to Hamilton?

Some of Aaron's words from earlier rolled through her mind. *Whoever killed their father killed their parents. If the father's murder was the catalyst, it's a foregone conclusion.*

Is that what Susan meant about Alex killing *her* parents? Did he do something to his father? If that were the case, then they would be related in some way. If so, how? Didn't Darwin say he only found records of Alex having a brother? That meant there were no other siblings.

But Susan said she loved Benjamin. She even said something like, *With Benjamin gone, Alex was alone.*

Was Alex alone?

"We've got a lot to talk about," Alex said. "But there are more important things we must do first."

Susan stared up at him. "Like what?"

"We have to find your daughter." Alex glanced at Sarah. "Will you help?" His eyes found Aaron and Parkman. "Will all of you help?"

The emotional plea in his voice tore at Sarah's heart. "Of course, Alex. We'll do everything we can to bring Susan's daughter home."

Alex pushed off the wall and moved in front of the hotel TV. He now stood between them all.

He gestured at Susan, then pointed at Sarah, Aaron, and Parkman.

"Susan, I'd like you to meet my new family. Sarah, Aaron, and Parkman." He faced Sarah. "Guys, I'd like you to meet my sister, Susan Russell, now Susan Nelson."

Sarah gasped and clutched at her chest. "Holy shit ..." she whispered as Aaron ran over and hugged Alex tight.

Parkman followed suit. When they released, it was Sarah's turn.

"I'm shocked," she said several inches from his face.

"Me too," Alex whispered in her ear as he pulled her close again. "Me too."

# Chapter 23

BLAIR'S PHONE WOULDN'T STOP ringing, so he placed it on vibrate. Turning it off would be better, but he didn't want to miss a call from that woman.

Morgan had brought them to the same abandoned warehouse from the previous night. He killed the engine, then turned in his seat.

"Guys, we need to figure out our next move."

Pruitt nodded rapidly. "Yeah, running around like this while every cop in the city is looking for us won't work if we're aiming for a pension."

"Agreed." Morgan looked at Blair. "None of us has done anything wrong. We're good cops."

"Easy for you to say." Blair stared out the window. "I'll get suspended at the very least."

"Why?" Morgan asked.

Blair turned to look at him. "Because of my interest in the Wagners. That crossed a line. I knew it, but was blinded by what I thought was a righteous fight for our two boys on trial."

"Well, when new evidence comes to light, and it proves the Wagners had nothing on their recording, *and* they've got the serial drug dealer killer in custody, no one will care two shits about you and the Wagners."

"How does anyone know about my interest in them, anyway, outside of our boys in Vice?" He frowned as he contemplated the dilemma. "My wife dropped Tracy off at a birthday party. Now my stepdaughter's missing. Of course, I'd go to the house looking for her.

How could I know that's where the Wagners were being sequestered?" He shrugged. "It makes sense, though. The Mounties bought the house last June. The deed is in the name of Baker, and the Wagners move in. When they leave town after court, they can keep it as a safe house or sell it."

"Anyway, once the Mounties know that Tracy is missing, they won't pursue anything with you." Morgan slapped Pruitt's arm, and Pruitt nodded.

"The only thing stopping me from—" Blair stopped talking when Morgan's phone rang.

Morgan fished in his jacket pocket and pulled it out. On the third ring, he looked up at Blair. "It's the captain."

"Answer it, but I'm not here. You haven't seen me. Isolate yourself from my problems."

Morgan stared at him for a long moment, then answered.

"Hey, Cap. What's up?" He stared at Blair. "No, haven't seen him." Morgan nodded. "Yeah, I heard. I'm out looking for him now." Then he frowned. "Me? Why me?" Morgan looked from Pruitt to Blair. "Okay, I'll get there soon—" He paused. "Really? Now? What's the emergency?" His mouth hung open. "Well, can't some other Vice cop handle it? Maybe Murphy?" Morgan ran a hand through his hair. "Okay, I'll come in." He ended the call.

Blair grabbed the back of the seat and pulled himself forward. "What's going on?"

"The captain wants me at the station."

"Why?"

"Some bullshit made-up thing about a perp they apprehended who has a connection to a dealer."

"How do you know that's made up?" Pruitt asked.

"Because we know all the major players in Hamilton, and the name Quincy isn't ringing any bells. The captain just doesn't want me out here helping you."

Pruitt pulled out his phone. "You think he's going to call me?"

"Probably, and you know why?"

Blair swung his head back and forth, watching each man as he spoke.

"Why?" Pruitt asked.

"Because he's pulling all Vice off the road. He doesn't want anyone on Blair's crew to throw a lifesaver to Blair here."

Pruitt's phone rang in his hand. "One second," he said to Morgan and Blair. "Stay quiet, guys."

Pruitt answered, and the call went the same way. "Can't you call Morgan in on something like this?" Pruitt listened to his answer, then said, "On my way, Cap."

He hung up and stared out the windshield. "Same thing."

Blair and Morgan shared a look.

"What did he say about me?" Morgan asked.

Pruitt looked at him. "When I told him to call you about it, he said he couldn't reach you."

"What?" Blair blurted. "He lied to you?"

Pruitt nodded, then swiveled in the front seat to face Blair. "Dude, what the hell is going on?"

Blair sat back with a heavy thump, his shoulder blades smacking into the seat hard.

"Why would the captain lie to you guys?" Blair spoke as if he were talking to himself.

An idea slowly dawned on him.

He snapped his fingers, making Morgan jump. "I've got it."

"Got what?" Morgan asked.

"I know who we can call."

"Who?"

"Sarah Roberts."

Morgan frowned. "Have you gone off the deep end?"

Pruitt faced him. "I think you've lost the plot, dear friend. Why call her?"

"Because I think she's the woman with the deep voice." He snapped his fingers again. "It has to be her."

"How often do you speak with that psychic witch in Toronto?"

Blair frowned. "Like never."

"Okay, then, why would she disguise her voice for you? Why not use her normal voice? I mean, how would you recognize the difference?"

"Because I called her around four this morning."

The men in the front seat exchanged a glance, then looked back at him.

"Why did you call her at four in the morning?" Morgan asked.

"You know that Russell kid the captain released today?"

Morgan nodded.

"He's part of Sarah's inner circle. I thought she was here, operating in Hamilton. It turns out I woke her up at her apartment in Toronto. She was nowhere near Hamilton last night. Alex Russell was working on his own."

"Then why call her now? Doesn't make any sense."

"You're not listening." His voice deepened as his patience ebbed. "I think it was Sarah who called earlier, and we don't have the luxury of time to wait until she calls again. Soon, she'll know that I don't have Alex, so there's no trade, and both of you need to head to the station soon, or the captain will have your heads."

"Works for me." Pruitt rolled his hand in a circle. "Make the call."

Blair looked at Morgan.

He nodded. "Let's get you Susan back at least."

Blair grabbed his phone, scrolled through to Sarah's number, and hit the button to call her.

# Chapter 24

"WAIT," SUSAN SAID. "WHAT are the charges you're facing? How did you get out of holding? Did they make you sign a promise to appear?" Before Alex could answer, Susan glanced sheepishly at Sarah. "You guys are willing to help with my daughter. I can't have my brother up on charges on my account. I'll tell my husband to drop any charges they file against him."

Alex sat on the edge of the bed and stared at the wall like he had something to say, but knew it would be difficult. "All the charges are already dropped."

"What?" Susan leaned forward to get a peek at Alex's face. "Why would they do that?"

Alex met her gaze. "One of the officers wore a body cam during the arrest. Sure, they found me in the bushes, but that by itself isn't a crime." He paused, inhaling deeply. "The camera picked up how startled I was when Officer Darrow went to grab me. It caught my reaction—"

"Did you karate chop him?" Susan asked. "You and Benjamin got into that martial arts thing so young. It's no wonder you work at a dojo now."

Speaking about Benjamin had to tear at everyone's heart. Susan saw it on their faces.

Alex's shoulders slumped. "I defended myself, but when I saw his uniform, I released his wrist without breaking it and surrendered to the handcuffs. The thing is, he didn't identify himself first. Captain Simmons said he doubted it would hold up in court."

"You spoke with Simmons?" Susan stared at him. "Wait, you *spoke* with Simmons as opposed to remaining silent? What did you say to him?"

"I told him the reason I'd been hanging around you." Alex cleared his throat. "That you were my sister and how I'd kept that from Inspector Nelson, your husband, because I felt it was your place to tell him. I explained why I thought we needed to talk. You know, because we'd lost a brother."

"And he took sympathy on you," Susan said softly. She placed a hand on Alex's shoulder and rubbed it. "Simmons is one of the good guys. We've often had him and the entire Vice team over for barbecues. I know him well."

Sarah moved closer. "Guys, we need to get moving. We need to find your daughter. But I have to ask something first."

Alex and Susan stared up at her.

"Why is there no record of you being his sister? Darwin said the files were sealed. What's that about?"

Susan looked at Alex. "When you tell them the whole story, I can't be in the same room."

Alex nodded. "I understand."

"Don't lie to them, but gloss over it for now."

Sarah looked over at Aaron, who was getting to his feet.

"Hey." Sarah raised a hand, stepping back. "I don't mean to pry, but your shared past seems murky. There has to be a reason for that."

"My father was a terrible man." Alex's voice had hardened.

Susan nodded at Sarah, then looked away.

"He was mean and did horrible things. When I was fifteen, Benjamin and I wanted to teach him a lesson. It went further than we expected. He died because of what we did. It wasn't our fault directly, but it was our fault *in*directly."

Alex's sister listened to Alex as she placed her hands over her face.

"I can go into more detail when we get home, but his death destroyed our mother. There was a court case. Our mom shot herself, and the court case died. She was the star witness. After that, our lawyers, for specific reasons of which I can't go into now, requested that the case files be sealed. I imagine their reasoning was based on allowing the rest of the family time to heal from this tragedy. The request was granted, and later, we learned that Susan had changed her name and had her birth records sealed. I don't know how she achieved that, but after what happened all those years ago, Benjamin and I accepted her wish. We were no longer a family."

Susan wiped her face and stared at the wall. "I hated my *family* in those days. My dad for what he did. My mother for her part in it. Then, my anchors, my brothers, for their part in everything else." She faced Sarah, her eyes bloodshot and wet. "I thought my bloodline was filled with poison. So, I filed motion after motion to erase myself, my name, my existence from the Russell cult—I mean, *clan*."

"Well." Sarah spread her arms wide. "Alex is one of the most stable, well-mannered men I've ever had the pleasure to know. But with him, your family gets much larger. You get us, too." She lowered her arms. "We don't hurt those we love here. We protect them. We take care of them. So, enough with the memories for now. Let's go find your daughter."

Susan nodded. *"Please,"* she whispered.

"But we'll need your husband's help."

"Call him. I can give you the number."

Sarah retrieved her phone. "I've already got his number."

Susan frowned. "Is that the psychic thing I've read about?"

Sarah gave her an odd stare and then produced a business card from her pocket. "When we got in the car at your place, you handed me this."

Susan snapped her fingers. "Oh, right. Forgot."

The phone rang in Sarah's hand. "Guess who it is." She tapped a button on the phone, then placed it to her ear. "I'm listening." She waited a moment, her brow twitching. "We have Alex with us. There is no need to trade." She faced Parkman, then looked at Aaron. "Inspector, just meet us." One more pause, then, "Okay, it's off Parkdale. We'll find it. See you in an hour." She waited a moment. "Yes, I'll bring Susan. Come alone. We have something to tell you."

She hung up and stared at Susan. "We're meeting him at an abandoned factory off Parkdale that's set for demolition. He said you'd know the place."

Susan nodded. "I know the one. But why not meet him at home?"

Sarah frowned. "I'm not sure. He sounded stressed. What does he know that we're missing?"

Susan shrugged. "Our daughter is missing. Since Alex didn't speak with him, maybe he thinks Alex had something to do with it. Then Alex gets released from custody by Blair's boss." Susan brushed the hair out of her face. "He's overtired, I'm sure. Stressed too. Once we meet him, we can talk it all out and go from there."

"He was up all night with me," Alex added. "He's likely exhausted."

Sarah turned and headed for the door. "Let's go, then. When this is over, and your daughter is home, we'll stay the night in this hotel, then drive home in the morning."

"You really think we'll find Tracy today?" Susan asked, her voice weak with hope.

"We won't find her inside this hotel room. We need to move."

Susan understood Sarah. The woman wouldn't promise something she couldn't guarantee.

However, Susan didn't know how meeting with Blair would help, but she was willing to tag along for now.

No one else seemed as determined to find her daughter as this group, and they had a reputation for dealing with the criminal element.

From what she knew of Sarah, if anyone could find Tracy, this woman might be her best chance.

She got up off the bed.

Finding her daughter might fill the vast hole that had opened in her heart like a giant maw. Without Tracy, how could she go on? Without Tracy, life held no meaning.

She followed them out of the hotel room, wiping at the tears that seemed to never stop.

# Chapter 25

BLAIR HAD LAID OUT the plan, which entailed taking Alex back into custody. But since Sarah might only be coming with his wife, getting to Alex was questionable, so they'd arrest Sarah. Once Blair spoke with her in the same chair the CI sat in last night, with the same powerful lamp on, he'd know more about his missing stepdaughter.

An interrogation in the factory would be much more effective than one downtown. Here, they could rough up suspects. Downtown, there were rules to follow, and people were listening.

Blair didn't think of himself as a rogue cop. Not in the least. He got results. And if he crossed the line a few times, it was only by inches and with the best intentions.

After he got Sarah's confession, he would take his wife and head to the station. Then and only then would he decide if he needed a lawyer to speak with Homicide.

"Everyone understands what's at stake here, right?"

Morgan nodded, his gun in his hand. He racked the slide on his weapon.

"What are you doing?" Pruitt asked.

"I'm trying to clear an obstruction."

"An obstruction?" Pruitt turned to Blair. "We gonna need our weapons?"

Blair gave him a fake smile. "With people like Sarah?" He shrugged. "One never knows. She could bring backup. She's already kidnapped my wife. She's got that martial arts expert Alex with her." He wrapped an arm around Pruitt's shoulders as they watched Morgan fiddle with his gun. "We'll probably need our guns, but I doubt we'll need to fire them."

Pruitt pulled his out, checked that the chamber was empty, and left it that way for safety reasons.

"Fuck," Morgan said. "Mine's jammed." He holstered it. "You guys have an extra? I'm going to stick mine in the trunk of our car."

Blair grabbed his and handed it over. "Take mine. When Sarah shows up with my wife, not being armed would pose less of a threat."

Morgan took it, racked the slide, nodded once, then replaced his with Morgan's in his shoulder holster and walked over to the car. He popped the trunk and placed his service weapon inside the spare tire compartment.

"Guys." Blair spun in a circle. "I'll stay here, right out in the open, by the car. They expect me to be alone, so I'll be alone." He pointed at the second-floor steel walkways. "I want Morgan up there"—he shifted his aim—"and Pruitt up there. You'll be forty meters away. Close enough to hear everything and still close enough to act as backup."

"Works for me." Morgan grinned.

Pruitt still seemed jittery.

"You okay, man?" Morgan asked him.

"Yeah." Pruitt avoided their gaze. "With all the heat coming down on you," he tilted his gaze toward Blair, "I just think we should head into the station and have a dozen cruisers surrounding this place. You know, do it the right way."

"Pruitt, this is the right way. We're not doing anything illegal. Sarah abducted my wife and called me to do a trade for a man held in custody —Alex Russell. When she realized Alex was released, she wanted to hand my wife over. No harm, no foul." Blair shook his head. "Shit doesn't work like that. She broke the law, and now it's all, *well, I don't need my captive anymore. You can have her back.*" He spoke those words in a high-pitched mimic of a whiny woman. "Fuck that. I'm waiting here to get my wife back and to arrest Sarah Roberts for the abduction of a Hamilton Vice inspector's spouse. Then we will take Alex downtown to find out who knows what happened to my stepdaughter. *And* then I'll speak with the captain and Homicide."

Pruitt kicked at something on the ground. "Sure, I get it, and I'd be angry, too. Something just feels off about this still."

"Let me ask you a question." Blair raised a hand to shield his eyes from the afternoon sun. "Did I kill that CI?"

"No, of course not."

"Did I do anything wrong, *procedurally*, with the Alex Russell arrest?"

Pruitt frowned. "Not if those uniforms arrested him."

"Exactly." Blair lowered his arm and stepped sideways into Pruitt's shadow to see his face better. "Lastly, did I meet with the Wagners? Did I compromise any of the witnesses in the trial I have been sitting in all week? No, I did not." He raised his hands to the side. "I've done absolutely nothing wrong. I'm not the bad guy here."

"Yeah," Morgan chimed in. "That's why I'm here. Gotta protect our boy."

Pruitt nodded. "You guys are right. I can't say I like this, but you're right."

"Like it?" Blair's voice rose. "Who likes this shit? But I have to stay. I need my wife back. One thing at a time."

Pruitt was still nodding, his eyes on the entrance.

"Don't forget, my man," Blair said. "The road to a diamond mine is always unpaved."

Pruitt glanced at him, his face scrunched in confusion. "What does that mean?"

Morgan scoffed. "Dude, it means you only get to the gold by going through some shit. Sometimes, you have to get your hands dirty."

Pruitt raised a finger. "Just not so dirty that it doesn't wash off."

"What?" Morgan stared at him, dumbfounded.

"Meaning, we can't go too far with this interrogation shit. I won't go to a place we can't come back from. I want my pension, man."

Morgan laughed, glanced at Blair, then laughed again. "Hey, I want my pension, too. Nothing's gonna jeopardize that. Not today."

"Guys." Blair went over to the car and opened the driver's side door. "Disappear. Get in position. We get my wife, ask Sarah some questions, and then head to the station. Easy peasy. We'll be home free in half an hour."

He dropped into the driver's seat and closed the door. Morgan and Pruitt started toward the factory. A minute later, he watched them ascend the stairs to the second level, and then they disappeared into the shadows.

Blair turned on the car, drove it in a circle until he was aimed at the entrance, and then killed the engine.

He brought up the game called Hearts on his phone and settled in for a few rounds while waiting for Sarah to arrive with his wife.

Idly, he wondered if Sarah would be surprised by Morgan and Pruitt in hiding. Or would she *know* they were there?

She was psychic, wasn't she?

He barked a laugh as he picked up the queen of spades and collected thirteen points.

"Fuckers," he whispered to the game.

# Chapter 26

SARAH DROVE THIS TIME, with Susan navigating beside her. Parkman, Aaron, and Alex sat in the back seat, staring out the windows.

As they rode over the Burlington Skyway, Sarah listened to them talk about Alex's time at Taco Bell and his fantasy about owning a franchise one day.

Susan directed her onto Parkdale, which seemed to have more potholes than the other streets she'd driven in Hamilton.

Susan gripped the dashboard with one hand as the car jostled over the bumps. "This is the older section. Heavy trucks wreck these roads."

After a few blocks, Susan instructed her to take a right.

"There it is." Susan pointed at a building about four stories high. The facility was wide open at the front, exposing large circular tubes, pipes, and what looked like vats for oil. Steel walkways and stairs traversed the front like a giant-sized *Snakes and Ladders* game.

Sarah pulled to the side and stopped. The back doors opened, and the boys piled out. The trunk opened, then closed.

"What's going on?" Susan asked.

"We don't know what we're walking into."

"What?" Susan seemed offended. "We're meeting my husband to discuss ways to find my daughter."

Sarah turned to her, placing her left forearm on the top of the steering wheel. "Then why are we meeting at an abandoned warehouse?"

Susan stammered momentarily, glanced at the warehouse, then back at Sarah. "I don't, I don't know. I didn't really think about it."

"Could it be your husband thinks I'm a criminal? Could it be he wants to do me harm?"

She frowned so hard her face morphed into a sneer. "Absolutely not. My husband's an inspector. He wouldn't dare touch you. Not as long as I'm there."

"Well, that's not something I'm willing to bet on."

Sarah put the car in drive and eased along the side road until she got to the entrance of the large factory parking area. One car sat in the parking lot near the building itself.

She eased in and stopped.

"What are you doing?"

"Giving the boys a moment to get into position and ensure we're not walking into an ambush."

"Oh, my hell." Susan gasped so hard she almost choked herself. "This is too spy-like for me." She ripped open her door. "That's an unmarked cruiser, just like my husband's. I'll walk from here."

"Susan. Wait." Sarah lunged across the seat for her, but she was already gone.

The door slammed shut, and Susan marched across the wide-open gravel lot toward the lone vehicle.

Sarah pulled to the side of the building in the shadows and then turned off the car.

"You good back there?" she asked.

"Yeah." Alex's voice was muffled coming through the back seat.

"I'm heading over now. Her husband has exited his car. They're embracing. I can't see anyone else around."

"Move away from the car first, then walk toward them. Keep him focused on you."

"Got it."

Sarah exited the vehicle, shut her door, and walked toward the center of the gravel parking lot. She scanned the pipes, the walkways all the way to the third floor, and the stairwells, but saw nothing. There was no movement anywhere. For all she could tell, Susan's husband had come alone as instructed.

That didn't mean he *was* alone, though.

Once she reached the center of the parking lot, she angled herself to walk toward the cruiser. Susan and her husband were locked in conversation, only glancing her way once or twice.

The closer she got, she could hear them talking about Tracy and how Sarah wanted to help.

Blair Nelson turned to Sarah when she stopped ten feet from them. He opened his suit jacket and gestured at his empty holster.

"Nothing to worry about here," he said. "I chose this spot so you would be safe."

"Me?"

He sighed. "Abducting a cop's wife and then calling me for a trade might seem highly criminal to some of my colleagues. Doing this here keeps everyone out of our business, making it safer for you." His smile was probably meant to comfort her, but something about it seemed cocky.

"A trade?" Susan did that sneer-grimace thing again as if she'd bit into a lemon. "What sort of trade?"

"Oh, Sarah didn't tell you?"

"Tell me what?"

"That she took you from our house to trade you for Alex. She planned to force me to release him."

"But he'd already been released by the captain. I heard everything from Alex himself."

"Right, but when Sarah took you from our house, did *she* know Alex had been released?" Blair looked her way. "No, she didn't." Then he blinked and gripped her by the upper arm. "Wait, what? You were with Alex?"

Susan stared at Sarah, ignoring her husband's last question. "What's this all about?"

"It's about everything we already covered. You know why Alex was hanging around your house. He's not a criminal. He shouldn't be in custody. And we want to help you find Tracy."

Blair chortled. "That's rich, Sarah, coming from you."

"Oh my ..." Susan gasped hard like she had in the car moments ago, forcing herself to swallow several times. Her eyes widened.

"That's how Blair called your phone."

"It would seem so," Sarah said, stepping closer.

"Because you'd called him for this *trade* stuff with Alex."

"Well, not exactly. Blair already had my number." Sarah averted her eyes to stare at Susan's husband. "Because he called me at four this morning."

Susan turned to her husband. "Honey, tell me what's going on."

Blair's eyes didn't leave Sarah. "That's what I'd like to know."

Susan pulled him closer. "Honey, there's something I need to tell you."

He met his wife's gaze. "It can wait. Right now, I need to speak with Sarah, and then we have to go to the station downtown together. Something else came up that I need to deal with."

"What came up?"

"Just stuff."

"What stuff?" Susan smacked his arm. "Seriously, honey, I need to find Tracy. I can't handle any more *stuff.*"

"Okay." Blair sighed. "It's about that drug dealer who was murdered last night in the park by our house."

"What about him?"

"Homicide wants to talk to me about that."

"Why *you*?" Her voice became shrill on the last word.

"Please, calm down." Blair rubbed her arm soothingly. "I was at the station all night. They don't want to talk to me as a suspect, but there are rumors that it might be a cop. They're interviewing everyone."

Susan exhaled heavily. "Okay, okay, but we have to find Tracy today. I can't handle another night without her."

"We will, we will." Blair fixed his gaze on Sarah. "However, I could just ask Sarah where she is."

Sarah shook her head slightly. "My abilities don't work like that."

"I'm not referring to your *psychic* ability."

She blinked once, then caught on to what he was saying. "You know as well as I do that I'm not involved with what happened in Hamilton yesterday, as I was in Toronto. You called me yourself."

"Right, but you sent people to do your dirty work, didn't you?" He moved away from Susan and closer to Sarah by two steps. "Just tell us where Tracy is, get in your car, and drive away. It's that simple. I'll forget we ever met. You're free to go."

Sarah stared over his shoulder at Susan, whose eyes were frantic now.

"Blair, I had nothing to do with your daughter's disappearance, and neither did Alex."

"Inspector Nelson to you." His voice had hardened.

"Honey," Susan pleaded. "What are you doing? Sarah has already agreed to help us."

"Stay out of this." Blair waved a hand behind him. "I need Sarah to confess. Once she's done that, I won't arrest her. Failing that, she'll be arrested and remain in custody until she returns our daughter."

"What makes you think she's involved?" Susan's voice cracked as she was shaking now.

"This is elementary, my dear. It's obvious what this bitch is up to. I'm the inspector here, and I'm the only one qualified to determine who is guilty and who isn't gui—"

A gunshot pinged metal somewhere behind them, cutting Blair off mid-sentence.

They all ducked and spun around.

"Who else is here?" Sarah forced the words through clenched teeth, moving closer to Blair's car for cover.

Blair popped his trunk and grabbed something from deep within. He stood back up with a gun in his hand.

"Stay here," he ordered.

Sarah ran over and wrapped an arm around Susan.

Someone shouted something above them. Another weapon was fired.

Returning to her car would expose them—it was too much in the open. The closest place to hide until this was over was a brick wall fifteen meters away. It likely housed the main office when this factory was in business.

"Come on," Sarah said. "We have to get out of the line of fire."

She pushed Susan along with her toward the brick wall.

Gunfire erupted from behind them, kicking up dirt a meter away.

"*Run!*" she shouted. "Someone's shooting at us."

They broke into a full sprint, getting behind the brick wall in seconds.

"Are you hit?" Sarah yelled, turning to examine Susan.

The woman shook her head in a panic-stricken, agitated manner. "I'm ... fine," she stammered.

Two more shots were fired. One kicked up dirt beside the wall they hid behind, and the other chipped a brick.

"Come on." She grabbed Susan's arm. "We have to get inside and find somewhere to hide until your husband can deal with the shooter."

Susan nodded and followed as Sarah dragged her deeper into the bowels of the factory, then up some stairs toward a row of offices with broken windows and missing doors.

They found a short corridor that contained a tiny room with a door near the end of the hall.

Clutching Susan's wrist, she dragged her into the small rectangular room that once held a mop and bucket—the janitor's closet.

Sarah closed the door and whispered, "Get your breathing under control. When they come looking for us, we need to be quiet."

Susan jerked her head up and down in understanding as she inhaled deeply, then exhaled slowly.

All the while, Sarah wondered what the hell went wrong.

She fired dozens of questions at Vivian.

Every question was left unanswered.

# Chapter 27

BLAIR MADE IT TO the second floor, his head on a swivel. Morgan was to his left. He ran toward him as the man's hand moved back and forth like he was searching for something to shoot with Blair's gun still clutched in his sweaty palm.

He moaned as Blair stepped closer, edging around a thick pipe at least a meter in diameter.

Morgan was on the walkway, his right hand covering a bleeding wound on his arm slightly below the shoulder.

"Fucker shot me." Morgan grimaced.

Blair surveyed the immediate area, fearing how out of control things were getting. No one was supposed to be shooting no one. "Who shot at you?"

"Alex Russell. That asshole jumped out of nowhere like Batman. Did some crazy Jackie Chan shit, then shot Pruitt and me and jumped over the railing."

"*What?*" Blair lowered to his knees. "It can't be. How could this happen? Weren't you guys watching each other's backs?" He was going to lose his mind.

Morgan stared up at him, his eyes blazing with the pain. "So this is our fault?"

Blair waved off his comment, then quickly assessed the wound and saw it was already clotting. The bullet barely cut him more than a small knife might. "I'm not *blaming* you or Pruitt. Just thought you'd see that asshole coming. You guys are the best in Vice."

"Dude," Morgan said, kicking him lightly in the thigh. "Go help

Pruitt. He got a couple in the chest."

Blair's eyes widened as he stared at Morgan. "The *chest*?" What had he walked his men into? They weren't prepared for an attack like this. There would be hell to pay when their superiors got wind of their private meeting that got a cop shot.

"Where's Pruitt?" Blair asked. "Tell me he was wearing a vest, *please*."

Morgan edged away to rest his head on the walkway's steel-grated floor. "A vest? Are you delusional? We chatted by the car. Did you see a vest on that boy?"

"Where is he?"

"Hey, is that my gun?"

Blair looked at the weapon in his hand and nodded. "Yeah. After I moved the car, I grabbed it from the spare tire where you'd hidden it. Even if it was jammed, I didn't want to have nothing on me in case Sarah was packing."

"Give it to me. I'll work on unjamming it." He used his right hand to point. "Here's yours."

Blair handed over Morgan's gun, then grabbed his. He checked the chamber and magazine, then stared at Morgan. "It's empty."

"I shot at Alex but missed each time. I told you, the guy's like Batman or something."

Blair lowered to his knees, listening to the cavernous factory. "I hear nothing."

"Everyone's hiding."

"Tell me where Pruitt is again."

Morgan jerked his head, indicating further along the walkway. "He's that way. I'll make it down to the car. Meet me there in a few minutes. We have to get the fuck out of here to take Pruitt to the hospital."

"What about you?"

"I'm fine. Might need stitches, but it's fine now."

Blair got to his feet but remained bent over. Like in a trance, he plodded along the length of the catwalk, already contemplating the trouble they were in when the captain caught wind of this.

Shots were fired at an abandoned factory where they were to exchange his abducted wife for information on his kidnapped stepdaughter.

"How fucked up is that?" he asked himself.

It took two turns on the walkway before he saw a man's shoes jutting out from behind a cylindrical vat.

Pruitt's shoes.

He raced over without regard for his safety and ran around the circular wall.

Pruitt's eyes were wide open and unblinking.

Two holes were neatly placed in the center of his chest.

He didn't have a chance.

Suppressing the tears was pointless. His eyes filled, blurring his vision, as he took on the weight of a dead cop, a dead *Vice* cop, at his feet. A friend. One of his team. Such a heinous act. How could Alex murder someone so coldly, without feeling anything whatsoever?

He wiped at his eyes and lowered to his knees beside Pruitt's body. Once he blinked away enough tears to be able to see better, he closed Inspector Pruitt's eyelids.

"*Motherfucker*," Blair whispered. "I'll kill him for you, my friend. He won't make the night. I'm going to *fucking* kill that man."

"*Blair!*" Morgan shouted from forty meters away. "I got him."

A weapon fired.

Even as Blair jumped to his feet, his gun sweeping for enemies, he wondered whose gun had discharged. Wasn't Morgan's gun jammed? That was why he had requested to use Blair's, which likely saved his life.

Maybe he cleared the obstruction.

Blair ran the length of the catwalk, turned at a junction, and headed toward the area where he'd left Morgan.

Sure enough, Alex stood there with his hands up. Morgan had his gun aimed at the young man's face.

Blair raised his weapon as he approached. From two feet away, staring into the asshole's face, he added pressure to the trigger.

Then he pulled it hard.

The gun clicked empty, but it was enough to make Alex's entire body jerk.

"One bullet stood between life and death, you motherfucker. If I only had one bullet left. But hey, I've got more in the car. Let's go." Blair shoved Alex so hard that the kid bumped into a railing and bent over it.

"Where are we taking him?" Morgan asked. "I'm not letting this asshole go to jail. Not after what he did to Pruitt."

"I didn't do anythin—"

Blair shoved his weapon into Alex's cheek, cutting him off. "He's not going anywhere near a jail cell. I've got another idea for this cop killer."

"Let me just shoot him in the face now. Right here. I can empty my gun in his mouth so he can taste death on his tongue."

"No." Blair's tone was firm. "My plan involves more suffering." He waved for Morgan to get up while keeping his gaze on Alex. "If we shoot him here, forensics will lead back to us. Trust me. I've got a plan that'll never come back to haunt us."

Morgan seemed to contemplate that, then eased his finger off the trigger of his weapon, resting it against the trigger guard.

"Cuff him so we can manage him better," Morgan said to Blair. Then, to Alex, he whispered, "Please resist. I want you dead so bad I can taste it."

Blair took a set of cuffs from Morgan and snapped them onto Alex's wrists without protest.

"Why are you always so quiet?" Blair asked. "Not whistling like you did earlier for the captain?"

Alex said nothing.

"What next?" Morgan asked, placing the tip of his gun against Alex's chest.

"Bring him down to the car."

"Where's that witch and your wife?"

"I don't know, nor do I care. We'll send a dozen cars here for Pruitt and explain how Sarah did it."

"But it was Alex," Morgan protested. "I saw him kill Pruitt."

Alex twisted around. "I didn't shoot anyone—"

Morgan lunged forward and elbowed Alex in the side of the mouth, cutting him off.

"Save it for Lucifer when you get to Hell."

Blair headed toward the stairs. "I'm saying Sarah did it because Alex will have disappeared by the time the investigation starts."

"Oh. Right." Morgan followed, with Alex being pushed along, blood seeping from his mouth.

When they got to the car without interruption, Blair stared over at Sarah's car.

"Wait here," Blair said. "I've got a better idea." He ran to the other car and glanced in the driver's window.

The keys were in the ignition.

"Perfect," he said to himself. "That's exactly what I would've done in case of trouble." He waved for Morgan to bring Alex over.

Blair opened the driver's side door and pulled the small trunk tab.

"Put him in the trunk."

"What are we doing, man? Why can't I just execute him here? We got no witnesses. Your gun is empty. Put it in his hand. Call it a righteous kill."

Blair leaned against the car, the adrenaline leaving his body making him feel weak now. "You have to trust me on this. They won't ever find a body where he's going, or at least for a long time. We use Sarah's car, so there's no DNA in ours."

The look on Alex's face hadn't changed.

"Hey, you okay over there?" Blair asked him. "Are you having a near-death experience? Because you're so close to death, you feeling euphoria or something?"

Morgan shoved the scrawny guy toward the trunk. Alex bumped into the side of the car, then rolled against it to stay upright.

"Get in." Morgan shoved him again.

Alex stared at Blair. "You're making a mistake you'll have to live with for a long time."

"Since it's my decision, asshole, it's my mistake. Let me make it good."

Alex bowed his head to enter the trunk, but Morgan rammed his good shoulder into him, and he dropped into the trunk hard without his hands to break the fall for him.

Morgan holstered his weapon and used both hands to jam Alex's feet inside, then slammed the trunk lid down.

"What now?" Morgan asked.

"I take this car. You follow in yours."

"Where are we going?"

"You know the old pier? By the boat launch that isn't used anymore?"

"Yeah, Pier 14. They built that new one. Now teenagers just park at Pier 14 to make out on weekend nights."

"No one is there during the day. Let's see how long he can hold his breath."

"Are we talking about something permanent?"

Blair nodded. "Permanent." He took a deep breath, his eyes watering. "After what he did to Pruitt? This world isn't big enough for the two of us. He's got to go."

Morgan shrugged. "Are you sure you're not just being nice to him? After what he did to Pruitt, I should fill this trunk with holes."

Blair grabbed Morgan's gun hand. "I can't run the risk that he knows where my stepdaughter is, so we can't kill him too fast. Before he goes for a deep swim, we can question him. Then you do with him whatever you please."

Morgan smacked the trunk twice. "Okay, let's see how this boy swims. But first, give him a chance to talk. Got it. Oh, and I want my cuffs back."

Blair laughed as he dropped into the driver's seat and turned on the car.

Morgan jogged to his vehicle and jumped in, and a moment later, headlights on, he pulled in behind Blair.

Something struck Blair as odd as he turned onto Parkdale to head toward the water.

Morgan had told him to go check on Pruitt. When he returned, he didn't immediately confirm whether Pruitt was alive or dead. Morgan acted as if he already knew Pruitt's fate—but why did Blair have to check on him if he already knew their friend was dead?

And now Morgan was determined to kill Alex for what he did to Pruitt. Yet, Alex tried to deny it twice.

Something wasn't adding up, but Alex was the odd man out no matter how he calculated it.

Sarah must have dropped him off before pulling into the factory parking lot. She set up this ambush from the beginning.

When he was done with Alex, he'd come for Sarah.

Eventually, he'd get his wife and stepdaughter back, and life would return to normal in his city of Hamilton.

Alex was guilty. He could feel it in his bones. No one acted like Alex unless they were guilty of something. The guy barely protested his innocence. And when Morgan jammed the gun in his chest, finger on the trigger, Alex didn't flinch.

He wanted to die. Plain and simple.

And Blair was going to grant that wish.

# Chapter 28

AARON CALLED SARAH'S NAME several times, but still didn't get an answer.

"This looks bad," he said. "I'm scared, man."

"Me too," Parkman said. "We should have found her by now."

They were on the third floor after covering the first and second floors of the factory. Other than pigeons, garbage, and a stained mattress on the third floor, they hadn't found Sarah or Susan.

That cop's body had grown cold by the time they discovered it on the second floor. His ID revealed him to be Inspector James Pruitt of Hamilton Police Service. Parkman handled the ID wallet with the edge of his shirt, careful to avoid leaving prints.

"We need to check on the main floor again."

"Wait." Parkman pointed. "Look!"

Sarah and Susan were standing by a brick wall on the ground floor, staring up at them.

She waved. "Are we clear?"

Sarah had to assume they were because both vehicles were gone now.

"Wait there for us," Aaron shouted as he bounded down the nearest set of stairs.

Parkman followed, doing his best to keep up.

It took a full minute to get to them.

"Where's Alex?" Sarah asked. "Tell me you guys saw him."

Aaron and Parkman exchanged a glance.

"We did," Parkman said. "I'll be honest. Things aren't good."

Aaron recited everything they'd witnessed as succinctly as he could.

"They cuffed Alex and put him in the trunk of *our* car?"

Aaron nodded. "At gunpoint."

"But why would they do that?" Susan asked. "My husband's a good cop. Worked his way up to inspector over the years. He's earned everyone's respect. This doesn't sound like him at all."

"They think he shot and killed Inspector Pruitt."

"Inspector Pruitt?" Susan gasped. "Is he dead?"

Aaron nodded. "I'm afraid so."

She touched Parkman's shoulder, leaning heavily on him. Parkman didn't seem to mind as he wrapped an arm around her.

"I've got you," he whispered.

"Was Alex armed?" Susan asked. "I mean, why kill Pruitt? I've known that inspector for over a decade. He was kind, gentle."

"Susan, Alex didn't kill Pruitt."

"Then who did?"

"We saw Morgan creep up on him and shoot him in the chest. Twice."

She covered her mouth with her hand, her eyes wide. "How did you know it was Morgan? I mean, where did you get that name?"

"Because Pruitt asked what he was doing with the gun aimed at him. Called him Morgan."

"Let me guess what happened next," Sarah said. "That's when Morgan told Susan's husband that Alex killed Inspector Pruitt?"

Aaron and Parkman nodded.

"Before that, though, Morgan shot himself in the arm."

"We couldn't stop them," Parkman said. "They had guns. We didn't. They were trigger-happy, too. Morgan wanted to kill Alex on the spot —"

"Of course, because Alex would speak the truth—"

"Guys!" Susan jumped in. "Wait, wait. Blair told me something about the captain wanting to speak to him. Homicide wanted a word. A dealer was murdered in the park by my house last night." She stared at them all. "Blair said they suspect someone on the force is killing these

654

dealers."

"One case at a time." Parkman ran a hand through his hair. "However, that could probably lead to Morgan. Especially if he can pull the trigger on one of his own so easily."

"Susan, I need you to think." Sarah shook, wrung her hands back and forth, obviously worried about Alex. "Where do you think your husband would take Alex?"

"I have no idea." She had a blank look on her face. "The police station? I mean, other than that, I don't know where cops take their prisoners."

Parkman shook his head. "Alex isn't his prisoner. This won't be routine, by the book. They're taking him somewhere to sweat him. Alex is his captive."

"No," Susan said, shaking her head. "Not my husband. He doesn't cross that line."

Those words were spoken with an ounce of disbelief mixed with conviction. She meant every word, but she wasn't sure if those words were true anymore.

"I thought I heard the word *swim* but disregarded it." Aaron waved a hand as if swatting a fly. "Could that mean something?"

"Maybe." Sarah turned to Susan. "Is there somewhere along the lake where they could take Alex? Somewhere without witnesses?"

She looked up to the left, stared at nothing for a long moment, and then refocused on Sarah, her head shaking slightly.

"I'm sorry. I have no idea. Nothing is coming to mind."

Sarah turned and headed for the side road.

"Hey," Aaron asked. "Where are you going?"

"They will call in about Pruitt. We have a dead cop up there. I don't want to be around when the cavalry arrives. We can think and talk elsewhere."

Aaron nodded and started after her. Halfway across the large lot, he turned to walk backward to face Susan. "Why would your husband leave you here with no car, especially if he didn't trust Sarah?"

Clearly, by her expression, she'd thought of that already.

"No answer?" Aaron asked.

"Aaron," Sarah said. "Her daughter is missing. Let's go easy—"

"Yeah, well," Aaron snapped. "Her husband has Alex now."

"You won't like the answer," Susan said.

Parkman moved closer to her. "You've come to some sort of conclusion?"

She nodded.

Aaron turned around to avoid looking at her. "Tell us what you're thinking."

"My husband is sure that Alex killed one of his cops. Morgan said he saw the murder happen, right?"

Aaron nodded. "He told him that Alex is a cop killer. That's right."

"Precisely."

Sarah glanced over her shoulder. "So, dealing with Alex meant more to him at that moment than making sure you were safe with me?"

Susan eyed her. "That's my guess. The boys on the force don't take kindly to anyone hurting one of their own. I can't imagine how they'll deal with a cop killer."

Parkman's facial muscles were tight as he stared straight ahead. "We have to find them before he does something insane. Alex is no cop killer."

"Call him." Sarah slowed to a stop, gesturing at Susan with her phone. "Call your husband. Tell him what we saw. Warn him about Morgan."

Susan grabbed the phone and dialed, placing it on speaker. Everyone gathered around as the phone rang five times, then went to voicemail. It said the voicemail was full, so she couldn't leave a message.

Susan wiped at her face. "Everyone, the RCMP, his captain, and I have been trying to reach him. He's avoiding a lot of calls. It makes sense. No one can leave a message."

"Keep trying. If he does something to Alex—" Sarah stopped talking to catch her breath. "I won't be able to control what I do to him."

"My husband isn't like that." There was a pleading tone to Susan's voice now. "He may occasionally walk a fine line and even cross it, but he's no murderer."

They got walking again.

"Where are we going?" Susan asked.

"Your place," Sarah said.

"My place?"

"My sister told me the RCMP are there waiting for Blair. We'll speak with the Mounties and try to end this nonsense."

"The Mounties?"

"I suspect they will know where your daughter might be, and they will help us get to Alex."

Susan jogged to keep up. "What makes you think that?"

Sarah lifted one shoulder. "We need help finding Alex. If everything else fails, at least at your house, eventually, your husband will come home. Unless my sister pops in for another visit, that's the best plan I can come up with."

They'd lost Alex again, but this time under worse conditions. Aaron clenched his fists at his sides. If Susan's husband hurt Alex or, worse, killed him, he would have no choice but to make Susan a widow.

They thought Alex was a cop killer, but they were wrong.

Aaron would be the cop killer.

# Chapter 29

ALEX CURLED INTO THE fetal position in the trunk, his mind racing about how to extricate himself from this problem.

They weren't taking him back to the police station. They weren't letting him go. He was expected to swim, which likely meant they intended to drive him to Lake Ontario.

Finding a way to extricate himself from this situation without hurting Susan's husband would be challenging. He'd already damaged their family enough. She was all he had left. And now that they were on the brink of repairing some of the damage, maybe even having a relationship again, he couldn't jeopardize that.

It was crazy how people had to die—like Benjamin—to bring others together.

The decision not to hurt Susan's husband extended to the other guy. Injuring another cop would definitely see him in jail for a while. That Captain Simmons guy wouldn't have sympathy for him twice.

Why would that man claim he shot someone else? All Alex had done was come and see if he needed help. The man was holding his arm and bleeding.

Now, they planned to make him disappear. He couldn't allow that.

So, anything he did to these men to get out of this mess was in self-defense.

They rode on clean pavement for some time, then slowed and turned onto a rougher road. Finally, the car slowed again, moving onto a gravel road.

Throughout the entire ride, he breathed with his mouth as the temperature increased in the darkness of the trunk.

About a minute later, the brakes squeaked briefly as the vehicle stopped. The door opened, the car moved as Blair got out, then the door closed.

Alex detected whispering by the side of the car. His partner in crime had arrived.

Moments later, the trunk popped. He squinted to avoid the sun in his eyes as Morgan lifted the lid.

"Turn around," Morgan said.

Alex stared at them as a wave of cool air made him shiver. He'd been sweating profusely in the trunk. It had been like a sauna on the ride over.

Somewhere nearby, he detected the sound of waves lapping a shoreline.

"You don't want to do this."

Morgan pulled his weapon and aimed it at Alex's throat. "*Don't* tell us what we want, asshole. You killed Pruitt. Cop killers don't live to tell."

"I didn't kill anybody—"

Morgan leaned in and smacked him in the mouth. "Go ahead. Open that mouth again. *Please* open that mouth again." He hovered over him, gun hand raised and ready to strike. "Now, turn around. I want my cuffs back."

Alex glared at Morgan for a long moment, tasting blood in his mouth. He opened his lips to let the blood drip freely, then maneuvered himself to turn around. If Morgan took off the cuffs, that could be good. He needed his hands if he was going to do anything.

The man didn't know how to be gentle. Alex winced twice as the cuffs were torn from his wrists.

He spun back around, massaging his left wrist. Morgan had the weapon aimed at his abdomen.

"We need to end this," Morgan said.

Blair glanced around as if looking for anyone watching them. "Put it away."

"There's no one out here." Morgan appeared ready to fire as he gritted his teeth and leaned closer, his other hand up as a shield to ward off blood and bone.

Alex tensed, ready to act on a second's impulse.

"*Wait!*" Blair said, his voice brokering no argument.

Morgan paused, his finger massaging the trigger. He looked sideways, up at Blair. "Why, man? I pop the guy, then we bury him."

It was time.

Alex shoved the gun's aim away from him by clamping onto the man's wrist. He pulled Morgan's arm up and then yanked it toward him.

Morgan jerked forward when Alex pulled, smashing the side of his face on the open trunk lid. He grunted with the impact.

When his hand squeezed to maintain his grip on the gun, it fired.

At such a close range, Alex's ears rang loudly inside the trunk. The bullet punched a hole in the back of the seat, inches over his left shoulder.

Morgan wrenched his hand out of Alex's grip and jumped back. The men stood outside the trunk arguing about something, but their voices were drowned out by the ringing in his ears—how long he'd be unable to hear worried him. Could the weapon at that range do permanent damage?

Morgan aimed his gun at him again.

Alex squirmed to get away, even swinging one leg over the edge of the trunk, but Blair forced him back inside.

"You will die," Morgan leaned closer to shout at him, mouthing the words as he realized Alex couldn't hear a thing yet.

Blair stared down at him, shaking his head. "We will find my stepdaughter without your confession."

He placed a hand on the trunk lid, gave Alex the finger, spat a gob of saliva at him, and then slammed the lid closed.

Back in the dark, his ears ringing and blood dripping from them, Alex curled up at the side of the trunk in case they wanted to fire their weapons through the lid.

He breathed rapidly, trying to calm his racing heart. That was *so* close—too close.

They didn't end up firing blindly into the trunk of the car.

Instead, the car started rolling. But the engine wasn't on. It moved faster, then tilted downward.

Alex braced for impact.

There was a moment of freefall where his gut rose to his throat, and he pushed into the upper part of the trunk. Then the car hit something soft, the impact minimal, and he dropped to the floor of the trunk.

The lake. The car was in the lake. They wanted him to sink to the bottom.

The vehicle swayed like he was on a boat now.

It didn't take long for the trunk to take on water. It seeped in around the edges.

Alex did what he had to do, closed his eyes, and focused on remaining calm.

He gasped for air at the bitterly cold water circling his right side. Less than a minute later, he was angling for the last air pockets to breathe and take on as much oxygen as possible before completely submerging. Then, he tore up the carpet to access the spare tire. Could the air in the spare be relied upon to breathe underwater?

In less than three minutes, the trunk was full.

Alex floated inside the dark trunk, mouth closed, eyes wide, unable to breathe now. He couldn't hear anything, but his thumping heart beat a rhythm in his inner ear.

The car lowered through the depths of cold water, softly touching the silt on the bottom.

In the final moments before he opened his mouth to breathe, panic overcame him.

# Chapter 30

INSPECTOR BLAIR NELSON DROPPED into the passenger seat of Morgan's car as Morgan got behind the wheel. A wave of exhaustion had enveloped him.

"No one needs to know about this," Morgan said. "Alex shot Pruitt, then disappeared. That's it. That's the end. That's the story. Got it?"

Blair rubbed his arms like he was cold. He just wanted to get the filth of the deed off him somehow. "He didn't get out." Trying to quell the nervous shake in his voice was pointless. "We watched. He didn't get out."

Morgan looked at him. "Of course, he didn't get out. How could he? You left the keys in the ignition. The trunk was locked. The car was under in minutes."

Blair stared at the grass billowing in the wind to the car's right. What had he done? *How* could he have done it? He just killed a man.

Images of Inspector Pruitt's body on the factory floor came to him.

He was a cop first. They protected their own. It was necessary—part of their code.

Was he lying to himself? Trying to justify murder?

There were no takebacks on this one. He would have to live with what he'd done. As long as Morgan kept his mouth shut, they could survive this.

Blair lowered his window slightly and placed his mouth at the opening, unable to breathe inside the car. "We stood there for close to ten minutes." He inhaled deeply, then turned to Morgan. "You saw, right? He didn't come up?"

"Hey, man, don't hyperventilate on me." Morgan started the car. "Let's go back to the factory and call it in."

"He didn't come up for air, right?" Something frantic had entered Blair's voice, and he didn't care.

"No, he didn't come up for air." Morgan glanced at him quickly, turned back to the road, then looked over again. "Dude, get it together. All that happened was that he disappeared. We have no idea where he went. We chased him from the factory. That was it."

"Wait." Blair faced him, twisting in his seat. "Can people hold their breath for more than ten minutes?"

Morgan shook his head, then rubbed the growing red spot on his cheek from where he had hit the trunk lid with his face. "No. That asshole is dead. No doubt in my mind. Free divers are known to do six minutes, some more, but that kid ain't no free diver."

"Is a free diver one of those maniacs who swim in deep water without a breathing apparatus?"

Morgan nodded. "Those are the ones."

Blair stared at Morgan's face. "Is that sore? You know where Alex injured you with the trunk?"

"I don't mind this small reminder from that dead cop killer. He got what was coming to him." Morgan slapped Blair's arm. "But remember, if you want to survive this, that skinny punk did not do this with the trunk."

Blair frowned. "What?" Was he in some zombie state where everything was glazed over with a slice of dread?

Morgan slowed the car at the entrance to the gravel road, then stopped. They were on the same route that took them to the grassy area where they dumped the car.

"Talk to me, man." Morgan rested an arm on Blair's seat. "Are we cool?"

"Like a cucumber."

"You've got to get it together, Inspector Nelson. Alex shot Pruitt, then shot me in the arm, smashed my face into a steel bar, and then ran. We couldn't find him after that. Cool?"

Blair stared at him for a long moment before nodding.

"I need to hear you say it."

"We're cool."

Morgan clucked his tongue. "No, not that. I need to hear you tell me the story. It's too important to fuck up."

"Alex shot Pruitt. He shot you, hit you, then ran. We never found him."

Their eyes locked for a long moment. Morgan nodded. "I'm counting on you, man. If we get through this, the next barbecue is at my place."

"You don't even own a barbecue."

"I'll buy one." Morgan put the car in gear and headed back toward Parkdale, which would take them to the abandoned factory. "When we get to the factory, we call it in."

Blair's phone rang for the hundredth time.

"Didn't you hear it ringing by the water?" Morgan asked.

Blair shook his head as he pulled out the phone. The battery was under twenty percent, which was plenty for another hour or two.

"It's an unknown number."

"Wait until we get to the factory to answer—"

"Hello?" Blair wasn't waiting anymore. He was too tired to wait. The running and the lack of sleep had to stop.

"Inspector Blair Nelson?"

"That's me. Who's this?"

"It's Detective Demetrius Robinson with the RCMP."

Blair shot a worried glance at Morgan. Could they already know about Alex? "How can I help you, Detective?" He'd never worked so hard to sound normal as he did with those few words.

"Well, sir, I'm afraid I've got bad news. Can you come into our regional office to discuss it?"

Blair's frown deepened. "Bad news? No, I can't at the moment. I'm busy working a case." He shot a glance at Morgan. "Just tell me what the bad news is?"

"Sir, this is highly unorthodox—"

"I'll make time to sit and chat with you boys next week." Making sure his voice didn't succumb to his nerves and falter or waver grew easier as a fresh irritation settled over him. "Or tell me what it is you called about right now. I'm a big boy. I can take it."

"Sir, if you insist. But, for the record, this isn't something we'd normally do over the phone."

"I'm listening."

"There was a plane crash in the woods near Dundas last night."

"And? What's that got to do with me? I work Vice. You guys found drugs on the plane?"

"No, nothing like that, Inspector." The man cleared his throat. "The RCMP handles witness protection. A young family of four was being removed from the area as there was suspicion they had been identified as—"

"Wait. What? Family of four?" Something wasn't adding up. Was he talking about the Wagners? They were a family of three. "Why are you telling me about this?"

"Inspector, it was the Wagner family here in Hamilton for the trial this week. I'm afraid they'd been placed in a safe house several blocks from your house. That's an oversight that's still being investigated. We apologize to inform you—"

"Several blocks from my house ..." Blair mumbled, his drowsy mind slowly fitting the pieces together.

"When they extricated the family in a hurry," Robinson continued, "I'm afraid they took a young girl who was in the house with them at the time. There was a birthday party. One of the mothers took a photo of our men sitting out front, watching the house."

"No," Blair whispered. "It can't be." He was talking to himself now as his stomach filled with what felt like chunks of lead, and his eyesight clouded over with tears.

"Hey, man," Morgan said beside him. "What's going on?"

"I'm sorry, Inspector." The caller was still talking. "Investigators at the crash site have done positive IDs on the passengers and the crew. Your stepdaughter, Tracy Nelson, was on that fateful aircraft."

Blair moaned and leaned forward, clutching at his stomach. He jabbed the end call button and handed it to Morgan. "Please," he cried. "Call my wife."

"What happened?" Morgan slowed the car again, then pulled into a short strip mall and parked by a McDonald's, angling the car near the exit to leave quickly if needed. "I'm not calling anyone until you tell me what the fuck just happened."

Blair rocked back and forth in his seat, his arms crossed over his stomach. "I deserve this, I deserve this. Karma, karma, karma—"

Lights flashed briefly throughout his vision as what felt like a wall crashed into the side of his head. It hit him twice, though, because whatever collided with his face on the left shoved him to the right so hard that his head bounced off the car window.

He slumped in his seat, groaning at the pain while rubbing the side of his head. "What the fuck, man?" He peered at Morgan sideways.

"Talk to me," Morgan shouted. The man grabbed Blair's suit jacket and yanked him close to his face. Morgan's breath smelled of stale mushrooms and onions mixed with bile. "What was that call about?"

"Why'd you punch me?" he yelled.

"Because you were babbling, talking about karma and shit." Morgan released Blair's jacket. "What was that call about?"

Blair wiped his face, his jaw producing a dull ache. "The RCMP called—" He hiccupped and gasped for air. "They called to tell me Tracy was killed in a plane crash," he wailed. "She's *dead*, and it's all my fault. My wife's fault, too. She snapped that picture of the security detail in their car watching the witnesses who were under their protection."

"Did you run their vehicle through the system?"

He nodded, slumping lower in his seat, his arms crossed over his gut.

"It's not your fault, man," Morgan said. "Did *you* kidnap her? Did *you* put her on that plane? No, you didn't." Morgan glanced around like they were being watched. "Look, man, talk like that will get us locked up in the slammer."

Morgan produced a gun. He kept it low, aimed at Blair's waist.

"What are you doing?" Blair's voice rose to an embarrassing falsetto.

"I'll pop you now if I think for a second that you'll cry like a baby to the feds. We have a story to keep. That's first and foremost. After that, live your life, grieve Tracy, fuck your wife, I don't care. Just don't *ever* say karma again."

"Okay, okay, man. Lighten up. Give me a break. The RCMP has been trying to reach me all day. I had no idea why. They even went to see the captain. Then he was trying to reach me. Remember what Pruitt said? Put that thing away and call my wife. I'm not the bad guy here."

Surprised he could get all that out, he sobbed against the door, his shoulders hitching with the tears. How could this be happening? Ever since Alex showed up, his life had turned upside down. So, Sarah and Alex had nothing to do with Tracy's disappearance. He would've never seen that coming.

At least that asshole was dead. There was zero chance Alex survived. The entire time they watched the car sink into the depths of Lake Ontario, the trunk remained closed. They studied the area for over ten minutes. Nothing but bubbles from the car rose to the surface. Nothing.

"What's her number?" Morgan was flipping through his phone.

"Hit contacts." Blair hitched in a breath. "She's under the name Nelson."

"Got her. I'll put it on speaker."

The phone rang once, then he heard Susan's voice. "Blair?"

"Honey," he cried.

There was a pause. "Where are you?"

Morgan cut in. "You're on speaker. We are about five minutes away from that factory. I think Blair has something to tell you." Morgan extended the phone closer to Blair's face.

"Wait," Susan said. "I've got something to tell you first. Perhaps it's better to do it on the phone rather than in person."

Blair nodded but didn't trust his voice now.

"Go ahead," Morgan said. "He's listening."

"I don't know where you took Alex Russell, but I hope wherever you went that he's safe." She paused, then added, "Sarah's still here with me. We ran to hide when we heard gunfire. She kept me safe."

Blair and Morgan exchanged a frantic look. What would Morgan do now that there was a witness to them taking Alex from the factory? When they threw Alex in the trunk, wasn't his wife hiding somewhere inside the building—out of sight? How would she know they *took* Alex anywhere?

"Didn't Alex's last name ring a bell?" Susan asked.

"Russell?" Blair murmured. "Russell? What?"

"My maiden name before my first marriage to Tracy's father."

Blair's eyes widened. He sat up straighter. "Wait, what? Were you related?"

Morgan punched him so hard that Blair wondered if he had broken his wrist. He covered the mouthpiece. "Not *were*. It's *are*." He leaned all the way across the seat. "You're not supposed to know he's dead, remember. He just ran away."

Morgan uncovered the mouthpiece as Susan finished saying something.

"Honey, did you hear me?"

"No." Blair rubbed his wrist, wincing at the pain. "Please say it again."

"Alex is my brother. He came by to talk to me because my other brother, Benjamin, was murdered in Toronto. He didn't speak with you last night at the station because he wanted me to tell you about the family connection. When Alex told Captain Simmons he was my brother, your brother-in-law, he ironed everything out and dropped the charges."

Heat rose on Blair's face. He'd go mad. That was all there was to it. He wouldn't make it through the night. He thought his world was upside down before. Now, it just went nuclear. He fought the sudden urge to scream.

"Blair, honey?" Susan's voice rose a pitch. "Are you still there? Where is Alex? Where's my brother, honey?" There was a crying plea in her voice now. "Okay, you said you had something to tell me. Go ahead. I'm listening."

"We'll call you back," Morgan said into the phone, killing the call as Susan shouted something.

They sat in silence for a long minute as Blair sobbed, leaning into the door. "I need to die. Go to Hell to burn. Get it over with. Living with this is worse."

He found tissues in the glove box and wiped his face with them. When he glanced over at Morgan, the man had the gun on him again.

"Go ahead," Blair said. "You'd be doing us both a favor." Blair lay his head back on the seat and closed his eyes. If he died in the next moment, he'd deserve it.

The car shuddered as it got underway. Blair opened his eyes and stared at Morgan as he pulled up to the exit and looked both ways.

The gun was in Morgan's lap, harmlessly aimed at the lower part of the dashboard.

Someone's tires squealed in front of them, drawing Blair's attention to the road.

A large pickup truck raced across two lanes and aimed at them head-on. It stopped inches from their grill as they jerked back in their seats, anticipating impact.

"What the hell!" Morgan shouted, both feet on the brakes and smacking his horn.

More vehicles surrounded them from the back and sides.

Cars roared in from everywhere, completely boxing them in.

"If you're going to shoot anyone, now's the time," Blair said. "This appears to be the end of the road for us."

Morgan was spinning in his seat, looking for a way out. His door wouldn't budge as an unmarked cruiser was shoved up against it.

"Hands where I can see them," someone shouted from behind their car.

Blair raised his hands to the top of the dashboard, but Morgan kept a hand on the weapon in his lap.

"Either use that thing or don't. These boys are serious. You won't need your gun if they don't see your hands soon."

"Hands up," the man outside the car shouted again. "*Hands!*"

Morgan grunted something, then released the weapon and raised his hands over the steering wheel.

"Remember the story." Morgan glanced at him. "Or I'll have you executed on the inside."

"Nothing you say scares me now. I'm already dead." Blair lowered his head. "There's nothing left for me. I killed my wife's daughter and her brother."

Someone was smashing on their windows, trying to break them.

"Just fucking remember the story. If not for your own sake, do it for Pruitt."

Blair lowered his head to stare at his lap and wait to be dragged from the car.

The men outside didn't take long to get to them.

And they were dragged.

# Chapter 31

THEY'D FOUND A TAXI quickly, and the ride was relatively short. When they turned on Maple Avenue, Sarah touched Susan's forearm.

"I need an army surplus store. Is there one local?"

Susan frowned as the taxi slowed in front of her house. "Army surplus? What are you looking for?

Now everyone was staring at her, even the driver.

"I need a Kevlar vest. Where would you recommend I get one in Hamilton?"

"I don't think they sell those things over the counter," the driver said. "What would you need one for, young lady? Gun violence is rare in Hamilton."

Sarah kept her attention on Susan. "I'm running out of time—"

"Out of time?" Susan asked. "For what?"

"My sister told me to do something, and I need a vest. It's not for me. I just need one."

Susan stared off to the side momentarily, then refocused on Sarah. "I think we have one."

"What?" Sarah leaned back. "That would be great."

"A few years back—"

"Guys?" Aaron broke in. "The meter's running. Are we done with the taxi?"

"Oh, right." Sarah cracked open her door. "Let's get inside the house."

Aaron paid for the taxi as everyone got out.

Susan's phone rang when the cab pulled away from the curb. She stopped on the front lawn to stare at the screen.

"It's my husband." She glanced up. "Blair's calling."

"Answer it." Sarah waved a hand at the phone. "We have to find Alex."

"Blair?" There was a pause. "Where are you?"

Sarah listened to Susan's side of the conversation, imagining what her husband was thinking when she told him that Alex was her brother. Wherever they were, whatever they were doing—it would likely stop now. Susan's husband would start damage control. Their daughter was missing, and now he just learned Alex was his brother-in-law. What a day for Inspector Nelson.

Sarah checked the time. It was getting late in the afternoon. Maybe an hour or two was all she had left to get that Kevlar vest to a dealer.

Why she had to do this task was beyond her. Vivian let her think it would end everything.

Wouldn't letting a dealer get shot end everything, so to speak?

"Blair, honey?" Susan's voice rose a pitch, catching Sarah's attention. "Are you still there? Where is Alex? Where's my brother, honey?" She sounded like she was pleading with them for answers. "Okay, you said you had something to tell me. Go ahead. I'm listening."

She blinked twice, then lowered the phone.

"What'd he say?" Sarah asked as Parkman and Aaron moved closer.

"That he'd call me back."

Aaron stared at Sarah, worry creasing his forehead. "If something happened to Alex, something he can't take back ..." Aaron left the rest unsaid.

Susan didn't need to hear that her husband would be found decapitated and dismembered in a ditch one day soon.

"Vest?" Sarah said, snapping Susan out of her reverie.

"Basement." Susan used the one-word response, mimicking Sarah, as she trudged up to her front door.

It sat open.

She turned to frown at Sarah, then went to push the door all the way open, but Parkman had moved in and stayed her hand.

"Let us," he whispered.

Susan nodded, stepping back.

Aaron took the lead. He crouched low, easing the door open slowly.

"*Guys!*" Sarah said loud enough for neighbors five houses away to hear her in their kitchens.

Aaron and Parkman spun around quickly.

Sarah stared as five men converged from either side of the house, weapons in hand. Ten armed men formed a semi-circle around them.

"Police! Let's see those hands."

Everyone raised their arms.

"Step inside," the same man said. "The door's open."

Aaron pushed it all the way, then moved slowly inside, followed by Parkman, who led Susan.

"What's this all about?" Sarah asked, still standing outside. How the hell was she supposed to deliver a Kevlar vest to a dealer now that they were being detained?

"Inside." If a word could be barked, this man achieved it. "Now."

Sarah lowered her hands, turned around, and entered the house.

There were another half a dozen men in suits standing around the living room of Susan's house.

"What's going on here?" Susan asked.

"Ma'am, we'll need you to take a seat." The tall man with a handsome face, whose smile reminded Sarah of Tiger Woods's smile, gestured at the single chair by the window.

Parkman helped Susan into the chair and then stood by her side like a sentinel.

"Why are you in this woman's house?" Parkman asked. "Are you aware that her husband is an inspector with Hamilton Police Service?"

The Tiger Woods look-a-like stood at least six feet two, weighed an easy two hundred and fifty pounds, had thick arms, and looked like the kind of man who could lift the back end of a car.

He nodded at Parkman. Several men flipped open IDs, showing them to Parkman and Susan.

"I'm Detective Demetrius Robinson with the RCMP. We are aware of Inspector Nelson's identity. Our presence here is for multiple reasons, of which we'll get into." He moved to stand directly in front of Susan, the hardwood floor creaking under his weight. "During our investigation, something came up involving your husband."

Aaron stood beside Sarah in the front foyer, their backs to the coat closet. Neither of them had been searched for weapons, nor was there any talk about being detained. Maybe she'd still have time to go to Susan's basement, get the inspector's extra vest Susan said he had, and leave. She had a drug dealer delivery to make.

"What came up involving my husband?" Susan asked, sounding skeptical. Then, "Have you found my daughter?"

Robinson raised a hand, asking for patience. "A drug dealer was murdered earlier today in Montgomery Park."

Parkman glanced over his shoulder at Sarah.

Was she too late? Was that supposed to be the dealer who got the vest?

"We found the victim's cell phone in your bedroom closet upstairs."

Susan frowned. "Here? In my house? Why was it here?"

"Ma'am, there's been a recent development in the murder of a dealer in the park from last year. In addition to that, we have several questions for you."

"For me?" Susan looked up at Parkman for support. "Unless you're here to tell me about my daughter, why would I care about cop business?"

"Guys," Sarah said, stepping forward. "We need help finding our friend, Alex. He was last seen in the trunk of a car driven by Susan's husband. Any chance you can call somebody?"

"We are in the process of apprehending Inspector Blair Nelson at the moment. Please, give us a few moments with Mrs. Nelson."

Robinson took a step back to offer Susan some space. "Mrs. Nelson, why did you take a photo of those two men parked out front of the Baker house yesterday when you dropped your daughter off at the birthday party?"

Susan seemed confused by the question, staring at several of the men crowding her living room.

"This is about a picture I took? Wait, how could you know about that? Did my husband tell you?"

"We know about that because we were protecting the Baker family. When my men ran your license plates after you snapped their photo, we discovered who you were. At the same time, an alert came up that your husband was running our plates." Robinson crossed his arms. "Ma'am, did you know that there's been suspicion for some time that an officer in Vice might be connected to the murders of drug dealers? That your husband has been in court all week, professing to whoever will listen that his men are innocent?"

"Did you say murders, as in plural?" She gasped, a hand wrapping across herself, resting on her clavicle. "There's been more than one?"

"We only connected it recently. Seven across the city have had roughly the same MO, two of which were in Montgomery Park."

Susan's face had gone from a scowl to a grimace as if what she was thinking didn't taste good at all. "And you think my husband has been killing these dealers?"

"Let's take a step backward." Robinson moved to the side to look out at the street as the sun lowered, causing late afternoon dusk.

"Wait," Parkman said. "Should Susan call a lawyer?"

"And you are?"

"Parkman."

"Got a first name?"

"Yes."

They stared at each other for a long moment.

"Are you going to provide it?"

"No."

Robinson moved back to stand in front of the coffee table. "Mrs. Nelson can call a lawyer if she would like, but it isn't necessary as she isn't a suspect. We are merely informing her of why we are in her home." He faced Susan. "May I go on?"

Susan glanced at Parkman, her face softened, and then she turned to Robinson. "Please."

"Due to the suspicion in your husband's department and you taking that photo, your husband's actions came into question. Were you aware that he barged into the Baker house? We had to remove him from the premises forcefully. And, of course, our witnesses needed to be relocated."

"Witnesses?"

"The people in that house were not the Bakers. They were under our protection regarding a case before the courts this week."

"A case before the courts this week? Is it the one my husband has been attending each day?" She scoffed. "That makes sense. It's two of my husband's fellow officers on trial. Those guys are the cops in Vice who allegedly killed the dealers."

Robinson waited for a moment, then shook his head. "I'm afraid not. Fresh evidence came to light recently. Someone else was supposed to be arrested for that crime. We now have proof that evidence was planted. Those officers will be released this coming week."

It looked like Susan had stared at Medusa. Her face hardened to stone, unflinching, unmoving. Then she asked, "Are you saying you are going to charge my husband for those crimes? If so, how do you know that the drug dealer's cell phone in my upstairs closet wasn't planted?"

"Ma'am, I fear we're getting ahead of ourselves."

"Susan," Parkman said, placing a hand on her shoulder. "This sort of thing doesn't fall into their jurisdiction. They're here for another reason."

It was Robinson who turned rock solid now. He glared at Parkman. "I'm afraid you are correct. We are here because of your daughter." He jolted when his phone rang. "Excuse me." Robinson turned away and answered it. He spoke in hushed tones, moving through the dining room closer to the kitchen door, his men separating to give him room.

The urge to leave overcame Sarah. She thought of her own daughter and didn't want to hear what they would say next. But it wasn't just that. Vivian screamed she was running out of time. She had to leave *now*.

Sarah leaned closer to where Susan sat. "Susan, I need to leave. You remember what I mentioned in the car? I have a vest to deliver." She glanced at the RCMP men watching her. "Am I being detained?"

"We would like it if you stuck around here in order to—"

"Am I being detained?"

Robinson stared at her for several heartbeats, the phone still at his ear. He shook his head back and forth rapidly. "He's in custody?" Robinson said into the phone. Then, "Does he know what happened?"

*Know what?* Sarah wondered, although she wasn't sure she wanted to know.

"Susan, you said those old vests were in the basement?" She hoped Susan knew what she was talking about without having to spell it out in front of all these law enforcement officers.

"They're in storage." Susan spoke without looking up at Sarah. "Tell me about my daughter." Susan's eyes hadn't left Robinson, who was just ending his call.

Sarah elbowed Aaron in the side. "I'm heading downstairs, then leaving. Vivian told me I have to go now."

"I'm coming."

Sarah whispered her intentions to Parkman, told him to push to locate Alex, and then shoved her way past the men standing around them. They located the basement door, ran down the stairs, and flicked on the lights.

"Where would he stash something like that?" she asked out loud.

"Over here," Aaron shouted.

He led her to a pile of boxes with months and years written in black marker on the side.

"I don't need tax returns."

"No. Look." Aaron pointed at six large plastic containers that appeared to be stuffed with clothes. He tore open one lid, lifted out the sweaters and track pants, and tossed them on the floor. After going through the first container, he opened the second one.

Someone wailed something upstairs.

They stopped to listen. "Is that Susan?" she asked.

Aaron nodded. "C'mon, we have to find a vest, right?"

They were moving on to the third one when Sarah was struck with the notion that they were looking in the wrong area.

She spun around and spied an old TV stand and cabinet shoved into a corner. Nothing indicated that a Kevlar vest would be hidden there, but she marched over anyway, drawn by psychic magnetism—intuition inspired by Vivian.

When she swung open the drawer, she encountered three vests, one piled on top of the other.

"Found them." She grabbed the thinnest one and ran for the stairs.

Aaron bolted up the stairs, staying close behind her.

At the top, Sarah paused at the sound of Susan crying. However, it was more sobbing and gasping enthusiastically.

"What the hell did they tell her?" she asked no one in particular. Then she turned and jogged toward the back door.

Aaron followed her out into the backyard and over the fence.

When the streetlights came on, they entered Montgomery Park.

It was time to find a drug dealer.

"Point me in the right direction," she said to Vivian.

But her sister was gone.

# Chapter 32

MORGAN SAT IN THE back of the four-door sedan while officers chatted among themselves outside the vehicle. They'd handcuffed Blair and placed him under arrest, stashing him in the back of a police cruiser.

All they told Morgan was that they'd give him a ride to the hospital to get his arm looked at. They hadn't relieved him of his weapon or cuffed him like they did to Blair. Being in the back seat, he didn't catch what the charges were. Did they nail Blair for that dealer's murder?

The burning question on Morgan's mind was: would Blair talk about what they did to Alex?

Without an answer, Morgan had to make a decision. He had money. He could bolt, flee the country. Nothing held him here anymore.

Regrets? Sure, he should have killed Blair when he had the chance. If Blair talked, Morgan would spend the night in holding and probably many more nights behind bars—like maybe the rest of his natural life.

He stared through his window at the figure in the cruiser's back seat, his head down. How could he get to Blair now that the man was in custody?

Blair raised his head. Their eyes met.

Morgan tapped his finger against his lips in the universal *shhh* gesture.

Blair watched him for a moment, then shook his head. Morgan frowned at him as if to say, *What*? Then, more forcefully, Morgan pushed his finger against his lips again and said, "*Shhhh …*"

They stared at each other from across a ten-meter distance before Blair shook his head again, stating emphatically that he would not remain quiet.

"The balls on you," Morgan whispered inside the empty car. "I'll fuckin' kill you."

Blair lowered his head to stare at the floor, their eye contact severed.

As Morgan watched with antipathy brewing in his chest, an idea dawned on him. Once he fleshed it out, his mind was made up. He could manage it. He *had* to manage it. Blair wasn't giving him a choice.

Five minutes later, one of the two RCMP officers in suits dropped into the front passenger seat. He turned around to offer his profile. "Once we're done at the hospital, we need you to come with us to give a statement."

"Hey, man. I just want to thank you guys. Fuckin' Blair was talking shit the whole time."

"It's no problem." The Mountie sat staring forward now.

"How did you guys find us?"

"We got approval to track his cell phone."

He felt heavy, as if something had pushed down on his shoulders, and realized it was fear. A foreign emotion, akin to walking the streets of a foreign city—everything felt off somehow, different, weird.

The fear stemmed from thoughts of being in a cage. No animal should be in a cage, least of all humans.

Morgan would rather be dead than in a cage for decades. He would *never* go to prison—*ever*.

"You tracked his cell phone and were able to mobilize enough vehicles to surround us all within an hour." Morgan clapped twice. "Bravo. You Mounties show us up."

The man in the front seat adjusted the air conditioning. "Well, it was more than an hour, but I get your point. We were going to corner him at a factory off Parkdale, where he seemed to be spending some time. But we were late getting prepared. We monitored his phone going to the lake, then when he left there, we saw you pulled in by this McDonald's."

"Yeah. The lake. That's where our fight started. I pulled over here because I was trying to escape the wacko. He had a gun on me."

The guy spun around to stare at him. "Seriously?"

Morgan nodded, putting everything into his gaze. "I think he went to that factory to meet Inspector Pruitt. When I got there, Pruitt was gone, supposedly. So was Alex."

"Alex?"

"Yeah, his brother-in-law. When I asked where he'd gone, Blair was evasive."

Another man in a suit moved toward the driver's side, then dropped into the car and put it in gear.

"What were you two chatting about?" the new guy asked.

"I was just thanking you boys for stepping up," Morgan said.

The driver twisted in his seat. "Thanking us?"

Morgan stole a glance at the cruiser holding Blair as it left the parking lot. "That guy has lost his mind. I also suspect he's the drug dealer killer." Morgan faced forward, shaking his head. "Two murdered in the park by his house. And now Inspector Pruitt is missing. I fear I'd be dead if you guys didn't show up when you did."

The RCMP men exchanged a glance.

"That's a serious allegation." The passenger stared at his partner.

Morgan nodded to himself. "Blamed his life on his brother-in-law, and now he's missing, too."

The driver got them moving onto Parkdale. "We've got officers at the lake to see why he stopped there for so long. We'll pick up his trail and end whatever rampage he's been on."

"Well, hey"—Morgan tapped the back of the front seat twice—"thanks for getting me away from him."

"No problem." The passenger stared straight ahead.

"Guys, is there any chance we could stop and get some coffee and donuts before we go to your detachment? My blood sugar's a little low."

They shook their heads in unison. "We've got orders to deliver you directly to the hospital, *then* the station. But don't worry. We'll rustle up something sweet while you give your statement."

Morgan leaned back and placed his hand on his weapon. He didn't want to do it, but he would. There was zero chance he would leave whatever building they were taking him to. He may not be a suspect, but once Blair started talking, asserted his alibi, and they found a dead Alex in the lake, he'll be held as a suspect. At a minimum, they'll get him on some accessory charge.

"Look, guys, cut me some slack. I need a coffee—"

"We're not stopping, Inspector Morgan. We've got orders."

He huffed once, reminding himself of when his mother said no to him. "Okay, the truth now. I have to take a piss. Stop at a donut shop. I'll take a piss and buy a few dozen donuts of whatever you guys want. Coffees, too."

No one spoke for a few moments.

Morgan eased his weapon out, then placed it against the back of the front seat, at the center mass of the passenger.

Killing someone meant nothing to him. We're all animals. They do it in the animal kingdom without guilt. Why would humans be different? Because we're self-aware? Fuck that. How will self-awareness help in the afterlife of nothing? There is no afterlife. There's the here and now. Get while the getting's good.

Morgan had always rationalized that if a God existed, he would strive to be a better human. The last thing he would want to do is face the Almighty after the life he'd lived.

But as Nietzsche said, "God is dead." This was it—you get one life, one chance to enjoy yourself. Feeling guilty was a waste of time. *Feeling* was a waste of time.

Killing. Now, that was something Morgan could sink his teeth into, and he had countless times. But he only killed assholes with money. This was why he had the money to head to Thailand, Nepal, or maybe even Andorra, where they had no extradition treaty with the United States.

He could prove beyond a doubt that there was no God by walking through a children's hospital and hearing tiny humans wail in pain. Walk through a war zone like Gaza or Ukraine and sift through the rubble after a missile strike to see a dead child in their pajamas, still holding a teddy bear.

Is there a God? Yeah, right. If so, then life was science fiction. And since it wasn't, he had created his own drama—Play? Thriller? Horror?

—he didn't care. He would do whatever he wanted or needed since there was nothing to live for but the pleasures this current life offered.

And now, it was time to leave Canada for good.

"Guys," he said. "Last chance before I take a piss in your back seat."

The men glanced at each other at a red light on Main Street.

"We'll be there in five minutes," the driver said. "Be a big boy and wait."

He turned onto Main Street.

Morgan pulled the trigger.

He reared back, aimed at the driver, and pulled it again.

Half of the driver's face shot up against the window in a smear of blood, cartilage, and bone.

The car had only gotten to about fifteen kilometers per hour on Main Street. It bumped against the curb twice, then rolled onto it, and stopped abruptly against the bumper of a parked vehicle, its back end still in the road slightly.

Morgan jumped over the seats and relieved the men of their weapons as the passenger moaned. He had a massive exit wound in his abdomen, and blood completely covered his crotch now. The man wouldn't make it to the hospital with that sort of blood loss.

"Should've stopped for donuts, assholes."

Once the weapons were stowed in his jacket, Morgan opened the back door to exit the car, feeling only joy.

Vehicles honked behind them. He slammed the back door shut and waved for drivers to go around them.

Then he jogged down the street to the lights.

He lived seven blocks away.

Once he got home, he would collect all his cash and bolt for the airport. He'd be out of the country by midnight.

Before all that could happen, he needed to see Reggie first. The man had been his personal CI, providing him with information on where the dealers with the most money were always located. Reggie *knew* things that he couldn't leave behind for the ensuing investigation, and Reggie had cash—Morgan wanted all of it.

He pulled out his phone and dialed Reggie's number.

"Hey, man, how's it hangin'?"

"I got no time for small talk." Morgan panted into the phone.

"You runnin' or somethin'?"

"Yeah. Listen, meet me at my house. Half an hour, okay?"

"Aww, man. I just be talkin' to this pretty girl. I'll come later tonight—"

"Come *now*," Morgan said. "Or I'll find a dozen charges to arrest you on."

"Okay, okay, if you put it like that. Fuck man. Chill. I'm on my way."

Morgan tossed his phone into the back of a passing dump truck one minute later.

He was five blocks away from salvation.

It was almost over.

# Chapter 33

SARAH RAN FROM THE baseball diamond to the basketball courts, but couldn't see anyone who resembled what she thought a drug dealer would look like. Yellow police tape was strung up around the crime scene, where two men were still scouring through the grass with flashlights. They steered clear of that section—dealers wouldn't be doing business over there tonight.

Aaron ran alongside her, but they found Montgomery Park was mostly empty except for six guys playing basketball under the park lights and the couple they passed walking their dog.

"We could use some help, Vivian."

They stood with their heads on a swivel, watching all corners of the park, Inspector Blair Nelson's Kevlar vest draped over Sarah's arm.

"What now?" Aaron asked.

"We give this to the dealer. Save a life."

He stared at her. "I know, but what dealer?"

She grinned. "If I knew that, would I be …" She waved off the sarcasm, her grin faltering. "What I am trying to say is, if Vivian wanted me to do this, she needed to tell me more."

Aaron stared at her a moment longer, sizing her up. She felt it in his gaze.

She'd decided to go easier on him. He was trying to make things work, where she hadn't been trying too hard. Maybe if she tried, too, they might find their way back to each other.

Aaron cleared his throat. "If Vivian isn't around, our luck is in limited supply."

Sarah studied him for a moment. "And?"

He gestured at the six guys on the basketball court. "How about I go make some luck?"

"*Make* luck?"

"Watch." Aaron trotted off in the direction of the basketball court.

"This oughta be good." Sarah crossed her arms as she moved toward a tree to lean against it.

Aaron made it to the six men, approached one, and whispered something to him. Sarah couldn't hear the exchange of words, but it looked like the guy told him to get lost.

Aaron asked someone else, but he pulled money out of his pocket this time.

The second guy glanced over at the yellow tape, then back to Aaron.

When he pointed at the street along the park's southern side, Sarah followed the man's finger.

Two men were chatting under the shadows of a bus stop shelter. When they'd seen them before, Sarah had assumed they were waiting for a bus.

She pushed off the tree and started that way, glancing over to see Aaron heading there, too. They'd meet roughly ten meters before the bus stop.

She ran at a slight angle to reach Aaron earlier.

"I need to do this," she said from ten feet away. "Alone."

"What?"

"Hang back. Let me talk to him."

"What if he's armed?"

She sneered at him, then exhaled heavier than she intended. "It's important." Were those two words enough for Aaron? Or did she need to resort to sarcasm and say something snarky or order him to stand back?

Aaron slowed his walking and then stopped. He nodded once. "I'll be listening."

That was easy. See? He's trying.

Sarah walked backward momentarily, spun around, and strode for the bus stop.

The second person was moving away now. This left one man at the stop, mumbling something to himself.

Sarah stepped into the waiting area and took a seat beside him. "I need something."

"Hey, baby girl, everybody need somfin." He spoke with an accent she couldn't place.

Sarah wrapped the vest so the man couldn't see the back, which had POLICE stenciled across it, and laid it on her thighs.

"I need a favor." Without a preamble, she got right to the point. This man's life hung in the balance.

"I ain't in the favor bidness, lady." He studied her. "I know you or somfin?"

Sarah faced him and shook her head. "I don't think so, but what I have to tell you is important."

The man frowned, then slid a few inches along the bench away from her. "What you be talking 'bout?"

"I know something about the man who will call you—"

The man's phone rang. He raised a finger for her to wait and answered it with a scowl of concern at what she said.

"Hey, man, how's it hangin'?" He paused. "You runnin' or somethin'?" Now, he frowned. "Aww, man. I just be talkin' to this pretty girl. I'll come later tonight—" The man stared at her, then hung his head and turned away. "Okay, okay, if you put it like that. Fuck man. Chill, I'm on my way."

He ended the call. "Boss man calls. I gotta run."

Sarah grabbed his arm and stopped him when he got to his feet. "Wait." She got up to stand beside him. "Take this."

The man looked down at the Kevlar. "What's that for?"

She thought the answer to that question was self-evident. "I see things."

He stared at her without expression. "You *see* things? Like what?"

"Your future."

His eyes widened slightly. She might have missed it if she hadn't been staring directly into them.

"My gramma could see things."

She held out the vest.

"That's one of those bullet stoppers, or somfin, right? What sort of things you seein' in my future?" He raised a finger again. "Now, don't freak me out, lady. Just tell me about my future."

"You don't have one."

The air thickened between them.

"Well, shit." He took the proffered vest.

"Wear it now. Under your jacket. Whoever you're going to see doesn't need to know you're wearing this."

The man inspected it, holding it up to the light. "Where'd you get this?" He pointed at the single word stenciled across the back. "I don't want to be charged for theft or nothin'."

"Here, take my cell number." She fished her phone out of her pocket and brought up her contact information. "If anyone gives you trouble—or shoots you—call me. I'll explain everything."

The man nodded and snapped a photo of her contact details page.

A minute later, after introducing himself as Reggie, he was wearing the vest under his jacket.

"I gots to go, lady. I'll call."

She waved at him as he walked backward. "I see you have a future now," she called after him.

He grimaced, then spun around and trudged up the street.

"Well, you did it," Aaron said, stepping out of the shadows.

"I sure wish we knew where he was going."

"You didn't think to ask?"

She shook her head. "He wouldn't tell me anyway."

"How do you know if you didn't ask? The answer is always a *no* until you ask."

"Vivian told me it doesn't matter."

"Oh." He stared at her. "Your sister's back?"

"No."

Sarah turned around and started walking toward Susan's house. "I feel sick."

"Why?"

"We don't know what they did to Alex, and Vivian is extra quiet about it."

"What could they do? I mean, it's Alex we're talking about."

She glanced at him as they exited the park and stepped onto Maple Avenue. "He's an extraordinary man, but he's not Superman."

Aaron nodded. "Yeah, true."

They walked in silence the rest of the way.

# Chapter 34

INSPECTOR MORGAN STRODE UP his street in the dark, keeping to the shadows. Calls were being made about him. Those dead RCMP officers would have been found by now. Responding officers would arrive on the scene where he had left the bodies. He had twenty minutes, perhaps thirty, before a dozen cruisers roared up his front walkway.

That was enough time to grab his stash of cash, take Reggie to his place, grab his money, and then drive Reggie's car to the U.S. Border, about an hour south. After that, he'd buy a plane ticket at the nearest American airport en route to Europe.

By tomorrow, he'd be a free man.

Life would start anew, filled with drinks, good food, and hot women.

Yet, even though he couldn't see a stakeout vehicle on his street, there was a palpable feeling that he was being watched.

If time were a currency, he was nearly broke. He needed to get inside his house. Reggie was usually in the park, which was a fifteen-minute walk. He could be in and out with time to spare.

So, where was the internal trepidation coming from? What made him falter?

He moved slowly from car to car, avoiding the direct streetlights, keeping to the shadows.

Nothing looked suspicious or out of place. As far as he could tell, no one was watching his house.

If law enforcement agents, Mounties, or cops approached him, he'd wait until they were a meter or two away. Then he'd kill them, without doubt, without hesitation. There was no alternative now. This was the only way out. He had determined his new path and was already approaching the point of no return.

That liberating feeling of finally being who he truly was lifted his spirits with a sense of euphoria. He didn't want that feeling to go away. Ending someone's life always gave him a rush, but killing so many people within the last twenty-four hours, three of them in law enforcement, gave him a rush that would compete with some of the best illicit drugs on the market—and he still wasn't done with the killing! Reggie's heart would stop beating within the hour, along with anyone who got in his way.

Without waiting a moment longer, his hand on the butt of his weapon, Morgan trotted up his walkway, inserted the key in the front door, spun the handle, and burst inside, closing the door behind him.

He scanned the street through the door's peephole without turning on the interior lights. No one exited a car; no one rushed the door. The sidewalk remained empty, the street vacant.

He leaned against the door and stared down the dark hallway. Streetlights out front shone through the windows to give him enough light to see where the furniture was—plenty of light to navigate.

This was a rental with a year still on the contract. The furniture was bought used. Worn-out lounge chairs that he'd worn out further. Leaving it all behind to be discarded by the landlord didn't bother him. Well, except for his photo album from when he was a kid. After he buried his parents, he kept that album.

Morgan shrugged. Maybe he'd pack it. Maybe he wouldn't.

His hand moved to the light switch, then stopped. Lights meant someone was home. It meant someone could see his movements from outside the house.

When the authorities arrived, he figured it would be better if they encountered a dark house. That would give him a fighting chance to get lost before they broke in.

But that was a big *if* they got there before he left.

Morgan pushed off the door and ran for the stairs, but stopped suddenly when he heard a thump above him.

*What the fuck was that?*

He stood on the second stair, gazing into the darkness on the next landing, contemplating what he heard as sweat beaded on his forehead.

With his back to the wall, he scanned the main floor hallway and the little he could see of the living room. The silhouette of the big screen TV was different somehow, but he couldn't quite place why.

Could someone be in the house? What a time to get robbed. They could move a truck up and empty the place for all he cared. Just let him grab his cash first, and then he'd be gone.

When he looked back up the stairs, trying to keep his heart from leaping into his throat, he went through the details of how someone could've gotten inside. The front door was locked. He hadn't noticed any broken windows.

By itself, that didn't mean someone *wasn't* inside the house. He'd been to enough crime scenes to know better.

Did they gain access using a back window? The basement?

Morgan eased his service pistol from its holster, checked quietly that one was in the chamber, and then gazed upstairs again.

There had been no more sounds while he stood on the second stair. Nothing from inside or outside the house—not even a car going by on the road.

He moved onto the third step, then the fourth, being mindful to place his foot near the wall because the fourth step squeaked.

Then he paused and listened.

Nothing.

He exhaled long and hard, unaware that he had mainly been holding his breath.

"Hello?" His voice echoed throughout the house, surprisingly giving him goosebumps. A cool sweat had broken out around his collar and armpits, too.

He shook it off and climbed several more stairs, the gun held out in front of him.

From somewhere at the back of the house, in the darkened area of the master bedroom, a floorboard creaked.

He stopped moving, stopped breathing, tightened his lips together to suppress any sound of surprise escaping them, and listened. The house seemed preternaturally silent, like he'd entered a soundproof room with foam walls.

Someone was in the house. He felt it, knew it. There was no debate now.

Gravity might have won when it came to a bottle of cologne or a hairbrush placed precariously on a dresser or countertop, making it fall at the most inopportune time. But that creak on the old wooden floor needed body weight.

But who was it? What was their purpose? Why the second floor in the dark?

It couldn't be cops. They would've identified themselves by now.

His racing heart forced him to breathe, but he did it with his mouth open to keep from making a sound.

Why hadn't he turned on any of the lights? Looking back, that made no sense now.

How long had he been on the stairs? How fast could he deal with the intruder and still get his shit and get out of town?

*Time's a-wasting.*

Reggie would be there at any moment.

He lacked the patience to deal with this shit. This wasn't the time.

Anger rising, quelling the unease coursing through him, he moved up the remaining stairs in the dark and stepped into the hallway facing the back bedroom, a scream hovering in his throat.

Pistol aimed forward, his arms shaking with adrenaline, he moved a few feet to the light switch and flicked it upward.

Nothing happened.

He frowned in the dark, flicking the switch up and down.

The power was out.

That made complete sense. When he'd looked into the living room while standing on the second stair, he hadn't seen the red light on the bottom corner of the TV or any lights from the power bar. Now he knew why it looked different.

The fuse box was in the basement, which is the likely area where his intruder entered the building.

So, whoever was up here didn't want to be seen.

Ten minutes. That's all he wanted to spend in the house.

What a colossal waste of time this had turned out to be.

"Hello?" he called again, without the goosebumps accompaniment. "Hamilton Police," he added. "You broke into the wrong house, asshole."

He moved toward the back bedroom. It was a mass of darkness, completely without light. The windows had shutters, and the curtains were pulled for when he worked night shifts and wanted to sleep well past sunrise.

Living here was over. Caring about the condition of the house had ended.

Killing his way to the U.S. Border was all he could think about, so he pushed the gun past the threshold of the bedroom door and randomly fired five times, hoping to hit something.

The sound in the enclosed space was deafening, contrasting with the absolute silence from moments before.

He fished out his phone and snapped on the flashlight option, then held it up to the interior of the bedroom to see who he hit.

The room was empty.

Morgan frowned. Could he be hearing things? Was the house settling or just getting old?

When he moved to turn around, something was behind him.

And it came quickly. There wasn't even time to react.

Whatever it was plowed into him so hard and fast that he lifted off the floor and flew into the side of the dresser.

His head bounced off the wooden top, snapping something somewhere inside his neck.

A prolonged moan escaped him as he lost consciousness.

# Chapter 35

SARAH AND AARON RETURNED to Susan's house as the authorities were escorting her to a waiting police car.

Parkman stood speaking with two men in suits. That large detective, Robinson something, was nowhere in sight.

Sarah moved closer to Parkman and waited for him to notice they were back. Aaron stayed by the sidewalk, his eyes on the police car pulling away from the curb with Susan in it.

"Sarah?" Parkman called, stepping toward her. "They've arrested Blair, Susan's husband."

"What about Alex?" She clutched onto his arm, a sick feeling in her stomach. "Was he with him?"

Parkman shook his head, staring into her eyes. He placed his hands on her upper arms. "We haven't heard anything about Alex yet."

"Tell me they've at least *asked* Blair where he took Alex?"

"They have Blair in holding now. The questions are about to start. We should be there, so we're all heading to the station." Parkman moved with the two suits toward a waiting unmarked cruiser. "You coming?"

Sarah waved Aaron over. "We're going to the police station."

"Sarah," Aaron said, catching up to her. "You know how you hate hospitals?"

She glanced his way. "Yeah."

"I feel the same about police stations. They're not good for me."

Sarah grabbed the top of the car's back door. "Why?"

"We never know if we'll leave."

"I understand, but it isn't about us this time. We're guests. We aren't there to be questioned. They have Blair in holding. He'll lead us to Alex."

He nodded once and got in behind her. Sarah sat between Parkman and Aaron.

Aaron leaned closer once they got moving. "I feel the same about being in the back of a police car," he whispered.

She bumped him with her shoulder. "I don't like it, either, but Blair took our car. We're car-less for now."

He sat up straighter. "True."

The ride was short, and once at the police station, they learned Susan was already inside. They were told to wait in an ugly room with metal chairs.

"This is great." Sarah dropped onto a chair and stared at the ceiling. "They have Susan and her husband, but no one's telling us about Alex." She grabbed her hair. "I'm going to lose my mind with worry."

A door popped open, and the detective from Susan's house stuck his head out.

"Come this way." Robinson gestured at them. "All three of you."

They followed him to a larger room with a chalkboard and about twenty chairs. Sarah counted three men in suits and two uniformed officers. The suits were in front of Susan and her husband. The uniforms were behind Blair, flanking him.

From Sarah's angle, Blair Nelson's arms appeared to be secured behind his back.

Detective Robinson made the introductions quickly, and everyone took a seat.

Susan had been crying, her eyes swollen and puffy now.

Blair's expression remained stoic.

Had they found their daughter? Is that what this was about?

Or did they bring them in here to tell them Alex was dead?

Robinson turned to Sarah and Aaron. "Susan asked that you be part of this debriefing as it affects you three." He turned to where Parkman was sitting.

Sarah nodded and turned her gaze on Blair. She jabbed a thumb toward Aaron and Parkman. "They saw you leave that warehouse with Alex." She leaned forward as he turned to face her. "Where is he?"

Robinson raised a hand, palm facing her. "We'll get to that in due time."

"No," Blair said. "She deserves an answer."

"But we don't have an answer to give her yet." Robinson's tone was firm. He didn't want Blair to respond.

Blair kept talking anyway, his eyes on Sarah. "Inspector Morgan tricked me from the beginning. He lied to me. Convinced me of things that weren't true."

"Just tell me where Alex is."

Susan's sobs turned to weeping.

Robinson sighed.

"We left him in the lake."

Sarah sat back in her chair and crossed her arms. "*In* the lake? He can swim."

"He was in the trunk of your car. The trunk remained locked."

Sarah gasped, her arms unfolding. "The car—" She swallowed. "Is in the lake?"

Blair eyed her for a long moment, then nodded. "I'm sorry. Alex is dead."

Sarah jumped so fast that her chair shot backward. Before anyone could grab her, she dove at Blair like she was trying to steal home plate.

Her arms wrapped around his neck as she sailed past him, and they tumbled sideways as the room lit up in a cacophony of shouts and screams.

# Chapter 36

MORGAN FLOATED BACK TO consciousness as if underwater on his back and staring up at the shimmering surface. He blinked, rolled his head, closed his eyes, then moaned.

Where was he? What had he been doing?

He opened his eyes. It was dark. Had he fallen asleep on the floor?

The pain reminded him that he hadn't. He was in his house—his *dark* house. Someone had cut the power. They'd fooled him into thinking they were in the bedroom.

He felt around him, but the gun was gone. A sour feeling coursed through his abdomen. Would they shoot him now?

A quick search of the two guns he stole from the Mounties produced one of them, still tucked in the back of his pants.

Pushing up from the floor took effort. How long was he out? Could Reggie have come and gone? When would the police be here?

He needed to grab his money and run. Prison didn't fare well for cops. Locked in a cage—he hated the thought.

On his feet now, wavering slightly, he leaned against the wall, pulled out his last gun, and moved into the hallway.

What the hell had hit him? It was like it came out of nowhere with such incredible speed.

Anyway, it didn't matter now.

He moved along the hall and entered the bathroom, where he knelt, using the counter for support. He opened the cabinet under the sink and swung his arm to remove all the bathroom cleaners and extra bottles of shaving cream. They piled out onto the floor around him. With one firm flick, he unlocked the left side of the cabinet's base, then did the same with the right. The bottom of the bathroom cabinet lifted out of place to reveal several hundred thousand dollars, neatly stacked in five-thousand-dollar bundles.

A bag.

He needed a bag.

"Shit," he mumbled as he got back to his feet and moved to the hallway linen closet. He kept a large black duffel bag in there in the event of an emergency—like today.

Keeping a watch over his shoulder, the gun still in hand, holding the edge of the bag, he stuffed the duffel with the cash, left everything else where it was strewn across the floor, and headed for the staircase.

Before he touched the first stair, there was movement behind him.

When he spun around to see what it was, the weight of something crashing into him forced him downward.

The stairs were unforgiving as he toppled head over foot to the bottom, ending up in a heap in the foyer.

He stretched his arms and legs through the pain, hoping nothing had broken, and angled his head to look up the stairs. Above him, nothing but darkness could be seen.

*The bag. The cash. The gun.*

He tried to right himself, but lights flashed in his vision when something whacked the side of his head, making him spin around and land on his back.

A deep moan escaped him as he blinked at the foyer chandelier above him.

Whoever gained entry to his house had just kicked him in the face. But from where? How are they moving around?

"What the fuck, man?" He groaned the words.

The doorbell rang.

Reggie was here. Reggie was always armed, just in case someone tried to rob him.

"Door's open," Morgan called from the floor, feeling around for the gun he'd dropped.

Reggie said something from the other side of the door, but it was unclear.

Morgan sat up slowly and looked around. The hallway was empty. Even his black duffel bag was gone.

"No, no, *no*!" Each word rose in crescendo as he spoke them.

Reggie was saying something again.

"Come in!" Morgan shouted as his hand found the gun.

The door opened, and Morgan swung the gun around to aim at the door.

"Oh, it's you," he said, lowering the weapon. "Get your gun out."

"Why?" Reggie asked, already reaching for it.

"Someone's in the house. They shoved me down the stairs and stole my duffel bag. I need it back."

"You called me to help with an intruder, man? You da poh-lice. You ain't need my help."

"Just shoot the fucker when you see him."

"What's he look like?"

"Don't know."

"What?"

"I *don't* know. Haven't seen him yet. He's like a fuckin' ghost."

Reggie backed up to the doorframe. "Whoa, I ain't doing ghost shit."

"Get in here." Morgan raised his voice and immediately regretted it, wincing with the pain in his head.

Reggie tapped his chest. "Damn, that girl was onto somfin here. She a psychic bitch—"

"Shut up," Morgan said in a forced whisper. "Listen for the asshole. He's still in here." He turned slowly, feeling the pain in his thigh and in his ribs where one might be cracked.

He moved toward the kitchen, then stopped. When he turned back around, Reggie had the front door wide open now as if he wanted to make a run for it, the gun in his hand aimed at Morgan.

"Can you please aim that elsewhere, dickstain?"

"Oh, right. Yup." Reggie moved the gun to aim at the wall.

Morgan studied the area. The only place the intruder could've gotten to quickly was in the main living room. He would've heard their footsteps if the asshole had run for the kitchen.

The entrance to the living room stood between him and Reggie now.

He motioned for Reggie's attention.

"What?" Reggie asked out loud.

Morgan scowled and shoved a finger to his lips. He gestured at himself, and then he pointed at the living room. He raised his weapon and pointed at it.

Reggie nodded, understanding that Morgan was about to jump into the living room and attempt to surprise whoever was hiding there.

Morgan took a step forward, then another.

A soft thump, like someone bumping a knee against the sofa, came from the other side of the opening to the living room. Then something large and black sailed out of the living room, coming right at Morgan's face.

His weapon tracked the item by reflex, firing blindly at it.

Something punched him in the shoulder, then again in the stomach.

It seemed like weapons were firing everywhere.

He lowered to his knees, gasping for air. What the hell had just happened?

The black duffel bag sat at the bottom of the stairs.

Whoever was in his living room had thrown the empty bag at him.

*Empty? Where was the cash?*

When he stared straight ahead, he saw Reggie on the front porch, clutching at his chest.

*Shit, I shot Reggie.*

He glanced down to see why breathing was so hard as he leaned against the wall.

There were several new holes in his body now. One on his left shoulder and one above his stomach. He touched one as the pain wasn't too intense yet. Blood poured from it like a small spigot was left on.

"What now?" he gasped, and blood dripped from his mouth.

"You shot me, man," Reggie said, pushing himself up. "That woman from the park was smart, man, but it hurts somfin awful."

*What woman was he babbling on about?* Morgan's strength ebbed from his body in waves. He tilted forward and fell to the floor on his face.

"Oh shit, I shot you, man." Reggie dropped the gun like it was hot. "I shot a cop." Those last words were spoken with disbelief.

Morgan caught all this because his eyes were still open.

Breathing was becoming a problem. He tried to cough, but the pain increased tenfold.

Sirens wailed in the distance—multiple sirens.

He was done for. They caught him. He'd made a misstep somewhere along the way.

He blinked, his eyes heavy, but he didn't miss the movement like a shadow slipping past him.

Reggie was getting to his feet, wincing. Now he was taking off his shirt.

Morgan wanted to ask him what the hell he was doing, but didn't have the strength.

When Reggie turned around, Morgan saw the Kevlar vest.

*You motherfucker. I should've killed you.*

Reggie undid the Velcro straps, slipped the vest over his head, and then dropped it beside Morgan. He grabbed his shirt and turned back to Morgan.

"Sorry, man. But you shot me, too. And it hurts my ribs somfin awful."

Reggie stepped out of sight and was gone.

Morgan closed his eyes as the sirens neared.

Something moved in the house again.

Morgan forced his eyes open. Unable to move, unable to fight back, he watched the intruder jam his cash back into the duffel bag. The man got to his feet, looked at Morgan, and ran toward the rear of the house.

Cars screeched to a stop out front, their flashing red and blue lights bouncing off the dark interior of Morgan's house.

The look of shock and surprise at who had bested him remained on his face when his heart stopped.

He had time to hear a cop pound up the front steps.

But then the power went out inside him.

Never to be turned on again.

# Chapter 37

THEY PRIED SARAH OFF Blair before she could choke the life out of him, with Robinson physically lifting her over his head and setting her in a chair by the wall.

"Stay," he shouted. "Or I'll cuff you and place you in holding." He was panting with the effort of detaching her from Blair's neck. "This is 2024—we don't exercise frontier justice anymore." Robinson turned back to Inspector Nelson and his wife, Susan. "Do you want Sarah removed?"

Susan shook her head. "No. She needs to be here for this."

Robinson faced Sarah. "See? Even after you attacked her husband, she wants you to stay."

Sarah eyed him, the large man that he was, knowing he was right yet still wanting to break several of Blair's bones.

Pain made her angry, and grief was a form of pain, making her seethe with rage.

Robinson's phone rang. He raised a finger near Sarah, tempting her to break it off. "Will you stay?"

On the third ring, she hadn't answered. Her lips were tight, her hands on her thighs, as she contemplated getting to Blair around Robinson.

Aaron moved behind her and placed his hands on her shoulders. "She'll stay."

Robinson answered his phone on the fifth ring. "What?" He stared at his men, then moved his gaze to the floor as he listened. "A what?" Then he faced Blair. "Seriously? Police-issued?" A moment later,

Robinson nodded and hung up.

"Everyone, your attention, please." Robinson paused, then stared at Blair. "Inspector Morgan is dead."

*Finally, some good news*, Sarah thought as she allowed Aaron's hands to pull her back into the chair.

The look on Blair's face wasn't relief.

Robinson continued. "And they found Inspector Pruitt's body at that factory."

"We can testify to that," Parkman said. "Aaron and I witnessed Morgan shoot Pruitt in the chest. It wasn't Blair."

Robinson snapped his head in Parkman's direction. "You *saw* that?"

Parkman nodded. "I thought you knew. We were all at the factory. We were going with Alex to introduce him to his brother-in-law." He gestured at Blair.

"How is Morgan dead?" Blair asked, his voice raspy after being choked by Sarah.

"Shot in the front foyer of his house."

"By who?" Sarah asked.

Robinson lifted his thick shoulders. "Whoever it was wore a police-issued Kevlar vest. They left it on the stoop."

"Sarah?" Susan said. "Is that the one you borrowed from my basement?"

Everyone in the room stared at Sarah.

Aaron raised his hands. "Hey, we didn't shoot Morgan. We went to the park and handed that vest to a dealer—to someone who never gave us his name."

Robinson raised his hands as he frowned at what Aaron had just said. "Okay, everyone. Let's start at the beginning." He stared at Blair. "What was your interest in the Bakers on Weir Street?"

He shrugged. "Seems trivial now."

"Tell us anyway."

He cleared his throat and raised his head to look at Robinson. "I understood they had evidence that would put two good cops away for a long time. I didn't believe it. That's why I was in court all week. I wanted to see this evidence for myself. It became an obsession. I let it slip that I wanted the witnesses located before court." He closed his eyes, then stared at Robinson. "It was all talk. Just jabbering amongst the boys." He nodded at Susan. "When my wife sent that photo of your boys parked in front of the Weir Street house, I ran their plate because she'd left Tracy at a birthday party there. That was it."

"So you thought a little witness tampering would help those officers on trial? Perhaps some intimidation of the witnesses, too?"

Blair shook his head and looked at the floor. "I said shit about how I wanted to see the evidence, that I didn't believe it. Would I act on what I said? No. Would I step in and speak to them beforehand?" He scanned the faces in the room. "Never."

"Yet, your wife snapped their picture when they were watching the house." He pointed at two men in suits who leaned against the wall.

Susan wiped her eyes, then lowered the tissue. "Wouldn't you?" she asked him. "I was dropping my daughter off at a place where I hadn't met the parents. When I saw two men out front, I just thought my husband would reassure me that I could leave my daughter there."

"Well, that's what started this whole mess." Robinson began pacing. "Once we saw Hamilton Police Service running the plate and heard rumors that Vice wanted to speak to the Wagners, we set up an extraction order. We worked on getting them out of that house and sending all the kids home. Then we took the family of three and your daughter to another safe house. Neither of you was there in time to pick up Tracy, and we couldn't wait."

"I was late getting there." Susan rubbed the tops of her thighs. "And now you're bringing her home, right? To me?"

Blair jerked his head toward her, his eyes filling with tears.

Sarah felt something in the room change.

Robinson stopped pacing to stare at Susan. "Yes. She will be here within the hour."

Blair's head shot up to stare at Robinson. "What? She's not dead."

Susan glared at him. "How could you say such a thing?"

His handcuffs rattled behind him. "Because the Mounties called me and said she died in a plane crash."

"Inspector Nelson," Robinson said. "You had gone rogue. We tried everything to bring you in and show you the evidence we had against you and Inspector Morgan. When we figured out you were together in Morgan's car, it was decided that a drastic measure was the only thing effective enough to separate you and get you to come in. We had the captain tell all his men to *bring you in* and even had him call Morgan, lying about how he was worried about you, that he wanted you at the station."

"I remember when Morgan took that call as we pulled up to the factory." Blair blinked away sweat from his eyes.

Sarah leaned forward, but Aaron held her back, pressing on her shoulders. "You guys told him his daughter was dead? That was your version of a *drastic measure*?"

"It worked, didn't it?" Robinson got pacing again. "Once Susan called him to explain that Alex was her brother, Blair was distraught. He had Morgan pull over in that strip mall, and we were able to mobilize a response from Morgan's cell phone."

"Don't *ever* imagine for a moment you can call me or any other mother and use those kinds of *drastic measures*. I'd kill someone for less."

"Sarah," Aaron whispered, a cautionary tone to his voice.

"So," Sarah went on, ignoring Aaron. "How is it that Morgan was at home and not in here? Why wasn't he in custody?"

Robinson turned to Sarah. "That's an error on our part. A grave error." He shuddered when he exhaled. "One we will have to live with."

"How so?" She leaned back, and the pressure from Aaron's hands eased on her shoulders. "Some of us aren't following."

"We thought Inspector Nelson here was killing drug dealers around town, with two murdered in the park close to his home, where he lived with his twelve-year-old stepdaughter. We even found the victim's cell phone in Blair's house. Nothing pointed to Morgan, so two of my men were driving him to the hospital to patch up a bullet wound. Those men are dead now."

The room descended into silence for a moment.

Blair shook his head, then whispered, "Why would I keep incriminating evidence like a victim's cell phone in my house?"

"We're assuming Morgan planted that."

Blair nodded. "Morgan told me Homicide called him and that they found the phone in my place." Blair shook his head. "We checked. No one from Homicide called Morgan. He knew it was there, so he planted it."

Parkman nodded. "That adds up."

As if they were watching a play, the law enforcement men against the wall stood like sentinels, taking it all in. Sarah saw no emotion on their faces at losing two of their men today. That would come later. The funeral would be huge.

"When I rushed home to meet Susan," Blair continued, nodding at Sarah, "you guys had already left, but the front door was unlocked. Because Morgan had just been there."

Robinson jumped in. "By then, we suspect Morgan figured we were already onto him."

Blair nodded. "Morgan lied to me again when he said something like, 'someone is trying to paint a picture of me as an accessory.'" Blair shook his head. "I wasn't an accessory. If anyone was painting anything, it was him that entire time. At the factory, he claimed his gun jammed. I gave him mine, and he shot Pruitt with it." Blair looked at Detective Robinson. "Ballistics will show that it was my weapon that shot Pruitt, but it wasn't me. That asshole was setting me up from the beginning. Even that note about the kill being for me, which was found on the victim in the park, was another one of his ways to connect me to the murders."

Parkman flicked his toothpick from one side to the other. "It wasn't Blair." He repeated. "Morgan shot Pruitt."

Aaron nodded. "We saw it."

"As you already said." Robinson moved over to a chair and dropped into it. "During all this shit, we had an information glitch. We were still looking at you, Blair, because of your focus on the Baker house. We were so blinded by you that we didn't see Morgan's role in any of this until the very end." He stared into empty space. "And now we've lost two good men." Robinson turned to Sarah with saddened eyes. "Two of our men, good Mounties, were told to drive him to the hospital, then bring him in to give his statement. He shot one in the back and one in the face. He stole their weapons and left the car on the side of Main Street for Joe Public to find, like they were human garbage. We sent officers to his house. That's who just called. Someone beat Morgan up and shot him. Then left a Kevlar vest on the front porch."

Sarah leaned forward again, but Aaron didn't try to stop her. "Beat him up?"

Robinson nodded.

Sarah thought back to the dealer she met in the park. She gave him a vest. He took a call from someone who told him to come over immediately. The man put the vest on as per instructions. Then they parted company. In her opinion, that man couldn't beat up Morgan unless he shot him first.

The door to the room burst open. Everyone looked over as a young girl ran into the room.

"*Mommy!*"

Susan launched out of the chair and wrapped her arms around her daughter. "Oh, honey," she cried. "I missed you."

It made Sarah miss her daughter. At least Willow was safe with Daniel in Toronto, far away from all this carnage.

Blair cried now. Tears rolled off his cheeks, likely relieved she was alive after being told Tracy was dead.

Sarah got up and moved to the side to stand with Parkman. Aaron followed her over. "We need to find Alex," she whispered.

No one added *if he's still alive.*

Detective Robinson directed Susan and her daughter to leave the room so they could be alone and talk. When the teenager was leaving, she asked about Blair and why he was tied to the chair, and then they were out of earshot.

Before they started talking about anything else, Sarah asked, "What about Alex? I need to know where he is."

Blair's mouth opened, but he remained silent when Robinson raised a finger. "We pinged Morgan's cell phone to several locations. One of them was near the water. I had officers attend the location, but they were off by fifty meters. They found nothing."

"Where is this place?" Sarah moved closer to the door. "We'll go look around."

Robinson continued as if she hadn't spoken. "Once Blair was in custody, we asked about the location at the water. Why did they go there?" Robinson glanced at Blair, then back to Sarah. "He told us the exact spot. We now have a team on-site working on getting access to the submerged car. By the morning, we will have it lifted out of the water."

The two uniformed officers flanking Blair moved in front to protect him if Sarah went after him again.

She struggled to find her voice, her lips quivering. Aaron grabbed a chair to hold himself up.

"Is that where you buried my Alex?" Sarah asked.

"He was in the trunk," Blair whispered. "I'm so sorry. I thought he was a cop killer. Morgan told me he shot Pruitt without regard."

"So you *murdered* him?" A dizzy spell hit her as her blood pressure shot up. Her legs had weakened, and her resolve cracked.

Alex was dead. There was no coming back from that.

"He was in the trunk." Blair was talking. "We watched for more than ten minutes. He didn't surface."

Aaron's shoulders hitched. Sarah sought a chair to collapse into. When she turned away from Blair, unable to look at him any longer, she watched Parkman's face. His toothpick had fallen to the floor, and he hadn't replaced it. The man's face had reddened, and a vein throbbed in his neck.

How would they survive this? Alex was their backbone, their secret weapon. But most of all, he was their family.

This was all her fault.

Vivian had warned her. She'd said Sarah had to do something specific, or Alex would die. She hadn't known that particular thing, so she hadn't done it.

And now Alex was dead.

She would quit. She would tell her sister she was done. No more lives would be lost because of her. Sure, Alex had come on his own to Hamilton, but they were there trying to help him.

Yet, they were too late.

The door opened, and a uniformed officer stuck his head in. "Apologies for interrupting, but is Sarah Roberts here?"

Sarah raised her head and wiped at the tears that had fallen and wouldn't seem to stop. "I'm—" She choked on the word. "I'm Sarah."

The officer stared at her. "Someone's here to see you."

She looked around for a tissue but couldn't find one. "Did they give a name?"

"He said Daniel and that you would know him." The officer backed out and held the door open for her.

Aaron nodded, telling her in his own way that she should go. When this was done, they would all leave.

It was over.

Vivian was over.

Sarah didn't have to be psychic to know she could never handle the grief of losing Alex. This was one of those things that would never mend, never be reconciled.

She got to her feet, wavered, and then stepped toward the open door.

Someone was crying to her right. Before exiting the room, she looked over to see Blair weeping. That bastard had done this, and now he was *upset*? He wasn't grieving Alex's loss. The selfish prick was mourning the loss of his future as he'd be charged with murder and sentenced to life in prison. His liberties were over.

"Sarah." There was a warning in Robinson's voice as she stared at Blair. It was enough to make her snap out of it and turn to follow the uniformed officer out to the front area to meet Daniel.

Her mind turned to Daniel and what he might be doing in Hamilton. Did he bring Willow? Why come without messaging or calling them first?

As she emerged into the front waiting area and saw the hooded figure standing by the door, she wondered how Daniel knew to come to the police station to find them.

"Daniel?" she asked, walking up to the man.

He seemed too small to be Daniel. His stature was different.

She paused her step, unable to identify the man from the way he stood, with his back to her, a hood covering his features.

When he turned around and met her gaze, Sarah screamed.

# Chapter 38

THE DOOR IN THE waiting area banged open behind her as Sarah hugged him.

"Hey," Aaron shouted, running up to her. "What's going on?"

Sarah wept in his arms, locking them tight around him, unwilling to let go.

Hands pulled at her. Then someone tore the man's hoodie back.

Aaron gasped, and Parkman let out a short yip.

"Hey, guys," Alex said, easing out of Sarah's arms as she cried, clinging to his sleeve.

"How?" Aaron asked, his voice raised in alarm and surprise. "Just. *What?*"

"Guys," Robinson said from behind them. "You want to bring it in here?"

Parkman nodded and ushered them all inside, Sarah still holding Alex's sleeve fiercely. Like if she let go, he'd float away.

Once they were all seated, with everyone holding Alex as if he'd disappear again and Blair staring like he'd seen a ghost, Detective Robinson clapped his hands once to get everyone's attention.

"And you are?"

"My name is Alex Russell. I'm Susan's brother." He nodded once at Blair. "I'm his brother-in-law."

"We were told you were in the car—scratch that, in the trunk—when someone drove the vehicle into the water." Robinson stared at him. "Is that true?"

Alex nodded, rubbing Sarah's hand. "Yes. Morgan and Blair left me locked in the car's trunk as it was submerged in Lake Ontario."

"How did you get out?" Blair asked, his voice low and altered, unlike his usual cadence. "Although, I have to say it's great to see you."

Alex eyed him for a long moment. "Is it? Quite the change of heart from what you said by the lake."

Sarah rested her head on Alex's shoulder, wiping at her tears that refused to stop.

He rubbed her head now. "It was Sarah who saved me."

Her head jerked up to stare at Alex. Did she do that *specific thing* Vivian talked about? "How did I do that?" she managed to ask.

"Do you remember before we went to the factory? You'd placed me in the trunk and gave me the—"

"Trunk remote," she finished for him. "Then I parked in the shadows, and you let yourself out once I diverted their attention to me."

Alex nodded. "I still had the trunk remote when the car hit the water. I pressed the button, which popped the trunk, but kept it closed so they wouldn't see it open and shoot at me. Then I breathed in the pockets of air inside the trunk until there was no air left to breathe. By this time, the car was sitting on the bottom. It sat in murky water about fifteen to twenty feet deep. I held my breath on the last inhale of air and waited another minute, then eased the trunk lid open and swam away from the car toward shore, making sure to remain near the bottom. I came up in some bushes and waited until I heard them leave in their car."

"Then what did you do?" Robinson asked. "You didn't call us for help. I would've known."

"I dried off as I walked back to my sister's house. When no one was home, I asked a neighbor if they knew anything. I was told about all the police cars and how Mrs. Nelson—my sister—was ushered out to the cruisers. That was it." He shrugged. "I assumed those cars brought her here."

"You weren't worried about bumping into Inspector Morgan?" Robinson glanced at Blair. "Or him?"

Alex shook his head. "That's why I wore the hoodie and said my name was Daniel. I thought Sarah could update me, and then we'd decide what to do next." Alex shrugged. "I don't know, like maybe call his boss and see about pressing charges."

Robinson stared at him for a moment. "Tell me something."

"Sure."

"Were you at Inspector Morgan's house?"

Sarah jerked her gaze at Robinson. Everyone was staring at him.

Alex frowned. "Morgan's house?" He pursed his lips. "Where does he live? I mean, how would I know that sort of thing? I'm new to Hamilton. I just wanted to visit my sister to talk about our brother, who died in Toronto. This guy arrested me"—he pointed at Blair—"and when I was released from custody by Captain Simmons, with an apology, I might add, this guy tried to kill me."

"Okay, that about sums it up for now." Robinson got to his feet. "Alex, I'll need a full statement if you don't mind sticking around. I'm sure your sister will also want to talk to you." He turned to face Blair. "Well, murder charges will be reduced to *attempted* murder, so there's that." He waved one hand. "Gentlemen, take him back to holding."

Alex leaned in close to Sarah. "As soon as I'm done with my statement and I've met with my sister, I'm ready to head back to Toronto. Will you take me home?"

Sarah nodded. "Anything. I want to go home, too."

"You can say that again," Aaron echoed, tapping Alex on the shoulder.

"It's so good to see you, brother," Parkman said. "You're like a fucking cat with nine lives."

"It's either that, or I'm immortal, and I haven't told you guys about it yet." He chuckled.

"Immortal?" Aaron whispered the word. "If you told me that, I'd believe you."

Sarah lightly punched his upper arm. "Don't ever die on us again, or I'll kill you."

"Don't plan on it."

Then he pulled her in for a long, tight hug.

"We love you too much." Sarah felt Aaron's arms wrap around them. Then Parkman's.

No one wanted to let go.
Ever.

# Chapter 39

FIVE DAYS LATER …

Sarah took the offered wine glass from Aaron as he sat beside her on the sofa. They stared across the living room to the recliner where Alex sat, a glass of water in his hand.

Willow had gone to bed thirty minutes before. Aaron had just checked on her and then refilled their glasses.

"She's fast asleep," he said.

Sarah nodded, then sipped from her glass. After a moment of silence, she got up and went to the small stereo. She found the soft piano classics she was looking for, adjusted the volume to ensure it remained in the background, and then retook her seat.

The music, the soft lighting, and the wine allowed her to relax more than she had in nearly a week. She needed to remain calm because she suspected Alex would come clean on some of his past, and it wouldn't be easy to hear or tell.

Aaron leaned forward and set his glass down. "How did you get Morgan's home address?" he asked. "I mean, from the near drowning to when Morgan was beaten up in his foyer—geez, that wasn't more than a few hours."

Sarah frowned. Why was Aaron assuming it was Alex at Morgan's house? Didn't he already tell them he walked to his sister's house and then to the police station? When would he have time to find Morgan?

Alex sipped from his water and set the glass on the table beside him. "I bought a cheap phone, signed into my WhatsApp, and contacted

Darwin on a donut shop's WiFi."

Sarah stared at him incredulously. "Darwin and Rosina got you Morgan's address?"

Alex nodded. "Within fifteen minutes."

"Did you shoot him?"

Aaron jerked sideways. Sometimes, he didn't appreciate her being direct.

"I did not shoot the inspector. I injured him." Alex picked up his glass again. "I wanted to hurt him badly. Maim him for trying to kill me."

"But you were interrupted." It wasn't a question. Sarah drank more wine. "By a man wearing a Kevlar vest."

Alex nodded.

Sarah explained what Vivian had told her to do and how they had given that man the vest.

"Morgan was armed," Alex continued. "So I tossed an empty duffel bag in his face to distract him. I jumped at him, attacked, weapons fired, I wasn't hit, and both men dropped." Alex shrugged. "I got lucky. You know the rest."

The soft piano played in the background. After several moments, Alex sat up straighter and cleared his throat.

"There's something I have to tell you."

Sarah nodded. Aaron stared at him. They waited.

"My sister blames me for what happened to our parents."

"We know." Aaron sat back. "She said you killed them."

"Maybe I did, maybe I didn't."

"That's confusing." Sarah looked from Aaron to Alex. "Isn't murder something more concrete?"

"I'll explain. But I have to start at the beginning."

Sarah eased back onto the sofa and waited.

"Our dad was a disciplinarian—strict, by-the-book rule follower. We were disciplined physically from an early age. I learned to manage it. Benjamin, not so much. Susan ..." He glanced away, and Sarah wondered if Alex would cry. "Susan was managed differently."

"How so?" Aaron asked.

"Kinder, gentler."

"Are you saying creepy without saying creepy?"

Alex nodded slightly. "But we didn't know what creepy was in those days. We were too young." He refocused on them. "At least not until she told Benjamin and me that Dad was touching her where he shouldn't be."

Sarah drank more wine, then coughed. "I'm sorry. We've hit the hard-to-hear part. I'll control myself."

"It was hard to hear for us," Alex said. "Benjamin and I came up with a plan. We wanted to hurt him back for all the beatings he administered on us, and now we had to protect Susan."

"So, what did you do?" Aaron asked.

"We knew where he worked at the steel plant. On Thursdays, he worked late for a shipment-related task. So, we waited for him in the parking lot by his car."

"Did Susan know what you were going to do?"

"Yes. We told her he wouldn't be able to touch her again. Not after that night."

"Was she with you?"

"No, we left her at home."

"What happened next?" Aaron asked.

"We wore something similar to ninja suits, covering our identity completely, and we jumped him in the parking lot when he walked to his car."

"And you didn't kill him?" Sarah asked.

Alex shook his head. "We did not kill him, although we wanted to." He sipped his water. "We broke both his hands and a few fingers. He touched our sister, and now he wouldn't be touching her again. We broke other things, too."

He stopped talking, and Sarah wondered if he didn't want to tell them how bad the injuries were.

"How bad?" Sarah asked. "What state did you leave him in?"

"Unable to walk for months. Couldn't feed himself. About fifteen broken bones. Some mild internal bleeding."

"Holy shit," Aaron whispered.

"Hey, he had it coming. He beat defenseless children and was grooming his own daughter. Benjamin and I made a pact that if he touched her again, we'd bury him up north somewhere."

"Good for you," Sarah said, her heart racing as she held up her wine glass.

"So, then, how did he die?" Aaron asked.

"It was two hours later."

"Where? In the hospital?"

Alex shook his head. "At the back of the parking lot."

"I'm confused." Aaron momentarily looked at the wall behind Alex as if trying to work something out. Then he refocused on Alex's face. "All that happened, yet you claim *you* didn't kill him."

"When we left him, he was breathing just fine. We fucked with his arms and legs. Broke a few ribs. Other than a couple of jabs at his cheeks, we left his throat and head alone."

"But when the cause of death came back …" Sarah said, leaving it unfinished.

"Someone had stepped on his throat, collapsing his trachea. Whoever it was pulverized his neck."

"Stepped?" she said to herself. "Pulverized?"

"Okay, stomped might be a better word."

They fell back into silence.

Alex adjusted himself in the seat as if he were uncomfortable. "Maybe I'll have some of that wine after all."

Aaron bolted to his feet, grabbed a glass from the kitchen, and poured a generous amount. He handed it to Alex, who drank it like cherry juice.

"Did they ever learn it was you guys who beat him? Or did they find who stomped on his throat?"

Alex shook his head. "To this day, it's an open police file. We never confessed. No one ever came forward. It's been over a decade. It's done."

"What happened to your mother?"

Alex drank the rest of his wine.

"Want more?" Aaron asked.

Alex waved him off. "Our mother grieved hard. She couldn't handle losing the bastard. Co-dependency ruined her. We tried to help, but nothing worked. In the end, she stayed in bed all day, wouldn't leave the house, had long baths that worried us, and eventually cut her wrists in the tub one night."

"Oh, Alex," Sarah said. "I'm so sorry."

"It's been a long time. I've grieved her but carried the weight of what happened for some time."

"That's why that Joseph guy in North Bay got to you."

Alex stared at her. "I wanted to kill him myself." He looked away from them, opened his mouth, closed it, then opened it again. "I don't think either of you could understand the restraint I undergo when we meet the Josephs of the world. If I had grizzly bear claws, I'd rip the heads off every groomer out there. Castration doesn't work, but decapitation certainly will."

Sarah held her wine glass in the air in a mock toast again, then drank the rest of it as Alex and Aaron lightened the mood by discussing other things. They discussed sports, the current movie in the theater, and who had signed up at the dojo last week.

"Wasn't there some sort of court case?" Sarah asked. "Sealed files?"

Alex turned to her. "Benjamin and I felt that was what pushed our mother over the edge." He stared at his empty glass. "Susan wanted out of the family after what happened to her. She wanted her birth records sealed. She filed motion after motion to get removed from what she called a cult." He looked up. "You have to understand. She was traumatized by our father. Later, it all came out in court in front of our mother. Her lawyer told the courts everything, and they granted her most of what she wanted. She met a guy, got married, changed her name, and had Tracy. They divorced when Tracy was young, but she kept her new name until she met that asshole Blair." He stared off at nothing for a moment. "After it was all over, Benjamin and I had each other, and we kept tabs on Susan." He refocused on Sarah. "Susan is a strong woman, determined. Reminds me of you. Looking back, I have no regrets. My father didn't deserve to live. My sister did. And so the courts granted her a new life."

They talked about Willow, life in general, and how amazing it was that Alex lived to tell this tale. Sarah made him promise he'd never disappear like that again.

Life would return to how it was, and they'd all soon fall into a routine.

However, Vivian had dropped in recently, telling her to watch over Parkman. Something was happening to him, and he may need their help.

*Parkman* was Vivian's new word lately.

The words *Parkman* and *Susan* came up as Aaron and Alex were talking, making Sarah return to the conversation.

"Wait. What was that about Susan?"

Aaron turned to her. "Susan and Parkman are spending a lot of time together now that she left Blair."

"Oh." She grinned, staring sideways at Alex. "How do you feel about that?"

"I have mixed feelings."

"She's suing Blair for a divorce, right?"

Alex nodded. "Yeah, their marriage is over. He's still in custody, facing a slew of charges."

"So, she's free to date, isn't she?"

"Yeah, but it's so soon."

"Hey, Parkman is charming. And they're adults. He deserves this."

They stared at Alex for a few moments.

"What?" Aaron asked.

"Yeah, what is it?" Sarah chimed in.

"We never found out who stomped on an injured man's throat."

"So?"

"Susan was out when Benjamin and I got home that night."

"Did she tell you where she was?"

"Sure, she had an alibi. But we suspected—"

"That she finished off her father."

Alex nodded.

"Oh …" Sarah thought about Vivian's focus on Parkman. Her warning to watch over him. "Do you think Parkman is in danger?"

Alex stared at her. He lifted his right shoulder. "I don't know. I just don't know. Consider the profile of someone stepping on another person's throat. The damage that will be caused."

"Yeah," Aaron said. "Someone driven by hatred works."

"Shit," Sarah said. "Is her ex-husband alive?"

Alex nodded. "He is."

"I need another drink." Aaron got up and left the room.

Sarah told Alex about Vivian's warning regarding Parkman.

"I'll watch out for him." Alex sat forward in his seat as if he were ready to go. "I'll keep an eye on both of them."

"Make sure he's safe."

He winked. "I got this."

But now Sarah was worried.

Could Parkman be romancing a murderer, even if she agreed with the murder in this case? If he were, could she be a danger to Parkman?

Vivian seemed to think so.

"Shit," she said again and got up from her seat. "I need another drink, too."

"Hey, Alex." Aaron pointed at the black duffel bag by the door. "What did you bring with you?"

"Yeah. That." Alex got up and walked over to the bag. "We need to discuss this."

He showed them the contents. They both gasped.

"About that drink," Sarah said and walked into the kitchen.

# Afterword

DEAR READER,

Now that we've finished with *Alex* and dealt with some of his mysterious upbringing—there's more that will come out in time—we haven't finished with his sister.

In the next novel, *Parkman*, we'll see more of Susan Nelson.

But before we head over to read that tale, I'd love to tell you why I chose Hamilton, Ontario, for this novel.

I lived in Hamilton for a year back in 1992. The cross streets of Kenilworth and Main were close to my house. I also lived on the mountain off a road called Garth for a spell. I've driven the Sherman Access hundreds of times. The Taco Bell mentioned in this book, the one Alex used to work at, was a place I visited often (to this day, I still love Taco Bell). I have fond memories of Hamilton. Even that mall where Susan goes shopping while Tracy is at the birthday party is a mall I've shopped at many times.

Popular advice for writers stressed that an author should "write what you know." Well, I write *where* I know. I rarely offer a location in a novel I haven't seen myself. I've done it, but only on rare occasions.

I wanted to feature Alex as much as possible in this novel, hence the book's title. Yet, at the same time, this is the Sarah Roberts Series, so understandably, she needed to play a pivotal role. I've tried my best to balance that, and I hope to continue doing so with the next three novels as we explore *Parkman*, *Darwin*, and then *Aaron*. Book forty is called *Remains To Be Seen*. I'll adjust the focus to Sarah again by then, but she'll still play a key role in those other books.

I also wanted to place Alex in a situation where he didn't have many options for escape, leading me to the trunk in the lake scenario. Giving him the trunk opener fob before the factory was something I didn't want the reader to see. It was there, though. How else would he extricate himself from the trunk when left alone in the car? And, upon hearing gunfire on the factory's second floor, of course, Alex would be the first one on the scene, standing over Morgan to see if he needed assistance.

When Alex popped the trunk but held it closed until the vehicle was fully submerged in the lake—that's something I wanted to gloss over as well. Since I couldn't lie to the reader, and we were in Alex's point of view as the car descended through the murky water of Lake Ontario, I wrote this line, "Alex did what he had to do, closed his eyes, and focused on remaining calm."

My goal, as sadistic as some might think, was to convince the characters and, by default, the reader that Alex didn't make it.

So, I'll leave you with this: how could I ever kill off a character like Alex?

Wait. Don't answer that.

We've lost Benjamin. It may happen again.

I hope it's never Alex. Or Sarah. Time will tell, though. The last book in the series, book fifty, already has a title. It's called *The End*.

I want to send out a special thank you to Demetrius Robinson for allowing me to use his name in this book—much appreciated!

Thank you for coming along on this journey with me. I look forward to the next one. And I look forward to meeting you all one day —come to Greece in June! We can chat about books! I'll be at a Reading Retreat on the island of Amorgos in Greece. It will be a fantastic time, and everyone is welcome to join. Please email me for details.

Until the next book …

Take care of each other and yourself.

Get caught reading.

All the best,

Jonas Saul

# About Jonas Saul

Jonas Saul is the bestselling author of the Sarah Roberts Series—
over two million copies sold—and more than sixty published
thrillers. His work has outranked Stephen King and Dean Koontz
on Amazon and has been optioned for television and film by
MadRiver Pictures.

A sought-after speaker and teacher, Jonas has presented at
international writing conferences and film festivals around the
globe. He is the creator of Imagine Greece Retreats, hosting
annual writers', screenwriters', and readers' retreats on the sun-
drenched shores of Greece, where he now lives. His teaching
focuses on creating unputdownable tension and emotion, building
a sustainable writing career, and avoiding the pitfalls of the

publishing industry.

An acclaimed freelance editor, Jonas works with several publishers and offers private editing services to authors worldwide. His editing site features glowing testimonials from clients who credit him with elevating their books to the next level.

For speaking engagements, jury work, or to connect:

✉ jonassaul@icloud.com | jonas@imaginegreeceretreats.com

🌐 Linktree – Find me here | Amazon Follow | BookBub Follow | Facebook (most active)

www.ingramcontent.com/pod-product-compliance
Lightning Source LLC
Chambersburg PA
CBHW030837030726
47495CB00005B/1258